ETHELINDE

ETHELINDE,

OR THE

RECLUSE OF THE LAKE

BY
CHARLOTTE SMITH

―――――

Edited with a new introduction and notes by
ELLEN MOODY

―――――

VALANCOURT BOOKS

Editor's Dedication: For the memory of James Andrew Moody, my
beloved husband

Ethelinde, or, The Recluse of the Lake
First published in 5 vols., London: Cadell, 1789
First Valancourt Books edition 2016
Reprinted from the second edition of 1790

Introduction and Notes © 2016 by Ellen Moody
This edition © 2016 by Valancourt Books

Published by Valancourt Books, Richmond, Virginia
Publisher & Editor: James D. Jenkins
http://www.valancourtbooks.com

All Valancourt Books publications are printed on acid free paper
that meets all ANSI standards for archival quality paper.

ISBN 978-1-943910-54-0
Also available as an electronic book.

Set in Dante MT

CONTENTS

INTRODUCTION

While in the last quarter century almost all of Charlotte Smith's original fictions have been published in more than one affordable and/or scholarly edition, her second and at the time (1789) highly influential *Ethelinde; or, The Recluse of the Lake,* has not. As yet the novel exists separately only in five-volume reprint sets, where the typeface is a facsimile using the long "s." It also fills Volume 3 of Pickering and Chatto's fourteen-volume edition of all Smith's works. One result is that in the criticism of Smith's novels, of novels of the era, and in modern histories of the novel, *Ethelinde* is repeatedly the Smith novel the writer chooses not to deal with in depth (though it often gets a mention). Its innovative, important, and absorbing content has thus been lost from view.

Ethelinde is centered on a depiction of adulterous love more sympathetic and true to experience on the sides of both the novel's hero, Sir Edward Newenden and his once loved wife, Maria, Lady Newenden, than what is found in Tolstoy's *Anna Karenina.* It is the story of Newenden's gradual falling in love with Ethelinde Chesterville, the novel's primary heroine, his physical as well as emotional need for her in the face of his wife's increasing distaste for him, for his idealistic and ethical values, and for his children; of his efforts to repress his longing for the congenial, sensitive, readerly Ethelinde; and of the final thwarting of his intensely compelling and sexual desire for Ethelinde. The novel's several stories are about women driven by persuasively told economic, social, legal circumstances to live with men outside marriage. The way British society has rejected these women and their children pivotally shapes the destiny of several of the book's central characters, most often the tale's teller. The story of Mrs. Douglas, who once widowed turns to Lord Pevensey, is told by Mrs. Caroline Montgomery, her legitimate daughter from Mrs. Douglas's first marriage and the recluse of the lake; her mother's past and her own resulting present poverty causes Mrs. Montgomery to live in a cottage in Cumberland with her legitimate son, the novel's secondary hero, Charles Montgomery, also in love with Ethelinde. Ethelinde's own mother died long ago, like Mrs. Douglas in her first marriage disdained by a high-ranking and rich family, and Ethelinde's bonding with Mrs. Montgomery causes Ethelinde to support Mrs. Montgomery's hesitant plan to send her son to India to provide more money for them and any children she and Montgomery may have after they marry.

Tellingly, Ethelinde and Montgomery end up living with Mrs. Montgomery based on income given her by one of her mother's illegitimate sons, Mrs. Montgomery's half-brother, Mr. Harcourt, mostly the result of enormous profits from West Jamaican plantations based on slave labor, which he gained by marriage. The present tense and dramatized stories which occur across the novel and cause Montgomery's many or impinging separations from Ethelinde, are dramatizations of internal ethical conflicts and emotional traumas brought on by his need to accept and obey the behests of corrupt patronage (parliamentary, imperial, sexual); by the imprisonment of her selfish indulged brother, Harry Chesterville, for debt and bankruptcy (from gambling and the extravagances he requires to maintain his upper class life with cliques of friends, followers, and business associates), and by life-threatening duels, and sea-voyages moving across oceans to the East and West Indies, to the coasts of Africa and ports of Portugal, and inland from Scotland to France and Germany. This is the male-centered side of Smith's depiction of her contemporaries' experience of life and includes graphic descriptions of murder and death from horrible wounds on war-torn landscapes, of what's left of people after bouts of killing in real battles (e.g., Minden, in Northwest Germany, in August 1759, a date which helps situate the novel's chronology). Before the book opens, Mrs. Montgomery had rescued her nearly mortally wounded husband from the field, but he had to continue to earn his living as a soldier, and while he lived for some years afterwards, his strength gave out, he died, and she was cheated out of a portion of the pension he intended for her (Volume 1, Chapter 6).

There is an unusual double gender perspective at work in many of the book's central events. For example, we experience how an attempted rape of Ethelinde (towards the close of the novel) could have been carried out successfully because the rapist, a mean-minded vain foppish fool, Tom Davenant, the ward of Sir

Edward, resents Ethelinde's continued rejection of him when she is a dependent near-pauper after her father has died. Davenant can enlist the servants in his friend's house, and men from its stables, because this rakish gambling and horse-racing friend, Jack Woolaston, is himself debtor to, and thus preyed-upon, by characters like Davenant, whom Woolaston preys upon. Ethelinde is helped to flee by two tenant-servants who ignore threats made by Woolaston (to fire them, to throw them off the land); these threats do not deter these servants because they are good men and have no faith in any continued support from Woolaston or Davenant anyway.

Men, especially younger sons, are as vulnerable as most of the women in this novel. We experience from an interior standpoint two marriages prompted by the desire or need of a male to obtain large sums of money, where Smith pays attention to monetary aspects of such arrangements not usually focused upon. Sir Edward Newenden married Maria because he needed her father's fortune, and he endures castigating, harassing harangues by Mr. Maltravers about specifics of money to the effect that nothing Sir Edward has is morally his. Mr. Maltravers's pointed arguments at length about who owes who what (Vol. 4, Chapter 6) form an instructive parallel to and show how mild in comparison is Austen's famous second chapter in *Sense and Sensibility* where a wife's arguments convince her husband he need not help his step-sisters after the death of their father at all. In the case of Sir Edward's sister, Ellen Newenden, a horsewoman, deceived by Woolaston's pretense of love into marrying him, we read a full depiction of the pressures of the lifestyle of Jack Woolaston; his successful lying neatly ties the exemplum of a duplicitious marriage into the depiction of the near rape of Ethelinde, as well as the card-table gambling scenes where Ethelinde's father, Colonel Chesterville, and her brother, Harry Chesterville, lose their and her fortune. *Ethelinde* is thus as much a "condition of England" novel and corrosive social satire as her much-praised *The Old Manor House* (1793) and the corrosive, bitter, less-noticed *Marchmont* (1796) (it too is similarly inaccessible due to lack of an individual modern edition). Smith's uses of King's Bench prison near the Thames anticipates Dickens.

As Stuart Curran and Lorraine Fletcher demonstrate, in *Ethelinde* there is as much space and time given over to depictions of the activities of opulent and strained middle-class town life in drawing-rooms (specifically, London and Bristol) with brief excursions into impoverished genteel existences in provincial lodgings (e.g., Devonshire where there is a coach road) as there is intense gratification in the landscapes of northern, southwestern and coastal England. The novel's leading rake, Lord Danesforte, early on seducer and lover of Maria, Lady Newenden (by Volume 2, Chapter 3), maintains a kind of open house at Danesforte Castle in Gloucestershire, where amateur plays are regularly put on and gambling dominates the long night hours; by the end of the book his expenses exhaust his estate, and the resulting alienation of all social circles from him ends in his death from a disease brought on by his lifestyle. Danesforte is likened to Lovelace more than once in the novel; Smith's depiction derives from her response to women who read Richardson's novel and were allured by Richardson's depiction of Lovelace. Ethelinde's cousin, Clarinthia Ludford, wishes she could have a suitor like Lovelace; Maria carries on a clandestine correspondence with Danesforte when she is taken to the Newenden modern mansion, Denham, and her parents' home in Berkshire due to her mother Mrs. Maltravers's vicarious enjoyment of this rake's behavior (Volume 4, Chapter 9). *Ethelinde* also contains several harsh burlesques of fashionable "ton" life, of one of its practitioners' inane soulless poetry of sensibility (her cousin, Rupert Ludsford). Smith's novel is fueled by loathing (it's not too strong a word) for groups of characters' mercantile vulgar ostentation and taste and snobberies interwoven with justified exposure of the miseries and injustice rank-based hierarchies and admired male sexual power inflict on others.

Smith's one depiction of a woman driven to become a governess, Miss Milward, an impoverished "accomplished" Englishwoman who ships herself to the West Indies, stresses Miss Milward's susceptibility to sympathized-with sexual and emotional advances on the part of Mr. Harcourt. Here social satire is replaced by another two stories of women's sexual vulnerability to the advances of men who behave generously to them financially and emotionally. Both women, Miss Milward and her illegitimate daughter, Victorine, live with men outside marriage. We see the limits of Smith's feminism when she forgives Mr. Harcourt as an illegitimate son of Mrs. Douglas with few connections and thus no economic opportunities but marriage to a rich woman. Smith blames Mr. Harcourt's wife's mean and ill-tempered jealousy as an older woman who knows her husband married her for her wealth. The second phase of this tale (or second story) parallels the central Newenden one, with the emphasis falling finally on the fate of the illegitimate daughter, Victorine, who becomes Ethelinde's brother Harry's mistress; perhaps unexpectedly to a modern reader, his father, Colonel Chesterville and Ethelinde would have been against this marriage on the grounds of the young couple's poverty; he married her in order to rebel, to assert his manly egoistic self-image (and thus is supported by Montgomery who would have married Ethelinde before the end of Volume 1 if she had agreed to it), and only by chance do they meet Mr. Harcourt, whose eldest legitimate son has died in circumstances which recall those of Austen's Tom Bertram in *Mansfield Park*.

Smith explores intense marital disappointment leading to adultery as well as the economic frustration and inescapable exploitation of subalterns such marriages still depend upon. She seems to let off lightly some of the males whose conduct hurts her females irreparably in this novel, but if we examine our feelings towards both Chesterville males, and Montgomery's incessant haranguing of Ethelinde, we may see that they are blamed as individuals as much as the social order everyone across the wide world of the novel exists in. Perhaps her treatment of Maria, Lady Newenden is the most disappointing area of the novel. Maria was coerced (we are made to feel) into marriage by her parents, who miseducated her into choosing for his rank a man who bored her; we are never permitted to see inside her mind and only hear her bitter ripostes and see instead her loyal father Mr. Maltravers's painfully false position when he attempts to persuade her to value her position, children, and Sir Edward. She is taken by her parents and Sir Edward with their children to Italy, but we learn only some time later from Sir Edward that she has fled with Lord Danesforte. Smith's language seems to indicate that Maria died of a miscarriage in circumstances where she has no one to care for her (Volume 5, Chapter 12), but that it has been taken by Fletcher to be simply a suicide (116; see also Fry 45) shows how little care Smith has taken to account for her. Maria is guilty of the one sin Smith cannot forgive in her novels: a cold indifference to her children.

The texture of the book's language, its set-piece poetic passages, landscape reveries, tempest and grief-drenched migrations are arresting and absorbing, and their unearthing of uncanny archetypes worth the scholar as well as reader's careful perusal. There are many passages of delicately felt pictorial beauty. Smith pours into the novel memories of reading Thomas Gray's journal and Oliver Goldsmith and William Cowper's poetry and displays a convincing exactitude showing her knowledge of landscape, botany, and birds. Her technique is one where her heroine glimpses what is nearly invisible and just manages to hear sounds few would notice. Here is Ethelinde gazing on the Sussex downs:

> And before her the sea appeared so clear that she fancied she could distinguish the gentle undulations of the waves. Numberless small vessels were scattered on its calm surface; the white sails of some caught the full rays of the sun, others were in shadow, and appeared like dusky specks hanging in the air. Scarce a cottage or a haystack arose as a sign that it was inhabited; and Ethelinde sat in mournful … reverie … some hours passed away … No sounds but the wind sighing through the leafless hawthorn under which she sat, or the whistling of the Stone Curlew, the wild and solitary inhabitant of open countries, broke the silence. (Volume 5, Chapter 2)

Buildings are used symbolically. There are two gothic sites: the novel begins at and returns to the Newenden family mansion, Grasmere Abbey, which one must assert is completely fictional (there was no such abbey in Cumbria; Lake Grasmere is in Westmoreland), and which may have influenced Wordsworth's choice of home. Grasmere Abbey may look like but is no haven; a great deal of money from Mr. Maltravers's successful trading businesses has been needed to maintain and hold onto it. One of the most powerful sequences of the novel occurs in Abersley, the Chesterville ancestral gothic-style home in Worcestershire, which belongs to Ethelinde's father's oldest brother, Lord Hawkhurst, who refused him support of any kind when he lay dying; in a visit to the family's mausoleum near a church, Ethelinde's (by now) severe depression, the result of believing Montgomery dead, and her wandering isolated condition becomes a lack of perspective that turns into a terrified encounter with what she imagines is the longed-for presence of her father come as a phantom to meet her (Volume V, Chapter 10).

Scattered throughout the novel are bourgeois households, mansions and town houses which mirror their owners' moral values and lifestyle. The oppressive Ludford House is maintained by Mr. and Mrs. Ludford (Mrs. Ludford was Ethelinde's mother's sister), who have similar homes in Southampton and London; they snub and mortify Ethelinde until they meet Mr. Harcourt and realize his bond with Mrs. Montgomery has led him to become Ethelinde's generous friend; then they turn sycophantic. There is the corrupt Member of Parliament Royston's London townhouse (his wife attempts to seduce Montgomery into becoming her kept lover). Ellen Newenden's home is Brackwood Downs (Sussex) where no one is safe, not even the horses she attempts to care for. Clare Park is the country house of Mr. Harcourt (in Gloucestershire and thus near Abersley, the Hawkhurst castle), but it is not a good place of rest when it is occupied by Harry and Victorine Chesterville who first seek out Mr. Harcourt in the West Indies, and then when they realize he is in England, follow and live with him to carry out a dissipated gambling life. Only at the very end of the novel does Mr. Harcourt's illness and near death somewhat improbably effect a reform in these characters sufficient to control the worst aspects of their bad educations, Harry from imitating Colonel Chesterville, Victorine from having been put in a convent after her mother died. A kind of ricochet from one of these houses to another occurs at the end of the novel when Montgomery, having obeyed the wrong-headed but understandable pressure of his mother and Sir Edward to go to India to wrest an income, but unable to behave with the required ruthlessness, finally returns to his mother's cottage in Cumberland where the novel began. His trip is at first a zigzag where he lives as a company agent or in servitude across the Indian and Atlantic oceans, and then appears as a beggar refugee within England. He travels from one house to the next, each time shut out after being given false information that Ethelinde and Sir Edward Newenden are either living together without marriage or have married, and thus (as he would see it) have betrayed him.

If *Ethelinde* is so good, why then this sad lack of a printing history? Charlotte Smith belonged to that circle of pro-revolutionary reformers whose books were marginalized in the early 19th century; her much-criticized openness about her life made her work more socially unacceptable even if she was sympathized with (Butler, Ty, Johnston). Paradoxically the books that readers felt attracted to, despite anti-Jacobin rhetoric, were her later, more overtly politically centered books, and it has been these that the feminist movement which first brought some of her novels back into print have turned to first: *Desmond*, the first English novel to treat of the French Revolution (1792); *The Old Manor House* (1793), with its depiction of the Seven Years War (1754-63) as fought in North America; and *The Banished Man* (1794), about emigration and set in the war-torn countryside of Europe, read as a partial recant of *Desmond*. *Emmeline, the Orphan of the Castle* (1788) was among the first to be reprinted in the twentieth century because it was her first novel and thought to be influential on Austen's *Northanger Abbey*. Recently critics have shown a preference for her very dark brooding novel, *Montalbert* (1795) and the wide philosophical issues debated in her last, *The Young Philosopher* (1798).

Ethelinde's title and length has probably put readers off; it announces itself as a heroine's text, a female novel of sensibility. But had Smith called her book *Newenden* that probably would not have overcome a fatal flaw in the text itself. There is just too much weeping, too frequent hysterical fits on the part of the heroine— however understandable in the circumstances, one must say of a number of them. The male protagonists are critiqued for their refusal to contain or control their egoism (as are the heroes of *Emmeline*), but that does not make these passages any the more endurable when the characters let go. The excess of obsessive grief and mutual self-berating makes the wry phlegmatic commentary of Ellen Newenden a funny relief. She is oblivious to anyone else's troubles unless it affects one of her horses. But she says truly, "In real life such *things are not*" (Vol. 5, Chapter 9). Still arguably the most brilliant study in the novel is that of the layers of Sir Edward Newenden's depression; in a replay of a scene shocking to contemporaries, one which still provokes readers' censures, in Madame de La Fayette's famous late 17th century novel, *La Princesse de Clèves* where the princess confesses her adulterous love to her husband, Sir Edward explains his interior urges to Montgomery. There is more real feeling in Sir Edward's quiet or prosaic marriage proposal to Ethelinde than in many a modern novel; at the novel's close when he is refused by her, they have the most believable dialogue in the book. Smith was never as daring again, for he is the first of a series of male surrogates for her; his inner life explains the great dark sonnets of Warburton in *Montalbert*. We may choose to understand all these passages as a release for the author's despair (and a depiction of her uncontrollable husband's behavior), but, taken together, they hurt her book.

Eighteenth-century scholars may nowadays be generally aware of the causes of Charlotte Smith's deep melancholy, but not the general reader. She was born Charlotte Turner in 1754; her father was a well-to-do squire in Sussex, who after Charlotte's mother's death and after his own poor management of his estate (he gambled like Colonel Chesterville), he married a wealthy younger woman at the same time as he sold his daughter, not yet sixteen, "like a legal prostitute" (Charlotte's words) to a very wealthy bidder in the form of a London merchant who wanted his grandchildren to be gentry. Charlotte found herself tied to Benjamin Smith, a violent (in later years she said her life was unsafe when she lived with him), extravagant and unscrupulous eldest son (before his father's death he embezzled a great deal of the money he was to inherit) who impregnated her ceaselessly (she endured twelve live births between 1766 and 1784), and was openly sexually unfaithful. In 1783 she felt constrained to accompany him to debtors' prison; in 1784, taking all her children, like some gothic heroine, she followed him to a remote mansion in France to escape his debt and live cheaply, where she gave birth for the last time in dangerous circumstances.

She returned to England by 1785 and began almost immediately to produce novels for publication and money. She finally separated herself permanently from Benjamin in 1787. But by law, custom, and pressure from other people, she could not free herself from his determined incursions into whatever place she lived in and wresting from her as his all the income she had made and he could find. I think her husband hated her for the respect her writing soon gained her, and for her dissimilarity to and justified scorn of him. In the mid-1790s he seems to have been able to present himself plausibly to some of her supporters who may have been embarrassed by her politics and open attacks on lawyers and the British court system. Her father-in-law had died in 1776; in an effort to keep his considerable legacy from his son and leave it to the grand-children, he had written such a complex series of provisions in his will (without legal advice it was said) that it was not until well after her death in October 1806 that any money came to those of her children left alive. Her resulting tireless demands, ceaseless need for money to support in genteel circumstances the nine children who survived childhood and provide career opportunities for her sons, and bitter unflinching complaints of how she was victim-ized, alienated needed patrons and some friends and readers. It was to publishers and booksellers she had to turn for the income she managed to earn to support herself and her family (Stanton, Wolfson). As her health failed, and she stopped writing the novels that brought in livable wages, she signaled how bad things were by telling of how she finally had to sell her beloved collection of 500 books. There had been some respite in February 1806 when Ben-jamin died, for some money did then revert to her from him, but it was too late for her to set up the home on Lake Leman she had dreamed of, for she died in October of the same year.

Different aspects of Smith's character, life, and work are stressed as context for her novels. Though written after *Ethelinde*, some of Smith's extraordinary poetry, including her series of original mourning poems, especially those written after the death of her favorite daughter Anna in 1795, her protest poetry, and the female georgic *The Emigrants* (1793) offers the reader an accurate groundwork of *Ethelinde* (Labbe, *Romanticism*; Hawley). As liter-ary influences, I would single out Prévost (whose *Manon Lescaut* Smith translated and published in 1785) and Rousseau's at once subversive and aggressive erotic and individualistic agendas (e.g., his *Reveries of a Solitary Walker*) as keys to *Ethelinde*. There is ever in her an active desire for satisfying adult male as well as female companionship which her life seems to have almost completely frustrated. I would bring out also an element not often empha-sized in the literature on Smith: the source of the ferocious anger fuelling her presentation of the forcing of Montgomery abroad to steal from others even more vulnerable than he, risking prob-able disease and death to be able to support Ethelinde in a town manner. Her quotation of Rousseau's famous outburst in *Julie, ou La Nouvelle Héloïse* is unironic, quite sincere (Volume 4, Chapter 11). At the root of this novel is her grief for her children, her ruined hopes and hard struggles for them, how she regretted that they had to go abroad apart from her to perform tasks she regarded as reprehensible.

She nonetheless in good faith threw herself into this book as a seriously intended depiction of the world she knew. That is why it is as long and nuanced as it is. Smith was working with a sense of hope that this book would be valued and speak to readers. *Ethelinde* contains a weight given to interior life that I miss in some of her more respected later books. I found this book painful to read; I worried about central characters in the way I worry for Doris Lessing's in her realistic, subjectively told novels. Sir Edward anticipates Sydney Carton (of *A Tale of Two Cities*): he consciously works towards a life of personal fulfillment based on modest expectations (like Austen's Edward Bertram in *Mansfield Park*). While money is central to the book, it seems by its end that the Montgomery and Newenden circle have enough to live quietly, on that competence that Austen's Elinor and Marianne Dashwood found so difficult to pinpoint, in rural retirement.

Around the time of the publication of *Ethelinde*, Smith had set up a home in the form of a cottage for herself and her children in Wyke (Surrey), and wrote a poem , "Thirty-Eight" (1792) (Fletcher 89), to a friend looking forward to an "independent middle-age" with these concluding stanzas:

> No more shall Scandal's breath destroy
> The social converse we enjoy,
>   With bard, or critic, *tête-à-tête*—
> O'er Youth's bright blooms her blights shall pour!
> But spare th' improving friendly hour
>   Which Science gives to—thirty-eight!

> Stripp'd of their gaudy hues by truth,
> We view the glitt'ring toys of youth,
>   And blush to think how poor the bait;
> For which to public scenes we ran,
> And scorn'd of sober sense the plan
>   Which gives content at—thirty-eight!

> Tho' Time's inexorable sway
> Has torn the myrtle bands away
>   For other wreaths 'tis not too late;

> The Am'ranth's purple glow survives,
> And still Minerva's olive thrives
>   On the calm brow of—thirty-eight!
>
> With eye more steady, we engage
> To contemplate approaching age,
>   And life more justly estimate;
> With firmer souls, and stronger pow'rs,
> With reason, faith, and friendship ours,
> We'll not regret the stealing hours
>   That lead from thirty e'en to forty-eight! (Curran, *Poems* 92-94).

I compare *Ethelinde* to Austen's *Mansfield Park* once more. Smith had gained a place in the serious literary world with her poetry, and had had two financial successes with her redaction and translation of a selection of court cases from François Gayot de Pitaval and François Richer's collection *The Romance of Real Life* (1787) and *Emmeline*. Austen was in a similar position: two fine successes (*Sense and Sensibility* and *Pride and Prejudice*) and hope for a future for herself as a somewhat independent writer produced the masterwork *Mansfield Park*. Neither could know what lay ahead: for Smith, a number of her children died, one was crippled, she earned insufficient economic returns for her and their and their children's needs. But by 1806 Smith had created a full shelf of masterly novels and more remarkable poetry and prose, and it is hoped that *Ethelinde* can yet take its place among them.

Ellen Moody

A longtime lecturer at George Mason University and now teaching at American University, Dr. Ellen Moody has published on early modern to 18th-century women writers, film, and translation. She has produced e-text editions of Isabelle de Montolieu's *Caroline de Lichtfield* and Sophie Cottin's *Amelie Mansfield* and has introduced Eleanor Sleath's *The Orphan of the Rhine* for Valancourt Books.

SELECTED BIBLIOGRAPHY

Albrecht, Françoise. "Charlotte Smith et Rousseau: De *L'Émile* au *Jeune Philosophe*." In *Le Continent Européen et le monde Anglo-Américain aux XVIIe et XVIIIe siècles*. Reims: Presses Universitaires, 1987.

Bray, Matthew. "Removing the Anglo-Saxon Yoke: The Francocentric Vision of Charlotte Smith's Later Works," *Wordsworth Circle*, 24:3 (1993): 155-158.

Butler, Marilyn. *Romantics, Rebels and Reactionaries: English Literature and Its Background, 1760-1830*. Oxford: Oxford University Press, 1981.

Ellis, Katherine. "Charlotte Smith's Subversive Gothic," *Feminist Studies* 3 (1976): 52-55.

Fletcher, Lorraine. *Charlotte Smith: A Critical Biography*. London: Macmillan, 1998.

Fry, Carroll. *Charlotte Smith*. Boston: Twayne, 1996.

Garnai, Amy. *Revolutionary Imaginings in the 1790s: Charlotte Smith, Mary Robinson, Elizabeth Inchbald*. New York: Palgrave Macmillan, 2009.

Hawley, Judith. "Charlotte Smith's *Elegiac Sonnets*: Losses and Gains," *Women's Poetry in the Enlightenment*, edited by Isobel Armstrong and Virginia Blain. New York: St. Martin's Press, 1999: 184-198.

Johnston, Kenneth. *Unusual Suspects: Pitt's Reign of Alarm and the Lost Generation of the 1790s*. Oxford: Oxford University Press, 2013.

Keane, Angela. *Women Writers and the English Nation in the 1790s*. Cambridge: Cambridge University Press, 2000.

Labbe, Jacqueline. *Writing Romanticism: Charlotte Smith and William Wordsworth, 1784-1807*. New York: Palgrave Macmillan, 2015.

———. *Charlotte Smith: Romanticism, Poetry and the Culture of Gender*. Manchester: Manchester University Press, 2003.

———, ed. *Charlotte Smith in British Romanticism*. London: Pickering and Chatto, 2008.

Moody, Ellen. Review of Mary Trouille, *Wife Abuse in Eighteenth-Century France*. *The Intelligencer*, NS 25:3 (October 2011):11-15.

Scott, Walter. "Charlotte Smith," *On Novelists and Fiction*, edited by Ioan Williams. New York: Barnes & Noble, 1968: 184-192.

Smith, Charlotte. *Ethelinde, or The Recluse of the Lake* [1789], edited and introduced by Stuart Curran. Vol. 3 of *The Works of Charlotte Smith* (London: Pickering & Chatto, 2005).

———. *Selected Poems*, edited and introduced by Judith Willson. Manchester: Carcanet, 2003.

———. *The Poems of Charlotte Smith*, edited by Stuart Curran. New York: Oxford University Press, 1953.

————. *Ethelinde, ou la récluse du lac par Charlotte Smith*, traduit de l'anglais
    par M. De La Montagne, auteur de plusieurs ouvrages dramatiques,
    4 vols. Paris: Fuchs, 1796.

Stanton, Judith. "Charlotte Smith's 'Literary Business': Income, Patron-
    age, and Indigence," *The Age of Johnson* 1 (1987): 375-401.

Ty, Eleanor. *Unsex'd Revolutionaries: Five Women Novelists of the 1790s*.
    Toronto: University of Toronto Press, 1993.

Wolfson, Susan. "Charlotte Smith: 'To live only to write & write only to
    live,' *The Huntington Library Quarterly* 70:4 (2007): 633-659.

NOTE ON THE TEXT

Ethelinde, or The Recluse of the Lake was originally published in five
volumes by T. Cadell, London, in 1789. The second edition, also in
five volumes, appeared the following year. The textual differences
between the two are mostly minor: Smith corrected a small number
of textual errors for the second edition, and the punctuation, particularly commas and semi-colons, was modified throughout. Not all of
the changes to punctuation were improvements, so while the present
edition uses the second edition as its source text, in some cases the
punctuation from the first has been preferred, such as where a dash or
semi-colon has clearly been inserted in the wrong place. The text has
been edited as lightly as possible. No attempt has been made to regu-
larize alternate spellings (e.g., honor / honour, increase / encrease), nor
to modernize common eighteenth-century spellings (e.g., choaked,
cloaths, chuses, head ach). A small number of silent emendations have
been made in order to avoid reproducing obvious errors: for example,
though Smith spells "lest" correctly sometimes in the text, it is also
sometimes written "least", and "to-night" and "to-morrow" are sometimes printed without the hyphen ("to night"). These have been corrected for this edition for the sake of clarity. Smith often writes "her's"
or "your's", which though considered incorrect today were common
at the time and have been retained; however, the misuse of "it's" for
"its" has been corrected throughout. The goal, hopefully successful,
was to produce a text as close to the original as possible and with the
flavor of an eighteenth-century text, but without reproducing unnecessary or distracting errors.

ETHELINDE,

OR THE

RECLUSE OF THE LAKE.

BY

CHARLOTTE SMITH.

IN FIVE VOLUMES.

VOL. I.

LONDON:
PRINTED FOR T. CADELL, IN THE STRAND.
M.DCC.LXXXIX.

Title page of the first edition (1789).

TO HER ROYAL HIGHNESS

THE

DUCHESS OF CUMBERLAND

MADAM,

As Dedications have been too frequently disgusting to the Patron and disgraceful to the Author, it is my Ambition, in dedicating these little Volumes to your Royal Highness, to express only the Dictates of Gratitude in the language of Respect.

My own Heart would reproach me should I fail to declare my deep Sense of that gracious Condescension with which you deigned to interest yourself in the Situation of my Children, whose opulent Relations and future Prospects prevent them not from being at present wholly dependent on their mother.

While the Motive that induced your Royal Highness to allow me the Honor of prefixing your name to this Work has evinced the Goodness of your Heart, I must confess that the Distinction so graciously conferred upon my Book has considerably encreased the Diffidence and Apprehension of its Author. It is impossible for me to present to the Public a second Novel, under Circumstances so flattering, without fearing that any little Merit it may have must appear inadequate to the Favor it has received.

I have the Honor to be,

MADAM,

Your Royal Highness's

most obliged and devoted Servant,

CHARLOTTE SMITH.

VOLUME I

CHAPTER I

On the borders of the small but beautiful lake called Grasmere
Water, in the county of Cumberland, is Grasmere Abbey, an old
seat belonging to the family of Newenden.[1] The abbey, founded by
Ranulph Earl of Chester, for forty Cistercian monks, was among
those dissolved by Henry the Eighth; by whom it was given, with
its extensive royalties, to the family of Brandon, from whence it
descended by a female to Sir Edward Newenden, its present possessor.[2]

His father, a man of boundless profusion, at his death left every
part of his property deeply mortgaged: but Sir Edward, on succeeding to it, had married the heiress of Mr. Maltravers (a gentleman who had acquired an immense fortune in the East Indies,)
and he had retrieved the fortune of his house, and disembarrassed
his estates by this opulent alliance.

Though much attached to Grasmere Abbey, which he vener-
ated as the abode of his ancestors, and loved as the scene of his
early pleasures, Sir Edward had not seen it for above four years.
Lady Newenden had never been farther from the metropolis than
to some of those places of public resort where all its conveniences
and amusements are to be enjoyed; and her Ladyship had conceived a dread of a journey into Cumberland, which Sir Edward,
to whom her slightest wish was a law, had never earnestly pressed
her to conquer: but in the summer of 1784, as his presence there
was absolutely necessary, he besought her, as a favour to accompany him thither; and as a favour, granted with the most perfect
consciousness of its value, she at length deigned to consent.

It was however almost the end of July before her Ladyship gave

1 Grasmere is a village in the center of the Lake District, until 1974 in Westmoreland, now part of the county of Cumbria. There is a lake there associated
with romantic poetry. Wordsworth lived there for fourteen years and said it
was "the loveliest spot that man hath ever found".
2 There is no record of a great abbey in this area. Ranulph, 4th Earl of Chester
(d. 1153) founded religious houses, but not Cistercian ones; he was a wealthy
landowner-politician who helped instigate wars to serve his own and family
interests.

this reluctant acquiescence; and then, as she had persuaded herself that she was to be condemned for two months to a desart, she had accepted the offer of Miss Newenden, the sister of Sir Edward, to accompany her, and she had invited her cousin Ethelinde Chesterville, and Mr. Davenant, a young man not yet of age, who was distantly related to Sir Edward and was also his ward, to be of her party.

This gentleman, who was still at Oxford, arrived from thence at the house of Sir Edward, near Windsor, the evening preceding the day on which they were to set out from thence to London, on their way to the North. About twelve the next morning therefore he handed Lady Newenden to her coach, after she had taken leave of her three beautiful children. But Sir Edward lingered behind: he kissed repeatedly each of the lovely little creatures, earnestly recommended them to the care of their attendants; and when on the point of quitting them, again returned, renewed his caresses, and repeated his entreaties that they might have every attention shewn them during the absence of their mother. Then reluctantly tearing himself from them, he proceeded with his wife and Mr. Davenant to the house of Mr. Maltravers, her father, where they dined; and in the evening arrived at their house in Hanover Square, where they were to meet Miss Newenden and Ethelinde Chesterville.

They found Miss Newenden already there. As no great affection had ever subsisted between her and Lady Newenden, they met without any warm expressions of pleasure. Their characters and manners were indeed wholly dissimilar. But though there was little friendship between them, there was less rivalry: the indolent apathy of Lady Newenden was not disturbed by the boisterous vivacity of her sister-in-law, who, occupied almost entirely by the stable or the kennel, considered her Ladyship as a pretty, insipid doll, whose mind was a mere blank, and whose person was fitted only to exhibit to advantage the feminine fineries which she herself despised—her own dress being usually such as was distinguished from that of a man only by the petticoat.

The first short compliments had no sooner passed, than Miss Newenden, addressing herself to her brother and Mr. Davenant, lamented that she had been prevented sending forward her horses the day before, as she had intended. "That devilish fellow, Jack Wildman's groom," said she, "put a confounded kicking horse into the stable with Meteor, the day before yesterday; and the dear soul, in kicking at him in his turn, has got a strain in the back sinews. I am wretched about it; for I am sure he must be fired.[1] He'll be of no use to me all the summer, and I question if I shall get him sound by next season." Sir Edward heard her with more civility than interest; but Davenant, listening more attentively to her distress, they immediately began to consult on the probable advantages of a cold charge; and it was agreed that, as soon as a celebrated farrier arrived, who was to be consulted, they would go together to the stable to inspect with him the condition of Meteor.

Their discourse was interrupted but not broken off, by the entrance of Colonel Chesterville and his daughter, neither of whom Mr. Davenant had ever seen before. Sir Edward introduced him to both. He bowed slightly to each; and then turning immediately to Miss Newenden, he continued with her a dissertation on the nature and consequences of a strain in the back sinews.

Colonel Chesterville, now near fifty, had been remarkably handsome man. Military service in various countries, and sorrows suffered in his own, had had more share than time in marking the strong lines of his sensible and manly countenance with something of peculiar dejection. His manners, though perfectly those of a man of fashion, had yet a too visible coldness towards persons for whom he felt no particular esteem; but when he conversed with those for whom his heart owned an interest, especially when he spoke to or of his daughter, all that fire and energy which had been the leading feature of his character in the younger part of his life, seemed to return. His affections were almost entirely centered in his children. His son, who had entered early into the army, and was now with his regiment at Gibraltar, had by some youthful indiscretions taught the Colonel the anxieties of a father; but Ethelinde was in his opinion the most perfect of human beings; yet those who knew her best found but little of partiality or exaggeration in the exalted opinion he entertained of her.

Few girls of her age, for Ethelinde was not yet eighteen, can be said to have any decided character at all; but the circumstances of her life had taught her to think and to feel. In her twelfth year she had lost her mother by a lingering decline, and the deep melan-

---

1 Treating an injured horse's leg by "burning, freezing, or dousing it with acid or caustic chemicals." Today considered a cruel treatment.

choly into which her surviving parent had fallen in consequence of that event, the thoughtless conduct of her brother, and the increasing anxiety which her father felt either from that or from some other cause, had obscured her natural vivacity, without diminishing her personal charms; and had given her a taste for solitude and reflection without lessening the natural sweetness of her temper. Her father's sorrows had redoubled her attachment towards him; her affection for her brother was increased rather than diminished, since his imprudence had made him unhappy. To her he had disclosed his entangled circumstances, even before he dared make them known to his father: and it was by her intercession that the Colonel had so easily pardoned him a second time, and had parted from him when he went to his regiment without any marks of displeasure.

Ethelinde however saw with great concern, that since that period her father had been more than usually unhappy; and that though he was less at home than was his general custom, he could with difficulty conceal, when they were together, the anguish that preyed on his heart.

Conscious of his own dejection, and fearing for the health and spirits of his daughter, which were evidently affected by it, he had, however unwilling to part with her, promoted her going to Grasmere Abbey with her cousin, Lady Newenden; and when she objected to it, because she was unwilling to leave him alone, he told her that he should take the opportunity of her absence to pay a visit of some months to his friend General Sandys, in the neighbourhood of Bath. Ethelinde and her father were now to part; for a few months only, but even so short a separation, at the moment it was to take place, appeared so terrible to Colonel Chesterville, that he lost all his fortitude when it arrived. He had continued a very insipid conversation with Lady Newenden till a late hour, because he had not resolution enough to bid adieu to his daughter; but finding that the longer he delayed it the more painful it became, he at length arose, and approaching her, he kissed her and bade her hastily farewell. He trembled while he spoke; and Ethelinde, who felt and shared his emotion, found her eyes fill with tears, and her hand involuntarily clasped in his, as if to detain him; while he, turning to Lady Newenden, said—"to you, Madam, and to Sir Edward, I confide almost the only good I

have on earth."—Lady Newenden curtseying, said something in
a low voice; but Sir Edward advancing, cried with mingled politeness and tenderness—"We accept the trust, my dear Colonel,
with the utmost pleasure; and we consider it as an high honor
and happiness that we are thought worthy of a charge so precious."

Ethelinde held out her hand to her father; he pressed it to his
heart; and then bowing to Miss Newenden and Mr. Davenant
(who gazed at him with an unmeaning stare), he hurried down
stairs, and left the house.

Ethelinde finding it impossible to stifle her concern, or stop
her tears, hastily left the room. She was no sooner gone than Lady
Newenden, who had thrown herself on a sopha, from which
she had arisen on the Colonel's departure, cried, in her indolent
way—"I wonder now what occasion Colonel Chesterville has to
make such a fuss about parting from Ethy, as if she was never to
come back again; it is really almost alarming to undertake the care
of a person who is made of so much consequence."

"Surely, my love," said Sir Edward, mildly, "it is very natural to
be attached to such a daughter, who is not only extremely amiable
and interesting, but is, as he told you, almost the only good he has
on earth."

"Lord, brother!" exclaimed Miss Newenden, "it is amazing to
me that you can think her so handsome. I don't know whether it
is quite civil to dispute the beauty of Lady Newenden's relation,
but really now I have wondered an hundred times what you can
possibly find in her; and I am surprised," added she, turning to
Lady Newenden, "that your Ladyship allows Sir Edward to express
these violent partialities."

"It is quite indifferent to me," answered she, with a sort of languid haughtiness. "For my own part Ethy seems to me to be just
like other misses; I see nothing extraordinary in her, either one
way or the other, though her father has always made such a racket
with her, that it is surprising she is not more pert and vain than
girls generally are. If she had been entitled to a great fortune, he
could not have lavished more expence upon her, nor could there
have been more rout about her beauty and her wit."

"Has she no fortune, then?" said Davenant, who had been
drumming on the arm of the sopha, and whistling a few bars of

an hunting song. This question, by his turning half round towards Miss Newenden, seemed to be addressed to her.

"Upon my soul I don't know. Lady Newenden, what is Miss Chesterville's fortune? Here is Tom Davenant enquiring; perhaps he is smitten, and means to make proposals."

"Indeed," said Lady Newenden, "I cannot inform him: her mother was my father's sister, and I have heard that she and Chesterville ran away together, when he was an ensign, a great many years ago. She was dead before we came to England, and I never enquired much about them."

"Colonel Chesterville," said Sir Edward, who seemed very little pleased with the conversation, "is a younger brother of a noble house. While yet very young, he married one of the sisters of my wife's father, against the wishes of his own family, and indeed of hers; for he had only an ensigncy[1] in a marching regiment: all his hopes of promotion depended on the interest of his father; and there was reason to fear that those prospects would be blasted by his marriage. His father, however, though he never was thoroughly reconciled, failed not to promote his interest in the army; and gave him at his death the same portion as he left to his other younger children: since which, some of his brothers are dead, and of their shares he participates; so that, besides his regiment, he has an handsome income. Were however his circumstances such as you, Nelly (turning to his sister), seem fond of representing them, he might still claim the respect and veneration of the world for the goodness of his heart, as well as for his long military services."

"Dear Sir Edward," cried Miss Newenden, "I don't want, I am sure, to represent him as being in bad circumstances; only you know that he has had the character of playing monstrous deep."

"I own I have heard that he plays; but I never saw any reason to believe, since I have known him, that he indulges that propensity to the prejudice of his fortune: and I know him to be so passionately fond of his children, particularly of Ethelinde, that I am persuaded he gratifies himself in nothing that is likely to be prejudicial to them."

Supper being now announced, Sir Edward sent a servant to summon Ethelinde, who instantly attended the table: her eyes were were red and swollen, and frequent sighs stole from her

---

1 An ensign was a low-ranking, low-paid commissioned officer.

bosom, but she struggled to cover the pain she felt, and would have taken some share in the conversation, had not Miss Newenden and Mr. Davenant almost entirely engrossed it, and talked on subjects quite unknown to her—such as racing and hunting. Sometimes Davenant looked for a moment at her, as if trying to discover the beauty in whose praise Sir Edward had spoken, but he otherwise noticed her very little. Miss Newenden seemed not to know that such a person was in the room, and Lady Newenden, who never spoke much, did not appear to consider herself obliged to make any unusual exertions for the entertainment of her own relation; and feeling less and less contented with her northern journey as it more nearly approached, she sat in an indolent yet somewhat sullen way, till the cloth was removed, and then retired to her own apartment.

The easy and affectionate attention which Ethelinde ever found in the behaviour of Sir Edward, made her more than amends for the indifference of the rest. He had now however some business to settle with his steward, before he went into the North, which obliged him to leave the room immediately after supper. Ethelinde soon retired to her chamber, and Miss Newenden and Mr. Davenant went together to the stable, where they remained in conference with the grooms till it was time to separate for the night.

The next morning they began their journey, during the first two days of which, nothing remarkable passed. Lady Newenden, in proportion as she left London more distant, seemed to leave her good humour also; and she failed not to express her dislike of the roads, the country, and the inns, as if to remind her husband at every stage of the greatness of the sacrifice she was making— while he endeavoured, by the most attentive and tender manners, to oblige and entertain her; and with the most patient endurance of her pettish arrogance, and childish caprice, tried to convince her that he was sensible of her condescension in undertaking the journey. But he too often found that all his endeavours served only to increase her discontent; and that the more earnestly he attempted to please her, the more difficult she became to please.

Her Ladyship, whose delicate frame and irritable nerves suffered extremely from the fatigue of travelling, usually retired to her bed as soon as they arrived at the inn where they rested for the night; Miss Newenden and Davenant then sat down to piquet; and

Sir Edward and Ethelinde were left to entertain each other with a book, or such conversation as the occurrences or remarks of the day afforded them.

CHAPTER II

A few of these conversations convinced Sir Edward that the winning manners and lovely person of Ethelinde were her least perfections. The solidity of her understanding, the gentleness of her temper, and the softness of her heart, interested, while the vivacity of her conversation entertained him; and as she every day gained on his good opinion, he could not help reflecting with some concern on her situation. He had heard, in general conversation, that Colonel Chesterville had only a very small fortune; and from some circumstances which had occurred, he feared that his son's extravagance, if not his own propensity to gaming, had considerably diminished it; and Sir Edward could not without great pain represent to himself the probability there was that this young woman, so lovely in mind and person, might be left a necessitous dependant on the family of Maltravers; while all his tenderness for Lady Newenden prevented him not from feeling that she had not that temper which was likely to soften or diminish the miseries of such dependence.

Mr. Maltravers, like most men who accumulate sudden and opulent fortunes, was wrapped up in the contemplation of his own consequence, and in the project he was ever forming to aggrandize his family by procuring an higher title for Sir Edward Newenden. Mrs. Maltravers had been a celebrated beauty; but of an obscure family, and destitute of fortune. She had therefore gone to the East Indies early in life, where those personal advantages had induced Mr. Maltravers to marry her, though he was many years older than she was. At the age of forty-two or three, she still retained much of her beauty; and, though a grandmother, was extremely unwilling to believe that she must relinquish all pretensions to admiration. This disposition did not greatly tend to enlarge her heart towards the young and beautiful: those indeed who have so great a partiality to their own perfections, being rarely found capable of doing justice to the perfection of others.

The other relations of Ethelinde were an uncle, who inherited the small paternal estate of his ancestors in the West of England; and who, retaining the rustic simplicity of an English yeoman, had brought up a numerous family to rural œconomy. Her only surviving aunt was the wife of a rich merchant at Bristol.

Of these relations, Mr. Maltravers, since his return from the East Indies, had taken little and reluctant notice; Ethelinde herself owing the preference which had been shewn her to her alliance with a noble family on the side of her father.

Colonel Chesterville's elder brother, now a peer, had married an extravagant woman of fashion. Embarrassed in his circumstances, and supporting his rank with difficulty, he had little power, and less inclination, to interest himself for the family of his brother; and his wife, having several daughters whose establishment depended entirely on their personal attractions, could not help seeing how much Ethelinde excelled them, and therefore she gave little encouragement to her to be often with them. Thus, in the midst of numerous relations on both sides, Ethelinde, amiable as she was, had few friends; and though she complained not of the little affection she found from them, Sir Edward saw that she felt and lamented it.

The gentle sensibility of her heart, thus forbidden to extend itself towards her relations, centered more warmly in her father and brother. Next to them, she had learned to love Sir Edward Newenden, from whom she always received attention, tenderness, and respect. She considered him as an elder brother; and was always happy in his company, and delighted with his praises; while, in cultivating so fine an understanding, Sir Edward found a new source of pleasure and gratification. During the journey, they read together in Italian and Spanish; in the first of which Ethelinde was a tolerable proficient, and in the latter he had been her instructor. Lady Newenden, on whose education great sums had been lavished, had learned everything, but could do nothing; nor had she the least ambition to be any thing but a very pretty woman. As long, therefore, as Ethelinde disputed not with her the palm of beauty, she was content to leave her all the praise that should be due to knowledge; and her Ladyship beheld with great apparent indifference the preference which Sir Edward sometimes too evidently gave to the society of Ethelinde.

Davenant had a mind which, resembling the imaginary qualities of the cameleon, received its predominant colour from the
object which was most immediately near it. Deficient in that
strength of intellect which gives determinate character, he was

"Every thing by turns, and nothing long."[1]

At Oxford, he drank, without loving wine; and kept hunters,
without loving violent exercise. In town, he sauntered about all
the morning, without pleasure of pursuit, and went to a gaming
table at night, though he always lost his money—an operation to
which he had a very great aversion.

He was the mere creature of the day: his dress, his expences,
his pleasures, his sentiments, being regulated by the opinion of
others, rather than by his own inclinations.

From that facility of temper, which at an early period had been
remarked in him, Sir Edward had been taught to hope that he
might be rendered a useful, if not a brilliant member of society.
But his guardian soon found, that the same easiness of disposition which would, if he had fallen into good company only, have
rendered him respectable, now laid him open to the influence of
numberless debauched and dissipated young men, who without
having more sense, had more vivacity than himself. Of these he
became the copyist; and committed folly with no other hope and
to no other end than to obtain the suffrage of fools.

His fortune however was not yet hurt; and Sir Edward, who
had seen but little of him since the preceding year (because he had
passed the last vacation in another part of England), still hoped
that, by detaching him from the society which had misled him,
and opening to him new pursuits of domestic comfort and literary
amusements, he might give new energy to his mind, and greater
rectitude to his morals. Davenant however had not been three days
with Sir Edward, before he saw the fallacy of this hope, and of that
which had for a moment led him to suppose that his ward might
become worthy of the honor of being the lover and the husband
of Ethelinde Chesterville.

1 A common misquotation from Dryden's *Absalom and Achitophel*: "Everything by starts and nothing long . . .", part 1, line 454; see Daniel Defoe, *The
English Gentleman Justified* (1701), ch. 22, p. 186.

Occupied entirely by Miss Newenden, Davenant noticed her
very little. Yet neither the person nor manners of Miss Newenden
were calculated to attract esteem or admiration: her person, without being tall, was hard and masculine; her features, though not
large, were sharp and harsh; and from being constantly exposed
to the air, her complexion had contracted an unpleasant redness,
particularly about her nose and forehead, and gave it a certain
coarseness, which, without adding to the general spirit of her face,
certainly increased the fire or rather the fierceness of her quick,
grey eyes. She had lost her mother when she was not more than
ten years old; and from that period had been left entirely to the care
of a governess, who found it more to her own interest to gratify
than to contradict her. Her father, himself a keen sportsman, was
pleased with the courage and agility she shewed on horseback,
and had been accustomed to indulge her in following the hounds,
while yet a child. Animated by the praises that were then bestowed
upon her, she had imbibed a notion that to possess a good horse
was the first point requisite to human happiness; and to be able to
ride well, the first of human perfections. Her father dying when
she was about sixteen, she became entitled to the whole of what
was at his death to descend to younger children; as she was an only
daughter, and had no brother but Sir Edward. This sum amounted
to about sixteen thousand pounds; a fortune which would probably have procured her a respectable establishment;[1] but Miss
Newenden, far from having any views of that sort, immediately
on becoming of age, furnished her stables with valuable hunters,
doubled her number of grooms, and took a small hunting seat in
Dorsetshire; where, though she sometimes prevailed on a maiden
aunt to reside with her, she oftener passed whole winters alone.
Sir Edward, who would have loved her extremely if he had met
with any affection in return, often pressed her to take up her abode
part of the year with him; but she seldom accepted his invitations,
unless for a few weeks at a time, either during an hard frost, or
some capital sale at Tattersall's.[2] As she advanced in life (and she
was now near eight-and-twenty) her passion for field sports, for the

1 Establishment here means marriage with all the upper class accompani-
ments of house, carriage, servants, and the ability to entertain expensively.
2 A club at Hyde Park Corner, founded 1766, for sporting and hunting men;
auctions for horses were held there.

stable and the kennel, increased rather than diminished. Many who knew that her fortune would be convenient to them, had, during the first years of her being mistress of her actions, addressed her with offers of marriage; but she had without hesitation dismissed them all; and though she still suffered some of them to attend on her in her favourite amusement, and shewed frequent preference to those who best understood the merits of an horse, or who displayed the most judgment in the hunt, she never thought of marrying, and soon ceased to be considered as an object of pursuit. Nothing indeed but her fortune had ever made her appear so; and the gentlemen who had with that view addressed her, were easily repulsed, and desisted, without any great pain, from addressing a young woman who had little other merit, and no other language and manners, than those of a stable boy.

The vapid and vacant mind of Davenant, ever open to momentary impressions, was amused with her singularity, and he fancied himself instructed by her skill in horse flesh. To keep up a conversation with Sir Edward, demanded more knowledge than he had acquired, and more attention than he was willing to exert: from him therefore he generally tried to escape. Yet in despite of that imbecillity of mind, which ever required that he should be told what he was to like or dislike, he was often struck with the animated beauty of Ethelinde; and as she conversed with Sir Edward by the table where he was at cards with Miss Newenden, he insensibly neglected his game while he gazed at her. But from these short fits of absence he was generally recalled by Miss Newenden, with "Come, Tom! what the devil are you thinking of? If you cannot attend, I'll play no more." Startled by this reproof, Davenant again attended to his cards, and seemed to have forgotten the object that had thus momentarily drawn his attention from them.

As they travelled very slowly, lest Lady Newenden should be too much fatigued, it was not till the afternoon of the sixth day after quitting London that they arrived within a few miles of Grasmere Abbey. As soon as the tall blue heads of the fells were very distinctly seen, Sir Edward, who was then in the coach with Lady Newenden, his sister, and Ethelinde, expressed forcibly the pleasure he felt in seeing them. "They are," said he, delighted at the view, "as the sight of old friends; and bring back to my mind the pleasant days I used to pass when, at the holidays, I went down to

Grasmere Abbey with my father. On that towering hill to the left, which at this distance seems an immense pile of purple rock, the first grouse fell by my gun. I was not more than ten years old; and the delight with which I saw Humphrey, my old servant, put it in the net, the triumph with which I shewed it, on my return to my father, I shall never forget. Look, my love," continued he, "at the wild grandeur of that varied and bold outline; observe the effect of the sun's rays on the summits of the craggs, while the large and swelling clouds that pass over seem almost to touch them and give them numberless shades in their progress."

"I see but little beauty in those dreary looking mountains," answered Lady Newenden; with a cold and disdainful smile. "Perhaps you had better apply to Ethelinde. You may teach *her*, as she is a young lady of *sublime taste* you know, to admire what I, who am a creature without any, really want faculties to enjoy."

There was something in this speech more disobliging than usual; but Sir Edward, turning to Ethelinde, said, with assumed gaiety, "Well then, my fair cousin, I must have *you* for my pupil; and you must learn to admire my country, for admired it must positively be. And you, Ellen," addressing himself to his sister, "have you acquired, by absence and refinement, a dislike to the scenes where you passed your early life? and do you prefer the flat uninteresting country round London?"

"No," answered she, "not exactly the country round London; but I like many countries[1] better than I do this, to be sure. Great part of Dorsetshire, for example, and Hampshire; where one may gallop upon turf for ten or twelve miles an end, without check or leap. This is well enough for the eye; but I own, for myself, I cannot think it very desirable otherwise."

Sir Edward, smiling at an objection so strongly in character, then dropped the conversation, and soon after got on horseback. Miss Newenden, however, who sometimes rode with him, now remained in the coach; where, as they advanced among the fells,[2] a deeper gloom fell on the countenance of Lady Newenden; Miss Newenden took out of the coach pocket the Sporting Calendar, where she was endeavouring to trace the pedigree of an horse,

1 18th-century people referred to counties as countries.
2 A fell is a hill or stretch of mountainous moorland, especially in the North of England.

about which she held an argument with Davenant the evening before; and, as neither of them spoke to Ethelinde, she contemplated without interruption the novelty and grandeur of the scenery around her.

She had been much accustomed to travel with her father; who, having himself an elegant and enlightened understanding, had improved that turn for observation which genius had given to the mind of his daughter; and she had learned to see the face of nature with the taste of a painter, and the enthusiasm of a poet; while to Lady Newenden all was a blank, which offered nothing to gratify either her personal vanity, or the consequence she assumed from her splendid fortune.

Their road became now more slow by the necessary of winding among the hills; and every mile presented some new beauty, affording to Ethelinde the purest and most exquisite delight. At length they came within view of Grasmere Water, and passing between two enormous fells—one of which descended, clothed with wood, almost perpendicularly to the lake; while the other hung over it, in bold masses of staring rock—they turned round a sharp point formed by the root of the latter, and entering a lawn, the abbey, embosomed among the hills, and half concealed by old elms which seemed coeval with the building, appeared with its gothic windows, and long pointed roof of a pale grey stone, bearing every where the marks of great antiquity. The great projecting buttresses were covered with old fruit trees, which from their knotted trunks seemed to have been planted by the first inhabitants of the mansion. In some of the windows the heavy stone work still remained, and they were totally darkened at the top by stained glass; in others, sashes had been substituted and the windows had been contracted by brick work to make them appear square within; but, even in these, the stained glass had been replaced, which generally represented the arms of Newenden surcharged with those of Brandon.

When the coach stopped, Sir Edward appeared at the door of it; and, taking the hand of Lady Newenden, he led her into an hall, saluted her tenderly, and bade her welcome to Grasmere Abbey.

Instead, however, of attempting to gratify him by expressing any pleasure at that which evidently gave him so much, she turned abruptly away and exclaimed—"Don't keep me, Sir Edward, in this great, cold place; it strikes as damp as a family vault. I hope you have ordered fires. I assure you that my departure will be a much fitter subject of congratulation than my arrival."

Sir Edward, a good deal hurt, led her without speaking into a long and old-fashioned, but well-furnished parlour, where he left her, and returned towards Ethelinde and his sister. He met Ethelinde in the hall; but Miss Newenden was gone with Davenant to the stables to chuse which she would have for her own horses.

A settee of rich cut velvet, with massy gilt feet, was in the room; which seemed to have in its time supported many of the venerable figures, and fair but faded forms, which were represented in the great portraits that covered the wainscot. On this settee or sopha Lady Newenden sat down; and, wrapping her cloak round her, complained of the excessive coldness of the house. By this time an old house-keeper, who had lived many years in the family, appeared, and in the broad dialect of the northern country, enquired—"Wat my lady wad please to have aufter her journey?"

"Have!" exclaimed her Ladyship, with evident marks of disgust; "why I would have a little warmth, good woman, if it is possible in these rooms. Do make a fire instantly; and if my own people are come, send Powell to me."

"Your servants," said Sir Edward, "are yet at some distance, one of the post horses of the chaise lost a shoe about two miles from hence, which has detained them. Dickenson however will execute any orders you may have to give her."

"She can do nothing for *me*," sullenly replied his wife. "I should be glad indeed to have my own bed made up; but I must wait, I see, till Powell comes."

Mrs. Dickenson, who had long served the mother of Sir Edward, one of the best tempered and mildest of women, began to find herself extremely hurt at the haughtiness of her new lady; and spreading out her clean white cloth apron, she with a sort of half curtsey approached nearer, saying—"Indeed, my Lady, I shud ha ben glad to ha known as your Ladyshep weshed for to have fires, and then sure they shud ha ben leeted all aboot the hoose, bot my leet lady she niver hud fires tull aboot the eend of Siptimber ur begennen of Ooctoober, an I cud na knaw your Ladyshep wud leek of um, for my leet lady she—"

"Tell me not of thy late lady, Mrs. Nicholson," said Lady Newenden, wilfully mistaking the name; "but since I am condemned to remain in this comfortless and dreary place, do prithee bestir thyself, to save me if possible from dying of an ague."

"Go, Dickenson," said Sir Edward, "and send in the housemaid to make a fire here; while you yourself see that others are made immediately in Lady Newenden's dressing and bed rooms."

The housekeeper immediately obeyed. Sir Edward, more vexed with his wife than he desired to appear, walked about the room in silence; and Ethelinde, depressed by the ill humour of her cousin, and concerned at the effect it had on Sir Edward, seated herself in the window, and looking at the surrounding hills, recollected how very far she now was from her father; and in that recollection felt deserted and forlorn.

By this time Miss Newenden joined them, and being better satisfied with the stable than her sister was with the house, she came gaily into the room with Davenant, who enquired of Lady Newenden how she found herself?

"More than half dead, I assure you, Davenant," said she, with her usual languor; "and all that amazes me is, how any creature can take such a journey as this for pleasure."

"I am very sorry, Lady Newenden," said Sir Edward, unable any longer to conceal his chagrin, "that *you* have undertaken it at all."

"Indeed, Sir Edward, so am I," answered she.

"I can't imagine why," cried Miss Newenden, with quickness, "for I am sure you are no worse for it."

"Not the worse, Ma'am? why I am shaken to death, dislocated in all my joints, and after having been martyred the whole way with jolting in extreme heat, I come into this cold damp, desolate place, which really is fit only for the nuns and friars that you told me, I think, used to inhabit it."

"Its inhabitants since that, Madam," said her sister-in-law with increased tartness, "were persons, of whom I may venture to say, that few of our present nobility are so *well*, certainly none *better* born. They were of a family with which at least *mere modern opulence* may be proud to boast its alliance."

"Dear Miss Newenden," answered her Ladyship contemptuously, "nobody disputes it; I only wish that the last and present possessors of the place had been contented to remain as quiet here as the owners did who lived at it two or three hundred years ago;

then I suppose they would not have spent so much money as has obliged them to have recourse to *modern opulence* to prevent these dreary rooms from being made into barns or granaries, or tumbling quite down."

"My dear cousin!" exclaimed Ethelinde, unable to repress her astonishment at this speech.

Sir Edward, finding that all his tenderness for Lady Newenden could not check the anger which this proud and contemptuous spirit provoked, now hastily left the room. Davenant, always an indifferent spectator of scenes where no kind of dissipation bore a part, strolled into the garden; but Miss Newenden, whose family pride (the only pride she had) was now roused, returned to the charge.

"Most women, let me assure your Ladyship, whatever may be their fortune, would think themselves too happy to share it with such a man as *my* brother."

"Not *too* happy surely," with a malicious smile, answered Lady Newenden, "if part of their lives was to wear away in banishment in the nunnery of Grasmere."

"But let me inform you, Lady Newenden————"

"Not to-night, dear Ma'am—do not inform me to-night; for I am really fatigued to death, and cannot keep myself awake to hear any more about your ancestors. Doubtless they were all knights and esquires of high degree; only I wish their old fashioned nunnery had fallen into the lake before I had been dragged a thousand miles to catch my death in it."

At this moment her woman, Mrs. Powell, and her Indian servant, entered the room.

"Ah! Powell," exclaimed she, "it is comfortable to see you. Get my drops[1] and my chocolate. I shall go instantly to bed. Why, what a while you have been coming!"

"Good Heaven! my dear Lady," drawled out her attendant, "I thof that to have got here at all was a thing impossible. Gracious me! I thof of all things we should have been killed by one of them there great large *ills*, and then squish squash through such a deal of water! I am sure your Ladyship must be quite tired out of your life."

[1] Drops: medicinal, probably containing an opium tincture, said to relieve pain; she is probably taking them to calm her irritation and promote sleep.

"Tired indeed! I hope every thing is ready for me?"

"Oh yes! I got every thing ready as soon as I came in for your Ladyship."

"Help me then," cried she, with redoubled languor, "help me to my bed. Good night, Ethy. Your humble servant, Miss Newenden. I congratulate you both on being so very robust, that even the fatigue of *such* a journey does not disable you from taking a pleasant rural walk, or an evening ride perhaps, over those sweet hills, to see prospects. You cannot fail of entertainment; so I shall make no apology for leaving you."

She then, leaning on her two attendants, left the room.

CHAPTER III

Miss Newenden, who, with some asperity of temper, had much of the pride of ancestry about her, now expressed to Ethelinde in very bitter terms the displeasure she had conceived against her sister-in-law for her ill breeding and haughtiness.

Ethelinde attempted to soften her, by reminding her that something should be allowed to health generally very delicate, and to present fatigue. "My cousin," said she, "has never been contradicted in what she desired to do, or desired to do anything to which she expressed the least dislike. Even Sir Edward, till this journey became necessary, has never requested anything of her but what he knew to be her own inclination."

"Hang such whimsical nonsense!" exclaimed Miss Newenden; "it puts me past all patience. My brother is a fool to give way to it as he does; for the more he humours her ridiculous affectation, the more insupportably tiresome she becomes. Oh! if I was a man and plagued with a whining conceited, capricious wife, I would run away to the end of the world to avoid her."

"You mean ride away," said Ethelinde, smiling.

"Yes, that I would indeed," answered Miss Newenden, taking good-humouredly this little joke at her own hobby horse. "I wish Ned had any spirit; I am sure I could put him in a way to cure her Ladyship of these insolent airs." Then seeing Davenant looking at her brother's brood mares, which were grazing in the park, she ran away to join him; and Ethelinde wandered out towards the plantation which fringed the feet of the hills that surrounded it. She was no sooner alone, than losing the impression of the unpleasing conversation she had heard, she gave way to the solemn but melancholy species of pleasure inspired by the scene around her. It was now evening: the last rays of the sun gave a dull purple hue to the points of the fells which rose above the water and the park; while the rest, all in deep shadow, looked gloomily sublime. Just above the tallest, which was rendered yet more dark by the wood that covered its side, the evening star arose; and was reflected on the bosom of the lake, now perfectly still and unruffled. Not a breeze sighed among the hills; and nothing was heard but the low murmur of two or three distant waterfalls, and at intervals the short soft notes of the woodlark, the only bird that sings at this season in an evening (it was the middle of August). Ethelinde having traversed a considerable part of the plantation, principally among tall firs, planted by the grandfather of Sir Edward, now stopped to observe the river, which flows from the lake in a deep and smooth current, and keeping its way under the foot of an enormous mass of rock, suddenly crosses the park, and takes its course near the abbey, where it once filled what is now a fosse of turf, but was formerly a moat; from which being diverted, it wanders away through green inclosures, till other hills conceal its further progress.

A rude stone bridge crosses the stream, and Ethelinde, leaning over the wall, looked pensively at the water, and listened to the rippling current, which was in unison with other soothing and agreeable sounds, while by this time innumerable stars were reflected on the lake.

> Qui, se spiega la notte il fosco velo
> Nel mare emulo al Cielo
> Piu lucide, piu belle
> Moltiplicar le stelle.
>
> METASTASIO.[1]

While she remained here, Sir Edward, who to dissipate his vex-

1 Pietro Antonio Domenico Traspassi, known as Metastasio (1698-1782), Italian poet and popular writer of *opera seria* libretti; from the tenth cantata of *La Pesca* (*The Peach*): "Here night is displayed over a gloomy body of water, which mirrors the brilliant sky, and multiplies the stars" (my translation).

ation had rambled round his plantations, overtook her. "Whither wanders my lovely cousin," said he, in the pleasant accents of affection, and taking her arm within his: "and why stays she out thus late?"—"I have not the least inclination to return to the house," replied Ethelinde; "the evening is uncommonly mild, and I have been admiring the beauty of the lake, and of those old rocks which form its bason. How calm, how beautiful is its surface, spangled with stars, and deeply contrasted by those dark tufts of evergreens which crowd over it!"

"Those trees," said Sir Edward, "were planted by my father when I was a boy. You like the scenery then, Ethelinde, and see nothing so terrible in passing a few weeks at Grasmere Abbey?" He sighed, and, as if waiting for Ethelinde's reply, was silent a moment: then making an effort to conquer the pain which the recollection of Lady Newenden's different taste impressed, he added, "Where did you leave Lady Newenden?"

"Her Ladyship retired to her own room with her servants before I came out to walk, and Miss Newenden went with Mr. Davenant to look at some of your horses."

"It is well," said Sir Edward, still trying to shake off his concern, "that Nelly has found in Davenant a companion who can participate in her pleasures, and it is not less lucky for me, that Davenant's happy facility of temper, ever falling into the whim of those he is with, serves to keep *her* at least in good humour."—Unable to help adverting thus to the petulance of his wife, he yet tried to drive it from him by other topics. "How do you like Davenant?" continued he.

Ethelinde, who had thought very little of him, and without any degree of good opinion, answered with some hesitation, "Very well."

"He has," said Sir Edward, "great good nature, and is not without understanding."

"Not absolutely without."

Sir Edward, smiling at the archness with which she delivered these words, said, "But you think that he has not much?"

"Certainly, Sir Edward, you must be a far better judge than I am; and as I always wish to discover the good qualities of those I am with, I wish you to point out those of Mr. Davenant."

"You are satirical, Ethelinde."

"I hope not, but own I have observed some features in his character that by no means impress me with a favorable idea of his heart or his understanding."

"You surprise me! What have you observed?"

"First, that though he knows not what in the world to do with his time, and is ever in an evident dearth of ideas, he never takes up a book or enters with any kind of interest into the most instructive conversation."

"Allowed. But what have you to say of his heart?"

"I have only to say of it that it seems to me deficient in feeling, in generosity, in tenderness. He acknowledges that he has a widowed aunt, his mother's sister, old, indigent, and deprived by death of her children, whom he has never noticed since he became old enough to assist her. And did I not observe that, when at the inn at Boroughbridge, your acquaintance in that town introduced to your pity a poor woman with five infant children, whom an horrid accident had robbed of their laborious father, Davenant, far from attending to her distress, went to the window, and looked out of it till she was about to withdraw, as if to avoid the necessity of taking out his purse. And when you reminded him of it, and desired him to give the little boy a guinea, he gave it indeed, but not like one who loves to give. Ah, Sir Edward! If a man so young; a man abounding in money, which all his superfluous expences hardly diminishes, is thus deaf to the voice of misery, and wants to be reminded of the assistance he owes his fellow creatures, what shall he be, when time, which blunts even the keenest sensibilities, shall have rendered him yet more insensible and unfeeling of every thing but the gratification of his own narrow and selfish tastes?"

"Indeed," said Sir Edward, "I did not know what a severe observer you are, Ethy, or I should have taken care of myself."

"Ah, no, Sir Edward! the less your actions are guarded, the more you must be beloved: they arise from the noblest impulses of the soul. Believe me, an heart like yours cannot be too much seen, and seen as it really is."

This artless but warm praise gave to Sir Edward a sensation of delight more exquisite than he had ever before felt. His voice trembled as he attempted laughingly to answer what he termed an extravagant compliment: then, as they walked towards the house together, he became quite silent. On entering the eating parlour, they found Miss Newenden and Davenant waiting supper: during which repast Sir Edward continued pensive, answering he knew not what to the questions Miss Newenden asked him about the horses she had seen; and as soon as the cloth was removed, they all separated.

Ethelinde, with a bosom unruffled by any uneasy passion, soon tasted the calm slumber of the innocent. But Sir Edward carried to his pillow thoughts and reflections that suffered him not to sleep. He had for many days learned, that, should he lose the conversation of Ethelinde, he should be deprived of that which in the absence of his children was the greatest pleasure of his life. But he had to-day caught himself making involuntary comparisons between her and his wife; and felt all the ill-humour and pride of the latter aggravated, while the sweetness, the spirit, the sense of Ethelinde proportionably rose in his mind. Then blaming himself for indulging an idea to the disadvantage of his wife—of the mother of his children, he fancied that he must himself have been in the wrong, and had not sufficiently allowed for the fatigue of body and mind Lady Newenden had suffered, nor for the little capricious humours to which the best women are subject; and he determined to think of it no more. With equal sincerity did he resolve to think less of Ethelinde; but as that was very difficult to accomplish, he persuaded himself that he thought of her only as a fond brother thinks of an amiable and beloved sister.

Every day, however, of the first three or four they passed at Grasmere Abbey, brought with it some new instance of Lady Newenden's uneasy and perverse spirit; and driven from her by haughty reserve, or petulant retort, he was compelled to resort for consolation to the mild and reasonable conversation of Ethelinde. An hour's reading with her, a walk with her, or some little poem repeated by memory as they rambled together on the banks of the lake, restored to his wounded spirit its wonted composure, yet instilled into his heart a slow and secret poison, which he detected not till it was no longer in his power to expel it.

Ethelinde, perfectly unconscious of the effect of that tender and innocent familiarity in which she lived with him, thought only how to soothe and amuse him in the many hours which they passed almost entirely alone. Lady Newenden, because she knew that it mortified Sir Edward, frequently dined in her own apartment, under pretence that the lower part of the house gave her cold; while he was continually harassed by the complaints and murmurs of her London servants, who regretted the luxuries they had left behind them, and hoped by their own discontent to irritate that of their lady. The women quarrelled with the old housekeeper, and saw ghosts in every passage of the abbey; the men bewildered the steward by their London assurance, and distracted him by their extravagance. Every appeal was made to my Lady; and every attempt of Sir Edward to check their impertinence was sure to be resented by her Ladyship, and to be followed by reproaches, complainings, tears, and fits. Miss Newenden, never without resource in fine weather, amused herself tolerably well by riding out, and renewing her acquaintance with those families within ten miles of the abbey whom she had formerly known. At one of those visits she met a party of six of her London friends, who had come down on a tour of pleasure to visit the lakes. She eagerly invited them to Grasmere Abbey: they accepted the proposal, and two days afterwards arrived; fortunately for Sir Edward, who, though his business was by no means finished, would not on other terms have been able to have detained Lady Newenden another week.

The acquisition of such a party restored to her Ladyship some degree of good humour. She again heard the soothing voice of adulation, and again felt the consequence given her by fortune. Cards were introduced of an evening, and *ennui*[1] was for the present forgotten.

Ethelinde too felt greatly relieved by their arrival; for she was now no longer expected to listen to Lady Newenden's complaints, to bear her ill humour, or to labour in the vain attempt of amusing her. Happy to be thus restored to some degree of liberty, she took immediate advantage of it; and the first day, as soon as dinner was over, and the ladies withdrawn, she went out unperceived, and taking with her that volume of the works of Gray, in which he, with the clearest simplicity, describes this small lake, she pursued her way, now over "eminences covered with turf, now among

1 Ennui, *ennuyé*: dissatisfaction arising from boredom. The connotations of the French word (annoyed, weary) are here intended to characterize Maria Newenden as a self-indulgent woman longing to be in "the world" (*le monde*).

broken rock," till she reached the village which stands on a low promontory projecting far into the lake.[1]

In this hamlet, the abode of cheerful labour and contented poverty, she observed one house distinguished from the rest by a small sash window at the end of it, looking into a little court and garden, surrounded with a quick hedge, and filled with flowers. The whole cottage, for it was still merely a cottage, had about it a look of neatness and comfort, which convinced Ethelinde it belonged to a labourer: but nobody appeared about it; and as dark clouds, gathering on the tops of the hills, and a ruffling wind arising, made her apprehend a storm, she returned immediately by the path she came. Having however passed much more time than she was aware of, and the sky being extremely overcast with dark red clouds, which scowling over the lake, gave to that and the surrounding rocks a peculiar gloom, she was afraid of being entirely benighted, and quickened her pace as much as possible. But the increasing obscurity, and the unevenness of the way, made her progress slow; and she had yet a quarter of a mile to the abbey, when a scattering shower was followed by several loud claps of thunder, which, echoing among the fells, were returned again and again in repeated vibrations. Ethelinde, not without some degree of fear, walked on, keeping on her hat with difficulty; when her eyes, which were fixed on the ground, that she might discern her way, were quickly raised by the sudden appearance of a tall young man with a fishing net on his shoulder, and a boat hook in his hand, who, coming from the water, met her in a path so narrow that they both stopped. The stranger, who though in a dress calculated for the amusement he had been pursuing, had the air and look of a gentleman, seemed extremely surprised at meeting a young person of Ethelinde's appearance at such an hour, and in such a place; yet immediately recollecting that she must come from Grasmere Abbey, and seeing that she stepped on fearfully, while the storm continued to increase, he followed her a moment after he had passed her, and said—"You will not I hope think it imperti-

1 The poems and *Journal in the Lakes* of Thomas Gray (1716-71) include descriptions of Grasmere; see "To Grasmere," 8th October 1769, "The bosom of the mountains spreading here into a broad bason [sic] discovers in the midst Grasmere-water, its margin is hollowed into small bays with bold eminences: some of them rocks, some of soft turf that half conceal and vary the figure of the little lake they command."

nent, Madam, if I enquire whether I can be of any use to you? The storm is likely to be violent. Will you allow me to wait on you to the abbey? I fear you find it very difficult walking."

Ethelinde, who had been a good deal alarmed at his turning to follow her, was convinced the moment he spoke that he was a gentleman; and answered without hesitation, though in a voice that yet trembled with fear, "that she was much obliged to him; but that, as she was very near the abbey, she could not think of giving him the trouble of going out of his way in such a night."

"My way," answered he, "is any in which I can be of the least service to you; I beg you will allow me at least to see you safe to the gate."

At this moment a tremendous burst of thunder made the rocks tremble to their base; Ethelinde started, and almost fell, from the suddenness and violence of the shock.

"I must hope," said the stranger, perceiving her terror, "that you will take my arm, without being deterred by the dirt of my dress, in which indeed I have been fishing since morning."

Ethelinde, who was almost unable to walk, now accepted his offer; and with his assistance soon reached the gate of the lawn; where the moment they arrived Sir Edward and a servant appeared, though it was by this time so nearly dark that Ethelinde only knew it was the former by his calling aloud the moment he perceived somebody approach—"Is that Miss Chesterville? Is it Ethelinde?"

"It is, Sir Edward," answered she, as she held out her hand to him.

"Where have you been?" cried he, with great agitation. "I have been—we have been extremely terrified on your account."

"I merely walked farther than I intended, and was overtaken by the thunder before I could get back. This gentleman has been so obliging as to take care of me part of the way."

"I thank him," said Sir Edward, with some degree of reserve. "Sir, will you do me the honour to walk into the house?"

"I am obliged to you, Sir," replied the stranger; "but it is late, and I live at some distance."

Then without waiting for farther invitation, seeing Ethelinde safe, he disappeared in a moment.

As the wind continued extremely high, and the thunder yet

muttered among the hills, Sir Edward, with his arm round her waist, hurried Ethelinde into the house as quick as possible. When they got thither, he enquired if she was much terrified, or if her clothes were wet. The rain however had been slight, and her terror was almost subsided; declining therefore any assistance, she went immediately into the room, where they were all at cards, and where she found that the party had been that evening still farther augmented by the arrival of Lord Danesforte, a nobleman who, having been on a visit in Scotland, had heard that Sir Edward and Lady Newenden were at the abbey, and had unexpectedly paid them a visit.

The curiosity of Lord Danesforte had been strongly excited to know who Miss Chesterville was, about whom Sir Edward had been the whole evening so restless that he had with visible constraint acquitted himself of the honours of his house; and after sending four or five servants different ways, he had at length left his company, and gone out himself in search of her.

This Ethelinde, the object of so much anxiety, now appeared before him in a blaze of beauty which turned his Lordship's curiosity into admiration. Her complexion, which was frequently too pale, was raised to a deep blush. Her fear had given way to pleasure at the kindness and attention of Sir Edward, and her whole countenance was animated by good humour; while the disorder of her hat, and her dark auburne hair, set off her face to more advantage than could have been done by the exactest arrangement or most studied ornament.

Sir Edward led her towards the table where Lady Newenden and Lord Daneforte were at cards, saying—"Help me, Maria, to quarrel with your cousin, and prevent her in future from rambling about of an evening, to the alarm of all her friends."

"Settle it with her yourself, Sir Edward," answered her Ladyship, coldly. "I never take upon me to argue with romantic young ladies on the peculiarity of their taste."

Ethelinde, accustomed to these sort of repulsive speeches from her cousin, now went towards the next table; while Lord Danesforte, who followed her with his eyes, said to Lady Newenden—

"Miss Chesterville is then your Ladyship's cousin?"

"Yes, my Lord."

"I should have guessed so. She possesses a portion of the family beauty, so very conspicuous in Lady Newenden."

"Do you think so?" replied she, with a forced smile; "I really cannot think there is much resemblance. Not that I disclaim it on account of any compliment it conveys, for in my mind Ethelinde is any thing but handsome."

Lord Danesforte, finding that to praise one lady was to offend the other, turned the discourse by some delicate and well-pointed compliment; but however he affected by words to give the preference to her Ladyship, his looks were again in quest of Ethelinde, who had sat down alone in a corner of the room. Sir Edward, disengaging himself from cards as quickly as he could, soon after joined her, and talked to her till supper was announced. He enquired who the person was who had taken care of her home? Ethelinde related simply how and where she had met him; while Sir Edward, gently chiding her for venturing so far as the village alone, made her promise that she would never again alarm him by the same kind of indiscretion.

During supper the discourse took a turn in which Ethelinde could bear very little part. Lord Danesforte had no opportunity of knowing whether her conversation and understanding answered to the spirit and intelligence which flashed from her eyes: his Lordship, seated near Lady Newenden, had not even an opportunity of addressing himself to her, who was next to Sir Edward, at the bottom of the table. But as the latter frequently spoke to her, he saw a variety of expression in her face, which increased his inclination to be more acquainted with her. He could not but observe the marked attention of Sir Edward; which, in addition to the extraordinary anxiety he had shewn while he believed her exposed to the thunder storm, put some notions into the head of Lord Danesforte not very favourable to that uniform and tender attachment which Sir Edward had always professed and supported towards his wife. As his Lordship was upon the turf,[1] and had several horses with him, hunters and poneys, with which Miss Newenden was well acquainted, the conversation during supper ran principally on their various merits; and a match was made at her desire between him and Mr. Davenant, who were each to ride their own horses in the park the next day; and on the day following a party on the lake

1 i.e., he races horses frequently.

was proposed, which Lady Newenden consented to join, at the earnest entreaty of Lord Danesforte; but she declared that if the day was not perfectly warm, and the water perfectly calm, nothing should induce her to venture.

CHAPTER IV

Lord Danesforte inherited from his ancestors an immense fortune; and was one of those who seem, by the consent of their cotemporaries, to be the acknowledged leaders of fashion, and arbiters of taste. His houses, his equipages, his horses, his mistresses, his dinners, were the theme of the day; and had for some years made a conspicuous figure in those fleeting annals, which give, in the eyes of trifling imbecility, a temporary consequence to dissipation and vice. He had received from nature a good understanding, and an handsome person; but he sacrificed the former in becoming the slave of opinion; and his intemperance had at the age of seven-and-twenty robbed his person of all the lightness, grace, and activity of youth, while his constitution was proportionably impaired. He plunged early into every species of debauchery, to shew his spirit; and it was now become an invincible habit. But that facility of gratification which his great fortune gave him, made even his pleasures satiate and disgust him; and amid the luxuries with which he was surrounded, some new pursuit, some project which might pique and animate by the difficulty of success, was ever become necessary to his existence. When he had no such scheme before him, he hurried from place to place, weary of himself, and was now very slightly gratified by that species of fame, which his morals, his health, and much of his fortune, had been sacrificed to obtain.

Sir Edward Newenden, whose temper, morals and conduct were exactly the reverse of his Lordship's, had first known him at Eton, where the difference of their characters and ages (for Lord Danesforte was four years his junior) had prevented any intimacy between them. They met afterwards abroad, where their acquaintance was renewed; and they had since occasionally visited, but without any particular friendship. The present visit of Lord Danesforte was paid rather because he knew not what else to do with

himself, than from any regard for his hosts, and it was received by
Sir Edward with more politeness than pleasure.

Lord Danesforte however found more attraction at the abbey
than he expected, and determined to remain there for some days.
Davenant, fitted by his vanity for a pupil, and by his ignorance
for a dupe; Lady Newenden, lovely in her person, and vain in her
disposition, with a mind open to the insinuations of flattery, and
an heart insensible to every thing but the impression received
through that medium; were subjects, fitted at once to entertain
him at present, and promise him those pursuits in future in which
he most delighted to engage. Flattered as he was by the silly imitation of weak and unexperienced young men; and eager after that
sort of fashion which arises from supposed intrigue.

His Lordship however no sooner saw Ethelinde than every
other motive was forgotten which had on his first arrival recommended Grasmere Abbey. Youth, beauty, spirit, sweetness, understanding; every charm which could attract admiration, he found
in her; but marriage was no part of his scheme of life: and as soon
as he knew who she was, he knew also that she was too well protected by her father, her brother, and Sir Edward, to give him
much chance of getting her into his power. But the difficulty of
carrying any favourite point was never an inducement with him
to relinquish it; and he was seldom so happy as when engaged in
some project which occupied those talents that were given him for
very different and more worthy purposes.

Notwithstanding the attention he was obliged to pay to Lady
Newenden, he found several opportunities of conversing with
Ethelinde, and was convinced that her understanding was at least
equal to her personal charms: the pensive softness which at first
appeared the leading feature in her character, frequently yielded
to the most animated vivacity; and her manners and conversation soon made indelible the impression which had been received
from her captivating form. In making these observations, it was
impossible to help remarking that Sir Edward Newenden had
made them before: Lord Danesforte indeed immediately saw that
he was much more strongly attached to her than their alliance by
his marriage with her cousin authorised; and he fancied that Ethelinde knew and was not insensible of his partiality. A mind like his
was incapable of feeling the variety and innocence of those affec-

tions towards an amiable man, which might have place in a bosom so ingenuous and untainted as hers. Esteem for his character, gratitude for his kindness, and the tenderness of a sister for his person, were blended in her heart, and she loved and preferred him to all other men (after her father and her brother), with the same purity as an angel might have loved him. Far from attempting to conceal this affection, she spoke of him on all occasions as the first of men; delighted in calling him her dear friend, and in repeating how well and how fortunately her cousin had chosen, when she rejected higher titles and more splendid fortunes for happiness and Sir Edward Newenden.

Alas! of this happiness her cousin was entirely insensible. Her ample fortune had drawn around her a number of lovers, among whom were three noblemen, whose rank was their only recommendation: at the same time Sir Edward Newenden being obliged to sell two of his estates immediately on the death of his father, entered into treaty with Mr. Maltravers, who was then making considerable purchases in the neighbourhood; and by that means was introduced to his daughter, then about seventeen. However embarrassed his father had left him, he had determined never to attempt retrieving his affairs by a marriage made merely with that view; but when he saw in Miss Maltravers a person and a face which would have attracted his notice, had their possessor been destitute of fortune, he could not help reflecting on the great advantage which would arise from a union where his interest and his taste would at once be consulted. With diffidence however he made his proposals, apprehending that the disarranged state of his fortune would be an insurmountable objection; but Miss Maltravers, who thought him infinitely the handsomest man she had ever seen, accepted him without hesitation: and her father, who had no will but hers, immediately complied; gratified perhaps with the power of restoring an ancient family to its original splendour; and more flattered by the prospect of raising the rank of him to whom he married his daughter, by the power and influence his fortune gave him, than by uniting her with a man already of a superior rank. Mrs. Maltravers, glad to have her daughter disposed of, that she might herself be under less restraint, acquiesced willingly; and after a very short courtship Sir Edward carried off the opulent heiress from his numerous rivals.

Lady Newenden entering on a world of which till then she had seen very little, found herself every where the object of admiration and envy. Her vanity alone was more powerful than the habitual indolence of her temper; and the only thing which did not fatigue her, was flattery. Dissipation soon became necessary to her vacant mind, and estranged her from that domestic style of life in which only Sir Edward was happy. He saw with pain that even his children failed of detaching her from those frivolous pursuits which were to him not only uninteresting, but disagreeable, yet he continued to gratify her in every wish she formed; and though he was himself unhappy, relinquished his own satisfaction to her content. This painful sacrifice she considered as no more than what she had a right to exact; and Sir Edward, who really loved her, forbore to complain even to her father, though compelled to pass every winter in London in a perpetual hurry of engagements, and the summer at some of the various places of public resort, instead of being suffered to enjoy the company of his children at one of his own houses. His love however was long proof against these differences of taste; the children, of whom he was passionately fond, endeared their mother to him; and though his plan of happiness was destroyed, his tenderness had survived almost undiminished, till the observations he was forced to make during this journey, when repeated malignity towards Ethelinde, and attempts to inflict pain on himself, had shewn such a general deficiency in those feelings which only can secure either love or esteem, as obliged him internally to acknowledge, though still reluctantly he acknowledged it, that his Maria had no heart.

Conscious of this decrease of his affection, and, almost fearing to ask himself whether the attractions of another object had not too much contributed to it, while every principle of honour reproached him for indulging the partiality he felt, he determined not only to attempt conquering his fondness for the company of Ethelinde, but most carefully to avoid every occasion of shewing it had ever existed. He had been so much off his guard on the evening when he apprehended she was exposed to the thunder storm, that Lady Newenden had remarked it with some asperity, and he now wished to appear as indifferent about her as about the most uninteresting person of the party; but he succeeded so ill, at least before the penetrating eyes of Lord Danesforte, that his Lordship was only amazed Lady Newenden noticed it so little. The trembling sensibility with which he heard her praises; the expression of his eyes whenever they were turned towards Ethelinde; all testified how deep and tender an interest he felt in whatever related to her.

The gaiety, the assiduity and adulation of Lord Danesforte, had not only restored Lady Newenden to her good humour, but engaged her to enter into the amusements which the neighbourhood of Grasmere Abbey afforded; and the party made for going in boats on the lake remained fixed. The day was extremely favourable; a gentle wind, sufficient only to fill the sails, fluttered on the surface of the water. In one of the boats Lord Danesforte's servants formed a concert: in the other the ladies sung, while the gentlemen sometimes joined them, and sometimes interrupted them with fine speeches. Laughter seemed more the object, than the pleasure arising from surveying the surrounding scenery; and, after remaining about an hour, Lady Newenden complained that the wind was cold, and desired to be put on shore. Sir Edward, one of the gentlemen, and two of the ladies, accompanied her: Miss Newenden, Mr. Davenant, with Lord Danesforte and the rest of the London party, remained in the boat, into which two of the servants were taken, who were directed to put the boat back into the middle of the lake, it being the purpose of the gentlemen to fish.

The servant however who managed the boat was inexpert; and Lord Danesforte, particularly impatient in trifles, seized the boat hook, and swearing furiously at his people, pushed it off with such violence that the sail was entangled in the boughs of a tree which grew over the creek where they landed; and he continuing to force the boat on, the sail was suddenly disentangled with such a shock, that Ethelinde, who had involuntarily arisen, was dashed instantly into the water.

Sir Edward, as he saw her fall, was about to rush in after her; but recollecting that with boots on he could not save her, he called to the servants who were on shore to tear them off while he disengaged himself from his coat. In the mean time Lord Danesforte with a torrent of oaths ordered his servants to save her as they valued their own lives. The men however hesitated; and Sir Edward had already thrown himself in, when a person was seen to approach the landing place, swimming with one arm, while with the other he bore Ethelinde, to all appearance dead. Sir Edward assisted him in bringing her on shore, where the stranger seated himself on the grass, and supported her. Though she had been hardly five minutes in the water, she was quite insensible, and Sir Edward, concluding she was dead, forbore with the utmost difficulty to express the violence of his grief and despair.

Lord Danesforte and his servants were by this time landed and surrounding her; while the stranger, seated on the grass, supported her in his arms; and Sir Edward collected presence of mind enough to give orders for a chair to be brought, that she might be conveyed into the house. The ladies of the party, affecting great terror, thought more of expressing it in the most becoming manner, than of assisting her who had occasioned it. Lady Newenden insisted upon fainting; but as nobody seemed disposed to attend to her, she very prudently contented herself with the appearance of it only. Miss Newenden, who on most occasions preserved her composure, collected from the rest their smelling bottles, which she never carried herself, and applied them to the temples and nose of Ethelinde, who, "like a fair lily overcharged with rain,"[1] reclined her lovely head on the shoulder of the stranger, while Sir Edward continued chafing her hands, and giving a thousand orders in a moment.

In a short time several servants arrived from the abbey; Lady Newenden's women attended on her; but Mrs. Dickenson, the housekeeper, applied herself to have Ethelinde conveyed to the house, which by means of an armed chair was easily accomplished; and the motion, together with the application which had been used, restored her to some degree of sensibility. She opened her eyes, but seemed unconscious of the surrounding objects, and immediately closed them. Sir Edward, satisfied that she yet lived, recovered some degree of recollection, and enquired after Lady Newenden, who was however much offended with the solicitude he had shewn about Ethelinde, and the risk he had incurred by his attempt to save her, that she deigned not to answer his questions; but bidding him go to those whose life was of more consequence than hers, haughtily retired to her own apartment. Sir Edward

---

1 "like a fair lily over-charged with rain," a common trope from the Renaissance through the Romantic era, from Shakespeare's "like bending lillies overcharged with rain" to Byron, "when the lily lies / o'ercharged with rain" (*Don Juan*, Canto 4:59).

then recollected the young man who had shewn so much courage and activity; who, unnoticed and uninvited, had followed the chair into the house, and now waited in the hall to hear the event of an accident, which but for him would probably have been fatal. Sir Edward, who as well as the gallant stranger remained trembling in wet clothes, now went in search of him; and, taking his hand, expressed in the warmest terms his gratitude and esteem.

"Allow me to ask, Sir," said he, "the name of the gentleman to whom we are so much obliged, and where I may offer him my repeated thanks?"

"My name is Montgomery, Sir. I live at the village on the lake."

The young stranger, bowing, was then about to depart; but Sir Edward pressed him to come into the house, change his clothes, and take some refreshment; adding that he could not think of parting so early with a person to whom he was so much obliged.

"Pardon me, Sir," replied Mr. Montgomery, "if I now decline staying. As to my clothes, their condition is of little consequence. I am almost an amphibious animal. But my mother will perhaps hear some indistinct account of the disaster, and may be alarmed. I dare not therefore stay to hazard giving her that pain. Any other time I shall consider myself highly honoured in being allowed to pay my respects at Grasmere Abbey."

He then enquired into the situation of Ethelinde, and hearing she was much restored, he expressed his pleasure at so favourable an account, bowed, and disappeared across the lawn.

Sir Edward then again went to the door of Ethelinde's apartment; and hearing she was in bed, much recovered and tranquillized, he became more easy; and having changed his clothes prepared with some degree of calmness and resolution to meet the reproaches and ill humours of Lady Newenden. She received him with mingled contempt and anger, reproached him in the bitterest terms for his rashness in attempting to save Ethelinde, and for his disregard of herself; and concluded with accusing herself of extreme folly in having encumbered herself with Ethelinde, who was accustomed, she said, to be made of so much consequence by her infatuated father, that she was become troublesome to every body else, and spoiled every party into which she was admitted.

Sir Edward was not less astonished at the violence than at the unfeeling injustice of this accusation; but, to avoid any argument on a subject which he feared he might not discuss with temper, he withdrew, only desiring her to compose her spirits, and dismiss her terror. The truth was, that Lady Newenden, sufficiently piqued at the attention Sir Edward gave to her cousin, which her pride prevented her from noticing to him, was yet more displeased at observing that though Lord Danesforte affected to be very assiduous in his attendance on her, he extremely admired the beauty of Ethelinde, and though her Ladyship would not then have cared, had she been assured that she should never have seen him again, yet could she not endure that a connoisseur in beauty should find charms in another while she was present; and irritated against Ethelinde, whom she had never loved, by her thus monopolizing admiration, she could no longer prevail upon herself to treat her with even the slight share of civility she had hitherto shewn her.

At the time of the hazardous accident that had befallen Ethelinde, Davenant had been so far from shewing any lover-like solicitude, that his whole attention had been occupied by the care of avoiding any disaster himself; for making his way on shore with as much care as expedition, he buttoned up his coat, tied another handkerchief over his immense neckcloth, and walked about with his teeth chattering and his hands in his pockets, without any attempt to assist the terrified party around him; till Miss Newenden, perfectly mistress of herself, gave him a smart blow on the shoulder with her open hand, crying, "Why, Tom! are you petrified, man? Come, come, prithee do something for these poor drowned wretches. Do run to the house, and hasten the people out with assistance." Willing to make his escape, Davenant gladly obeyed her.

The feelings of Lord Danesforte took quite another turn. As soon as he was convinced Ethelinde was not dead, his rage against his servants, for an accident owing wholly to his own unguarded violence, broke out anew. He loaded them with abuse, uttered against them the most horrid imprecations; particularly vented his wrath against his own gentleman, on whom he threw the blame of what had happened; and having sworn at him for above half an hour, he went to his apartment to dress.

Lady Newenden however appeared not that evening. The others, who, except Miss Newenden, were of that class of women who have no peculiar lines of character, but who dress fashionably, talk fashionably, and fill up public places, had each of them displayed her elegant attitudes and fine feelings, and now renewed their solicitude about the fair sufferer; though had they been assured of the impossibility of her recovery, not one of them would have felt the least concern.

Not so Sir Edward.—The accident had served to shew him all the violence of that attachment to Ethelinde, which he had so long and so vainly attempted to stifle. Thrown entirely off his guard by her danger, he feared he had betrayed to others the sensations he had felt with so much violence, but he could now only determine anew to check, if it was yet possible, this dangerous passion; or if that was no longer in his power, to conceal it for ever from those whose peace it might irreparably injure.

He was struck with the extraordinary coincidence of accident which had twice thrown Montgomery in the way of Ethelinde; as he immediately knew him to be the same young man who had attended her home in the evening of the storm. Whence he came, or to whom he belonged, Sir Edward was yet to learn; but it was impossible to see him without wishing to know more of him.

Ethelinde being the next day tolerably recovered by the care of Mrs. Dickenson, was able to sit up, but not to leave her room. Lady Newenden enquired after her only by a cold message; and Sir Edward, however desirous of seeing her, determined to deny himself that gratification; and to obliterate the memory of his past extravagant transports, by behaving now with as much calm civility as if Ethelinde had only on his heart the claim of a relation of his wife's; and in this resolution he had the forbearance to remain for four-and-twenty hours.

CHAPTER V

Davenant had heard Lord Danesforte repeatedly declare, that of all the women he had ever seen, Ethelinde was the loveliest.— "And if," said his Lordship, "I was a *marrying* man, I should prefer her to all others for a wife." These sort of speeches from a man whose taste was universally acknowledged, and whose manners and opinions were the objects of Davenant's imitation, had a great effect on him; and he began to consider whether he might

not himself obtain Ethelinde, whose beauty his eyes had acknowledged, though he was insensible of her superior attractions. In
consequence of this idea, he became suddenly very solicitous
about her health; and heard with great apparent concern, that
in consequence of her accident she had a cold, attended with a
great degree of fever. Sir Edward, whom these symptoms threw
into real agonies, had on their first appearance sent for the best
advice the country afforded; but Ethelinde, who by no means
believed herself so ill as his fears made him imagine, was notwithstanding glad of an opportunity to remain a few days in her own
room, where she was plentifully supplied with books; and where
Sir Edward, unable to resist the pleasure of being with her, and
fancying that Lady Newenden noticed it not, sat with her sometimes for an hour, and renewed those conversations which she so
much preferred to the mixed, desultory, and uninstructive trifling
of the large party below. On the accident she reflected with no
other sensation than that of gratitude to her gallant deliverer, and
concern for the terror her friends had on her account suffered. Her
acknowledgments to Heaven were rather for the preservation of
a life dear and necessary to her father, than because it appeared to
her to be of great value. The quickness of her feelings had already
taught her, that its pains were greater than its pleasures; and naturally cheerful as her temper was, a sort of presentiment of future
misfortune frequently gave a cast of sadness to her mind, and
oppressed a heart hitherto unconscious of those passions which
prey so forcibly on acute sensibility. This disposition she had made
a point of duty to check in the presence of her father; but now she
yielded to it almost imperceptibly; and the moments she passed
with Sir Edward were particularly tinctured with this tender melancholy—which, delicious as it was to both, was full of danger to
him; who, escaping from vapid and irksome company, found it
doubly delightful to lay out his whole soul in the soft and sensible
society of Ethelinde.

On the fourth day, however, she found herself well enough
to quit her room. Lady Newenden received her with her usual
haughty indifference: Miss Newenden, wholly engrossed by other
matters, hardly recollected that she was among them; while Lord
Danesforte, in her delicate and interesting languor, in the glow
which some remains of fever gave to her cheeks, and in the sub-

dued brilliancy of her eyes, had subjects of increased admiration, which he as much as possible concealed. Davenant, as if to make her forget the little attention he had formerly shewn her, was now officiously polite, and entered in form on all the assiduity of a professed lover. Lord Danesforte, who piqued himself on the deepest politics, had by this time persuaded him, that he had been long and violently in love with Miss Chesterville, and that he ought immediately to attempt securing an interest in her heart. His Lordship saw that she had conceived no favourable opinion of Davenant; but, as he heard of no attachment to any other person, he doubted not but the splendour of such a fortune as he would now in a few months be possessed of, would obviate every other objection; and that when she was the wife of such a man, she would of course be introduced into societies where she would soon be taught, that to love or respect him was by no means necessary;—and no longer under the protection of her father, of her brother, or Sir Edward, he had little doubt of being able to avail himself of the interest which he concluded he might then make in her heart.

While all he saw of Ethelinde increased the impatience with which he desired the accomplishment of this plan, she was solicitous for an opportunity of thanking Mr. Montgomery for the timely assistance he had afforded her. She had yet hardly seen him. On the night they had first met, it was almost dark; on their second meeting she saw nothing; and though the following day he had been at the Abbey to make enquiry after her, she was not then visible. The ladies, however, who had seen him; and particularly Miss Newenden (though much more conversant in the perfection of an horse, than in human beauty) had been warm in praise of his figure. One compared it to that of the Apollo Belvedere; a second to a young Mercury; Miss Newenden wished to see him on horseback, adding that she never saw so tall a man so perfectly graceful; and another lady, who was the best read and most romantic among them, repeated

> "His eyes are like the eagle's, yet sometimes
> Liker the dove's; and as he pleases, win
> All hearts with softness, or with spirit awe."[1]

[1] "His eyes were like the eagle's … as he pleas'd, he won/All hearts …" John Home, *Douglas, A Tragedy*, Act 4: Lady Randolph describing Norval's dead father to him.

It was impossible for Ethelinde to hear all this, and repress her curiosity, which now became even painful to her. Four days had passed since she left her chamber, and in every one of them she had flattered herself she should see him: but still he came not; and all the information she could gain about him was, that he lived with his mother at the pleasant cottage they had remarked in the village; that they were believed to be natives of Scotland; but were known to hardly any person in the neighbourhood of Grasmere, which, however, they never left but once a year, when they went for a few weeks to visit some relations in the Highlands. Ethelinde at length began to despair of seeing him, as the whole party were to go in three days, and Lady Newenden had determined to accompany them as far as Scarborough, where they proposed remaining some weeks. Her cold, which was accompanied by a troublesome cough, had detained her from her usual walks for the first four or five days; but at the end of that time she determined to renew them, not without a latent hope that, if she went towards the lake, chance might again throw him in her way. Davenant now took it into his head to be her constant attendant; Lord Danesforte, though he greatly wished it, dared not hazard losing his favour with Lady Newenden, and Sir Edward was compelled to be more than ever attentive to his wife, lest he should betray the real situation of his heart, and confirm the suspicions she had proudly and darkly hinted.

Ethelinde, with Davenant for her attendant, had advanced on a fine evening to the village; but no Montgomery appeared. As she came within sight of the cottage, she felt an irresistible inclination to enter it. "And why should I not?" said she, arguing it with herself, "ought I to quit the country without acknowledging the obligation I owe to Mr. Montgomery? Surely no. There can be no impropriety in my waiting on his mother; there will be an apparent want of gratitude, if without expressing it, I go where I shall never have an opportunity of saying that I am sensible of the obligation." In a few moments she had argued herself into the most perfect conviction of the propriety of what she was desirous to do, and pursued the path which led to the cottage. Entering the little wicket in the fence which divided the garden from the village street, she tapped gently at the door.

The moment they waited for admittance was employed by

Davenant in remonstrating against this visit. "Why should you visit this young man?" said he. "I do not believe he is a person of consequence enough to make it necessary. Besides, I should think it not quite correct: had you not better write to thank him, and all that sort of thing?"

"That sort of thing," answered Ethelinde, smiling, "is not the sort of thing that appears sufficiently expressive of my gratitude towards the man who has saved my life." The argument was put an end to by the appearance of a maid servant, who to Ethelinde's enquiries answered that Mr. Montgomery was not in the house, but that her mistress was in the parlour; the door of which she immediately opened, and a lady very plainly dressed, yet elegantly neat, rose at their entrance.

Ethelinde, with the grace and sweetness peculiar to her, approached, and desired she might have the honour of leaving with her the thanks she owed Mr. Montgomery, for a very seasonable exertion of his gallantry and good nature.

Mrs. Montgomery, who had felt a momentary surprise at the entrance of such visitors, answered, with all that ease which accompanies perfect good breeding, that her son was extremely fortunate in having had it in his power to be useful to her; then entreating her and Mr. Davenant to sit down, she entered into conversation with them; and if Ethelinde was at first surprised by her air and manner, in a place where she expected only rustic simplicity; or the over-acted complaisance of the last century, she was still more so at the knowledge of the world, the correctness of language, and the charms of address, which Mrs. Montgomery so eminently possessed. Her person was as interesting as her conversation, her figure, though she appeared to be four or five and forty, was graceful yet feminine; and her face, though wan and faded, was illuminated by eyes so full of expression, that it was impossible to help considering how dazzlingly handsome she must have been in the early part of her life. Ethelinde, more charmed with her than with any person she had ever seen, would have forgotten in a few moments that Davenant was with her, had not Mrs. Montgomery occasionally addressed herself to him. Davenant however felt awkward and constrained; and qualified to speak only on the passing trifles of the day, was out of his element with those to whom other topics were familiar; while Ethelinde was in that most congenial to her; and being every moment more pleased with her new acquaintance, near two hours had passed away almost imperceptibly, when Mrs. Montgomery exclaimed "here is my son," and he immediately entered.

"Charles," said his mother, "Miss Chesterville has had the goodness to come hither to thank you for the trifling service you were so happy as to render her."

"Miss Chesterville," replied he, advancing, "does me too much honor: the happiness of having been in any degree useful to her must ever be reckoned among the most fortunate occurrences of my life."

Prepossessed as Ethelinde was in his favor, his figure and address exceeded all that an imagination somewhat romantic had formed of his personal advantages. His face was indeed so uncommonly handsome, that had not his complexion been heightened by his manner of life, and by being exposed continually to the air, it would have had the blooming lustre of feminine beauty. His features however were strong without being harsh; his eyes dark blue, with a spirit in them unusual to that colour; and his luxuriant hair of the brightest brown. The expression of his countenance was so ingenuous, so interesting, and his form so perfectly answered every idea of an hero, that had her eyes only been consulted, it was impossible to deny him the preference to all the men she had ever seen. In addition to these exterior advantages, she beheld the most captivating address, and those manners which are produced only by a liberal education acting on an excellent understanding. She could not repress her admiration; nor help enquiring by what caprice of fortune it was, that a man so fitted to dignify and adorn society, should thus be concealed in a remote corner of the world, forgotten or neglected by those who ought to take a pride in cherishing his talents and producing his virtues.

The lapse of time was no longer perceived by Ethelinde. Mrs. Montgomery and her son seemed equally insensible of its flight. But Davenant, always apprehensive of personal inconvenience, seeing it quite dark, ventured gently to remind her that it was eight o'clock, and that they should have only the moon to conduct them home. Obliged to attend at length to a repetition of this remonstrance, Ethelinde arose, and, in taking leave of Mrs. Montgomery, entreated permission to pass another hour with her before she quitted Grasmere Abbey, which must now be in a few days. Mrs. Montgomery expressed her pleasure at the proposal, adding—"Indeed, my dear Miss Chesterville, your intention is particularly flattering. It is seldom the amiable and well informed are found in so remote a country as this; still more rarely that the young, the gay, and lovely, will voluntarily quit more lively society to pass their hours with those whom choice or calamity have separated from the world."

She pronounced these words in a tone which would have convinced Ethelinde, had she not by other remarks been assured of it, that the exile to which this amiable woman had devoted herself was rather of necessity than choice; and with increased curiosity, Ethelinde was anxious to know what had compelled her to abandon a world where her talents and virtues must have made her respected and beloved, and why her son was thus buried in obscurity. The lateness of the hour which had alarmed the delicacy of Davenant, who was more fearful of catching cold than the most tender woman, was an additional motive to Montgomery to attend Ethelinde home; and when she besought him not to take a trouble so needless, he answered—"Rather call my attendance a luxury which it would be extreme cruelty to deny me. A walk by moon light on the borders of Grasmere Water with Miss Chesterville is a happiness which no man can hope to enjoy above once in his life."

They proceeded then towards the abbey, Davenant offering his arm, which Ethelinde, as she usually did, declined; and almost immediately the irresistible inclination she felt to enjoy the conversation and secure the favourable opinion of Montgomery, so far conquered her natural good breeding, that Davenant, a being always indifferent to her, now entirely escaped from her mind; and while she listened to the remarks of Montgomery, replete with natural taste and poetical enthusiasm, she found them so much in unison with her own feelings, that the universe seemed to hold nothing else worthy of her attention: and when, on their arriving at the gate of the park Montgomery stopped, reminded her of her promise to see his mother, and, wishing her a good night, suddenly disappeared across the lawn, she had hardly courage to return his parting compliment; but feeling disheartened and unhappy, walked silently into the house, uninterrupted by Davenant, who, piqued at her neglect of himself; and mortified at the preference she had shewn to a young man whom he considered as a mere peasant, spoke not; but went sullenly to join the company, while she retired to her own room.

"Where is Ethelinde?" enquired Sir Edward of Davenant.

"She is come in," replied he; "and that young Montgomery walked home with her."

"And is he here now?" asked Sir Edward.

"No; he left Miss Chesterville at the gate."

"Well Tom, and what do you think of him?" said Miss Newenden; "is he not a pretty fellow?"

"As to that, Ma'am, I have no skill in judging of gentlemen's beauty."

"I'll swear," cried she, "Tom Davenant is envious of him. He knows that there is not any of his dressing, lounging, tonish friends half so well looking. As to Tom himself, he has no chance in the world. All the misses hereabouts are dying for this Adonis of the North."

"Upon my word, Ma'am," said Davenant, reddening with anger and vexation, "I never put myself on a footing in any respect with this person, who may or may not be a gentleman; and as for the misses you speak of, I have no ambition to rival him in their favor."

"Pooh," said Sir Edward, "you are not so very young I hope Tom, as to mind Eleanor's rattling. But where is Ethelinde? is she not well?"

At this moment however she entered the room. Sir Edward dared not express the pleasure which the sight of her always gave him; but not being able to forbear examining her face, he thought he saw in it a peculiar expression of sadness; and when Lord Danesforte addressed her, of confusion. His Lordship rallied her on her *gratitude*; enquired how she approved on land of the young man who had been so fortunate in another element; and enquired sneeringly what was Mr. Montgomery's establishment?

Ethelinde had no spirits to laugh away this attack, but answered with a languid and forced smile; and before supper came in complained that her walk had fatigued her, and went to her own apartment.

CHAPTER VI

The temper of Davenant, though it appeared to have no strong bias, was yet much tinctured with that mean jealousy, the infirmity of narrow minds, which cannot bear the success of another, even in points wherein they really feel no other interest than that which arises from the repining malignity of conscious inferiority towards eminent abilities, beauty or fortune. The praises which had been bestowed on Montgomery had imparted to the heart of Davenant this species of corrosive discontent. He neither loved Ethelinde or any human being but himself; but the envy he conceived against Montgomery, whom he considered as a man without fortune and without pretensions, prompted him with redoubled solicitude to pursue Ethelinde; and determined him, by professing himself her lover, to convince Montgomery that he must no longer presumptuously aspire to the honour of her notice. This resolution being strengthened by the advice of Lord Danesforte, Davenant addressed himself the next morning to Sir Edward, in some confusion owned his partiality to Miss Chesterville, and desired his interest and that of Lady Newenden to promote his suit.

Sir Edward who had long since ceased to think of this alliance, received this avowal with a good deal of surprise; and not being able immediately to determine on an answer, he begged Davenant to give him a day to think of it.

As soon as he was alone he began to reflect on the situation of Ethelinde, and to call his own heart to an account for the painful sensations he felt at the very idea of her being married to another. "Is she not likely," said he, "to be left in indigence if her father should die? Has she a mind capable of bearing dependance? What right have I to obstruct a marriage which would secure her affluence? and why should I obstruct it? Can she ever be mine? Do I even wish it? Am I villain enough to entertain any other designs; and is not my affection for her as pure as her own gentle heart? Let me then promote this marriage, since it will be so advantageous for her. Yet to whom would I give her?—to Davenant! Has *he* an heart capable of feeling her value? Is he a man with whom Ethelinde can be happy? And may I not, instead of promoting her felicity, betray her into the most insupportable of all miseries?" These reflections rapidly succeeding each other, still left Sir Edward undecided and unhappy; when a servant, who had been sent to the post, delivered to him the following letter:

Cleveland-Row, Sept. 4, 17—.

"My dear Sir,

"Particular and most unpleasant circumstances oblige me to solicit the favour of you to send my daughter back home as soon as possible. I will not, dear Sir Edward, attempt to conceal my situation from you—the unhappy conduct of my son, added to an unfavourable turn in my affairs, has involved me I fear beyond all recovery.

"I know not what it may be necessary for me to do, but at all events my Ethelinde will console and assist me. Do not however shock her by telling her my reasons for wishing her to return before her cousin; but rather give any that you think will be plausible, and save her at least some days of fruitless uneasiness. To your friendship I leave the regulation of her journey; only entreating you to restore, as expeditiously as you can, the blessing of her presence to your faithful and devoted servant,

H. CHESTERVILLE."

This letter completed the uneasiness of Sir Edward. It convinced him of what he had long suspected—that Chesterville's affairs were in an unhappy situation, and that Ethelinde would be portionless.[1] Unable to determine whether he should take immediate measures for complying with her father's request, or inform him of Davenant's proposal, his mind grew more perturbed; to have time to discuss this point at liberty, he ordered his horse and rode out.

Miss Newenden was gone out early; but Davenant did not as usual accompany her, and was engaged in a match at billiards with Lord Danesforte. Lady Newenden and some of the ladies

---

1 "Portion" is another word for dowry, her inheritance. A widow's "jointure" is a wife's provision, her legacy at the death of her husband. These sums were connected in people's minds, and were negotiated at the time of the marriage "settlement."

were looking on, but Ethelinde was as usual in her own room. The game was become very interesting; for Lord Danesforte, on whose success Lady Newenden had betted, had considerably the advantage, when the servants introduced Mr. Montgomery. Davenant, already vexed at his ill success, turned pale at the sight of him. The ladies received him with politeness; and Lord Danesforte, with that careless familiarity with which he generally treated his inferiors. After a slight bow, and "your servant, Sir," to Montgomery, he turned again to Davenant, and desired him to continue his play; and Montgomery advancing towards Lady Newenden, enquired whether he might be allowed the honour of speaking to Miss Chesterville? The haughty and insensible Lady Newenden could not preserve her coldness towards him, so very enchanting was his address, but answered that Miss Chesterville should immediately be summoned. She then rang the bell, and desired a servant to call Ethelinde.

At the idea of seeing Montgomery again, all her spirits were in alarm: her heart beat quick; her hands trembled as she would have opened the door of the billiard room. Conscious of her emotion, she stopped a moment to recover her spirits; but finding her tremor increase, she found it useless to hesitate, and entering, made to Montgomery, who immediately approached her, an inarticulate compliment about his mother.

"My mother, Madam," said he, "apprehensive that you might quit this part of the world before she can have the honour of waiting on you here, presumes to enquire whether, without her returning the visit with which you honoured her, she may really hope to see you again. The rheumatic complaint under which she has occasionally suffered, returned again last night with some increase, and prevented her from making any attempt to thank you for the favour you did her yesterday. Understanding that in a few days the family depart, she fears that she may see you no more: suffer me then, who am also deeply interested in the enquiry, to ask if she is likely indeed to be so unfortunate?"

"Indeed I never thought of standing on the ceremony of Mrs. Montgomery's returning my visit; but intended this evening to have waited on her again."

"And you still, I hope, intend it; and will suffer me to be the welcome messenger of such your obliging intentions. May I say to her, that at an early hour in the afternoon she may expect to see you?"

To this Ethelinde answering in the affirmative, Montgomery remained a few moments longer, which he passed in addressing himself to Lady Newenden and her friends, and then took his leave.

"What a very pretty young man!" exclaimed one of the ladies; "one wonders how he has acquired such manners here; or having elsewhere acquired them, how he came here."

"Probably," replied another, "a natural son of some man of fashion."

"Miss Chesterville then," said Lord Danesforte, malignantly smiling, "has made a fortunate acquisition in the acquaintance of his mother."

This remark, and the manner in which it was delivered, extremely hurt Ethelinde: such a suspicion had never occurred to her: and though she was persuaded it was false, yet could she not stifle or conceal the pain it gave her.

"Why does your Lordship believe—or why do you, Madam, believe—that Mr. Montgomery—that Mrs. Montgomery—" She hesitated, blushed, and was unable to go on.

"Nay, I believe nothing about it, and know nothing," replied his Lordship; "how indeed should I?"

"Nor do I," said the lady, "positively believe any thing about it; only such a young man seems not to be the son of a mere farmer or such a sort of person. He has had a good education, and certainly has something of fashion about him—that is—something that bespeaks him descended from no plebeian race."

"I thought," said Ethelinde, "that you had understood, as I did, that he was descended from a younger branch of the noble family of his name in Scotland, and that his mother was a native of that country."

"Did any body tell us so?" said Lady Newenden. "I really had forgotten it, but now I recollect, I think somebody said so to Sir Edward. As to myself, Ethy knows I never pretend to dictate, otherwise I should say that she runs some risque of repentance in thus engaging in an acquaintance with people in an equivocal situation."

"It is at least a proof of Miss Chesterville's liberality of sentiment," rejoined Lord Danesforte. "But you know that sometimes people of a certain style make acquaintance at water-drinking places,[1] which are almost always dropped the next winter; and Miss Chesterville becoming known to Mr. Montgomery and his mama nearly in the same manner, she doubtless means so to drop them."

This, which was intended for a lively sally, was received with much applause by the ladies, and by Davenant, who laughed louder and longer than any body at all his Lordship's bon-mots. Their mirth was not interrupted by the entrance of Sir Edward, whose air of chagrin and uneasiness was unnoticed, or at least unattended to, while the party repeated to him the very good thing which had dropped from my Lord.

Ethelinde however had left the room; and the company soon after dispersing to dress, Sir Edward was again at liberty to ruminate on the subject which had occupied his thoughts the whole morning, and to which the mention of Montgomery had added a new source of meditation.

He knew that Ethelinde had so much sense, and a mind too much under the dominion of reason, that there was less reason than with the generality of young women, to fear she would improperly fix her affections: yet he also knew that she had great sensibility, and a very warm and tender heart. When to the advantages of person which Montgomery possessed, the circumstance was added of her owing to him her life, a recollection which could not fail of producing the liveliest gratitude in her bosom, Sir Edward could not but dread the consequence of her frequently seeing him: yet he could neither determine earnestly to encourage her union with Davenant; nor had he yet collected courage enough to tell her that her return to her father was immediately necessary.

This uneasy indecision continued during dinner. Ethelinde came down in her hat, as if equipped for her walk; and, on something being said which led to it, Davenant asked her, with all the courage he could assume, whether he might have the good fortune to attend her.

"No, Sir—I thank you," was her only answer.

---

1 A spa, or holiday health resort where people mingled more freely, e.g., Bath, Weymouth, Brighton.

"You will not surely walk alone, Miss Chesterville?" said Sir Edward.

"Why not, Sir; what have I to fear?"

"The darkness of the evening, which now closes in very soon. Pardon me, but it seems to me very improper."

The gravity with which these words were pronounced surprised Ethelinde, who said, "Do you indeed, Sir Edward, object to my going?"

"Alone, I certainly do."

"Then if Lady Newenden can spare one of the footmen, I shall beg to borrow one for the walk."

"Oh! you may take which you will," answered her Ladyship: "but do not you pay Davenant a very ill compliment, when he so gallantly offers to attend you?"

"Not at all," replied Ethelinde, conquering her vexation: "though I hold myself bound to pay the trifling attention of a visit to Mrs. Montgomery, in consequence of the obligation I owe her son; yet, as Mr. Davenant feels no such necessity, why should I, by accepting of his offer to attend me, subject *him* to the possible inconvenience of forming an improper acquaintance?"

This answer turned the laugh against Davenant, who, thoroughly sulky, received it with a very ill grace. The footman was ordered to attend Miss Chesterville, and Sir Edward tried to see her depart without betraying farther symptoms of the real state of his mind; and forcing himself into the amusements that were going on in his wife's drawing room, attempted to pass the evening without thinking of Ethelinde. He attempted it however in vain, and all his efforts, though they seemed to conceal his pain from others, had no power to conquer its acuteness even for a moment.

When Ethelinde arrived at the cottage of Mrs. Montgomery, she found her alone, and delighted with the pleasure of seeing her young friend. The first interview indeed had been decisive. That irresistible attraction which the sensible and ingenuous feel towards a character congenial with their own, that secret sympathy which the selfish and narrow-minded frequently consider as the effect of romantic enthusiasm, had already attached them to each other; and this second meeting served to confirm the favourable impression of the first. With a form, over which the hand of time seemed to have passed in vain, and to a face, faded indeed and wan, but animated by fine eyes and an expression of melancholy resignation which made it infinitely interesting, Mrs. Montgomery possessed a superior understanding, and an heart which had acquired in the school of adversity fortitude to bear its own sorrows, with redoubled feeling for the calamities of others. Thrown into obscurity, the dignity of her mind supported her; and, amidst ill health and long misfortune, she had been not only resigned, but grateful that her sensibility yet remained, and that she had such a son for its object.

Ethelinde had not been long with her before he became the subject of their discourse. He had been that of Ethelinde's thoughts from the moment of his taking leave of her in the morning, and she now felt more uneasy than she was willing to own even to herself, at seeing that he was not with his mother, though he knew that she was to be there.

"Charles," said Mrs. Montgomery, "is absent on his usual amusement, but I hope he will drink tea with us. I would have detained him the whole evening, that he might have enjoyed the pleasure of your company; but he said that he should spoil our tête-à-tête, and that he had better deny himself a pleasure he should perhaps never enjoy again, than become subject to eternal regret, in having tasted and lost it. You will easily perceive, Miss Chesterville, that my son, young as he is, has not been always accustomed to the recluse life he now leads. Charles indeed was born not to the prospects which from his family he ought to have had, but to such as, however inadequate to his birth, were yet very different from those he now has before him."

"Since you encourage me, Madam," replied Ethelinde, "I will own to you, that merely to see either you or your son in a situation so remote and solitary as this, could hardly fail to render even apathy inquisitive. Judge then, whether curiosity is not raised after I have both seen and *heard* you. Indebted as I am to your son for the preservation of my life, is it possible for me to help wishing to know some particulars of persons to whom I have such obligations?"

"And you shall know; if the story of a life marked with much sorrow, without any uncommon adventures, will not fatigue you."

"Ah! believe me, that if its recollection and relation are not painful to you, you cannot confer on me a greater favour."

"Painful it certainly is, to carry back the memory to the past, where the death of the dearest of our friends, and the defection of others, have marked too many of our years. Yet let me say—and I hope I may say it with honest exultation—that I have also a satisfaction in re-tracing the past; since my calamities have been such as were incurred neither by folly—or guilt; and since I trust that He, whose pleasure it was to afflict me, has accepted of my endeavours to bear my afflictions with fortitude.

"My father was a native of Scotland, of the noble family of Douglas.¹ He was a younger brother of a younger branch, and married very early in his life a young woman as well born and as indigent as himself. In the year 1745 he was among those who joined the unfortunate Charles Edward; and he fell at Culloden,² leaving me then about twenty months old, and his wife, then not more than seventeen, entirely dependent on the bounty of his father, and overwhelmed with the greatness of her calamity; but when she held in her arms her unfortunate orphan, the sole legacy and sole memorial of a man whom she had fondly loved, she struggled against her unhappy destiny, and for my sake attempted to live.

"Though peace was at length restored to the wretched country, which had been too long the seat of devastation, many families found themselves totally impoverished, and none had suffered more than my grandfather, who having narrowly escaped with life, survived to lament the loss of three brave sons, and to see great part of his property in ashes. He lingered only a twelve-month afterwards, and then sunk into the grave, leaving his small patrimony to his only surviving son, who had himself a numerous family. My mother saw, or fancied she saw, that he could willingly

1 The Douglas were one of the earliest powerful clans in Scotland and held onto power and wealth into well into the 19th century.
2 The concluding pitched battle of the third full-scale 18th century Jacobite rebellion in England: the first occurred in the 1690s, the second in 1715, and the third in 1745. In each case the Stuart family's Roman Catholic claimant, James II, his son, James III (supposed king), and his, Charles Edward, led frustrated Scottish and disaffected English to overthrow the Hanoverian Protestant monarchy. The Scottish were decisively defeated at Culloden (near Inverness), and in an effort to prevent another uprising the English executed many Scottish leaders and a sampling of ordinary soldiers; they also instituted harsh repressive and retaliatory measures.

have dispensed with any additional burthen; and she determined to go to England, where she hoped to be received by a brother of her own who was settled in London. Thither she conveyed herself and me in the cheapest way she could and was received by her brother (who had sunk his illustrious birth for the convenience offered him of becoming partner with a merchant) with kindness indeed; but such kindness as a mind narrowed by perpetually contemplating riches shews to the poor who are dependent on them. His wife, by whose means his fortune had been promoted, convinced him that his sister and her child could not be commodiously received into his house. Lodgings were however provided for her in the neighbourhood, and she boarded with her brother; but the second month of her thus living was not passed, before the neglect she felt from him, and the pride and ill nature of his wife, taught her to experience in all its bitterness the misery of dependence. Born with very acute feelings; and at an age when every sensibility is awake, my mother found this situation every day more insupportable. Yet whither could she turn? She had neither knowledge of business, nor any means of engaging in it. She had no acquaintance in England, and not in the world any friend who had at once the power and the will to assist her.

"Almost the first circumstance which made any impression on my mind, was the agonies of passion with which my mother clasped me to her bosom, and wept over me, while she called on the spirit of her departed Douglas to behold the wretchedness of his widow and his orphan. At that age, however, it is only a slight sketch now and then of some violent passion or striking circumstance that rests on the memory of an infant. I have no recollection of anything else, till the scene was greatly changed, and in my childish eyes greatly amended.

"It was summer, and though at that period the mercantile inhabitants of London were less accustomed than they now are to go to country villas, yet my uncle, who was growing rich, had one near Hammersmith, where he usually repaired with his family on Fridays, returning again to town the beginning of the following week. The weather was uncommonly hot; and my mother, who was never of these parties, but was left in London to share the dinner of the solitary servant who took care of the house, fancied that I had for many days drooped for want of air; and alarmed by that idea, she took, after the family were gone, an hackney coach, and directed it to carry her to the gate of Hyde Park.

"Though the sun was declining, it had yet so much power, that in walking through the park with me in her arms, that I at least might not suffer, she became extremely fatigued. She saw people going into Kensington Gardens: thither she went also; and to avoid observation, betook herself to an unfrequented part of them, where, quite overcome with bodily fatigue and mental anguish, she threw herself on a seat; and straining me to her bosom, began with a torrent of tears to lament not so much her own hard fate as that which awaited the infant of her lost Douglas, whose name she frequently repeated, broken by the sobs and groans which a thousand tender recollections of *him*, and poignant fears for *me*, extorted from her. From this delirium of fruitless sorrow she was awakened by the appearance of a gentleman, of about thirty, who suddenly approached her, and enquired with great politeness, yet with great warmth, whether her distress was of a nature which he could mitigate or remove?

"Alarmed by this address from a stranger, my mother arose, and making an effort to conquer her emotion, and conceal her tears, she thanked him in an hurried voice for his politeness, but assured him that she was merely fatigued by the heat of the weather, and should now hasten home.

"He was not however to be so easily shaken off. If my mother had at first struck him as a very beautiful young woman, he was still more charmed when she spoke; and when, amidst the confusion she was under, he observed as much unaffected modesty as natural elegance, it was in vain that she entreated him to leave her, and assured him that she lived in a very distant part of the town with a brother, into whose house she could not introduce a stranger, and that she should be otherwise much distressed by his attention. He would not leave her; but taking me up in his arms, he carried me out of the gardens, and then delivering me to my mother, he ran towards the palace, to procure, as he said, a coach. My mother, who trembled she knew not why, at the politeness she could not resent, now hurried on in the hope of escaping from her new acquaintance; but she had not proceeded an hundred paces before he was again at her side, again took me in his arms, and under pretence that there was no coach to be had where he had been, but that one would probably be met with if they walked on, he engaged her to proceed, till a coach overtook them: not such as he pretended to have sought; but one on which was an earl's coronet, and the arms of Douglas, quartered with those of an illustrious English family.

"Now," said he, stopping as it came up, "here is a carriage, which shall convey you and this little cherub to your home. You will not, I think, refuse me the honor of accompanying you, that it may afterwards take me to mine."

"Again my mother urged every thing she could think of to prevail upon her new friend to desist from a proof of attention which could only distress her. He would hear nothing; and the warmth of his importunity forced her, in spite of every objection, to get into his coach; where he seated me in her lap, and himself by her side.

"He then attempted to quiet her fears by entering into discourse on the topics of the day; in which he exerted himself so effectually, his manners were so easy, and his conversation so entertaining, that the agitation of her spirits gradually subsided. The soothing voice of friendship, of pity, of sympathy, which she had not heard for many months, again made its way to her bosom and when he insensibly turned the discourse from less interesting matters to her own condition, the tears flowed from her eyes, softness pervaded her heart, and she confided to this stranger, whom she had not yet known above an hour, the unhappy uncertainty of her situation, the actual misery she suffered herself, and the anguish which weighed down her spirit when she reflected that she had no other portion to bequeath me than poverty, servitude, or perhaps dependence, more bitter than either. In making this avowal, she had named her family, and that of her father.

"Yes," interrupted her protector, "I heard, as I listened to you in the gardens, the name of Douglas. I am myself of the race; for my mother was a Douglas; such a circumstance, added to the captivating beauty of the fair mourner to whom I listened, made my curiosity invincible. Dangerous curiosity! to gratify it, I have I fear lost my peace!"

"Not to dwell too long on the recital, let me say that this nobleman professed himself passionately in love with the young widow; and though she insisted on his giving up so wild an idea, he

declared before he left her that he would by some means or other
introduce himself to her brother, since to live without seeing her
was impossible. It was with difficulty he was at length prevailed
upon to leave the house; and without extorting permission from
my mother, he was there again the next day, and every day, till the
family returned; after which he managed so adroitly, that in a few
days he made an acquaintance with my uncle, and was in form
invited to dinner; while neither himself or his wife at all suspected
for whose sake the acquaintance was so anxiously cultivated, but
were extremely elate at the notice which a man of rank took of
of them, and the compliments he paid to the respectability and
intrinsic worth of men of business.

"The attention however which he found himself obliged to pay
to the mistress of the house, and the few opportunities of seeing or
conversing with my mother which this method of visiting allowed
him, became very uneasy to him. And at length, after a long struggle with himself, he determined to hazard telling her his real situation. He probably knew that he had by this time secured such an
interest in her heart, that it was no longer in her power to fly from
him, whatever her honor might dictate. Having with some difficulty obtained an opportunity of speaking to her, he told her that
he knew she must long have seen his ardent and incurable passion;
"which perhaps," continued he, "I ought never to have indulged;
but alas! from the first moment I saw you, my heart was your's!
while reason in vain condemned me, and repeated the fatal truth
which you must now hear. I am already married—I am not villain
enough to attempt to deceive you; but listen to what I have to add
in extenuation of my conduct before you condemn me to despair."

"The indignation with which my mother received this acknowledgment, the attempts of her lover to appease and soften her, I
need not relate: having at length prevailed on her to hear what he
had to urge, he told her, that to gratify his family he had, when
little more than twenty, married the heiress of a rich and noble
family; plain, and even deformed in her person, with a temper
soured by ill health and the consciousness of her own imperfections, and with manners the most disgusting. For upwards of three
years he dragged on a life completely wretched with a woman
whose malignity of temper deadened all pity for her personal misfortune. At the end of that period she was seized with the small

pox, attended with the worst symptoms; but the distemper acting on a habit constitutionally bad, failed to deprive her of life, which would have been a blessing to them both; but left behind it violent epileptic fits, which continuing with increasing violence for many months, had deprived her of the slender share of reason she ever possessed, and threw her at length into confirmed idiotism, in which state she had invariably remained for the last six years. Thus situated, he considered himself, tho' the fatal tie could not by law be dissolved, as really unmarried; and at liberty to offer his heart to the lovely object who now possessed it, though the cruel circumstance he had related made it impossible for him to offer her that rank in which it would otherwise have been his ambition to have placed her, and to which she would have done so much honour.

"I was then in my mother's arms: he took me tenderly in his; and said, "Intercede for me, lovely Caroline, with your mother! Ah! soften that dear, inexorable heart, and tell her, that for your sake she should quit an abode so unfit for you both, and accept the protection of a man, who will consider and provide for her Caroline as for a child of his own." He then hurried away, leaving a paper in which he had repeated all he had before said, and protesting that his first care should be to settle a fortune on me. That evening, my uncle and his family, who had been absent, returned; and it happened that his wife, who was always rude and unfeeling, treated my mother with an unusual degree of asperity. Her brother too, whether from accident or from some intelligence he had received of his Lordship's visits, spoke to her with great acrimony, reproached her with having been now above twelve months a burthen to him, and advised her to try if she could not procure a place as companion to a lady or governess in a family; adding coldly, that he would in that case take care of me, and put me out to nurse, till I was old enough to procure a livelihood.

"Honour, and respect for the memory of her husband, had made in the breast of my mother a struggle, which this inhuman treatment rendered at once ineffectual. On one side, affluence, with the man whom she already loved more than she was aware of, and a certain provision for the infant on whom she doated, awaited her; on the other, poverty, dependence, and contempt: her child torn from her, and herself sent to service. The contrast was too violent: She retired to her room, and, without giving herself time for reflection, wrote to Lord Pevensey, and the next day quitting her inhospitable and selfish relations, without giving them any account of herself, she set out with his Lordship for Paris. A servant was provided for me: All that love and fortune could offer were lavished on her; and at an elegant house on the banks of the Seine she was soon established, with with a splendour which however served not to make her happy.

"Still conscious of the impropriety of her situation, she could never conquer the melancholy that preyed on her mind; though she sometimes thought, that to have the daughter of Douglas educated and provided for, as his Lordship's fondness educated and provided for me, was in reality a greater proof of attachment to his memory than she would have shown, had she suffered me to have remained in the indigence and disgrace to which the penurious and sordid temper of my uncle would have exposed me. The two sons, whom she brought my lord, shared her tenderness without lessening it towards me; and while the utmost care was taken of their education as soon as they were old enough to receive instruction, I had the best masters which Paris afforded; and, with such advantages, almost every European language at an early age became equally familiar to me. Lord Pevensey, who was as partial to me as if I had been indeed his daughter, and in whose fondness for my mother time made no abatement, saw with pleasure the progress I made, and flattered himself that he should establish me happily, though the situation of my mother (who, though she was treated in France with great respect, was well understood not to be the wife of Lord Pevensey) was a very unfavourable circumstance to me even in that country. The world however called me handsome, and I had received an education very different from that which is usually given to young women in France. On the day on which I completed my fourteenth year, Lord Pevensey came to me, as I was dressing for a little entertainment which he had ordered on the occasion, and wishing me joy of my birth day, he saluted me, and put into my hands a bank note of a thousand pounds. "Take it, my dear Caroline," said he, "as a trifling testimony of my affection for you: use it for your smaller expences; and be assured that I will not neglect to make your future prospects equal to the education you have received, and to which you do so much honour."

"I received this generosity as I ought. Alas! my benefactor went

in a few weeks to England, and I saw him no more. A strange presentiment of evil hung over my mother, whose health had long
been very uncertain. She could not bear to take the last leave of
his Lordship; and he, who lived but to oblige her, still lingered,
and delayed his journey, till repeated letters from those who had
the care of his estates compelled him to determine on it. His two
sons, one of ten, the other of eight years old, were by this time at
a public school in England; and he promised to gratify my mother
with the sight of them on his return, which he said should be as
soon as he could settle the affairs which called him over.

"When he was gone, however, my mother fell into a deep melancholy; and as we were almost always alone together, she talked
very frequently of the incidents of her past life, related the particulars I have repeated to you, and asked me whether I could forgive
her for having thus been betrayed into a situation, which, whatever it might be in the sight of heaven, would in that of the world
render me liable to eternal reproach. It was in vain I conjured her
to banish from her mind reflections which served only to destroy
an health so precious to us all. Still they recurred too often; and
her delicate constitution very visibly suffered. After Lord Pevensey,
who had been used to write by every post, had been gone about
six weeks, his letters suddenly ceased. My mother for some days
flattered herself that it was merely owing to his being on his journey back; but her hope gradually died away, and the most alarming
apprehensions succeeded—apprehensions too well founded. We
were sitting together one morning, when a sudden bustle of the
servants in the anti-room surprised us. I arose to enquire into the
occasion of it; and on my opening the door was shocked by the
sight of my two brothers, and their tutor, who had been attempting to prevent their sudden entrance. The poor boys on seeing
me burst into tears; and exclaiming, 'oh! Caroline! my father!'
they rushed by me, and threw themselves into the arms of their
mother; who, wild with terror, had no power to enquire, what
indeed they soon told her.—'Oh! Mama!' cried they, 'our papa, our
dear papa, is dead! They have sent us here to you—they have taken
him from us, and every thing that was his!'

"The tutor, who highly respected my mother, now attempted
to take the children from her; but she held them in her arms, while
with a look which I shall never forget, and with the voice of pierc-

ing anguish, she enquired what all this meant? The worthy man related, in a few words, that Lord Pevensey had been seized with a fever at one of his country houses, where, after a few days illness he died: that his brother, who became heir to his title, had instantly possessed himself of all his effects, and had directed the two boys to be taken immediately to France, and to drop the name they had hitherto borne. With reluctance the tutor added, that the present Lord intended in a few days being at the house we inhabited, in order to receive the jewels and other valuables which belonged to his brother.

"No tear fell from the eyes of the dear unhappy woman, no sigh escaped her heart. She desired me to tranquillise the poor boys (who still fondly clung round her, weeping for their dear papa,) and complaining that she suffered great pain in her head, desired to be put to bed. I remained by her; and endeavoured to excite her tears, while mine flowed incessantly: but the greatness and suddenness of the calamity overwhelmed her constitution, though it still left to her mind strength enough to reflect on the condition of her children.

"'Caroline,' said she to me, as I sat by her, 'I shall probably be in a few hours reduced to that indigence, from which, perhaps it were better I had never been relieved. But your brothers! for them I suffer! The proceedings of the present Lord Pevensey leave me little reason to hope that any will exists in England which secures them the ample provision their father designed for them. There are, in a box which my Lord left, several papers which he told me were of consequence: but they will be taken from me unless immediately secured. Send therefore for Mr. Montgomery, and deliver to him that box.'

"She then gave me a direction to him. I had never seen Mr. Montgomery, though he was a friend of my Lord's. I hastened to execute her commands; he flew to the house on receiving my message, and instead of a man of business, as I expected, I beheld a young man of about seven-and-twenty, in the uniform of one of those Scottish regiments which were received by the King of France after their master's affairs became irretrievable. He had been quartered for some time in a remote province; but being distantly related to and highly esteemed by the late Lord Pevensey, he had constantly corresponded with him, and had been entrusted with his intentions relative to my mother, my brothers, and myself.

"I cannot describe the person of Montgomery. Suffice it to say, that his figure was even finer than that of his son, who resembles him extremely. The warm and lively interest he took for my mother, the manly tenderness which he discovered when he saw our distress, and the trouble which he instantly undertook to encounter for us, were powerful incentives to me to admire and esteem him. I then thought him the noblest of human beings, and a few days convinced me that he deserved all the partiality my young heart had conceived for him. The new Lord Pevensey, who intended to have reached my mother's house before she could have notice of his journey, (and was prevented only by the zeal of the tutor who had the care of my brothers) arrived on the third day after she had received these fatal tidings. He was a man not much turned of forty, but with a harsh and stern countenance, a large heavy person, and a formal cold manner. He brought with him a lawyer from England, and engaged another in France to accompany him to the house; where, with very little ceremony, he demanded of my mother all the jewels and effects of his deceased brother. Summoning all her resolution, and supported by Montgomery, who never left her, she tried to go through this dreadful ceremony with some degree of fortitude. She delivered, with trembling hands, a star, a sword set with brilliants, and several other family jewels. She then opened a casket, in which her own were inclosed; and Lord Pevensey was taking them from her, when Montgomery interfered, saying that they were her's, and he should not suffer her to part with them.

"It would be tedious to relate the scenes which passed between Lord Pevensey, his lawyer, and Montgomery; who finding it necessary, engaged lawyers on the part of my mother. A will of the late Lord had been found among the papers which she had put in the possession of Montgomery, in which an annuity of eight hundred a year was settled on my mother, and all his estates charged with the payment of ten thousand pounds to each of my brothers, and two to me. This will the present Lord disputed, and the contending parties prepared for law, the circumstance of the case rendering it necessary that this contention should be carried on as well in England as in France.

"The spirits and health of my mother gradually declined.

The friendship, the unwearied kindness, of Montgomery alone supported her: but neither his attention or mine could cure the malady of the mind, or bind up the wounds of a broken heart.

"I will not detain you with relating the various expedients for accommodation which were in the course of the first month proposed by the relations of the family, who knew the tenderness the late Lord Pevensey had for my mother; that he considered her as his wife; and that her conduct could not have been more unexceptionable had she really been so. Still lingering in France, and still visiting an house into which his cruelty had introduced great misery, the proceedings of Lord Pevensey wore a very extraordinary appearance. My mother was now confined almost entirely to her room, and Montgomery concealed from her his uneasiness at what he remarked: but to me he spoke more freely, and told me that he was very sure his Lordship had other designs than he suffered immediately to appear. In a few days the truth of his conjecture became evident. I was alone in a small room at the end of the house, where I had a harpsichord which I had removed thither since my mother's illness. She was asleep. Montgomery, on whom my imagination had long been accustomed to dwell with inexpressible delight, had been detained two days from us. Those days had appeared two ages to me; and his absence, combined with the uneasiness of our situation, and the state of my mother's health, depressed my spirits, and I sought to soothe them by music. A little melancholy air, which I often sung to Montgomery, was before me: it expressed my feelings; and I was lost in the pleasure of expressing them, when the door from the garden opened, and Lord Pevensey stalked in his formal manner into the room.

"I arose instantly from my seat; but he took my hand, and with an air of familiarity bade me sit down again. Then drawing a chair close to me, he looked in my face, and cried—'Sweet Caroline! she will not refuse to sing to me! She does does not hate me; and will perhaps be the lovely mediatrix who shall adjust all differences between me and her mama.'

"'I have no power, Sir, to adjust differences,' answered I, much alarmed at his look and manner. 'Indeed you have, my charming girl,' cried he, attempting very rudely to kiss me; 'and if you will only be sensible of the same friendship for me, as your mother had for my brother, every thing he left in her possession shall be hers.

Nay I will make you sole mistress of my fortune, and she shall enjoy all she claims with her beloved Montgomery.'

"I cannot describe what I felt at that moment. I knew not what I said, in the first emotion of terror and anger. I flew to the door, but it was fastened. I then attempted to reach that which led to the garden, but he caught me in his arms. I shrieked, I struggled to disengage myself, while the wretch exclaimed—'Violent airs these, for the daughter of Mrs. Douglas to give herself! Pretty affectation in a girl who has been brought up on the wages of prostitution!' I heard this cruel insult, but unable to answer, I could only redouble my cries. The monster endeavoured to argue with me; but, incapable of hearing, I tried only to escape him, when the door was broke open with great force, and Montgomery burst into the room.

"Without staying to enquire into the cause of my shrieks, he flew at Lord Pevensey, whom he pinioned in a moment to the wainscot. A scene followed so terrifying, that I cannot do it justice. Lord Pevensey, far from apologizing for his conduct, had the brutish audacity to repeat to Montgomery his insulting sarcasm against my mother, and dared to intimate that he himself had taken the place of the deceased Lord. The agony into which I was thrown by the violence of Montgomery's passion, was the only thing capable of restraining it. Seeing me to all appearance dying on the floor where I had fallen, he quitted his adversary, and came to raise and reassure me. Lord Pevensey took that opportunity to depart, threatening however personal vengeance against Montgomery, and that he would redouble every attempt to ruin my mother, whom he again insulted with such epithets, that Montgomery was with difficulty withheld from following him, and demanding an immediate reparation. Dreadful as this scene had been, it was succeeded by one which would have made me forget all its bitterness, had not other consequences followed. When Lord Pevensey was departed, Montgomery returned back to me; and while I thanked him as well as I was able, for the protection he had afforded me, he confessed, with agitation almost equal to mine, that from the first moment he had seen me, he had loved me: that his affection, which had since increased every hour, had made him extremely attentive to every thing that related to me; and that he had been long convinced of the designs of Lord Pevensey, and foreseen that to obtain me, he would affect delays and hold out hopes of compromise. 'Ill however as I thought of him,' continued he, 'I could not have believed that his villainy would have gone such lengths, or have been so unguardedly betrayed. Now we have every thing to apprehend that money or chicanery can execute.'

"This was no time for reserve or affectation. I answered that I feared only what might affect his personal safety, that the threats of Lord Pevensey in that respect distracted me with terror, and that I should not have a moment's tranquillity till I saw a life secure which I very frankly confessed was infinitely dearer to me than my own.

"It would be uninteresting perhaps to you, my dear Miss Chesterville, were I to describe the raptures of Montgomery on the discovery of my sentiments. A scene too tender to be related followed; and we were recalled from the delightful avowal of mutual passion, by a message from my mother, who had been awakened by the confusion which had happened below, and whose servants had indiscreetly told her what they knew of its occasion. As she had been informed of so much, it was impossible to conceal from her any part of what had passed. Though Montgomery softened as much as he could the opprobrious speeches which Lord Pevensey had made relative to her, they sunk deeply into her mind: he saw how much she was affected, and ended the conversation as soon as he could. But when he had left us, my mother desired I would return to her and thus spoke to me:

"'Caroline, I will attempt no longer to deceive you. I feel myself dying. A few days I am convinced will terminate my life, and my sufferings. I leave my poor boys with few friends to contest the will of their father against all the weight of affluence and power. And you! oh child of my first affections! I leave you with all that fatal beauty, of which my weak heart has been so foolishly proud, to encounter not merely indigence, but the baseness of a world, where your mother's character, justified as I hope and believe it is in the sight of heaven, will expose you to the insolent addresses of the profligate; where you will be told that, as the mother deviated from the narrow path of rectitude, the daughter cannot pursue it. My errors will be urged to betray my Caroline to destruction, and when she reflects on the example of her mother, she will perhaps learn to desert her precepts.'

"The bitter anguish inflicted by these cruel reflections here stifled her voice. I was myself more dead than alive; yet as I hung trembling over her on the sopha on which she lay, I attempted to say something that might console her, and with difficulty articulated the name of Montgomery. 'Montgomery!' cried my mother, as soon as she recovered her speech—'oh! he is the worthiest, the most generous of human creatures! To him I have, in a will which this paper contains, given the care of my two boys. But you!—oh! Caroline!—is a man of his age a guardian proper for a lovely young woman of yours? I have therefore addressed myself in another paper to your father's family, and have besought them to pity and protect my Caroline. The present you received from my deceased Lord, on your last birth day, will preserve you at least from the indigence I once experienced.—To Providence, to your own good principles and strong understanding, I commit the rest.'

"I had not courage to say, that Montgomery desired only to have the strongest claim to become my protector, by receiving my hand. But in the evening, when I saw him, I told him all that had passed. Eagerly seizing on hopes so flattering to the ardor of his passion, he besought of me to allow him go to my mother, and propose our immediate marriage. She heard him with gratitude and delight; and though she knew he had nothing but his commission in the French service, and that being a catholic, he could never rise to that rank in England, which his high birth would have entitled him otherwise to expect, she hesitated not to give her consent. 'Yes, my dear child,' said she, at the end of this affecting scene—'In his virtues you will find fortune—in his honour and his courage, protection. In leaving you to the care of such a man, I die contented.'—She grew daily weaker; but was anxious, even to a degree of impatience, to see us united before her death. Montgomery therefore, to conquer every scruple and every difficulty, procured a clergyman of the church of England, who married us in her presence; and at my desire (who wished to shew Montgomery that I knew how to value complaisance) the priest who officiated in his regiment performed the ceremony a second time.

"But forms could do nothing toward uniting our hearts more closely; and the happiness of a marriage where love only presided, was perhaps too great for humanity: for those halcyon days were greatly obscured by the increasing illness of my mother, who declined rapidly for almost a fortnight, and then died in the arms of Montgomery, commending, with her last breath, her two boys to his protection. Her death, which, long as I had expected it, appeared utterly insupportable now it arrived, threw me into a state of languor and dejection, from which I was suddenly roused by hearing that Lord Pevensey, who had quitted France immediately after his disgraceful dismission from the house, was now returned; and, enraged to find that Montgomery was actually my husband, had determined to pursue, with all the eagerness that rage and hatred could inspire, the process by which he hoped to deprive me and my brothers of our legacies. Nor was this all: the personal affront that he had received from Montgomery he could not bear, though he had deserved it; and he now sent him a challenge, which Montgomery readily accepted; but, to evade the strictness of those laws which are in force in France against duelling, the place where they were to meet was fixed in the dominions of the Pope, a little beyond Avignon.[1]

"Montgomery, anxious only to conceal this from me, found a pretence for his journey; and telling me he had some military business to transact at Marseilles, which would detain him for some days, he darted from me, concealing with courage truly heroic the anguish he felt in knowing that we were perhaps to meet no more.

"Providence yet preserved him to me. He dangerously wounded his adversary, and returned himself in safety. Then he related the cause of his absence; and the happiness I felt at his safety was augmented, when a few days afterwards we received from Lord Pevensey, who believed himself dying, and was visited with the reproaches of a troubled conscience, an acknowledgment of the justice of my brothers' claims to the provision made for them by their father, and an order to his procureur at Paris to put an end to every suit depending against us. In a few months Lord Pevensey recovered; we were put in possession of our rights; and my beloved Montgomery, to whom I owed everything, studied not only how to make me happy, but to pursue as near as possible that line of conduct which my mother would have done had she lived. A war was raging with great violence between France

1 From the era in which Avignon was the papacy center (14th century), it had remained autonomous and so duellists could hope to escape laws against murder.

and England;[1] and I was unwilling to send the two dear boys to a country where it would be now difficult for me to see them. But as I knew it was the desire of my mother and my benefactor to have them brought up in the protestant religion, I sent them with their tutor to Geneva.—I had hardly recovered the pain of this parting, before one much more grievous was inflicted. The regiment in which Montgomery had a company, was ordered into Germany. The situation I was then in made it seem madness to think of following him; but I was convinced that I should not survive his departure. He was to me, father, brother, lover, husband! I had no other earthly happiness, and without him the universe was to me nothing. At first his fears for my safety made him resist my importunities: but he was compelled at length to consent; and I followed him, residing wherever he was encamped; and, however horrid the scenes were to which I thus became a witness, I feared nothing but for his life; that one dreadful apprehension having the effect of all violent passions, and making me forego, without missing them, every convenience to which I had been accustomed, and meet without apprehension from a thousand dangers to which I was hourly exposed.

"In a small village on the banks of the Weser, near the camp of Mareschal de Conrades, my dear Charles was born, towards the beginning of the campaign of 1759. But he had not above six weeks blessed my eyes, and those of his doting father, before that dear father went out to the fatal field of Minden.[2] I cannot describe what I felt during the action. My faculties were suspended by the most dreadful apprehensions that could agonize the human heart: this frightful suspense was terminated only by the certainty of all I dreaded. The English were victors; and the servant who had long attended on Montgomery, had only time to tell me that he fell at the head of his company, his arm broken by a musket shot, and

1 The Seven Years War between England and France (1756-63) fought (among other places) in the U.S. and Germany. At its close the disposition of territories in the Western Hemisphere between France and England was decided, and France ceded control of India to the English.

2 Smith misspells the name of a major battlefield commander, Marshal of France, Louis Georges Érasme de Contades; he commanded the French at the Battle of Minden, fought August 1759, one of the large battles fought in northwest Germany; the English and Prussians defeated the French. Montgomery is fighting on the French side.

receiving a thrust from a bayonet in the breast. The man added that, with a party of soldiers who adored their captain, he had attempted to bring his master off the field; but that they were cut down by a body of Hessian horse, who, driving every thing before them, had compelled him to abandon the enterprize. I believe that my senses for some hours forsook me, during the horrors of a night too terrible to be described. The English took possession of the village where I was; but, fortunately for me, a young officer of that nation was the first who, in endeavouring to prevent the excesses of the troops, entered the house where I remained with my infant in my arms.

"Roused by my fears for my child, I seemed suddenly to acquire courage. I demanded protection of the young officer, which, with the generous ardor of the truly brave, he instantly granted me: and, being himself compelled to quit me, he gave me a corporal's guard; recommended me to the men as an English woman; and, having secured my safety, promised to return to me when the confusion of the hour a little subsided. The stupor of my grief being thus shaken off for a moment, I recollected that, if I suffered myself to sink, my boy, deprived of the nourishment which sustained him, would perish miserably. I took therefore the sustenance my servants offered me; but I neither spoke nor shed tears, nor heeded any thing that was said to me; my mind dwelling on the plan I had formed to avail myself of the generosity of the English officer, and to engage him to assist me in finding Montgomery, whether living or dead. It was late before this gallant young man returned to me: the moment he entered, he enquired eagerly after my health and safety, I thanked him as well as I could for the preservation I owed to him; but added, that, to give it higher value, he must yet add another favour, and enable me to find the body of my husband, who had fallen in the field.

"He seemed amazed at my design, and represented to me that, besides the terrifying circumstances attendant on such an undertaking, so unfit for my age and sex to encounter, my endeavours would very probably be fruitless.—'Nor should you, Madam,' added he, 'so implicitly yield to grief: he, whose death you lament as certain, may be a prisoner.'

"This ray of probability would have cheered for a moment the blackness of my despair, had not the particulars related by Montgomery's servant left me nothing to hope. I related these circumstances to the English officer, with that gloomy desperation which precludes the power of shedding tears. He saw the state of my mind, and generously resolved not only to gratify me, but himself to protect me with a party of his men.

"With my little boy in my arms, for I refused to leave him as obstinately as to relinquish my project, I went forth on this dreadful errand; to a scene of death and desolation so terrible, that I will not shock you by an attempt to paint it—livid bodies covered with ghastly wounds, from whom the wretches who follow camps, making war more hideous, were yet stripping their bloody garments. Heaps of human beings thus butchered by the hands of their fellow creatures, affected me with such a sensation of sick horror, that I was frequently on the point of fainting. But Montgomery among them, left to be the food of wolves or dogs!—that beloved face, that form on which my eyes had so doted, disfigured and mangled by birds of prey!—this horrid image renewed from time to time my exhausted strength; and the pity of my noble conductor, more and more excited in my favour, suffered him not to tire in the mournful office of attending me.

"We had however traversed in vain so much of the bloody field, that my search seemed to be at length desperate; and my protector entreated me to consider, that by a longer perseverance I should injure my own health, and perhaps destroy my child, without a possibility of being of the least use to the lost object of my affection. It was now indeed night; but the moon shone with great lustre: and just as he had agreed to indulge me with ten minutes longer, on condition that I would then desist, the rays of the moon fell on something white a few yards from me, which glittered extremely. An impulse for which I cannot now account, made me suddenly catch it up: it was part of the sleeve of a shirt; and in it was a button set with brilliants, that had once belonged to Lord Pevensey; and which, as the diamonds surrounded a cypher formed of her hair, had been, after his Lordship's death, given by my mother to Montgomery.

"This well-known memorial convinced me of one fatal truth—that Montgomery was among the dead; but it revived the wretched hope of finding his body, which I imagined could not be far off. My conductor allowed that it was probable, and accounted for the remnant of his clothes being found, by supposing that it had been torn and dropped in a dispute for the spoil, which had happened among the plunderers of the deceased.

"Animated by this melancholy certainty, I more narrowly examined every ghastly countenance near the spot; and at length, half concealed by the blood that had flowed from his arm, which was thrown across his face, I discovered those well-known features so dear to my agonized heart.

"Then that grief which had hitherto been silent and sullen, suspended perhaps by a latent hope of his being a prisoner, broke forth in cries and lamentations. I threw myself on the ground; spoke to Montgomery, as if he was yet capable of hearing me; and in the wildness of my frenzy protested that I would never remove from the spot where he lay; but would remain there, and perish with my infant, by the side of my husband. The young officer, with all that humanity which characterizes the truly brave of every nation, bore with my extravagance; and with the most patient pity attempted to soothe and appease me, by calling off my thoughts from the dead, to whom I could be no longer serviceable, and fixing them on my child, to whom my existence was so necessary. But a new idea had now struck me—I insisted upon it that Montgomery was not dead; that I felt his heart palpitate and that if I remained there, and watched him, he would recover. I laid my head close to his mouth; I fancied that, though feebly, he still breathed. My generous friend, who imputed all I said to the delirium of extravagant sorrow, yet condescended to humour, in hopes of assuaging it; but when, in compliance with my earnest entreaty, he enquired into the reality of my hopes, he fancied, with mingled astonishment and pleasure, that he really found a slight pulse in the heart, and that the body had not the clayey coldness of death. Fearful, however, of indulging me in an hope which if found fallacious, might drive me into madness, he only said, that though he thought it improbable any life remained, yet that to satisfy me, the body should be removed into the house where I lodged, where a surgeon should attend to examine it; and if, as he greatly feared, there was indeed no chance of the vital powers being re-animated, I should at least be gratified in seeing the last offices performed, and should, as long as I remained where I was left, receive, both in regard to executing that mournful duty, and to my own safety, every good office he could render me.

"The guard which he had directed to follow us through the field, approaching on his signal, they were directed to raise the body he pointed out, and to carry it to the village from whence we came. Fatigue and terror were now equally unfelt; for though I had been too much agitated to discern those symptoms of life which my protector had really found, and had merely asserted it as an excuse to remain by the body of my husband, I was now sure that I should be indulged in my grief, and that Montgomery would receive the rites of sepulture. The body was no sooner placed on a bed in the room I inhabited, than throwing among the soldiers my purse, unseen by their commander, I hastened to give myself up to the dreadful luxury of sorrow. I found the young Englishman already there, gazing attentively on the disfigured face, with looks rather of doubt than of despair. On my entrance he retired; saying, 'Though I would not have you, Madam, too sanguine in encouraging hopes which will make a painful certainty doubly cruel, yet I cannot wholly discourage them: that wound on the head, which seems to have been done by the hoof of an horse, gives me the most apprehension, for the rest appear not to have been mortal: but the surgeon, who shall attend you the moment he can be spared from his duty, will be better able than I am to tell you whether you have really any reason to flatter yourself.'

"Before the surgeon arrived, I had, with the assistance of the French maid who attended me, washed the blood from the face; and from the various wounds he had received. The ideas which had occurred only in the ravings of a distempered imagination, now became real hopes; a slight pulsation appeared in the artery of the temples; his heart certainly, though languidly, beat. Ah! imagine my transports, for words cannot paint them—imagine what I felt, when the surgeon, who soon after arrived, declared that Montgomery was not dead! Far, however, was he from pronouncing that he would recover. Besides the fracture in his arm, which was a very bad one—a wound made by a bayonet in the breast, which was not however very deep— and a violent wound on the head, where the skull had narrowly escaped a fracture— he had lost so much blood; that it was almost impossible to suppose he could survive it; and his weakness was so excessive, that he remained wholly insensible, supported only by drops of nourishment, which I conveyed into his mouth with a spoon, and the surgeon dared not proceed immediately to the necessary operation of setting his arm, lest the shock should dismiss the feeble spirit which seemed every moment ready to depart from its mangled abode.

"Let me be brief in an account which I see has affected you too much.—At the end of a week, Montgomery, restored from the grasp of death, recovered his recollection, and knew *me* and his boy; and as the surgeons could not conveniently attend him where he was, my generous friend had him removed, as soon as it was possible, into Minden, now in possession of the English. There, at the end of a month, he was out of danger, but yet confined to his bed; and there, at the termination of that period, he parted from his noble preserver (for whom he felt all the friendship his generosity and personal merit deserved), as he was then ordered to another part of Germany, and soon after returned to England. Before he went, he assisted Montgomery to procure his exchange; which was attended with some difficulty, because there were doubts of his being a British subject. Having, however, by the instruction of this excellent friend, procured sufficient testimony of his being, though the son of Scottish parents, a subject of the French King, his exchange as such was admitted, and at the end of five months we returned to Paris. But Montgomery returned a cripple; for his arm, which had been with difficulty, and only by the extraordinary skill of the English surgeon, saved from amputation, was rendered wholly useless, and he wore it always in a sling. The extraordinary circumstance of his escape from death, as well as his great military merit, procured him the notice of the King of France, who gave him, with a pension, considerable at that time, and in that service, the cross of St. Louis.

"It was now that I reasonably hoped for some portion of happiness. Adoring Montgomery; having been the fortunate instrument, in the hands of Providence, to rescue him from death; with a lovely boy, on whom we both doted, and a fortune equal to our wants (for, with what arose from the interest of Lord Pevensey's gift to me, and Montgomery's pension, we had near four hundred pounds a year)—I seemed to have nothing left to wish for; and some years did indeed pass, during which my felicity could hardly admit of increase. The early promise of merit which Charles's infancy gave, every year seemed to confirm: it was the principal pride and pleasure of his father to be his instructor in every liberal science, as well as in tactics; for, born in a camp, he seemed a predestined soldier. Though brought up himself in the Catholic religion, Montgomery was so little of a bigot, that he suffered me to educate my son a Protestant; and that circumstance only had prevented his early entrance into the French army. Measures, however, were taken to procure him a commission among the Swiss in that service, when a violent and sudden illness deprived him of his parent and protector, and me of the most beloved of husbands and the tenderest of friends.

"Pardon me, my dearest Miss Chesterville! Though I have long been familiar with sorrow; though almost five years have passed since this lamented event; I cannot always conquer these unavailing tears. But wherefore should I distress you? I have only to add, that, at the death of my husband, a great part of our income ceased; and though I solicited a continuance of at least part of his pension, I found that under a new reign his services had been superseded by newer claims. So many difficulties arose, and so uncertain seemed my success, that after an expensive application at Paris and Versailles for some months, I gave up all hope, and determined to go to England; which, notwithstanding my long separation from it, I still considered as my country.

"On my arrival in London with my son, I made myself known to some of my own and of Montgomery's relations, who were established in employments about the court; and they, having understood my situation, promised that they would immediately apply for a commission for my son in the army, where I was compelled to suffer him to be placed; not only because his own inclinations led him to prefer a military life; but because our income, now reduced to less than two hundred a year, did not enable me to support him without a profession.

"Allured by these promises, and piqued at the neglect I had met with in France, I relinquished all thoughts of returning to that country. But, if I found solicitation and attendance irksome there, these circumstances were at least equally painful in England; and, after many months of fatiguing and incessant endeavours to obtain a confirmation of these promises, I was weary of the task, and went to my friends in Scotland. My *relations*, at least, were very numerous there; but many of them looked upon me and my son as foreigners and aliens, about whom it no longer concerned them to be interested. I staid however a few months among them; and then determining to fix on some cheap retirement, I found this cottage; to which, expending a small sum of money on it, I removed my books and effects: and I have ever since lived here with my son, regretting nothing but that his talents and his virtues are lost to society.—Yet why should I regret it? He here still cultivates his excellent understanding; the virtues of his heart are preserved in all their purity; and his passions, naturally too warm and violent, have here no objects likely to render them too powerful for his reason. From the little I saw of modern young men of fashion during my short stay in London, perhaps I ought rather to rejoice that my son is thrown at a distance from the contagion of their example; and that, with all their spirit, he is free from their vices. Far from murmuring at his lot, his whole study is to make me happy, by convincing me he is so himself. As we equally understand several languages, our reading is pretty extensive; and books are almost our only indulgence. Charles is a proficient in music. He understands tolerably every other science; and in drawing is almost a master: and by these resources he contrives to pass without weariness those hours when the weather forbids his going abroad. We have been twice to spend a few weeks with my relations in Scotland: but I shall own to you that society, such as I generally meet with, serves only to make my return to this solitude more delightful; that my heart is now wedded to it; and that I have no wish for any other enjoyment than that I have found? indulging in this remote hermitage the tears which the memory of Montgomery render sacred; and fulfilling, at least as well as I am able, though not so well as I wish, my duty towards our beloved Charles."

Mrs. Montgomery, seeing her son now enter the little court, wiped away the tears, which in repeating this last sentence had again filled her eyes, and received him with a melancholy smile. He bowed gravely to Ethelinde, tenderly spoke to his mother; and desired that his entrance might not interrupt so delightful a tête à tête. But it had now been some time nearly dark; and the appearance of candles reminded Ethelinde that it was time to return to the abbey, and that there were other beings in the world besides Mrs. Montgomery and her son; a circumstance which had for some hours entirely escaped her recollection.

The narrative she had heard had drawn many tears from her eyes. Those of Mrs. Montgomery bore testimony to the mournful story she had been relating, and when lights were brought, Montgomery instantly perceived what had been the subject of their conversation.

Ethelinde at length reluctantly rose to go. With pain more acute than she had ever felt before, she bad an adieu, perhaps the last adieu, to Mrs. Montgomery; and, softened too much to be able to restrain her tears, she sobbed out, "God bless you! all happiness await you, dearest, dearest Madam!"

Mrs. Montgomery, not less affected, but more accustomed to sorrow, pressed her fondly in her arms; and giving her hand to her son, said, "Heaven protect my lovely, my amiable young friend! Charles, you will wait on Miss Chesterville."

Ethelinde faintly requested him not to give himself that trouble. But he insisted on being allowed to attend her; and proceeding with her along the side of the Lake, he walked silently by her side for near half the way: at length he summoned courage to enquire when the family of Sir Edward Newenden left Grasmere Abbey.

"In a few days, I believe."

"This then," said Montgomery, in the most mournful accents, "is probably the last opportunity I shall ever enjoy of seeing Miss Chesterville?"

"I hope not," said Ethelinde faintly.

"Alas! I dare not hope ever again to be so happy! You, Madam, are destined to adorn the most brilliant circles; my lot is obscurity—obscurity, however, in which I was well content to remain, till I beheld excellence, and learned to feel the power of beauty, when united with goodness and understanding."

This was too much for the full heart of Ethelinde, who was already more strongly prejudiced in favour of this young man, than she had ever yet been for any human being. She dared not trust her voice with an answer. Another long silence ensued, broken only by a deep sigh from Montgomery, who then again spoke.

"My mother, Madam, has perhaps been relating to you the events of her past life?'"

"Yes, Sir, she has."

"She told you then, perhaps, that the English officer, to whose humanity my father owed the prolongation of his life, was of the name of Chesterville?"

"Of Chesterville?"

"Of Chesterville—Captain Henry Chesterville. Ever since I came to England I have anxiously desired to know if he yet lived, that I might find him; but I failed in my enquiries, the little while I staid in London; and since having had no means of information, I despaired of ever having the gratification of seeing him; till, hearing that your name was Chesterville, I flattered myself he might be of your family; and I determined to take the first opportunity of asking you."

"Good God!" said Ethelinde, "it was my father!—Unaccustomed to talk of the events of a war in which he bore an active part, I never heard him name this particular circumstance, but I am well persuaded it was himself."

"I am convinced of it too," replied Montgomery, "for methinks our families have been long acquainted.—I dare not trust myself to say, how proud my heart is of the idea that we are to renew an acquaintance so enchanting, so flattering to me. I hope Mr. Chesterville will not so far have forgotten his own beneficence, as to be offended if I still consider myself as known to him, and take the first opportunity of assuring him that the son of Montgomery values himself on inheriting the obligation owed by his father. Will you, Madam, intercede for me, that I may become known to Mr. Chesterville?"

"My intercession will not, I am persuaded, be necessary.—My father will be happy to repeat to you, that whatever benefit his good fortune once enabled him to confer on your father, has been more than overpaid by your having hazarded your life for mine."

They were by this time arrived at the gate of the lawn, where they had before parted. Montgomery stopped.—"Is it then indeed," cried he mournfully, "the last time I shall have the happiness of seeing you in this country, and do you really leave it in a few days?"

"I believe so," replied Ethelinde , "yet I think not *so* immediately as to preclude the possibility of your seeing Sir Edward and the family again, if you are disposed to take that trouble. Lest, however, I should see you no more, accept once again of my thanks, and ever of my good wishes!"

In saying this she almost involuntarily held out her hand to him: Montgomery seizing, carried it to his lips; and kissing it with an eagerness which forced her hastily to withdraw it, he turned away and disappeared—while Ethelinde, heart struck, and feeling lost to all the rest of the world, returned to her own room; and sent an excuse to avoid joining the company, among whom she was unfitted to appear.

CHAPTER VII[1]

The next morning Ethelinde, summoning as much resolution as possible, endeavoured to drive from her thoughts the image of Montgomery, which perpetually pursued her; and to appear at breakfast with her usual cheerfulness. Sir Edward, however, who had so long and anxiously studied her countenance that he could guess at almost every emotion of her heart, easily discerned that all was not right there. Her gaiety was forced; she affected an interest about things to which he knew she was entirely indifferent; and, as soon as she could without rudeness escape, she made a pretence to hasten away from the company.

Sir Edward could no longer delay informing her of her father's wishes for her return: yet he dreaded the explanation; but he now determined to follow her. He saw her go out; and, taking a shorter way, he met her in a copse that terminated the park on the opposite side from the Lake. A winding path led through it; in which, some time before he approached her, he saw her walk slowly along, in a thoughtful and melancholy attitude. As soon, however, as she perceived him, she quickened her pace, and met him smiling. His looks were less gay: he took her hand, and enquired why she preferred solitude to the amusing party within doors.

"For no reason in the world, but because I am like nobody else; and if it were not for my father, I should like to renounce every

1 Misnumbered VIII in the 1790 second edition I used for my copy text. I have silently corrected chapter numbers.

scene I have yet been in, and to pass the rest of my life on the banks of the Grasmere water."

"Alone, Ethelinde?" enquired Sir Edward, fixing his penetrating eyes on hers.

She cast them down, and blushed. "Why not alone, Sir Edward? You know I have no fear of solitude."

"But Lady Newenden would say, that young ladies who have such a passion for rocks and woods, always associate with them the idea of some gentle swain—such, for example, as Davenant."

"*He* is, in truth, a gentle swain!"

"Or of Montgomery, the gallant Montgomery."

"Pooh! You know that I am hardly acquainted with him."

"And have hardly thought of him, Ethelinde?"

"I hope you do not believe me so silly and romantic, as to need this sort of raillery. Why should you suppose I think particularly of Mr. Montgomery?"

"Nay, I do not suppose it; nor will I, my dear Ethy, rally you; for indeed I have that to say to you, which makes me not only serious, but unhappy.—Your father——"

"My father!—Oh! what of him? he is not ill?"

"Do not alarm yourself thus. He is *not* ill; but by his letter seems not quite well: and he mentions a wish that you should return to him as soon as you can make it convenient."

"Dear Sir Edward, how long have you known this? Where is his letter? Let me set out to-day. I am sure he is ill; he is unhappy; why should I neglect a moment obeying him? I will go back to the house, and prepare instantly for my departure. Contrive it for me, I beseech you, so that I may lose no more time."

"Be more composed, I beg of you, Ethelinde. Reflect that nothing can hurt the colonel so much as your distressing yourself: nor is it in this case necessary; for you may believe that, had he been seriously ill, he would have pressed your immediate attendance."

"Cannot I see the letter? But at all events I will instantly set out."

"You shall, if you desire it, to-morrow morning."

"Why not to-day?"

"Because a conveyance cannot be procured, perhaps; besides, it is really unnecessary to hurry yourself.—I wish to speak to you on another subject. Mr. Davenant has desired me to offer you his heart and fortune. How are you disposed towards him? You must have seen enough of his intentions to have considered of your answer."

"Can you really, Sir Edward, ask that question seriously?"

"Very seriously: at least my commission was very seriously given me; I merely promised to execute it."

"Of Mr. Davenant's heart, Sir Edward, you already know my opinion; judge therefore, my dear Sir, whether his fortune, splendid as it is, will tempt me, thinking as I do, to accept it. I am obliged to him certainly for his good opinion, and for employing you to acquaint me with it; but no considerations shall influence me to unite myself to Mr. Davenant."

"He will, however, probably expect some reasons for a refusal so peremptory; a refusal for which, believe me, he is very little prepared."

"If he insists on it then, I shall give them. But, my dear Sir, why waste we time in talking of him, when my heart is with my father, and I am impatient to follow it?"

"And will you leave no part of it behind? will none of your good wishes remain on the banks of Grasmere water?"

"While you are here, you know they will," answered Ethelinde, with her usual frankness; and, putting both her hands into his, he pressed them gently, and stifling a sigh, said—"And your new acquaintance, Mrs. Montgomery, will *she* retain no portion of your regard?"

"Assuredly she will; and if I had time and spirits to tell you how much she deserves the regard of all the world——"

"You know then who she is? I own her manner of life, and the appearance of her son, has excited my curiosity."

Ethelinde then, unable to resist the pleasure of talking of Montgomery and his mother, and secretly flattering herself that she should create a friend for them in the noble-minded and generous Sir Edward, related, in as few words as she could, the outline of their history , but, though she passed over much of it, the vivacity with which she spoke, the animation of her countenance, and the warmth of her expressions, convinced Sir Edward, who watched her narrowly, that the young man had made an impression on her heart, to which it had hitherto been a stranger. The pang this conviction gave to his own, he immediately endeavoured to suppress, and, yielding to his natural generosity, he became really interested for the mother and the son.

Ethelinde had hardly finished her narrative before they reached the house, after going all round the plantation; and then her father, his possible illness, his certain uneasiness in her absence, recurring to her mind, all her spirits forsook her. She entreated Sir Edward to consider for her the means of setting out the next day; and wishing him also to acquaint Lady Newenden of the necessity of her leaving the abbey, she retired to her own room to indulge her tears; which, for the first time in her life, were not wholly for her father.

Montgomery, whom she was perhaps never to see again!—Montgomery, so amiable, so unhappy, and to whom she was so much obliged!—could she help lamenting the probability of their eternal separation? Accustomed, however, to scrutinize her own thoughts, she blamed herself for the sudden and powerful influence which the idea of this young man had gained over her mind; and she determined to check as much as possible a partiality so sudden and romantic, that she would assuredly have blamed it in another.

This resolution was easily made, but difficult to keep. All other conversation was importunate and fatiguing to her. She was restless, absent, unhappy; and, while her duty and tenderness to her father urged her to an immediate departure, the thoughts of seeing Montgomery no more, of being perhaps forgotten by him, added to the depression of spirits which the apprehended illness of colonel Chesterville occasioned.

She could not, however, avoid appearing at dinner. Sir Edward had already informed Lady Newenden of her intended journey, who received it with great indifference: but Davenant put on as melancholy a look as his vacant features could assume; and Lord Danesforte, the moment he could get an opportunity of speaking to her, lamented that the party was soon be deprived of its most amiable support; and asked if "she would allow him to see her safe part of the way?"

"By no means, my Lord; I entreat your Lordship not to think of taking that trouble."—She spoke this aloud; and Lady Newenden turning her eyes upon them with a look of displeasure, he found that, in hazarding too much with one, he might lose his ground with both; he therefore desisted for that time, and contented him-

self with animating the pursuit of Davenant, knowing that Ethelinde had rather a dislike than a partiality towards him; and that,
removed as she would be from any farther acquaintance with
Montgomery, little was to be apprehended from her affection to
another. He thought so lightly of the principles of women, that he
doubted not but that he should be able to triumph over her understanding, if opportunity was offered him, by the same means
which had enabled him to boast of his good fortune with many
others.

When the company dispersed after dinner, Davenant followed
Sir Edward, to enquire the event of the negociation he had been
entrusted with.—Sir Edward, hurt himself at being thus deprived
of the company of Ethelinde, and made uneasy at the unpleasant
prospect which the embarrassed situation of her father's circumstances offered to her, was ill disposed to be teized by Davenant
about an affair to which all his fears for her future fate could not
induce him heartily to wish any success: yet, ashamed of appearing out of humour with a man who had not really offended him,
he prepared with patience to listen to Davenant, who, with an
assured confidence, said, "Pray, Sir Edward, what was Miss Chesterville's answer? I hope she is not—I think indeed she cannot be
adverse to my proposal."

"She seems, however, averse to any proposals of marriage. At
present her thoughts are occupied by her father's indisposition:
you must wait, therefore, a more favourable opportunity."

"I cannot say, Sir Edward, that it is pleasing to be kept in suspense. With such a fortune and such settlements as it will be in
my power to offer her, I think she may not find it very difficult to
determine."

"If fortune was her only object, certainly she would not; but
Ethelinde unluckily expects many other qualifications in a husband.—She expects a heart capable of understanding her value,
and a taste which shall teach whoever she marries to appreciate
more than mere personal perfections. But in truth, Davenant, I
cannot advise you upon the subject: it is a commission which you
know I did not wish to undertake. It will be fitter for you to speak
to her yourself; you will then judge of the probability of your
success."

Davenant, though unwilling to suppose that a man of his consequence could meet with a refusal, began however to doubt anew whether some prepossession in favour of another had not produced the coldness with which she had received the overture made by Sir Edward. He went to Lord Danesforte, and scrupled not to tell him, with mingled sullenness and resentment, that his first advances had by no means been received with the complacency he had expected.

His Lordship rallied him on his pusillanimity.—"Faith, Davenant," cried he, "I thought you had understood women better. A beautiful girl, who like Ethelinde has been accustomed to be treated as a future goddess, and has been brought up with no other persuasion but that her person will make her fortune, expects attendance, adulation, and almost idolatry. You are as cold and as timid as if you had never conversed with any bed-maker at Oxford; and therefore expected a repulse, the very apprehension of which generally produces it. Let her fancy that you are madly in love with her; and that you are ready to fight for her—to die for her—or to live with her; and the angel will descend from her seraphics, and consider the substantial and terrestrial comforts of a fortune of five or six thousand a year. Speak boldly then your own pretensions, mixed up with a sufficient quantity of flattery; no matter how strong—she has been so much used to it, that you must season it high to make her attend. If she goes alone, ask to escort her yourself; and speak reason to her. Upon my soul she is a lovely girl; and is to be forgiven for a little pride. But believe me, whatever airs she may give herself, she has too much sense to have occasion to think twice about the final acceptance of you, though she may like to coquet a little, and teize you for a month or two, to shew her power."

Thus encouraged, Davenant felt his resolution revive. Though his heart was not interested, his pride was now deeply engaged; and of that pride which arises from the consciousness of wealth, he had a great deal. But conscious also of some deficiency which he had neither strength of mind to correct, or candour to own, there was ever about him a mixture of haughtiness and bashfulness, especially when he found himself in company with people in whose estimation he well knew mere riches were not an equivalent of cultivated understanding, or an ingenuous heart.

The intellectual perfections of Ethelinde were so far from

increasing her charms in his opinion, that he would have liked her better, if, with as lovely a person, she had possessed an understanding even inferior to the generality of women; since he had no inclination to encounter the scrutinizing eye of refined sensibility in his courtship, nor was he much disposed to acknowledge the superiority of his wife after marriage. But her beauty and her noble birth would gratify his vanity, and acquire for him some of that eclat[1] which he coveted in the fashionable world; while he imagined that his disinterested generosity, in marrying a woman without fortune, would secure not only her gratitude, but his reputation for liberality of spirit, for the rest of his life.

When he left Lord Danesforte, he enquired for Miss Chesterville, and hearing from the servants that she had walked out into the park, he followed her.—Encouraging, almost unknown to herself, an hope of once more meeting Montgomery, Ethelinde had gone out of the park; and instead of taking the well-known path towards Montgomery's house, which she fancied she desired to avoid, she took that which wound up the side of one of the fells, and which Sir Edward had caused to be cut through the rude surface, among brush wood and low trees; it led almost perpendicularly up to a little alpine spot among the rocks, whence a stream burst out, whose waters were accumulated probably on the top of the fell, and hurrying down its side, were precipitated from hence into the Lake below. Sir Edward had made a sort of cave under the masses of stone, supported by rude pillars; and though dark tufts of trees concealed it on three sides, yet on the fourth it opened to a view of the Lake, towards the village where the dwelling of Montgomery was situated. Sir Edward had, in one of their rambles, shewn the place to Ethelinde; and thither she now went, to indulge those thoughts which made her unfit for society, and to take a last and distant leave of the house which held those friends so newly acquired, yet so deeply regretted.

She sat down, faint and out of breath; turned her eyes towards the white cottage, glittering on the unruffled bosom of the Lake, and sighed deeply.

"Would I had never known these amiable people; since we are situated so wide of each other, that I shall probably never meet

1 *éclat* (French): ostentatious display, dazzling effect. Smith (or her printer) writes the word without the accent as if it were English.

them more! since they have given me a specimen of social pleasure which I cannot taste where I usually am, and yet cannot cease to regret! Among beings how different do my days move on!—with Lady Newenden, thinking wholly of herself, with Miss Newenden, who loves nothing but her horse; or among a crowd of insignificant women, eager after trifles, and occupied often in the cruellest defamation, to gratify either their malice or their love of talking. How much superior is Mrs. Montgomery, in her cottage, to the most affluent among them, surrounded with splendor! How much superior is her son—good God! how much superior to such a man as Lord Danesforte, with his title, his figure, his immense estate, and powerful interest! How much more respectable than Davenant, with his five thousand a year, his university education, his stud, and his ridiculous indulgences, is the unattended, unassuming Montgomery! the child of sorrow, born amidst blood and carnage! educated by a father who had seen and braved all the miseries of war, and cultivated all the arts of peace; and now supporting a widowed mother!—with talents which might raise him to the most enviable situations, but with an heart that sets him above them all!

"Montgomery has nothing! had he the fortunes of Lord Danesforte, or of the insignificant, selfish, narrow-minded Davenant, how differently would he use his power! Possibly he is happier as he is. Ah! may nothing ever disturb his happiness, or that of his beloved, his amiable mother!'"

Tears filled the eyes of Ethelinde, while these reflections passed through her mind. She held her handkerchief to her face; the rushing of the torrent near her prevented her hearing any other sound; before, therefore, she was conscious of his approach, Montgomery was at her side.

She started when she perceived him, and endeavoured to conceal that she had been weeping; while he, advancing, exclaimed, in the most animated accents, "I absolve Fortune for ever for all her cruelty! After being so happy as to meet you here so unexpectedly, I shall never complain again!"

"Unexpectedly indeed!" answered Ethelinde, hardly finding breath to speak, "I could not have imagined that any body but myself had frequented this lonely seat."

"Pardon me; it has long been a favourite spot of mine, and will now be more than ever haunted; for so strange a composition is the human heart that there is often a delight in indulging regret; and such will be my occupation here, when I remember that I here saw Miss Chesterville, perhaps for the last time."

Ethelinde tried to force a smile, and answered—"Did you not make to me the same speech when we parted last?"

"Ah! forgive then the tautology. How indeed can a man think of varying his expressions, when his heart is sensible only to one invariable impression of incurable unhappiness, and hopeless regret?"

Ethelinde still attempted to turn off this discourse, by affecting to consider such speeches as matters of course; but her voice and looks ill seconded her intention, that yielding to the tenderness and concern she felt, she turned away; and was obliged again to take out her handkerchief.

Montgomery, deprived of all resolution by these symptoms of sensibility, forgot that he had determined never to disclose to its object a passion inevitably hopeless; since his own circumstances were such as must make it madness in him to think of uniting himself with a woman who had no fortune. He had learned that Ethelinde was the daughter of a younger brother of a family not very opulent; and though his heart had on his first acquaintance with her acknowledged her perfections, and had since been more deeply interested at every interview, he thought he should have command enough over himself to conceal his partiality in the presence of Ethelinde, and philosophy enough in her absence to conquer it for ever.

But the sight of her tears, the idea of her feeling pain at their separation, overturned at once all these wise resolutions; and with an emotion which only true passion could produce, he ventured tremblingly to disclose the attachment which he now felt was invincible; and while he described its violence, lamented the probability of its being successless.

Ethelinde, as sincere as sensible, was incapable, in the present moment, of concealing that she shared this indiscreet passion.—"I cannot disguise it from you, Mr. Montgomery; my obligations to you, and your own merit, have made an impression on my heart which will never be obliterated. Conscious of the impropriety of indulging such a sentiment, I will own to you that I would gladly have forgotten it; yet why should I wish to do so? Though we shall perhaps meet no more, though our destinies seem to render a more permanent acquaintance impossible, I may surely cherish a friendship, a———"

Words were wanting; but her tears spoke more forcibly, than language could have done, the emotions contending in her bosom.

"Good God!" exclaimed the ardent and passionate Montgomery, "for what am I reserved? To meet the loveliest, the most amiable of women; to find her generosity and compassion awakened for me, and to be certain that I shall see her no more—no more hear of her, perhaps, unless that she has blessed some more fortunate man with that hand and that heart, which are all that I covet on earth. Poverty! Adversity! Obscurity! I have hitherto endured all without a murmur! But now I feel how bitter it is to be thrown out of that line of life, from whence I might have dared to look up to supreme happiness."

"I cannot bear this," said Ethelinde. "Let me leave this place; and let us endeavour to submit to that destiny which we probably cannot change. Remember the claim your mother has upon you, and suffer her not to feel the pain of seeing you unhappy."

"Believe me, Madam, I have used every argument with my own heart, which your considerate compassion can suggest; and you will recollect that, far from indulging this dangerous passion, by seeking the frequent pleasure of beholding you, I tore myself away on the afternoon you passed with my mother. Ah! fruitless precaution! it was then too late to suppress the admiration which I felt from my first interview, and which every subsequent one has contributed to heighten into an attachment that can end only with my life."

"I must not listen to this sort of conversation, Mr. Montgomery," said Ethelinde, rising to leave him; while she doubted whether her trembling limbs would carry her from the spot.— "Adieu, Sir! May all happiness await you! and may Mrs. Montgomery——" She could not finish the sentence, but, turning away, was hastening towards the path that led down to the abbey.

"Suffer me, however," said Montgomery, "to attend you home. I know I ought not to have spoken to you as I have done; but when I know not whether I shall ever see you again——"

An interval of silence ensued, and Ethelinde endeavoured to

recollect herself, and to summon some degree of fortitude and resolution. To have listened to a young man, almost a stranger to her; to have confessed a passion, perhaps so improper in itself, so repugnant to the duty she owed her father, shocked and distressed her. Yet when she turned her eyes on Montgomery, when she beheld the melancholy look that his fine features had assumed, and heard him complain of the obscurity of his destiny, only as it prevented his aspiring to her pity, tenderness, and affection, against which reason fruitlessly contended, again overwhelmed her; and to say adieu for the last time seemed to be so cruelly painful, that every uneasiness of her life appeared comparatively light. She ventured not to trust herself a second time to speak, lest she should more evidently betray the state of her heart: but trembling she pursued her way; while Montgomery, without presuming to offer her his arm, walked mournfully by her side.

They had thus advanced within a few yards of the entrance of the park; and as they were now near the gate, where they must take leave, the agitation of Ethelinde increased. She repented the girlish and romantic weakness which had tempted her to indulge herself with a farewel view of the cottage, blamed herself for having incurred so much needless anguish, and still more for having betrayed it to Montgomery.

While these thoughts passed through her mind, Montgomery was reflecting, not on the means of bearing better this cruel separation, but on those of seeing her again.

"Will you," said he, "suffer me to see you, if any circumstance at present unexpected should occasion my being in London?"

"It were better, perhaps——" Ethelinde was proceeding in a faultering voice to deny him; but, interrupting her, he cried—

"Ah! do not, I entreat you, forbid me; possibly I may never claim the conditional indulgence I solicit. After knowing that to the generous gallantry of colonel Chesterville, my father, when an enemy, owed his life, would it not be ungrateful were I to neglect an opportunity of paying for that dear parent the debt of gratitude, which no change of circumstance, no lapse of years, nor even death itself, can cancel?"

"Let your visit then be to him; and as for me——"

The conclusion of her speech was broken by a sudden whistle, and round an angle of the path, Davenant, suddenly turning, appeared before them calling his dogs. Never was an interruption more unwelcome; for though Ethelinde knew not what she was going to add, and had but a moment before prudently determined to conceal, as far she now could, the real sentiments of her heart, yet she never so thoroughly disliked Davenant as at this moment; and Montgomery, whose eyes were eagerly fixed on her half-averted face, now turned them towards the unfortunate intruder with a look of anger and scorn; while Davenant, whose narrow mind had conceived a mean jealousy of Montgomery, looked gloomy and offended at meeting Ethelinde with him; and slightly touching his hat, which salutation Montgomery as coldly returned, he said to Ethelinde—"I have been all over the park, Miss Chesterville—I believe twice over it, in search of you."

"And to what, Sir, do you owe having taken so much trouble?"

"To—to—my—nothing, but only I wished to have had the pleasure of being of your walking party."

"You are very good," answered she; "but I chose to walk alone." Immediately conscious, however, that he would remark Montgomery's being with her, she added—"and by accident met Mr. Montgomery coming to the abbey."

"Mr. Montgomery," said Davenant, "is always a lucky man."

"Yes," answered Ethelinde, with vivacity; "he has more than once met me very opportunely; and, had it not been for him, I should probably never have enjoyed the happiness I shall now have in a day or two—that of meeting my father."

They were by this time within the lawn, and Montgomery said something as if he meant there to take leave; but still lingering till the last moment, still deferring to take the farewell look, he went into the house with them, saying that he could not forbear, since he was so near, soliciting permission to pay his respects to Sir Edward and Lady Newenden.

Sir Edward received him with friendly politeness. The rest of the party, in their usual way, continued talking on trifling subjects, to which Montgomery was unable to give the slightest attention; and finding that to be merely in company with Ethelinde under such restraint was worse than not seeing her at all, he sat only a few minutes; and then hastily rising, paid his compliments round, without daring to distinguish her by any particular address (lest his emotion should become too evident), and withdrew.

Ethelinde had murmured something of sending her friendly wishes to his mother; but her words were inarticulate; her heart beat so violently that she breathed with difficulty; and, as she heard the great hall door shut after him, her spirits seemed so entirely to forsake her, that, though she would gladly have withdrawn, she knew not whether she could command strength enough to cross the room, and therefore sat down where she was; hoping that, as it was nearly dark, her agitation would pass unnoticed.

Lord Danesforte however approached her; and in a low voice, but with his usual vehement expressions, lamented that they were so soon to lose her.—"It is the most unreasonable thing in the world," said he, "for Chesterville to send for you to London at this time of the year. How does he think you are to exist there, or how are your friends to exist without you, who have once known you? Here will be hanging and drowning, I am afraid, when you are gone. As to Davenant, we must have a watch set over him, or we shall see him floating, like another Leander,[1] on the Lake; or pendant from some willow over it."

Ethelinde was by no means able to answer this trifling raillery; and was so near shedding tears, that she was afraid, if she spoke at all, her voice would betray her: she bowed therefore gravely, and Lord Danesforte went on—

"We shall be all undone without you. As for me, I shall fly off as soon as I can after we get to Scarborough. You will admit me to see you in London, as an old acquaintance?"

"I dare say my father would think himself honoured by your Lordship's visits."

She spoke this so faintly as hardly to be heard; and was much relieved by the approach of Sir Edward, who, as soon as Lord Danesforte turned towards another part of the room, sat down by her, and told her that his post-chaise, with four hired horses, was to be at the door at seven o'clock the next morning.—"But my dear Ethy," said he, tenderly taking her hand, "what am I to say to Davenant? He complains that he has in vain sought an opportunity of

---

1 Leander: A hero from Greek myth; in love with Hero, who lived on the other side of the Hellespont, he would swim across nightly to be with her, led to her by her light; one night a storm extinguished her light, and he drowned. Marlowe and Chapman were the first two poets to popularize it in witty Ovidian narratives.

speaking to you; that you repulse without hearing him; and he has been asking me if I will allow him to escort you part of the way tomorrow, that he may have an opportunity of explaining himself."

"I hope, Sir, you refused him?"

"I referred him to you."

"I am sorry you did, because it puts me to the pain of rejecting peremptorily a mark of attention, for which I am doubtless obliged to Mr. Davenant, but which I can by no means accept."

"Suffer him then to speak to you this evening, and let him hear your resolution from yourself. May I tell him that you will hear him?"

This was almost too much for Ethelinde, who, overcome by the pain of having parted probably for ever from the man who possessed her heart, was yet compelled to listen to proposals from another, for whom she felt only indifference bordering on contempt; and whom she found herself disposed to dislike the more; because he possessed all those pecuniary advantages, the want of which in Montgomery deprived her of all hope of being his.

Sir Edward had so far conquered his own inclinations by the force of his excellent principles, that he believed himself henceforth determined to act, in regard to Ethelinde, with the most disinterested friendship. He suspected her partiality to the young stranger as soon as she had herself been sensible of it: every day's observation confirmed his suspicion, but as he knew that Montgomery was entirely destitute of fortune, and was too well informed of the embarrassed situation of colonel Chesterville, he was convinced that, by giving way to such a passion, Ethelinde would be miserable either in its disappointment or its success; while, by accepting the offers of Davenant, she would be secure of affluence for herself, and of retrieving the situation of her father. To himself, though dearer than his existence, she could never be anything more than a beloved sister, and his generous and feeling heart stifled as much as possible every other wish than that of seeing her, if not happy, at least out of any hazard of suffering either the torments of hopeless passion, or the humiliation and inconveniences of indigence. He fancied that Davenant might, under her influence, become more worthy of her; and though he flattered not himself that she could ever love him, he trusted that her good sense, her good heart, and her filial piety, would reconcile her to a lot, which, though he would not in other circumstances have chosen for her, seemed now the best that was likely to offer.

In answer to his request that she would hear Davenant that evening, Ethelinde, collecting as much courage as she could, replied that she was much fatigued with a long walk; and, having preparations to make for the next day, should go immediately to her room.—"Excuse me therefore, dear Sir Edward, if I entreat you to take once more the trouble of conveying my thanks to Mr. Davenant for the honour he does me by his good opinion; and at the same time assure him that every application of that sort must, however flattering, be ineffectual."

"Davenant will not receive such an answer as final from me."

"He must then pardon me if I beg he will hear it from myself, should he unluckily remain in the same mind after he reaches London. Indeed, Sir Edward, I cannot see him this evening, pray do not press it; and if you have indeed the affection for me which I have always been so proud of, persuade him wholly to desist from a pursuit which persecutes and perplexes me."

Sir Edward, struck with her manner, and the resolution she seemed to have taken, was more than ever disposed to believe that she would not thus hastily have rejected one man without being sensible of a strong partiality for another. She immediately arose, and retired to her own room, where the image of Montgomery was immediately before her, and her whole soul lost in the tumultuous yet painful pleasure of knowing that he loved her; but, while she felt inexpressible delight in that conviction, the bitterest anguish seized her in recollecting that she had parted from him probably for ever.

The hope, however, that he would in pursuance of the hint he had given, follow her to London, lurked in her heart; but, if she for a moment indulged it, her reason reproached her for the folly and indiscretion of wishing to nourish a passion which must be so fatal to her own repose, to that of the man for whose happiness she would have sacrificed her life, and to the tranquillity of her father, hitherto her first consideration.

During a sleepless night, these contradictory and irreconcileable sensations passed alternately through her mind; and, by the morning, reason had so far gained the ascendant, that she fancied herself determined to think no more of Montgomery, to check every wish that led to a nearer acquaintance with him, and to give herself up as entirely as ever to her attendance and duty to the best of fathers, without suffering any other object to divide with him her tenderness and her attention.

CHAPTER VIII

Ethelinde arose the next morning, pale, languid, her eyes swollen with weeping, and her heart heavy. She went into the breakfast room, where the tea was made for her by the old housekeeper, and as she had taken leave of Lady, Sir Edward, and Miss Newenden, the evening before, as well as of the rest of the party, by the usual compliments on such occasions, she intended to have begun her journey without repeating a ceremony so painful with friends who are beloved, and so unmeaning with persons wholly indifferent. She had not, however, been many minutes below, before Sir Edward entered the room.—"Prepared already, my dear Ethy, to begin your journey? Ah! I see you are anxious to leave us! You are tired of Grasmere Abbey, though you have yet been here only five weeks."

"Not tired of Grasmere Abbey, Sir Edward, nor anxious to leave you; but very solicitous to return to my father, very uneasy lest he should be more indisposed than his tenderness for me will allow him to relate."

"I hope you will not find him so. Give him this letter; and tell him that, as soon as I return to London, my first visit shall be to him. When that will be, I know not; Lady Newenden will probably wish to stay at Scarborough, if she finds amusement there; and will then perhaps go to some other place of public amusement, since London will be without attractions for some months to come."

"Shall I not see my cousin before I go? It is however immaterial, as I took leave of her last night;"

"There is another person, however, whom you ought to see: Davenant has repeated his wish to be allowed to speak to you."

"Dear Sir Edward," answered Ethelinde with increased quickness, "how can you be so importunate about that young man! Indeed I can never like him, I can never esteem him; why then should I listen to him? Why should I suffer him a moment to be in doubt about my sentiments?"

"Then why not hear and dismiss him, if to dismiss him you are determined? But allow me, my dear Ethy, to say, that, however indifferent you may be to circumstances merely pecuniary, you should not hastily nor harshly refuse an offer, on which perhaps few young women would hesitate. Consider of it; see your father first."

"Good God!" cried she, "is it from *you*, Sir Edward, I receive such advice? To listen to a man who is so indifferent to me, merely because he is rich! My father, Sir, unless he is greatly altered, would never, I think, urge me to become the wife of Mr. Davenant, unless I felt for him that preference which I am persuaded I never shall feel. Dear Sir Edward, press me no more on this subject; and for-give—forgive the ungrateful petulance with which I have received your friendly but impracticable advice." She then gave him her hand; while her eyes, filled with tears, were fixed on his face. He found himself too much affected, and not daring to trust his own resolutions, he only kissed her hand, and said, with as much steadi-ness as he could command—"You will always command me, Ethe-linde; you know that I have no wish but to see you happy."

Davenant now entered the room in a travelling dress; and advancing, as if almost doubtful of his reception, towards Ethe-linde—"I hope," said he, "Sir Edward has been interceding with you, Miss Chesterville, for leave for me to wait on you the first stage."

"I should be very sorry," answered Ethelinde, "that you thought, Sir, of taking so much trouble—trouble which is entirely needless; as I shall be perfectly safe with the attendants, and in the conveyance, Sir Edward has provided for me."

Davenant however continued to urge his request, which Sir Edward did not discourage, nor could Ethelinde without rude-ness refuse. He prepared therefore to attend her: and after taking a melancholy leave of Sir Edward, who saw her depart with extreme reluctance, she got into the chaise; Davenant seating himself by her side, and having his servant follow with his horse. The pres-ence of such a companion did not serve to raise the dejected spirits of Ethelinde. To take leave of Sir Edward was sufficiently painful; but Montgomery still appeared the most interesting figure on the canvas: she saw him, in her imagination, sitting pensively on the banks of the Lake, or on the fragment of rock where they had last conversed; she heard him sigh over the recollection of the few but decisive moments they had passed together; she fancied him lamenting *that* destiny which tore them for ever from each other; and she beheld the concern with which his mother watched his desponding looks and altered spirits. Absorbed in these reveries, she forgot that Davenant was with her; she gave no attention to his attempts to entertain her; and her native politeness was lost in the prevalence of a passion, against which her prudence and her reason could make no effectual resistance.

She failed not, however, to call them both to her assistance. To feel herself thus strongly and suddenly attached to a person of whom she knew so little, was exactly that romantic infatuation which she had so often condemned as weakness when it had occurred in real life, and as of dangerous example when represented in novels. But it was in vain she felt all its impropriety; and her reason served to shew her the danger of her situation, without affording her the strength to extricate herself. She tried to think more of those to whom she was going, and less of those whom she left behind; and, by the time they had passed the first two miles, forced herself to give some degree of attention to the sort of discourse with which Davenant attempted to amuse her. They now entered a long and narrow valley, confined on both sides by enormous fells; the few trees that grew on some of them were already faded, and half leafless, the masses of grey rock which composed others, appeared more than usually dark, from a lowering sky; the deep gloom which hung over the face of nature seemed in correspondence with the heavy heart of Ethelinde, whose forced spirits being soon exhausted, she would most gladly have been alone, that she might have indulged the tears which were every moment ready to gush from her eyes: but Davenant, who had at first been offended by her silence, had been elated by her subsequent complaisance, and had at length collected courage to open to her his long-meditated proposals. In the midst, however, of his speech, to which he fancied Ethelinde lent the profoundest attention, she suddenly started; and hastening to let down the window of the chaise, exclaimed—"Mr. Montgomery! oh! Montgomery!"

The chaise was stopped; and from a tuft of brush-wood which

grew out of the rocks, in the narrow way they were then traversing, Montgomery stepped forward, and came to the window.

He seemed surprised at the sight of another person in the chaise: but Ethelinde, regardless of her companion, expressed her pleasure at meeting him; while he said, in a mournful tone—"Can you pardon me for stopping you on your way, to entreat once more the permission I before solicited? May I wait on colonel Chesterville in London? May I hope he will receive the grateful acknowledgments of the son of his old friend? I have not his address; I could not, when I last saw you, ask for it; may I now beg you to put it on this card?"

He then gave into her trembling hand a card and a pencil. She wrote the direction to her father, and returned it to him, saying—"We are to hope then for the pleasure of seeing you in London?"

"I hope so," answered he. "My mother has new expectations given her from her friends, and has consented that I should attempt to realize them. My hopes"—and his words were broken by a deep sigh—"are far less sanguine!"

"Fail not," said Ethelinde, as she gave him her hand, "to offer to Mrs. Montgomery my most affectionate compliments. If she also should be in town, she will suffer me to see her."

Montgomery pressed fervently, to his lips the hand she held out to him, and made an effort to speak; but finding that the longer the interview lasted the more severely he felt the pang of its conclusion, he suddenly released her hand; and, bowing, bade the postillions go on. They instantly obeyed; and Ethelinde, in again losing sight of him, fancied her being again about to be annihilated. Unable to conceal sentiments so strongly felt, she arose from her seat, and looked through the back window; where she saw Montgomery, standing like a statue where she had left him, his eyes earnestly fixed on the chaise, which however soon turned round a sharp rising ground; and when it concealed him from her view, she sat down, sighed from the bottom of her heart, and, when Davenant addressed her, seemed surprised, as if she had forgotten he was there.

"Mr. Montgomery," said he, "is, I see, so great a favorite, that if I trouble you again with what I was saying, I suppose I have no chance of being noticed now?"

"Mr. Montgomery," answered Ethelinde, "*is* a great favorite, but what were you saying? I beg your pardon—I believe you were making some very civil speech, to which I ought to have been attentive. But the sight of a friend one has a regard for——"

"Yes," replied Davenant, his gloomy humour returning, "this is not the first time I have remarked that that *lad* is much more listened to than I am; and I suppose if he had been talking to you instead of me, you would not have forgotten what *he* was saying."

"Possibly not, Sir," replied Ethelinde; "but you will recollect that I am not compelled to listen to you; and that the trouble you gave yourself in leaving the Abbey with me was equally unwished for and unnecessary." Gentle, and unwilling to give pain as she naturally was, she was so entirely engrossed by the idea of Montgomery, and so vexed to find that after his having waited to see her on the way, their last interview was interrupted by the presence of Davenant, that her habitual mildness forsook her, and she could not refrain from expressing the uneasiness she felt.

"I am sorry I intruded upon you, Madam," said Davenant, "and sorry to find that my hope of making myself acceptable to you is counteracted by your prepossession in favour of another person."

"You have no right to assert, Sir, that I have any such prepossession. For your favourable opinion of me I thank you; but it would be an ill return to mislead you: though I am sensible how much greater the advantages are which you offer me than any I have a right to expect, yet I have no wish to marry, and therefore must be permitted to decline the honour of your proposal—an honour which some person of greater merit will most undoubtedly be found ready to accept."

"And you refuse then, Madam, to let me wait on your father—a permission you just now gave so readily to Mr. Montgomery?"

"No, Sir; I do not refuse what does not depend on me. Mr. Davenant cannot fail of being welcome to every body whom he may favour with his visits as a friend."

Sullen silence on the part of Davenant, whose pride was more hurt than his love, and deep reflection on that of Ethelinde, made the rest of their way to the house where the horses were to be changed extremely unpleasant to them both. When they arrived there, Ethelinde, conscious that she had been too petulant, endeavoured to erase the recollection of it by forced civility, yet not wishing to awaken hopes which she never meant to encourage: but Davenant, who, in the proud consciousness of his own splendid fortune, had conceived a sovereign contempt for Montgomery, whom he looked upon as nothing better than an indigent peasant, was so extremely piqued by her former behaviour, that he disdained either to repeat his overtures, or renew his assiduous civilities; but, after staying a few moments, he mounted his horse, and returned in a very ill humour to Grasmere Abbey; hardly bidding adieu to Ethelinde, who pursued her journey alone, by no means repining at the loss of her companion since she could now indulge, unmolested and unremarked, the fond dreams which had taken possession of her fancy. She should see Montgomery again; he would visit her at her father's; perhaps her father might be of use to him, perhaps, with an introduction so respectable, added to his extraordinary merit, he might find friends. How delicious were these dreams! and how easily her soft and susceptible spirit, believing all it wished, had built a little fabric of visionary happiness, which soothed the anguish that had for some days preyed on her mind! Montgomery, the beloved Montgomery, was to become the *protegé* of her father, he was to be restored to the rank his family held; he was to rise in the army; to be noticed by his relations; to be the friend of Sir Edward Newenden. Affluence was to follow of course. She was sure of his love; sure of seeing him again; and, carrying these thoughts to her pillow, she enjoyed more quiet sleep than she had done for many preceding nights. She bore her journey, though rapid, without suffering much fatigue; and, as it drew towards an end, felt new pleasure in reflecting on the approaching meeting with her father. On the evening of the fourth day she was set down, at his house in Cleveland Row; and, flying eagerly up stairs, was instantly in his arms.

Tears were in the eyes of both, while he pressed her to his bosom, but as soon as the first transports subsided, and Ethelinde sat down to give her father an account of her journey, she was shocked by the alteration she observed in his countenance, as well as his manner. He was pale, and his eyes had lost their lustre; a heavy melancholy sat on his countenance; his clothes hung loosely about him, from his extreme thinness; and his air bespoke dejection and uneasiness of mind.—"My dearest Sir," said his daughter, taking his hand, "you have been indisposed, I am afraid, longer than you mentioned to Sir Edward. You look thin. How long have you been ill? and why did you not instantly send to me?"

"My illness," replied he, "is of little consequence, and is now, I think, going off; but my mind is disturbed, Ethelinde—cruelly disturbed by the conduct of your brother: his draughts have very much exceeded all bounds: I have paid all but the last, but now I cannot continue to do so. Perhaps my example has not been a good one: too much attached to play since the death of your beloved mother, I have given him cause to say that his father has sanctioned his indiscretions. Unhappy boy! my heart bleeds for him; for is he not the son of the most beloved of women? But I have already gone too far for him; and justice to my Ethelinde now withholds my hands. Alas! she has been already too much injured. To his last draughts I must refuse, nay I have refused acceptance."

"Oh! Sir!" cried Ethelinde, tears flowing from her eyes, "if you love your daughter, let her not be the means of distressing her brother! It is not yet, I hope, too late to save Harry from such a mortification. My dear Sir, let me intercede for him; and consider how much it will injure his credit, how much it may expose him to contempt. As for me, bestow not a thought upon me; there is no inconvenience I would not cheerfully submit to, rather than have my dear Harry made unhappy."

"By heaven you are an angel, Ethelinde, but the more generous and disinterested you are, the more it should have been my care to reward such excellence. Ah! my dear girl! Harry thought not thus of us, or he would not have acted so inconsiderately as he has done. But let me not deceive you, my love; nor, while I blame my son, excuse myself. I have been most improvident. Playing usually with such a degree of good success as authorised me to pursue it without self reproach, I foresaw not that a series of ill fortune might sweep away all the advantages I had ever gained. That evil hour came upon me at my late visit. Let me not lengthen a painful detail: I lost a thousand more than I could raise without mortgaging my pay. I have done so; and your brother's expences have swallowed up every other resource. In time my income will come round again; but we must live no longer as we now do. I have determined to quit this house immediately, and to go into lodgings at Bath. Can my Ethelinde forgive her unhappy, her imprudent father? can *she* submit to an humble way of life, whom palaces and splendour ought to await?"

"Think not so meanly of me, for God's sake, my dearest father, as to suppose me capable of murmuring. In any situation of life I can be happy with you, and regret nothing unless I see you uneasy; that indeed is too much for me. Let us, since this regulation is necessary, lose no time about it. Behold me ready to attend you to any place, ready to revere and love you always as the best and tenderest of parents; and, should it ever be necessary, to embrace with cheerfulness the humblest state of life, to relieve you from the burthen of supporting me."

"Oh! comfort of my soul!" exclaimed colonel Chesterville, embracing her—"image, in mind and in person, of that best of human beings, my other, my first Ethelinde! never torture my mind by supposing that the extremity shall arrive which shall tear thee from me; and while thou art left me; consoling and lovely as thou art, I cannot be quite wretched! We will quit London in a fortnight. I waited only for your arrival to arrange the necessary preliminaries."

"And my brother, Sir? his draughts?" cried the weeping Ethelinde.

"Alas! my love, I was compelled, with an aching heart compelled, to refuse accepting them; for, in truth, I had not the means of paying them; yet when I reflect that my poor boy will be so cruelly distressed—that, with infinitely more excuse, he has not been more indiscreet than his father—oh! Ethelinde, it breaks my heart; my rest, my strength forsakes me. I cannot survive the ruin of my children, which my own infatuation has brought on."

"Be not thus affected, or you will kill your Ethelinde! Dear Sir, if Sir Edward Newenden was here, you would have no difficulty. Till I can have recourse to him, which I will instantly set about, allow me to recal the draughts, and to find means to pay them."

"Dearest girl, what means can you have? I will, however, send after them; and cannot object to your application to Sir Edward, whose noble nature I know so well. Write to him therefore, my love, by the earliest post. To his generous friendship I shall not blush to be obliged. And now, my Ethelinde, try to compose yourself, call upon that excellent understanding to supply you with fortitude to bear, and upon that excellent nature to pardon your father for the temporary reverse of fortune which he has brought upon you."

Ethelinde, whose heart was too full to carry on a dialogue so affecting any longer, was glad, for both their sakes, to avail herself of this permission to withdraw. She recollected not till this moment the letter given her for her father by Sir Edward Newenden, on the morning they parted: she now gave it him; he begged she would stay while he read it. Its contents were most kind; and convinced the colonel that he might have a firm reliance on his generous friendship, in the present cruel exigence. This conviction served greatly to calm his mind; Ethelinde retired also with some degree of apparent composure. But the moment she was alone, all her fortitude forsook her: the lovely visions she had been painting were annihilated for ever! Far from any hopes remaining that her father would be able to serve Montgomery, she saw him in a situation of painful dependance; and she knew that the little fortune she might have expected was no more: but on that she would not have bestowed a thought, had not the loss of Montgomery inevitably followed. A night of the most uneasy dreams succeeded to the painful and fatiguing day she had passed, and she arose and met her father at breakfast, the next day with forced smiles indeed, and assumed cheerfulness, but with a countenance so wan, and eyes so heavy, that he started when he saw her, and throwing his arms round her, sobbed aloud, and exclaimed—"Oh! Ethelinde! these heart rending smiles, this languor which you vainly attempt to shake off, tell me, my child, too truly that you are unhappy; and my reproaching heart excuses me of having robbed those eyes of their lustre, and of suppressing those genuine smiles which were the delight of my soul!"

Ethelinde, seeing him extremely affected, declared that her looks, if indeed, she did look so ill, were merely the effect of the fatigue of a long journey, which would soon go off. She then exerted herself so effectually as to succeed in tranquillizing his mind. As soon as breakfast was over, he went out; and Ethelinde, anxious about the draughts of her brother, set about a plan she had formed the night before, which was to part with several valuable trinkets and jewels, some of which had been her mother's and some presents to herself, in order to raise money to take them up; for though she had no doubt of Sir Edward Newenden's instantly supplying the money, she dreaded the delay that must arise before she could have his answer, especially if he should have left Grasmere Abbey before her letter got thither, of which she was by no means certain; in which case it must follow him to Scarborough.

END OF THE FIRST VOLUME.

VOLUME II

CHAPTER I

An anxious week now passed, during which the Colonel applied to have his son's drafts restored to him, in order for payment; but found they had been sent back protested to Gibraltar: a circumstance which gave to Ethelinde the most cruel uneasiness, as she knew that her brother, warm and irritable as he was, would feel the mortification as well as the inconvenience arising from such a circumstance, with particular poignancy. By the return of the post she received a letter from Sir Edward Newenden, enclosing a draft on his banker for the sum Captain Chesterville had drawn for, and entreating her father to apply to him on every occasion without scruple; adding, that as soon as he returned to London he would be happy to be allowed to assist him in regulating his affairs, and hoped to see him again without embarrassment or uneasiness. A conduct so truly generous greatly affected the Colonel while it impressed on Ethelinde the warmest sentiments of gratitude and affection.

But the variety of sensations which her father's declining health and encreasing difficulties, her brother's dissipation, and Sir Edward's goodness, gave her, could not for a moment expel from her mind the image of Montgomery. Whenever she was alone, she indulged herself in the painful pleasure of thinking of him: and as she had related to her father the circumstance that introduced him to her acquaintance, and found that he was indeed the English officer to whom the elder Montgomery owed his life, she had sometimes an opportunity of talking of him who occupied so much of her thoughts. Colonel Chesterville spoke of the Mr. Montgomery with whom he had been acquainted, as the bravest and most amiable of men; and he described his wife as possessing to a great degree that eminent beauty of which Ethelinde had seen the remains, together with the most enchanting manners. He expressed himself pleased with the inclination Montgomery had shewn to renew their acquaintance, and thus unsuspectingly encouraged, in the heart of his daughter, a passion which was already fatal to her peace.

Montgomery, however, appeared not; and Ethelinde felt all the pain of uncertainty, and all the apprehensions that the idea of his having forgotten her brought with it; which, added to her domestic unhappiness, allowed her not to taste of peace. She confined herself entirely to her father; going only once out, to visit the children of Sir Edward Newenden at Denham House, about two miles from Windsor. She was by that visit enabled to give their father an account of them, and to make more supportable to him the long absence from them which all his letters lamented; for he had informed her, that he and Lady Newenden were at Scarborough with Lord Danesforte and a large party of friends; and that her Ladyship expressed an inclination to remain there at least another fortnight.

About four days after this visit, a servant arrived express from the governess who had the care of the little Newendens, informing her, that the eldest boy was suddenly and violently seized by a fever and that the apothecary of the neighbourhood apprehended him to be in extreme danger. She therefore besought Miss Chesterville to come down, and bring with her a physician; adding, that in a life of so much consequence she could not think of being answerable to Sir Edward for the event, and that Mr. and Mrs. Maltravers being at Bath, there was no other of the family in or near London.

Ethelinde, her heart torn by anxiety for Sir Edward, who doated on this child, hesitated not a moment to obey the summons. But her father, who dreaded lest she might be exposed to the danger of an infectious fever, suffered her with extreme reluctance to depart, and gave way to all the forebodings of evil which on such an occasion overwhelm the strongest mind, already depressed by misfortune.

One of the most eminent physicians in London went down with her; and on their arrival he found the little patient in a situation which gave him the most alarming apprehensions for his life. The fever being pronounced of a malignant nature, the other children were removed from that part of the house; and Ethelinde, that no communication might occur to affect them, ordered their governess and nursery-maids to remain with them, while she, with the assistance of one of the inferior servants, undertook to attend entirely on the sick child. While the sight of suffering innocence awakened all the tenderness of her nature, the obligations she considered herself under to Sir Edward animated her zeal. But in despite of her unwearied attention, and the skill of the physician, the poor little boy grew so much worse on the second day, that no hopes were entertained; and a messenger was sent off to Scarborough to acquaint Sir Edward with these distressing tidings.

Two more anxious days and two hopeless nights did Ethelinde yet pass at the bedside of the little sufferer, without taking any rest or quitting him a moment; every chance that remained of saving him depending entirely on the incessant application of medicines or nourishment. Towards the evening of the third day, the physicians thought that some favourable symptoms appeared, and the hope of his recovery gave new courage to his lovely nurse. The child, who was about four years old, and had always been very fond of her, was now, in every interval of recollection, pleased and soothed if he saw her, and when he had the power, refused to take any thing but from her hand, or to compose himself to sleep unless her arm supported him.

The flattering symptoms encreased, and a soft sleep into which the patient had fallen, strengthened the faint hopes that Ethelinde had yet hardly dared to indulge. She was kneeling on a cushion by the bedside; one arm, extended across the pillow, supported his head; with her other hand she held one of his, counting the feeble pulse; while her eyes watched the little faded face, and her whole countenance most forcibly spoke tenderness, anxiety, and fear. Precautions had been taken to keep the room as quiet as possible: somebody glided in; but, concluding it was the servant who attended her, she did not look up, till a violent burst of tears and the exclamation of "Oh! my boy, my poor boy!" made her raise her eyes, and she beheld Sir Edward at the foot of the bed. She was less surprised at his appearance, as it was time to expect him in consequence of the express, than shocked at the expression of grief and horror which she beheld in his face. His eyes were swoln and wild; his lips trembled; and with his hands clasped he seemed to wait in agonizing terror to hear, that his little darling was taken from him for ever, or that he was only come to see him die.

Ethelinde, in a low whisper, besought him to be composed, and assured him that the child was better, and that there were some hopes.

"O flatter me not, my dearest Ethelinde," murmured the

unhappy father; "that altered countenance! Oh I cannot be deceived. His mother! she is not here: she comes not!" In a transport of grief he struck his hand on his forehead, turned to the window, and wept aloud.

"Be patient, Sir Edward, for God's sake," whispered Ethelinde: "think not I would deceive you; but indeed there is a change for the better within a few hours."

"Oh! loveliest, kindest, best of creatures! you have supplied—more than supplied—the part of a mother to my poor boy! And should he recover!—But I dare not hope it," continued he, approaching the bed, on the side of which Ethelinde knelt—"Oh no! when I look on him I dare not hope it."

At this moment the two physicians, for another had by this time been called in, entered the room. Sir Edward, breathless with his fear, was unable to speak to them; and when they approached to examine the situation of the child, his anxiety grew so insupportable, that without knowing what he did, he ran out of the room, and into the garden, where he continued walking about, without having courage to ask the result of their enquiries.

After having suffered this dreadful suspence some minutes, one of the physicians came out to him, "Be of comfort, Sir Edward," said he, "we have hopes. Our little patient, tho' not, I am afraid, out of danger, is however better. His strength is greater than we could have expected; and the tender, the incessant care of Miss Chesterville gives us every advantage."

"Heaven bless her!" exclaimed Sir Edward, while the tears, which anxiety, had restrained, again streamed from his eyes. "Heaven bless and reward her! My boy then will live!—will be restored to me!"

"Of that," replied Dr. F——, "we cannot yet speak with absolute certainty. But this I will venture to say, that if no unfavourable symptoms appear before tomorrow morning, he will, tho' slowly, recover. Let me however hint to you, Sir Edward, that our lovely assistant risks her own health too much. The abstinence, the watching, the anxiety she has suffered, make her particularly liable to be attacked by an infectious distemper, which the disorder your son labours under undoubtedly is. Persuade her to attend a little to herself, lest she should be disabled from executing her kind offices before her little charge can do without her."

New anguish now struck the heart of Sir Edward: not yet secure
of the life of his son; he was assaulted by fears for another life,
hardly less dear to him. He hastened however, as soon as the physicians departed, to the room where Ethelinde yet remained with
the child, who was now awake and sensible. His father embraced
him with transport, heard with apprehensive pleasure every symptom related that promised his recovery; and then leaving him a
moment to the care of the servant, he besought Ethelinde to go
with him into another room.

She obeyed with difficulty, being so weak for want of rest that
she could hardly stand. He was shocked at perceiving it, as she
leaned gently on his arm; and having led her into Lady Newenden's dressing-room, and shut the door, he seated her on a sopha;
and then, unable to conquer the violence of the tenderness, gratitude, and solicitude which agitated his soul, he threw himself on
his knees beside her, and seizing her hands, he sobbed aloud, and
pressed them to his heart and to his eyes; while Ethelinde, overcome by these wild expressions of his concern, and worn out with
fatigue, wept also, and suffered him for some moments to remain
kneeling. His voice was at first choked; but as soon as he recovered it, he said, in trembling accents—"Ethelinde, you have, under
Providence, saved my boy! but at what a price, if your own life is
to be endangered! My Ethelinde, the fever is infectious, you have
taken no care of yourself! Oh God! if you should become ill—if
you should yourself suffer, what will become of me? Distraction
must be my portion!"

"Wherefore terrify yourself, dear Sir Edward, with these, perhaps groundless, apprehensions? Let us not look forward to future
pain; but rather rejoice in the favourable prospect of the little
angel's recovery; and do recollect how necessary it is that Lady
Newenden, who must be dreadfully uneasy, should be relieved
as soon as possible from the torturing suspense in which you left
her."

"Best and most considerate of human beings! Loveliest—dearest!—Oh! why are not all hearts like yours! Yes! I will send to Lady
Newenden; but—she feels not as you do!" Then, seeming to recollect himself, he added—"But undoubtedly I will dispatch a
messenger to her this evening. I can however have no courage to
undertake any thing till you consent to take rest and refreshment.

You are so pale, so languid, Ethelinde! If you would not render me the most wretched of mankind, and deprive me of more than half the comfort of my child's recovery, have pity on me by taking care of a life more dear to me, a thousand times more dear, than my own existence!"

"I want no rest, Sir Edward! I cannot rest till the little boy is out of danger. Neglect for a moment now, may destroy our reviving hopes. I feel no fatigue. Suffer me to return to my charge and be assured that my attendance on him, especially while we have favourable prognostics, does not affect me half so much as the sight of your grief and agitation."

She then returned with faultering steps back to the sick room; and having the comfort to find the little boy still sensible, and the promising appearances encreasing, she endeavoured to tranquillize her thoughts: but the vehemence with which Sir Edward had addressed her, the agony in which she had seen him, and the expression he had used in regard to Lady Newenden, dwelt on her mind, and encreased the tremor of her frame. That night however she lay down for a few hours, while Sir Edward watched by his son; but tho' extreme fatigue closed her eyes, her sleep was disturbed and uneasy; and she arose without being at all refreshed by the transient forgetfulness she had obtained.

On the arrival of the physicians the following day, they pronounced their patient to be out of danger; and Sir Edward, who had forborne to send an express while it was doubtful, now sent a servant off with a letter to Lady Newenden, in which, after informing her of the probability there was of her son's recovery, he spoke in the warmest praise of Ethelinde; to whom, he said, so great an happiness was, under Providence, owing; and he entreated Lady Newenden to return to Denham as soon as her health would permit. He wrote also to Colonel Chesterville; and besought him to come down and stay with him and Ethelinde, at least till the arrival of Lady Newenden; in consequence of which the Colonel, who had been wretched ever since his daughter's absence, arrived the same evening.

Though he was extremely hurt on first seeing Ethelinde, who looked like a beautiful spirit, so pale and thin was she grown, he became more easy when she assured him that the alteration in her appearance had been occasioned merely by the fatigue of sitting up, added to her fears for little Edward, and that in a day or two she should be perfectly well.

As the child's illness every hour abated, she no longer remained by his bed during the night, but was his constant attendant by day, and at all other hours; and in two or three days he was well enough enough to sit in her lap, and to return her caresses.

With what transport did Sir Edward hang over them both! and how difficult did he find it to check the effusions of love, gratitude, and admiration, which filled his heart! Since he dared not however express in words what he felt, he endeavoured, by kindness and generosity to the father, to gratify the beloved daughter, and having gathered from the Colonel what sum would redeem his mortgaged pay, and make him easy, he immediately gave it him; making himself his sole creditor, and taking his bond for the money; declining however to receive any interest upon it, till it was more convenient to him to pay it. The recovery of his beloved child, the presence of Ethelinde, and the peace he had thus restored to her father, drove for a few days every painful idea from the heart of Sir Edward; but after a time they recurred with great severity. Lady Newenden arrived not, tho' there had been time for her arrival, and he could not help reflecting on that want of feeling which could allow her in such a case to think of her own ease only. When to her coldness and insensibility was contrasted the generous tenderness of Ethelinde, he felt that she became every hour more dear to him: in her absence his thoughts dwelt perpetually on the means of making her happy; when she was present, his eyes watched every turn of her countenance, and his ears attended only to her voice: the languor and paleness which still continued, though her fear and her fatigue were at an end, alarmed him as much as it did her father. She insisted on it however that she was well; and refused to take either advice or medicine till the evening of the fourth day after the little boy was pronounced out of danger. She was then compelled to go to bed; to acknowledge that she felt herself very much otherwise than well; and before morning symptoms appeared which made it no longer doubtful that she had received the same illness which had been so nearly fatal to him.

The distraction of Colonel Chesterville and Sir Edward is not to be described. While the former insisted on remaining with her, the latter sent repeated expresses to London for physicians, and wandered from the door of her chamber to the parlour, from the parlour to the garden, incapable of resting any where, and asking of her attendant a thousand questions in a moment. In the midst of this painful suspence, and while he continued to hear only of encreasing fever and more alarming delirium, a coach approached. Sir Edward ran out, expecting the physicians he had sent for; but he saw his own servants and carriage, and assisted Lady Newenden into the house.

"I stopped in town," said her Ladyship, as he led her in, "and heard that Edward is out of danger. Your looks however do not confirm the news. How is he? how are the others?"

"He is better—he is, thank God, out of danger, and the other dear little ones are well. But Ethelinde, to whose attention we owe so much, was yesterday seized with the same disorder, which she has acquired in attending upon our boy; and I dread the event."

"Good God, then!" exclaimed Lady Newenden, "the fever is infectious?"

"Undoubtedly."

"And you have suffered me, Sir Edward, to enter the house! Upon my word, I am but little obliged to you! I certainly however will not stay; and as Ethelinde cannot I suppose be removed——"

"Be removed!—would you remove her?—her to whose generous and disinterested tenderness you owe the life of your child."

"I am obliged to her; but as my life is also of some little consequence, and I can do nobody any good by risking it, I shall remove myself to the house of my father. It would be wiser I think, Sir Edward, if you were to quit the house also."

"May I perish if I am capable of such selfish ingratitude. You, Lady Newenden, are at liberty to do as you please."

"I intend it," replied she haughtily, "and shall take the other children with me. Order back the coach therefore, let my baggage be replaced; and let the servants have orders to bring down the younger children and put them into the coach."

"And you depart without seeing Edward?"

"Of what use will it be to him since he is out of danger; and why should I hazard my own life?"

"As you please, Lady Newenden," said he, with an air of chagrin which he could not disguise. He then went up to hasten the

children; and as soon as they were ready, Lady Newenden got into
the coach; and without expressing any solicitude about Ethelinde,
and very little for her son, she departed for the house of her father,
which was about five miles from her own. Miss Newenden had
parted from her in town, and, as the hunting season had now commenced, was gone to her house in Dorsetshire. Ethelinde in the
mean time grew worse every hour, and continued either in heavy
dosings or wild delirium. Her father, in such distress as suspended
the power of complaint, sat by her, watching her when she lay
quiet with some degree of hope, and starting into the most agonizing fears when she broke into raving. The name of Montgomery was frequently repeated. She fancied that she talked to him,
heard his answers, and sometimes held imaginary dialogues with
his mother. At length the physicians arrived. Sir Edward attended
them to the door; and then beckoning the Colonel out, he led him
down stairs in silence.

Her situation was found extremely dangerous; and a dreadful interval was now to pass of the most torturing suspence, for
it was many days before they could tell how the disorder would
terminate. The skill, however, of the physicians, and the advantage of youth and a good constitution, at length enabled them
to pronounce her out of danger from the fever, but she was so
much reduced, that a decline seemed inevitable; and this dreadful
though more distant apprehension deprived both her father and
Sir Edward of all the comfort they derived from the absence of any
more immediate danger.

In a fortnight Lady Newenden returned, as every probability of
infection was then at an end. But Ethelinde, not yet strong enough
to leave her chamber, passed another week almost alone; her
father having been obliged to return to London; and Lady Newenden, whose house was now crouded with company as usual,
paying her very little attention. Her visits were short and cold; and
she seemed more disobliged by Ethelinde's having shewn a virtue
and tenderness she herself possessed not, than grateful for the restoration of her son, to which she had contributed at the hazard of
her life. More vain, capricious, and haughty than ever, Sir Edward
fancied that there was an evident change in her behaviour towards
him, and that towards her children she expressed less tenderness
than ever; while all the gentle affections she seemed to want, he

found in Ethelinde, and every comparison he made served only to shew him her superior perfections.

But the more his attachment towards her became confirmed and ardent, the more sedulously he endeavoured to conceal it, and the more uneasy he grew at the hints Lady Newenden frequently threw out of his too great partiality to her cousin; tho' they were given sometimes in raillery, sometimes with contemptuous bitterness. His peace however was effectually destroyed, his mind in a perpetual conflict; and one of the most painful circumstances of his suffering was, that he dared not see Ethelinde but in company with others; and that their reading, their conversations, their innocent and friendly confidences, so soothing to his heart, were of necessity suspended; and though he believed she was sinking into the grave, by a gradual decay brought upon her by her attendance on his child, he knew not what he could attempt to save her; and the embarrassed state of her father's affairs completed the distress of his mind on her account.

CHAPTER II

Lord Danesforte now added frequently to the number of visitors which the return of Lady Newenden had brought to Denham. Gaiety and amusement reigned in the house: and Mr. and Mrs. Maltravers, who were sometimes there, by no means checked the dissipation of their daughter; but seemed to consider it as one of the privileges of great fortune to be insensible of the weaknesses of humanity and the prejudices of the vulgar. Ethelinde, who from the circumstances of her father, which were now too well known, began to be considered as a dependent, was sometimes wholly neglected by the lady of the house; and when she was noticed, it was done in such a way as gave the other visitors to understand, that notwithstanding her noble birth, she had very little on which to value herself, but the protection and assistance of her opulent relations.

She would most willingly have quitted Denham; but her father had now parted with his house in town, and was in lodgings till he could settle his affairs by the assistance of Sir Edward; who, deprived of almost all other happiness, found his greatest consola-

tion in contributing to the ease and relief of the father of Ethelinde.
He was with him two or three times a week; paid many of those
demands which were most uneasy to him; put the rest in a way to
be discharged: and laid down a plan for the Colonel's future life,
which would, he hoped, not only retrieve his circumstances, but
enable him to leave an independence for Ethelinde, whose state of
health, however, was still such as made him dread that she might
not live to make such a provision necessary. In the extreme languor that her illness left, the idea of Montgomery, which had not
forsaken her for a moment even during her delirium, took if possible more forcible possession of her thoughts. Disguised by the
useless and unmeaning parade with which she was surrounded,
and weary of society where friendship and sincerity were forgotten, she suffered her imagination to wander towards scenes more
adapted to her taste, and more soothing to her heart: and fancied,
that if she could live with Mrs. Montgomery in her cottage, she
should be happy. To be the friend, the companion of that amiable
and interesting woman—how desirable, compared to her present lot! To be the wife of Montgomery!——She dared not trust
herself with an hope so romantic—so enchanting—so impossible!
She tried to drive it from her: but her busy fancy was still, in spite
of herself, employed in dressing scenes of visionary happiness,
from which she returned to feel with awakened anguish the melancholy and depressing circumstances of her real situation. Lord
Danesforte, who saw, in the faded delicacy of her face and form,
new attractions, took every opportunity of whispering to her
the most extravagant compliments; but she observed, that when
Lady Newenden was present he carefully avoided taking any particular notice of her; and she sometimes fancied that her Ladyship
shewed for him a preference, injurious to the affection she owed to
the best and tenderest of husbands. She checked these suspicions,
however, as soon as they arose; and comparing the mind, the manners, the person of Sir Edward with those of Lord Danesforte, she
believed it impossible that a woman who was by her own choice
the wife of the former, could bestow a thought on the latter. Sir
Edward, though the company of Lord Danesforte afforded him
little pleasure, appeared not to be displeased by his frequent and
long visits, and his Lordship had found means to make Mrs. Maltravers his warm friend and admirer. When Sir Edward therefore

was not of their parties to London or at home, Mrs. Maltravers almost always was; and the countenance and company of her mother precluded the possibility of her Ladyship's suffering from the envenomed tongue of scandal, though continually seen with a man so notorious for his licentious gallantry.

It was now the end of October. Ethelinde continued ill and languid. The pain of her mind prevented her frame from gaining strength: but she complained not; and in the many desponding moments wished that her life, which was not likely to be happy, might be short. Davenant, who had been left on a shooting party in Yorkshire, now arrived at Denham. At first he affected coldness and indifference towards Ethelinde. He seemed to resent what passed at their last meeting, and to talk of other beauties he had seen, who had vied with each other in their attention to him. Ethelinde, whose indifference his addresses had converted into dislike, gave less attention to him than ever; and the blustering airs of consequence which he had of late acquired, were more disgusting to her than his former insipidity of character, ready always to assume the tone of the company he was in.

Since Lord Danesforte had become his model, he had learned to talk nonsense with greater vehemence, to make bold assertions on things of which he knew nothing, to swear at his servants when he was not angry, and to boast of being well received by persons whom he knew only by sight. He fearlessly entered into arguments with Sir Edward, of whom he had till now been in some sort of awe, and advanced undauntedly those dissolute principles which his weak mind had received, as fashionable and liberal. Sir Edward, now ashamed of having supposed he could ever be acceptable to Ethelinde, and now trembling at the dreary prospect before her, which made some establishment absolutely necessary, sought at first to reason with him, and to stop the career of folly into which he was evidently plunging, in spite of his natural love of money: a passion which, however despicable, was the only one likely to counterbalance his passion for celebrity on the turf and at the gaming table. But reason was lost on him; and authority Sir Edward possessed no longer, as he had been some weeks of age, and Sir Edward had, the day when he came to Denham, settled the account of his minority with him; and having resigned into his own management his estates greatly improved, and amounting to above five thousand a year, he had transferred to him four and forty thousand pounds in government securities, being partly money left there by his father, but much more of it the amount of savings made by his excellent guardian during his long minority.

Colonel Chesterville, who had not for ten days seen his daughter, now arrived. The generous friendship of Sir Edward had greatly relieved his mind; and he came down in the comfortable hope of finding her much better, and of taking her with him to Bath in encreasing health and spirits. But when she appeared to him, all these pleasing expectations were succeeded by the most painful apprehensions: her pale lips, heavy eyes, her colourless cheeks and emaciated hands, made him start in terror as she approached to embrace him; and on questioning her he found, notwithstanding her attempts to conceal it, that far from having regained any portion of strength, she had grown every day more weak and languid.

He would not alarm her by expressing all the fears this certainty inflicted on him: but seeking Sir Edward as soon as he returned from his morning ride, he communicated to him all his fears; and found sympathy in a warm and affectionate heart, as much attached to Ethelinde as his own. But consolation was not to be found for either, when she appeared to be in danger. It was however determined that she should go immediately to Bristol:[1] and the Colonel fixed to depart in three days.

Lady Newenden was that day absent; accompanied by her mother and a female friend, and escorted by Davenant, she was gone to a magnificent ball, given by a woman of fashion to a very numerous party of guests, where Lord Danesforte was to meet them, and from whence he was to accompany them home. Sir Edward had declined going, on pretence of expecting Colonel Chesterville, and for the first time for many months he enjoyed the pleasure of being with Ethelinde in company only with her father, to whom all the tenderness and attention he shewed to her, seemed no more than what was her due from every human being. Checked only by his fears for her health, the pleasure Sir Edward enjoyed in being with her, made the day imperceptibly glide away. When he could see her smile, and hear her soft but sensible voice;

---

1 Like Bath's warm waters, Bristol's Hot Wells at Clifton were thought to help the sick.

when she sat surrounded by his children, who never were so happy
as when they were hanging about her; he drank intoxicating
draughts of passion, and neither his reason nor his morality were
strong enough to prevent his making comparisons as unfavourable to his wife as destructive to his own happiness.

Lady Newenden and her party returned not till four in the
morning. The night had been rainy and tempestuous; and her
Ladyship, in quitting the crouded rooms, and travelling seven
miles in such bad weather, caught a very severe cold. A violent
cough succeeded. Mr. Maltravers, on whom the pallid looks and
sunk features of his niece had made no impression, was extremely
alarmed at the indisposition of his daughter. Advice was immediately sent for, remedies of every kind applied with the most impatient solicitude; but as the complaint yielded not immediately to
them, Mr. Maltravers told Sir Edward that he could not be easy
unless his daughter went to Bristol; and as whatever he said Sir
Edward was accustomed to attend to, the journey was immediately proposed, with pleasure on his part, as Ethelinde would be
with them; and he should, without the appearance of singularity, still be indulged with the happiness of seeing her. As London
was yet dull and empty, and nothing offered more entertaining,
Lady Newenden objected not to the scheme which her father
was so eager to promote. She even asked Ethelinde and Colonel
Chesterville to delay their journey till they could all go together,
and pressed Davenant to accompany them. Mr. and Mrs. Maltravers proposed also to be of the party; and at their request the little
Newendens were to go with their parents. The journey was now
fixed for the following Friday, and every body seemed contented
with it but Ethelinde, who equally disliked being carried where
Davenant was to go, and where she should be precluded from the
possibility of seeing Montgomery, if he should arrive in London.
But this circumstance she dared not communicate; and attempted
by forced cheerfulness and assumed smiles to hide from the view
of others, particularly from that of her father, the little delight that
any party, however pleasurable, was now capable of affording her.

The day before that fixed for their departure, Colonel Chesterville received a note as he was sitting after dinner; and was told
by the servant who brought it in, that a messenger from London
waited for an answer. He opened and read it; then giving it to his

daughter, said,—"Ethy, my love, it is rather to you than to me, since the young man who writes it is rather your acquaintance than mine."

Ethelinde changed colour, and with trembling hands read the letter, which was to this effect.

> "Sir,
>
> "The son of that Montgomery who once owed his life to your generosity, has now an opportunity of paying his respects to the preserver of his father; and will be most happy if you will allow him to wait on you any day this week on which you may be disengaged. Allow me to offer my compliments to Miss Chesterville; and the honor of remaining,
>
> "Sir,
> "Your most obedient humble servant,
> "Charles Archibald Montgomery.
>
> "Oct . 27, 17—."

The emotion with which Ethelinde read this, was too violent to be concealed. Her faded cheek glowed for a moment, and then grew paler than before. Without speaking, she returned it to her father, who, unsuspecting her partiality, asked her what answer he should send? "I should be very glad," added he, "to see the young man. I loved his father, admired and respected his mother, and am much obliged to him. It is unfortunate that I should be from London."

Sir Edward, who guessed by the tremor into which the receipt of this letter had thrown Ethelinde, that it came from Montgomery, wished for her sake (as he believed) that every future interview might be avoided with a man whose circumstances made the success of his pretensions to her so impossible, and he fancied that he was willing to save her from the pain of an hopeless passion—pain of which he was himself too conscious to make this design appear even to his own heart quite disinterested, though he endeavoured to persuade himself that he sought only the welfare of a beloved object.

Colonel Chesterville however, who knew nothing of this internal conflict, said after a moment's consideration—"Sir Edward, will you and Lady Newenden permit me to ask Mr. Montgomery hither? To a young man, the distance will be nothing, and I own I should be sorry not to see him, though it is hardly possible for me to go to London before we begin our journey."

"Pray, Sir," replied Lady Newenden, with more than her usual civility, "invite him hither whensoever you please; if you mean the Montgomery we saw at Grasmere: we are, you know, also his acquaintance, and can have no objection to his visit."

"I conclude, Sir Edward, that I have your leave," said the Colonel, rising from table. "You will therefore permit me to step into your study to answer this, and so appoint to-morrow for seeing him here."

The ladies now leaving the room, Ethelinde retired to her own with spirits so fluttered that she could hardly breathe. To the emotion which the thoughts of seeing Montgomery gave her, was added that which arose from her observations on Sir Edward's behaviour, who had watched her looks while she read the note, changed countenance at her father's request, and had given no encouragement to the invitation sent to Montgomery. "He knows then," said she, "the weakness of this poor heart. He knows and condemns it. At Grasmere I recollect a thousand circumstances that assure me he then suspected it, though he has since carefully avoided the subject. He must think me an unhappy romantic creature, caught by mere personal beauty. He must despise me, for he has never conversed with Montgomery."

Solicitous to conceal an inclination which, she was compelled to own to herself, her slight knowledge of Montgomery hardly authorized, she determined to behave so as to give no reason for further suspicions on the part of Sir Edward, or to awaken them on that of her father. But then the idea of Montgomery, dejected by her coldness, depressed by receiving mere common civility where he had too much reason to expect the tenderest friendship, struck her imagination; and she dreaded lest her resolution should be unequal to the painful task of mortifying with repulsive coldness him to whom her heart was irrevocably, though perhaps indiscreetly given. Fortunately Davenant did not dine at Denham, but was gone to meet a party of friends at Salt Hill,[1] with whom he

1 Salt Hill, on the road to Bristol, was a scenic spot whose name reflects its origins in ancient ceremonies dating back to the 16th century; see Daphne Phillips, *The Great Road to Bath* (Bristol: Countryside Books, 1983): 120-126.

was to stay till the day appointed for their proceeding all together
to Bristol. Ethelinde had always perceived more of mortified
pride than of love in his address to her. Having been once persuaded by Lord Danesforte to become a candidate for her favour,
he was piqued to see that Montgomery, a northern peasant, as he
insolently called him, was preferred to himself, who possessed
so large a fortune; and he pursued Ethelinde rather to show the
superior claim to consideration which he supposed that fortune
gave him, than because he felt for her any real preference. When
this despised competitor appeared no longer, he shewed very little
recollection of his former proposals, except resentment that they
were not received with the gratitude they merited: but Ethelinde
feared that Montgomery, by now following her to London, and by
his visit at Denham, would again urge the narrow spirit of Davenant to press on her the pre-eminence of riches; and that, situated
as she was, her father, though the tenderest and best of parents,
would consider it as a point of duty to influence her acceptance of
a man whose ample fortune would place her above all those inconveniences that she was even now in same degree exposed to; but
which would probably become actual indigence, if she should be
deprived by death of her father's protection. Feeble as her frame
was in consequence of her long illness, it was dreadfully shaken
by these reflections. The painful pleasure of seeing Montgomery,
and a thousand wild conjectures whether his visit was merely to
see her again, or to offer proposals, which she knew too well must
be fruitless, kept her spirits in continual agitation; and a night so
passed contributed but little to amend her looks; which she was
conscious were so unlike those she wore at Grasmere Abbey, that
as she looked in her glass she doubted whether the meditated visit
of Montgomery might not relieve him from his unfortunate passion, by the mournful alteration of its object.

CHAPTER III

Overpowered by oppressive sensations, Ethelinde prepared the
next day to meet Montgomery: sometimes determining to receive
him with so much apparent indifference as to convince him she
repented of the imprudent half avowal she had made; and some-

times melting into the tenderest compassion, and relinquishing all pretensions to that discretion, which could be exerted only by giving him pain.

She wandered round the gardens, and about the house, listening to every noise; and now sent anxious enquiries over the paling that bounded the pleasure-ground near the road; now walked into the hall, and looked towards the entrance, wishing yet fearing to see him; sometimes dreading lest he should be unable to come so far from London on account of other engagements; and at others feeling half angry that at near one o'clock he was not yet arrived; though her father in his note had named the morning as the most commodious time.

In the midst of this suspence Lord Danesforte, in his phaeton and four, drove up to the door. Lady Newenden was not yet visible, remaining long in her own apartment on account of her indisposition; and though he was not unfrequently admitted there, he now sauntered into the garden, where perceiving Ethelinde, he came forward in his assured way to meet her. She attempted, but vainly, to avoid him; he took her hand, and staring confidently in her face, cried—"Are the roses still absent from those lovely cheeks? Hasten, my charming Ethelinde, to regain them; and shew what it is to rival with genuine beauty, the poor copyists who are compelled to have recourse to art."

She struggled to get her hand from him, but he held it fast, and, as she gave no answer to his compliment, went on—"I believe, upon my soul, that the fates intended me a favour when they robbed you of your bloom. You were too enchanting with all your blazing attractions; but as the devil will have it, you are only grown more bewitching by your illness.—You then dazzled my eyes, and took my heart by storm; now, you steal upon it with such languid loveliness, that I am ready to die at your feet."

Ethelinde had often attempted to repulse with unfeigned coldness and dislike the troublesome and fulsome compliments with which Lord Danesforte persecuted her, whenever they were alone: she now felt, in addition to her natural dislike of him, redoubled impatience, lest her meeting with Montgomery should be interrupted by his intrusion. "I beg," replied she, "your Lordship will release me. These sorts of speeches are so common, that they are much beneath you to utter; and so extravagant, that they are disgusting to me to hear."

"Upon my soul they are not compliments, but what I really think. Do you suppose I should pass so much of my time here, you little enchantress, were it not for the pleasure of being with you?"

"Really, my Lord, I never considered your motives, and I must entreat your Lordship to think better of my understanding, than to suppose I can listen without pain to such discourse."

"You listen, however, not only without pain, but with pleasure, to Sir Edward Newenden, though he is a married man."

"What does your Lordship mean?"

"I mean, that you are vastly too charming to be seen with impunity even by the moral, the married Sir Edward; and that he is too agreeable, too interesting, to leave a fair chance of success either to poor Davenant or to others, who, did they not see such a prepossession, might be tempted to throw themselves and their fortune at your feet."

"Good God!" exclaimed Ethelinde, bursting into tears, "what have I done to provoke this insult? and what, to give rise to suspicions so cruel, so injurious? Leave me, Sir—I beg you will leave me. I must quit the house if such ideas are entertained as may make my stay in it destructive to the peace of Lady Newenden. But suffer me, my Lord, to say, that only a heart the most depraved could conceive them—only a spirit the most cruel and malignant give them utterance."

"My sweet weeping marble!" resumed he, again seizing her reluctant hand, "now might that fine formed head serve as a model to a statuary, Don't alarm yourself about the peace of your cousin; for to my certain knowledge her peace is out of the reach of any such trifling accidents. Why, suppose Sir Edward is in love with you, you are not to blame."

"In love with me?" said Ethelinde indignantly.

"Absolutely in love with you. Do you think I did not see it at Grasmere Abbey? Do you think every body did not see it when you met with that accident?"

"Cruel!—cruel!" cried Ethelinde, "that friendship so disinterested, so brotherly as his, should call forth suspicions so injurious, so inhuman. My Lord, you must allow me to repeat to my father what you have said, that he may at once and for ever remove me from a family where I am liable to them."

"Ridiculous! What would you tell your father?—that I suspect, nay, that I know Sir Edward prefers you to all women: and is the Colonel to call me to account for the assertion, or Sir Edward for the involuntary trespass?"

"Neither, my Lord," answered she, trembling at the question; "and perhaps I was wrong to think of troubling him on a matter which I still hope your Lordship spoke of only in raillery. Be so good as to forbear naming it again, and I will endeavour to forget that you have named it at all."

"Bribe me to silence, then, or I do not promise it," said he, rudely kissing her. She endeavoured to disengage herself; and ready to faint through weakness, terror, and vexation, she hastened into the house as soon as she could effect it. As she entered the hall from the garden, Montgomery came in at the opposite door. He advanced eagerly yet respectfully towards her: but her wan countenance, the tears that were in her eyes, and the agitation in which she appeared, struck him with astonishment and terror. The sight of him helped to overcome her, and she sat down in one of the hall chairs, faint and breathless, unable for some moments to answer the enquiries he made, with a faultering voice, and eyes expressive of the tenderest concern; adding, "I am afraid I do not see Miss Chesterville in her usual health?"

Ethelinde, struggling to conquer her confusion, answered that she *had* been ill, but was now much better. Her voice was however so low and tremulous, that it could hardly be heard: and on the appearance of a servant she with difficulty arose, and desiring him to let Colonel Chesterville know that Mr. Montgomery was arrived, she led the way into one of the parlours; where; being again seated, she acquired courage to ask him after his mother.

"I left her well; and brought from her a thousand wishes and compliments to Miss Chesterville; whose enchanting society she almost regrets having tasted, since she must hope for it no more. Had it been possible for her to have come to London——"

"And was it *not* possible?"

"Ah, no!" answered Montgomery in a mournful voice. "It was with difficulty that I could come myself. But my mother, ever generous and attentive, is anxious that I may make one more effort on the recollection of those whose promises induced us to quit France. And—dare I own, that—her consent—her wishes—were added to the invincible inclination I felt to pay my respects to Colonel Chesterville, and to renew an acquaintance with you, Madam, which has formed, since its first commencement, the happiness and torment of my life."

"I will not," replied Ethelinde, "affect to misunderstand you, Sir: but I beseech you, if any unfortunate prepossession remains, try rather to conquer than to indulge it. I am in a few days going to Bristol with Lady Newenden. We shall probably meet no more. Pursue your fortune, and may success, may happiness attend you! The remembrance of *me* can serve only to retard your progress, and repress your military ardour: and though I own I should be hurt to suppose that you forget me, yet I would willingly sacrifice the gratification of my own vanity and self-love to your tranquillity: and as it is impossible——"

"What is impossible?" exclaimed Montgomery eagerly—"what is impossible to the man who adores *you*? It is true, I have now nothing! But were I assured that you yet feel for me any of that generous pity which you once expressed, difficulty and danger would vanish before the inspiration of such hope, and I would directly embrace that line in which I have the earliest prospect of success. I will enter into the service of the East India Company, and embark with the troops now preparing for India. I have expectations of preferment already. I am not without hope that Mr. Chesterville or Sir Edward Newenden may strengthen those expectations, at least I shall not fail to ask them, however reluctantly I ask favors, if you do not forbid me."

Montgomery had hardly, in an hurried but vehement manner, finished this sentence, when Colonel Chesterville entered. His daughter with the utmost difficulty commanded her voice enough to introduce him. The Colonel received him with the warmest expressions of friendship, and seemed extremely pleased with his address and appearance. Montgomery, with as much modesty as if he had never before quitted his northern retirement, yet with as much ease as if he had been always an inhabitant of the great world, received his politeness; and Sir Edward soon after entering, Mr. Chesterville taking Montgomery by the hand, desired Sir Edward to consider him as a friend of his own, as the repre-

sentative of that Mr. Montgomery for whom he had formerly so
sincere a regard. Sir Edward received him with politeness, complimented him on the circumstance of their former acquaintance;
and though Ethelinde observed not that generous warmth with
which he met those to whom he was partial, yet he invited him to
dinner, and seemed involuntarily pleased with him. The conversation soon becoming general among the three gentlemen, she took
the opportunity to withdraw to her own room.

The presumptuous behaviour of Lord Danesforte, and the suspicions he had openly avowed in regard to Sir Edward, shocked
and alarmed her. She now remembered numberless insinuations
which had before fallen from him, and was afraid that he had
not confined these unworthy suppositions to his own breast, but
had disclosed them to Lady Newenden. Yet of late her Ladyship
had been less cold and haughty than usual towards her, and in
better humour than since her journey into the north. Ethelinde
dared not suffer her mind to glance towards the visible partiality
of her cousin for Lord Danesforte. Yet in despite of her natural
candour, she could not but consider an intimacy with a man of
such a character, as improper for the mother of a family, for her
in whose hands were intrusted the honour and happiness of Sir
Edward Newenden. Lord Danesforte intended, she found, to join
the Bristol party; and she dreaded being frequently liable to hear
conversation, the impertinence of which her displeasure seemed
incapable of repressing, and which she dared not openly resent,
lest her father or Sir Edward should be embroiled with this unprincipled and rash man, whose fortune and rank had impressed him
with an idea that he might do any thing with impunity.

Her father's immediate difficulties had been relieved by the
generous friendship of Sir Edward, but the weight on his mind
had only been transferred. He was before harassed by the importunity of his creditors; he now sunk under the sense of obligation
too great to be repaid. Sir Edward was the most generous of men,
but Colonel Chesterville had been used to confer rather than to
receive favours, and his independent spirit shrunk from the painful recollection of so large a debt. Ethelinde saw with concern
his uneasiness, and that his state of mind, usually melancholy,
yielded now to hopeless dejection: he was kept only by his tenderness for her from giving up every thing, and hiding himself in

another country or in the grave. His son had not written to him; and whenever Ethelinde looked that way, a dark and portentous cloud seemed to hang over her fate in regard to her brother, which redoubled the pain of her actual situation; and now the appearance of Montgomery, the irresistible partiality she felt for him, the imprudence of her indulging it, and the impossibility of their ever being united, seemed to add to the poignancy, and variety of the distresses which at once assaulted her heart.

Her health was yet far from being re-established; and the sufferings of her mind encreasing her weakness, she with much difficulty acquired resolution to appear at dinner. Lord Danesforte and several others who came to take leave of Lady Newenden were there; and Montgomery was barely noticed among the croud, except by Sir Edward and Colonel Chesterville. His figure, however, was so striking, that the strangers enquired of each other who he was; but learning that he was a young man from the north whom nobody knew, he was suffered to remain unnoticed. The dinner was a cruel trial to Ethelinde. Once or twice she ventured to steal a look at Montgomery; then glancing her eyes towards Sir Edward, she found his fixed upon her with a look of enquiry so penetrating that blushes immediately dyed her cheeks, and she would most willingly have concealed herself in her own room, fearing every moment lest her encreased emotion should betray her. At length the tedious dinner was at an end: she withdrew with the ladies; and being long accustomed to appear or disappear without being remarked by her cousin, she seized on the first moment it was possible to retire, and indulge her reflections in solitude. She could not forbear however going to the window to watch if Montgomery departed. She knew that he must return to town that evening; in two days they were to go to Bristol; she should therefore never see him more—never again behold him; and her heart sickened at the idea of passing a life that without him must be a blank. His wild project of making a fortune that might entitle him to pretend to her, of which he had given her an hasty sketch, afforded her no consolation; every prospect before her was dreary; and as she sat at the window listening to every noise, and watching every light that moved in the distant stables, of which she had a view from her windows, the world seemed to offer nothing to her reflection but pain, mortification, and disappointment. From this gloomy reverie she was awakened by a summons to tea. The hope that Montgomery was not yet gone, made her conquer her reluctance to appear below. She went down therefore, and found in the drawing-room various groups assembled in different parties of conversation; but neither her father nor Montgomery were among them. A new alarm now found its way to her thoughts. High-spirited, sanguine, and conscious of his noble birth, Montgomery might perhaps impart his impossible project to her father. He might even say that that project was not disapproved by her. This idea so strongly agitated her mind when she began to make the tea, that it was with the utmost difficulty she sent it round the first time. But after almost half an hour, seeing that they did not appear, and having been told on enquiry that the Colonel was busy with Mr. Montgomery in Sir Edward's library, her courage and presence of mind could hold out no longer; and having filled the cups with hot water, and poured the cream into the sugar bason, her confusion became so visible to Sir Edward, whose eyes were never long diverted from her, that he approached, and asked her in great concern if she was ill?

"I am, indeed," said she, "so ill from the heat of the room, that I must beg Lady Newenden to excuse me."

She hastily arose, and Sir Edward took her hand, and led her towards the door. She trembled, and only by an effort reached it. "Good, God," cried he as he supported her, "what is the matter? How long has this been?"

"Ask me not," answered she as she got to the door, "nor give yourself any trouble about me. I am merely weak and low."

"Weak and low!" exclaimed he as they reached together the bottom of the stairs. "You are not able to walk.—Lean on me—let me assist you to your room."

At that moment all that Lord Danesforte had been saying to her in the morning rushing on her memory, she cried—"No, Sir Edward, I earnestly entreat you will not. I am very well able to walk—indeed I am."

"You earnestly beg I will not! Is it indeed thus, Ethelinde?" Montgomery, and her partiality for him, forcibly struck him, and he fancied her rejection of his own services arose from her partial fondness to her fortunate lover. Then recollecting that he had no right to blame her if it was so, he checked the sudden anger he felt, and bowing left her, saying—"I hope however you will soon be better."

Instead of returning to the company, he went to his own dressing-room, to recover his serenity, and call himself anew to an account for his unhappy and criminal passion, which every day encreased, and which he every day attempted to conquer, but which all his efforts served only to render more incurable. He was very little aware of the use that was made of his absence. Lord Danesforte, who had by the most insidious, and almost imperceptible degrees possessed himself of the confidence of Lady Newenden, had artfully encreased in her mind those suspicions of her husband's fondness for Ethelinde which had originated at Grasmere; but the anger and disdain which they might have excited; and which would have broken out in a way that would have obliged Ethelinde to have left the house (a circumstance his Lordship by no means desired) had been so artfully counteracted by oblique yet unequivocal declarations of his own devoted attachment, that her Ladyship felt as much pity as anger towards a man who could for so inferior a being as Ethelinde neglect for a moment a woman whom Lord Danesforte declared to be, in face and in figure as well as in every perfection of mind, the first of created beings.

A few days study had made him master of her character, and he was now able to guide at his pleasure that capricious temper which had never yet submitted to the dictates of another. But she was herself so far from being conscious of his power over her, that she fancied he lived only to admire and obey her; and she triumphed in being able with an unsullied character to bear away from the unmarried of the fashionable world, him, whose notice would have exalted into pre-eminent fashion the vainest among them.

"Ethelinde is ill," said his Lordship, "and Sir Edward is gone out to take care of her."

"Sir Edward is extremely kind," scornfully answered Lady Newenden; "and if he could cure Ethelinde of such extreme affectation, his assiduity would really be serviceable to her family, to which it is a great nuisance. Somebody—Sir Edward himself, I suppose, has said that that elegant languor becomes her features; and since she has heard so, she disdains the appearance of health, and will hardly make use of her limbs."

This ungenerous and cruel reflection Lord Danesforte

answered only by a smile, which signified at once approbation and assent. He saw that the bitterness which Lady Newenden had harboured against Ethelinde, was not the less likely to answer his purpose by being mingled with contempt, which prevented her from declaring openly the jealousy she felt, but which she was ashamed of suffering to appear towards an object whom she had always affected to consider as so very inferior.

He never openly declared his suspicions of that passion which he believed Sir Edward to have; but by distant hints and significant looks had more forcibly impressed it on the mind of Lady Newenden: at the same time intimating, that the dignity of her own character required that she should neither notice nor resent it; and that it was exaltation of spirit to let Ethelinde remain in the house without appearing to observe, or at least to be angry at it.

By conversation of a still more dangerous tendency, he imperceptibly erased from her feeble understanding those principles which should have secured her inviolable tenderness to her husband, and that true greatness of mind which ought to have made her the protectress of her cousin's character, and to have excited resentment on any attempt to prejudice her against Sir Edward. Having once carried those points, he knew he might with impunity presume to propose to her any deviation from rectitude which his own dissolute morals might induce him to suggest. Her person had at first been indifferent to him; but as his project of gaining Ethelinde had advanced but little since he had first imagined it, and as in its pursuit he had acquired so many advantages over the judgment and affections of Lady Newenden, he had now no inclination to recede, and scrupled not to add the destruction of Sir Edward's honour and happiness to that of the numerous trophies in the same way which he had already obtained.

Still, however, he made his approaches so gradually, threw into his manner so much of the undesigning ease which exists among people of the same rank, and so carefully avoided before him any appearance of unwarrantable attachment to his wife, that Sir Edward, naturally candid and unsuspicious, felt no alarm; and though he had no particular friendship or esteem for Lord Danesforte, he was not uneasy at the frequency or length of his visits, since they seemed agreeable to Lady Newenden, and were never particular, because the house was generally filled with other parties, who lived in it in equal freedom. Possibly the passion prevailing in his own mind prevented his scrutinizing too narrowly what passed in the minds of others. Lady Newenden had long since ceased to impress him with that idea of perfection which he had first fondly cherished: his scheme of domestic felicity, the "life of reason" which he hoped to have passed, had vanished, and having no taste for what his wife had substituted, his mind had unhappily found for itself another occupation, and was now employed in contemplating the loveliness of Ethelinde, and in studying to contribute to her happiness while he despaired of his own.

In about half an hour Sir Edward returned to the drawing-room, and found there Colonel Chesterville, whose looks intimated that some extraordinary occurrence had agitated his mind. Sir Edward knew that he had, at Montgomery's request, withdrawn with him; and the subject of their conference darted into his mind, and gave him the most uneasy sensation he had ever felt: for though he had in some degree encouraged Davenant when he fancied it was for the interest of Ethelinde to marry him, he found that a lover whom she approved would appear to him in a very different light; and though he dared not ask more than her friendship, he felt that he should be unable to see another avowedly in possession of her love.

The painful suspence he was in, was soon put an end to: Colonel Chesterville requested to speak to him in his study; and there in great emotion related to him the conversation which he had held with Montgomery.

"I was far from being aware, my dear Sir Edward," said he, "of the purport of Montgomery's visit; and though I tremble for the consequence of it on my daughter, for I fear he is not indifferent to her, while I feel with renewed bitterness the injury I have done her in depriving her of the fortune I might have preserved for her, I cannot blame the young man; I cannot help reverencing his open and manly conduct. He has told me that he loves, that he adores Ethelinde; that he has said so to her, and she has heard it without displeasure: but having nothing to expect but the reversion of a very small fortune after the death of his mother, whom he describes as the best of parents, and whose life is as dear to him as his own, he dares not think of now aspiring to an alliance with my daughter: all, therefore, he has to ask of me is, whether I will refuse him permission to consider himself as making an effort in life, not merely to possess himself of affluence, but to obtain such a fortune as may give him that hope to which he now presumes not to raise his eyes. "Believe me, Colonel," said he, "that was I possessed of millions, it is a connection which I should glory in forming. But I have nothing; and so little value have pecuniary possessions hitherto had in my eyes, that I should probably have continued most contented in that obscurity in which concurring circumstances had placed me, had I never seen your angelic daughter. She has awakened in my soul that ambition which had long been dormant; and I feel animated with new life when I believe that it may possibly be passed in rendering myself worthy of *her*. But misunderstand me not: I mean not to bind her; I request no engagement, no promise, and I would scorn to sully the lovely purity of her gentle and ingenuous mind, by asking of her to encourage my hopes clandestinely: therefore it is, that finding the happiness of my whole life depending on her; being convinced, after a long struggle, that the impression she had made on my heart was decisive of my destiny, I came hither: I open that heart to you without reserve; and trust to the noble and candid spirit of a soldier and a man of honour, to see my conduct in its true light."

"What," continued Colonel Chesterville, "what could I say to this romantic but interesting boy? Though I listened to him with pain, I could not with displeasure: his father seemed to be restored again to life, and to be present before me. Yet how could I encourage a pursuit so wild, so extravagant, which may embitter the life of my poor Ethelinde by a hopeless passion? It is madness to think of it."

"And what then did you say to him?" enquired Sir Edward.

"What *could* I say to him?" replied the Colonel. "His family is not only unexceptionable, but illustrious. His grandfather, by a political error only, lost one of those titles which have long been in it, and which is now gone to a more distant branch. His person is such as I suppose no woman can behold without acknowledging its superior beauty. In his openness of heart, in that proper courage which makes him, though so long lost in indigence and obscurity, fearlessly speak to a fellow-creature; in that candour which forbids his using a deception, even to gain the point on which his happiness depends; I find much, which while I cannot but approve and admire myself, makes me tremble for Ethelinde; who has exactly that mind and that heart which generosity, courage, and candour, must deeply affect. Yet nothing is more romantic than his hopes, nothing more impossible than their union! Had Ethelinde a fortune——"

"You would not hesitate."

"Not a moment—if she thinks of this young man as I believe she *must* do."

"And what are these projects of his for acquiring a fortune?"

"Such as I cannot believe he will succeed in—He proposes going to India."

"As a soldier? Will that be consistent with such principles as he professes; at least if the ideas are just which we Europeans entertain of the means by which fortunes are in that line accumulated?"

"I told him it was inconsistent with his feelings, with his principles; but he fancies with the warm enthusiasm of his age, that he can preserve his integrity amidst temptations the most powerful; and acquire opulence, not by being the plunderer but the protector of the people among whom he proposes serving."

"And with what answer, my dear Colonel, have you at length dismissed him?"

"I objected, I remonstrated against his attaching himself to my daughter. I represented that she was now without fortune, that my death would very little enrich her; that by my having married at a period as early as his present age, my children were grown up while I was yet but in the middle of life; that therefore the little she could ever claim, she might not for years possess, and that he certainly had too much generosity to wish to engage the affections of Ethelinde on a remote hope that the impediments between them might be removed: and that though I wished him in his pursuit all the success his merit deserved, I could not think of entering into any promise that Ethelinde should, in the event, be his. He declared that he expected no such promise. All he desired was my assurance that whenever he had a fortune acquired with honour, I should not on any other account object to him: then, without waiting for me to form an answer to a proposal so eccentric, he departed, desiring to leave his compliments for you, and my permission to breakfast here to-morrow. He is gone to-night to Windsor."

"I am afraid," said Sir Edward, hesitating, "that in the state of health Ethelinde is in at present, this may greatly injure her. Unless

Montgomery had been convinced that she did not disapprove his opening his mind to you, I cannot suppose he would have done it; yet surely she has an understanding which would prevent her from encouraging a project so imprudent, so impossible!" He could not repress his emotion, though too conscious of its source, and without being able to determine on what it would be proper to do to stop the progress of Montgomery's pursuit, Sir Edward and Colonel Chesterville parted for the night, equally unhappy.

CHAPTER IV

Ethelinde passed not her time with more tranquillity. She was obliged to excuse herself from supping below; which, as she often did so, was the less remarkable. The night brought to her no repose; or such as was too much broken by uneasy dreams to afford her any refreshment. Her father came not up to her room, as he usually did the preceding evenings; but early the next morning, as soon as he heard she was dressed, he came into her little dressing-room, and sitting down, said with a deep sigh that he had just received a letter from her brother.

"And what, my dear Sir, does it say?" eagerly enquired Ethelinde.

He gave it into her hand.

It contained complaints of his unpleasant situation in consequence of his bills having been returned; and though he did not actually reproach his father, there was, throughout the letter, a style of impatience and regret, which made the heart of Ethelinde throb with pain as she read it.

"You see," said Colonel Chesterville, after she had run it over—"you see, my love, how I am situated. The money for these bills, you know, I have since sent; and have been enabled to do so through the generous friendship of Sir Edward Newenden: but where—where am I to find money to supply new demands? I cannot, I will not again apply to my friend: I am already too much obliged to him: I would I were in my grave; for troubles to which I am unequal multiply around me."

Before the conclusion of this speech, the face of Ethelinde was bathed in tears. "Pray, my dear Sir," said she, sobbing, "give not way thus to despondence. Think, if your melancholy wish were fulfilled, what would become of your daughter."

"It is for my daughter that I would live!—And I dare venture yet to hope that my daughter will be my blessing."

"Yet to hope!" exclaimed Ethelinde: "Has then my father ever doubted that his daughter's endeavours at least have been to contribute to his happiness?"

"I never have had reason a moment to doubt it: and yet—"

"Wherefore do you hesitate, dear Sir?" said the trembling Ethelinde.—"If I have given you a moment's pain, it has been undesignedly, and I desire only to repair my fault."

"No, my Ethelinde, thou art incapable I know of giving me pain intentionally. I will be ingenuous with you: Montgomery has opened to me his mind.—He has told me that you do not discourage his wishes, wild and romantic as they certainly are. His merits I acknowledge; but situated as he is in regard to fortune, ought my dear girl to suffer her mind to be influenced to the injury of her peace?"

Though from the opening of this dialogue Ethelinde had suspected to what it would tend, she could with the utmost difficulty support herself. Pale and trembling, she dared not raise her eyes to her father; still less dared she own all she felt for Montgomery; yet too ingenuous to deny her preference of him, she remained silent, and seemed, in breathless expectation, to attend to her father's farther pleasure. He perceived her agitation, and was convinced that Montgomery had not deceived him.

"I will not, my love, distress you," continued he: "I will leave you now to recollect yourself, and in half an hour I will return to know what you would have me say. I would have you indeed consider what I *ought* to say to Montgomery, who is to be here at breakfast, and who will then expect my answer."

"Your answer, dear Sir! What then has he said to you?"

"He wishes to be received by me as your lover; and to go to India in the hope, that if he is there successful he may on his return receive your hand. I conclude that these proposals were not made to me, till your assent to them, had been obtained."

"I will not be disingenuous, Sir. Mr. Montgomery did mention to me yesterday the visionary plans he had formed. I thought them so entirely chimerical that I gave them no encouragement."

"But tell me, Ethelinde, is your heart free from prepossession in favour of this young man?—If it is, he is presumptuous in proceeding so far with me. Nay, be not thus distressed, but consider me, my love, as one who lives only in the hope of seeing you happy. Ethelinde is above dissimulation; and has not, I trust, a thought that she should wish to conceal from her father."

"I will not, Sir, attempt it," answered the faultering Ethelinde; "but—though I cannot deny that Mr. Montgomery has perhaps been thought of with indiscreet, with unguarded partiality, though I have not concealed from him the weakness for which I have condemned myself; yet believe me, dearest Sir, believe me when I protest to you, that it shall at least never offend you; and that if I cannot conquer it—and indeed I will try—I will at least conceal it, and never voluntarily indulge a wish to have any will but yours."

"Good God!" exclaimed Colonel Chesterville, walking in an agony about the room, "I cannot bear this! Ethelinde, have pity on me and on yourself! Tell me not of what you will attempt, to make me happy, but rather what I can do to contribute to your felicity. If Montgomery had a competence, and if your heart is irretrievably his, I would not hesitate a moment: but can I justify it to myself to encourage his hopes, situated as he now is? Can I suffer my daughter to engage herself to a young man, who, whatever may be his merit and his birth, is in other respects only an indigent adventurer? Must her youth wear away in waiting for his precarious success? her health decline in the languor of hope long delayed? and possibly, after years so passed, if indeed her constitution enables her so to pass them, may she not fall a victim to the bitterness, of disappointment? My dearest girl, consider well what it is Montgomery asks; consider not only his request, but your own situation, If I die—alas! I need not say how unhappily destitute of fortune you will be. Where will you live?—how be supported to attend the return of your lover?"

The tears and sobs of Ethelinde were now redoubled. To give her feelings utterance was impossible, and her father proceeded in a lower and more tremulous tone—

"I did indeed flatter myself, that before I died, the merit, the loveliness of Ethelinde would have placed her in the protection of some man of honour and of fortune: this unhappy prepossession blasts all my hopes, and I shall die doubtful of that my heart most ardently wishes—the happiness of my dearest child: or perhaps, more wretched still, I shall die in the certainty of her being miserable. Death will then be indeed terrible!"

Ethelinde, now making an effort to speak, said—"Hear me then, Sir—hear me when I solemnly declare—that—if it will be any satisfaction to you, I will forbid this unhappy young man to think of me again—I will put an end for ever to those hopes which I ought not to have given him—I will desire him to tear me from his heart for ever!"

"Not so, Ethelinde," answered her father, greatly moved—"I expect not a sacrifice so painful. But I would make one request to my daughter; and she must, with so excellent an understanding, see the propriety of what I ask."

"Name your request, Sir, and be it what it will, it must have with me the force of a command."

"It is then, that you will positively promise me to enter into no engagement with Montgomery, however he may urge it."

"I give you my word I will not."

"Is it, do you think, proper that you should see him, at all, since he may perhaps press you to give him at least more hope than, situated as you are, you ought to give him?"

"I will not see him Sir," said Ethelinde, in a voice that betrayed the violent struggle she underwent, "if you desire that I should not." But she had no sooner uttered these words, than her heart rebelling against her duty, represented the sorrow, the despair of Montgomery; and finding herself unequal to the cruelty of inflicting it, she added—"Yet I must say that I shall for the first time in my life obey you with reluctance. I am obliged, greatly obliged to Mr. Montgomery. I admire, esteem; and reverence his mother beyond any human being—and—"

"And you love him!—Ah! my child, I see it too plainly. Yet trusting to your understanding, to your delicacy, to the promise you have given me, I will not press you farther; you shall act as you please in regard to seeing him; and I will leave you to recollect yourself before an interview in which I know the softness of your heart will be rectified by reason, by regard for my peace, and for that of the young man himself." Colonel Chesterville then left the room; and Ethelinde, who had no power to carry on the dialogue, tried to acquire as much strength as he seemed to expect she should exert.

While she blamed Montgomery for the haste in which he had disclosed to her father schemes so little likely to be realized, she was deeply affected by this proof of his warm and serious passion for her. Far from finding, on examination of her heart, that she had strength enough to reject him, her enquiry served only to make her fear, that though she should part with him for ever, it would be impossible for her ever to forget him. But to make her father unhappy, by appearing to persist; to seem so weakly romantic, as to attach herself to a young man of whom she could yet know so little, and to give up her reason to the indulgence of a passion so imprudent, so girlish, and so contrary to her duty!—her pride, her good sense, her tenderness towards her father, all forbade it; and for a few moments the thought she could command herself enough to represent to Montgomery the impossibility of their ever being united, and to entreat him to relinquish—nay to insist on his relinquishing every hope of it: but when she had as she believed brought herself to this resolution, the noise of some persons entering the courtyard drew her suddenly to the window, and she saw Montgomery spring from his horse in all the hurry of impatience, and enquiring eagerly for Colonel Chesterville, he hastened into the house.

Her late-formed determination was in a moment forgotten. Her heart acknowledged his power over it; and without knowing what she should say to him when she met him, she walked about her room, dreading the summons to meet him which she every moment expected to receive, yet being sensible that if it did not soon arrive, the violence of her agitation would deprive her of the power to obey it.

Near half an hour was passed in this way: then, a servant came up with Mr. Montgomery's compliments, and his request to allow him a few moments of her time in the breakfast-parlour. She had just voice enough to enquire whether Colonel Chesterville was with him; and hearing that he was, she crept with trembling feet down stairs, stopping several times to recover her breath, and trying to argue herself into some degree of fortitude to meet what was before her.

CHAPTER V

On entering the breakfast parlour, Montgomery was sitting alone by the table, where every thing remained untouched. On the sight of her he started up, and flew towards her; but his countenance expressed only solicitude and pain. He took her hand, led her to a seat, and sat down by her: both seemed unable to speak; and their silence was broken by a deep-drawn sigh from the almost convulsed bosom of Ethelinde. Montgomery, with agitation, the violence of which was encreased by his efforts to speak with calmness, at length said—"I await my destiny from you! I have ventured to speak to your father of hopes which he does not encourage; but if you forbid them not, I will not despair!"

"Why *did* you speak to him? Why force him to forbid that to which there were always so many impediments—but—I know not what I would say——"

"Good God! is it possible that having once harboured an hope, however remote, I should, without an attempt to realize, resign it? Say only that you repent having given it, that I have forfeited all pretensions to that generous pity which you once deigned to afford me, and that it will contribute to your peace to know that I drag on, in hopeless wretchedness, a life which from that moment will have lost all its value."

"That it would contribute to *my* peace to see you wretched! Ah, Montgomery! you know that had we met under more propitious circumstances, the happiness of *my* life, for I cannot if I would dissemble, would have consisted solely in making you happy; but obstacles, unconquerable obstacles, are between us: in attempting to surmount them, you have precipitated the certainty of their being for ever invincible. My father, the tenderest of fathers, does you justice, and owns that you deserve a more fortunate lot than it is possible for you, situated as I am, to find with me. Go then, Montgomery; forget that we ever met: go; pursue that prosperity which you cannot fail of possessing."

"And what will prosperity do for me? Alas! if you disclaim all interest in my destiny, I shall grow careless of it. Animated by the delicious hope of making myself worthy of you, I might realize all the prospects which I have drawn; but if you thus send me from you unheard, unguarded, unpitied! if I go to be forgotten for ever by one of those two beings in whose tender remembrance only I wish to exist; shall I have spirits to encounter the difficulties before me? Will any thing be worthy of my present attention, when I know that no part of my future life will be yours."

He stopped, from incapacity to proceed. Ethelinde was silent, for the conflict of her soul was too great either for language or for tears.

After pausing a moment, he recovered his voice and went on.

"You are so generous as to say that had we met under more propitious circumstances, my happiness would be yours. Let it be the glory of a passion like mine to surmount circumstances. He who is favoured by Ethelinde Chesterville, should be more than mortal, and for such a prize—oh, what spirit of enterprize might it not awaken in the calmest breast! In mine, should it not produce all that shall enable me to forget difficulty and danger. I feel a conviction that I shall repair the caprice of fortune if I go out with the hope of removing the cruel obstacle between us. Or if I fail, the recollection of your pity, of your tenderness, and the certainty of being remembered by you, will make death itself infinitely happier than without that hope, it is possible for me to find the most prosperous life."

"But who," said Ethelinde, collecting all the resolution she could to recal him from this wild effusion, "who shall teach your mother to be reconciled to your departure; and if you fail, who shall console her for the loss of her only son?"

"You know not, my Ethelinde," answered he, "the fortitude of soul which that dear mother possesses. With the softest sensibility, she blends the most heroic courage. It is true, that till she had seen and conversed with you, I was the only object of her fondness; yet she kept me not with her to indulge a weak parental fondness, but because nothing offered which I could with honour or indeed with advantage accept: but when she beheld you; and learned that the perfections which had attracted her tenderest esteem, had made an impression never to be erased on the heart of her son, she was too generous to desire me to linger another moment in the obscurity where I had long been content, but bade me pursue that road which might raise me to affluence, and justify, as well in fortune as my birth has done in noble blood, my pretensions to the loveliest of human beings."

"There is no person on earth," replied the trembling Ethelinde, "whose good opinion I so eagerly covet. Let me go farther, and say that to be related to Mrs. Montgomery would be the most desirable connection the world could offer me; but when her partial opinion of me, and her tenderness for you, engaged her to give her sanction to your wishes, she knew not, she could not know, the insuperable objections there are; she could not suppose that she was embittering the misery of this impossibility, and depriving me of the little fortitude I could perhaps have exerted, by shewing me all the value of what I might have possessed in acquiring a stronger claim on her affection and regard."

The tenderness of this speech was ill calculated to reconcile Montgomery to the inevitable necessity of their parting for ever, which Ethelinde fancied she was endeavouring to impress on his mind.

"Merciful heaven!" exclaimed he; "and is it thus that you would subdue my mind to this fancied, this cruel prudence, by such enchanting, such overwhelming softness! No, Ethelinde, since you deign to own that I am not indifferent to you, I cannot, I will not resign my hopes. I ask not to bind you by any promise—I only ask of you not to forbid my loving, my adoring you; because it would be impossible for me to obey you. Yes, one other request I have, it is that you will suffer me to write to you while I yet remain in England, and will allow my mother to correspond with you when I am departed."

"I cannot," said Ethelinde, "comply with the former request; the latter will be a great pleasure to me."

"And do you refuse to receive one letter from me? No, I will not be refused. You are going, I find, to Bristol—going with as large a party as were with you at Grasmere Abbey. Amid such a circle, may I not venture to remind you of the unhappy man who is compelled by his inauspicious fate to become part of his life an exile, in the hope of rendering some future period of it more fortunate? You will not, you cannot deny me such a request; for perhaps—before you return, I may be gone to a region from whence I cannot often importune you."

Tears had been restrained by the extreme perturbation of her mind; but, melted by the despondent tone in which he spoke, Ethelinde now gave way to all the melancholy softness which oppressed her heart. Montgomery, unable to sustain the sight of her grief, and torn with with those contending passions, which he was from his disposition accustomed to feel in all their violence, feared that if he remained he should commit some extravagance, and therefore he hurried out of the room, entreating of Ethelinde to compose herself, and allow him to see her again for two minutes only, before he took leave of her.—"I will go," said he, "and try to collect resolution enough to undergo the most insupportable moment of my life."

Ethelinde saw him pass the window, and go into the garden; and then, feeling herself quite unequal to the task of bidding him farewel for ever, dissatisfied with herself for the little resolution she had hitherto shewn, and conscious that every moment she was with him added to the reluctance with which she must part from him, she determined to quit the room while she was yet able, and not see him again only to renew the mutual agonies of their separation.

She went therefore as well as she was able to her own room. But, when she reflected on what he must feel at her refusing to see him again before he departed, she summoned strength enough with trembling hands to send down by the servant who usually attended her, the following note:

"Sir,

"After the weakness I have betrayed, it were in vain to attempt concealing from you the fatal prepossession which prudence, reason, and duty equally forbid me to indulge. Since our parting is inevitable, why should we lengthen its pain? and I do intreat you to spare me the repetition of a scene to which I own myself altogether unequal.

"Accept of my truest wishes for your prosperity, for your happiness, wheresoever you may be; and believe, that I must ever retain a proper sense of the flattering opinion with which you have honoured me, as well as of the obligation I owe to you, and to Mrs. Montgomery, whose recollection of me will still consti-

tute the greatest part of the small share of happiness which can
now ever be the lot of,

Sir,

Your most obedient,

and most humble servant,

ETHELINDE CHESTERVILLE."

Having sent down the letter, she waited with trembling anxiety to hear him depart. It was impossible for her to remain tranquil; she traversed the room with hasty steps; now watched at the
window; now listened to the noises within the house. In a few
moments she saw her father, who had, to shew his perfect reliance
on her prudence, been out during their conference, return into the
house with Sir Edward. She listened on the great stair-case that led
to the hall, into which the breakfast-parlour opened, and distinctly
heard the Colonel, who had parted from Sir Edward, enter the parlour and speak to Montgomery: but the door was then shut, and
she could not afterwards distinguish what was said. So violently
was she now affected, that weak as her frame yet was, she had no
longer any power to struggle against the agitation of her mind;
but feeling herself very faint, she was compelled to lie down on the
bed; and again tried to reconcile herself to the idea of having seen
the last of Montgomery.

In about a quarter of an hour, the servant who attended her
came in to look at the fire. She started up, and enquired with
eagerness where her father was, and who he had with him. The
maid answered, that the handsome young gentleman who had
breakfasted there was just gone; and that the Colonel was with Sir
Edward in his study.

Montgomery then was gone: gone for ever! She reposed her
head again on her pillow; sighed from the very bottom of her
heart; and without any farther attempt to check the acuteness of
her grief, was satisfied she had acquitted herself by the effort she
had already made, and with a melancholy and gloomy kind of satisfaction gave herself up to regret and tears.

Sir Edward, to whom Colonel Chesterville had communicated
what had passed with Ethelinde, waited in a state of mind the most
disturbed and uneasy for the result of her meeting with Montgomery. He was afraid of asking himself why he so earnestly desired

that she might have strength of mind to dismiss him for ever, and ashamed of the reluctance he felt to acknowledge that, considered in every other light than that which related to pecuniary circumstances, Montgomery was without exception. The noble and candid spirit of Sir Edward made him sedulous to hide, though he could not conquer, the jealousy which narrowed his heart; and he determined to interest himself for Montgomery with as much zeal as if he had not dreaded his influence on Ethelinde. Yet he persuaded himself that it was better to limit his services to that line in which Montgomery himself seemed most desirous to succeed; and to apply to Mr. Maltravers for his assistance in procuring him an appointment to India, persuaded as he was that neither Ethelinde or her father would think of forming with him any engagement which could be fulfilled only at the remote and uncertain period of his return.

This idea he had communicated to Colonel Chesterville during their walk, by whom it had been eagerly embraced. On the return of the latter to the parlour where Montgomery was, he was struck with the appearance of the unfortunate young man; who, while his heart refused to obey the reasons Ethelinde had given in her note for their meeting no more, yet felt all their justice; and though he could not determine to relinquish his hopes, dreaded to press them on Ethelinde, whose health seemed already too much shaken, and whose tenderness for him redoubled his love and embittered his despair. Colonel Chesterville, too considerate to have forgotten the time when for the mother of Ethelinde he had himself hazarded the loss of fortune and family interest, felt more pity than anger; and when Montgomery shewed him the note he had received from Ethelinde, and related in animated language what had passed, the Colonel found his concern and tenderness for both, such as he dared not discover to either. He besought Montgomery therefore not to insist on seeing Ethelinde again; represented the cruel effects of repeated struggles on a constitution so weak as her's had long been; and by arguments urged rather as a friend solicitous for the true interests of both, than as a father who had a right to be obeyed, he prevailed on Montgomery to leave the house at least with some apparent composure; but he could obtain from him no promise that he would forbear to write to Ethelinde; none, that he would for a moment attempt, by the force of reason

or of despair, to wean his mind from the recollection of that preference that alone animated his resolution, and created the spirit of
enterprize, by which, with the sanguine imagination of a young
man, he still determined to believe he might at length obtain all
his wishes.

CHAPTER VI

When Montgomery was departed, Colonel Chesterville went
again to Sir Edward, who waited for him in his study. He related
the conversation between Montgomery and his daughter; the
note which Ethelinde had sent him; and what had afterwards
passed with Montgomery. With mingled pity, sorrow, and vexation, Sir Edward heard the relation: he now felt too certainly what
he had hitherto only suspected—that the affections of Ethelinde
were fixed on Montgomery; and he saw that her father, moved
by his tenderness for her, and his pity and partiality to Montgomery, was doubtful whether he ought to oppose a passion which he
could not disapprove, and to the propriety of which only fortune
was wanting. The Colonel remembered his own conduct and
found it difficult to blame that of Montgomery: and naturally of a
temper somewhat warm and romantic, the military life he had led
had added more to his honour than to his prudence. Sir Edward
found therefore that a very little encouragement would persuade
him he was acting right in suffering his daughter to give herself to
the man she loved; and that he reproached himself with extreme
bitterness for his own indiscretion in having deprived her of that
fortune, which, however small, would have diminished somewhat
of the extreme indiscretion she would now commit, in marrying,
portionless herself, a man who had neither income nor profession
of any kind. In the course of his conversation, Colonel Chesterville had not only dropped enough to convince Sir Edward that
such were his feelings, but had touched on the possibility of procuring a commission in the English army for Montgomery; and of
the young people's living with him till they could afford an establishment of their own. As these were rather hints than proposals,
Sir Edward attempted not to convince him of their impracticability; but contented himself for the present, with beseeching him to

reflect on Ethelinde's illness, and to save her as much as possible from the repetition of scenes likely to encrease it. He said, that he would consider of what could be done for Montgomery; and, would recommend it to the Colonel to suffer nothing to delay the journey to Bristol; and to say as little as possible to Ethelinde of Montgomery, but to appear as if he considered the affair to be at an end.

The unequivocal marks of friendship which Mr. Chesterville had received from Sir Edward, as well as his exalted understanding and excellent heart, gave him great influence; and his present advice seemed so perfectly proper, that the Colonel determined implicitly to follow it. He thought it however better to have some conversation with Ethelinde before he saw her in mixed company and therefore went to her room, leaving Sir Edward to reflect alone on what he had heard; to call himself, as he repeatedly did, to account for an inclination of which he found it impossible to divest himself; and to make new resolutions in regard to that rectitude of conduct which he determined to observe, in spite of the whirlwinds of passion, which, becoming more frequent, seemed threatening to overturn the integrity of his upright heart.

Whenever he thus scrutinized the internal conflicts with which he was agitated, he believed that by mere dint of reason and resolution he should be able to get the better wholly of a prepossession which might be as fatal to the repose of its object, as it was, and must be, to his own happiness: but whatever fancied strength he acquired in her absence, he no sooner saw her, no sooner heard her speak, or believed either that another would win her, or that she was herself unhappy, than all the weakness of his soul returned; and he again yielded to the predominating influence of a passion, now become part of his existence.

Colonel Chesterville, on his entering the apartment of his daughter, found her at her toilet, where she was adjusting her hair, and endeavouring to compose her looks so as to appear at dinner. She had, ever since the departure of Montgomery, been trying to consider him as given up for ever; and to fortify her mind to bear this eternal and inevitable separation, with at least so much apparent resignation as might at once prevent her father from suffering by the sight of her uneasiness; and others, who would ridicule her concern, from perceiving it all: flattering herself, that by forcing herself into company, she should for at least some moments of the day be compelled to call off her thoughts from the dangerous object on which they too fondly dwelt. Her heroism even went farther; and she thought she could prevail on herself to listen to Davenant, disagreeable as he had hitherto been to her; not with an intention really to encourage his addresses, and with as little to mislead him by coquetry, but merely with that degree of attention which should erase from his mind, and from that of Lord Danesforte, all impressions they might have received of her partiality to Montgomery; whose name, uttered in a sort of malicious raillery, as they frequently uttered it, gave her the most unpleasing sensations of impatience, and sometimes of resentment. Her father, finding her much more tranquil than he had ventured to hope after the scene that had passed, said very little to her; but taking her hand, and pressing it to his bosom, he let her see how much he thought himself obliged to her for this effort to obey and relieve him. This silent acknowledgment affected Ethelinde more than any language could have done. She dared not speak, lest the subject which still so greatly affected her should renew that emotion she had been struggling to stifle; but carrying her father's hand to her lips, she kissed it; a tear fell upon it; and deep sobs were bursting from her overcharged heart, when her father, unable to remain with her, broke suddenly away and left the room.

In a few minutes, however, she had again argued herself into tolerable calmness; she finished her dress; bathed her eyes, which bore too evidently the marks of tears, with rose water: and then, that she might not remain a moment alone in her room, was going to walk with the children in the garden; but seeing at that moment Sir Edward meet them, she was deterred from executing her intention—for, convinced that he knew of her partiality for Montgomery, and disapproved of it, she dreaded, in her present faultering spirits, even the gentle representation which she thought his brotherly tenderness might urge him to make of its weakness and indiscretion.

A very numerous party attended Lady Newenden at dinner; a circumstance now rather pleasant than otherwise to Ethelinde, as she hoped to escape unremarked among the croud. The next day they were all to set out for Bristol; and Mr. and Mrs. Maltravers with their servants were already arrived. Lord Danesforte, whose assiduity was almost equally divided between Mrs. Maltravers and her daughter, Lady Newenden, was not to go with them, but to join them in a few days; and among other pleasurable schemes proposed, one was, that the whole party should, as soon as her Ladyship had received the benefit she expected from the water and change of air, go to the magnificent seat of Lord Danesforte near Gloucester; where he proposed by that time to collect a set of theatrical friends:—a scheme which appeared so pleasant to Mrs. Maltravers, that she bore better than she would otherwise have done, the less pleasant view of getting among Mr. Maltravers' relations; one of whom, his elder brother, lived in Somersetshire; and his sister, the wife of a very opulent merchant at Bristol, would of course expect some notice from such near relations; whose figure was too conspicuous to allow their passing any time in the immediate neighbourhood without being well known.

Lady Newenden, too much above the vulgar prejudices of middling life to give much attention to the claims of relationship, had made up her mind as to any trouble her uncles, aunts and cousins, might give her. The amusements Lord Danesforte had pointed out to her in this tour, had made her still willing to undertake it, when the necessity for it existed no longer, even in imagination; for her Ladyship was in truth quite well. Mr. Maltravers, aware that many of his family; and of the acquaintance of his early life, would now be witnesses of his splendour, failed not to direct every preparation ostentatious vanity dictated; and that his generosity might in some degree keep pace with his magnificence, he presented to Ethelinde a bank note of an hundred pounds, requesting of her to expend it in cloaths and ornaments for her appearance at Bath and Bristol.

Ethelinde, of whom he usually took no more notice than common civility required, would willingly have declined this present, because she neither coveted ornaments, or desired to be considered as meaning to enter into amusements which her state of health, and still more her state of mind, made her incapable of enjoying: but her father, who thought that such a present from a man so affluent as Mr. Maltravers to the daughter of his sister, was not an obligation that ought greatly to oppress him or Ethelinde, directed her to accept it. Instead however of disposing of it in the manner her uncle proposed, she sent, before her departure from

Denham, fifty pounds to her brother at Gibraltar, without communicating what she had done even to her father.

The day now arrived when they were to begin their journey. It was the third from that on which Montgomery had parted from Ethelinde. Her mind had since dwelt on every word that had passed; and her memory, faithful to her passion, had brought back his tones of voice, his look and attitude, so that he was ever present to her mind. She was sure that she had given no second refusal to his request of being allowed to write to her; and however contrary to the prudent resolutions she had made as soon as he left her, she had almost unconsciously cherished a latent hope that this letter, half prohibited and yet anxiously expected, would arrive. His temper, equally warm and persevering as his mother had described it to be, and of which she saw so much in his application to her father, and in his conversation with her, made her suppose that he would not easily relinquish the advantage he had gained in being assured of her attachment to him; and while she believed she was doing the utmost in her power to submit patiently to a separation so necessary, she would have been extremely mortified at the certainty that he quietly acquiesced. She determined most heroically to shew whatever he wrote to her father; but still wished he would write. The instant of her departure however came, and nothing arrived from him: a circumstance which failed not to make yet heavier the oppressed heart of Ethelinde, and to add to the fatigue of a journey which she now made with the extremest reluctance, reflecting that had she continued in or near London, there would yet have been a probability of her seeing Montgomery, or at least of hearing from him.

Sir Edward saw her dejection; and, no longer doubting of its cause, made it an additional argument with himself against indulging the passion which now had gained so strong an ascendance over him, that it was with the utmost difficulty he commanded himself enough to conceal it from Ethelinde herself, who was not unfrequently startled at the warmth with which his friendship was expressed. But though it sometimes gave her pain by reminding her of what Lord Danesforte had dared to hint at, and made her fear that Lady Newenden might be made uneasy, she was far from having any of that vanity which would, to a less pure and ingenuous mind, have given a very different interpreta-

tion of Sir Edward's behaviour. Her father, who had seen a great
deal of the world, who had lived much abroad, and who fancied
that Ethelinde was an object of universal admiration and esteem,
saw nothing extraordinary in an attachment which he thought
her merit demanded; and far from discouraging it, he recommended his daughter on all occasions to Sir Edward; and put into
his hands a will, in which he left her in case of his death entirely
under the protection of this generous and affectionate friend. Jealous in honour as Colonel Chesterville was, the least hint of the
suspicions which Lord Danesforte so cruelly presumed to harbour
would have made him wretched; and have rendered all the favours
he had received from Sir Edward more painful than the difficulties he had been relieved from: but though Lord Danesforte, to
answer purposes of his own, had already circulated the injurious
calumny as far as he could with safety, Colonel Chesterville was
the last person likely to hear it, except Sir Edward himself; who,
had he known by what arts Lord Danesforte had already tainted
the mind of his wife, and was proceeding to destroy the reputation
of the innocent Ethelinde, would have no longer suffered him to
mix with the parties, where to practise all this mischief was possible; and would probably, before the ill effects became irremediable, have checked his career.

On the arrival of Sir Edward's family, with Mr. and Mrs. Maltravers, and Colonel and Miss Chesterville, at Bristol Hot Wells,
the two latter would have retired to a separate lodging; as Ethelinde was really ill, and desirous of more quiet than could be
obtained in an house where so much company as Lady Newenden kept, were continually received; but Sir Edward pressed Colonel Chesterville so warmly to remain with them, and seemed so
uneasy at the idea of their separation, that the Colonel gave up the
plan. Ethelinde had an apartment in the house, where she could be
perfectly quiet, and her father a room near her's. Lady Newenden,
having chosen her own apartments, was indifferent whether they
went or stayed. Another house immediately adjoining was taken
taken for Lord Danesforte and Davenant; and Mr. and Mrs. Maltravers, on account of their large suite of attendants, had a large
house for themselves.

During the first few days after their arrival, nothing very material occurred. Lady Newenden, desirous of getting over the visits

to their Bristol relations before the arrival of her noble friends, proposed to Sir Edward and her father to go to them some morning, but desired that no invitation to dinner might be accepted— "If once," said she, "we get into eating parties, those city folks will be in their element; and we shall be more *ennuyé* than by going through a rotation of London aldermen." Mr. Maltravers, though Mrs. Ludford was his sister, not only acquiesced in Lady Newenden's plan of sinking the relationship as much as he could, but would have been still more pleased could he have evaded acknowledging it at all.

This however was hardly possible. His sister, conscious of the opulence of her husband, and valuing herself on her own family, was high-spirited, and would, he knew, loudly complain of the affront, should he totally neglect her: and as the wealth of Mr. Ludford was great, though not equal to his own, his children, consisting of a son and a daughter, were well received in all companies, and could not therefore be avoided.

Ethelinde, from the extreme weakness to which her fever had reduced her, as well as from depression of spirit, was unfit to attend her cousin, her uncle, and Mr. Maltravers, in this visit; and therefore excused herself. Colonel Chesterville, ever desirous of shewing attention to the family of a wife whose memory was most dear to him, accompanied them; and as by his going Mr. Maltravers' coach was full, Sir Edward was glad of the excuse to remain at home also. The visit, which was to be a morning one, was announced by sending a servant the evening before; and on their arrival, the party found Mr. and Mrs. Ludford, and their daughter, Miss Clarinthia Ludford, ready to receive them.

The lady of the house, her ample person dressed in a gown of fine muslin, a fashionable hat surmounted with a plume of feathers, and her whole appearance displaying more wealth than taste, rose to receive Mrs. Maltravers; who was, though less gorgeously, at least as youthfully drest. Mr. Maltravers saluted his sister, and his niece. Lady Newenden, after the first introductory words, remaining silent, the conversation was divided between Colonel Chesterville, Mrs. Ludford, and Mr. Maltravers; but though the visit was short, it evidently languished: the ladies, moving in different circles, had little in common that might serve for discourse; Mr. Maltravers was not interested in the commerce which wholly

engrossed the ideas of his brother-in-law; and Colonel Chesterville addressed himself sometimes to the elder and sometimes
to the younger lady on the news of the day: but his was of the
London world; and their notions wholly confined to the people
among whom they lived, and where they felt and enjoyed that consequence which was obscured among the more brilliant luminaries of the hemisphere of the metropolis.

Miss Clarinthia Ludford, however, was a young lady of science,
and, unlike some of that description who are so cruel as to conceal
their talents from their friends, she was always generously communicative. Drest like the Shepherdess of the Alps, the tender and
unfortunate Adelaide,[1] her bosom was as full of sympathy, and
prone to love. No object, however, offering in the present group to
call forth those gentle sensations (for Colonel Chesterville, though
a very handsome man, was near fifty, and her uncle by marriage),
she contented herself with making to her cousin, Lady Newenden, some advances towards conversation; and having tried two or
three topics on which she met with no encouragement, she ventured to ask, "whether her Ladyship had read the last new novel?"

"No really, Ma'am," replied Lady Newenden, with her usual
cold languor, "I seldom read those things."

"Dear!" exclaimed the gentle Clarinthia, "I thought every body
had read those sort of fashionable books. All the time I can spare
from my masters and my filligree,[2] I dedicate to reading. Your
Ladyship, perhaps, reads history, or is fond of poetry?"

"Not particularly."

Almost discouraged, Miss Clarinthia now ventured another
question. "Does my cousin Ethelinde read much? I am told she is
very accomplished."

"Oh yes," replied Lady Newenden with a contemptuous smile,
"Miss Chesterville reads, I fancy, every book that is to be had at a

1 The reference could be either to Jean-François Marmontel's (1723-1799)
popular tale from *Les Contes Moraux* (1755-59), from which *The Shepherdess of
the Alps* appeared as a separate translation (1790, 92, 97), which text prompted
numerous illustrations; or Charles Dibdin's popular comic opera, *Shepherdess
of the Alps*, first produced at Covent Garden in 1780.
2 Masters means tutors, probably in music and dancing, though she seems to
read. Filligree is a delicate form of jewelry in metal, twists of gold and silver in
the form of beads or threads.

circulating library; and as for accomplishments, I believe, but I am no judge, that she is what is called highly accomplished."

"Oh heavens! how infinitely happy I shall be in cultivating the acquaintance of so amiable a relation! I am sure I shall like her extremely. My mama wishes me of all things to make acquaintance with people of taste and knowledge, and I shall account myself doubly fortunate in finding so delightful a friend in my own family."

Lady Newenden, who feared that this predilection in favour of Ethelinde would produce exactly what she had been labouring to avoid, the frequent visits of the Ludford family, only bowed in silence; and by that time Mrs. Maltravers, who was heartily tired, arose, and they departed as formally as they entered.

Lady Newenden threw herself into the coach; and but for the presence of Colonel Chesterville would have declared her dislike of the people she had seen; but contenting herself with scornful silence, her mother began by saying to Mr. Maltravers—"Your sister is strangely altered since we saw her last. She is as fat as a landlady, and how very much her complexion is changed!"

"We none of us grow younger, Mrs. Maltravers," gravely answered her husband.

"No, that is very true; but I hope we don't all alter quite so much neither."

"What signifies it," peevishly replied Mr. Maltravers, "how old women look?"

"Old women, Mr. Maltravers! I don't know what you reckon old."

"But I know what you reckon young. You account yourself young; and are fonder of being admired than a girl of sixteen."

"I, Mr. Maltravers, fond of admiration! I might perhaps be excused if I were—but—"

"Thirty years ago you might—but not now."

"I am sure, Sir, you know not what were my pretensions thirty years ago; for I was then a little child in England. But I was talking of your sister, and not of myself."

"And thinking of yourself, more than of my sister."

"How so, Sir?"

"Why you was considering how much younger you look than she does, though you are I suppose about the same standing."

"You know to the contrary, Mr. Maltravers."

"I know that she is fifty, gaily as she now chuses to dress, and that you are very little less."

The lady now grew too angry for a reply. Colonel Chesterville, to change the discourse, mentioned Miss Ludford—"She is rather pretty," said he, "and has something of the family countenance."

"Family countenance! Colonel," said Lady Newenden indignantly—"is it possible you can think so?"

"Indeed, Colonel," added Mrs. Maltravers, "you pay the family countenance no great compliment; what with such a nose! and such a complexion!"

"The girl is well enough as to figure and face," said Mr. Maltravers, "but she is over-run with affectation and folly. A sort of something Mrs. Ludford has got in her head about education, has made her stuff this girl's memory with scraps of every thing; she has a fine romantic name for an adventure; and will probably, by dint of reading plays and romances, fancy herself the heroine of a novel, and. find one of her father's clerks for the hero."

Lady Newenden smiled at this satyrical remark of her father on his niece. But when she heard, in the sequel of their conversation, that Mr. Ludford had insisted on their fixing a day for dining there, and that it had been impossible to evade it, she grew more out of humour; and meditating how to escape, sooner than she proposed at first, to complete the engagement she had made with Lord Danesforte, she sat silent the rest of the way.

Ethelinde and Sir Edward Newenden had passed their time much more pleasantly and rationally. As soon as the coach drew from the door, he had taken his three children, the little one yet in arms, and the two boys, the elder of whom Ethelinde had so lately, under Providence, rescued from death, and to whom she was particularly attached, and had carried them himself into the room where she sat. The little girl was in her lap, the others playing at her feet; and while Sir Edward contemplated her soft countenance with tender admiration, he could not repress a deep sigh, excited by the contrast between her and Lady Newenden; who, never sensible of great maternal affection, had lately shewn towards her children, indifference, which wounded the heart of Sir Edward more than the coldness or haughtiness he frequently met with himself. Surrounded with company at home, or engaged in parties abroad, she only saw the little ones when they were brought to her for a few moments while she was dressing. When she arose, it was so late, that when breakfast was over some party was ready to engage her, from which she returned but to dress for dinner; then she was completely occupied for the rest of the day, and generally till three or four the next morning: and this mode of life, against which Sir Edward at the beginning of their marriage had gently but fruitlessly remonstrated, was now so settled an habit, that no probability remained of her ever adopting any other; particularly since the intimacy of Lord Danesforte at the house introduced later hours and deeper play. Of domestic happiness Sir Edward was entirely deprived: but he had not the least suspicion that any other attachment subsisted between Lord Danesforte and Lady Newenden than a league of fashionable idleness and dissipation. Yet the long visits his Lordship made, and his following her wherever she appeared, began to make him uneasy lest the world should judge more harshly; and the frequent demands for sums of money, larger than she had usually called for, gave him cause to apprehend that she might not only injure her reputation, but the fortunes of her children, by the acquaintance and style of life she had chosen. This uneasiness he had long concealed, knowing too well that complaint might irritate the temper, but not change the conduct of Lady Newenden: but he longed, yet dreaded to lay open his heart to Ethelinde; her gentle sympathy he thought would soothe and console him; and her advice direct him: but in exciting the one, or obtaining the other, he feared that he might betray more than he had already done, the situation of his heart in regard to herself; and not only alarm her delicacy by the discovery, but shew her that if he had lost the affections of his wife, it was not till he had in some measure deserved it by suffering his own heart to wander to another object. The consciousness of his partial and encreasing fondness for Ethelinde often checked the murmurs that Lady Newenden's manner of life gave rise to; and when of late he had once or twice found it difficult wholly to suppress them; and had remotely and very gently touched on his dissatisfaction, she had received his hints not merely with coldness but with scorn, and had enquired sneeringly whether, considering all the condescension she shewed in gratifying him with the company of *persons he preferred*, he had any right to dictate to her? or to complain of the way in which she chose to pass that time, which her rank gave her leave to use as she pleased; and that fortune, which she had not hitherto objected to *his* having a considerable share of, to bestow on his *peculiar favourites.*"

Sir Edward, though far from being ashamed of what he had done for Colonel Chesterville, had yet never spoken of it: not only through delicacy to the feelings of a man already too cruelly wounded, but because he knew that Mr. Maltravers would object to such a disposition of a large sum of money, and think he had the greater right to object, because it was advanced to his relation. But these speeches of Lady Newenden convinced Sir Edward that by some means or other the transaction had become known to her; and he was not only disturbed by that certainty, but greatly hurt at those expressions which he knew must allude to Ethelinde, and which he dreaded lest in some fit of capricious ill humour his wife might repeat to her. The few days that they had been at Bristol had been passed by Sir Edward in extreme uneasiness from these causes: yet could he not determine to let Ethelinde quit the family; nor could he forbear at every opportunity seeking her company, and indulging that tender admiration which, since her attendance on his child, seemed hardly less the effect of taste than the off-spring of gratitude.

When he had sat with her about half an hour, talking to and of the children, who were playing round them, the youngest fell asleep on her lap; and that her brothers might not awaken her, Sir Edward sent them to their maid, and then returning, he sat down by Ethelinde; and enquired if she knew when Lord Danesforte and Davenant were expected?

"To-morrow, I believe," replied she; "at least I understood that the house they have taken is preparing for them to-day."

"Adieu! then to the short calm we have enjoyed! Deep play begins again; day and night inverted; and every real and rational enjoyment of society annihilated. You know, Ethy, how reluctantly I ever say that to Lady Newenden which may give her pain; but I think this goes too far. Good God! that I should be thus unfor-tunate!—That your cousin's taste and mine should so essentially differ! I wish—but what do wishes avail—that she could be con-tent with less dissipation, or that I could find pleasure in the pursuits which please her. As it is, I grow more and more uneasy at the course of life she is in."

To this, Ethelinde knew not what to reply. To deny the justice of his observation, or the propriety of his complaint, was impossible: yet she was equally unwilling to say any thing that might, by acquiescence, irritate his uneasiness or condemn her cousin's conduct. She remained silent therefore, and Sir Edward re-assumed his discourse.

"Mr. and Mrs. Maltravers, who are the properest persons to check this extravagant career, are exactly those who add to the velocity with which she pursues it. Her mother, more volatile, more vain, more inconsiderate than herself, encourages her in amusements by which she is equally gratified; and her father; who is by disposition as well as habit so prone to judge severely of all the rest of the world, is blind to her errors; and would resent any attempt to convince him that she has any——" He paused, and deeply sighed. Ethelinde spoke not, and he again went on.

"There *was* a time when I *did* hope that I and my children had some interest in the heart, some power on the affections of Lady Newenden. But that is all over! Other pleasures than domestic, other demands more forcible than duty, influence her. She is lost to me—to her unfortunate children!"

Tears now filled the eyes of Sir Edward, and deep sighs burst from his heart. Ethelinde, extremely distressed, was inclined rather to weep with him than able to console him. But still apprehensive of encouraging by her participation an impression so fatal to his peace, she tried to reason with rather than indulge him.

"Surely, my dear Edward," said she, "you see this matter in too serious a light. Consider how Lady Newenden has always been indulged; reflect a little that her manner of life is no other than is adopted by other women of equal rank and fortune, and assure yourself that tho' the routine of fashionable life may for a while engage her, her heart is not less your's, nor affections are not less her children's."

"You judge generously, my Ethelinde. Does Lady Newenden adopt equal candour in her judgment? I fear not! There is, among the people she frequents, a style of living, of thinking, which makes me tremble; and 'tis not merely time and money sacrificed, but principles and feelings of infinitely more consequence. You will not own it; but your discernment is too quick, your sense too solid, not to see that she holds in contempt the opinions of the rest of the world, and forms all her ideas to the standard set up by a particular set of people; of whom Lord Danesforte, one of the most profligate and unprincipled young men of this dissolute period, is the leader. Is he exactly the man to whom my wife should entrust the choice of her friends, and the regulation of her opinions?"

"Possibly not; but of this I am convinced, that if you expressed any disapprobation to my cousin, she would suffer the acquaintance to drop rather than give you a moment's pain."

"Ah, no! Ethelinde!" sighing from the bottom of his heart, replied Sir Edward—"I have already made but too many unsuccessful experiments on the tenderness of Maria. Much may be allowed to the boundless indulgence of her education, much to the possession of youth, beauty, and affluence; but nothing can excuse the want of natural feelings—of the tenderness of a mother.—— Do not however imagine that I feel, or have ever felt, any thing like suspicion of her personal fidelity. I think too well of her to have such an idea. Yet I am unhappy.—I want a companion, a friend, a rational being—and I meet only a fine lady, who sacrifices, to the opinion of the weak and vicious, her health, her time, her fortune, and the peace of her husband. Alas! she may perhaps flutter on a few years; the defects of her mind, the errors of her character concealed by the blaze of equipage and of title; but where, when the delusion is over, where will she find friendship, tenderness and gratitude, to fill the dreadful vacuum which must remain? How unlovely, how unloved if not despised, will she be turned over to

"An old age of cards!"[1]

Nor is this the worst consequence. Innocent of all that is usually called evil, as she undoubtedly is, yet you well know, that the world will not scruple to put her fondness for Lord Danesforte's company to the most disgraceful and odious account; already I doubt not the tongue of slander has been busy with her fame. Should this be?——Advise me, Ethelinde—young as you are, your excellent understanding will be a better guide to me than my own disturbed and distracted reason."

1 Alexander Pope, *Epistle II: To a Lady*, l. 244

Ethelinde, more and more concerned at the deep impression he seemed to have so suddenly received of Lady Newenden's misconduct, still hesitated, and looked at him with eyes expressive of what she felt at the sight of his unhappiness; at length she faintly said—"Perhaps if you were to share your objections to Mr. Maltravers, he might see the propriety of them, and represent to his daughter the ill consequence of cultivating too eagerly the acquaintance of Lord Danesforte."

"I must," said he; "for I foresee nothing but circumstances to which I cannot submit, in its continuance. I have silently, yet incessantly lamented having allowed it to go on so long. Yet I could not suppose, after our leaving the Abbey, but that it would have dropped. Our journey to Scarborough however cemented this improper and dangerous connection; and so pleasant was it become to my wife, that I saw—with what bitterness saw, that even her child's illness, the expected death of that dear little boy, whom you, with Heaven's favour, preserved to me, was hardly attended to with common humanity.—Lady Newenden had not strength to set out post with me, to attend her son during his illness, or to receive his last sigh, had Heaven robbed me of him; but she was not fatigued by the perpetual vigils of loo and hazard. To those her nights were given; and in such wretched resources she found a remedy for maternal solicitude—for maternal sorrow!"

Tears, in spite of the indignation he felt, now filled the eyes of Sir Edward. Reflection on the different conduct of Ethelinde, softened him into a tenderness he could not repress, and taking her unresisting hand, he held it to his eyes, and sobbed in the severest agony of spirit.

Ethelinde wept also; and was extremely shocked at all that had passed, but without believing that the affections which Lady Newenden had thrown away, were unhappily fixed on herself, she entreated him to be calm; and, since the acquaintance of Lord Danesforte was painful to him, to put an end to it rather than lament it. But the sense as well as the softness of her remonstrance were so far from calming the tumult of Sir Edward's soul, that it added new poignancy to the afflicting comparison he was making between her and Lady Newenden, and new bitterness to the regret which had so long possessed his heart in reflecting that Ethelinde could not only never be his, but that it was breaking through every barrier of reason and honour even to wish it or suppose it possible.

His transports were now so truly alarming, that Ethelinde, in whose arms the infant Maria was yet sleeping, found it better to disengage herself; and telling Sir Edward (who still, with his head on the table, his handkerchief to his eyes, and her hand grasped in his, continued in a convulsive fit of crying, and seemed incapable of hearing her), that the baby was awake, and that she must ring the bell for its nurse, she at length, by beseeching him to consider that the servants might see how violently he had been affected, and make strange comments, roused him from the state he was in. Suddenly starting up, he pressed her hand to his lips: "Angel of goodness and purity!" cried he, in a trembling and wild tone. Then turning away, he went to the door, and was hurrying across the hall with his handkerchief still in his hand, and the tears too visible on his face, when Lord Danesforte and Davenant, entering at the opposite door, met him.

Lord Danesforte was beginning a salutation in his usual easy style, when, struck with the singularity of Sir Edward's appearance, he stopped, and said—"Why what the devil's the matter, Newenden?—Nobody is sick, or dead, I hope?"

Sir Edward, to whom his sight was sufficiently irksome at that moment, could not command himself to speak to him; but passed silently by him, leaving both his Lordship and Davenant to make their way into the room, where Ethelinde was found with a countenance likely to encrease their surprise.

"Why what ails every body today?" cried Lord Danesforte. "Have you had a funeral in the house? Miss Chesterville, you seem to have been a party *concerned*. Pray tell me what ails Sir Edward?"

"Nothing, my Lord, that I know of."

"Nothing! Oh, I suppose he has been reading a tragedy with *you*. Is it not so? Your gentle hearts have been sympathizing together. I'm glad 'tis nothing worse. Come, come, tears are becoming to fine eyes; and susceptibility, you know, the most winning of all attractions. But prythee smile a little now. Here's Davenant languishing for a kind look."

The sneering expression which sat on the countenance of Lord Danesforte while he uttered this speech, left Ethelinde little doubt of the malice of his meaning; but so much had the scene which had passed affected her, that she was totally incapacitated from answering or evading his cruel raillery: making therefore a pretence of the little girl who was in her arms, she hastened away, not doubting but that his Lordship, whose influence on Lady Newenden now appeared in a more dangerous light than it had ever yet done, would represent what he had been witness to in his own way.

CHAPTER VII

In a few moments after Lord Danesforte's arrival with Davenant, Lady Newenden, Colonel Chesterville, and Mr. and Mrs. Maltravers, arrived from their visit. Her Ladyship seemed much elated by this acquisition to what had been before "a dull family party." The chagrin she had conceived at being compelled to make a visit to the family of Ludford was forgotten; and the extreme coldness and visible displeasure of Sir Edward, unnoticed; or being noticed, scorned. Dinner was no sooner over than the loo table was introduced into the drawing-room. Other company came in; deep play began; and Sir Edward, not only suffering under his own uneasiness, but grieved to remark the avidity with which Colonel Chesterville joined those who played, went out to conceal his concern; and that he might enjoy that solitude which his present temper of mind required, he went towards St. Vincent's rock.[1] Ill health, which was more than a pretence, made the retirement of Ethelinde easily accounted for. Glad to escape, she seized the first moment in which the whole party were deeply engaged; and in her own room sat herself down to reflect on what had passed in the morning, which had rather left on her mind a tumultuous and confused sense of pain, than any distinct sentiment of particular unhappiness. All, however, when she began to investigate it, appeared to offer only sources of encreasing calamity. She knew too well that Lady Newenden was so haughty, so high spirited, and so much impressed with an idea that her fortune set her above

1 St. Vincent's Rock was a famous sublime scene in this era: it is the cliff just above the Bristol Hot Wells seen above a turn in the Avon. J.M.W. Turner was among those who drew and painted it in 1793 (*The Rising Squall—Hot Wells from St. Vincent's Rock, Bristol*, exhibited 1793).

the common forms of life, that there was little hope of her feeling any thing but rage and resentment on the slightest remonstrance from Sir Edward. She knew that Mr. Maltravers, far from allowing her to be wrong, would feel nothing but indignation at the bare hint of its possibility; and, making her quarrel his own, would be sensible only of indignation at Sir Edward's want of confidence and liberality of mind; while Mrs. Maltravers, as much bigotted to Lord Danesforte and his parties as Lady Newenden herself, would with impatience hear, and with anger resent, any attempt to put an end to the acquaintance.

But she saw the mind of Sir Edward so embittered, and his feelings so outraged, that he was determined to attempt to break the connection; and she thought it very probable, that in the anger this attempt would excite, Lord Danesforte would call forth all the malignity of his character, and that the injurious suspicions he had dared to hint to her with so little reserve, would be communicated with all the aggravation of ingenious malice to Lady Newenden, who would gladly adopt them as an excuse for her neglect and ill humour towards him, who was not only the husband of her choice, but so estimable, so amiable, that nothing but the depraved taste of insatiable and exorbitant vanity would have found pleasure in seeking the adulation of others to the ruin of his happiness. Besides this apprehension, of itself sufficiently mortifying and alarming, she suffered extremely in reflecting on her father's situation, and still more on his passion for play, of which she had seen too much since they had been with Sir Edward. The certainty of never seeing Montgomery again, and his failing to write to her, completed the number of corrosive reflections that preyed on her heart.

Of these latter, however, she tried to get the better by the exertion of her reason. "Wherefore," said she, arguing with herself, "wherefore should I so weakly give way to a prepossession which is certainly imprudent, and probably may be fatal? Why not check it while yet in my power; why not conquer heroically a partiality I cannot indulge without a breach of duty and prudence? Untried, what is virtue? or what is that nominal virtue, which, contented with profession, with speculation only, suffers the first violent partiality to take possession of the mind, and to overturn at once all its resolutions and principles? I, who have so often heard my companions talk of this violent, this predominant love, and have laughed at the chimeras which idleness and inexperience have engendered; who have so often shut the novel in disgust where such romantic passions were described and applauded—shall I fancy myself so madly in love, as to sacrifice my own health to the idea; or, what is yet more precious—infinitely more precious—my father's repose?"

Animated by this idea, and the feelings which related merely to herself blunted by the concern she felt for Sir Edward, she believed for a few moments that she could effectually divest herself of her attachment to Montgomery. Perhaps his not availing himself of the tacit acquiescence, or at best the faint refusal of permission to write to to her, was not without its share in strengthening this resolution; in which she very earnestly attempted to confirm herself, till the following letter, in the midst of all her heroism, was delivered to her from Montgomery.

Harley-street, Oct. 29.

"Madam,

"You will pardon me I am sure for thus intruding myself upon you, when you learn that which will I know give you pleasure; I presume not to say on my own account, but from the general humanity and tenderness of your character, and, from the particular interest you deigned to take in favour of Mrs. Montgomery.

"Soon after that day when I took, as I feared, a last leave of you and of happiness, I met, by an accident with which it is unnecessary to trouble you, a gentleman who married a relation of my mother's, and who possesses a very large fortune of his own, as well as a still larger in right of his wife, who was an heiress. This gentleman, on being made acquainted with my situation and my prospects, has been so far from approving my project of going out in the military line to India, that he has insisted on my accepting an apartment in his own house; and has undertaken to procure for me such a situation in this country as one of the descendants of the noble house of Montgomery need not blush to be placed in. I applied immediately to my mother, without whose approbation I ever make it a point to do nothing. You will not wonder to hear, that any plan which keeps me in England has her warm concurrence. May I without presumption add, that to remain in the same country with Miss Chesterville, hopeless as I am of seeing her, is yet most consolatory to the heart of her ever devoted,

obedient, and obliged servant,

Charles Archibald Montgomery."

P. S. "I know *I* dare not ask, dare not expect *one line* from you; yet should your generosity ever prompt you to enquire after me *on my mother's account*, I am to be heard of at John Royston's, Esq. Harley-street."

Ethelinde, having tremblingly perused this letter once, began to consider its contents. It was too respectful to offend her. That Montgomery left not England avowedly on her account, as had been his original design, gave her the truest pleasure she was capable of tasting; yet that he should enter on a state of dependence with a gentleman, who, though allied to his family, seemed to have been known to him only by accident, appeared to be a plan somewhat inconsistent with his high spirit, and those notions of independence which he had sometimes expressed with a warmth that his youth and high birth rendered at once interesting and alarming;—alarming since they were but too likely to impede that species of success in life which his circumstances made requisite, if not to his actual support, at least to his ease and comfort. Concluding, however, that the prospects offered him, were superior to his former visions of advantage, and very certain that he would do nothing unworthy of himself, she was not only much consoled by the letter, but forgetting the resolutions she had made a few moments before, the idea of Montgomery returned to her mind as amiable as ever, and soothing herself with an hope that fortune might favour them, and that they were finally destined for each other, she attempted no more to argue herself out of a passion so well justified by the merit of its object, and which she hoped she might yet without indiscretion indulge.

But though she was relieved from that uneasiness which she had felt at the thoughts of seeing Montgomery no more, she had still much to pain and distress her. The change of air however, aided by her youth, gradually conquered the remains of weakness and languor which her illness had left, and in about ten days from her arrival at the Hot Wells, she was almost as well and quite as beautiful as ever. The late hours which Lady Newenden kept, she had never been in an habit of complying with; and as she never played, and the house was usually in a tumult of company, among whom she was not missed, she had an opportunity of passing much of her time alone, and of avoiding the impertinent freedoms of Lord Danesforte, and the proud but troublesome attentions of Davenant, who, seeing her admired by others, retained still his wish to become acceptable, but could not prevail on himself to hide the anger he felt at the little satisfaction his preference seemed to give her. She avoided him as much as possible; but fled with yet more solicitude from Lord Danesforte, who failed not, whenever he could get an opportunity, to insult her with hints of Sir Edward's affection for her, and not unfrequently to press his own. Fearing to exasperate him by great severity of retort, (for innocent as she was, she dreaded his unprincipled malice), and equally alarmed at the resentment her father would not fail to shew if he had the least idea of his style of conversation, she passed half the time she was in his company in forming devices how to escape the whole day without suffering him to exchange a word with her; and as he never attempted it but when he was sure of being unobserved by Lady Newenden, she generally succeeded in avoiding him wholly. With Lady Newenden she now never met but at table or in the drawing-room; so that it was seldom any conversation passed between them: but when it did, there was something of cold contempt in her manner which made Ethelinde extremely unhappy; and every circumstance concurred to make her wish the time was arrived when the rest of the party were to go to Lord Danesforte's house in Gloucestershire, and when she should go to Bath to remain with her father the rest of the winter.

Sir Edward, however, was determined to put an end to a scheme which he had never approved, and the ill consequences of which became to him every day more apparent. The more he observed of Lady Newenden's conduct, the more dissatisfied he grew; yet to appear jealous would throw ridicule on himself, and suspicion on his wife, which perhaps she might not deserve. His tenderness for his children made him tremble at doing any thing which was likely to injure the fame of their mother: yet she was herself every day detracting from its purity; and he feared that, though he had not heard it, the tongue of scandal had already been busied in its destruction. These reflections, the careless haughtiness with which his wife treated him, her boundless expences, which he could not check, and the irksomeness of having his house filled with people whose society was disagreeable to him and dangerous to her, together with his hopeless tenderness for Ethelinde, made his life a perpetual conflict of contending passions—passions which, as he could not safely reveal, preyed on his mind, and disturbed his temper. The only consolation he once had, was to seek out Ethelinde, and forget for a moment every thing but her gentleness and her perfections: but since the innuendos Lady Newenden had repeated on every attempt he had made to detach her Ladyship from her present connections, he no longer ventured so frequently to sit with Miss Chesterville; but when the whole house was in the hurry of amusement, he retired to his study, and there indulged the anguish of his spirit without observation. Mr. Maltravers and Colonel Chesterville had not failed to remark the alteration so evident in his behaviour: but the former, who could never suppose it arose from his wife's conduct, had hitherto forborne to notice it; and the latter knew not whether Sir Edward might not be hurt at its being noticed, and therefore forbore to enquire into what it was possible he wished to conceal. A few days only had passed in this way, when Mr. and Mrs. Ludford, their daughter, their son, and a friend of his, a young counsellor of great reputed abilities, came in form to return the visit they had received from Lady Newenden, Mr. and Mrs. Maltravers, and Colonel Chesterville. Their equipage was a coach and four; very shewy, and attended by four servants in liveries equally gaudy: for Mr. Ludford, though still in business, had no longer any occasion to adhere to the economics of mercantile life; but, having purchased an estate about three miles from Bristol, had commenced country gentleman; and his son, though his name was in the firm of the house, never sullied his dignity with any attention to that which, though it had procured him all the consequence he boasted, he considered as much beneath the attention of a man of spirit, a man of fashion, and a *bel esprit*. He had established his claim to the first title by spending a great deal more than his father's liberal allowance; to the second, by emulating the company and imitating the manners of dissipated young men of rank, to whom he often lent money while he borrowed their vices; and to the third, by having got by heart all the most offensive passages he could pick up against the religion of his country, and by having written certain somethings which he was assured by his friends were specimens of uncommon and original genius, and which the world of taste had in sundry newspapers been called in to admire. On these, and on prologues and epilogues written for private theatres, which the same friends declared to be *full of point*, his fame was established; and Mr. Robert Ludford was reckoned a young man of infinite talent.

This reputation for wit gave but little pleasure to his father, who knew that he had himself accumulated a great deal of money without any. But his mother was of a different opinion; and if there was any thing that gave her more delight than shewing her own finery, it was seeing her son's genius displayed in print, and hearing him accounted among the luminaries of the age. His person was short, and extremely thin; a perfection on which he highly valued himself, and which his whole dress was calculated to shew to advantage. He had two little black eyes, with which he practised, at the glass, the sparkle of spirit and the languish of tenderness and these, with two sleek black eye-brows, carefully adjusted, assisted much in the expression which he endeavoured to throw into his countenance. His paleness, or rather sallowness, he could occasionally remove; and he had made graceful attitudes his peculiar study. Still, however, there was something constrained in his manner: his hair was generally so preposterously dressed, that his head appeared too big for his body; which, together with his high cape, took up so much of his whole person, that his face would have escaped the view, if his nose, somewhat long and sharp, had not fortunately rescued it from oblivion. Such was the young man, who, leaping out of the phaeton in which he had driven his friend Mr. Emmersley, presented himself in the parlour, where Sir Edward Newenden, Colonel Chesterville, and his daughter, had just received Mr. and Mrs. Ludford and Miss Clarinthia. Lady Newenden was not yet visible; and neither Lord Danesforte, Davenant, nor Mr. and Mrs. Maltravers, appeared at their usual rendezvous till about an hour before dinner. The few minutes conversation which the weather and the usual enquiries after health supply, was already nearly exhausted, when this fortunate arrival relieved Sir Edward from the heavy task of renewing it. Mr. Ludford, animated by the presence of his cousin Ethelinde, of whose sense he had heard much, and whose improved beauty (for it was some years since he last saw her), he was extremely charmed with, called forth all his vivacity: but Sir Edward, who saw that his particular address to her greatly disgusted and distressed her, drew off his attention by entering on a subject of literature, on which he knew the vanity of the little *bel esprit* would infallibly induce him to descant. Sir Edward succeeded: Mr. Robert Ludford and his friend entered eagerly into the conversation; while Mrs. Ludford sat in admiration of her son's talents, Mr. Ludford, whose thoughts were now called from the ledger to the plough, began a calculation on the number of cabbages necessary to fat fifty oxen; and Miss Clarinthia, who, though extremely well read, was by no means equal to her brother, took this opportunity to begin a conversation with Ethelinde.

"It is inconceivable, my sweet cousin," said the gentle Clarinthia, "how fondly I have languished to see you! My heart told me I should not be disappointed in meeting with a tender and agreeable friend in so near a relation."

Ethelinde only bowed.

"I now hope, my dearest creature, that we shall be vastly together. I am told that you read a great deal, and play divinely! Oh! do you know that music is the passion of my soul, and that I perfectly doat upon poetry! Are you not vastly fond of it yourself? I am sure I need not ask;—you seem to be all made up of harmony and tenderness. But tell me, do you not live upon, doat upon poetry?"

"Some poetry assuredly," said Ethelinde, "gives me very great pleasure."

"Have you ever seen any of Rupert's? Robert is such a common name that I soften it into Rupert. You cannot imagine what delightful verses he writes. And Mr. Emmersley, he has another turn; graver indeed, but very sublime. I long to shew you some of their compositions. You will be delighted with them. As to myself, I have now and then tried a little thing in verse; but I dare not shew them, unless to you. In prose perhaps I may succeed better; indeed I study it more."

Ethelinde now found she was expected to speak, and therefore said—"What, then, do you principally read, Madam?"

"Don't call me Madam, my dear cousin, I beseech you; but

remember I am your Clarinthia, and you my lovely Ethelinda.[1] There is a vast deal in name, don't you think so? I should have been miserable if Mama had not insisted on my being called as I am. Only think of my father's wanting me to be named Judith!"

Ethelinde had little occasion to enquire farther into the nature of her cousin's studies: but as it was necessary to say something, she repeated the question—"You read history, perhaps?"

"Oh yes, a great deal of history. One must, you know, be acquainted with those things, or else one appears ignorant. But after all 'tis fatiguing enough. To tell you the truth, my great delight is in novels."

"Novels," said Ethelinde, "are certainly very entertaining."

"Oh yes, delightful! and the only fault I find with some of the latest is, that they are too probable, and I fancy myself reading what is true. Now the thing I like is to be carried out of myself by a fiction quite out of common life, and to get among scenes and people of another world."

"In that I should think you might easily be gratified."

"Whenever I am so happy as to see you at Ludford House," continued Clarinthia, elated at the attention Ethelinde lent her, "I will shew you a little sketch I have drawn up myself. My heroine falls in love with a young man: quite a divine creature of course, who is obliged to go Ambassador to Tripoli. She knows not what to do; but at length determines to hire herself into the family of the Tripoline Ambassador here, to learn the language, and accompany her lover as his valet de chambre. This plan, by the help of walnuts to change her complexion and a pair of black mustacios, she accomplishes; then she meets with an amazing number of adventures in France; where she kills two or three men in defence of her lover; and her sex being discovered, a French nobleman becomes enamoured of her, and carries her away by force into a chateau in a wood. But I will not tell you a word more of it, because I will surprise you with the catastrophe, which is quite original; only one event is borrowed from the *Arabian Nights*, and one description

1 The "a" turns Ethelinde's name into the sort of unreal, pseudo-classical name given to heroines of romance. The problem with this joke is Ethelinde is itself an exotic name.

from *Sir Charles Grandison*. Rupert indeed says, that with a little application my pen will become truly Richardsonian."[1]

She now stopped, rather for want of breath than of subject; and Ethelinde enquired of how many volumes the novel was to be.

"Only two volumes," replied the fair authoress; "and I believe I have got writing enough to make them. But you know now 'tis the fashion to have little books, with a wide margin, and a vast deal of white paper; then people read them so easily while their hair is dressing, that it is quite comfortable."

Ethelinde was thoroughly tired of her literary cousin; and for the first time in her life not sorry to see Lord Danesforte enter the room; who, finding ample subject for that ridicule in which he delighted and excelled, was much pleased with the group, and exerted his talents to obtain that notice which his title alone would from such a party have secured him.

He listened for a moment to the arguments with which Mr. Robert Ludford was overwhelming Sir Edward; applauded every thing he said with great gravity; and having done enough to persuade him he was an admirer of his eloquence, he passed across the room to Ethelinde, and with a sly look, which she perfectly understood, desired to be introduced to her amiable companion.

Clarinthia, delighted with this compliment from such a man, instantly recollected all the instances she had heard of love at first sight, and flattered herself that hour was now come when her fair form and ornamented mind was to captivate a peer; so celebrated in the annals of gallantry—so unrivalled in those exploits and accomplishments that give ton and eclat to a modern man of fashion. Lord Danesforte understood her character instantly. Vain of her person, which was not above mediocrity, and vainer

1 The first European translation of *One Thousand and One Nights* was by Antoine Galland into French and published between 1704 and 1710; it was enormously popular. Samuel Richardson (1689-1761), the author of *Sir Charles Grandison* (1753-4) was one of those who centrally transformed earlier romances into realistic, psychologically revealing novels; his original use of epistolary techniques was imitated everywhere; his other two novels were *Pamela* (1740) and *Clarissa* (1748). Like her brother, Clarinthia has aspirations to be considered learned, to be admired. Tripoli, the capital of Libya and located on the Mediterranean, was a place where Barbary pirates found a port; Clarinthia is aware that "Moors" and/or black African people live there; all this makes it an exciting site for romance.

of her understanding, which was beneath it, his affected admiration gratified her predominant foible. She became immediately
acquainted with him. Ethelinde most willingly yielded to her the
delight of entertaining a Lord; and in the quarter of an hour in
which they were together, Miss Ludford was more charmed than
she had ever been in her life, and her mama so much elated with
the notice taken of Clara by Lord Danesforte, and the attention
given by Sir Edward and Colonel Chesterville to her son, that she
was solicitous only to strengthen these favourable impressions
by more frequent interviews, and therefore urgently pressed the
whole party to dine with her on the following Friday. To Lady
Newenden, who soon after entered the room with her usual cold
and reserved manner, she warmly urged this request, with which
Sir Edward had before complied. Her Ladyship, by a glance from
Lord Danesforte, understood that it would not be disagreeable to
him, and therefore, however ungraciously, she assented. The visit
had now been prolonged beyond the usual limits of a morning
visit. With a profusion of fine speeches to their relations therefore,
among which those of young Ludford to Ethelinde were distinguished by their ominous absurdity, the family of Ludford ordered
their equipages and departed.

CHAPTER VIII

That poignant ridicule in which Lord Danesforte excelled, and
which made him generally accounted extremely entertaining,
he now exerted to place the departed visitors in the most absurd
light. Ethelinde, though the ostentatious vanity of her aunt, and
the affectation of her cousin, were extremely displeasing to her,
and though she saw all the absurdity of the young mercantile *bel
esprit*, was yet hurt that Lady Newenden considered little that they
were nearly related to herself, and that much allowance should be
made for different modes of life. That they all seemed desirous of
stepping out of their's, rendered them undoubtedly ridiculous; yet
did not Ethelinde love to hear her cousin, who had hitherto much
disliked visiting them, declare that she should enjoy the dining
there of all things—a change occasioned solely by the pleasure she
found in gratifying the satyrical talents of Lord Danesforte with

such ample matter for their display. Before his Lordship and Lady
Newenden had exhausted all the amusement the group afforded
them, Ethelinde was more weary of them than she had been of
the objects of their ridicule, and left them to enjoy it alone. Sir
Edward had long before retired; and again Lord Danesforte had
occasion, though obliquely, to point out to Lady Newenden that
neither of them remained in company a moment longer than they
could possibly avoid.

"Don't you, my Lord, envy their tête-à-têtes?" said she. "Don't
you think the sentimental, the delicate, the even prudish Ethelinde
vastly in character, in listening to the soft speeches of a married
man?"

"I am glad you see it in so proper a light. It is indeed ridiculous.
Since your understanding is too good to allow such folly to give
you a moment's pain, I may venture to say that the affair becomes
so notorious that it will soon be the public talk."

"With all my heart. I shall not even then figure in the ridiculous
character of a jealous wife. I am provoked at Chesterville, who,
having borrowed money of Sir Edward, will not see what is so visible to every body else. I suppose he expects a farther loan as the
price of his silence and complaisance."

"*Tant mieux, ma belle amie:*[1] for as we win the money as fast as he
borrows it, the advantage you know is finally ours."

"But whose will be the advantage when we quit this place?"

"*Que cela nous importe?*[2] Shall I invite the Colonel and his fair
daughter to Danesforte?"

"Certainly, if *you* find amusement in their company."

"That is out of the question. But it is always a point with me to
gratify my friends. The golden rule, my dear Lady N. do as you
would be done by. Therefore if Sir Edward would be made happy,
and our parties be made up, you know."—

"You are mistaken as to Sir Edward. He goes not to Danesforte."

"Indeed!"

"No—and he has been at a distance attempting to dissuade me
from going."

1 So much the better, my fine friend, with "amie" having erotic connotations
in the French.
2 What does it matter to us?

"Impossible!"

"True, I assure you.—But I gave him no manner of applause."

"Why, what can he possibly mean by it?"

"I am indifferent as to that. He has contrived, however, to per-suade my father to think as he does, that it would be improper to go: but my mother, who is seldom determined on a point she does not carry, insists on his not breathing a word to you. In order, however, to put the matter out of dispute, I shall fix on this day se'nnight[1] for my departure. My father and Sir Edward may stay here if they will, enjoying *les delices du sentiment* with the *family party*, of which we are to have a second *echantillon* on Thursday."[2]

Her Ladyship then went to her toilet, and Lord Danesforte as usual attended her.

Ethelinde passed the next two days as she had done so many others, in thinking with tender regret of Montgomery, with pain-ful solicitude of her father and her brother, and with encreasing disgust of Lord Danesforte and Davenant. The latter was now become professedly a man of ton:[3] he seemed more disposed to vilify and ridicule her for not accepting his proffered regard, than again to renew his offers; but in doing the first he would have hazarded incurring the resentment of Colonel Chesterville; in the second, his talents were so slender, that he seldom ventured beyond a repetition of some *confounded* good thing that he had heard uttered by Lord Danesforte, which, interlarded with many oaths, and somewhat marred in the telling, sometimes passed for his own.

He had now learned, with little change of countenance, to lose his thousands; to get every night so extremely intoxicated, that the small share of understanding he possessed he had never perfectly at his command; to swear vollies of oaths for every trifle; and to dress sometimes like a dirty groom, and sometimes like a ridicu-lous *petit maitre*;[4] to say every thing to every body; to be careless of

1 Seven nights and seven days or a week.

2 "The delights of sentiment:" Lady Newenden is mocking the cult of sensi-bility; *échantillon* means sample or pattern, they are to be a pattern of a family. She mocks the popular sentimental idea of a family party as fashionable cant.

3 The phrase "man of ton" refers to someone who behaves and dresses as a member of the most fashionable society; Davenant is self-identifying as part of the class-conscious elite of his society (gentry, aristocracy, royalty).

4 Davenant behaves like a fop (a stock character in the drama) or dandy. See

the opinion of half the world, or rather to despise it, that the other half might pronounce him a man of the very first style.

Thus qualified to obtain applause, he no longer solicited but demanded it; and far from treating Ethelinde with the humility of a lover, in hopes of some change in his favour, he seemed haughtily to resent that want of discernment, which had made her refuse an offer he was no longer in a humour to repeat.

Lord Danesforte, who had found him an admirable scholar, and whose instructions had been repaid by very considerable winnings, now saw that his purpose would be effected quite as well without promoting the match with Ethelinde; for it was evident that Colonel Chesterville was undone; that he had been a while saved by the interposition of Sir Edward Newenden, but that nothing could cure him of his propensity to play; and that the time was rapidly approaching, when Ethelinde would probably be deprived of her father's protection by the embarrassment of his circumstances; and of that of Sir Edward Newenden, by the invidious light in which the eye of designing malignity chose to behold his affection for her. Then he doubted not but that, deserted and impoverished, her reserve, her pride, and her feelings, would be levelled to her circumstances, and that his partiality to her would be received with gratitude instead of being repulsed with scorn.

The day had now arrived when the whole party, in which Lord Danesforte was of course included, were to dine at Ludford House; and Ethelinde knew that there was no hope of her being excused, however unfit she was in spirits, as she could no longer plead illness. Lady Newenden went in an undress, to shew her contempt for the magnificence which she supposed would be lavishly displayed by her monied relations; but Ethelinde, who knew that they expected that sort of compliment, went rather more drest than was her usual custom. Ornament could add nothing to her interesting and beautiful face; or a figure which was at once femininely soft, and commandingly graceful: tho' not yet in high health, she never was more lovely. Sir Edward, who would have beheld the fairest form with indifference, unanimated by such a soul as her's, gazed at her as a model of perfection, sent on earth "to shew what

---

Ellen Moers, *The Dandy: Brummell to Beerbohm* (New York: Viking Press, 1960), an excellent introduction to types of people and characters associated with the world of the "ton."

angels are;"[1] and Colonel Chesterville, little imagining that he was adding to the torments of his friend, yielded to the tender and enthusiastic admiration with which he beheld his daughter, and broke forth in her praise. He was sitting with Sir Edward, waiting for the ladies, when Ethelinde came down dressed; but having forgotten to put on her cloak, she went back to fetch it. As she left the room her father exclaimed—"How charmingly Ethy looks! how much within this fortnight is she recovered!"

"She is indeed," answered Sir Edward, suppressing a sigh, "a very charming young woman."

"Such," said Colonel Chesterville, his eyes filling with tears as he spoke, "such was her mother five and twenty years ago. Yet even of her, celebrated as she was for beauty, my daughter has the advantage."

"Exquisite as is her person," reassumed Sir Edward, "her mind is even superior to it; and the lovely blooming Ethelinde we just now saw dressed as for a scene of gaiety, is in my mind a less soul-attracting object, than the Ethelinde I beheld a few weeks since, hanging over the bed of a dying infant at the risk of her own life, and performing the tender offices of the parent who was, but who ought not to have been, absent."

This image affected Sir Edward as much as the remembrance of his wife, and his fondness for his daughter, had before affected the Colonel; and the latter, uneasy to see (not for the first time) that Lady Newenden's conduct, in regard to her child, had made an unfavourable and lasting impression on Sir Edward, was ready to cry out, "Consider it not so deeply,"[2] when their conversation was put an end to by the entrance of Lady Newenden and Ethelinde, who were ready to depart.

A very short time brought them to Ludford House; built by its present possessor, in a situation the very worst he could have chosen on the estate. The building was substantial and expensive; but heavy and inelegant. Servants, whose appearance bore testimony to their good living, were seen in unnecessary numbers;

1 From Henry Baker's "To a Deaf Young Lady." In the context of the poem Smith conveys the idea that Ethelinde silences others and so becomes like a deaf young woman, saved "from mankind's impertinence."

2 From Shakespeare's *Macbeth*, Lady Macbeth to Macbeth shortly after the murder of Duncan, Act 2, scene 2, line 30.

and their liveries, though ill fancied, were sumptuous; it being an established maxim with Mrs. Ludford to have "the best of every thing."

The dinner, which was in the same style of the house, consisted of such a profusion of good things as would have entertained the whole corporation of Bristol.[1] Mr. Ludford, who now fancied himself a country gentleman, informed the company that the beef was fatted on his own farm, and in a peculiar manner; that the mutton was of a breed, whose flesh had a finer flavour than that of common sheep; and that the pork was fed on Indian corn, from the West Indies. The Lady of the house exerted herself in doing the honours of the table with a zeal more ardent than is now very usual. But Miss Clarinthia, delighted with Lord Danesforte's attention to her, thought only of securing a conquest she was persuaded she had made. Coronets and titles had taken strange possession of her brain; and ever since she first saw, and was noticed by him, a young West Indian, a ward of her father's, for whom she had long entertained a gentle sympathetic affection (not the less tender for its being disapproved by her papa), was entirely forgotten, or thought of only with pity; for this divine nobleman appeared in her slumbers, and occupied her day dreams. She little imagined that he addressed to her the most extravagant compliments with no other view than to amuse Lady Newenden; while her Ladyship found a counterpart for this entertainment in the assiduity and foppish gallantry of her little smart cousin, Mr. Rupert Ludford, who, placing himself between her and Miss Chesterville, said a thousand ridiculous things, mingled with scraps of French, on the happiness of his present situation, and of the pride with which he contemplated beauty to which he was so nearly allied. The dinner, however slowly and heavily it passed, being at length over, and the ladies retired to a magnificent drawing-room, Mrs. Ludford took an opportunity of addressing herself particularly to Ethelinde, towards whom she had hitherto behaved rather as a new acquaintance than as so near a relation.

"So, my dear," said she, taking the hand of her niece, "you are at present with your cousin? Pray how long have you been with her?"

1 A reference to ritual dinners given the Mayor and Alderman of Bristol (perhaps originally tradespeople), a prospering city (out of trade). Smith reveals her own snobbishness.

"Almost the whole of the past Summer, Madam."

"I am glad of it, child; for a young person is awkwardly situated without a *chapperoon*.¹ I have wondered sometimes that Mr. Chesterville did not place you somewhere or other."

"Place me, Madam?" said Ethelinde, somewhat surprised.

"Yes, my dear," continued her aunt, "place you with some female friend, or some lady who would like you for a companion. A single man like your father, who is so much out, must have found it *illconvenient* I should think, and besides not so prudent for you, at your time of life, to be living about."

"I believe, Madam, there are few fathers more attentive, as I have ever found mine, both to general propriety and to the particular happiness of his daughter."

"Oh I dare say so, my dear; but gentlemen in the army are used to that sort of life that is not I think quite the thing for a young woman. Indeed I often wondered how my poor sister Ethy could submit to it; but she cared for nothing but a red coat. Poor dear girl, she suffered enough going about from place to place; never a settled home, and every thing always at sixes and sevens; and died at last I believe because of her long stay in those places in Spain and Turkey,² and I don't know where abroad, that quite ruined her health. Pray, my dear, where's your brother? I hope he turns out a good sort of a young man."

"Yes, Ma'am," said the piqued and disgusted Ethelinde.

"He does, does he? I am glad to hear it—I haven't seen him I believe this nine year. He's older than you, e'n't he?"

Ethelinde, more and more hurt, as she knew this affected pity and affected forgetfulness was the mere insolence of purse-proud prosperity, answered more coldly, "Above five years older, Madam."

"Ay true, so he is; I remember now, all the rest of Ethy's children died. 'Twas well they did; though I recollect, poor soul, that she

---

1 The first of several malapropisms, the use of an incorrect word in place of one it sounds like (sometimes with the effect of absurd comedy); the original is a character Smith might be thinking of: the aspirations and ignorance of Mrs. Malaprop (Sheridan's *The Rivals*, 1775), lead her habitually to utter nonsense.
2 Smith's text reveals the global reach of British colonialism and how it affects the lives of those related to men in the military and middling to upper classes (there to find position and fortune).

pined sadly about it; but with Mr. Chesterville's small income to be sure a large family would have been mighty difficult to support."

Ethelinde could no longer conceal her vexation. Her aunt perceived it, and went on:

"I don't mean, my love, to make you uneasy; far from it. Nobody should value themselves upon their affluence, as I often say to Miss Ludford, but should be thankful for it; especially when they see that let people have what birth and beauty they will, 'twill not make 'em respectable without money; and that made me sorry when Mr. Chesterville refused to let your brother come 'prentice to Mr. Ludford some years ago; when to oblige me, and because he was my nephew, my husband would have taken him with a low premium, and have given him a chance for a share of the business with Bobby."

Ethelinde, instead of expressing gratitude, answered only by a cold bow; and Mrs. Ludford kindly continued:

"I believe however the truth of the matter was, that your father did not care that a lad who had an Earl for his grandfather should be a merchant; so rather than see him rich in a counting-house, he has sent him to wander about the world, as he did himself, with a knapsack behind him."

It was with the utmost difficulty Ethelinde repressed the tears of vexation and anger which this gross and unfeeling conversation excited; but, contempt assisting her to subdue them, she listened still quietly to the rude and unpleasant discourse, which thus proceeded:

"I suppose, since you are in this country, that your father will let you go see your eldest uncle Maltravers."

"Certainly, Madam; it is my father's wish and mine to shew all respect to every part of my mother's family. I believe Lady Newenden and Sir Edward intend to go, as well as my uncle John Maltravers and his lady."

"I hope so; for I've no notion of people's being above their original. Besides I assure you, though when your mother married she thought it I believe a great thing to marry an *honourable*,[1] yet her own family was far from contemptible; and though brother

[1] As the son of an Earl, Ethelinde's father would be called the Honorable Mr. or Colonel Chesterville.

John has had such great luck in *Ingee*,[1] yet I dare to say that he's not so set up with it, or with a bit of a title that he has married his daughter to, as to think it derogating to him to remember Burton-Maltravers, where he was born and bred, and where his grand-father and great great grand-father have lived time out of mind."

"Assuredly not, Madam."

"Well I'm glad of it. So you are to live with Lady Newenden, are you?"

"No, Madam; when her Ladyship leaves the Hot Wells, I go with my father to Bath."

"To Bath do you? What!—I suppose your father likes Bath on account of the *sort of society* so easy to meet with there?"

Ethelinde could not be ignorant that Mrs. Ludford alluded to the Colonel's love of play; she was too much hurt to command her feelings, and would probably have answered with a tartness which would have been very displeasing to her aunt, had not Miss Ludford, who had been the greater part of the time in conversation with Mrs. Maltravers and Lady Newenden in another room, now fortunately relieved her.

The relief was not less felt by Lady Newenden and her mother, who had been worn to death with the sight of all Miss Ludford's ingenious productions, in shell work, in wafer work, in filligree and coloured paper. These she fancied had greatly amused *them*; for Ethelinde, of whose taste and talents she had heard much, she reserved her music, her poetry, and her essays in prose. No sooner therefore were the other two ladies engaged in conversation with her mother, than poor Ethelinde was fated to undergo a new spe-cies of torment. Miss Clarinthia, having invited her into her own dressing-room, thus began:

"My dearest girl, you cannot figure to yourself how delighted I am to get you for a moment alone; for I have ten thousand ques-tions to ask you, and ten thousand things to tell you. What is the matter, my dear creature? You look out of spirits."

"Nothing in the world," said Ethelinde, "but that at times I still feel the effects of my late illness."

"Dear, how sorry I am! Do you know that, ill or well, you are excessively charming, and have made two conquests already?"

1 Slang for India.

"Indeed!" answered Ethelinde, to whom no such intelligence, even better authenticated, would have given the slightest emotion.

"Yes, indeed; my brother, the discerning, the critical Rupert, declared the moment he came home the other day, that you was the prettiest creature he ever saw."

"Really!"

"And that animal Emmersley, though almost a profest flirt of mine, has the assurance to say he is dying for you."

"Nonsense. Pray don't repeat such silly common-place speeches, but shew me the the drawings and work you were talking of."

"No, no, I have other business for you. Tell me, for I long to know, is there nobody you are partial to? have you no *penchant*? no little affair of the heart?"

"No, indeed!" cried Ethelinde, blushing deeply.

"My dear Ethelinde, it is not easy to believe you. So lovely, is it probable you should not be beloved? so gentle, is it possible you should not be susceptible of the tender passion?"

The tone and air with which this was said exciting the risibility of Ethelinde, conquered for moment the fretfulness which so much absurdity produced; she could not help smiling, and answered, that she really thought it time enough to consider of love affairs, and that hitherto she had found sufficient occupation in learning what her father chose to have her taught, and in attending on him.

"You are a dear good soul; but you cannot make me believe you have never felt a partiality. What do you think of Lord Danesforte?—Is he not charming?"

"Very much otherwise, in my eyes."

"What! don't you think him one of the highest bred, most elegant, enchanting men in the world?"

"No."

"No!—Pray where will you find any body like him?"

"Not easily I believe. But singularity is with me no recommendation."

"Lord, that is vastly odd! Now I think he's quite a modern Lovelace. So much wit! so much vivacity! such a vein of pleasantry!—"

"That you long to be a modern Clarissa, by way of companion."[1]

1 We are first made explicitly aware that Maria Lady Newenden has been

"No, in truth; I am not quite so vain neither. But cousin——tell me, if Lord Danesforte is not the thing, who is?"

"Sir Edward Newenden. With a much handsomer person, he has a finer understanding and a more worthy heart."

"Pooh! but he is married, you know."

"Is he therefore less estimable?"

"No, I believe not; but one never thinks of those grave cooped-up people as being agreeable or otherwise. Besides, whatever power of entertainment Sir Edward has, he either keeps to himself or bestows on the gentlemen. Lord, how tiresome he talked with my father to-day about Scotch cattle and Welch cattle, as if he had been a drover!"

"Because he saw the conversation acceptable to your father."

"Then he entered into a dissertation on the Roman law with Emmersley, and I am sure 'twas not acceptable to him, for he left him, poor dog, behind in a moment; and the good self-sufficient little man, who thought to have set forth his knowledge to amaze us all, looked presently like a simpleton, and was glad to get off the ground. All that is very clever I believe, but it is also very tiresome: now I like a man, who, the moment he comes into a room where ladies are, has no eyes, nor ears, nor thoughts, but to contribute to their amusement, and to persuade them he is amused himself."

"Lord Danesforte then is well accomplished to charm you?"

"He is, and if I could wholly divest myself of one little, one unfortunate *penchant*, I protest I should be half in love with him."

"You had better keep to your old *penchant*, my dear cousin, for I

---

seduced into full sexual intercourse by a later satiric remark of Ethelinde: her comparison of Danesforte with Richardson's Clarissa provides perspective on Danesforte who, like Lovelace (in the novel, *Clarissa*, 1748), has the manners and education of a gentleman, but (as the reader was expected to notice) has not had to rape Maria Lady Newenden. The explicit identification is held off until Lady Newenden and the whole Newenden party are to go Danesforte Castle. The important line is this in Volume 2, Chapter 3: "he had now no inclination to recede, and scrupled not to add the destruction of Sir Edward's honour and happiness to that of the numerous trophies in the same way which he had already obtained." Foolish Clarinthia says she is not so "vain" as Richardson's heroine, Clarissa, who was difficult to seduce (thus Lovelace was forced to rape her). Accusing Richardson's heroine of too much pride begins with the novel's earliest readerships. Smith broaches the topic of rape again in Volume 5.

assure you Lord Danesforte is a Lovelace in more than his outward behaviour."

"And to such a man you think Clarinthia Ludford has, can have no pretensions?"

"Pardon me, I was far from meaning to say that, if you allude either to his title or his fortune; but I do not think Lord Danesforte the man whose moral character entitles him to the good opinion, of my cousin."

"Oh! would to heaven he would try that opinion! But probably he is engaged to some woman of quality?"

"Really I do not know; but if you are so desirous of seeing more of him, suppose you were to join the party who are going to Danesforte, where there are to be I know not what amusements?"

"How I should like it! But I am sure my mother would oppose it! Besides, 'tis not likely I shall be asked."

"If you wish really to go, I am persuaded my Lord would be rejoiced to have your company."

"My dearest soul, do you really think so? Lord, how vastly delightful it would be!"

"There are to be theatrical exhibitions, balls, and I know not what else."

"Dear, how charming! I dare say Rupert will get asked, and will write the prologues and epilogues so delightfully! I am half wild with the thoughts of it. Don't you long for the time?"

"I do not go."

"Not go——and survive the certainty of not going!"

"With the most perfect composure," replied Ethelinde, "and not only survive it, but am much happier than if I did go."

"Lord, you are the strangest girl!—And pray why do you stay away?"

"Because my father wants me with him at Bath; and because I do not love such tumultuous parties."

"Well, that is amazing. But, Ethy, we shall meet again, shall we not, to talk this matter over before the time?"

"Certainly; and in the interim depend on the party, for I am sure Lady Newenden will be glad of your company."

A summons to Miss Ludford to go down to make tea, now put an end to the dialogue. The gentlemen were assembled, in the drawing-room; Mr. Ludford had again engaged Sir Edward in a discourse on farming; in one corner of the room Mrs. Maltravers was relating the luxurious magnificence to which she was accustomed in the East to Mrs. Ludford, and inflaming her ambition by the detail of shawls and embroidered muslins in which even her slaves were dressed: another group was Mr. Maltravers impatiently and testily defending the slave trade against the judicial knowledge of Mr. Emmersley, and the sentimental oratory of Mr. Robert Ludford;[1] while Davenant and Lord Danesforte had taken a pack of the cards which lay on the table ready for whist, and were eagerly set in on a corner of it to lansquenet.[2] The entrance of the tea-table and the young ladies broke the chain of argument into which Mr. Robert was just entering, and he declared that he must leave the defence of the liberty of others while he found his own in such imminent danger; and with this gallant declaration he placed himself behind Ethelinde, and thus addressed her, leaning over the back of her chair:

> "Well might, alas! the threaten'd vessel fail,
> "When winds and lightning both at once prevail!"[3]

She turned suddenly towards him, with a look expressive of some surprize.

"Exactly in that situation," said Mr. Rupert, "I find myself. The wind is my natural affection for you; a sort of sense which stifles every other idea; the lightning, those brilliant eyes, which give me the exact sensation of being electrified."

There was in this speech something so grotesque that Ethelinde could not help smiling. The young man took it as a symptom of her approbation, and went on:

"It is rather cruel upon me to be attacked thus both ways: as

1 The first organized protests against slavery had begun by 1790; Bristol's position in southwestern England on the Avon made it the second most important port city (after London); it was one of the points of the triangular trade between Africa and the West Indies; enormous profits were made.

2 Lansquenet is a card game whose procedures offer much opportunity for high play and cheating.

3 From Pope's "Imitations of English Poets:" "Waller: A Lady Singing to Her Lute," lines 3-4. Meant by Smith to suggest the insipidity of young Mr. Ludford's taste. He is a poseur, at once salacious and affected and insincere in all he professes.

my cousin, you know I must have felt a sympathetic affection, amounting however only to tender friendship; but as the loveliest woman I ever saw, my friendship amounts to adoration."

"If I knew at all," said Ethelinde, "the sort of answer you expect to these compliments, I would endeavour to give such as might convince you I am sensible of their value; but really I am so little accustomed, to hear any thing *so* sublime——"

"Make room for me by you," cried the elated beau, whose excessive vanity prevented him from seeing that he excited in Ethelinde only pity and contempt, "and let me talk to you."

To exercise at once his agility and his talents, he now jumped over the chairs on which his sister and Ethelinde sat, and placed himself with great composure between them. "Now," said he, taking the hand of Ethelinde on one side and of his sister on the other, "here is a little constellation of talents. Methinks I feel like Apollo, with a Muse on each side. But, my dear cousin, you have too much of the Melpomene: do you never smile?"[1]

"Oh, very frequently."

"I wish I could see it; though you would be vastly too enchanting if you were divested of that pretty prudish air. Did you ever see the verses that I wrote on a lady—a very fine girl, upon my honour—who was much celebrated here last year?"

"Never, that I recollect."

"I wonder at that; for they were in all the newspapers and magazines. A friend of mine—friends, you know, will be indiscreet— stole a copy, and sent them to all the prints, under the name of 'the modern Petrarch.' I am almost tempted to repeat to you one stanza."

"You will oblige me."

> "Lo! Sensibility with *iron fang*,
>   Doth on my palpitating heart-strings hang,
>   As more and more thy dulcet charms appear;
>   And *tiptoe* Admiration's ardent gaze
>   Counts all thy beauties o'er in much amaze,
>   And strikes my heart, and *rouses to a tear.*"

1 Apollo, popularly thought of as the god of reason. It was Hercules, a classical divine hero (one parent a god and the other an ordinary mortal), who was often seen as torn between the figures of Vice and Virtue. Melpomene was the muse of tragedy.

"Are they not exquisite?" said Miss Ludford. "You cannot imagine what applause Rupert got for them; till it was known who did them, the most celebrated names had the credit of them, and the papers were full of conjectures."

"Oh a trifle," interrupted Mr. Rupert, "unworthy Miss Chesterville's attention, but as they are applicable to beauty yet more eminent than that they were intended to celebrate."

Ethelinde was by this time so extremely weary, that she found the utmost exertion of her complaisance hardly equal to the task of concealing it; yet to smile and appear pleased at the folly and vanity of her cousins, was less irksome and uneasy than to listen with attention and good-humour to her aunt's insulting kindness. Lord Danesforte now approached the young mercantile poet; and seizing with avidity the ridiculous traits of his and his sister's characters, he gave them such ample opportunity to display them, that, intoxicated with his attention, they became more absurd than ever; and Ethelinde, though she could not thoroughly approve his conduct, could not forbear smiling at the admirable effect of his flattery. But he was not long suffered to be amused with it; for Mrs. Ludford, not willing, perhaps, that she should share with Clarintha any part of his Lordship's admiration, now left Lady Newenden and Mrs. Maltravers, and again addressed herself to her niece.

"Pray, child," said she, "have you any scheme of life after you leave Bath?"

"Madam!"

"I say, niece, what does your father propose doing with you?"

"Nothing more, Madam, than what he has hitherto done."

"But I understand that his affairs are not in a good *sitiation*. I hope for your sake, child, that I have been misinformed."

"Whatever is their situation, Madam, I shall be content with any manner of life which may be necessary for my father to embrace: so long as I am with *him*, I shall not only be content but happy."

"Well, I am glad you're so resigned. However, niece, if he should find it *illconvenient* to have you with him at any time, I shall be glad to have you here for a month or two, as I always wish to be kind to my relations."

"I thank you, Madam," said Ethelinde, bowing with great coldness.

"One thing more let me say to you—As your mother's eldest sister, I have some right to give you my advice."

Again Ethelinde bowed: and speaking lower, the good lady proceeded—

"Lady Newenden is quite, you know, in high life, and lives among the great, that think nothing of gaiety and odd connections, but you are a young woman, and having your fortune to make, should be more careful of the opinion of the world, especially of prudent discerning people."

"I hope, Madam, I have done nothing to render such a caution particularly necessary to me."

"I hope not, niece Chesterville: but a young person in your *sitiation* cannot be too careful. Sir Edward is a man, to be sure, of good character and all that; yet too much notice taken of a young woman who lives in the house with him, by a *married* man, is not much to her advantage in the *idears* of people of reflection."

Ethelinde at these words grew pale and trembled; so possible is it for innocence to wear the appearance of guilt. All that Lord Danesforte had hinted at now came into her mind; and shocked to find that he had gone farther and dared to utter to others what no heart but his own would have conceived, she could not conceal the torturing uneasiness which the fear of such a report gave her; she could not immediately speak; and while she was meditating, her aunt reassumed her lecture.

"I don't wish, child, to make you uneasy, as I told you before; but it is my duty, as you have no other woman relation older than myself, to tell you that people don't scruple to say strange things not only of Lady Newenden, with whom Lord Danesforte it seems lives almost always, but of Sir Edward and you."

"I am sure, Madam—I am"—hesitated Ethelinde.

"Nay, it will go no farther for me, of course. But one cannot hear such things of one's own family to be sure without speaking about it; so if you leave the Newendens, as I suppose you will, and chuse to come to me, I repeat to you, niece, that I shall be glad to have you, and so will Clary."

This insulting pity, as well as the imputed error, served to overcome the spirits of Ethelinde. She would hardly have concealed the painful emotion she felt from the notice of the company, if the arrival of the coaches at the door, which Lady Newenden had ordered early, had not fortunately relieved her. They now hurried away; and when Mrs. Ludford pressed her Ladyship to give her the honour of yet another day at Ludford House, she answered, that it would hardly be in her power, as in two days she left the Hot Wells and was going to Danesforte Castle in Gloucestershire.

Ethelinde, who went with Sir Edward and Davenant in the last coach, hardly spoke the whole way: Davenant talked of the house they had just left; condemned its taste; and told Sir Edward the advice he had received from an eminent improver about his own, which he intended to alter in the modern method. But he had the whole conversation to himself: Sir Edward, whose uneasiness at Lady Newenden's conduct grew every day more insupportable, had heard, in his constant attention to Ethelinde, great part of what her aunt had said to her: he appeared to be listening to a long history of the importation of ginger and aloes to the port of Bristol,[1] which Mr. Ludford was giving to Mr. Maltravers; but the change of Ethelinde's countenance made him attentive to a very different subject; and his pain on her account could only be equalled by the indignation he felt at being assured that the indiscreet and improper intimacy of his wife with Lord Danesforte had already exposed her conduct to constructions most fatal to her honour and his own.

CHAPTER IX

Sir Edward, who had for some time determined to put an end at once to the project of going to Danesforte (and who found Mr. Maltravers averse to any interference, so accustomed was he to indulge his daughter in all her wishes), now meditated how to accomplish his purpose. He had already attempted to dissuade Lady Newenden from it; but was by the attempt only rendered more sensible that he had no longer any power over her affections. He had then recourse to her mother; but far from finding from her either consideration or reason, she told him that she was amazed at his attempting to contradict Lady Newenden, who had so good

---

1 Aloes is a tropical plant (imported from Africa) whose thick leaves make it useful in medicine and cosmetics. It can be used with ginger for skin care. Again Smith stigmatizes young Mr. Ludford as a fop or effeminate dandy.

a right to please herself; that there could be only one reason for his objections, originating in a ridiculous jealousy, not more injurious to her daughter than unworthy of himself; that as she should be with Lady Newenden, he need not himself go, if it was unpleasant to him, but might go back with Mr. Maltravers and the children; "unless," added she, "you prefer staying with *your friend the Colonel and his fair daughter.*"

Contempt stifled the anger rising in the bosom of Sir Edward, and he turned silently away, resolving more decidedly than before to leave his honour no longer in the power of a woman educated under a mother so weak and vain, that time had diminished her personal advantages without giving her sense enough to discover their diminution, or to replace them by reason and reflection; but who was still persuaded of their potency, that she hazarded even the reputation of her daughter, and the peace of her family, to the ridiculous gratification of hearing herself told, as she frequently was by Lord Danesforte, that beautiful as Lady Newenden was, she was herself still handsomer; that one was the dazzling brightness of morning, the other the glowing splendour of meridian day. When speeches so soothing to her reigning passion were opposed to the harsh truths with which Mr. Maltravers loved to mortify the vanity of his wife, it is not surprising that to a mind like her's, all improprieties were overlooked, and that the honour and peace of Sir Edward were light in the balance, if indeed she ever at all considered either.

Besides the arrangement which had long since been made with Lady Newenden, Lord Danesforte had another very conclusive reason for wishing a continuance of a party so profitable as he had found her's; having by bets and various other modes won of Davenant above ten thousand pounds since they had been so frequently together; and while he had still so much ready money remaining, his Lordship had no inclination to let his young friend pass into other hands. As Davenant was now his own master, Sir Edward had no other means to prevent this than remonstrance and entreaty; but Davenant seldom gave him an opportunity to try the efficacy of either; for they now never met but in mixed company, though Davenant was almost always at the house; and of late Sir Edward had fled from the society which had destroyed his peace and shut himself up in his own room; which, whenever his absence was remarked, gave occasion to Lord Danesforte to observe to Lady Newenden, that the inseparable cousins no longer kept up any appearance of reserve.

These hints however, and these suspicions, were carefully concealed from Colonel Chesterville; who, though he was too frequently of their parties, had not the most distant idea either of the attachment formed between Lady Newenden and her noble friend, or that which they so unjustly affected to believe subsisted between Sir Edward and his daughter. The Colonel, whose unhappy fondness for play, was the only blemish in his character, had yet notwithstanding all its sad consequences, the propensity as strong as ever; and under the idea of a family party he had indulged it, without however in the present instance suffering by it, for he was in some degree a winner; but Sir Edward could not without extreme concern behold the fatal infatuation which, in spite of reason, experience, and conviction, impelled him to gratify this passion at the hazard of his happiness—of happiness yet dearer to him, that of his daughter.

Every circumstance therefore concurred: his just apprehensions for his own honour, for the honour of his children, his indignation at Davenant's losses, and his concern for Colonel Chesterville, to determine Sir Edward against suffering the continuance of this dangerous, this improper connection. He had already tried all reason that tenderness could effect, in vain; and he now, with whatever reluctance resolved on that which appeared the only method left to crush it at once, by assuming, what he had never yet done, the authority of an husband.

The morning after their visit to the family of the Ludfords, Mr. and Mrs. Maltravers and Lady Newenden all assembled about half past eleven to breakfast; Ethelinde, though she had before breakfasted, attended to make the tea. Colonel Chesterville, who had taken his breakfast with her, was gone out on horseback. The remaining party were already round the table; and regulating their journey for the next day, when they proposed setting out for Danesforte, when Sir Edward entered the room; and without speaking to any body, but slightly bowing to Mr. and Mrs. Maltravers, seated himself at the table.

Lady Newenden continued to speak—"I imagine we shall get there by Friday. Saturday and Sunday will be requisite for a little rest; and on Monday we begin rehearsing a play. Sir Edward, do you intend to go with us, or come after us?"

"Neither, Madam."

"Then we must do without you. My Lord wished you to have taken a part."

"The part I *have* taken already, Madam, is sufficiently ridiculous."

"To be out of humour certainly is ridiculous enough. 'Tis really curious to find you giving yourself such airs, by way of making, if you can, my party unpleasant to me."

"Lady Newenden," said Sir Edward, in as firm a voice as he could command, "I dare venture to appeal to Mr. and Mrs. Maltravers now present, whether I have ever, since we were married, contradicted any one wish of your heart. Your will has been my law. You know best, Madam, in how many circumstances, essential to happiness, our tastes and tempers have differed; but my happiness and my peace I have sacrificed without a murmur. Excuse me if I go no farther; my honour——is not to be so tamely yielded."

"Your honour, Sir!—Pray what do you mean?"

"My meaning, Lady Newenden, is simply this—that Lord Danesforte's intimacy at my house is disagreeable to me; it is scandalous in the eyes of the world; and I am determined to put an immediate end to it."

"I beg, Sir Edward," said Mr. Maltravers, with great agitation, "that this may be explained. Maria, my angel, be not so affected. Sir Edward is too warm. Sir Edward, I beg you will explain yourself."

"No, Sir," said Lady Newenden, finding her father thus ready to defend her—"no explanation of my conduct is necessary. I scorn his odious suspicions, and despise his meanness, which dares—" (and passion almost choked her utterance)—"dares to cast thus fearlessly a blot on *my* character, to hide his own odious and infamous partiality to a young woman whom I have so simply suffered to remain in my house——to you, Miss Chesterville!"

The sudden accusation, and the violence of voice and gesture which accompanied it, amazed and shocked Ethelinde so much, that she let fall the tea-cup she held; and trembling and pale as death, she awaited to hear who should next speak, quite unable to speak herself.

"Don't discompose yourself, Maria," said Mrs. Maltravers,

half weeping——"don't flurry yourself, child. Sir Edward, I am shocked and ashamed——"

"And I, Madam, am shocked and ashamed that Lady Newenden should be so lost to all feeling, to all delicacy, as to attempt to excuse her own foibles by this aggravating, base accusation of the innocent—of her own relation!"

A convulsive laugh compounded of contempt and rage now broke from Lady Newenden, and with a smile, where indignation and scorn were mingled, she cried—"I thank you, *good* Sir Edward, for all your *attention* to *my relation*—all arising, no doubt, from pure love to *me*—your long tête-à-têtes; your constant solicitude for her; your total neglect of every body else; and last, not least, your generously and properly lavishing the money *I brought you* on this favourite cousin and her father."

Ethelinde was now so much terrified, that she no longer knew what she did, but ran hastily out of the room without knowing for what; and in the hall meeting her father, who was that instant returned, she threw herself into his arms, and fell into an agony of tears, as astonishing as distressing to him. "Good God! my love, what is the matter?" cried he extremely terrified, "tell me what has happened—tell me—Your brother, have you heard any thing alarming of him?"

"Oh! no! no! Take me from hence—Ask nothing—but take me instantly from hence!"

"What can this possibly mean?" exclaimed Colonel Chesterville, more and more amazed. "Sit down, Ethelinde: compose yourself and tell me."

Ethelinde knew that an explanation must be attended with the most distressing circumstances to all parties, yet saw that to evade it was impossible; and before she had time to deliberate, or to recollect herself, Sir Edward, his eyes inflamed, his look confused, and his step hurried and faultering, rushed across them. Colonel Chesterville caught his arm. "My dear Sir Edward," cried he, still supporting the weeping Ethelinde, "tell me, I beseech you, what has happened?"

"Your daughter," sternly and aloud he answered, "has been cruelly, infamously insulted and traduced—and I am—the most miserable of men."

He would then have passed on, without being conscious of

any particular design, so cruelly was he agitated; but Chesterville, high-spirited and warm, with the most trembling sensibility in whatever related to his daughter, still detained him, and eagerly exclaimed—"Insulted, Sir Edward! Who has dared—who shall dare to insult her?"

"I blush to tell you, Colonel," replied he; "I am ashamed of myself that I have so long born, from the same quarter, injuries equally poignant; and perhaps more irreparable. Give me your company in my room, for I have much on which to consult you. Ethelinde"—and his voice faultered with contending passions)— "I conjure you to compose yourself. For the sake of the unhappy woman who has thus dared to traduce you, be calm, or I cannot tell to what an excess my just anger may arise. We must part: Lady Newenden and I must part: yet in taking such a measure I wish to do it calmly; I wish still to remember how I have loved her—to remember that she is the mother of those beloved children—— whom she has forgotten!"

His voice was now quite lost. He turned away and wept bitterly; while Ethelinde, whom the violence of her sensations had at first overpowered, acquired reflection enough to remember that the longer this scene continued the more noise it would make, and the more publicly the unhappy dispute become known. She therefore besought her father to go with Sir Edward; while departing with faultering steps to her own room, she reflected with dreadful anxiety on all that had passed; thought with fearful apprehension of the violent passion and unconquerable obstinacy of Lady Newenden; and found, from all her recollection of her temper in trifles, too much reason to apprehend that she would not only refuse to relinquish her favourite project of going to Lord Danesforte's, but would, in her resentment against Sir Edward, assert his partiality to her cousin, as a reason why she would keep no terms with him; and Ethelinde doubted not but that her character would be injured, and perhaps her father's life endangered. It was easy for her to see, from Lord Danesforte's former conversation, that this cruel suspicion had been communicated from him to Lady Newenden. There was reason to fear that, equally void of principle and humanity, he would hesitate at nothing that design or malice could execute; and that whatever he dared do, he dared justify by the usual appeal to the pistol or the sword. The longer she dwelt on all this, the more wretched she became; but on one thing only was she able to determine, which was on instantly quitting the house; and she waited impatiently till she could see her father, and urge the immediate necessity of their going to Bath.

Near an hour, however, she waited in the most painful suspence. There seemed to be much noise and confusion in the lower part of the house. The servants were running about in consternation. At length one of the maids passing by the door of her room, she heard that Lady Newenden was very ill; for that Lord Danesforte having been peremptorily refused admittance, by order of Sir Edward, had afterwards been let in by Mrs. Maltravers; and that a contention between Sir Edward and his Lordship had ensued; which was ended only by Mr. Maltravers and Colonel Chesterville forcibly separating them; in consequence of which Lady Newenden had gone into fits.

All her terrors redoubled by this account, Ethelinde could stay no longer alone.—"Where is my father?" cried she, as she wildly ran down stairs—"Where is Sir Edward? There will be mischief——Oh God! there will be murder!"

She had now nearly reached the bottom of the stairs, still in breathless agony calling on her father, when her flight was stopped, and she became rivetted to the place, where she clung for support to the balustrades, by the sudden appearance of Montgomery.

His hair was dishevelled, his eyes were wild and haggard; his clothes covered with dirt; and he seemed quite worn-out with fatigue or born down by same recent calamity. He spoke not to her——he seemed not to be able to speak. "Where—what"—exclaimed she, unknowing what she would ask. Her strength forsook her; and she sat down on the stairs, and looked at Montgomery with eyes that expressed terror too great for utterance.

"I have frightened you, I am afraid," said Montgomery, as he tremblingly took her hand. "Would I could have avoided it. Let me see Colonel Chesterville instantly."

"Have you not seen him then?" stammered Ethelinde.

"No," replied he, raising and supporting her, "I have been able to see nobody. The servants seem in alarm; the house in confusion. They told me you were above stairs, and left me to find my way to you. You tremble—you are agitated! Alas! I fear the evil tidings I bring have already reached you!"

"What tidings? what new misery is coming upon us?"

"Let me place you in a chair," cried Montgomery, who had by this time led her into a little breakfast-room where Sir Edward used to read, but which was now deserted. She was obliged to comply, and then again conjured him to tell her what he had to communicate. "I will try," said she, "to bear it: at least I can bear any thing better than this suspense."

"Your brother"——he hesitated—he stopped.

"My brother!" shrieked the terrified Ethelinde—"What of him? Is he dead? My God! is he dead?"

"Not so," said Montgomery—"but—a disagreeable—a very disagreeable circumstance has befallen him."

"At Gibraltar?"

"No; in England. He is arrested—he is in prison."

"Returned unknown to my father—arrested—and in prison! Oh! my poor Harry!—My father!—what will become of him when this is known?"

"Yet he must know it!" cried Montgomery, affected beyond all endurance by her agonies; "and I came to entreat of him to go with me immediately to London. It may soon be too late to save poor Chesterville. I dread—indeed I dread the effect which the consciousness of having done wrong, and the poignancy of despair, may have on a disposition like his. He gave me his promise that he would be calm—but—"

The nature of Montgomery's apprehensions, in all their dreadful extent, now rushed into the mind of Ethelinde. Her brother, her beloved Harry, perishing by his own hand, was present to her. Her heart was before in torture; this idea drove her almost to phrenzy. "Let me go instantly—instantly, for my father," said she, as she darted by Montgomery and fled across the passage, "or it will, as you say, be too late to save him!"

She hardly felt the ground, yet knew not whither she was running. Montgomery followed her, with looks and gestures equally wild; and in the passage they met Colonel Chesterville, who had that moment left Sir Edward Newenden.

"Ethelinde! Mr. Montgomery!" exclaimed he in astonishment.

"Oh! Sir," cried Ethelinde, seizing his hand with the eagerness of phrenzy—"come, for God's sake, come, or my brother will be lost—lost for ever!"

"Come whither?——your brother!—What am I to understand? Mr. Montgomery here!"

"He comes to tell us——that poor Harry——"

"Speak, Sir, I beseech you," said Chesterville. "What of Harry? —Where is he?"

"He is living, Sir, and I hope well; but he is at present confined."

"Under the arrest of his commanding officer?"

"Alas! no; he is in London. He is in a place of confinement at the house of a sheriff's officer. "

"Then," cried Chesterville, in a voice that terrified Ethelinde— "then I am undone indeed!"

He now walked, in the calm anguish of settled despair, into a parlour. His daughter, more alarmed by the solemnity of his grief, and by the look of speechless distress which his convulsed features wore, than she could have been by the most violent declamation, hung on his arm, but could find nothing to console him. He looked at Montgomery; who with clasped hands stood before him, as if for farther information, which he was yet afraid to ask. Montgomery understood him; and thus related the circumstances of his meeting with Captain Chesterville——

"I had business," said he, "with a person in Westminster which detained me till near eleven o'clock. I was then returning to Harley-street; when in passing near Charing Cross, I saw a young man of military appearance before me. Three very ill-looking men had followed us both for some hundred yards: they now passed me; and I saw two of them seize the gentleman before me, who with his stick knocked one of them down; the third immediately fell upon him. It was impossible for me, had I known their office, which I did not, to behold without indignation the unworthy treatment the unknown gentleman received. I stepped forward; and with my assistance he soon disengaged himself from the ruffians: then I besought him, as by that time I suspected their business, to make his escape immediately, and leave me to settle the matter with them as well as I could: but this he refused; and in the confusion which followed, the men, who had by this time summoned constables and watchmen to their assistance, pronounced the name of Chesterville. I found that it was your son; and my anxiety to deliver him increased: it was now, however, impossible, as we were surrounded by peace-officers. The men would have dismissed me; but I insisted on going wherever Mr. Chesterville went, and we were both immediately lodged at an house in Carey street, Chancery-lane. An explanation soon took place. I learned that Captain Chesterville had been three weeks in London; that he had been in that time trying to settle some demands that had long made him uneasy; in which failing, he had been thus arrested."

"For what sum, Sir?" enquired Colonel Chesterville.

"I am afraid for a large one."

"And his commission, Sir?—By what means did he obtain leave of absence, if—But it is impossible!—he cannot have sold his commission!"

Montgomery knew that this was unhappily the case: but he saw the Colonel so extremely hurt at the idea of it, that he had not courage to tell him it was so. The speaking eyes of Ethelinde were fixed on his, and understood too well the answer they gave to her mute enquiry. Colonel Chesterville became more and more distressed. Ethelinde was now seated by him; one of his hands grasped her's, the other he held to his forehead, as if unable to support the pain that darted through his brain. "Let me go to Sir Edward," said Ethelinde, faultering—"perhaps—" then recollecting the reproaches of Lady Newenden for the assistance her father had already received from her husband, she hesitated and stopped; all the cruel scene of the morning rushing with accumulated pain on her memory.

"No," replied her father, "go not to Sir Edward. Sir," continued he, turning to Montgomery, "I must bear this heaviest of all calamities, for Ethelinde deserves that I should live for her. Tell me, with what hope to serve my son you undertook this journey, and what you think think may be done for this unhappy boy. My dear girl, go to your own room: leave me with Mr. Montgomery: the detail of your brother's fatal, and I must say inhuman conduct affects you too much. Oh! Ethelinde! if you would not have me sink under my wretchedness, preserve that health so dear to this tortured heart. My hopes have been long concentered in my two children. One fails me—oh God! how cruelly!—but in thee"—(and he wildly caught her to his heart)—"I still seek for comfort—still contemplate perfection!"

Ethelinde, who found his emotion grew too violent to be endured, and that her presence rather irritated than assuaged his transports, now hurried out of the room while she was yet able; oppressed with sensations so numerous and painful, that she could hardly be said to possess her reason. But in the midst of all her sufferings, the generous friendship of Montgomery for her brother, which assured her at once of the goodness of his heart, and that his heart was her's, infused a soft and salutary, yet melancholy delight, which supported though it could not console her.

CHAPTER X

When Ethelinde had left the room, Colonel Chesterville, collecting all his fortitude, heard with a sort of desperate resolution all that Montgomery had to relate of the unhappy young man his son. His imagination had not gone beyond the truth: Chesterville had not only sold his commission, but owed more than double what that would raise. All the money he had received from his father he had paid away to satisfy debts of honour; but many still remained unpaid, besides heavy sums to tradesmen; and to complete the wretchedness of this unfortunate father he heard, that far from bearing with fortitude the evils he had thus brought on himself, Chesterville seemed to be rather desperate than resigned; and to hold it for a maxim, that when a man could no longer support his rank, it was time to quit the world.

When, in addition to this, Colonel Chesterville reflected on all that had passed in the morning; on the misery which tore the bosom of his best friend, Sir Edward Newenden; on the duel too probable between him and Lord Danesforte; and on the barrier which Lady Newenden's calumny had put between them, by which every hope of assistance was cut off even if he could determine to accept it; he saw nothing but complicated unhappiness—perpetual imprisonment for his son—perpetual despair for himself—penury and calamity for Ethelinde. Sharp as was the anguish inflicted by so desolate a prospect, all its pangs were aggravated by the consciousness, that he had himself given to his son a dangerous example, and sacrificed to his fatal love of play the fortune of his daughter. Montgomery saw with extreme concern that a stupor had taken possession of his faculties, and that in the severity of his sufferings he was incapable of determining in what way to attempt a remedy.

This young man, not less warm in his affections than solid in his understanding, determined on trying what he could yet do for the relief of the brother of Ethelinde; though his first efforts, which had been to engage another friend to become bail with him, had been fruitless; Mr. Royston, the gentleman who had professed himself so warmly his friend and patron, and to whom, in the unsuspecting generosity of his heart, he had applied, not having merely refused him, but signified to the persons concerned that Mr. Montgomery, who so liberally offered to become security for another, was himself worth nothing; in consequence of which every farther attempt was rendered abortive; so that it was with great difficulty, and in consequence of having paid as a consideration almost all the money he had, that Montgomery had obtained a respite of three days before the unhappy Chesterville was to be conveyed to the King's Bench Prison. Of these three days the second was wearing away; and nothing but speedy and decisive measures were likely to save him from confinement for life. Heedless of ceremony, where his heart was so deeply affected, Montgomery now left Colonel Chesterville, and went in search of Sir Edward. On enquiring of his gentleman whether he could speak to him, the man said he believed not, as his master had given orders not to be disturbed. Montgomery however sent in his name, and was immediately admitted. The countenance of Sir Edward expressed surprize at his arrival, mingled with something of deep concern and recent agitation. Montgomery was struck and hurt by it: he thought Sir Edward received him coldly; he knew not that he was agitated by unhappiness too great to be concealed or endured; and that what he had himself to communicate would with redoubled anguish oppress him.

Montgomery briefly related the reason of his journey; and without attempting to palliate or disguise any part of the truth, as he had done in pity to the sufferings of an unhappy father, he represented the certainty of young Chesterville's ruin, if some measures for his release were not instantly pursued.

Sir Edward heard him with distress hardly to be described: the situation he was in with Lord Danesforte, with whom something little short of a direct challenge had passed, the confusion in which his family were, and the cruel insinuations which Lady Newenden had thrown out relative to Ethelinde, made it almost impossible for him to follow the first impulse of his heart, and go himself to London to the release of her brother; but not to suffer one so near and dear to Ethelinde to become a prisoner for life, was his determination. He started up, as soon as Montgomery had related all he knew, and went to Colonel Chesterville, where he endeavoured to calm the violence of his grief, and declared that he would not only immediately procure bail for the young man, but would take measures to relieve him from every difficulty. He therefore besought the Colonel to compose himself, and to recollect the necessary of instant exertion.

Chesterville, whose senses had been locked up through the excess of his concern, now grasped the hand of Sir Edward, and burst into tears. "No, never, never, Sir Edward!" cried he, as soon as he was able to speak. "No, never will I suffer *you* to do more for me and mine. Had I not been already too much obliged to you—obliged beyond all power of returning the debt, I ought to consider your own peace. Lady Newenden's conversation of this morning is sufficient to determine me. I will never hear again that her money has been squandered on us, nor endure that the spotless purity of my Ethelinde's name shall be exposed to the tongue of slander, in consequence of my necessities, or the follies of her unhappy brother. I must suffer, I have deserved it; Harry has deserved it too; but who will pity, who will protect my poor girl? You, her generous, her disinterested friend, can do it no longer. I go to share the poverty and imprisonment of my son; but where shall I find for her—for that innocent, suffering angel—protection and consolation?"

The image of Ethelinde, deserted in indigence, or confined with her father within the hideous walls of a prison, had already taken strong possession of Sir Edward's imagination; and such was his tenderness for her, that every sorrow of his own became light compared to that of not being able to shelter her from the evils of her destiny. That ardent affection however now lent him strength to consider what should be done; of which consideration Chesterville was himself incapable. It seemed necessary for Ethelinde and her father immediately to go to London. But a pang arose when he remembered that Montgomery, before too much beloved, and now endeared to her by his active friendship for her brother, would be with them; and that distressed as Chesterville was, and already inclined to favour Montgomery, of whom he now spoke in the warmest terms of approbation, it was not impossible but that he might give to him his daughter, and believe, that situated as she was, he acted right in despite of pecuniary considerations when he gave her a protector in the man she loved.

Ethelinde could certainly never be his. He knew that after what had passed, he must be for ever denied the delight of seeing her, the comfort of contributing to her ease, of sharing her grateful friendship, and her innocent affection. But to see her irrevocably another's, to know that she was married without an adequate support; and that her whole life might be exposed to trials he could not soften, to difficulties he could not alleviate; all his sense, his morality, his resolution, hardly supported him when he considered it; and he sometimes fancied he could rather bear to destroy her, and then himself, than endure the certainty of that, the very idea of which inflicted anguish so acute.

To pain so involuntary and so unconquerable, every consideration would have been opposed in vain which related merely to himself; but when he thought of her; when he recollected that his unguarded admiration had already exposed to the shafts of envious malignity, and haughty jealousy, the sanctity of her character; and that, innocent as she was, she might be rendered liable to the imputation of guilt; he found strength to determine, that whatever it might cost him he would stifle the anguish that consumed him, and act in regard to Ethelinde exactly as he would do for a beloved sister, had he a sister so situated.

This resolution did not preclude him from opposing a match for her so indiscreet as would be that with Montgomery; but it forced him, if he was able to persevere in it, to promote the interest of this indigent but fortunate Montgomery, and to attempt so to serve him as might remove the only barrier between them. Thus at war with himself, this generous heroism now supported, and now deserted him; but as nothing could be done till young Chesterville was released, the most immediate step to be taken was to enable his father to procure his liberty. For this purpose he wished to go with him to London; but he could neither leave his wife to follow Lord Danesforte, which she still seemed determined to do, without appearing to yield implicitly to the dishonour which such a measure would bring on him; nor could he easily content himself without an explanation from that nobleman, which the dialogue that had passed between them rendered necessary. Colonel Chesterville, who had been extremely hurt by the uneasiness of Sir Edward, and by the whole scene of the preceding morning, had before the arrival of Montgomery been labouring to persuade him that his wife, however carried away by the prevalence of modern customs, and by a desire to appear above the prejudices of the crowd (a vanity common to so many young and beautiful women), had yet really been guilty of nothing that should influence him to recur to harsh measures; and that nothing could be really so destructive to his peace and honour as the noise of a rupture with her, unless it was a public quarrel with Lord Danesforte.

Chesterville had a very good heart, and very good sense; and when unobscured by one fatal propensity, nobody had a better judgment or clearer notions of real honour. He believed himself, what he endeavoured to impress on Sir Edward; and though his indignation and anger were excited towards Lady Newenden by her attempt to injure the character of Ethelinde, he was too candid to suffer that anger to influence him against her in other respects; and as he thought her more weak than wicked; malignant towards others, but not guilty of any actual offence against the honour of her husband: he thought it, not only on account of himself but of his children, wrong in Sir Edward to carry his resentment at once to such extremities as would preclude the possibility of saving her character, or of her returning to a reasonable mode of life, if she should see her error. His arguments had their weight; but Sir Edward was yet undecided, when the arrival of Montgomery opened new sources of vexation, and divided his concern between his own situation and that of a family so dear to him.

While he yet deliberated, Mr. Maltravers, from whom Sir Edward had parted in displeasure, had considered more coolly the circumstances of his daughter's conduct; and though he could not determine to blame, he was afraid of defending it. He saw that there was now no alternative; a separation between her and her husband was inevitable, unless he could himself prevail upon her to give up, at least for the present, an acquaintance, to which, with some justice, Sir Edward had taken an aversion, and determining to attempt to move her, he was admitted to her bed-chamber, where he represented to her, with tears, the disagreeable consequences of her refusing to comply with Sir Edward's wishes; which were, that she would immediately renounce the plan of going to Danesforte, give up her continual parties with his Lordship, and return to Denham to remain there till after Christmas.

Lady Newenden, who had been in fits all the morning, and was now sunk in languor, listened very quietly to all her father had to say. When he concluded, she raised herself on her arm, and turning to Mrs. Maltravers, who sat in a very ill-humour on the other side of her bed, she cried—"Do you hear, Madam, what is expected of me? Do you see my father himself urge me to give up everything to the ill-humour and caprice of a man whose fortune I have made—to him, who, while he desires to restrain me from acquaintance proper for my situation in life, and from amusements I have a right to, scruples not himself to make scandalous connections with my own relations in my own house?—And shall I be so meanly tame as to bear it? No; Sir; you may tell, Sir Edward, that I will not be checked in my acquaintance, to gratify his ridiculous prejudice; nor limited in my expences, to enable him the better to supply those of his Ethelinde. Tell him I will perish first!"

Poor Maltravers, whose shaken nerves, and long habit of humouring his daughter, equally unfitted him now for contending with her, was sorry for her distress; and frightened at her vehemence. His wife he sometimes contradicted, though, as his temper was rather peevish than peremptory, she generally teized him at last to her purpose, but Maria had governed him ever since she was six years old, and nothing appeared to him so dreadful as opposing her will. "Well, but Lady Newenden—Maria—my dear child—consider," said he, "consider what a noise the matter will make—consider, pray do, what people will say."

"And am *I* to be made miserable do you think, lest fools and vulgar folks should gossip? People of real fashion will only ridicule Sir Edward, I promise you; and to the opinion of other people indeed I shall not sacrifice one hour of satisfaction."

"No, indeed," said Mrs. Maltravers, bridling with anger, "I have no notion why one should. I am surprised at Sir Edward, for daring to suppose that *my* daughter can even think of an impropriety; and

I am sure I cannot see why he should be humoured. The next thing will be, I suppose, shutting her up from all society whatever."

"Yes," added Lady Newenden, with an acrimonious smile, "and he will teach me doubtless to walk tamely about one of his houses (Grasmere Abbey perhaps), while my fortune is lavished on his amusements and his sentimental friends. I am surprised, Sir, you do not see his motive. 'Tis not for me and for his children he is anxious——I tell you, 'tis for Ethelinde Chesterville."

"Dear Maria, I declare I can hardly believe it."

Another scornful smile was raised by her father's incredulous simplicity.

"Not believe it, Mr. Maltravers!" said her mother——"No, to be sure; men are always in the right."

"Don't be absurd, Mrs. Maltravers, I desire," cried he in some anger, which, not daring to shew itself to his daughter, broke out against his wife.—"don't be absurd. You don't believe yourself—you know you don't—that Sir Edward has any improper attachment to my niece."

"My mother is convinced of it," said Lady Newenden.

"Then if you are," said he, still addressing himself to his wife, "you've acted a monstrous part, I must tell you, in letting her be with your daughter so long. But you know 'tis no such thing; and I am sure if Sir Edward had thought his kindness to her cousin gave my Maria any uneasiness, he would never have done any thing in Chesterville's concerns."

"Gave *me* uneasiness, Sir!" said Lady Newenden—"Pray don't mistake me so egregiously; I never suffered an uneasy moment about it. The man whose vitiated taste could find attractions in that face of faded wax, that maypole-like figure, and that mawkish affectation of literature and refinement, is in my mind an object of pity and contempt, but certainly not of resentment."

"Well, but, Maria, Sir Edward is resolute. He declares, that if you persist in going to Danesforte, his house receives you no more."

"Then I will have an house of my own, Sir, to receive me."

"But the world—what will the world say?"

"The vulgar world may say what they please: the world of fashion and sense will say that Sir Edward is ridiculously jealous of me, and dissolutely attached to Ethelinde. I shall live as I please, and have nobody to dictate to me, or to fancy they have authority to controul my most innocent actions."

"But your children, Lady Newenden!"

"Oh! Sir Edward will of course take care of them. Besides, I dare say his intention is to have a little arrangement with Miss Chesterville; and you know he is continually praising her for the goodness of her heart and the tenderness of her nature, and talking of her attention to Edward when he was ill; so that it will be quite the thing to have her superintend his nursery."

Mr. Maltravers, who was very fond of his grandchildren, now found that his blind attachment to his daughter was not proof against her insensibility and want of natural affection.

"Maria," cried he, in a harsher tone than he had ever yet used towards her, "I must insist upon your giving up these improper ideas of resentment: I will have you comply with Sir Edward's wishes. You are to renounce Lord Danesforte's acquaintance! It must—nay it shall be so!"

Lady Newenden now threw herself into an agony of passion, which ended in an hysteric fit; while Mrs. Maltravers, weaker than her daughter, exclaimed, half crying and half scolding, against his cruelty. Mr. Maltravers, equally tormented with fears for the health and the character of her who had been the sole object of his pride and solicitude for so many years, knew not what to do to preserve both; but in order to attempt it, he left his daughter to the care of her mother, and went in quest of Sir Edward Newenden.

To the unhappiness of a man, who, whatever might be the other features of his character, was a fond and generous father, Sir Edward could not be insensible. Mr. Maltravers represented the situation in which he had left Lady Newenden; related her suspicions, or rather gave them as the reason of her angry coldness; and hiding the obstinate asperity with which she had still refused to give up her acceptance of the invitation to Danesforte, or relinquish the acquaintance of the inviter, he tried to palliate the evil which he almost despaired of curing; hoping, however, that by a little condescension on both sides the difference might for the present be adjusted without the report going forth to the world, to whose opinion he was by no means so indifferent as was Lady Newenden; and who would, he believed, see her conduct in a very different light from that in which she flattered herself it would appear.

Sir Edward heard him not merely with attention, but with pity and regard.—"Believe me, Sir," said he, "that Lady Newenden's happiness has hitherto been my first object. Had she candour and generosity, she would own, that to her's, my own gratification has in every instance been postponed. You must recollect, Mr. Maltravers, that from the instant of our union, my own plans of of life, my taste, my amusements, even my friends have been invariably given up, till I saw that one predominating connection was likely to injure her character, that one dangerous amusement would probably ruin her children. Then it became time at least to explain to her my sentiments on both. I did so. With calmness, with tenderness I spoke; and even then regretted the necessity of giving her a moment's pain. But I received only contempt; I excited only scorn. Yet I had patience: till the world, less blindly indulgent, talked so loudly of Lady Newenden's society, that I could no longer forbear to use that authority which only can save her from farther ill consequences, and which, having once been compelled to exert, I will not now resign. Yet do not mistake me, Mr. Maltravers:—did I for a moment believe that my wife had really sacrificed my honour and her own, I should without hesitation cast her off forever. That I take any pains therefore to direct and reform her conduct, ought to be a proof that I think her yet innocent of all real crime, and am determined to save her from the appearance of it. As to the ridiculous charge of my being improperly attached to her cousin, I despise its folly, while I own its malignity hurts me; and I tremble to think how deeply depravity must have entered that heart; which can, to gratify a momentary resentment or excuse an evident error, blast, irrecoverably perhaps, the character of an innocent young woman, so nearly allied in blood, and so unfortunate in many respects that she has a double claim on the tenderness and protection of her relations. That I love Ethelinde, is very true: that I admire, revere, and esteem her, I never denied; for I have rather gloried in it. The ungenerous interpretation Lady Newenden has put on my friendship for her, is one of the most convincing and most painful proofs of the influence that unprincipled man, Danesforte, has cast over her mind; for of herself she never could have imagined it; or having mistaken my friendship for love, would never have borne calmly that its object should remain with her. It is too evident therefore to me, that in his dissolute and designing conversation originated the suspicion; and that arguments of the most pernicious tendency were brought forward to reconcile her to the conviction, which he spared no art to impress. When a man has thus the power to pervert the heart, what shall become of the principles of my wife, if the connection is longer endured?—What shall become of the reputation of your daughter, Mr. Maltravers?—of the honour of my children's mother? You are too reasonable, I dare believe, to blame me for resolutely breaking through this improper acquaintance: assist me, therefore; and to the power of an husband add the authority of a father."

Maltravers, who felt all the force of Sir Edward's argument, and who could not help recollecting that all he asserted of his tenderness and indulgence to Lady Newenden was true, now readily assured him, that he would leave nothing unattempted to persuade her to acquiesce immediately in everything he wished:—"But, Sir Edward," said he, with marks of deep concern, "this unhappy affair has already created fears of worse consequences. Yesterday, when my wife's extreme folly introduced Lord Danesforte into the house, contrary to your directions, the few words that passed between you were of anger and defiance. I am told that his Lordship is fierce, violent, and haughty; should he think proper to resent what then passed—"

"My dear Sir, I am no duellist; but if Lord Danesforte's fierce and violent temper chuses to break forth, and urges him to call me to decide our difference by the sword or pistol, I must certainly meet him. Be assured, however, that unless he insists upon it I shall not; for I should be sorry to take his life, or to hazard mine against such a man: a consideration not less strong is, that such a meeting, however it might terminate, would inevitably expose the fair fame of Lady Newenden; which, however careless she is herself of it, must ever be necessary to my peace and to our future comfort, if indeed there be any hope of domestic comfort after what has passed."

Mr. Maltravers, still fearing lest Lord Danesforte should resent the reception he met with in the morning, and despairing of his daughter's compliance with what her husband made the condition of their re-union, left him in great uneasiness, and went back to

Lady Newenden, thinking only of this beloved daughter, without giving the slightest attention to the situation of his nephew, young Chesterville, and the unhappiness of the father and sister of that luckless young man, which Sir Edward had as forcibly as possible represented to him, in hopes of procuring his assistance: absorbed entirely in his affection for his daughter, his heart was strangely contracted towards every other object; and unless reminded that he had other claims upon him, he never thought of them, and even then with coldness and reluctance.

CHAPTER XI

The day was wearing away. Dinner was announced, but nobody seemed disposed to partake of it. Lady Newenden remained in her bed-chamber, and Mrs. Maltravers attended her; Ethelinde, with an heart breaking through anxiety and incertitude, had hardly strength to get down stairs; Chesterville was lost in the contemplation of his own misery; and Montgomery so restless at the loss of time, that he neither had spirits or appetite. They all however attended at table at the request of Mr. Maltravers, whose solicitude seemed to be to stifle as much as possible the reports which he feared would go forth of the transactions of the morning. Lady Newenden was so frequently indisposed, that her absence, and that of her mother, appeared not extraordinary to the servants. Chesterville could neither eat, nor force himself into conversation; being wholly occupied by the situation of his son, and of the journey he proposed to begin immediately after dinner for his relief. Ethelinde, with fearful apprehension, the tears frequently rising to her eyes, watched the looks of her father, and could not throw any degree of cheerfulness into her own; Sir Edward appeared calm, but his face sufficiently told that he was ill at ease; he endeavoured however to keep up something like a conversation with Mr. Maltravers, who now frequently addressed himself to Montgomery, whom at another time he would probably have overlooked or neglected.

Sir Edward turned the conversation on Montgomery's family; and reminding Mr. Maltravers that he was the young gentleman for whom he had solicited his interest for an appointment to the

East Indies, he contrived to engage Montgomery in a relation of the events of his father's life and his own. This narrative must, he thought, interest Maltravers in his favour. Colonel Chesterville, to whose generous behaviour towards his mother, and of whose preservation of his father, he spoke with the most animated gratitude, was so much affected with it; that it wholly overcame the little resolution he had till then been able to command; he hastily left the room without speaking, and his daughter, in greater emotion, followed him.

Sir Edward, who saw the fine eyes of Montgomery turned towards her, as she went, with a look of tender alarm, besought him to go on; and, the servants being by this time withdrawn, said—"They are so unhappy at this moment, that it were cruelty to wish them to remain in company. Colonel Chesterville too has preparations to make for his departure. You have, I apprehend, no preparations to make; favour us therefore with your conversation till they are ready."

Montgomery then, suppressing a deep sigh, continued to relate the death of his father, and the subsequent disappointments of his mother, which had determined her to come to England; and when he paused, Maltravers, who had heard his narration with no interest, but with sufficient complaisance, said—"And so, Sir, you wish, it seems, to be sent out to India?"

"Such, Sir," replied Montgomery, "were my wishes till I had other views offered me by Mr. Royston."

"By Mr. Royston, the member of parliament, Sir?"

"Yes, Sir; he is, by his mother, my relation; and seems much disposed to be my friend."

"I am glad to hear it, Mr. Montgomery, both on your account and his; for he is not much accustomed, I think, to do generous actions."

Montgomery felt the blood rise to his cheeks. There was something rude and unfeeling in this speech; but he said, as calmly as he could—"I am sorry that is your opinion of him; you are then acquainted with him?"

"Yes, Sir, I think I am; for I bought my seat in parliament of him, and now sit for his borough."

"Well, Sir?"

"Well, Sir; all I have to say is, that he is a man who loves parade very much, but money more; and that in order to support the former at little expence, there is no meanness he is not capable of in regard to the latter. With all this, he has abundance of family pride; and while he talks of the blood his ancestors have shed in the cause of liberty, he blushes not to sell his own freedom of speaking, and even thinking, to the minister of the party by whom he thinks he can get most."

Montgomery, who had of late discovered much in the manner of his relation which convinced him he had been too sanguine in trusting to his professions, wished, however painful it was, to hear more of his character; he therefore remained silent, and Maltravers, after a short pause, went on:

"I am by no means desirous, Sir, to discourage your reliance upon him; perhaps you have good reason, from your own experience of him, to contradict mine, and the general opinion of the world. I do not wish to be inquisitive, but pray how long have you been under his patronage?"

"It is near a month, Sir, since I have been in his house."

"And pray, Sir, what are his views for you?"

"To procure some place under Government, for which he imagines my knowledge of languages qualifies me."

"You understand languages, Sir? Pray which?"

"The French, Italian, Spanish, and German."

"Mr. Montgomery, you are a young man; I am somewhat farther advanced in life, and have made a fortune without patronage. Go to the East Indies; there your talents will avail you. I have no quarrel, I assure you, with Mr. Royston, but I know him so well, that as you are a friend of Sir Edward's, I do advise you not to depend upon him too much; for besides that he is held very cheap by Ministry, who are aware when he opposes them that it is only till some new *douceur* can be obtained,[1] and that his talents are contemptible, I know he is at this time negotiating for himself; and will make no other attempts to serve you than perhaps a faint mention of you; and on that he will afterwards doubly pride himself; for he will have had the satisfaction of boasting that a Montgomery is his relation, which will raise his family pride; and on the other

---

1 "douceur" refers to gift; bribery; this metaphor for patronage derives from the idea that plums are sweet.

hand, of having attempted to serve him, which will do credit to his generosity."

"Is it possible," said Sir Edward, "that Mr. Royston *can be* such a man?"

"Is it possible, Sir Edward," replied Maltravers, "that you do not know him to be such a man?"

"No, I have hardly ever seen him; never above once, I think; and from common report I take no man's character."

"I speak not of him from common report, but from my own knowledge; and will give you one instance of his venality, which will convince you common report is sometimes to be trusted. During a late administration he held, as the price of his own vote and another which he could command, a considerable place under Government; but in the peevishness of his self-consequence, he wanted some addition to it, which was refused him. The next day he went down to the House, determined to exert all his oratorical powers against the Ministry, who were thus unmindful of his eminent services. He spoke. The House laughed; and some, who knew not the unsuccessful negotiation, wondered. The all-sufficient politician went home elate, and persuaded that the dismayed Premier would send to him, deprecate his wrath, and grant his demands with apologies and excuses. A messenger was indeed sent to him; but it was to say, that Ministry had no farther occasion for his services. Thus cruelly disappointed, he flew to the Secretary from whom the dismission came, deplored his hasty and unguarded speech, besought forgiveness, and offered, as the price of his restoration, to unsay every word he had uttered."

Neither Sir Edward nor Montgomery could help smiling at this anecdote, tho' both were concerned to find that the hopes of the latter rested on no better foundation than the promises of Mr. Royston. After a short silence, Sir Edward said—"If then Mr. Montgomery should find his expectations from this gentleman vanish, I am sure you will assist me in endeavouring to procure him some situation in that line he originally thought of."

A variety of uneasy passions kept Montgomery silent, while Mr. Maltravers answered—"What, to the East Indies? Yes, I will do all I can for him; and I should be glad Harry Chesterville would employ me in the same office; for by all accounts he's in a bad style.

He was always, I thought, a giddy, unpromising boy, and now it turns out to be as I thought."

Montgomery, who knew not that this quickness to see the faults of others, and thus bluntly to speak of them, while he could not perceive that his own daughter had any, was one of the prominent features in the character of Maltravers, blushed with anger and resentment at this harsh condemnation of his friend; yet, ingenuous and modest, he, in consideration of Maltravers' age and relationship to Chesterville, repressed his feelings, and only said— "I wish indeed he was in a more fortunate situation than he is at present; but surely, Sir, you judge too rigidly of my friend?"

"Your friend! I admire at[1] the friendship of young men. Pray what do you know of him?"

"Not much, I must confess, since I have been acquainted with him only a short time; but—"

"Pooh, pooh! you have been at drinking parties together, I suppose, and encouraged each other in idleness and debauchery, and now you fancy you have a great friendship for him. Believe me, young man, if you would make your fortune, you must avoid such patrons as Royston, and such friends as Harry Chesterville."

So saying, without expressing any other concern for his nephew, or appearing at all sensible of the pain he had inflicted on Montgomery, he arose from the table, and left the room.

Sir Edward easily perceived how much Montgomery was hurt. "You must not," said he, "mind the blunt, and sometimes rude manner of Mr. Maltravers; he has acquired them by being much among people obliged to him, and dependant on him. He does not mean to hurt you, nor is at all conscious that he does; and as to poor Harry, he loves him as well as he does anybody, except Lady Newenden."

"But will he not assist him, Sir?" enquired Montgomery; who, in his zeal for his friend, forgot the offensive speeches to himself.

"I am afraid not," replied Sir Edward; "or if he does, it will be only with his interest to procure him some appointment abroad. Mr. Maltravers parts with money very reluctantly, unless it is to his daughter; and young Chesterville formerly offended him by refusing to go to India, as he offended his aunt, Mrs. Ludford, by declining to be a merchant. He preferred the army, in which he had been

1 "Admire at:" wonder at (an older but not yet obsolete connotation).

brought up, and which was indeed natural enough. Would to God he had so acted as to have done credit to his choice; and that he had not thus brought misery on his father, himself, and his sister!"

Sir Edward concluded the sentence with a sigh, which Montgomery echoed back; and then said, in a melancholy voice— "Would he had! But, Sir Edward, on what has Colonel Chesterville finally determined? Time presses. If he goes not to London this evening, I must at all events set out."

"He intends it, I believe," said Sir Edward, rising; "but I will go to him, and you shall know in a few moments." Sir Edward then left the room; believing that if mention was made of Ethelinde, he should betray himself. He saw that Montgomery did not imagine she was to go with her father, and he feared lest in speaking of it, any thing should be said which might give him any reason to suppose that Lady Newenden's jealous malignity compelled her at such a time to quit an asylum so much more proper for her than the scenes to which she was to be exposed with a brother actually imprisoned, and a father who was unable to release him.

Sir Edward now went in search of Colonel Chesterville, whom he found in his daughter's room, sitting with fixed eyes, and a calm yet alarming expression of grief on his countenance; while Ethelinde, who had dismissed the servant, was employed in putting his clothes into his travelling trunk; now wiping away the tears that blinded her, now unconsciously indulging them; and sometimes asking her father's directions, as if to rouse him from his mournful contemplations.

"Why will you so fatigue yourself, Ethelinde?" said Sir Edward, when he saw her thus employed.

"Because," answered she smiling thro' her tears, "it is a pleasure to me to wait on my father; and those who are unable to keep servants, should learn cheerfully to become their own."

At this reply her father sobbed aloud. "'Tis I," cried he, in a convulsive tone, "it is I who have undone thee! I, whose cursed infatuation has deprived thee of the conveniences of life, and am now dragging thee to poverty and a prison." He now became so violently agitated that Ethelinde, terrified, caught his hand, hardly able to articulate, "My dearest Sir, for God's sake spare your daughter. Indeed nothing would be an hardship to me if you would be easy."

"Easy!" exclaimed he, striking his forehead with his clenched hand, "can I be easy? No, never, never!" His voice was now choked, but his looks were wild and convulsed. Sir Edward who saw in the pale countenance of Ethelinde her extreme concern and alarm, took the hand of her father, which he had snatched from her, and cried—"For God's sake, Colonel Chesterville, have more fortitude, and think more of your daughter."

"Think of her!" cried he, vehemently interrupting him; "I *do* think of her; and 'tis thinking of her that distracts me. My dear, dear friend, if this dreadful stroke overwhelms me, as it surely will—" He stopped, and again lost his voice; but recovering went on—"be a friend, be a protector to my desolate Ethelinde."

"I will defend and protect her with my life," cried Sir Edward eagerly. "In spite of the world, I will guard her person and vindicate her innocence."

Ethelinde now sat down, and, leaning on a table, fell into an agony of sorrow. Sir Edward, thrown almost off his guard by the solemn charge given him by her father, made yet an effort to check the vehemence of his emotion, and went on in a calmer tone— "Yes, my dear Chesterville, I will, fearless of malignity, and scorning falsehood, which ever counteracts itself, accept the sacred trust, whenever you are yourself disabled from its execution; but exert yourself, and remain still the protector, the friend of your daughter. The lassitude of despondence, the ravings of despair, are equally unworthy of you. Consider how unable your Ethelinde is to support the sight of either; and consider also, that to indulge these transports can avail nothing. Ethelinde," continued he, tenderly taking her almost lifeless hand, "let me conjure you to have better courage. Trust in that Providence which forsakes not the innocent and good; and let me entreat you to have some reliance on me, who will never suffer either malice or folly to shake my affection—yes, I glory in saying so—my warm, my faithful affection for you; let me add, my pure, my brotherly tenderness, which never can end but with my life."

Ethelinde found it quite impossible to speak, but she gently, almost involuntarily, pressed the hand which held her's. Sir Edward understood more of her sentiments than words could have uttered; and was about again to speak, when Ethelinde took the handkerchief from her eyes, and fixed them on his with a look so expressive of gratitude, tenderness, and grief, that, unable to bear it, he turned from her, and sat down on the other side by her father.

"My dear Colonel," said he, in the gentle accents of pity and benevolence, "call forth, I beseech you, your fortitude, and repress this fruitless concern, which is so destructive to us all. Mr. Montgomery is anxious to set out tonight. Perhaps your journey may be, without inconvenience to your son, delayed till to-morrow. Then you, and our dear Ethelinde, may be better able to undertake it."

"Oh! no," cried Chesterville, deeply sighing, "I will not, I ought not to delay it. I mean immediately to go, and have ordered a chaise."

All Sir Edward's terrors for Ethelinde now returned; he saw her weak, languid, overcome with grief, and her father unable to support her. It was night; it was November; and the weather was cold and comfortless. To complete his objections to her going, Montgomery, to whom in every other character than that of the lover of Ethelinde, he wished well, was to be her guide, her protector, her consolation. He dared not himself go with her, lest calumny should have new subject for its malevolence; he dared not propose her stay, for he knew that it would be interpreted to her disadvantage, and indeed that she would not, after what she had heard in the morning, consent to stay.

A new and most severe struggle now arose in his bosom. He remained silent awhile; then believing he had conquered his anxiety by dint of reason, he fancied he could with calmness see her depart; and therefore said, but in a low and reluctant manner—"Since then you must go, I will send a servant to finish your packing, with which Ethelinde must not fatigue herself, and if you will come with me, Colonel, I will trouble you with two or three commissions which I want to have executed in town."

Chesterville then arose, and left the room with Sir Edward. Ethelinde remained alone, and for a few moments was unable to collect her spirits enough to think steadily. Tears still flowed from her eyes and sighs burst from her heart: yet Montgomery— the beloved Montgomery, to whom she was so recently obliged, whom she more tenderly than ever loved, was to be with her. His presence would soften every calamity, the certainty of his affection, strengthen her resolution; and his tenderness, his friendship, his approbation, counterbalance all the evil with which her destiny seemed, from other quarters, to threaten her.

CHAPTER XII

Ethelinde having acquired more composure before the entrance of the servant whom Sir Edward had sent to assist her, now saw the remainder of the baggage they were to take with them packed and carried down; and being herself ready to depart, was on the stairs when a carriage stopped at the door. She concluded it was the post-chaise her father had ordered. On her entering the parlour, she found Montgomery there alone. Foreseeing and dreading the subject on which she supposed he would speak, she hastily said—"I thought my father was here. It is late, is it not better to call him?"—She was then hurrying away, when Montgomery stopped her. "One moment only, Miss Chesterville; I would not be importunate, but I may have, I can have, no other opportunity."

"Whither then are you going?" said she, somewhat amazed.

"To London," answered Montgomery; "and I leave you here!"

"Indeed you do not; I am also going to London."

"Is it possible?" cried he, in a transport of joy; "can I be so happy as to be allowed to attend you? Oh! joy unexpected!"

He passionately kissed the hand he held, which Ethelinde attempted to withdraw; but before she could prevail upon him to release it, the door opened, and Mrs. Ludford marched into the room, followed by her son, her daughter, and Mr. Emmersley. Ethelinde, in some confusion, welcomed her. She stiffly said— "Your servant, child;" and then seated herself with great dignity and formality, while Miss Clarinthia, running up to Ethelinde cried in a half whisper—"My dearest Ethelinde, how are you? Lord! my love, I'm afraid we interrupt a tête-à-tête. Who is that excessive handsome young man?"

Ethelinde had hardly time to answer that his name was Montgomery, before the little *bel esprit*, Mr. Rupert, exclaimed in an impromptu produced with a facility upon which he highly valued himself,

> "Ye balmy breezes come! who brush,
> The blossoms of the blackberry bush;
> Nor yet refuse to waft my song;
> 'Tis not tedious, 'tis not long,
> But full of fire; for I'm inclin'd
> To praise my charming Ethelinde!"

With an heart loaded with anxiety, Ethelinde was little able to bear this buffoonery; she cast a look expressive—too much expressive, perhaps, of contempt, on the poet; and without otherwise noticing his intended compliment, sat down; but Miss Ludford, impatient to be heard, thus addressed her:

"Dear child, why what is the matter to-night? You seem out of spirits; and Rupert's Muse itself, sportive and elegant as she is, cannot even raise a smile."

"I am going from hence," said Ethelinde, hardly able to speak.

"Going! whither?" enquired her cousin.

"To London," replied Ethelinde.

"And immediately?"

"Immediately—to-night."

"With whom do you go, Miss Chesterville?" asked Mrs. Ludford, whose temper was greatly ruffled to perceive the little attention Ethelinde lent to her son.

"With my father, Madam."

"Does Lady Newenden and Sir Edward leave Bristol also?"

"No, Madam, not immediately."

"Does her Ladyship know I am here?" reassumed Mrs. Ludford, swelling with the sense of her own importance, which she began to suspect made less impression upon others than on herself.

"Her Ladyship, Madam, is ill in bed."

"Ill in bed, is she! and you going to leave her! That is not methinks quite so friendly."

"Indispensable business, Madam, obliges me to go to London."

"Business obliges you, does it?—humph! I should not have suspected you of knowing much of business."

"Does your business relate to matters of property, of law, or of negotiation?" said the pert young counsellor, strutting up to her; "if to law, pray retain me. Next to pleading to you, I should like to plead for you."

"I have no occasion to trouble you, Sir," said Ethelinde with great coldness. "The business on which my father goes to town is a matter of no importance to any but his own family."

Thus repulsed, the barrister was not however abashed; but addressing himself to Mr. Montgomery, began to ask him as many questions as if he was likely to become witness on a trial. Montgomery, who was perfectly well bred, was extremely disgusted with his confident and forward manners; yet he answered him with great temper, that he came from the North of England, that he had business with Mr. Chesterville, and that he was going back the same evening to London.

Mrs. Ludford, while her daughter and Ethelinde were talking in a low whisper, listened to these answers, and immediately imagining that Montgomery was the lover of Ethelinde, and that they were going to London to be married, she determined at least to have the satisfaction of mortifying her niece. In this generous intention, she turned towards her, and said so loud that Montgomery could hardly escape hearing it—"Pray, Miss Chesterville, who is the young man that is going to London with you?"

Ethelinde, deeply blushing, remained awhile unable to answer a question so rude and abrupt; and in that moment Sir Edward Newenden and Colonel Chesterville entered the room.

Nothing could be more inconvenient to both than this visit. Sir Edward, though he had so settled matters by a letter to his banker that Chesterville was to receive a sum on his arrival in London equal, as was supposed from Montgomery's account, to the release of his son, had yet a thousand things to say to him, and a thousand charges to give Ethelinde. His heart was too full to enjoy any society; and the visitors whom he was now compelled to entertain were particularly irksome to him. Colonel Chesterville, whose soul had been torn with agonizing passions the whole day, and who knew that every moment was of importance to his son, was in haste to depart; and he dreaded taking leave before so many witnesses, as he could neither command nor conceal his emotion. But the chaise was now at the door which was to convey him and his daughter from thence. Montgomery, who had arrived post, and who came forty miles that morning, would have returned by the same mode of conveyance, but Chesterville could not help asking him into the chaise; and after a few cold compliments to the unseasonable visitors, while Mrs. Ludford seemed very much offended by their departure, Colonel Chesterville got into the chaise, having wrung the hand of Sir Edward, unable to speak to him. Sir Edward, almost equally speechless, took the hand of Ethelinde, and seated her by her father: "God bless you, Ethelinde—may good angels guard you! Remember me ever as your friend! and never scruple applying to me when you think you can give me the happiness of being useful to you!" Sobbing audibly, she attempted unsuccessfully to thank him, to return his good wishes; but her voice failed. Sir Edward bowed to Mr. Montgomery as he followed her: he would have wished him well; but he could utter nothing: the chaise-door was shut; it drove speedily away, as they intended, late as it was, to go three or four stages that night. Sir Edward felt the separation as if his heart had been torn from his bosom. He stood at the door as long as he could hear or see the chaise; then remembering that he had appearances to keep up, and duties to fulfil, he went mechanically back to the parlour, from whence he began to fear his visitors never intended to depart.

"So, Sir Edward," said Mrs. Ludford, who piqued herself on what she dignified with the name of sincerity and plain dealing, but which the rest of the world called ill-manners and ill-nature— "So, Miss Ethelinde has left you?"

"To return no more Miss Ethelinde, I fancy," said Miss Ludford. "Mr. Montgomery I suppose is a lover, and my cousin is going to be married, is she not?"

"I do not know that she is," replied Sir Edward, very gravely.

"I suppose 'tis a secret into which only part of the family are to be admitted. This Mr. Montgomery—pray who is he? I suppose he has a great fortune? for expensively as the girl has been brought up, no man in his senses, in middling circumstances, would like to marry her."

"Miss Chesterville's merit, beauty, and family," said Sir Edward, "render her an eligible object to men of the most distinguished birth and splendid fortune, but at present I do not believe she is likely to alter her situation."

"Nay, Sir," cried Mrs. Ludford, rising to depart, "you are, I doubt not, *better informed* than anybody. I am sure I wish Miss Chesterville very well; and can only say, that in general people's being above their family, and above their fortune, does not answer.

I suppose *we* shall see no more of Lady Newenden or of Mr. and Mrs. Maltravers?"

"Lady Newenden," answered Sir Edward, "is ill, and Mr. and Mrs. Maltravers are not here to-night; but I am sure they will all, if possible, make a point of paying their respects at Ludford-House before they leave Bristol."

Mrs. Ludford then left the room in her usual stately way, followed by her son, her daughter, and their friend; all equally mortified at the coldness with which they thought they had been received, and all lavishing on the innocent and unhappy Ethelinde every cruel and satirical reflection that malignant vanity in its disappointment engenders. Miss Clarinthia alone, with assumed softness, affected to defend her; and imputed her cold and pensive manner to the situation of her heart; of which, however, she knew nothing. When they were gone, Sir Edward went back to the room where he usually sat; and there, in contemplation on the fate of her whom he so adored, in bitter regret that he was deprived of her society, and that another might probably soon claim an exclusive right to it, while he found no domestic comfort to soothe the sickness of his soul, or to wean him from his fatal attachment, he painfully wore away the hours till it was time to go to rest: his heart then softening towards his wife, he sent to enquire after her; she returned a cold answer that she was very indifferent; but as she did not request to see him, nor signify any intention to make those concessions which he still resolve to insist upon, he went not to her apartment to bid her good night, but to the nursery; where having kissed his sleeping children, and let fall a tear on the cheek of little Edward, whom Ethelinde so fondly loved, he retired, sad and desponding, to his own.

END OF THE SECOND VOLUME.

VOLUME III

CHAPTER I

The visit of the Ludford family to Sir Edward and Lady Newenden that evening, had been principally at the desire of Mr. Rupert and Miss Clarinthia, who flattered themselves that they might be included in the party to Lord Danesforte's. Mrs. Ludford, while she affected to despise every thing but the substantial comforts of riches, was yet very solicitous to be noticed by "people of quality;" and was never so well pleased as when she compared that affluence acquired by trade, to the more brilliant but frequently ill supported splendor of such of the nobility as believed themselves obliged to make an appearance more equal to their rank than to their fortune. Every opportunity therefore of making this comparison she eagerly seized; and when they afforded at once gratification to her pride, and occasion to display the talents of her son, every thing was obtained that could make her eager for the party.

With avidity she engaged with her son and daughter in the project of going to Danesforte; where Mr. Rupert was to write for the theatre, and Miss Clarinthia take a part: so had they arranged it in their imagination; and infinite was their mortification neither to meet Lord Danesforte or to hear anything of the intended party; but to be received, if not with coldness, at least without any pleasure, and to observe throughout the house symptoms of confusion which, while it disappointed their expectations, piqued their curiosity.

During their journey home, they made various conjectures on the cause of Ethelinde's journey to London. " 'Tis some affairs I suppose of her father's," said Miss Ludford. "We all know how terribly embarrassed he is. Poor dear girl! She is much to be pitied."

"Pitied, for what?" cried the elder lady. "I dare say she would be much affronted at being pitied. She thinks herself rather an object of envy, I suppose: and as to this journey, I dare say it happens because Lady Newenden has found out at last that every body talks of her and Sir Edward."

"Indeed, mama, I am convinced that was mere scandal; besides, it looks, I think, more like a wedding than any thing else. I am sure that Mr. Montgomery is a lover."

"Perhaps he may. He has nothing, I suppose; most likely some dependant on Sir Edward. 'Twill be convenient enough to have Miss Chesterville married. There are ways great people have of settling matters very commodiously; and Chesterville will be glad to get his daughter off, that he may have nothing to interrupt him at his beloved gaming-table."

"Dear ma'am," exclaimed the gentle Clarinthia, "I declare I do not believe any harm of Ethelinde; and I understand that Mr. Montgomery is a man of family."

"Of family!" answered her mother; "and what good does family do? Chesterville was a man of family too; and my sister Ethy never considered that his family would not support her and her children. I am sure she made a bad history of it with her honourable connections; and I dare say her daughter will do the same, or worse; for, like her, she sets up for a beauty."

"The girl is certainly handsome," said young Ludford, conceitedly; "but in my mind that is all. 'Tis a pretty inanimate creature; I have tried to make something of her, but she seems totally to be deficient in spirit and discernment."

"The world supposes," said Mr. Emmersley, "that Sir Edward has been more successful, Ludford; and if that is really the case, her predilection in his favour must excuse her blindness to you."

"Oh! I forgive her from my soul," replied Mr. Rupert. "I never think your fine misses worth much trouble; nor should I have thrown away a thought on this, had not she had the reputation of an understanding in a superior style."

"I wonder how she acquired such a character," said Mrs. Ludford.

"Why, by being puffed by Sir Edward," replied her son, "to be sure; he is reckoned a man of sense and reading, and his word was taken for that of his great favourite. 'Tis nothing but puffing that gives people character. Then the girl is handsome; and a very, very small share of wit will make a pretty woman in fashion."

"And I suppose a fashionable carelessness of her reputation too is one reason for her fame: for my part I should, as she is related to me, be much better pleased if she was either less talked of, or talked of more to her advantage."

While this party was indulging their spleen on the subject of poor Ethelinde, Mr. Maltravers was labouring to adjust matters between Sir Edward and Lord Danesforte: the former of whom was very desirous of avoiding every measure that might expose the reputation of his wife; and the latter, even more anxious to evade relinquishing his arrangement with Lady Newenden, and his future projects in regard to gaming parties with Davenant, both of which he apprehended would be broken if he resented the conduct of Sir Edward. Though his Lordship possessed courage or rather fierceness enough to have no apprehensions of the event of a meeting, he yet found little inclination to hazard it, when it made him every way liable to danger and inconvenience, without promising any possible advantage. His personal courage nobody doubted; and he therefore determined rather to make the apology, at which Mr. Maltravers gently hinted, than become liable to fall by the hand of Sir Edward, or to be obliged to quit the country, should he himself have the advantage. Lady Newenden obstinately refused to make any concession; and the day after Ethelinde's departure, continued to keep her room. But Sir Edward, as he sat at breakfast alone, was surprised by the entrance of Lord Danesforte, who, gaily and carelessly approaching him, took his hand—"My dear Newenden," said he, "we strangely misunderstood each other yesterday. The devil, I believe, was in you. Prithee, Newenden, what has got possession of your head? If it had been any body else, I can tell you, I should have set about obtaining an explanation in a different way; but I know you are my friend, and that your conduct of yesterday was a mere fit of ill humour. Why the devil would you desire to put an end to our party; it is impossible but what you must think better of it."

Sir Edward withdrew his hand, and calmly, but coldly, answered —"My Lord, I cannot think otherwise of it than I did before; nor should I, without long consideration and very substantial reasons, have desired Lady Newenden to have given it up. My Lord, I will be explicit with you; I have too good an opinion of my wife to believe her capable of offending against her honour and mine; but the appearance of such great familiarity with any society I disapprove——"

"Cæsar himself not more nice, ha? My dear Sir Edward, one would really think you had been born and educated an hundred and fifty years ago. Ridiculous! If it was known that you had this whim in your head, and of a woman too whose conduct is so irreproachable as Lady Newenden's, upon my soul you would be laughed to death, and be held up as the Mr. Strickland of the modern world."[1]

"I should be very indifferent about that—my own happiness, the honour of my family, is of some consequence to me; the opinion of those whom you call the modern world, of none."

"Why, upon my soul, you grow worse and worse: 'tis so absurd, Newenden, that we will not argue upon it. Lady Newenden goes surely to Danesforte. I have every thing prepared; and it will be the damnedest thing in the world to disappoint us. Besides you will go with us yourself, and Mr. and Mrs. Maltravers. Surely in point of propriety, you may defy all the old cats in Europe to find fault; but why the devil you attend to their gossip, I cannot guess, and why, having lived so long in the world, you have not yet acquired courage fearlessly to please yourself."

"Pardon me, my Lord, I have acquired that degree of resolution, and therefore it is that I shall please myself in the present instance; and instead of going at this inauspicious season a longer journey, shall return with my family to Denham."

"Since that is the case, Sir Edward," said Lord Danesforte, gravely, "it becomes necessary for me to enquire what are your objections to accepting an invitation to my house."

"Simply, my Lord, because I dislike the dissipation in which Lady Newenden has been of late too much engaged; and, above all, I dislike deep play, and will suffer it no longer."

"Do you mean, Sir," said his Lordship, looking more and more displeased, "to say that I have engaged your wife in deeper play than has been her former custom?"

"My opinion on that matter," replied Sir Edward, "I shall not give when it is thus asked, nor do I conceive that your Lordship has any right to interfere in my domestic arrangements. I do not like my wife should go to Danesforte, and therefore your Lordship must excuse her."

"You cannot however, Sir, prevent my thinking this conduct very extraordinary."

1 Mr. Strickland is the leading character in a popular comedy by Benjamin Hoadley, *The Suspicious Husband* (first acted 1747).

"I embarrass myself very little with your Lordship's thoughts."

"By heaven, Sir Edward Newenden, this is behaviour I do not understand."

"Any explanation that you wish shall be at your service, my Lord."

Maltravers, who had been in an adjoining room listening, not without apprehension, to the progress of the dialogue, now entered; and dreading lest the dissention should become too violent for accommodation, he could not conceal that he had heard what had passed.

"My dear Sir Edward, Lord Danesforte," said he, addressing himself to both, "here seems to have been some misunderstanding. Let me beg that it may go no farther. Let me entreat of you, Sir Edward, to think better of me and Mrs. Maltravers than to suppose we would suffer Maria to persist in a plan really improper; but indeed you mistake the thing. My Lord, excuse Sir Edward's warmth; the little difficulty will be cleared up. Allow me——"

"My dear Mr. Maltravers," said Lord Danesforte, "I cannot but feel infinitely obliged to you; to Mrs. Maltravers too I am deeply a debtor. Thus flattered by your good opinion, it is, I own, doubly mortifying to me to find that Sir Edward Newenden, whose friendship I so highly prized, should have conceived an opinion that the scheme of domestic felicity he prefers has been by my means disturbed. Damn it, I could not have supposed Sir Edward capable of such an idea."

"Nor did I, my Lord, name such an idea. Your Lordship is pleased to enquire why I object to Lady Newenden's going to Danesforte. Without discovering that it is an enquiry you have any right to make, I answer that I chuse to put an end to the deep play and perpetual dissipation in which my wife has of late been unusually involved. Why you, my Lord, should find yourself offended by such a resolution, I cannot imagine; but be that as it may it is irrevocable." Sir Edward then left the room; and Lord Danesforte, with a great oath, protested it was the damnedest rudeness he had ever experienced. "What the devil does he mean by it, Mr. Maltravers? Pray has he had many of these amusing humours?"

"Really no, my Lord; for I don't remember that he ever contradicted Lady Newenden before; and now I am persuaded he will think otherwise of the matter. Lady Newenden, I must say, was wrong; she said, in her warmth, some things of my niece, Ethelinde Chesterville, which has piqued Sir Edward, and—"

"I don't wonder at his being piqued," said his Lordship, with a smile of great meaning.

"Not wonder at it?" asked Maltravers. "As how?"

"Why, my dear friend, you know that nothing hurts, nothing wounds so deeply as an incontrovertible truth."

"Truth! Why do you suppose it is truth?"

"Aye to be sure I do; and I really thought that it must have passed for such to every body who were not wilfully blind. My good friend you have not seen so much of the world to wonder now at any circumstances of this kind."

He then related some passages between Sir Edward and Ethelinde, with such observations upon them, that Maltravers, who had imputed the charge merely to the passion and spleen of his daughter, began to see Sir Edward's partiality to his niece in a different and very unfavourable light, and to believe what his Lordship laboured to impress, that the objections Sir Edward had to Lady Newenden's going to Danesforte, originated not in his dislike to her connections, but in his own reluctance to go where Ethelinde was not; and in his apprehension that her Ladyship's demand for money would prevent his supplying Ethelinde and her father to the extent he wished.

It was now that Maltravers, glad of any excuse which vindicated his daughter, thought it was his turn to be angry; but still the scandal such a rupture must occasion, and the ruin it would probably bring to all his ambitious schemes for his daughter's family, made him determine to smother this resentment, and palliate rather than inflame.

Lady Newenden still proudly persisted in being left mistress of her own actions; and talked with so much acrimony of Ethelinde, that Sir Edward, finding her father much inclined to join in her resentment and aggravate her suspicions, and her mother, violent as weak, maintaining her Ladyship's right to please herself, was at length compelled, or rather harassed, into a compromise, and after two days of debate and contention, it was settled that he would himself accompany his wife, her father and mother, to Danesforte for one week only; and in return for this effort of complaisance her Ladyship was to consent to go immediately afterwards to Denham, and remain there till after Christmas. Sir Edward, in pursuance of this arrangement, sent his children to his own house, and reluctantly prepared himself for a journey which nothing but his apprehensions of the evil reports that might be raised against their mother, joined to his fears for the fair fame of Ethelinde, could have induced him to have undertaken. He now regretted that he had taken a resolution which it was impossible to keep; but as prudence governed him, and not an obstinate adherence to his own opinions merely because he had once formed them, he was convinced, after long deliberation, that his children's honor and his own demanded this sacrifice. They might be irreparably blemished by his resentment if it was carried farther; they might be saved by his giving the sanction of his presence to this contested expedition; and the world, who knew his principles, and that no man, with a nicer sense of honor, had more resolution to defend it, would never suppose that he would accompany his wife to the house of a man to whom she was improperly attached; and while he thus hoped to stifle all reports that might have circulated against her, and gradually to dissolve the intimacy, which, though he believed it innocent, was very offensive to him, he thought to obtain of Lady Newenden an act of oblivion in regard to Ethelinde, and that he should still be permitted to serve and befriend her without being liable to the evil interpretations which that friendship had hitherto met with from his wife, her father, and her mother. Thus without being at all satisfied with the disposition he had been compelled to make, he determined to appear so for one week, to conceal the uneasiness which Lady Newenden's conduct, though more circumspect than before, still gave him; and to endure, as well as he could, the more corrosive reflection that Ethelinde was unhappy, and that another had the power which he was denied, of succouring and consoling her.

CHAPTER II

While these scenes were passing at Bristol Hot Wells, Ethelinde and her father, attended by Montgomery, reached London. The attachment which had been forming ever since the first moment of their acquaintance between these young people, encreased

every moment that they were together. In the mind of Montgomery, the beauty of Ethelinde was, however interesting and captivating, forgotten in contemplating the sweetness of her disposition,
and the tenderness of her heart. Her attention to her father, her
anxiety for her brother, the fortitude which she assumed in the
hope of alleviating the wretchedness of the one, and the sacrifices she prepared to make to relieve the pecuniary distresses of
the other, were such proofs of genuine goodness and greatness
of soul, that Montgomery, who was all spirit and generosity, must
have loved such qualities wherever he had met them; but when he
discovered them in a young and lovely woman, and knew that in
an heart so noble and yet so soft he had himself the tenderest interests, his love amounted to adoration. A passion so violent, acting
on an ardent temper, and encouraged by the sympathy raised in
the bosom of her who was its object, could neither be concealed
or restrained. Montgomery spoke openly of it to Colonel Chesterville, who, depressed as he was by the calamitous situation of his
son, and oppressed with pecuniary embarrassments of his own,
could hardly with prudence listen to a passion which promised
only a continuation of distress to his daughter. He could not but
see that it was mutual, and therefore knew that to repress it must
be fatal: he could not but feel that to encourage it was wild and
romantic, and that every way unhappiness must attend it; yet so
partial did he find himself towards Montgomery, so winning was
the open candour of his manner, so attractive the warm generosity, the manly spirit, and genuine integrity of his temper, that
Chesterville found it impossible to deny him his esteem and affection; and while he dared not encourage the elevated and sanguine
hopes which he yet formed of making his fortune, he lamented
that one fatal and apparently insurmountable object would make
it impossible for him to give his daughter to the man, who, had
he possessed only a competence for her support, he would have
preferred to the most splendid fortune, and the most elevated connections.

The heart of Ethelinde had long been irrecoverably Montgomery's; but too well persuaded that it was impossible she ever could
be his wife, she endeavoured, not to conquer her affection for him,
for that was not in her power, but to subdue her mind to her situation; to dedicate her life to the service of her father and her brother,

and her heart to Montgomery; never to marry, since death would
be preferable to an union with any other man; but to content herself with loving him and seeing him happy, which she was well
persuaded he might be, if he could, by adopting the same plan,
address some woman of great fortune, and by that means procure
an establishment equal to his birth, without seeking it in another
country. She fancied that passionately as she loved him, it would
hurt her less to see him the husband of another, than not to see
him at all; and she was assured that the greatest heiress would be
unable to refuse him, when, with such a person and such a heart,
the splendor of his birth, and the brilliancy of his talents were
considered. In this temper of mind Ethelinde reached London.
As Colonel Chesterville had no lodgings there, they drove to an
hotel; where, as it was late in the evening and the weather bad, he
would have left Ethelinde, while he and Montgomery went to the
place where the latter had left young Chesterville in confinement;
but she was so anxious to see and to console her brother, that she
besought her father with tears to take her with him. He reluctantly
consented; and after a slight refreshment, which was however
hardly tasted, they got into an hackney coach, and proceeded to
the place whither Montgomery directed them.

The unhappy father was silent the whole time, trying to prepare his mind for a meeting with a son whom he at once condemned and pitied, and whom he felt disposed to reproach with
anger and to embrace with tears; but he could acquire no fortitude; and his heart sunk within him when he reflected that he was
now going to visit, in imprisonment and in disgrace, him who had
been the darling of his mother's heart, who had been blessed by
nature with every perfection of person and understanding, and
adorned with every advantage of education which expense could
procure; but who, wanting only steadiness and principle, was the
misery instead of the blessing of his father, the disgrace instead of
the pride and the protector of his sister.

These tormenting thoughts deprived him of all resolution.
Ethelinde, whose hand was grasped in his as he sat by her, felt its
convulsive pressure, and heard his deep and heavy sighs; but knowing too well that she had no consolation to offer, she remained
silent, yet repressing her tears, which, if they once began to flow,
would, she knew, serve only to encrease his distress, and rob her of

the strength that was necessary to support them both through the scene they were entering upon.

Montgomery, suffering both for them and the poor young man who had occasioned their unhappiness, was equally silent and dejected till they got within a few yards of the door; and then he said to Colonel Chesterville—"My dear Colonel, we are now near the melancholy confinement of your son; let me entreat you to meet him without any appearance of anger and resentment; they may drive him to despair, but can remedy nothing. Think only how you may shorten or end his distress, and I will venture to say your generous forgiveness for the past will have more influence on his future conduct than the sharpest reproaches."

"I will do all I can," said Colonel Chesterville, with a deep sigh. The coach by that time stopped. Ethelinde trembled, and inclined towards her father in terror of the dismal-looking mansion, lighted by a distant lamp. Montgomery, who perceived every sensation of her heart, besought her to be composed, and saying he would go up first to apprize young Chesterville of their visit, he opened the coach door and leaped out.

On rapping at the door of the house a fierce and hideous figure appeared, demanding his business. He answered, that he must speak with Captain Chesterville. "I don't believe," answered the man in a surly tone, "that there is any such Captain here; but you may go in and speak to my master." Montgomery then disappeared. The bailiff's follower still stood at the door; and in trembling and breathless suspense the unhappy father and daughter remained three or four minutes.

Montgomery then returned to them; but instead of assisting them into the house, he put his hand on the coach-door, hesitated a moment, and then said, in a faultering voice—"Be not alarmed—but—"

"But what?" exclaimed Colonel Chesterville in an agony.

"My poor friend is removed from hence."

"Whither?"

"To the King's Bench prison."[1]

1 These scenes have autobiographical roots. King's Bench Prison was a old prison (founded in the medieval era), located in Southwark, south London. In the King's Bench Court, cases of bankruptcy, defamation and other misdemeanours were heard. Smith's husband was remanded there in December

"And why? Good God! did you not say that you were secure of his remaining here till my arrival?"

"I hoped I was; but other circumstances have intervened that I did not foresee or apprehend. The hazard became too great for these people to run."

"Larger debts then came in?"

"Alas! yes; and they carried him from hence yesterday evening."[1]

Momentarily stunned by this blow, Chesterville now recovered himself enough to say—"Well, my dear Sir, what is to be done?"

"We must immediately go thither," said Montgomery, "if we would see him to-night; for I understand by the people here that after a certain time we cannot be admitted within the prison walls."

"Prison walls!" cried Ethelinde, hardly knowing what she said. "Oh God! my brother! my dear, dear Harry!"

"We will go however," said her father, with some degree of calmness. "We will go. Get into the coach, Montgomery. Oh Ethelinde! what scenes are these for you!"

Ethelinde could not speak; Montgomery stepped into the coach, and they directed the man who drove it to proceed as fast as possible to the prison.

On their way they were all silent. The faculties of Colonel Chesterville were absorbed in the greatness of a calamity that now seemed without remedy; his spirits, which under any other pressure than that occasioned by the misfortunes of his children would have been tolerably supported, now sunk at once; and the man who had so often seen, with an equal eye and an undaunted heart, death in all its most terrible forms; who had bled in Germany, amid fatigue, alarm, and famine; who had traversed the desolate wilds of America, and beheld with firmness the savage scenes of slaughter from which humanity recoils, shrunk in despondence and dismay from the spectacle of the confinement and degradation of

---

1783 for debt and embezzling his father's trust fund, and she lived there with him and their children.

1 Ethelinde's brother was held first in a sponging house, a place of temporary confinement, a private house, until an arrangement to pay the debt could be paid. For this the landlord and the bailiff who brought the debtor there received fees (for rent, for food). Her brother's debts are too large for any compromise.

him from whom he had hoped for the reward of his parental tenderness, and the consolation of his declining age.

Ethelinde, trembling, and sick at heart as she was, attended less to her own sensations than the agonies of her father. When the coach stopped at the door, she heard him gasp for breath; she felt his hand tremble as he held hers; he tried to speak to Montgomery but could not. Montgomery however understood him, and went into a place called the lobby of the prison, where two or three turnkeys stand to admit the persons who enter. The first man he spoke to told him, that in less than half an hour the doors would be shut. Montgomery hastened back to the coach with this intelligence, and proposed that he only should see young Chesterville that night, and inform him of the intention of his father and sister for the morrow. "No," cried the Colonel, in a faultering voice; "no; I will see him if it be but for a moment." He then made an attempt to open the coach-door, but could not. Montgomery assisting him, he at length left the coach; and Montgomery lifted Ethelinde out in his arms, and as he yet held her there, he said, in a low whisper—"For God's sake recollect and support your own fortitude, in mercy to your father, to poor Harry, and if I may say so, to your Montgomery!"

"I will endeavour to have courage," replied the trembling Ethelinde, "but this is very terrible."

They by this time had ascended the steps, and were in the first entrance. The fierce and stern faces of the keepers who filled it, the noise of riot and wrangling from other figures, who were by the gloomy light discovered among them, all gave a new shock to the unhappy party. Ethelinde, who leaned on her father, found him hardly able to support her or even himself; and as the men who surrounded her looked with inquisitive and attentive eyes into her face, she was terrified, and eagerly caught the arm of Montgomery, who was a little before her. He put his arm round her.—"Be not frightened," said he, as he assisted her down the steps which lead into the area of the prison, "you are safe."

They now proceeded across the space in which the dwellings of the imprisoned are built. The night was cold and wet; the rain, or rather an heavy fog, fell murky and gloomy on a few wretched-looking persons, who were carrying their scanty suppers from the places where they had been making their melancholy market; yet in the place where liquor is sold, the voice of merriment and even of riot was heard, that aggravated rather than relieved the dismal appearance of the wide court, which, as it was extremely dirty, Ethelinde did not traverse without being wet quite through her feet; her hat too was wet, her hair hung negligently over her face; her complexion was wan, and her eyes swoln with tears. Yet still was she lovely and interesting; and in all these appearances of grief and languor, Montgomery not only saw the power of expressive and delicate beauty, which ornament can do little in heightening, but beheld new instances of what he more fondly adored—her sensibility and tenderness of heart.

The Colonel, who could not shed tears, who could not complain, but whose soul was saddened as by the stroke of death, ascended the dark stone stairs first; Montgomery supporting Ethelinde, who was compelled to stop several times as they went up. At length, after mounting two flights of stairs, they arrived at the place whither Montgomery had been directed; and having found the number on the door of the room which they were told young Chesterville inhabited, he tapped at it.

It was opened, without any question, by young Chesterville himself; and the first figure he beheld there was his father.

Unable to speak to him, he flew back. "Oh, Harry!" cried the unhappy man as he leaned against the side of the door. He could articulate no more; and Ethelinde, rushing by him, threw her arms round her brother, and fell into a violent passion of tears.

Montgomery, who alone preserved any presence of mind, and who beheld with deep concern the still and speechless sorrow which sat on the countenance of the agonized father, took his arm and led him in—"Come, dearest Sir," cried he, "be composed, be calm. You see Chesterville is well; you are sure of soon seeing him in an happier situation. Sit down, and tranquillize your spirit."

"I will," said the Colonel, sighing as if from the bottom of his heart, "I will!" Montgomery, having seated him, went to Ethelinde, who still hung weeping on her brother.—"I beseech you," said he, as he took her hand, "I implore you not to give way to this immoderate grief. My dear Harry, speak to your father."

Montgomery then disengaged Ethelinde from him, and sat down by her on a little tent bed which was in the room. Colonel Chesterville spoke not: he looked on his son "more in sorrow than in anger."[1] Young Chesterville, whose high spirit had been shocked and abashed by the sudden appearance of his father, and the violent agitation of his sister, now seemed to recover some degree of resolution. He advanced a step or two towards his father; but his eyes were fixed on the ground, and he said nothing, while a crimson glow, arising from the mixed sensations of shame, pride, remorse, was on his cheeks. His dark auburn hair was undressed, unpowdered, and hung loosely over his face,[2] and he wore a long military great coat over a white waistcoat, his whole appearance indicating that kind of neglect which is the effect of hopeless despondence. A moment he stood hesitating whether to deprecate the anger he merited by imploring pardon, or evade it by escaping from the room. His pride prevented his doing the one, his remaining tenderness for his father the other; yet he dared not meet his eyes, and he knew not how to speak. While he yet underwent this struggle of contending passions, Chesterville, whose eyes were mournfully fixed on his figure, was struck with the resemblance he at that moment bore to his mother. At her idea, at the idea of her son in prison and in poverty, a flood of grief and tenderness overwhelmed him; and forgetting for a moment that his son had been the author of his own misfortunes, he caught his hand with an eagerness like phrenzy, and carrying it to his eyes, he burst into tears.—"Oh! my boy! my poor boy!" cried he, deeply sobbing; "my lost, unhappy Harry!"

Young Chesterville, proud and violent as he was, could not bear this; he threw himself on his knees before his father, and in an hurried and inarticulate voice said—"I do not ask you, Sir, to forgive me, because—because—I know you cannot—you ought not!"

"He will forgive you," exclaimed Ethelinde; who, disengaging herself from Montgomery, was in an instant kneeling by him; "your father will forgive you, my dear brother, and your Ethelinde will join in imploring him to pardon you, and to spare himself."

Neither the father nor the suppliants now knew any longer what they said. Agitated beyond all power of recollection, Colonel Chesterville could only give way to the deep groans which seemed

1 *Hamlet* I: 2: 231-232.
2 Harry is in a dishevelled state to the point he no longer has the usual marks of his caste or class, which includes combing and whitening powder on a man's hair.

to swell his heart even to bursting; and his son, throwing his arms round his sister as she still knelt by him, cried—"No, I deserve not your affection, dearest and most generous girl! I deserve to be deserted—to be detested. Agonize me not thus by the sight of sorrow which I am not worthy to excite, but attend to your own health; and let the daughter be a blessing, a comfort to him, who has reason to curse the hour that gave him a son!"

"I do not curse you," said the Colonel: faulteringly and feebly he spoke. "No, Harry, you have broken my heart, but I bless you still! Still dear to that heart is the son of a woman I adored."

"Curse me rather! A thousand times better could I bear to hear you execrate my name than to see you thus," cried young Chesterville, starting up in the wildest phrenzy. "Fool! villain! monster! parricide that I am! I will not live to bear this! Leave me!" shrieked he in the most furious tone, stamping and striking his forehead with his hand; "leave me this instant! for I am mad! I am tormented! more tormented than the damned! and I cannot answer for myself!"

Montgomery had, during the former part of the scene, in sympathizing solicitude hung over Ethelinde as she knelt on the ground. She still remained there, leaning her head on her father's knee, while the paroxism of passion which had seized her brother redoubled her sobs, and converted the softening grief of her father into horror. Montgomery, trembling for its effect, seized young Chesterville's arms as he seemed attempting to dash himself to pieces, and saying, without meaning at that moment, a dramatic quotation, "are you a man?"[1] he forced him to forbear these frantic actions and to hear him; though he yet struggled to disengage himself, and said, in a convulsed voice——"Leave me, Montgomery! Unhand me, Sir! D——n! am I to be fettered like a boy? Go, Sir! I disclaim your officious friendship, and will be master of my life!"

"Be rather master of your reason, Chesterville. Is it manly thus to alarm your sister, thus to aggravate the concern of your father? Surely it is as inhuman as it is absurd. You know, you must see, that he came not to reproach nor to distress you, but to labour for

[1] A literary sounding phrase. It can be found in *Macbeth*, III: 4, 57 and *Othello*, III: 3, 347. Smith does not want to call attention to these texts so much as the melodramatic feel of the young man's posturing, which Montgomery attempts to stop.

your release. It is so late that he can stay but a moment. Recollect yourself; and add not thus to concern which you see annihilates his faculties, and will shake his frame perhaps to its destruction, if you are not more rational."

"Will it?" cried young Chesterville, staring wildly at his friendly monitor;—"Do you think it will? Then it were better for me to go to sleep and not know it. Why should I live? Am I not a curse to him?—am I not a fool who against conviction have trespassed, till I am sunk into an abyss myself, but whither it would be infamous to drag my father and Ethelinde? No! no!" continued he, shaking his head with a wild and convulsive motion, "I can bear any thing myself—But they—they must forget me!"

"They cannot forget—they came to help you."

"They *cannot* help—they must forget me!" quickly answered Chesterville, starting away from Montgomery and stepping to his father: then suddenly assuming a graver and more composed tone—"Sir," said he, "I thank you for coming to me: but it hurts you—it hurts my poor Ethy here"—(he took her hand)—"and it can be of no use—for nobody can do me any good. Leave me, Sir, to my destiny, and think only of your daughter. It is late. You seem not well. I have behaved with such premeditated folly that I deserve to be abandoned. You know not the extent of my headlong infatuation. It is too late to recede: I must go on and finish here (for I can never be released) a life which I am sorry you ever gave me!"

"Almighty God!" cried Colonel Chesterville, whom this speech distressed more than his most extravagant transports—"what do you mean?" Then rising and embracing his son as he stood before him, he cried—"Harry! I forgive you—forgive you every thing! All I have, all I can command, is yours! Sir Edward Newenden will assist me. We will labour, we will accomplish your release: and with my soothing Ethelinde, with my repentant, my ever dear Harry, I will contentedly leave England, and go where, if we cannot enjoy the luxuries of the world, we shall at least escape the contagion of that example, which only, and not his own disposition, has misled my son."

"You are very good, Sir—very good," said young Chesterville, quitting his father's arms, and walking with an hurried step to the other end of his small apartment; "but I neither deserve it, nor can it avail me. I owe more, much more than you possess. I do indeed. My honour itself is forfeited; for I have contracted debts of honour which I can never pay. I never can appear again. I am disgraced; I am undone. There is but one step left for me to take. Reconcile yourself to it, and forget that you ever had a son. Oblivion—long, long, eternal oblivion is best—it is best for us all!"

He sat, as he said this, on the bed, and tried to speak calmly; but his words seemed often stopped in his throat. Ethelinde, who leaned on the chair from whence her father had risen, had, while he spoke, been raised by Montgomery; and quite exhausted by grief and terror, she was unable to support herself, but reclining on his bosom, was sustained by his arms, which were thrown round her. The frightful idea of suicide, which all that her brother said served to impress, froze her blood with terror. But she could only sigh; she could not speak. The fatigue of a long journey operated with the anguish of her soul to render her lifeless and almost senseless: yet the calm, the manly spirit of Montgomery, his ardent love, his disinterested friendship, were present to her. They shed one ray of hope on the gloomy horror of all around her, and saved her from sinking into despair equal to that of her brother.

Colonel Chesterville, who grew every moment more wretched, now made an effort to reason with his son. "Let me know, my dear Harry," cried he, "the extent, then, of your indiscretion. I have on the friendship of Sir Edward Newenden the strongest reliance. I have other friends who will, perhaps, assist me. Matters may be mitigated with your creditors. Means may be found to soften some of them—to pay others."

"Impossible! Impossible! I have nothing to hope! I have a weight here," (pressing both his hands on his heart,) which nothing—no, nothing can remove! Hark; there is the bell which summons strangers to depart. Go, my dear Sir; go, or the gates will be shut. To-morrow Montgomery will come to me, and we will talk farther of these things, and he will let you know. Come Ethelinde," continued he, approaching his sister and taking both her hands, which he eagerly grasped, "rise and leave me. Montgomery and my father are going. I will not have you come here again. This is no place for my sister. So God bless you, dear Ethy; good night to you. Montgomery, you will be so good as to go to-night with my father and sister; and come to me, Montgomery! come again to-morrow!"

There was a breathless impatience in his voice, a wild anxiety in his eyes while he thus spoke, that redoubled the terrors and apprehensions of his auditors. They were all, however, silent, till a rap at the door obliged Montgomery to rise and open it. A squalid and unhappy-looking man entered, and said to young Chesterville—"an please you Captain, the last bell has gone, and your honour's friends will be shut in." "There, there," cried he, as if solicitous to avail himself of this intelligence, "I told you so. My dear Sir," addressing himself to his father, "you will be much inconvenienced, indeed you will, if you do not instantly rise and go. Come, come, be quick, pray do. Run, Gilham," said he to the man who yet remained at the door, "run down to the turnkey and beg two minutes, or it will be even now too late."

"If I never go from hence at all," said Colonel Chesterville sternly and resolutely, "I will not quit you while you are in such a temper of mind."

"Nor will I," said Ethelinde, in a faint yet determined voice.

"You must, you must," replied her brother, speaking with yet more hurry. "There are no beds here for you; I have hardly one even fit for my father to repose upon. You must neither of you, you shall neither of you stay."

"I will stay with him, my dear Sir," said Montgomery, addressing himself eagerly to the Colonel, "and do pray hasten hence with your daughter."

"*You* stay with me? For what? Indeed I have no room for you nor any desire for a companion. I am best alone—I *will* be alone!"

"No, Chesterville," said Montgomery, bearing with the most patient calmness the seeming rudeness of his friend;—"no, Chesterville, you are not fit to be alone, and I will sit by you all night."

"It is very strange, Sir," exclaimed Chesterville with an oath, "that you will think of intruding thus upon me. Curse me if you shall stay!"

Ethelinde, now almost dead with terror, and fearing that Montgomery would not keep his temper when thus provoked by obstinate ingratitude, pressed his hand, and said in a whisper—"Oh, Montgomery! bear with him, forgive him; he knows not what he says; he is not himself!"

"Be satisfied that I cannot resent any thing he says now," answered the noble minded young man, pressing her hand to his lips; "but at all events he must not be left."

"You will not refuse to let me remain here however," said his father, looking at him with eyes where fear and affection were mingled; "you will not turn your father out of your room?"

"No, Sir; no;" replied young Chesterville, "I certainly cannot; but wherefore stay? to what purpose?"

"Simply because it is my pleasure—let that satisfy you."

"And my sister, Sir—what is to become of my sister?"

"Your sister will, I am persuaded, be in safe and honourable hands." Then turning to Montgomery, he said—"Montgomery, I commit her to your protection; and let it convince you that I know the nobleness of your soul when I confide to you the last hope of mine. Take care of my daughter to the hotel we left; protect her there to night; early to-morrow come to me here, and we can then judge better of what is to be done. Good night, dearest Ethelinde! in the care of Montgomery, in your own purity, in the protection of heaven, you are safe."

"I will as religiously watch over her," said Montgomery, "as if she were my orphan sister. Chesterville," added he, applying to her brother, "your father gives me a sacred deposit, which I will to-morrow restore to his guardianship, and I expect that you will not, by your ungovernable and useless passions, disable him from undertaking it." The man who had before appeared, now entered hastily to say that the turnkeys were actually barring up the doors; and Ethelinde, kissing her father's hand in breathless agitation, and then that of her brother, was hurried down the stairs by Montgomery. They arrived just as the last door was about to be irrevocably closed. Montgomery, taking some silver from his pocket, prevailed on the turnkey not only to facilitate the opening of the outward one, but to assist them with a light to the hackney coach that yet waited; in which having placed the breathless and frighted Ethelinde, he seated himself by her, and ordered it to be driven to the Adelphi Hotel.

Ethelinde, during the incoherent and hurried dialogue which had passed relative to their departure, had no time to oppose the proposal her father made of sending her away with Montgomery; nor had opportunity been allowed her, would she have done it; since to have expressed any objections would have been to acknowledge that she mistrusted either him or herself. In truth she did neither; yet to be consigned at such a time in the evening, and in such a conveyance, to the care of so young a man, and to have no place to receive her but a public hotel, struck her as a great impropriety; and the cruel situation she was reduced to, anxiety for her father, and fear for her unhappy brother, added to all the fatigue and all the alarming circumstances she had encountered within the last six and thirty hours, quite overwhelmed her; and hardly could she sit up in the coach, hardly in a low voice answer the tender but most respectful enquiries of Montgomery; who, now they were alone, would not even touch her hand, lest it should appear as if he took advantage of her situation, and of the confidence by which she and her father had honoured him; but with the most acute pain he remarked the excessive dejection of his lovely, his adored charge; tried with anxious solicitude to soothe and reassure her; and having, on their arrival at the hotel, prevailed on her to take some refreshment, he was gratified on seeing her retire for the night in rather better spirits than from the occurrences of the evening he dared flatter himself with expecting.

CHAPTER III

When Ethelinde was alone in the apartment prepared for her, she found herself too much tired to recall with clearness the transactions of the day. A confused but acutely painful recollection rested on her mind; the soothing idea of Montgomery's love and protection only tranquillizing in some degree the tumult of her spirits and the anguish of her heart. Secure that no new evil could for that night befall her brother, she courted a transient but welcome forgetfulness, and at length sunk into repose; which, though not unbroken by the fearful though half-retraced images of the preceding day, yet refreshed and relieved her; and when she awoke the next morning, she thought, that supported by the tender friendship of Montgomery, and firm in the consciousness of innocence and rectitude, she should have resolution enough to endure with serenity the bitterest destiny that might await her, if it affected not the lives and health of Montgomery, of her father, of her brother, and of Sir Edward Newenden, for of the latter she ever retained the tenderest recollection with the truest gratitude.

She believed that any other calamity she could meet, not merely with courage, but with cheerfulness. Never having flattered herself with any sanguine hopes of being united to the only man whom she ever could love, she fancied that the cruel change in her situation would make no other alteration in regard to him, than as it called forth all the nobleness of his nature, it encreased her attachment without raising her hopes. Every other establishment but that which she might in happier circumstances have shared with him, would be not only indifferent but hateful to her; she had nothing therefore to regret in the certainty, as she believed, that she should never marry; and to alleviate the misery of imprisonment to her brother, or to sacrifice every thing she actually possessed, and every future advantage, to release him from it, seemed so much her duty, and was so truly her inclination that she did not think the determination to do both any sacrifice; and she felt that having done so, she could submit to any mode of life which, while it supported her father and her brother, might not degrade her in the opinion of Montgomery.

She met him at breakfast, with more composure than she had apparently possessed since they left Bristol, yet she was rather languidly resigned than certainly calm; rather endeavouring to acquire fortitude than having obtained it.

Montgomery felt the ardour of his attachment to her every moment encrease; he saw, with the most poignant regret, that her constitution was unequal to the temporary strength of mind that the ardour of her affections lent her; and while he looked despondently towards what she had to encounter, and saw only bitterness and anguish in store for her, he dreaded lest its pressure should destroy so soft a frame and so tender an heart.

He feared to give her hopes which he felt not himself, lest disappointment should be embittered: yet he attempted to appear cheerful, and affected to talk of present calamities as dark clouds which would probably be dispersed. But Ethelinde saw that he thought not so sanguinely as he spoke; yet afraid of enquiring into the extent of his fears, she said little, and seemed solicitous only to preserve her resolution and firmness, that she might neither dissolve into tears, or by any other indulgence of sorrow give a new reproach to her brother, or another pang to her father.

When their breakfast was finished, Ethelinde expressed her impatience to return to the melancholy confinement where they were; and Montgomery, ever attentive to her comfort, as well as the propriety of her situation, then asked her (not without hesitation), whether it would not be better to pay the people at the hotel, and that evening to place herself in a lodging?

Ethelinde, ignorant of his reasons, but concluding them just, desired he would act as he thought right. He paid the bill therefore, and about ten o'clock they departed together in an hackney coach.

Still shuddering at the prospect of a prison, Ethelinde readily accepted the arm of Montgomery; and more dismayed if possible than the evening before, she, with his assistance, reached the room inhabited by her brother. On its being opened, she eagerly approached her father, whose figure first struck her—pale, languid, and faint, sitting at a little deal table, on which he rested the arm that supported his head. Her brother, who had opened the door, looked less dejected, but more wild and unsettled. His eyes betrayed the total want of sleep; his manner was abrupt and disturbed; and all his features seemed inflamed with that sharp despair which corrodes and irritates a young, ardent, and proud spirit, unused to misfortune, and conscious of having merited the misery it cannot resolve to sustain.

Ethelinde approached her father with quickness. He held out his hand to her. "My dear child!" said he as she kissed it, while tears fell from her eyes—"My dear Ethelinde!" She would have asked him how he did; but her voice failed; and afraid of affecting him too much, she suppressed her sobs, wiped away her tears, and sat down.

"Montgomery, my friend!" said Colonel Chesterville, "Harry would speak to you." The two young men went down together, and Ethelinde and her father remained alone.

As soon as the door was shut, he seemed trying to assume courage to speak. He sighed deeply; and then, after a long pause, said—"My daughter! the extent of our misfortune is greater than I could have supposed! We are utterly ruined! My child—thy father, thy brother, have undone thee!——Ethelinde is a beggar!"

There was a sad solemnity in his manner which made her tremble. She would have said—"Never can your daughter repine at her fate, whatever that fate may be, while she is rich in your tenderness and safe in your protection;" but she could only pronounce inarticulate sounds; she murmured rather than spoke , and her father, in a voice now steady through forced resolution, now faultering from the bitterness of his reflections, went on.—"To extricate your unfortunate brother is impossible; I therefore must share his prison. Had his debts amounted only to what I could have raised by the sale of my commission, by what else I can otherwise dispose of, and by the loan offered me by Sir Edward Newenden, he might have been released; and though deprived of every thing, I could, I believe, have lived for you."

"And you will live for me now, Sir!" cried Ethelinde. "Oh! talk not of leaving me! While you are with me I fear not poverty!"

"Ah! dearest girl! you have never tasted its bitterness; and there was a time," continued he, sobbing, "when it was very unlikely you ever should!" He stopped; deep groans impeded his utterance; yet he could not weep, but his face was convulsed by the passions contending in his soul. "Yet a little—a very little—and I shall probably be at rest. Ethelinde—it is for you only I wished to live; for you—had it been to secure your happiness—could have been content to die! But to leave you, lonely and defenceless as you are in such a world!—is a prospect so insupportable to me, that it renders dreadful the approach of dissolution; and makes me die a coward!"

"For God's sake, my dearest father," said Ethelinde, grasping his trembling hands, "have pity upon me, and do not talk so!"

"I thought I could have prepared you," answered he, "for what is, I feel, inevitable. Ethelinde, my heart is broke—quite broke! Against every thing else I *could* have struggled, but this stroke is decisive."

"I hope, dearest Sir," said Ethelinde, in a weak and faultering voice, "I hope that your uneasiness prompts you to see things in the worst light; Sir Edward Newenden's friendship——"

"Be not deceived, my child, with groundless hopes; Harry owes four thousand pounds more than I can by any means raise, even taking advantage of the letter Sir Edward has given me on his banker. I will perish here myself rather than make a farther demand on his generous friendship."

"Let me write to him, Sir," cried Ethelinde; "I am sure he will do any thing for you; his fortune is large, his spirit yet more noble than his fortune."

"And shall I therefore tax it so heavily? and for what?—to pay the extravagance of a gamester? God forbid! Sir Edward's fortune, brought to him by his wife, is the property of his children, and ought to be sacred. I am already deeply—too deeply indebted to him; and I charge you, my child, think not of applying to him. For a few days, while the temper of Harry's mind remains what it now is, can my Ethelinde submit to remain near this place with her father, to watch over the hours of a brother, whose hand seems every moment armed against his own life? I intend to procure a lodging in the immediate neighbourhood if my Ethelinde does not object to it."

"Is it possible, Sir, you can suppose that I will not with avidity attend you wheresoever you may be? Ah! do more justice to the heart of your daughter; and believe that her life is devoted to you and the dear unfortunate Harry."

"Goodness and generosity were ever thine, my angel," cried her father, tenderly wrapping his arms round her; "oh! what a destiny is that which is likely to be the lot of excellence almost beyond humanity!" He now for the first time for many hours was softened into tears. They seemed to give great relief to his swollen and oppressed heart, and having indulged them, for some moments in the arms of his daughter, he became more calm; and though his countenance yet bore an expression that terrified Ethelinde, yet she was somewhat comforted to find that the darkness of his despair a little abated; and by the time Montgomery and her brother returned, he had collected himself enough to talk with some composure of the immediate regulations necessary for fixing himself and his daughter in the neighbourhood of his son's confinement.

It was then settled that Montgomery should go in search of a proper lodging whither they should remove in the afternoon. When he was gone, young Chesterville went away also under pretence of ordering a dinner for them; but he remained absent much longer than it could be necessary to do on that account, being unable to bear the mournful though tender looks of a sister he had injured, and of a father in whose breast he had planted a dagger never to be withdrawn; but who yet, much as he had learnt, knew not the most painful and insupportable of those tortures which corroded the bosom of his son—tortures with which he had but just acquired courage to entrust Montgomery. In about an hour Montgomery returned; and young Chesterville, who watched for his entrance went up to the room with him. The Colonel had remained silent almost the whole time they were absent; and Ethelinde, having nothing to offer likely to give him comfort, had been trying to argue herself into that state of calm composure and chearful fortitude which was the most likely to prevent his feeling on her account aggravated pain.

A melancholy dinner now passed, at which none of the parties had either conversation or appetite. Ethelinde however exerted herself in the hope of prevailing on her father to eat; and Montgomery spoke with some degree of chearfulness, in that of sustaining her spirits. The Colonel, to gratify his daughter, attempted to swallow what he put on his plate; but after a fruitless effort or two, sent it away; while his son now eat eagerly for a few minutes; then suddenly starting up, filled a tumbler of wine, and drank it; after a moment in which he seemed totally lost in reflection, he again rose from table, and brought wine to his father, to his sister, and to Montgomery; and, affecting to laugh at his own absence, the laugh was so convulsive that it made Ethelinde shudder. He poured out for himself a second bumper, and drank it as eagerly as before.

Ethelinde, who could read in the eyes of Montgomery all his thoughts, now looked earnestly at him, and saw but too plainly that he beheld her brother's behaviour with concern and even terror. Their repast being at an end, Montgomery said—"Miss Chesterville, I take the liberty of recommending it to you and the Colonel to go to your lodgings before it grows late. The night is wet and stormy, it seems likely to become worse, the walk across this place is always inconvenient; let me therefore have the happiness of seeing you safe out of it before it is dark."

"Yes," said the Colonel. "Go first, Ethelinde. Mr. Montgomery will conduct you, and I will stay with Harry till he comes back."

Ethelinde now therefore tenderly took leave of her brother, and Montgomery attended her, defending her by an umbrella from the rain as well as he could, to a small but decent lodging in the

Borough.[1] He there gave orders for every thing that he thought would contribute to her accommodation, and having seen her safely seated by a good fire, and having received her promise that she would attend to her own health, he imprinted on the hand she gave him a kiss, that seemed to repay him a thousand times for all the trouble he was engaged in; and then returned to her father and her brother.

He found the former more deeply dejected than ever; but Harry Chesterville had by this time drank so much and so rapidly of wine, probably not very pure, that he was no longer master of his reason, and was in a vehement and almost frantic manner dis-coursing to his father of the right which he affirmed every man of spirit possessed and ought to exercise, of shooting himself through the head when life became unpleasant to him.

The poor Colonel, who, had his son been in a situation to hear reason, had no spirits to reason with him, surveyed him with looks of silent terror, while tears extorted by the memory of his mother, rolled slowly from his eyes. He seemed glad of the return of Mont-gomery; and rising immediately, he wrung the hand of his son, and said—"Go, Harry—go to bed and recover yourself; you are only wounding me and yourself more deeply." Then the reflection of where he was about to leave this unhappy, still most beloved son, stung him with insupportable sharpness, and his tears were not to be restrained.

Montgomery had dreaded more from the petrifying and immovable grief which the first shock had occasioned, than from these softer emotions; he was therefore glad to see him able to indulge them; and consigning him to the care of the runners[2] who waited on young Chesterville, that he might be conducted to his lodgings, he returned back, at the earnest request of the father, to attempt to tranquillize the son.

"Well, my friend!" said he eagerly, as soon as Montgomery entered the room, "and now you will go in search of Victorine? She is by this time in town. I am mad, by heaven, till I hear of her, till I see her, till I have her in my arms."

1 Southwark.
2 The term used for people who made money by carrying messages and buying supplies for people in prison.

"Mad you certainly are, my friend; so mad indeed that I do not think you in a condition to be left to yourself."

"Not left to myself!" exclaimed Chesterville. "What do you mean by that? Do you intend poorly to fly from your word? Do you mean to refuse going to her? Would you drive me mad indeed, and compel me to shoot the keepers of this damned place rather than not force my way to her myself?"

"This is extreme folly, Chesterville," said Montgomery; "folly, which nothing but your situation can excuse. If *you* will go to bed quietly, *I* will go to the place you have named, and will enquire for the person about whom you are so anxious; but be not, I beseech you, so impetuous; and if she is not yet come, as may very probably be the case, do not therefore give yourself to the devil, or threaten to cut my throat."

"Forgive me, my dear fellow," cried Chesterville. "Pray make allowances, I have been all day enduring the tortures of the damned; and I have drank to forget them till I have forgot myself."

"I am glad," rejoined Montgomery, "that you are conscious of your condition, I wish, however, you had not got into it, as it has served to render your father more uneasy."

"Has it?" said Chesterville. "Upon my soul I am sorry, I do not mean to hurt him; but this girl, this dear deserted girl has occupied my whole heart, and I believe my senses will go quite if I do not hear of her."

Montgomery, who felt himself the excess of that passion which tore the bosom of his unhappy friend, promised, now he became more rational, to go out in search of the object of his solicitude, but Chesterville, who now found his head ach violently, and his pulse beating as if his veins would burst, was first prevailed upon to go to his bed. Montgomery then removed every thing by which he could injure himself if a violent paroxysm of passion, aided by intoxication, should return; and having desired the man who waited on Chesterville to give some attention to him, he set out on a new undertaking of knight errantry, in search of a distrest damsel.

Colonel Chesterville, in the mean time extremely hurt by the wild conversation and indiscreet intoxication of his son, felt every moment's reflection on the present situation of his children encrease the anguish of his mind and diminish the strength of his body. Cold shiverings succeeded each other; he complained that his head seemed to have irons passed round it; and no common remedies gave him any relief. Ethelinde persuaded him however to send for an apothecary; who having understood from her that long fatigue and extreme anxiety had preceded the complaint, sent him a composing medicine; and Ethelinde, after sitting two hours by his bed, had then the comfort to find by his breathing that he was asleep. At first his rest was interrupted by sobs and groans; but at length he seemed to enjoy calmer slumber; and Ethelinde, quitting softly the side of his bed, retired to her own; where composing herself to rest, since now she knew, as she believed, the worst, her mind was soothed by the fond image of Montgomery—an image which, with her reliance on heaven, rendered her able to sustain her many and unmerited sorrows.

CHAPTER IV

Montgomery was directed by young Chesterville to the house of a person who let lodgings near the Haymarket; where he was to enquire for a lady lately arrived from abroad, by the name of Madame de Lerida. He was told that such a lady had come to town two days before:—"and you Sir," said the woman of the house, "are, I suppose, the young gentleman she expected, and has been so uneasy about? Poor gentlewoman, she speaks hardly any English." Montgomery followed the woman of the house, who went up stairs as she said this, and opening the door of a small dining room, cried—"Here, Ma'am; here's the young Captain come at last." She retired; and Montgomery advancing a step or two, beheld, approaching eagerly towards him, a young and very lovely woman, who, on perceiving it was a stranger, and not him whom she expected, started back, and threw herself into her chair in evident terror and dismay. Montgomery, who guessed instantly that he had been mistaken for Chesterville, approached her, and said in French—"Be not alarmed, Madam, that a stranger addresses you instead of Mr. Chesterville. It is at his desire that I have the honour of waiting on you."

Re-assured by hearing that he came from Chesterville, and by his manner and voice, the fair stranger now ventured, though tremulously, to enquire why Chesterville came not himself! "Alas!" said she, "he promised to be here to receive me; but I found him not; and two long, long days have I waited for him!—yet even now I do not see him!"

Montgomery knew not what to answer. From her languid looks, and the anxious and trembling solicitude with which she enquired after him, he thought her by no means in a situation to be told abruptly of the distress and imprisonment of her lover: yet to impute his absence to illness would probably be more alarming to her tenderness, and if he suffered her to believe it owing to neglect or inattention, it would possibly wound her still more cruelly. Hesitating and alarmed, yet unable to decide on what was best to be done, Montgomery at length said—"The reason you do not see him is, that his father is at present in town, and he feared——"

"He feared!" exclaimed the beautiful foreigner—"Wherefore did he fear? Did he not promise that I should be received by his father—by his sister—and his family—and has he already forgotten that I have hazarded all for him?"

"Believe me, Madam," said Montgomery, yet more distrest by the earnestness of her manner and the tears which filled her fine dark eyes—"believe me you will have no reason to complain of my friend. He loves you with the truest affection; and I have seen him almost distracted at not being able to come to you to-night. Would I could explain to you the barriers which force him to remain at a distance; but believe me, upon my honour, they are not imputable to him: and in a day or two——"

"A day or two! Can he then yet leave me a day or two in this situation?"

"I hope he will not be compelled to do it."

"Oh! my God! there is certainly something extraordinary in this. Are you, Sir, his relation?"

"No, Madam, but I am his friend; and as such I do most earnestly conjure you, for his sake and for your own, to tranquillize your spirit, in the assurance that Chesterville will soon be with you and satisfy all your apprehensions."

"But when?" cried she eagerly and apprehensively. "He promised to receive me, to protect me here. He has broken his word. How shall I trust to him again? Surely, Sir"—and she fixed her penetrating eyes on those of Montgomery,—"surely there is in this something more than I am to know; for unless Henry is greatly changed, it must be sickness or death only that I think could keep him from me: or if he were even on the bed of sickness, would it not be Victorine who should soften his sufferings, and soothe him with affection and pity?" Tears now streamed down her cheeks; she seized eagerly the hand of Montgomery, crying in an animated tone—"Sir, you seem to have an heart, such as the friend of my Chesterville should possess; tell me then, I conjure you tell me, and relieve me from this insupportable suspense—where is Chesterville?—and what has befallen him?"

Montgomery now saw that to keep her longer in this tormenting uncertainty would be equally cruel and useless, he therefore told her, softening the matter as much as he could, that Chesterville had unfortunately been indiscreet and thoughtless, and before his last departure for Gibraltar, had contracted some debts, which being unable to discharge immediately, he had been arrested, and was now imprisoned.

It was some time before he could make her comprehend the terms he used: for having been educated in a convent, she knew nothing of the customs or manners of the world; and found it difficult to understand that, among a people piqueing themselves on their liberty, it was the custom to shut a man up in perpetual confinement, to enable him to pay his debts. At length, however, the nature of Chesterville's situation being explained to her, she melted anew into tears; which Montgomery would not endeavour to stop. But when she had a few moments indulged them, she checked their course, and said to Montgomery, with sudden vivacity—"Well, Sir! since it is so—since my unfortunate Chesterville cannot come to me, have the goodness to shew me the way to his confinement?"

"Not to-night, surely," said Montgomery, much alarmed at the quickness of her manner—"You will not, Madam, think of going to-night?"

"And why not to-night? Wherefore should I lose a moment? Come, I will now immediately prepare myself." She then arose to fetch a cloak; but Montgomery taking again her hand, and soothing her with the most friendly pity, at length persuaded her, though not till it had cost her many tears, of the impossibility of her executing her purpose that evening. She then reluctantly relin-

quished it; but extorted from Montgomery a solemn promise that
he would at an early hour the next day come to her, in order to
convey her to her lover.

He then took leave of her; penetrated with concern for her
situation and with admiration of her beauty and sensibility. He
yet only knew that she was a native of the West Indies, but had
been educated in a convent in Spain, where she had some relations; from whose house Chesterville had taken her in his way
from Gibraltar, in which he passed through that country instead
of coming on ship board; and that (for reasons which he had not
explained) she had been left at Calais, under the care of a brother
officer, a man beyond the middle of life, who had undertaken to
convey her to the lodgings Chesterville had provided for her, after
his arrival in London.

As Montgomery went down stairs, he again encountered the
talkative owner of the apartment, to whom he said—"Madam,
my friend, the husband of this young lady, is prevented coming to
meet her so soon as he expected: have the goodness to see that she
has every accommodation and convenience, and you may depend
on having every expence discharged."

"Why yes, Captain, to be sure I don't at all doubt about that; but
howsever as the lady it seems is a *farringner*, I should be glad to be
sure to have a little item of where I *mid* look for her *frinds* and so."

This request quite staggered Montgomery. To give a direction
to Chesterville was impossible: and his own was improper, as he
lived with Mr. Royston, and much error and inconvenience might
arise from it. For a moment he hesitated; but at length said that
he should be there the next morning, and then would give her an
address to respectable people with whom the young lady was connected. Then, with an aching heart, he left the house; and returning to the King's Bench prison, he reached the apartment of young
Chesterville about nine o'clock. Chesterville was asleep; but at the
noise his friend made in entering, he started up; and seeing him,
cried eagerly—"Well, Montgomery—is she come?—have you
seen her?"

Montgomery then related to him all that had passed: and Chesterville, far from considering that he had brought this unfortunate
young creature into a scene of misery and distress, in which he had
not even the means of supporting her in the necessaries of life,

expressed a wild and frantic delight at the certainty of her being arrived. Montgomery, equally warm in his temper, but infinitely more considerate, attempted not to argue with him on his impetuosity, but agreed to find some pretence for absenting Colonel Chesterville and Ethelinde from the prison the next day, in order to obtain an opportunity of introducing to her lover the amiable object of his solicitude.

Having settled this matter in the best manner he could, he took leave of his thoughtless friend, and went to the lodgings of the unhappy father; who was, he found, in bed, and that Ethelinde had also retired to hers. He contented himself, therefore, with leaving a note to inform them that he had left his friend Chesterville tranquil and reasonable; and requesting them both to make themselves as easy as possible, he promised to be with them early the next day. This done, he went, extremely fatigued and exhausted, to his present home, at the house of Mr. Royston in Harley Street, from whence he had been five days absent. The moment he found that the young man whom he had seen arrested in the street was Chesterville, the brother of his adored Ethelinde, he had determined to hazard every thing for his relief; and therefore though Royston had charged him with several petty commissions, he had neglected them all; and only leaving a note to say he was going into the country for a few days on business, he had departed for Bristol.

On entering the house, he heard Mr. and Mrs. Royston were both out; and feeling himself glad to be released from any attendance on them that night, he went to his own room, where he found a letter from his mother, full of anxiety on account of his unsettled situation, and entreating him to write by every other post, as the only means to lighten to her the uneasiness which, while he remained without any establishment and absent from her, almost overwhelmed her. "Yet," added this excellent parent, "if you were once, my dear Charles, placed to your advantage, the murmurs of your mother at your absence should be confined to her own bosom. Now, I own myself very wretched; and weak and foolish as I know it to be, I am become strangely low-spirited and even superstitious. In my short and melancholy walks, I fancy your father often attends me, and demands of me his son—demands of me wherefore I have taken him from the country for which he himself bled, to throw him into precarious dependence on people unworthy of the trust. Methinks his exalted and independent spirit is rendered uneasy at the idea; and so forcibly has this image pursued me both in my incoherent dreams and waking reveries, that I cannot a moment divest myself of the impression. My dear Charles, in a few, a very few weeks, you will probably know whether the promises of Mr. Royston will be realized; and if you are still only amused with vain offers which signify nothing, return to her whose whole hope is in heaven and you. A competence is ever yours here; and with that I know my son can find content. Where is the lovely interesting young woman for whose sake we both learned to wish for more? You spoke not of her in your two last short letters, and now it is eight days since I have heard. My dear Charles will not surely neglect for a moment to satisfy the doubts and solicitude which have, during this longest silence I ever experienced from him, taken possession of the heart of his affectionate mother,

"CAR. MONTGOMERY."

The heart of the son smote him on the perusal of this, which contained a draft for ten guineas; his mother being always attentive to supply him with money to the utmost extent of her power. Fatigued as he was, he sat down instantly to write to her; and as he never concealed any thing from her, he gave her an account of all that had happened in regard to the brother of Ethelinde, and having explained the reason of his not writing, and spoken warmly of that passion which his mother so generously encouraged, and of the excellent qualities of its lovely object, he sealed his letter and went to bed; beseeching the fabled powers of pleasurable dreams to send to his weary imagination the tender and amiable image of his adored Ethelinde.

Early the next morning he arose, mindful of his promise to Colonel Chesterville to enquire for an attorney, to be employed in soliciting and managing the affairs of his son. But Montgomery, who knew no such person, and hardly where it was likely to meet with one, was compelled to await the levee[1] of Mr. Royston; who having many estates to manage, and being by nature somewhat litigious, was likely to give him immediate information.

1 Early morning general reception; Mr. Royston presents himself to the world as a patron who is ready to welcome clients.

After waiting till the man who ostentatiously called himself his patron had breakfasted, Montgomery was admitted to his study, while he was dressing to go down to the house, where he now took a part with opposition, and fancied that his feeble support of their opponents added greatly to the terror and alarm of the Ministry, who had disobliged him.

"Your servant Mr. Montgomery," was his answer to the first compliment of his young relation. "So!—you have been absent all this time on *business?*"

"I have Sir."

"Well Sir!—You have completed it better then, I hope, than you have the commissions which you did me the honour to undertake for me."

"Commissions, Sir!"

"Yes, Sir, commissions! I did suppose that you would have deigned to have given some attention to the requests made you by me and Mrs. Royston, and to have called, in your walks, on Mr. —— and Mrs. —— and Lady ——, whom, you know, we wanted to see: but other claims—claims from persons more likely, perhaps, to raise you and serve you in the world than I am, have, I suppose, made you neglect *me* to serve other patrons."

Royston, whose caprice was equal to his ostentation, had never talked to him in this way before; and for a moment the surprise of Montgomery prevented his reply. At length his high spirit kindling at the contemptuous manner in which Royston spoke, he repeated with amazement and indignation—"Patrons! Mr. Royston?"

"Aye, Sir; patrons. A man of *my* fortune and interest, let me tell you, Mr. Montgomery, does not always trouble himself with the claims of relationship. I *thought* I might be of use to you: you have found those, I hope, who may be of more."

"I don't know, Sir," said Montgomery, blushing with vexation— "I really do *not* know what *you* mean; and I doubt whether I ought to explain *my* meaning to a man who cancels all obligations by thus——"

"A man, Sir!" cried the pale and mortified Royston, while his lips quivered with passion—"What do you mean by calling me a man?"

"Are you *more*, Sir," said Montgomery contemptuously, "or *less?* When I say a man, I mean a human being of courage, reason, honour, candour, generosity! If I have miscalled you—pardon me."

"I have a fortune, Sir,"—said the enraged senator—"a fortune that sets me above——"

"The feelings and claims of humanity, Sir? If it does, I am sorry for it."

"Why pray now," cried Royston, putting on in his turn the semblance of contempt—"what do you think my fortune may be?"

"I never heard, Mr. Royston; and certainly never thought of enquiring."

"But you can guess, Sir—you can guess!"

"No, really Sir, I have no data on which to form any conjecture whatsoever."

"Hazard a conjecture, Sir, however."

"Perhaps five thousand pounds a year."

"Add two other fives! Mr. Charles Archibald Montgomery—two other fives! and you will even then fall short of the truth!"

"Well, Sir, I congratulate you on the possession of wealth, to which the generosity of your spirit doubtless does so much honour."

"I think indeed it does"—said Royston, stretching out his little white face, and becoming taller upon what he mistook for a compliment—"I rather think it does. You, however, being young, and having seen much of the world among the highlands of Scotland or the fells of Cumberland; or perhaps before you honoured Great Britain with your residence, among the noblesse of Normandy or Picardy;—you, I say, having doubtless an extensive acquaintance and enlarged experience, have discovered persons of larger fortunes and more powerful connections, to whom you make your court."

"Mr. Royston," said Montgomery, with the coolness of a man who despises his adversary too much to be angry—"I am under obligation to you it is true; inasmuch as it is now almost a month since I have inhabited your house at your earnest request. I will not suppose you mean to insult *me*; and to convince you I see your behaviour in its true light, I will tell you, that I have not been to engage the favour of a patron, but to relieve the distress of a friend."

"To relieve the distress of a friend, have you? well that is kind;

and pray, if your secrets are not sacred, what species of distress
may it have fallen in your way to relieve?"

Montgomery was now greatly embarrassed. He had no right
over the secrets of Chesterville; and where he had no hope of
relief from the confidence, could not think of betraying him to a
man so unfeeling, so fond of money and of himself, as Royston.
He hesitated therefore, and only said—"That species of distress
which too often befalls the young and inconsiderate; and such was
some days ago my reliance on your generosity, that, had I not been
undeceived to-day, I should have applied to you for your assistance
to extricate him."

"Really! What you think then that a man of *my* fortune has no
other employment for it, than to lend money to disappointed fortune hunters and distrest gamblers? No, Mr. Montgomery; my
relations you know, who have no fortune, may have some little
claim on my assistance, so far as parliamentary interest goes; but
on my purse—for their friends!—no, no, that will never do!"

"Nor have I, Sir," said Montgomery, "any inclination from
this moment to trouble you for either the one or the other. For
the kindness which you have shewn me, by giving me an apartment in your house, and about half a dozen dinners and suppers,
though they were kindnesses pressed upon me, I thank you;—I
trust that your great fortune is less hurt by such an exertion, than
my feelings by being obliged to a man, who—pardon me—is not,
I find, a man to whom I am fond of owing an obligation. Sir, I wish
you a good day; and shall give you no farther trouble than to send
for my portmanteau this afternoon, which your servants will of
course deliver." Montgomery thus speaking, left the room; to the
great amazement of Royston, who saw the young man escape him
whom he intended to have kept some time longer, for the double
gratification of his pride: first, by insulting him with the supercilious superiority of a patron; and then, by boasting to all the world
how generously he acted in "taking up a relation, who though one
of the noblest families in Scotland, was actually without any support but what was derived from him."

The earlier visions of Montgomery, offered by this connection, had long since vanished. He found that Royston, so far from
being able to procure him an advantageous post by his interest,
was really in opposition, and of so little consequence, that no

attempt would be made by the then Administration to induce him to change his party. But this discovery had been gradually made, and Montgomery knew not, when he had made it, how immediately to disengage himself from Royston, and while he deliberated on what he ought to do, his encountering the brother of Ethelinde in distress, and the subsequent events, had driven every thing that related merely to himself from his mind.

He now, however, left the house; first enquiring for Mrs. Royston (who was not at home), that he might pay her his parting compliments. Since he could not see her, he left a note for her, thanking her for her numerous civilities, and simply informing her, that circumstances had arisen which prevented his availing himself longer of Mr. Royston's obliging offer of an apartment in his house.

Having done this, he dismissed them as much as possible from his mind; and sending a porter from a coffee house for his clothes, he took an hackney coach and went into the Borough; where, at the distance of about a quarter of a mile from the lodgings of Colonel Chesterville, he provided himself with a second floor in the house of a tradesman; and then having called to know how the Colonel and Ethelinde did, and having heard they were tolerably well, though he saw neither of them, as he said he was in haste, he hurried to the apartment of the unhappy Chesterville in the King's Bench prison, to consult with him on the introduction of the desolate and afflicted Victorine, which he had promised her should take place on the morning of that day.

CHAPTER V

The generous and anxious Montgomery found his impetuous friend impatiently attending his arrival. The moment he saw him he enquired eagerly for Victorine. "Have you not brought her? when shall I see her? where have you left her? and why are you so late?" were questions articulated without waiting for an answer to either.

"For heaven's sake, Chesterville," said Montgomery, "for heaven's sake be more calm and reasonable. You know best what reasons you have for wishing to keep your attachment to this young foreigner concealed from your father and your sister; if they are very forcible, is it possible you should not consider the probability there is of its being discovered if she comes hither?"

"I did wish indeed," replied Chesterville, "I did wish that my father might not know yet that I am married, because——"

"Married!" exclaimed Montgomery, "are you married then?"

"Yes, upon my soul I am; and I suppose you think I'm a d——d fool, for it."

"Not at all. If you loved Victorine (or what am I to call her?) you did well to marry her; that is, if her character was such as brought no disgrace on you from the connection; but unless she has a fortune, I own I tremble at the effect which such intelligence may just now have on your father."

"Fortune? not a shilling. She is the natural daughter of an Englishman; her mother, a Spanish West Indian, whose father was a rich planter in Cuba. In the war before the last, the father of my goddess attended his brother, who was wounded, and carried, by a circumstance not necessary to relate, to the house of Don Julian Gomez de Lerida; there both the brothers were kindly entreated by a generous enemy; but the younger, though he survived for some time the wound he had received, became a cripple; and the elder, who was fondly attached to him, procured leave to attend him to Jamaica, as he could not be carried to England; where he lingered some weeks, and then died. The tenderness of these brothers for each other, and their own amiable qualities, greatly endeared them to the inhabitants of that part of the island among the high lands, whither they had been invited to remove on account of the salubrity of the air. Among others who were interested in the fate of the surviving soldier, was the widow of one of the most opulent men of the country. She was not very young, nor very handsome; but she was very tender, very rich, and so truly sympathized with the inconsolable young man on the loss of his brother, that he became sensible of her attention, and was not perhaps entirely indifferent to the splendour of an income of sixteen or twenty thousand a year that his kind widow was in possession of, though he had of his own an handsome fortune, and inherited his brother's, which was also considerable.

"The ladies of the torrid zone have very little prudery about them; and the enamoured widow soon made to the amiable wanderer such overtures as were not to be withstood. He married, therefore; and resigning his commission, sat down in one of the finest places in Jamaica; and losing by degrees all inclination to revisit England, where he had no relations or family, he became a settled inhabitant of an island in which he possessed all the luxuries and splendour that an immense fortune could procure; and his wife, who was fond of him to excess, felt still less desire to see England, where she knew her own consequence would be lessened, and where she apprehended that a thousand hazards would be incurred of losing her husband's heart by the attractions of European beauty. It was her business therefore to render his present home as pleasant as possible, by collecting the best society, and by every variety of amusement which could there be procured; but loving him as she did, she was not free from the fatal attendant of excessive passion, jealousy; and though conscious that it might produce the very evil she apprehended, she could not always help teizing him with suspicions, and fatiguing him with reproaches and ill humour.

"The first four years of their marriage brought them three children: the youngest died soon after its birth. As the other two grew up, their father was very desirous of procuring for them an English education; but their mother could neither resolve to part with them, or to go herself to England; and after a year or two of debate, it was at length settled that a learned tutor should be procured in England for the boy, and a governess well accomplished for the girl. The lady, now near fifty, dreaded extremely the appearance of this accomplished governess, tho' she had taken care to instruct her English correspondent to send her one who should not have any pretensions to beauty. To find one who was without those pretensions, was more easy than to discover a well educated and sensible person, willing to undertake a voyage to Jamaica. At length the daughter of a deceased officer, pleasing in her person, but not handsome, who had received an excellent education, and was capable of teaching what she had learned, was found, who consented to go; and a tutor being also procured by the very high terms offered, they arrived at the habitation where their instructions were required.

"As the governess was certainly not a beauty, and was found very advantageous to Miss, the mama was for a few weeks tolerably contented: but the yellow-eyed monster at length seized her with cruel violence; her husband, himself a military man, felt pity for the indigent daughter of one who had lost his life in the service; he felt compassion for a young woman, compelled by her situation to quit her friends and her native country for a precarious dependence on strangers so far from home, and he felt respect for her talents, and for that strength of mind which enabled her, under such circumstances, to exert them. All these considerations gave to his manner, whenever he addressed Miss Milward, a tenderness which his wife, who was always watching him, construed into love; and though she could not immediately resolve to dismiss the governess by whose instructions her daughter profited so much, yet she made her husband so very uneasy by dark hints when they were in company, or by open reproaches whenever they were alone, that he grew weary and disgusted; and though he had still so much gratitude and affection for her as to be unwilling to quit her entirely and return to England, yet he found himself so worn and harassed, that he determined on making a short excursion to Cuba, to visit his old friend Don Julian; with whom, though he had not seen him for eight years, he had still continued at intervals to correspond.

"To this plan his wife dared make no opposition, lest he should adopt one less supportable to her; nor was she sorry to have him for a time removed from the dreaded attractions of Miss Milward, little imagining that an object would be thrown in his way infinitely more dangerous.

"Don Julian had a daughter, who at his former visit was about nine years old; she had since been sent to Spain, and received her education in a convent, and within two months had returned to her father, whose only child she was, to be married to the son of the Governor of Cuba, a Spanish Grandee. To this little ugly, but proud Spaniard, Donna Anthonietta had an invincible aversion. Though very dark, she was extremely handsome; for with the most expressive eyes, she had the finest black hair, the most pearly teeth, and the loveliest shape that could be imagined. Sprightly gaiety was the character of her countenance; yet she could throw into it the most bewitching tenderness. With all these outward attractions, she had more knowledge than most Spanish women; and as much spirit and vivacity as is to be found on the other side

the Pyrenees. As she was soon to be married, she was under very
little restraint; and the English gentleman soon became so great
a favourite, that she could not live without his company, and
took very little pains to hide her partiality from others, while she
wished he might himself perceive it, and of course she succeeded.
Mr. Harcourt was a very young man when he married, and was
now not thirty. He had a fine person, which, though not improved
by eight or nine years residence in an hot country, was yet handsome and interesting. To the daughter of his host—an host to
whom he had been so much obliged, he paid every attention; but
still only the attention and admiration which a married man, and
her father's friend, could with propriety express towards her; but
her affection for him, animated as it was by the vivacity of her
character and country, soon broke through every restraint which
European virtue or European customs might have produced, and
Harcourt had soon to reproach himself with having betrayed in
the tenderest point the confidence placed in him by Don Julian,
and broken the laws of hospitality towards his friend.

"Nobody however seemed to perceive the terms they were
upon; for the little Spanish lover, her intended husband, had so
good an opinion of himself, that he never supposed it possible for
an Englishman, or for any man, to supplant him. Nobody therefore was uneasy at Harcourt's long stay in Cuba but his wife, who
had twice sent over a yacht he had built to fetch him, and had twice
had the mortification to see it return with excuses that he yet staid
at the pressing instances of Don Julian.

"The unhappy Mrs. Harcourt had by this time learned that the
Spaniard had a young and beautiful daughter, and all the agonies
of jealousy seized and tormented her. Again she sent a pressing
message to her husband to return; but the tenderness and beauty
of Anthonietta had now attached Harcourt to her with a passion
equal to her own; and she was besides in a situation in which he
could not bear to leave her to encounter the rage of an incensed
father, and perhaps the revenge of a disappointed lover, who only
waited the arrival of some papers from Spain to complete their
marriage. Anthonietta, who determined never to become his wife,
now pressed her English lover to elope with her; but this, fondly
as he loved her, he could not determine upon immediately. He
dreaded the effects such a step might have on her father; who,

though of a milder temper than the Spanish creoles usually are, was jealous of his honour, and adored his daughter, on whose approaching illustrious union he greatly prided himself. Nor could Harcourt divest himself of all concern for his wife; who besides the tie their children had formed between them, had no fault but that of not being young, and of being too fond of him. Distracted by his love on one hand, and these reflections suggested by honour on the other, he yet hesitated, though the circumstances of Anthonietta became every day more critical. At length her tears and entreaties conquered; and he determined to go with her to Spain, as he could not carry her openly to England; and leaving her there in safe hands, to return to Jamaica, and make all the atonement he could for his error, by fulfilling the duties of a father and an husband.

"It was extremely difficult to contrive this: but at length, by means of the captain of a merchantman on whom Harcourt had conferred great obligations in the way of his employment, Anthonietta was with her anxious lover conveyed ship-board, and carried to Barcelona, where she was soon afterwards delivered of my little Victorine. Harcourt, while his tenderness encreased for her mother, could yet not divest himself of affection for his son and daughter in Jamaica, nor of pity for *their* mother, whom he had left in ignorance of what had become of him, and with whose misery he could not help reproaching himself. He wished therefore to return to them; and Anthonietta reluctantly consented, on his promise to stay only a twelvemonth, and then to rejoin her in Spain, and to take her finally to settle in England. She went into a convent during his absence, and called herself his wife. She had taken care to conceal from her unfortunate father where she was; but all the circumstances of her flight were by some means known to him; and he had not only loaded her with his malediction, but had disinherited her, and sent for the son of his sister from Spain, on whom he intended to bestow all his great possessions.

"This news reached the tender unhappy Anthonietta soon after the departure of her lover. Had he been yet with her, she could have bore every thing with resolution, but he was gone—gone perhaps, for ever! and her love, her pride, her filial affection all equally suffering, a lingering illness ensued. The hope of hearing from Harcourt, of hearing that he meant to return to her, awhile supported her; but letters were long in coming; they were sometimes lost; and what did come she fancied were cold, and rather civil than tender. He spoke with fondness and with anxiety indeed of the little girl he had left in Spain; but with pride and pleasure of the two children whom he had rejoined in Jamaica. Of their mother, he said little or nothing; yet Anthonietta fancied that habit and gratitude had conquered a transitory and vague attachment to her, and that she should see Harcourt no more.

"Violent in her passions, the mortification, the misery this idea inflicted, was too much for her; and in a sudden fit of enthusiasm, the offspring rather of disappointment than of piety, she put herself into the hands of artful priests, who persuaded her that her salvation could no otherwise be secured, than by renouncing for ever the wicked heretic who had seduced her, giving all she possessed to a convent, and taking the veil. The money and jewels she had of her own were considerable enough to tempt the avarice of these people; and having once possessed themselves of the confidence of the fair reluctant penitent, they at length prevailed upon her to send from her even the child on whom she doated, and of whom one of the priests undertook the charge, and boarded it in a remote convent; while the unhappy mother, calculated neither by temper or habit for the life she was now thrown into, lingered yet a few months, and then died, leaving Victorine, about fourteen months old, to the mercy of the persons who had torn the infant from her bosom, and persuaded the wretched parent it was a crime even to wish to see this innocent creature, and to bless her in her last moments.

"She wrote however a short billet to Harcourt, which was probably never delivered; and to her father, Don Julian, who, in consequence of receiving it, ordered the child a small pension for its support, and gave a large endowment to the convent where his once loved, but renounced Anthonietta, expired.

"Victorine was long supported by the pension—so long indeed as to become old enough to enquire into and to gather from her mother's papers, which were among her clothes, and from a female negro servant who had attended her mother, and was yet about her, all the particulars I have related. At length, however, the pension paid by her grandfather suddenly ceased. He was dead. His nephew succeeded to his fortune; and the deserted Victorine was left without resource, unless she would become a servant in the religious house where she was brought up. She wrote to her father, Mr. Harcourt, but had no answer. In all likelihood, her letters never were sent: and the distress of this lovely and unfortunate young creature could only be equalled by the acuteness of that sensibility with which she felt her misfortunes. In the same convent were educated the two daughters of a merchant at Barcelona: they had conceived some degree of affection for the desolate orphan; and prevailed on their father whose notions were somewhat enlarged by commerce, to suffer them to invite her to their house when they returned home. There, as I was at Barcelona some weeks, I saw this lovely girl, living as a dependant, and not always kindly treated. The Spanish merchant, to display his own generosity and liberality, related to me some parts of her history. I found that her father was an Englishman, and with a degree of Quixotism for which you will laugh at me, I fancied I could assist her applications to him for support. On this subject we had frequent conversations, and her beauty, her understanding (which is of the first rank, though she has been brought up in ignorance), her innocence, and her calamities, all conduced to inspire me with the most violent passion for her: but native dignity and prudence defended her from all the artful means that passion inspired to obtain her consent to go with me to England; till at length finding myself, or fancying myself unable to live without her, we were married by a Spanish priest, according to the rites of her religion, and set out together across France for Calais; where I was prevailed upon by an old brother officer, whom I met there (waiting for his wife and daughters, who were coming from the South of France), to leave her in his care, and reconnoitre my situation in England a little, before I exposed her to the inconveniences to which he knew I should too probably be liable. I was to take a lodging for her, and write to her at Calais. I did so, and sanguinely fancied that I could conceal my being in England equally from my father and my creditors, till some method could be found, though I knew not what, to settle my affairs. How I was deceived, my dear Charles, and all the distressing sequel, I need not repeat."

Montgomery had listened attentively to this narrative. "Well, my dear Harry," said he, when his friend had concluded it, "there is nothing to be said to all this but that we must either conceal the matter wholly from your father, or manage so to inform of it as to soften the shock it may give him. I will attempt for you either the one or the other; not the less willingly because I suspect that your Victorine is a relation of my own."

"Of your's? How do you mean?"

"Why some parts of my genealogy, highly as I value myself on my family, are a little awkward. My maternal grandmother, after she became the widow of one of the family of Douglas, who was my mother's father, lived many years with one of the Lord Pevensey's; the elder brother of him who still enjoys the title: by him she was the mother of two sons, who bore the family name of Harcourt, and to each of whom he gave ten thousand pounds. They both went into the army. The younger died in consequence of wounds received at the Havannah, and the elder is certainly the Mr. Harcourt to whom your Spanish fair one owes her birth; so that she is, you see, my cousin."

"Oh God!" exclaimed Chesterville, in a transport, "is it possible? Perhaps then, my dear, dear Charles, you can help me in applying to her father. A new ray of hope—of hope the most flattering to my imagination, darts upon me from this most fortunate discovery. Do you ever hear from Harcourt? Are you in habits of friendship and correspondence with him?"

"It is now, I think, near two years since my mother last heard from him. He then mentioned that his son was solicitous to come to England, and that he believed he should himself accompany him. My mother, as I recollect, immediately answered his letter; and has often expressed her surprise that she has not since heard of him: yet she observed that if he were dead, the decease of a man of so large a property would be known, or if he had arrived in England, she should certainly have heard of him. For these reasons we have concluded that our having no letters from him was the effect merely of that indolent disposition which grows on the inhabitants of the tropical climates when they have passed the meridian of life."

"Well, but you will write to him for me, will you not; and forward to him a letter of mine and of his daughter's?"

"Assuredly I will. I will do more, and prevail on my mother to receive and acknowledge her niece; nay I am persuaded she will want no entreaties of mine; for to a mind the noblest and most generous that ever was possessed by woman, she adds the tenderest recollection of her brother, and has a thousand times lamented that their destinies had thrown them so far from each other."

After some farther conversation, it was agreed that Montgomery should persuade Colonel Chesterville and his daughter not to visit the prison that day, under pretence that it was too much for them all, and that it was necessary for young Chesterville to be left alone to collect his thoughts and tranquillize his mind: then, being secure that they would not be with Chesterville that day, Montgomery was to conduct Victorine to her husband; and this being arranged, he went from the prison to the lodgings of the Colonel.

CHAPTER VI

On his entering the little sitting room he was struck with the figure of Ethelinde at a table, on which she leant the arm that supported her head. Her face was pale; terror and anguish were impressed on it. Montgomery hastening to her, she took his hand and said, bursting into tears—"Oh! my dear friends! my father is so ill—so very ill!"

"How! when!" cried the alarmed Montgomery. "They told me, when I called this morning, he was pretty well."

"I thought him so when first I saw him, and therefore sent that message to your enquiry. He had some quiet sleep during the night; he was able to eat a little at breakfast; and he spoke calmly. The apothecary who visited him thought him without fever, and I began to hope another night's rest would quite restore him. But I fear"—(and she sighed deeply)—"I fear indeed I was too sanguine; for about two hours ago, he attempted to write a letter, which he said was on poor Harry's affairs; I entreated him not to do it, lest it should fatigue him; he answered—"Alas! my Ethy, no time is to be lost."—"Let *me* then write it, Sir?"—"No," replied he mournfully, "it must be in my own hand." He sat down, and began his letter; but after he had written a line or two I saw the muscles of his face working; his eyes filled with tears; a deep groan seemed to issue from the bottom of his heart; and he threw away the pen. "I cannot write," said he, in a voice broken by agony—"I cannot solicit these people for pecuniary help. I am heart-struck—and why should I struggle against destiny? why not rather submit to it like a man, than poorly cringe for a remedy to those I despise, and by whom perhaps I may be contemptuously refused."

"Dear Sir, cried I, approaching him, give up for the present every application but to Sir Edward Newenden. I was going on, when he suddenly stopped me—'Ethelinde,' said he, in a voice of less tenderness than he usually speaks to me—'Ethelinde!—shall it be said that to the exigencies of my unworthy son, I have sacrificed the honour of my daughter? Never! Let *him*—Let us all perish first!' The tears and sobs of Ethelinde now impeded her utterance; but she tried however to conquer them, and went on.

"I told my father that nobody would say or think of the odious compromise at which he hinted but the base and worthless, whom it was absurd to fear. He gave me very little answer, only said, with more mildness, that he would not apply to Sir Edward; that he knew not what to do: then he put his hand to his head; complained that it ached, and that he was very cold. I desired him to lie down; and he said, languidly, that he was best on his bed. I led him to it; he still complained of the cold, and desired me to cover him with his great coat. When I had done it, and drawn the curtains round him, I desired to fetch him a glass of warm wine and water: he drank it; thanked me; gave me back the glass; and then catching my other hand, he fell into an agony of tears so terrifying, that I, almost deprived of my senses, besought him to let me send for a physician. 'A physician, my angel!' cried he with a convulsive kind of laugh—'No, no, I have no money for physicians, besides *they* cannot cure a broken heart. Send therefore for no physician; but leave me—leave me now; I shall be more composed presently, and will try to sleep. Don't come in till Montgomery comes; and then awaken me, as I want to speak to him.'

"He held my hand a moment or two longer; his tears seemed to have relieved him; he grew more quiet; and again saying he thought he could sleep, bade me await your arrival in this room."

"Well, my dearest Ethelinde," said Montgomery, attempting tenderly to console her, "what is there in this that should so extremely alarm you? All that you have described is merely the effect of vexation and uneasiness. The first shock of his son's disaster, your father has not yet conquered: but in a few days he will acquire more strength of mind; we shall then set jointly about the release of poor Harry, and all will yet be well."

"Don't attempt to deceive me Montgomery. Alas! it is mistaken kindness. It will only lend new horrors to the fatal event which must, oh God!—which will happen! My father cannot long survive this dreadful stroke; his heart is, I really believe, broken; I see it in his looks, I hear it in his voice, I feel it in his manner, in his sentiments, in his solicitude for me! Oh! Montgomery! ever since this dreadful conviction has overwhelmed my mind, it has been my earnest prayer to heaven that I may die too!"

"You die!" cried Montgomery, whom the very idea had almost robbed of his senses—"You die! loveliest, dearest, most angelic of human beings! Ah! no! you will live, my Ethelinde will live to cherish the declining years of her father, and to bless her devoted, her adoring Montgomery."

As he uttered these words he threw himself on his knees before her, and wildly kissed her hands. She attempted not to take them from him; but softened by grief for her father, and gratitude and love for him, she wept over him, and was roused only by the sound of somebody coming up stairs, from indulging the delirium of tenderness, as pure as it was ardent. The entrance of the apothecary, whom Ethelinde had a little before sent for, obliged them both to recollect themselves; and she went into her father's room, to inform him of his arrival and that Mr. Montgomery was also there.

While she was gone Montgomery asked the apothecary his opinion of his patient. "My opinion is, Sir," said he, "that the gentleman is in a bad way; but to be honest with you, medicine can do little for his relief; the complaint is less in disposition of body than mind, or at least the latter is the effect of the former."

This by no means served to appease the anxiety of Montgomery; and the account the apothecary gave on his return from the Colonel, encreased it. He now hastened to the chamber himself, and approached the bed, where Chesterville held out to him his dry and burning hand.—"My dear friend," said he, as Montgomery took it, "I am obliged to you for coming, but there seems to be no end either to my misery or to your goodness. I have much to say to you!"

"Dear Sir!" cried Montgomery, startled, at the condition of the hand he had taken—"let us, I beg of you, talk of nothing now but of getting you well again."

"And do you know how that is to be done while my mind is in tortures. My dear young friend, if I could communicate to you—but words cannot do it—any part of my feelings—of the sensation I have here," (putting his hand to his heart) "you would know the folly of attempting to live by recourse to common, or indeed to any remedies; you would be convinced that I ought rather to use the small remainder of my days in thinking of the future welfare of her who gave life its only consolation, and to part from whom lends to death its only terror."

Montgomery now attempted to reason him out of his prepossession, but without effect; for though by degrees he spoke with more composure and cheerfulness, the idea of his speedy dissolution seemed to remain in its full force. He spoke much of the irremediable misfortunes of his son, and with yet more solicitude of the situation of Ethelinde. Montgomery with an aching heart endeavoured in regard to the former to inspire the unhappy father with hopes he was himself far from feeling, and of Ethelinde he said—"Dearest Sir, disquiet not thus your spirits, but believe that while I exist my life is hers. I am, it is true, without fortune; possibly I may never possess one worthy of your daughter; but I have youth, health, and strength, and I should glory in exerting them in the protection and support of that angelic creature, whether she deigns, by giving me her hand, to render me the happiest of human beings, or judging me unworthy of such exalted felicity, will only allow me the privilege of being considered as her guardian and her brother."

Chesterville wrung his hands. "Oh generous and excellent young man!" cried he in a faint voice, for his spirits were almost exhausted—"Ethelinde must be yours, for you alone can deserve her. With such a friend, such an husband, she cannot be unhappy, however humble may be her fortune; and in leaving her to your protection I shall die with more tranquillity."

Montgomery, elevated to rapture, yet melting into tears, could no otherwise answer this than by kissing the hand of him who had pronounced, in this sentence, a blessing upon him. After a moment's pause, however, he recovered voice enough to say—"Sacred be the delightful trust! for dear, more dear than my existence, will be the pledge of your confidence!"—then finding he was himself unable to proceed, and that the conversation too deeply affected his suffering friend, he only added, "But it is better not to say more on such an inexhaustible topic for my gratitude, at this time. Dear Sir, for the sake of her whose guide and guardian you must still be, even when you have given her to the happy Montgomery; of her, to whose happiness, to whose tenderness, your life is so necessary; yield not, I beseech you, to these gloomy thoughts; but by resisting conquer them, and let us rejoice in your returning health." Chesterville only shook his head and said—"It will not do, my dear Montgomery, believe me, it will not!"

Montgomery then promising to see him again before night, left him; and though he knew his presence was anxiously expected by Victorine, he could not forbear remaining a moment with Ethelinde—a moment the most delicious he ever passed. He related to her what her father had said; and sanctioned by such authority, she scrupled not, in the tenderest accents, mingled with tears, to avow to him all the softness of an heart which doated on him with an affection equal to his own. Montgomery, too happy to attend to reason, then pressed her to an immediate marriage.—"Wherefore should it be delayed, my dearest love, when our union would not only bless your Montgomery, but would tranquillize the last hours of your dear—I fear I must say, your dying father. He has told me that if he sees you mine, his heart in regard to you will be at ease."

"Ah! Montgomery!" cried the weeping Ethelinde, "and can you urge me to marry while my heart is bursting with agony? would you have the first hours of our union embittered by fear and distraction for a life so beloved; and shall our nuptials, and the funeral of him who gave me being, be kept together?"

"In any other situation," said Montgomery, "I should not indeed urge it; but——"

Ethelinde had now recovered more recollection and presence of mind, and interrupting him, she said—"Montgomery, I have shewn you the weakness of my soul; let me now convince you that it has, if not much, yet some strength to combat against itself: that I love you—fondly and truly love you—I have with too little caution perhaps acknowledged: I do not, however, regret it, persuaded as I am that I shall never repent any confidence I place in you. But fortunate as I should think myself in becoming your wife in any condition of life (however inferior such condition may be to that in which we were both born), yet I must not think of myself but of you; and I must enquire whether it will be indeed a proof of that tender love I bear you, to bring to your arms only indigence and misfortune, and to blast the brilliant promises and prospects of your youth, by uniting you to the sorrows and burthening you with the calamities that are overwhelming my family."

"Gracious God!" exclaimed Montgomery, with all the enthusiasm of passion, "Gracious God! is it possible that you can for a moment suppose such unworthy considerations can check the ardour of a love like mine? Ah! Ethelinde! if you loved as I do—you would know how poor in comparison of it——"

"I believe it," said Ethelinde, whose mind acquired firmness as she felt herself right—"I believe you love me: and without that persuasion I could not, I think, have lived till now. It is natural for you to fancy that in the success of that love you will find all happiness, but it is just in me to represent to you, both for my sake and for your own, that the consequence of marriages made under such circumstances is too often misery—misery created by the very tenderness which the parties retain for each other."

"Impossible!" cried the impetuous Montgomery, "that it can be so in my case! To be the husband—the beloved husband of my Ethelinde! what evil can reach the man who shall be so exalted above the rest of his species?"

"The evil, my dear friend, of seeing her you love in poverty, in misfortune—"

"But my health and strength will be exerted to avert that poverty, to guard her against those misfortunes."

"And do you think then that I could bear to see Montgomery, the descendant of so many heroes—himself the worthiest, the most truly noble of his race—degraded for my sake to the abject condition of labouring for bread, or humbling himself to the drudgery of a mechanic? No, my dear Charles (added she, her tears now refusing to be restrained), no! I can part from you—I *think* I can part from you: at least I am sure I can die—but to give you instead of a blessing, only a burthen, and to entail wretchedness on a life which may otherwise be the boast of your family and the glory of your country?—Never! never can we be united unless our destinies amend—and of that there is no prospect! We will, at least I *hope* we shall, still remain the tenderest of friends—but never think of marrying."

Montgomery, charmed by her genuine tenderness, yet alarmed by the firmness of her manner, while the excess of his passion would not suffer him to attend to the justice of her objections, now renewed his supplications; but she would not either give him a promise to name their early marriage to her father or allow him to press it at their next interview; and, finding her at length faint and overcome by struggling at once against her own affection and his vehemence, he left her; charging her to take care of an health so precious to him, and gently, yet with tears, reproaching her for the coldness and calmness with which she repressed the most violent and tender passion that ever glowed in a heart of sensibility for the most perfect work of heaven.

He then went to the less discreet and yet more unfortunate young creature who had, with less consideration, united her destiny to that of the poor prisoner; and, as he pursued his way, reflection on their condition brought the truth and justice of what Ethelinde had said on the probable inconvenience of such a marriage full in his view. "What will become of them?" said he as he recollected their situation—"They have no money for their daily support, and I am afraid the poor Colonel will suffer from a deficiency for himself and Ethelinde, if his illness lasts long. In the state he is now in, I cannot disclose to him the marriage of his son, yet how is his wife, poor young creature, to be supported? and what will they do? to whom can I apply, or what remedy can I administer to their necessities?" Before his active and generous mind had found any resource for them, he arrived at the lodgings of Victorine; who, as it was now between three and four o'clock in the afternoon, had long since given up all hopes of seeing him; and had abandoned herself to the emotions of horror and despair, which from the vivacity of her spirit she felt with uncommon violence. It was with difficulty he could calm her enough to venture to take her out, so extremely had she been agitated; at length however he led her down stairs in order to put her into an hackney coach, when they were met in the passage by the landlady.

"Your servant, Captain," cried she, dropping him an half curtsey; "so the lady is going out I find?"

"Yes, Madam," answered Montgomery, somewhat surprised—
"Have you any commands for her or me?"

"Why as to that, Captain; I *likes* for my part to speak plain and
above board, and the long and the short of the matter is this: this
here young *farringner* may be, for all I *knows* I am sure, a *parson* of
credit and that, or she may not be. I *stands* a little *partickler* on the
credit of my *ous* and doesn't much care to *av* lodgers as *beent* of *car-
reter*, so I should be obliged to you, Captain, to inform me whether
she is your lady indeed; or if so be you would acquaint me where
I may make *enquiration* after your *frinds* or *hern*, it would come to
the same thing."

Montgomery, without perfectly understanding the language in
which this harangue was delivered from the fine powdered, curled,
and bedizened figure before him, yet comprehended that it meant
to express doubts of the safety of the money she was to receive for
the board and lodging of his desolate charge. He should not, he
thought, do away these doubts by naming the King's Bench prison
as the residence of her husband; and hardly knowing what answer
to give, he said—"I thought, Madam, the person who took your
lodgings for this lady satisfied you in all those particulars."

"No such thing though, Sir," answered the landlady, whose
countenance expressed yet more displeasure—"and I don't think
proper to go on no longer without a little sort of satisfaction."

"Well Madam, what satisfaction do you expect?"

"Why, Sir, what I usually *has* in these here cases, where I take
strangers and that as *beent* recommended by my own *frinds*, is a
week's *arnest*; and Miss have been here now a matter of five days at
board, and have had the best of every thing; and you know I have
seen none of her money yet; and if I goes to speak to her she falls a
crying; so, this morning, thinks I, I'll get Mr. Grinly, our lodger up
two pair of stairs, to speak to her, being he can *parler vous* and that;
but when he began for to question her upon who she was and so,
she never so much as answered him good, bad or indifferent, but
fell a crying all one as when I spoke to her myself, and ran away like
a crazy body and locked herself into her own room."

"Well Madam," said Montgomery, who now began to see that
it would not be safe or proper to let Victorine remain with such a
woman, "I believe the most satisfactory method for us both will be

for me to pay you now for the week's lodging and for the board, and to seek another abode for the lady."

"As you like, Sir. To be sure I should be glad to be paid; and as to my lodgings, I've never no fear of not letting them to people of quality and that, being that they——"

Montgomery, dreading a new torrent of impertinence, then enquired with some impatience whether he might go into the parlour to settle the account; and being shewn in by the landlady; he desired her to take a pen and ink and make it out. This she instantly did; charging two guineas for the lodgings, two more for the board of the poor languid young creature who had hardly eaten a morsel of any thing but bread during her stay; and having by other articles run up the whole amount to five guineas, she delivered it with a smirk to Montgomery; who, though convinced of the extortion, would not wrangle about it, but threw down five out of eleven guineas he had in his pocket; and then assisting Victorine, who understood nothing of what had passed, into the hackney coach, he ordered it to drive to Black Friars Bridge, not chusing the inquisitive and unfeeling woman (who ordered her maid to bring down Miss's box) should hear whither he was going to conduct his unhappy charge.

Though his temper was somewhat ruffled by the behaviour of this woman, he presently conquered his vexation; and though he knew not what in the world he could do with Victorine, he exerted himself to comfort and reassure her: in which he succeeded beyond his hopes; for depending now on soon seeing Chesterville, and totally unconscious of the deplorable situation they were both in, her fine eyes reassumed their dazzling lustre; a smile was restored to her beautiful mouth; and Montgomery, who now perceived those charms which the agitation of her mind and the fatigue she had suffered had at their first interview in a great measure concealed, acknowledged that only Ethelinde had more personal beauty than Victorine. Of her mental perfections he could not judge, though he spoke the French and Spanish well enough to converse with her easily in either language; because her mind had never for a moment been at ease, and she appeared besides to be so very young (not more he thought than fifteen) that he could form no fair estimate of her understanding.

CHAPTER VII

While Montgomery was thus occupied in the service of the younger Chesterville, his sister, who yet knew not half the merit of that noble-minded young man, was overwhelmed by inquietude for her father and by her love for him, which she was more and more convinced she ought not to indulge at the risk of involving him in the ruin of her family. A strange stupor seemed at times to take from the unhappy father the acute sense of his sufferings. He no longer complained of his son, no longer reproached himself, but for the most part took in silence the medicines or nourishments offered to him by Ethelinde, and with a melancholy smile sometimes kissed her hand as she administered them, and sometimes a tear stole slowly down his cheek as his eyes followed her when she left his bed-side. Feeling himself altogether unable to visit his son that evening, and little dreaming how distressing his presence would have been if he could have gone, he said to Ethelinde that he was unhappy that neither of them could see him, and in perpetual anxiety lest he should relapse into the state of wild despair in which they had before beheld him. Ethelinde comforted him with assurances that Montgomery had represented her brother as much calmer and more reasonable; and for that night he became tolerably easy.

The next day, and again the next, passed nearly in the same manner. Colonel Chesterville, without much encrease of bodily complaint, was sinking gradually under his anxiety of mind; and still preferred the ease he obtained in his bed, and the solitude of his bed-chamber, to the effort which, in the presence of his daughter, he thought himself compelled to make, that he might conceal from her the rapid progress of that internal delay he was himself sensible of; still solicitous, though he knew he must die, to spare her, as long as he could, the conviction that he was dying. During these two days, Montgomery, occupied in finding an attorney to undertake the management of young Chesterville's affairs with his creditors, or in expedients to raise money for the support of him and of his wife, only called twice a day on Colonel Chesterville; who was, as well as Ethelinde, yet ignorant that he had left Mr. Royston, and had fixed himself in their neighbourhood. In the mean time, as the young men were too certain that Colonel Chesterville could not himself visit the confinement of his son, and that Ethelinde would not, without the escort of Montgomery, which he forbore to offer; Victorine remained with her husband, too happy to be with him even in a prison, and careless of the future while she possessed the present felicity of being restored to him.

As some minds, however acute their feelings may have been early in life, become by degrees subdued to the most humiliating situations, and seem hardly conscious of calamities which once appeared too terrible to be a moment endured, so there are others which sink without a struggle, and lose in despondency the power of resistance. Of this class was the spirit of the unfortunate Colonel Chesterville. He had sustained indeed the beginning of his misfortunes with some degree of fortitude; had now softened them by hope, now sought a transient relief against their recollection by the dangerous but seducing amusement to which he was addicted;—but the moment he believed the condition of his son irretrievable, his courage forsook him; and having cast one fearful glance on the possibilities of resource from his elder brother and from Sir Edward Newenden, he found, as he believed, that all failed him; there was only to linger through life under such circumstances as his pride and his affection rendered equally insupportable, or to quit it. To do the first he found impossible, and he now prepared himself to die.

On the third of the visits which Montgomery made to him and his daughter, he fancied that he saw in him a more threatening change than he had before perceived: his eyes were sunk and hollow, his forehead and temples tense and of a deadly sallowness, and his voice was weak and tremulous. When Ethelinde for a moment left him, he said, as he sat in an easy chair in the little dining-room—"Montgomery, I am going fast. I thought to have been of some use to poor Harry, but there will be no time for it; I shall be released by death from my troubles! My poor boy must probably await the same release from his prison." Montgomery was in no condition to answer him, and after a short pause, to recover breath, he went on—"I *did* think of writing to my brother; and I began a letter to him which I could not finish. He has a large and expensive family. It may not be in his power—it may not be in his inclination to assist my son; yet I have sometimes been tempted to try, because I would not willingly leave any thing undone; and he may say, perhaps, that I injure his family by not giving him an opportunity to rescue so near a relation from the disgrace of a prison; yet upon the whole, I believe it is better let alone."

Montgomery, who had often wondered that an application had not been made to Lord Hawkhurst on behalf of his nephew, eagerly caught at this hint.

"Let me go to him, Sir; I beseech you do. I am sure if he knew Chesterville's situation he would interfere. He is reckoned a good-natured man—a man of honour, and of feeling."

"True, my good friend; but he has a wife; a woman so imperious, so expensive, that my brother has no will of his own, nor any money, if he had that will, to employ in the assistance of his friends; then he has, you know, six daughters, all brought up to expect titles when they marry, and a son, the very son of such a mother. From my unconquerable dislike to her, and my brother's implicit obedience, we have long been on no other terms together than that of common civility. Shall I now solicit him for pecuniary assistance? Oh! Montgomery, I cannot."

"Indeed, Sir, I must take the liberty of thinking you wrong," said Montgomery. He then urged so many reasons why the experiment should at least be made, that Colonel Chesterville at length gave a reluctant acquiescence; and it was agreed that Montgomery should the next morning wait on Lord Hawkhurst, and represent the situation of his nephew. This being determined upon, Montgomery departed, more wretched than ever from the encreasing sorrows of his adored Ethelinde. He was too well convinced that her father could live but a very few weeks, he doubted even whether a very few days would not put an end to his existence. Her brother was not only imprisoned, but from the enquiries made by the attorney whom he had employed for him, his affairs were even more desperate than his father had imagined; and he was without the means of supporting himself or the unfortunate young woman whom he had, in his improvident love, brought over to share and encrease his misfortunes. Montgomery himself had expended in his service more than half of all he could at present command, and he knew not where to have recourse for a supply without distressing his mother, of which he could not sustain the idea.

Such were the corrosive reflections which filled his mind, when in the evening he called at the coffee-house in the neighbourhood of Harley-street, where he had ordered any letters that came for him to Mr. Royston's to be left.

He found one from his mother, filled with the tenderest solicitude for Ethelinde, and hinting that if her son could content himself to share, with the woman he loved, his mother's moderate income, that mother would embrace them both with transport, and be happy in the happiness of her son. He kissed, in a transport of filial gratitude, this testimony of his beloved parent's true affection, and without much curiosity for any thing else, he opened another letter, which to his great surprise ran thus:

Dec. 18th, 17—.

"If you had not been always as insensible as you are irresistibly charming, there would have been no occasion for me to have wrote what you must have seen. Ah! Montgomery! I little thought you so cold. You cannot fail to know who now addresses you, though you have been wilfully blind to a thousand tender proofs of my attachment. You must want money. Accept of the enclosed; and let me at eleven o'clock to-morrow, at——, in —— street, know, that you are not displeased with this small proof of regard from her, who hopes there is no occasion for her to sign any other name than

your devoted Friend."

In a piece of silver paper enclosed in this billet was a bank note for five and twenty pounds; which, as well as the letter itself, Montgomery contemplated for a moment in the utmost astonishment. He was so little conscious of his own personal attractions that he had not the least idea of having been particularly noticed by any woman; nor could he at all guess who was so well acquainted with his occasion for money, and so liberal both of that and of her character. He puzzled himself with conjectures to no purpose; he thought he had somewhere seen the hand-writing, which there seemed to have been no pains taken to disguise; but it was merely a confused idea; and he could fix on no person likely to have sent

such a letter, though his name both in it and on the direction left
him no reason to suppose it could be intended for another. He
was by no means disposed to keep the appointment; but wearied
himself with plans how he might return the present, which he had
determined not to accept. Having however no talents for intrigue,
and his whole soul being occupied by his concern for Ethelinde, he
determined to consult young Chesterville on this puzzling business, and returned to what only was near his heart, the relief of
Ethelinde, and the execution of what he had now his mother's
as well as her father's consent to—their immediate marriage. He
went that evening no more to visit her; but to the prison of her
brother, where he related to him what he had done among the
lawyers in the course of the day, deplored the encreasing illness
of the Colonel, and told him the arrangement they had made for
his going the next day to Lord Hawkhurst. Young Chesterville,
who had now had time to reflect seriously on his present situation,
seemed to hear him with more gratitude and with more attention than usual, and to feel with deeper concern the situation of
his father; but Montgomery, though he wished to make him feel
keenly, which the volatility of his temper sometimes prevented,
by no means desired to rouse his sensibility as to throw him into
one of those agonies of frantic passion in which he had once or
twice seen him; and therefore when he had gently told him the
worst of all he had heard, and what seemed to offer some prospect of remedy, he turned the conversation, and as Victorine, who
sat with them, knew not English enough to understand them, he
related the circumstance of the anonymous letter, and put it into
Chesterville's hands.

Chesterville, having read it with attention, returned it, and said,
with a smile—

"Upon my soul, Charles, you are a lucky fellow. How much did
your inamorata enclose to you?"

"A bank note," answered he, "of twenty-five pounds; which I
want you to tell me how I can return."

"Return! why, would you be such a devilish fool as to return it?"

"Certainly I will."

"You will! And pray why so?"

"Because I detest a woman capable of acting with such indelicate freedom; and will neither meet her nor accept of her money. "

"Hey dey! Mama's maxims I see still stick by you as if you had never moved out of the nursery. My dear Charles, is it possible such a handsome, sprightly fellow as thou art, can have more prudery than an old maid, or more hypocrisy than a parson?"

"I think I have neither, Chesterville; but you, who know my heart is devoted to your sister, can you suppose I can give a thought to a woman of intrigue, or feel for such a woman any thing but antipathy and disgust?"

"Ti tum ti ty, ti dy di dum—very fine indeed! and as well said as if you had taken it out of one of our sentimental comedies. Keep the money, dear Charles; be advised by me; keep the money, and visit the lady. How can you be so cruel as to let such a loving tender soul die for you, as I dare say she will!"

"Pooh!" cried Montgomery, hurt at his lightness of mind, "I ask not for your advice about the lady, I only ask if you can tell me how to return the money. "

"I wish," cried Chesterville, "I could get out of this cursed place, I would go to the appointment for you, and I dare say the generous fair one would be so pleased with my knight errantry, that, as I am not a very ugly fellow myself, I should have a few bank notes showered upon me."

"This is sad trifling, Harry," said Montgomery; "and if your wife understood you, which she luckily does not, would be worse than trifling. Prythee be serious if it be possible; and since you either cannot or will not give me any help in this business, let us drop it, and talk of your father. I do not wish to shock but prepare you; he is so ill that you ought indeed to be prepared for the worst."

Chesterville was one of those characters which feel acutely, but feel only for a moment; and whose temper, equally thoughtless and sanguine, never considers consequences, or despairs of evading them. He now shed tears for his father, then reproached himself for having been the origin of his illness; now tried to persuade himself that he was not so incurably ill as Montgomery represented him, and then that his illness was the consequence not of vexation, but of some constitutional decay. Montgomery, whose generous heart felt for the inconsiderate and unhappy son, as well as for the dying father, watched, with painful solicitude, all these varying passions as they passed thro' the bosom and influenced the behaviour of young Chesterville. He wished that the scene which he must inevitably pass through might have its effect in regulating his future life, but he could not think without anguish of the terrors that must embitter that life if his mind was for ever haunted with the idea of having killed his father by the most dreadful of deaths—a broken heart.

The innocent Victorine, who comprehended not why she was prevented from seeing this father and this sister, now in the most pathetic terms besought her husband to let her go and assist his sister in attending on his father. "Alas!" cried she in a *patois*[1] dialect, between French and Spanish, which she accustomed herself to use to her husband, who understood the latter imperfectly—"Alas! I never knew my own father, but indeed I shall love your's! and if he knows how much I always have loved you, he will let me be his daughter." Montgomery, who knew that to hazard such a discovery would be to hasten the inevitable event he so much dreaded, soothed her into the relinquishment of this project; but agreed with young Chesterville that he would settle with the Marshal of the prison, so as to get leave, with an attendant to guard him, that he might see his father whenever the latter desired it; and having furnished his friend, who could not bear to ask the Colonel for money, with two guineas out of the five he had in his pocket, he took his leave for the night, and retired to his own humble apartment extremely fatigued; yet forgetting every inconvenience in the reflection that the day had been passed in the service of Ethelinde.

CHAPTER VIII

The next day Colonel Chesterville grew still more languid; and Ethelinde, excessively alarmed, waited impatiently the arrival of Montgomery, as she now, unexperienced as she was in illness, fancied that his end was rapidly approaching. A universal tremor seemed frequently to seize him; his voice was hollow and feeble; and he was so weak as to be liable, on the least emotion, to faint away. His servant, an old soldier who had followed him in all his

---

1 A non-standard version of a language; often refers to a local dialect or native uneducated form of speech; it may combine languages. It is also used as a distinguishing class marker.

fortunes, and who had frequently seen the approach of death in its various forms, thought it now necessary to apprize Ethelinde of the imminent danger of his beloved master; but this the honest veteran, when it came to the point, knew not how to set about. He adored his young lady. How could he shock her, situated as she now was, by intelligence so fatal. "I can never do it," said he, as he opened the door of the room where she sat; "I shall kill my dear young lady." He looked at her, however, a moment in silence, and his eyes filled with tears when he considered how friendless she would be left. Ethelinde, who was at that moment sitting at the window, which she now and then opened to watch for the appearance of Montgomery, turned suddenly towards him; and perceiving his agitation, said—"O! Philip! what is the matter? For God's sake tell me! Is my father worse?"

"Don't be frightened, Miss," said the affectionate creature, "pray don't be frightened; Master is not worse, I believe; but—oh, Miss, he is bad enough, too bad, I fear, for either of us to have much hope of him."

Ethelinde, whose spirits were now in a state to meet every evil half way, instantly fancied that her father was dying; and springing across the room, she was opening the door that led to his, when Philip stopped her—"Oh! dear Madam," cried he, "have patience—pray have patience. Indeed my master is no worse that I know of. I left him a minute ago in a quiet sleep, but indeed, Miss Ethy, he is sadly changed within these last two days, and I hope—I hope I shall not frighten you; but indeed, indeed I am afraid he will not live many days more."

Ethelinde, now understanding that Philip wished rather to prepare her for some sad catastrophe, than to announce any tidings of lately encreased illness, stopped and sat down, but as if she had now understood this fatal intelligence for the first time, she fell into an agony of tears.

"Oh!" cried she, "where is Montgomery? why comes he not to support me at this dreadful moment; and without him how am I to endure it?"

Philip attempted in vain to appease the violence of her sorrow. "Ah! Miss," cried he, "pray don't take on so; it does poor master no good; on the contrary, I'm sure it would half break his gallant heart if he knew it; and for that noble lad, young Montgomery, he deserves that you should take care of yourself that you may live to reward him."

The simple eloquence of Philip, however, served only to make Ethelinde weep the more; but the poor fellow, while he wept with her, thought more of vindicating his own tears, than of drying hers—"Yes, Miss," continued he, "if ever there was another man as good as my poor master, 'tis Mr. Montgomery. He's just the same considerate, kind gentleman about servants. Yesterday, as he went down, he met me at the stairs foot—'Philip,' said he, looking at me with a face full of concern, 'Philip, what do you think of your master?' 'Ah! Sir!' said I, shaking my head, as who should say I think bad enough of him. 'Indeed,' cried he, for he understood me, 'he is indeed very ill! Philip, I must send him a physician; and till I do, I know the dear, young lady above stairs, and you will take all the care you can of him; but,' said he, just as I was going to answer him, 'methinks you look ill yourself, my old friend; will you accept this from a man who loves a soldier much, but a faithful servant more?' and, Miss, he put a guinea into my hand. I would not have taken it, but he said—'Come, come, no scruples. While the Colonel, your master, is ill, you cannot ask him for money; and perhaps you may want a few shillings to keep up your spirits in the fatigue of sitting up. I shall be affronted if you do not take it.'"

Thus ran on the zealous domestic; till Ethelinde, roused from the indulgence of those tears which flowed equally in grief for her father and tenderness for her lover, fancied she heard her father stir. She stepped softly in; but he heard her, and said languidly— "Ethelinde, my angel! I feel myself very faint, yet fancy I should be better if I could sit up."

Ethelinde, now calling to the servant, ordered for her father a glass of cordial wine; a few bottles of which Montgomery had sent for him the evening before. Philip then assisted him to rise, and led him into the little dining-room; where he was hardly placed in the easy chair before he fainted away.

Ethelinde, though she had twice been witness to the same alarming incident, was now in an agony of terror trying to restore him; but before she could succeed Montgomery arrived. He beheld with extreme pain the condition of Colonel Chesterville, and the alarm of his angelic daughter; who, while his servant supported him, chafed with trembling hands his pale and death-like temples and forehead. After a moment he opened his eyes; and seeing Montgomery, he held out his hand to him, saying—"My dear friend, you are come to be a witness to one of the conflicts between me and death; yet a few more and I shall trouble you, shall agonize my suffering Ethelinde, no longer."

Montgomery now tried to speak cheerfully. "You will be better, Sir—this was mere weakness. I have brought a physician to see you; you have neglected having good advice too long; do not, I beg of you, express reluctance, but gratify me in admitting him; he waits below."

"If it will gratify you, my dear Montgomery, I certainly will let the physician come up; but do not, Ethelinde, my love, fancy that because I admit him I have any dependence on his science, however skilfull he may be. I know I cannot live; but you may be the better prepared, by hearing from him how long it will be before my sufferings will be at an end."

Ethelinde, in mute but poignant sorrow, stood behind his chair when Montgomery and the physician entered. He was a man of feeling and judgment; but seeing at once the situation of his patient, he would neither give flattering hopes, or shock the beautiful and interesting mourner with tidings so painful. He desired therefore to be alone with the Colonel; who, asking him to be very sincere as to his condition, owned that there was every reason to fear he would not survive above three days. Chesterville, who had long been conscious of this, received the intelligence with firmness, and sending for Montgomery, who had retired with Ethelinde to another room, he desired that immediate means might be taken to procure him a sight of his son. Montgomery then, with the physician, departed; and the latter confirming at the door the dangerous state of the patient, Montgomery hastened to the prison to procure leave for young Chesterville to attend his father. This he at length accomplished; but it was not without difficulty that he prevailed on Victorine to part with her husband, whom she fancied she should see no more. Montgomery, however, having at last appeased her, they set out together, with an attendant sent by the Marshal; and Montgomery dreading the meeting, as well on account of Ethelinde as of her father, went up with him to the room, where she was now on her knees, on one side of his chair, rubbing his hands, which he complained were cold and numb, as if the blood no longer circulated through them. The Colonel held out his hand to young Chesterville, who, shocked at the dreadful alteration that had taken place since he last saw his father, and too conscious that he was himself the occasion, sprung suddenly back, and rushing by Montgomery, would have hastened away. "Whither are you going?" cried Montgomery, forcibly detaining him. "To hide myself," answered young Chesterville, "to hide myself for ever from a sight I cannot sustain. Unloose me, Montgomery! I cannot bear to look at him. Almighty God! I have murdered, I have destroyed my father!"

"Thus it is," said Montgomery, still holding him in the passage whither he had fled, "thus it is that you ever act when firmness and calmness are necessary. Is this a time to give way to such boyish excesses? If unhappily you have given your father pain, forbear to add to it in his last moments; convince him rather that you are become less rash, and let him at least die in the hope, that your future life will be more fortunate than the past."

Oppressed by grief and regret, young Chesterville heard this warm but friendly remonstrance with patience; and suffered Montgomery to lead him back to his father, who was now again so faint as to be obliged to lean on Ethelinde as she held her salts to him. Again he put forth his cold trembling hand towards his son; and attempting to speak words of comfort to him, they died away on his lips, and he could only utter—"Harry! my poor unfortunate boy!"

Young Chesterville now threw himself on his knees before him; and hiding his face, kissed in an agony of passion the hand which his father extended. "Oh, Sir! I deserve not to meet this goodness. I, who have undone you, who have reduced to this condition the best of men, the most indulgent of fathers!"

"We have both of us something to reproach ourselves with; I have not been blameless; but let us rather endeavour, my dear Harry——"

At this moment a noise was heard on the stairs; and Sir Edward Newenden, pale and breathless, ran into the room; but on beholding the scene before him, he stopped short, and seemed unable to express the painful astonishment he felt.

Young Chesterville saw his father quite overcome by the suddenness of his appearance, added to the affecting conversation he was that moment engaged in, and arose from his knees to support him; for Ethelinde, paler than death, seemed herself ready to sink. Sir Edward, whose looks perfectly corresponded with those of the melancholy group before him, was for a moment speechless, his eyes demanded of Ethelinde, not an explanation of the reason of their being where he found them, for of that he was already apprized, but what recent calamity had befallen them; while his own looks were so wild, his dress so disordered, and fatigue and unhappiness so evident on his countenance, that she dreaded to enquire after Lady Newenden or the children.

Colonel Chesterville, feeble as he was, was the first who broke this mournful silence—"My dear Sir Edward," said he, "you are very good thus to visit the prisoner and the sick."

"My friend!" exclaimed Sir Edward, "had I known your situation sooner, the visit would have been more useful, but my own affairs—my domestic affairs—I know not," added he, putting his hand to his forehead, "what I would say; but whatever is my private misery, my present business is to relieve your's."

Ethelinde, who found herself overcome with such a variety of painful sensations, that she feared every moment she should faint, now attempted to leave the room, hardly knowing why she wished it. Sir Edward and Montgomery at the same moment offered to assist her; but she faintly thanked each; said that she would return immediately; and merely wanted air. The eyes of Sir Edward eagerly followed her; but he sat down, and seemed trying to compose himself to hear from Montgomery, or from young Chesterville, particulars of their distress.

Neither however could venture to give him any account in the presence of Colonel Chesterville, who was soon so exhausted, that he desired Philip might be called, and that he might be replaced in his bed. Sir Edward remarked, with fearful solicitude, the extreme weakness to which he was reduced; and saw too evidently that his death was rapidly approaching. When he was gone, he expressed these fears to the two young men. Montgomery confirmed their being too well founded from the opinion of the physician; and young Chesterville bitterly reproached himself for that ill conduct which had, he said, broken the heart of his father.

"Would to God, Harry," said Sir Edward, "that you had had more discretion, or your father less sensibility; however, since it is so, let us not lament, but exert ourselves, let us try whether it be yet too late to take from the heart of the poor Colonel this dreadful weight, and there may then, perhaps, be a possibility of restoring his health."

"Chesterville," said Montgomery, who entered immediately into the feelings of those he conversed with, "perhaps this detail may not be very pleasant to you. I will undertake to inform Sir Edward of what he wishes to know. Perhaps," added he, looking at him significantly, to remind him of the impatience and uneasiness of Victorine, "perhaps it may be as well if you take leave of your father till to-morrow."

"To-morrow," said Chesterville, mournfully; "that to-morrow may never come for him."

"Be assured," replied Montgomery, "that you shall be sent for if any alarming symptoms occur; but I hope and believe the danger not so immediate."

Chesterville then withdrew; and after speaking a few words to his father and his sister, who sat by his bed-side, he returned with his unwelcome attendant to the place of his confinement.

Montgomery then related to Sir Edward the situation of young Chesterville, without however touching on the history of his marriage. Sir Edward appeared extremely hurt to find his affairs so much worse than he had supposed; but took a direction to the attorney whom Montgomery had employed in them; and having assured him that he would immediately set about his relief, Montgomery, who hoped to engage Lord Hawkhurst to assist those generous exertions in favour of his nephew, departed in order to wait on that nobleman; and in a few moments after he was gone, Ethelinde, who found her father had sunk into a quiet sleep, came into the room where Sir Edward remained. The moment she saw him again, she was struck anew with the dejection of his countenance; and still fearing to enquire its cause, she approached and sat down by him in silence.

He gazed at her a moment with so much pity and tenderness, that she was more and more affected, and at length said, in a faultering voice—"You have, I fear, Sir Edward, fatigued yourself too much by your journey to make this visit to my poor father."

"No, Ethelinde," replied he, "this visit is the only one that could give me a moment's relief, and teach me, while I am assisting those

I love so much as I do you and your father, to bear with patience my own incurable wretchedness."

"Good God!" exclaimed she, amazed and alarmed at the tone, as well as the words of this speech, "what is the matter? where are the children? are they well?"

Sir Edward seized her hand wildly, and cried—"My children are well; but they have no longer a mother."

"What can you mean?" demanded Ethelinde. "Is Lady Newenden then ill? Or——"

He hastily interrupted her.—"Lady Newenden is a worthless, a lost, an unprincipled woman. I have left her for ever. Name her not. Accursed be the hour that gave her to me—accursed the blind infatuation which so long prevented my seeing her infamy."

His vehemence of manner, the fire which flashed from eyes usually expressive only of benevolence, terrified Ethelinde so much, that unable to interrupt him, she continued in speechless horror to gaze on his agitated countenance and passionate gestures, as he walked, with hurried steps, backwards and forwards in the room; and then in accents, trembling through passion, he thus went on—

"I was persuaded not to insist on her giving up the visit to that infamous Danesforte. In a moment of weakness I yielded to indulge her. It was perhaps fortunate, or I might have yet been ignorant of my own disgrace, and of her scandalous conduct."

He paused a moment; and Ethelinde acquired courage to say, "surely you have judged too hastily—it is certainly impossible that Lady Newenden can have deserved——"

"Ah! my Ethelinde," said Sir Edward, interrupting her, "you know not the profligacy of such societies as Lady Newenden has of late been admitted into. The purity of *your* mind makes it impossible for you to conceive the unblushing effrontery of a woman who believes that her rank and her fortune entitle her to sport with the ties of duty and affection, and defy the opinion of the world. Ask not particulars; I am, as you well know, of a nature incapable of unfounded jealousy, and I hope incapable of judging rashly of my wife, the mother of those lovely children; but there no longer remains even a hope that I may be deceived. I have quitted Lady Newenden for ever, and have now no other business in this world than, while I redouble my tenderness towards her children, to endeavour to forget *her*. Yes; I have yet one other occupation that interests me—it is to be the friend and protector of her cousin."

At this moment all that had passed at Bristol, all the suspicions Lady Newenden had affected to harbour; and all she had expressed, recurred forcibly and painfully to the mind of Ethelinde; and she foresaw that since matters were come to such extremities between Sir Edward and his wife, the latter would, as an excuse for her own faulty conduct, urge this imaginary attachment of the former towards her cousin, which every thing he did for the liberation of her brother, or the consolation of her father, would at this juncture confirm. A thousand uneasy and distressing reflections passed rapidly through her mind, and prevented her speaking; though her eyes filled with tears, and fixed earnestly on the agitated countenance of Sir Edward, said more than the most expressive words.

He saw that she was greatly affected. "I make you miserable," cried he; "you, for whose happiness I would lay down my life. I cannot indeed console you by my stay; for I have nothing to speak of but misery, nothing to hope for but your compassion. I will go therefore, while I am yet able, and while it may yet save your father or console his last moments, I will set about the emancipation of Harry. God bless you!" added he, passionately kissing her hand; "God bless you! I do not ask you to make yourself easy, because I know it is impossible, but if you would not add to the weight of misery already almost too heavy for me, support yourself, and be as noble in fortitude as you are in tenderness enchanting."

Thus saying, he hurried away before Ethelinde had time to answer. She sat down when he was gone and tried to obey; but the more she reflected on her situation, the more dreadful it every way appeared; and she dwelled on the various distresses that surrounded her till her ideas were bewildered, and she fell into a sort of melancholy stupefaction, from which she was roused only by a summons to her father.

He now took the prescription of the physician, and for a while every other pain was absorbed in the mind of Ethelinde, by considering the hourly change that her father's emaciated form exhibited. What was now administered was a cordial, given rather in hope to render the pains of dissolution supportable, than with any expectation that it was in the power of medicine to delay it.

The intention in some measure succeeded; in a short time Colonel Chesterville found himself revived, and spoke more cheerfully than he had done for some days. The hope of Sir Edward's assistance, though he had declared against receiving it, had its weight; and he rejoiced that he should leave Ethelinde such a friend and protector. Of the late events in that family he was ignorant; and Ethelinde would not wound him by relating them: the Colonel therefore hoped that Lady Newenden, forgetting or repenting of her cruel and unjust suspicions, would receive his daughter, and be to her a sister, which, though it was in its pleasantest prospect not the situation his tenderness would have chosen, was yet, as he believed, greatly to be preferred to the desolate and helpless state in which she must otherwise probably remain. As the world receded from his dying eyes, his resentments were softened or forgotten; and gazing with interest only on Ethelinde and his son, he tried to see what related to them in such a point of view as might enable him to meet, without the agonies of apprehended evil and misery for them, that death, which notwithstanding a transient relief from medicine, he felt to be inevitable.

CHAPTER IX

Montgomery having dressed himself with more care than he usually gave to his appearance, was punctual to the hour on which he had been appointed by Lord Hawkhurst to attend him; for, to avoid delays and excuses, he had desired and obtained permission the preceding day to wait on his lordship.

On his arrival in Saville Row, he was shewn into the dining-room, and informed that his Lordship would immediately be with him. He employed the few moments he was alone in surveying the room, which was magnificent, and in examining the family pictures which hung round it; in most of whom he saw a striking resemblance to features so deeply engraven on his heart, that whatever bore any affinity to them was soothing, and relieved him from the pain with which his embassy was inevitably attended, unused as he was to solicit favours, and ill calculated to brook the supercilious coldness of those who have favours to bestow.

After waiting about half an hour, Lord Hawkhurst entered. He was, in figure and face, greatly resembling Colonel Chesterville: but his manners had less ease, and his countenance less openness. "Mr. Montgomery," said his Lordship, "I beg your forgiveness for having made you wait; but indispensible business detained me."

"I beg your Lordship will make no apologies. I should not, my Lord, have presumed, stranger as I am to you, to have waited on you, if I had not been persuaded that what I have to relate of your brother, Colonel Chesterville, ought to be communicated to you."

"Of my brother, Sir!" cried Lord Hawkhurst—"Do you come from my brother? It is very long since I have heard from him. Have you any letter from him for me?"

Montgomery then told him that Colonel Chesterville was very ill; and on his expressing concern, which however he did not seem to feel, said—"I hope your Lordship will make it convenient to see him, as I am convinced it will be a cordial to him?"

"To be sure, Mr. Montgomery—Certainly—And had I known sooner he was ill in town, I should assuredly have called upon him; but I give you my word of honour that this is the first intelligence I have had of him since he went to Bristol. I will see him this morning. Pray where does he lodge? I think he has given up his house in Cleveland Row."

Montgomery then began to relate the adventures of young Chesterville, whom he had no sooner named than his uncle exclaimed—"A bad history—a bad history I am afraid that young man has made of it. Why, Sir, I am told he has sold his commission, spent the money, and is gone nobody knows where."

"Where he is, Sir," said Montgomery, "is unhappily too well known, and will soon be more generally so." He then described his situation, sinking only as much of it as related to Victorine; and ended with saying that, in order to be near him, his father and sister were lodged in the Borough, where the former lay dangerously ill.

Lord Hawkhurst now found that his fraternal affection was expected to exert itself beyond the trifling ceremony of a visit. He found that money would be wanted of him; and where to get it, or how to part with it, without the concurrence of his wife, he was equally at a loss.

It was less difficult to blame than to relieve. "Upon my word, Sir," cried his Lordship, "I am very sorry—very sorry to hear all this. The more so—the more so, Mr. Montgomery, because I give you my word of honour that my own estate, and the places¹— the places I have the honour to be entrusted with—by my sover- eign—are barely, barely adequate—I say, they are little more than adequate to the support of my house. I am astonished—really astonished at the—what shall I call it?—at the very unfortunate turn—I say the unfortunate turn, Mr. Chesterville has taken. It was always against my advice—always, I give you my word of honour—that he was indulged in expences—I say in expences— greatly indeed beyond—yes greatly exceeding—the expectations his father judiciously—I say judiciously—should have entertained for him. I am sure I wish from my soul—I do indeed—from my soul I wish that it was in my power to aid—that is, to give effec- tual aid to—to remedy the disastrous state which—I say which Mr. Chesterville has unluckily brought himself into—but I give you my word of honour—that it really is not; and I must repeat, that Colonel Chesterville has been wrong, extremely wrong—he has upon my word—and has acted diametrically—I say diametrically opposite, to my advice and wishes."

"However that may have been, my Lord," said Montgomery, who by no means liked the inclination he observed to censure rather than to serve, "I persuade myself you will not suffer your brother to quit the world without having the consolation of seeing you, and of knowing that he leaves in your Lordship a friend to his children."

"Upon my word, Sir," replied his Lordship, "I should be extremely sorry—I give you my word of honour I should be much concerned—greatly so indeed—to appear unkind; and if my going would be of any real use—yet I own it is extremely inconvenient to me to-day—and——"

While he yet hesitated, and continued to meditate an excuse, Lady Hawkhurst, who was going out with her daughters, entered the room to speak to him. She curtseyed slightly to Montgomery; and her Lord, who seemed glad to avail himself of her presence to find a reason for not doing what he had no inclination to do; said— "Lady Hawkhurst, my brother, Colonel Chesterville, is ill, and this gentleman is so good as to come to inform me of it: how are my engagements for to-night? I hardly recollect."

1 Paid positions.

"You cannot go to-night, my Lord; you are to go to Lady —— and Lady —— and the Duchess of ——; or you may escape possibly a moment from one of them, as I suppose you have not far to go to your brother?"

"Well my Lord," said Montgomery, more and more disgusted and discouraged, "perhaps some other day, before it is too late, you may have an opportunity of seeing the Colonel. I conclude I am to give him no positive hope of it; and that as to my friend Harry——"

"Why I give you my word of honour, Mr. Montgomery, it is not at this moment in my power to say how far it will be possible for me to be of the use to him, which unquestionably I would be glad to be of—But really——"

"What does he want done, my Lord?" said Lady Hawkhurst.

"Why Mr. Chesterville has embarrassed himself, as you know I always foresaw; and I am sure, notwithstanding the little attention—I say the very little attention that has ever been, by any part of that family, lent to my opinion—I say, notwithstanding the little deference shewn me on all occasions relative to this young man, I would gladly, I give you my word of honour, contribute to his extrication; but in truth the claims—of my own family——"

"To be sure, my Lord," cried his Lady, taking the speech from him to finish it herself—"To be sure! your own family have, and ought to have the first claim, and I rather wonder that Mr. Chesterville should think of such an application. Pray, Sir," added she, addressing herself to Montgomery, "do not let him suppose that he has any dependance on my Lord. He ought not to have run through his fortune. My son, who has somewhat more pretensions, I think, never made more figure about town than young Chesterville, nor played deeper; and as to my daughters—Lady Sophia and Lady Helen, and Lady Amelia—neither of them have had half the expence lavished on them as Miss Chesterville has. 'Twas all very well if the girl had gone off; but you see it does not always succeed; I find she's not married yet."

Montgomery, at hearing Ethelinde thus contemptuously spoken of, felt the blush of indignation rise into his cheeks, and scorn and anger flashed from his eyes: yet he commanded himself, and answered—"No, Madam; she is now attending, with the most assiduous affection, on her father."

"A good sort of girl indeed, I believe," re-assumed her Ladyship, "The little I ever saw of her, I thought her really very tolerable, and prettyish I think in her person."

"She has every merit, Madam," said Montgomery, "which can render human nature perfect, and beautiful as she is, her mind is ten thousand times more lovely."

The three Lady Chestervilles, who had remained standing behind their mother while this dialogue passed, during which her Ladyship had not herself taken a chair, bridled at this, and each cast a disdainful look at Montgomery. Their mother, who was now more than ever determined to impede any friendship which her Lord might be disposed to shew his brother, answered only by a contemptuous smile, and then addressing herself to her husband, said—"My Lord, shall we put you down? We are going to Grosvenor Square."

His Lordship, glad to find the means of escaping from the importunity of Montgomery, answered that he was ready, and then turning to his visitor, said—"I am very sorry, upon my word of honour, Mr. Montgomery, that I am upon the instant obliged to go out on business that admits of no delay, but will you do me the favour to tell Colonel Chesterville, that I will not fail to embrace— I say I will not miss, he may rely on it, the very earliest occasion to call upon him, and shall sincerely hope to have the pleasure of finding him better. Lady Hawkhurst, I will not detain you; Mr. Montgomery, I wish you a good morning; I am sure you will forgive me; I am truly concerned at being obliged to leave you." His Lordship then departed with his wife and daughters, and left Montgomery to contemplate the force of blood, and the effect of sympathy in a man of fashion.

"Good God!" said he, as he quitted this unfriendly mansion, "is it possible that this man can be the brother of Colonel Chesterville and the uncle of Ethelinde? Can a being so callous; as void of common humanity as of natural affection, be of the same blood? I thank heaven, it is the effect of rank and fortune on the human heart, that I am indigent and obscure, for more worthy in my eyes is the humblest peasant who labours for bread, who has yet the feelings of a man, than this unmeaning, pompous, verbose, unfeeling peer!" Anger awhile occupied the mind of Montgomery; but anguish soon returned to it with accumulated force. He was conscious that Colonel Chesterville was dying; he knew not what would become of Ethelinde; he knew not whether, if he could gain her consent under such circumstances to marry him, he should himself be able to support her; for he was now farther than ever removed from all prospect of an establishment, and from his mother he could not bear the thoughts of taking what she was so ready to give him of her slender pittance. In addition to these fears for the future, was added the acute uneasiness of wanting money even for his support, for by having supplied young Chesterville, and paid the physician, together with the purchasing of some wine and other things which he fancied the weak condition of Colonel Chesterville made necessary, his finances were now reduced within a guinea; and could he have borne to have solicited a recruit from his mother, he was by no means certain it was in her power to have sent it to him.

The bank note which his anonymous correspondent had sent, was in his pocket book; but hurried as he had been by various emotions of uneasiness for persons so dear to him, he had thought no more of it after having once determined to return it, and the sender had never recurred again to his memory. Now, however, he was reminded of her by finding at the coffee-house, when he called for his letters, a second billet in the same hand, reproaching him for neglecting her first appointment, and assuring him that if he did not meet her at the same place on the following day, her anxiety to see him would be of ill consequence both to herself and him. In a postscript was added—"I deem it needless to sign a name to a letter written in an hand which you have seen too often to mistake." Again he fancied he had certainly seen it, but when or where he could by no effort recollect. The threat contained in the letter he disregarded; but his solicitude to return the bank note, which however he might want it he was resolutely fixed not to use, determined him, after some hesitation, to go on the following day to the place named, return the note, and decline any farther acquaintance with the sender.

He returned in the evening, in the utmost depression, to his lodgings; and as he had only painful intelligence to give to Ethelinde, he found himself altogether unequal to the task; but contented himself with seeing Philip at the door, of whom he learned that Sir Edward Newenden had returned in the afternoon, and that in consequence of some conversation which had passed with him the Colonel appeared more easy in his mind, but that he grew gradually weaker, and that Ethelinde had, at his earnest request, retired to bed immediately after dinner.

A very different scene passed at the house of Lord Hawkhurst. His Lordship spent the morning in attending the levee of the Minister and in political negociations. His Lady, before she set him down at the door of the great man's house, said—"Pray, my Lord, who is that young fellow that came with a message from your brother?"

"I know nothing of him. His name is Montgomery."

"He is either very officious," said her Ladyship, "or Mr. Chesterville is very indiscreet. Could he not write? And why must he employ a stranger to bring a message of that sort? But indeed his way of going on has always been very extraordinary."

"I don't know," replied the nobleman—"I think I ought to call upon him though."

"For what?" answered his unfeeling wife—"I don't see the use of it. If he is not very ill there is no occasion for it; and if he is, it will only make you feel uncomfortable."

Lord Hawkhurst, who while his conscience told him he ought to go, yet thought of it with reluctance, listened without conviction to so feeble an argument; but plunging into business for the rest of the morning, he endeavoured to persuade himself that he really had not a moment to spare to visit, in so remote a place, his brother in distress and calamity. His Lady and her daughters, who dismissed instantly from their minds the unpleasant idea of a poor relation, passed some hours in shopping and giving orders for clothes for the approaching winter's birth day;[1] in which all that fancy unchecked by œconomy could invent, was directed to be prepared for them. They then returned to dress for dinner at home; where at six o'clock a large party assembled, The news of the day was discussed, and all the powers of ridicule were exhausted to excite laughter. The young ladies who had been brought up fearlessly to speak on every topic, were the forwardest in pointing out the absurdities or foibles of every character which came in review before them, and the evening concluded with deep play, where

1 A day set aside for celebrations of the sovereign's birthday, in the form, among other things, as an occasion for ostentatious dress.

they betted with as much spirit as their mother. Lord Hawkhurst thought not of his dying brother, or thought of him with so little fraternal affection, that the efforts of his wife to drive him wholly from his recollection succeeded but too well; and her Ladyship and her daughters, who had an ill run of luck, lost in the course of the evening as much money as would have taken from the oppressed heart of so near a relation, the greater part of the concern that was weighing him down with sorrow to the grave. But to lose or win was, in a constant course of play, become a matter of indifference; while to feel for the calamities of others was a vulgar weakness, against which a constant application to the gaming-table is, among many other of its advantages, a sure antidote.

Ethelinde, languishing as she was, had attended the whole day assiduously on her father, and watched with acute anguish, which she yet stifled, the evident progress of death towards this beloved parent. Early in the afternoon Sir Edward came, and informed Colonel Chesterville that he had, in the three hours he had been absent, made such efforts in adjusting his son's affairs, that there were hopes of his being actually released the next day. This intelligence, though it could not prolong that life which was now ebbing fast away, lighted with a gleam of comfort the "gathering shadows of the grave."[1] Chesterville could not thank his generous friend; he could only press his hand, and say to his daughter, who, overwhelmed with gratitude and tenderness, sat weeping by him—"Ethelinde, be it the business of your life to shew to this most excellent of men, that the infinite obligations he is showering on you and your brother, are not bestowed on the ungrateful. I cannot thank him!" He then sent Ethelinde, who was too much affected, out of the room, and put into the hands of Sir Edward a will he had hastily written, in which he had left Ethelinde entirely to his care and guardianship. "I did think, my dear friend," said he, in a feeble voice, "that desolate and deserted as my Ethelinde was likely to be at my death, it were right to leave her in the protection of that wonderful young man who has been to me as a dutiful son,

1 A line that must have struck a chord in Smith as she also quoted it in her sonnet 64, "Written at Bristol in the Summer of 1794," "Here from the restless bed of lingering pain," where she denies that "health and hope" can disperse "the gathering shadows of the grave" when the mourner has despaired from "a broken heart." It comes from Smith's patron William Hayley's "Epistle to a Friend, on the Death of John Thornton, Esq." (published 1780), l. 190.

to her as the most affectionate of brothers. He loves Ethelinde; I believe that her affection for him has been restrained only by her consideration for me; but he is without fortune and without profession, and after having myself struggled through life with all the difficulties and mortifications incident to a narrow fortune, in consequence of a marriage where love alone presided, I think I ought not to encourage, in regard to my dear girl, a marriage yet more imprudent. To you, Sir Edward, I fearlessly confide her. If you can, for her sake, procure any provision for Montgomery I know you will do it, and then will promote her happiness, if it depends, as I believe it does, on her union with that deserving young man."

Sir Edward, though to see Ethelinde happy was the first wish of his heart, and though he felt for Montgomery the truest esteem, could not, however, prevail upon himself to engage that he would endeavour to effect this marriage. Noble and generous as his spirit was, it was yet an effort beyond his strength to promise that he would give to the arms of another the woman he had so long and so fondly adored, at a time too when there was a probability that the dissolution of his own marriage would leave him at liberty to address her himself. Though he was hardly conscious that this latent hope lurked in his heart, it undoubtedly influenced his feelings. He hesitated a moment, when Colonel Chesterville had done speaking, and then said—"My dear Colonel, believe that to the invaluable trust you honour me with, it will be my pride and pleasure to give the same unremitting attentions with which you have watched over your Ethelinde, and that I will make her interest and happiness my first object."

They were both affected. Sir Edward's voice faultered; and as he found that the conversation was too much for the Colonel, and very painful to himself, he abruptly broke it off; and promising to be early with him the next day, departed; Colonel Chesterville yet remaining ignorant that the conduct of Lady Newenden had left to Sir Edward no other hope of happiness than what he could obtain by his generous endeavours to promote the happiness of others, and above all that of the family of Ethelinde, to whom her father believed Sir Edward had no attachment, except that which every man of sensibility and honour must feel for such a young woman so situated.

CHAPTER X

At eleven o'clock the next day Montgomery hastened to the house where his unknown correspondent was to meet him. He was shewn by the person who belonged to it into a dining room, where he had not waited long before a chair[1] was brought into the house, and a female figure issued from it, who was by the same person conducted up stairs, and having entered the room, and taken off the hood which concealed her face, Montgomery with amazement beheld Mrs. Royston.

A sudden emotion of astonishment made him step hastily back. The lady, with the most perfect ease, advanced smiling towards him. "Why are you so surprised, Montgomery? Have you not often been told by my eyes what you now compel me to explain by words? So! you have at length left Miss Chesterville to Sir Edward Newenden, and deign to recollect that there are other people in the world."

"Left Miss Chesterville to Sir Edward Newenden, Madam?" said Montgomery, in yet more surprise; "to what can you possibly allude?"

"Don't affect ignorance of an affair about which all the world talks; and of which I, who have had an interest in watching you, am perfectly mistress. Come, come; we know that Ethelinde Chesterville has been the cause of Lady Newenden's quitting Sir Edward; we know that her brother has got into prison, and her father and she live near him, where you also have taken a lodging, and where you were the favourite of the young lady till Sir Edward came, who means to establish her mistress of his house."

The cheeks of Montgomery glowed with indignation. "Is it possible, Madam," said he, "that you can have listened to, or have believed falsehoods so scandalous? But wherefore detain you? I came hither merely to return this unexpected mark of a preference I am sorry you should feel, and which I am by no means solicitous to preserve. I must beg the favour of you to desist hereafter

1 This is an enclosed carried sedan which allows the identity of the rider to remain hidden.

from the trouble of watching where I am. It is greatly degrading a character which I wish still to respect. We will, if you please, mutually forget this interview, and the circumstances that led to it; and pardon me if I say that before we judge so hardly of the conduct of others, it were well if we were more cautious of our own. I wish you a good morning."

Montgomery was then hastening away, having thrown the bank note on the table; but Mrs. Royston, not easily repulsed, cried— "Stay, Montgomery, one moment. Don't expose me to the agonies of resentment that will know no bounds, remember

"Hell hath no fury like a woman scorned."[1]

"Oh! Montgomery! what must be the violence of that affection which could urge me to go such lengths. Alas! it has made me forget every thing—my honour, my children, my peace!" She then paused, affected to look tenderly on him; and as she found him unmoved by violent declamation, suddenly changed her battery, and dissolving into tears, threw herself on a seat and produced a very affecting hysteric.

But Montgomery, who as well on account of her conduct towards him as her defamation of Ethelinde, considered her rather as a monster than a woman, felt more abhorrence than pity, and telling her that he recommended it to her to be calm and to return home, he resolutely walked down stairs and left the house. Shuddering at the dissolute conduct of this violent and disgusting woman, he felt considerably relieved in having returned her money, and in having escaped, though with only a single guinea in his pocket, from the house and patronage of her husband. He now recollected several singular circumstances in her behaviour towards him, which his ignorance of the world, and the great freedom of behaviour among the veteran women of fashion who frequented her house, had made him regardless of at the time they occurred. He always thought her behavior very disgustingly forward, and had heard that her character had for some years been very equivocal; but she was one of those women who interested

1 First uttered in William Congreve's *The Mourning Bride* (1697): "Heav'n has no rage, like Love to Hatred turned / Nor Hell a fury, like a Woman scorn'd". The slightly altered line was by this time proverbial.

him so little that he gave hardly any attention to what he heard about her; bold, unfeeling, and daring, talking dauntlessly of every thing without understanding, and censuring acrimoniously the conduct of others without having herself either principle or virtue; totally indifferent to her husband, she did not openly ridicule him because her own pride might have suffered from his loss of consequence; having brought him a great estate, she knew he loved money so well that he could not notice her gallantries, lest in consequence of a divorce he should be compelled to return her fortune; and secure in that certainty, she threw out encouragement to every man she liked as fearlessly as she had done in regard to Montgomery, and very seldom met with any so insensible of her favours. She was now no longer young; and had never been handsome; her children, for she had several, she considered only as incumbrances, and restraints, and kept them in the nursery under the care of servants, while she passed whole nights at the gaming table, or in pursuit of some discreditable scheme; and Royston, occupied by his politics or his law suits, blinded by his imaginary greatness or restrained by his real littleness, suffered her unchecked to pursue her own way, taking care only that her expence should not exceed a certain sum, which yet left him to receive a very large portion of the income she had brought him.

Such was the woman whose vice and folly urged her to dispute the heart of Montgomery with the lovely, blameless, tender Ethelinde; and failing in her attempt, to pursue with insatiable malice the innocent and unconscious rival whose attractions had rendered her bold advances so odious in the eyes of a man, that from their first interview, she had beheld with unusual complacency.

Montgomery in returning to the Borough had dismissed Mrs. Royston wholly from his mind, and had thought only of Ethelinde, and of the approaching death of her father. On his reaching the door of the house where she lodged, he saw Philip standing at it, as if watching for him. "Oh Sir!" cried the faithful creature, as soon as he approached, "my master is going fast; but Sir Edward— that dear good Sir Edward, has released the Captain. Thank God my poor master knows that before he dies!"

Montgomery now hastened, in breathless agitation, up stairs; and entering the room, he beheld Colonel Chesterville sitting in his easy chair, supported on one side by Ethelinde, while on the other young Chesterville was kneeling before him; and Sir Edward Newenden stood by, surveying the affecting group with a countenance expressive of the deep interest he took in their sorrow. When Montgomery entered, nobody seemed able to speak to him but the dying man, who taking his hand from his son, held it out towards him.— "Welcome, ever dear Montgomery," cried he, in a voice which seemed to articulate only by the exertion of all the strength he had left—"you are come to rejoice with me in the release of my poor Harry; and to help me—for I, alas! can not do it—to help me to thank this most generous of men, who has taken all its bitterness from approaching death!"

"For God's sake," said Sir Edward, "my dear Colonel, let us hear no more of this; the only thing that is, that can be gratifying to me, is to see you revived in spirits and—"

"If generous, disinterested friendship could disarm the hand of destiny," answered the Colonel, with a placid, though faint smile, "I should still live; but that cannot be, I hardly know whether I wish it."

"Oh! attempt it, for God's sake!" cried young Chesterville, wildly, "attempt it my father—to save from eternal reproach, from eternal anguish, your wretched, your repentant son!"

"Poor boy!" said he, looking at him with the tenderest pity, "I would for thy sake that I *could* live; yet ought not my death to be imputable to thee——and if I am convinced that thy errors are abjured, believe me, Harry, my life will end more happily than it could have continued."

"And *I* shall live," exclaimed his son in a frantic tone, "to be reproached as the monster who murdered his father—such a father too as never man had! Oh! no! no! I cannot be forgiven— cannot forgive myself! It is impossible, for I have sinned even more than I have dared avow! my folly, my rashness, my wickedness, has involved the innocent, and my wretchedness is as irretrievable as it is insupportable!"

He now hid his face in the chair next to him. A faint blushing arose in the pale and sunken cheek of his father; his languid eyes were turned towards Montgomery as if to enquire the meaning of all this; but he had no strength to do it by words. He gasped for breath, and laid his convulsed face on the bosom of his daughter.

Every body was silent; and Montgomery, who hoped that the

secret of his marriage would not now be needlessly disclosed to embitter the last moments of his father, was less able to speak than the rest. At length, as he thought every moment of suspense shortened the fragile life of the unhappy Chesterville, he tried to say something that might give to this inconsiderate speech an interpretation which might at once palliate and evade; but before he could form his words to effect this purpose, a sudden exertion of resolution enabled the Colonel to say, though in a voice broken by convulsions into which this new stroke seemed to have thrown him—"Montgomery, you will not deceive me! If you know to what Chesterville alludes, tell me I conjure you; and tell me ere I die in dread of something worse perhaps than the truth."

Thus called upon, and the request enforced by the speaking though agonized look which Ethelinde cast towards him, Montgomery felt himself compelled to speak—"There is nothing, indeed," said he in a tremulous and hesitating way—"nothing at which you need be thus cruelly alarmed. Mr. Chesterville met in Spain with a young woman, of beauty and of merit; he loved, and has married her. Nothing but his own desperate situation, and your feeble health, could have induced him to attempt that concealment, which his present distress of mind has, you see, involuntarily broken."

"He is married!" cried his father; "Well Harry, let me then hope that you have another motive to steadier conduct. Where is his wife, Montgomery?"

Before there was time to answer this question young Chesterville sprang eagerly forward and prostrated himself at the feet of his father. "If you will but forgive me—if you will but receive her!" He could add no more. Montgomery, trembling at the situation into which his impetuosity had thrown the Colonel, who was now evidently convulsed, and seeing Ethelinde sit down supported by Sir Edward as if she was herself dying, was determined to shorten a scene so impossible to be long endured. "Mrs. Chesterville," said he, "is in the apartment in the prison, from whence, perhaps, it were better to fetch her."

"Certainly," said Sir Edward. "My dear Colonel, do you wish to receive the wife of your son?" He spoke not; but by a motion of his head and hand he signified his consent, and young Chesterville starting from his knees, would have flown out of the room; but

Montgomery stopped him, and holding his arm forcibly, said— "For God's sake, Chesterville, be more like a rational creature, or you will render it impossible for your best friends to do you any good. Are you in a situation to appear abroad? Ought you to leave your father if you were?" Chesterville, convinced in a moment that he was wrong, wrung the hand of his friend in silence, and suffering him to depart, he walked back and sat himself down as tranquilly as he could, by the side of his sister. "Speak, Harry, to your father," said Sir Edward; "and as I trust you have not given him a daughter unworthy of him, explain to him who she is, and prepare him for her reception."

Young Chesterville then, in a low and tremulous tone, related, as briefly as he could, her history, and when he mentioned that she was related to Montgomery, a gleam of pleasure lightened in the eyes of his father—"You need not, Harry, have concealed this from me. You have been indiscreet, but not dishonourable. I forgive you, because you have married a woman of honour; because she boasts of a portion of that blood which warms the generous heart of Montgomery; and because I know too well the force of that passion, which I once felt for that dear woman whom I hope soon to rejoin in Heaven.——Let me leave my blessing, it is all I have to give, to her children!"

"Stay, Sir," cried young Chesterville eagerly, and again falling on his knees, "'till she whom you deign to receive as your daughter can share it with us." At this moment Montgomery entered, leading Victorine. Her husband started up, caught her in his arms, and bade her prostrate herself at the feet of his father. Montgomery, dreading that such a scene might dismiss the feeble life which was so nearly extinguished, would have checked the impetuous eagerness of his friend; but the Colonel said—"I can bear it, Montgomery—It is a last effort—Let me die at least in doing what appears to be my duty." A cordial was now administered; he pressed his hand to his heart as if to stop its violent fluttering, and after a moment's pause, proceeded—

"Receive, Harry, my last blessing; and may my last advice be remembered!—You have married; let your future study be to make up in tenderness and attention to your wife, that want of fortune which now perhaps she does not feel—I charge you with my departing breath to act by her like a man of honour—She is young; I hope she is worthy; try to restore her to her father's remembrance; much is to be hoped for from Mr. Harcourt—As Sir Edward has nobly released you, let him direct what use you shall make of your liberty: and among the new duties which you will have to perform, remember the everlasting gratitude you owe to *him*."——He was now obliged to stop for breath; and the mournful pause was broken only by the sobs of Chesterville, who with difficulty supported the terrified and weeping Victorine. "Another duty," continued the Colonel, "you will share with Sir Edward Newenden and with Montgomery: it is that of protecting your sister; and I charge you, Harry, as you would give peace to my departing soul, consider this as what you are doubly bound to execute. I have only one word to say to you more—May it make a lasting impression.—I have committed numberless follies; fatal ones indeed too many of them have proved; but among the excesses of my youth, and amidst the contagion of very dissolute society, I never rejected the doctrine I was too weak to practice; and though I served not my God as I ought to have done, I never outraged his name. Believe me, Harry, it is this, though heaven knows it is but negative merit, that now enables me to die—to die with some degree of courage; to leave what I best love on earth to the providence of that gracious being, who will, I am persuaded, receive, forgive, and unite me to your mother. You are young—You have, I am afraid, been too much misled—Before you are settled by habit in impious defiance of Heaven, reflect on the last moments of your father; and wait not till you are reduced to the brink of the grave, ere you learn to brave terrors by its rectitude and religion."

Young Chesterville, unable to speak, kissed his father's hands, as if to promise all he desired of him. Victorine, who understood very imperfectly what passed, would have done the same: but he desired her husband to raise her towards him; and taking her in his trembling arms, he kissed her cheek and blessed her; then, after a longer pause, during which he breathed with great difficulty, he turned his eyes towards his daughter, who sat, almost lifeless, by him.—"Ethelinde," cried he—"source of my best hopes on earth!—image of her who is my mediatrix in Heaven!—I die and leave you indigent;—but not unprotected:—that power whom I have too much neglected, has yet pitied *me*; and has softened the horrors of this parting, by raising up for you a generous, a disinterested friend in Sir Edward Newenden. *He* will be your father—and your protector; and you have two brothers who will glory in acting with him—the dear repentant Chesterville, and the noble-minded Montgomery.—If ever it should be your fortune to possess such a competence as may enable you, without cruelty to him, to unite your fate with his, I believe your lot will be as happy as my fondness could wish for you; but if that should never happen, my daughter is too generous to carry poverty and sorrow into the bosom of the man she loves. Sir Edward, to you, as her second father, I bequeath my Ethelinde."——This was said so feebly that it was hardly heard. Sir Edward, whose manly countenance was covered with tears, could answer nothing; while he pressed to his lips the hand of Ethelinde, that Colonel Chesterville had put into his; but Montgomery, who saw his best hopes suspended, if not destroyed, by the injunction her father had lain on her, would have spoken if he could, or if there had been any hope of being heard; but the voice which had yet made another effort to thank him, was stifled by the hand of death; and the ear which had been soothed so often by his generous friendship, was closing for ever. A faint and deadly dew broke out on the forehead of the Colonel—a film covered his closing eyes—his pulse beat no longer—and in a moment after he had pronounced the name of Ethelinde, while still he seemed by the motion of his lips to invoke blessings on her, his gallant spirit fled.

No sooner was Chesterville sensible of his death, than, instead of calmly endeavouring to execute his last wishes by tenderness and attention to his sister and his wife, he started up like a lunatic, and shrieking out that at last it was all over—that he had now killed his father assuredly—he snatched his sword, and was running away he knew not why or whither. Victorine had fallen senseless from his arms on the floor; and Ethelinde, who saw and heard in the deep stupefaction of grief, without having a distinct idea of any thing, gazed without shedding a tear on the face of her dead parent.—"Stop that madman, for God's sake!" cried Sir Edward Newenden to Montgomery. Montgomery ran after him, overtook him on the staircase, and tried to force him back; but he struggled violently against his friend's efforts; and venting on him all the fury he meditated against himself, he would even have struck him, if Montgomery had not forcibly confined his arms. They were however so equal in strength, that the contention might have lasted some minutes, but Chesterville, absolutely frantic, threw his friend from him, and plunging from the top to the bottom of the stairs, he fell against the last baluster with violent force—stunned himself—and lay bleeding on the ground.

Nothing but the confusion this struggle occasioned, could have roused Ethelinde from her mournful contemplation on the countenance of her father. But she started at hearing the voice of Montgomery so loudly contending with her brother; and Sir Edward said to her with quickness—"Recollect yourself, Ethelinde;—my friend, your dear father, is gone!—We can now do no more for him.—Let me hasten you from hence with this poor young woman, who must I am sure excite your pity.—Let me see you in a place of safety—and let me try to calm your brother." At this moment Montgomery ran into the room.—"I believe," said he, "Chesterville has destroyed himself.—For Heaven's sake, Sir Edward, see what is to be done." Sir Edward then seized the hand of Ethelinde, and putting his other arm round her waist, he drew her towards the door; desiring Montgomery to attend to Victorine, who being absolutely insensible, he took in his arms, and with the assistance of one of the servants of the house, carried down stairs, ordering poor Philip, who had been a weeping witness of the whole scene, to attend to the remains of his deceased master.

Chesterville, who had received a violent contusion on his head, was now lifted from the ground, and carried into a little back room inhabited by the people of the house. Hither Ethelinde and Victorine were brought also; where, as soon as the latter recovered, a new terror awaited her. She saw her husband, his pallid face covered with blood, and his eyes closed, and concluding that he was dead also, she relapsed again into total insensibility.

By this time the reasoning and arguments of Sir Edward had prevailed over the torpid sorrow of Ethelinde: he made her feel that it was her duty to exert herself; he assured her that nothing else could prevent the frantic grief of her brother from driving him into some fatal excess, and that tho' at present his wild frenzy had not materially hurt him, there was no answering for future consequences, unless she had courage to interpose between him and his despair. Montgomery, who had been occupied in assisting

Chesterville and his wife, now approached her, and enforced these arguments. Ethelinde could not shed tears; their source seemed to be exhausted; but she sighed deeply, and giving an hand to each of her friends, she said, very faintly— "I will, indeed, do all that is in my power; I will try to do all I ought to do; and you will both assist me, I know:—you will both help to take care of my unfortunate brother and his wife:—you know I cannot stir from hence myself to attend them."

"Not stir from hence?" said Sir Edward—"Why not?"

"Because," replied she, "I will not leave my father. I know he is dead—but till I *must* quit him, I will stay by all that remains of him."

"Indeed you shall not," said Sir Edward.—"Pardon me, if the first exercise of my power as your guardian is to insist on your relinquishing a project so improper, and taking you, together with your brother and his wife, to my own house."

Montgomery, who doubted as little of the honour of Sir Edward as his own, could not oppose, though he could not approve this intention. To Sir Edward's care Ethelinde had been confided by the last words of her father, and nothing remained but to suffer him to exert that protection which he himself had no means of offering.

Ethelinde however still objected to being removed: but Sir Edward insisting firmly on it, and assuring her that Philip had the charge of the remains of her beloved parent, she reluctantly consented to depart: having however extorted a promise from both Sir Edward and Montgomery, that she should see her father once more before he was carried to the burial place of his ancestors. This point being gained, and Chesterville restored to some composure, to which the stupor from the blow and the loss of blood contributed more than all Sir Edward's arguments, an hackney coach was procured, in which Victorine, Ethelinde, and her brother were placed; and Sir Edward entreating Montgomery to give proper orders for the funeral, the expence of which he took upon himself, desiring that it might be such as became the rank and family of the Colonel, he conducted the mournful group to his house in Hanover Square.

CHAPTER XI

Montgomery having seen Ethelinde depart with Sir Edward, her brother and his wife, stayed to direct what was immediately necessary in regard to the remains of his deceased friend, and having acquitted himself of this melancholy duty, he retired, overcome with grief for the present, and sorrowful presages of the future, to his own little apartment; which he would immediately have discharged, in order to remove himself nearer to any place where Ethelinde might for the present remain, but he had no means of paying even for the little time he had been there, till he received another supply of money from his mother.

Absorbed in sorrow for her recent and irreparable loss, Ethelinde had for the first day no power to reflect on any thing else. Her brother, sinking from his furious and ungovernable paroxysm of despair into torpid and immoveable regret, sat for whole hours together without speaking; and then suddenly starting, would shut himself up, and admit neither his sister or his wife into the room. Sir Edward, ever solicitous for Ethelinde, was hurt to observe the effect this behaviour of Chesterville had on her already harassed spirits. He saw her with fruitless anxiety exert herself to inspire her brother with more fortitude; he saw her sinking under the weight of her own sorrow and his; and that she suffered more severely than he did, from looking forward, and from the sad conviction, that though no longer a prisoner he was in fact a beggar, and, without either fortune or profession, had a wife to support, and probably would have a family.

Nothing however could immediately be done; and Sir Edward, wretched as he was in his own situation, gave his attention principally to soothe and tranquillize Ethelinde. After having vainly attempted to dissuade her from the indulgence of an inclination which could serve only to shock her feeling and irritate her sorrow, he accompanied her himself to the room where the remains of her father were deposited; he saw her, without shedding a tear, imprint with pale and trembling lips a last kiss on the cold hand of that dear parent; then with a convulsive sigh she turned away, and was seated more dead than alive in the coach which had brought her thither; Sir Edward supporting her as they silently went together towards Hanover Square. In a few moments however she seemed to have recovered the shock and some degree of recollection and presence of mind were restored to her; she asked, in a tremulous voice, when Sir Edward proposed that the funeral should take place? and he told her, that he was that day going to Lord Hawkhurst, to know if he had any directions to give relative to the interment of his brother in the burial place of the family, near his Lordship's principal seat in Worstershire. "And this," continued Sir Edward, "I should have done sooner, but that I was unwilling Lord Hawkhurst should suppose that it is incumbent on him to exert those offices for his brother now he is dead, which when living he declined. His Lordship's unkindness to your father embittered his last moments. He complained not: but I saw that it sunk deeply into his mind. Now perhaps Lord Hawkhurst may think it necessary to conceal, by funeral parade, the unbrotherly neglect with which he abandoned the latter days of your father; but he shall have nothing to do with it, otherwise than what I am compelled to allow him." Ethelinde could not reply to this. Sir Edward saw her to her apartment in his own house, and left her with Victorine and Montgomery, who was waiting her return; and then his coach carried him to the house of Lord Hawkhurst.

On his arrival he found his Lordship on the point of getting into his chariot; he could not therefore be denied; but hearing that Sir Edward Newenden waited on him on particular business, he went back to his study, and Sir Edward followed him.

"I waited on you, my Lord," said he very coldly, "to desire to hear if your Lordship has any directions to give relative to the funeral of your brother, which is to take place on Thursday in Worcestershire?"

"The funeral, Sir?" said he, affecting or feeling great surprise and concern, "Is my brother dead?"

"Is it possible you can be ignorant of it? Did not Mr. Montgomery some days ago inform you, my Lord, of his desperate situation, and solicit you to see him?—There was then no hope of his recovery, and he has now been dead three days."

The heart of Lord Hawkhurst had not yet lost all its feeling, and his countenance now testified that grief and remorse had seized

it. "Good God!" exclaimed he, and his lips trembled as he spoke, "I
had not, I give you my honour, Sir Edward, the least notion—I say,
that I had not the least idea of his being so ill; none in the world;
and I never was so astonished in my life!—Really it is strange
that—that his—that his son—his daughter—never thought proper
to inform me."

"His son, my Lord, was, as you undoubtedly knew, a prisoner;
his daughter too much occupied by her attendance on him, to be
able a moment to leave him.—They thought, probably, that the
information Mr. Montgomery gave you, would have been sufficient to have excited your brotherly regard, had any remained for
the Colonel. However, my Lord, he is gone, and now wants nothing that can tax the kindness of his family. I thought, as his Execu-
tor, I ought to inform you that he desired his remains might be
deposited with his ancestors; but it is not my intention to give you
any farther trouble." Sir Edward then rising, was leaving the room;
when Lord Hawkhurst in great confusion detained him.—"Yet
a moment, Sir Edward—favour me—I give you my honour I am
really in extreme affliction—Pray tell me—what can I now do?"—

"Nothing, my Lord. The dead cannot be recalled, and your
concern is merely thrown away.—A few days since indeed a little
attention, though it could not have arrested the stroke of death,
would have mitigated its pain; and my poor friend might have left
the world in the hope that the kindness withheld from him would
be extended to the protection of his children.—But now all concern on your Lordship's part is testified too late, and can avail
nothing."

"But his son, Sir Edward," said Lord Hawkhurst, in yet encreasing embarrassment,—"can I contribute now to his release?"

"He *is* released, my Lord; he is at present with me.——If however you will hereafter consider him as your nephew, and assist in
procuring some provision for him, it will be well; in the mean time,
if your Lordship has no commands for me relative to the mournful
office that remains to be performed, I will not longer detain you."
Sir Edward then hastily departed; not without feeling some satisfaction in perceiving that he had left, in the callous bosom of Lord
Hawkhurst, pain which he was not likely soon to lose.

As soon as he was gone, Lord Hawkhurst went up to his wife's
apartment, where the change of his countenance immediately

announced to her and her daughters that something had made him uneasy: and he informed them immediately of the death of his brother, and the concern he felt that its suddenness had prevented his seeing him.

The proud, selfish, and unfeeling woman to whom he addressed himself, had many motives to urge her to stifle and counteract, as much as possible, these emotions in the mind of her husband. She dreaded the expence he might feel himself bound to engage in on behalf of the children of his brother, in order to reconcile his own mind to the neglect of him while he lived;—she dreaded lest Ethelinde should be taken to the protection most natural to offer her, for she was too handsome not to eclipse her daughters, and might too, probably, attract the notice of her son;—and she knew not to what extremes his Lordship might go in making reparation, if once she suffered him to consider it as a duty at all. For these reasons she heard very coldly the account her husband gave her, and then said—"Well, my Lord, but you could not possibly help what has happened.—I am sorry you are so much concerned about it; but I cannot see wherein you are to blame.—You cannot dispose of life and death."

"I wish, however, I had seen him the day Mr. Montgomery called here."

"Of what use would it have been? it would only have made you uneasy: and besides, how could you go to such a place you know, as where he had put himself. Really one has enough to do to attend one's own appointments, and cultivate acquaintance for the benefit of one's own family."

"He was of my own family," said Lord Hawkhurst very gravely: "the only surviving brother of four."

"Well, well, my Lord," said her Ladyship, much alarmed at his earnestness, "you always treated him as such I am sure while it was in your power without hurting your own children; which certainly no one can expect: I wish that you had seen him, since you fancy that you should in that case have been less concerned; tho' for my part I think it is better as it is, as it only shocks one to see sick people, and is besides hazardous to health, and surely quite useless. I hope you will not forget your appointment today at four with the Duke of —— who assured me he would grant the favour you wanted done for young Partington, the lawyer's son; and you know how much my son's election on the probable vacancy depends on his exertion. It wants now only a few moments to four.—Pray, my Lord, don't think of neglecting your appointment."[1]

"I might well be excused, Madam," replied he, "since the arrival of this intelligence. I rather wish to consider what is to be done with the children of my brother."

"Done with them! Why I suppose they'll be taken care of. I dare say he left something handsome; and I am told that they have a great many friends. You know, my Lord, that with such a family as you have of your own, you cannot in reason be expected to do more than assist any other friends they may have." She then rang the bell, and ordered her own carriage to go out with her daughters to buy mourning; and, with the most perfect apathy, left her husband to digest his regret and vexation as well as he could; having given him only to understand, that it was not her pleasure to offer an asylum to his niece, or to make up in kindness to his nephew the neglect his deceased father had cruelly experienced. But tho' she forbade his taking any measures to lessen his regret, she could not prevent his feeling it: the speeches of Sir Edward Newenden had sunk deeply into his mind; and natural affection, the recollection of his parents, the honor of his family, every thing contributed to impress him with concern so poignant, that the usual remedies of plunging into other pursuits, and drowning recollection amid the business and politics of the world, seemed wholly inefficacious. Unable however to bear his own reflections, his Lordship was compelled to have recourse to these remedies: and not daring to do what his heart dictated, which was, to have sent immediately an offer of protection to his nephew and niece, he went forth reluctantly and in pain, to see how far the miserable negociations he had engaged in to promote his parliamentary interest, and the success of the crooked politics by which his wife was ever urging him to promote the interest of his children, would repress the murmurs of his conscience, and obliterate the idea now predominant in his mind—that of his only brother, hastened

---

1 The Duke referred to is Lord Hawkhurst's patron: he has done some favor for the son of a friend and will help to bring the Hawkhurst son into Parliament. What is expected in return is Lord Hawkhurst's fawning presence as a means of increasing the crowd at the Duke's afternoon reception.

towards the grave by his unkindness, and perishing through grief, penury and neglect, in the precincts of a prison, to which his paternal tenderness had led him.

Sir Edward, without waiting for any assistance from the near relations of his friend, saw the last offices performed, and attended his remains to the burial place of his ancestors, where, having seen them deposited with the respect his rank and family demanded, he returned to town; miserable himself, to meet a family equally unhappy. During his absence, Montgomery had been every day with Chesterville and Ethelinde. His remonstrances, mingled with soothing pity, had softened the obdurate grief of the brother, who now began to look forward to his future life: but he had not steadiness enough seriously to contemplate a prospect which offered nothing but darkness and despair. He had no reliance but on Sir Edward; yet was already so much obliged to him, that he dared not expect farther assistance, or bear the thoughts of intruding on his goodness. Utterly without money and without profession, deeply in debt to Sir Edward, and with a wife to support, he knew not on what to determine; and frequently from mere inability to bear his own reflections, he had recourse to the bottle, to obtain a temporary relief from the wretchedness that pursued him.

This was an aggravation of the already insupportable sorrows of Ethelinde, nor could even the attempts of Montgomery to console and re-assure her succeed. She saw herself wholly destitute, and without dependance but on the bounty of a man to whose friendship she knew the most evil interpretation would be given by the world; and which, since his separation from Lady Newenden, she could not with any attention to her character continue to receive. Montgomery, equally indigent, had too long bestowed in attendance on her, that time and those abilities by which only he could hope to remedy the injustice of his destiny: his project of going to the East Indies she heard of no more; and in his anxiety and tenderness for her he seemed to have forgotten the necessity of attending to himself: yet she determined, whatever it cost her, to remind him of it; and to tear herself from him, while her heart was if possible more devoted to him than ever. The situation of her brother gave her more pain than she was capable of feeling for herself; she could not bear to think of his being supported wholly by Sir Edward Newenden, whose fortune, in consequence of the entire separation he meditated from his wife, must soon be much circumscribed; and the sums he had already paid for her father and her brother, she knew there was no prospect of his ever receiving: yet young Chesterville seemed at times so entirely to have lost all that manly fortitude which might yet have retrieved his affairs, and gave way with little resistance to the indulgence of all his former inclinations, that she despaired of every thing that related to him; and gave up the hope she had once entertained, that his marriage might, by giving a new turn to his mind and enforcing the necessity of prudence, become the means of entirely changing his conduct. When the violence of the first shock given him by the death of his father was over, and when the attentive friendship of Montgomery had roused him from the lethargy into which he afterwards fell, his manner appeared to her more wild than ever. Sometimes he talked rationally of his future prospects, and hinted at a project of going to India with Montgomery: but on other occasions he seemed either teized and offended by the solicitude and uneasiness his friend and his sister expressed; or, heating his imagination with wine, he laughed away their remonstrances, declared that he feared nothing but being preached to death; that he had a sure resource against distress, and should do well enough. Poor Victorine, too young to judge of his real situation in a country to the customs of which she was a stranger, wept when she found him unhappy; but, believing it impossible he could be wrong, smiled when she saw him gay; and fancying that with him she could never be sensible of any hardship, or need any other consolation than his affection, she often thought that Ethelinde and Montgomery were unkind to say any thing that vexed him; and instead of aiding their remonstrance, tried only to soothe him into forgetfulness that remonstrances had ever been made, or were in any degree necessary.

Such was the situation of the party at Sir Edward Newenden's town house, when he returned out of Worcestershire from the funeral of Colonel Chesterville; and in a sort of mournful fluctuation they continued above a week. Sir Edward, too well aware of the advantage Lady Newenden would take of his receiving Ethelinde and her family into his house, could not however determine to part with her; nor bear to think that when she quitted him she must be thrown entirely into the protection of Montgomery, and would probably avail herself of the necessity of her circumstances to excuse to herself the imprudence of a marriage where neither party possessed the means of procuring the necessaries of life. His mind, occupied by this idea, by the uncertainty of what he could do with Chesterville, and by his determination to live no more with Lady Newenden, was torn with constant uneasiness, and agitated by uncertainty how he ought to act: while his attachment to Ethelinde, and his fondness for his children, who were now with him in town, and under her care, alone softened with tender sensation the dark and confused chaos which obscured his faculties, while they oppressed his heart.

At those hours when Montgomery was not with them, and when Chesterville and his wife were accidentally absent, Sir Edward would bring his children into the room where Ethelinde sat, and placing himself in another part of it would pretend to be engaged with a book. But his thoughts were not on what he seemed to read, but on Ethelinde; and towards her his eyes were turned whenever he found her not likely to observe him. He no longer struggled to conquer a passion with which he had long thought it a point of honour to contend, but though he was content to suffer all its hopeless violence, he was so truly in love, that her interest, her happiness, her fame, were the first objects of his solicitude; to them he thought he could sacrifice even the delight of seeing and serving her: but when the image of Montgomery —the happy Montgomery arose, when he fancied that he was exclusively possessed not only of her love, but of her esteem and gratitude for his services to her father, his heart rebelled against his reason and his principles; and the conflict was often so violent, that he was on the point of telling Ethelinde the excess of his fatal prepossession, and entreating her to punish him by condemning him to eternal absence. The mournful silence of these meetings was seldom broken but by the sportive questions, or innocent playfulness of the children, who were much fonder of Ethelinde than ever they had been of their mother. One morning while Ethelinde and his father were sitting together, before the family assembled at breakfast, the eldest boy was displaying on the carpet variety of childrens books, which had been purchased for him the day before; and among the pictures with which they were adorned he was pointing out to his brother, a good boy and his mama.

"Yes George, and we had a mama once," said the sensible little Newenden; "but nurse says we must not ask for her now, for she is gone a great way off, and will never love us any more."—"I want mama," cried George; who was hardly three years old.

"Yes," answered Edward, "but mama—poor mama, is taken quite away from us; and now we have nobody to love us but nurse and papa and cousin Ethy."

Sir Edward, who at the beginning of this little dialogue had laid down his book and turned as pale as death, now burst into tears; and running to his two boys, he threw himself down by them, clasped them wildly in his arms, and became so agonized with passion that Ethelinde, who was not less affected, thought it necessary to interpose.—"For God's sake, Sir Edward," cried she, attempting to raise him, "give not way to emotions so useless and so distressing.—Be calm—be composed, I conjure you; these agonies are dreadful; and see how they affect these dear innocent creatures."

The voice of Ethelinde had ever a fascinating power on the heart of Sir Edward; it now owned her influence, but felt only encreasing torment; he looked up as she wrung his hand;—"I affect *you*," said he, "I affect even these unconscious little creatures!— pardon me— I know it is unmanly—to weep like a woman, over the errors of the worthless and unfeeling, who have dishonoured and forsaken me and mine!"—Again his voice faultered, and a paroxysm of grief and sorrow came over him, while he continued to grasp and to kiss the trembling hand of Ethelinde. For a moment she bore in silence these painful testimonies of his perturbed mind; then trying to collect all her courage, she again besought him to be appeased, and to suffer her to take away the children, from whom the sight of his agonies had by this time extorted the most piercing cries of infantine sorrow; and the youngest of them, a little girl who had just learned to walk, hung sobbing on the clothes of Ethelinde, though she was not old enough to understand that she had been abandoned by a mother whom she had hardly known.

"Take them away," cried Sir Edward, "I cannot bear this; but do not stay long from me, for you only can reconcile me to an existence so hateful—so hopelessly wretched." He knew not what he said; and Ethelinde, hurrying away the children to their nurse, returned to him, without having the power to collect her thoughts sufficiently to be able to reason with him.

Victorine and Chesterville entered the breakfast room at the same moment, luckily for Sir Edward, who was by their presence compelled to recall some degree of composure. Their breakfast passed in only such conversation as could not be avoided, and almost as soon as it was over Victorine went to her own room, and her husband went out. Sir Edward was again left alone with Ethelinde; who having been collecting her thoughts and strengthening her resolution during their short and melancholy meal, paused a few moments after the tea table was removed, and then addressed herself to Sir Edward, who, having seated himself on a sopha opposite to her, had thrown his arm over it and leaned his head on his arm, hardly seeming sensible of who was in the room, till her voice awakened his attention.

"Will you, my dear Sir Edward"—said she, speaking in a low and tremulous tone:—"Will you give me a few moments patient attention?"

"A few moments!" cried he, starting from the posture he was in, and fixing his swollen eyes on her face—"A thousand! a million! Oh! would to God my whole life could be passed only in listening to that soul soothing voice—only in gazing on that attractive, that softly bewitching countenance!"

Ethelinde had been two or three times, within the last few days, alarmed and distressed by speeches of the like nature; still, though they pained and confused her, she was willing to understand them only as the tender effusions of that warm and lively friendship Sir Edward had always profest for her.

"You are not patient—you are not composed, nor reasonable," said she, looking very grave—"Therefore it were better to defer what I have to say till another time." She then arose to go; but Sir Edward, hastily quitting his seat, took her hand.—"Upon my soul I am—I will be calm!" cried he.—"Pardon me, dearest Ethy; there are times when I think my reason is failing me; when I feel so wretched that I hardly wish its continuance;—pray forgive me—and sit down."—Ethelinde returned to her seat; he took his on the opposite side of the table; and after another short pause, "Sir Edward," said she, collecting all her courage—"it is I think a fortnight to-day since I saw my father expire!"

"Yes," answered he—"it is a fortnight: but to what purpose would you now recall that distressing scene to your mind?"

"For a purpose which I hope and believe I shall ever invariably pursue, that of recollecting all I have lost in him, and all I owe to your unexampled friendship. Absorbed as I have hitherto appeared in the first of these sentiments, believe me the last has never for a moment escaped me. Conscious that I owe every thing to you; the liberty of my brother, his support, perhaps his life, and what was yet dearer to my bleeding heart, the little peace that soothed the dying moments of my dear suffering parent; nay even the last mournful offices that could be performed for his beloved ashes, I would feign—"[1] She tried to go on, but finding it impossible, stopped and yielded to the grief with which these melancholy images overwhelmed her.

"I promised you my patient attention Ethy," said Sir Edward, whose voice was choaked with sobs; "I revoke my promise, if it is thus you mean to engage it: of what use is this fruitless retrospection, this fruitless regret which tears you to pieces? if you would afford me any pleasure from what I have done, shew me that it has been useful to you, and——"

"Do not revoke your promise," replied Ethelinde, recovering herself by an effort—"no, do not revoke it; but hear me, I beseech you, without minding the weakness which my woman's heart may betray me into, in the course of what I think it necessary, for both our sakes necessary, that I should say, and that you should hear."

Sir Edward, struck at once with the earnestness of her manner and the purport of her words, was silent, and she thus proceeded—

"The subject of your unhappy division with Lady Newenden is so delicate, so difficult to be touched with any hopes of accommodation, that I hardly know how to speak of it; yet let me, dear Sir Edward, conjure you by all your past affection for her, by all the tenderness you feel for your children, by all your hopes of tranquillity hereafter, consider well what you do, when you throw her off for ever, consider whether your anger has not been raised rather by transient and thoughtless indiscretion, than by confirmed and premeditated guilt. Remember the many instances there have been of groundless, unreasonable jealousy, followed by fatal consequences, and ask yourself whether you should ever forgive yourself if your suspicions should be found equally unfounded, and be followed by some deplorable catastrophe."

1 Possibly a misprint for "fain."

"Deception! Suspicion!" said Sir Edward—"Is it possible I *could* be deceived? am I so prone to suspicion? Alas! Ethelinde, far, very far, from being solicitous to learn that Lady Newenden was culpable, I was even mean and dastardly in shutting my eyes. As long as it was possible, I tried, I laboured to deceive myself, but the veil which my affection would to the last have thrown over her indiscretions, had they been merely indiscretions, was forcibly torn away by the daring hand of determined unblushing infamy. Lady Newenden, who shall no longer bear that disgraced name than till I can divest her of it by law, is, be assured, unworthy of your concern as much as she disdains your pity. The wretch who has robbed me of my peace and my children of their mother, has yet another account to settle with me; an account, which will not be the less heavy for its being delayed till my duty to those desolate children is fulfilled by a settlement of my affairs, and till I have done all I can for the estimable part of that family which my wife has disgraced."

There was a sullen and resolute resentment visible in Sir Edward's manner, which made Ethelinde tremble: she still would have urged the possibility of Lady Newenden's innocence, but he spurned the idea when she attempted to renew the subject, and said with impatience—"Speak of her no more, Ethelinde, lest you provoke me to curse her; press me no more on a topic so hateful— I cannot answer for myself."

"Well, Sir Edward, may I then speak of myself?"

"Do, and I will hear you for ever with delight," said he.

"Let me then say, that circumstanced as you now are, all the obligations I am under to you are of double weight. What we denominate the world, made up of persons who have either very bad hearts that prompt them to invent malignant calumnies, or of very bad heads which find occupation and amusement in believing and in spreading them, will, I have no doubt of it, misrepresent your kindness both to me and to poor Harry. Lady Newenden, my uncle Maltravers, and above all, Mrs. Maltravers, who never loved me, will take advantage of it; and while your generosity is imputed to the most unworthy motives, my character will equally suffer." She stopped, hesitated, and after a deep sigh went on.—

"I am well convinced, Sir Edward, that this reflection must have occurred to you; though *you* have never been offended with the remonstrances of Mrs. Ludford, or the sarcastic hints of Lord Danesforte."

"Mrs. Ludford!—Lord Danesforte!—what do you mean?"—

"That both," replied Ethelinde, blushing deeply, "had the cruelty long ago—so long ago as we were at Bristol, to insinuate, that your—your—friendship for me, was improper for you to feel and for me to allow.—"

"Curses light on his infamous head!" exclaimed Sir Edward, starting up, in a new agony of rage and resentment. "How dared he offend your ears with such a suggestion against me. May I perish in unlamented infamy if I wash not away all my injuries in—"

"Hold, Sir Edward," cried Ethelinde, terrified at the vehemence of a man whose temper was naturally as equal as it was excellent—"I conjure you, conquer these useless transports, or it will be impossible for me to disburthen an heart which still, in spite of malevolence and falsehood, feels that it may rest on your honour, and rely on your protection."

"I will be patient," said Sir Edward. "But name not again that detested villain!"

"What has been said when I lived with my cousin, and under the immediate guardianship of my father, is much more likely to be said now; when my cousin is no longer mistress of her house, and when my parent is gone!—for your own sake therefore, my dear Sir Edward, as well mine, it is absolutely necessary that I remove. During this last melancholy fortnight there was some excuse; for the deserted ward fell naturally into the immediate care of her guardian; but now it is time to seek another asylum."

Sir Edward felt the reason of all she urged; but his heart revolted. He could not bear to part with her, though conscious that she ought to go: and still dreading that love had more influence on her resolution than prudence, he was again torn with the conflicting emotions of jealousy, tenderness, grief, and despair.

"And whither would you go Ethelinde?" said he—"for whom would you quit the protection to which you were commended by the dying directions of your father."

"Indeed, Sir Edward, it is too true that I have no asylum. Among many and opulent relations I know of not one who will receive me: yet here I certainly ought not to stay: I cannot stay without being wretched."

Glad that the name of Montgomery was not repeated, of which he was in momentary dread, he said, with more calmness— "I think much of the objection you have raised against remaining with me chimerical; yet if it makes you for a moment uneasy, it has with me all the force of reality. Surely however much may be removed if I send for Ellen. The presence of my sister, of your brother and his wife, ought to silence the most prudish or the most malicious observer. Ellen knows what has happened in regard to Lady Newenden, and will undoubtedly come to me if I now send for her.—Tell me—will her presence make you easier?"

Ethelinde, not knowing how to persist in desiring a removal which she saw would be so painful to her benefactor and friend, and not knowing whither to go or how to remove, consented at length to this plan. Sir Edward instantly sat down to write to his sister; and recapitulating all that he had informed her of in a former letter (to which letter he had received no answer), he pressed her with great earnestness to come to him and to replace in his house the mistress who was to enter it no more. He slightly touched on the situation of Ethelinde, and named her brother and Victorine; but forbore to say that it was principally on the account of the former that he so earnestly solicited his sister's company. To this letter he received by the return of the post the following answer.

Brackwood Down, Feb. 17th. 17—

"Dear Ned,

"I had yours by to-day's post. I had also your former, dated a month ago. 'Twas of no use to send an answer as nothing was to be said. I was always afraid that you would have the worst of it, but I hope you have too much sense to take the matter much to heart. The money is, I think, the worst part of the business; as to the woman, such affairs are so common that I hope you won't care. I saw old Chesterville's death in the newspapers, and was sorry to hear it. To be sure I'll come up if you cannot do without me, though I can do but little good, and the weather is still so open 'tis a thousand pities to leave this place. My horses are all in a fine style, and Meteor leads the field as usual—I wish her Ladyship had run out of the course in the summer, for to go to London now is terribly inconvenient to me: however I will be with you about Tuesday, meaning to set out on horseback after Monday's hunt, and get as far as Dorchester, where I take post-chaise. Till then, dear Ned, farewell!—

Yours truly—

ELEANOR NEWENDEN."

CHAPTER XII

While Sir Edward and his friend waited the arrival of the lady whose letter concluded the last chapter, he listened attentively to the various schemes which Chesterville and Montgomery discussed for the future establishment of the former.

After various projects considered and rejected, it was at length agreed, that to go with his wife to the West Indies in search of her father would be the most eligible plan. Sir Edward highly approved of it, and that no impediment might remain, he signified to Montgomery, that he would supply Chesterville with a sum of money, and endeavour to procure him a commission in a regiment stationed in Jamaica. Ethelinde was much consoled by this arrangement, as she had hopes that Mr. Harcourt, who was reputed to be so immensely rich, would make for some provision for his daughter, and enable his son-in-law to repay his pecuniary obligations to his generous benefactor. Every thing then was done preparatory to the execution of this measure: on the day appointed Miss Newenden arrived. On her first entrance she shook her brother by the hand, spoke to Ethelinde, without much feeling, of her recent loss, and rather roughly rallied young Chesterville on his marriage. "You headlong boys," said she, "are all alike; caught with the first pretty face, you run your heads into a noose that the rest of your life is passed in struggling to get out of. Here's poor Ned, you see, forced to cut his at last, and I suppose in a year or two we shall have you as eager to send your Spanish wife back, as he is to get quit of his Asiatic. You had better by half have brought over a Barb; there would have been some sense in that."[1] Sir Edward was not pres-

---

1 Ellen Newenden speaks in the language of what we today call orientalism and that of a horsewoman who races her horses. By Asiatic she refers to a stereotypical image of the "East" as a place of luxurious idle magnificence; a Barb is the 18th century term for a Barbary stallion prized for its speed. Harry

ent to hear this speech, and Victorine did not understand English enough to be hurt at it. Chesterville, who was capable of rattling as wildly as Miss Newenden, answered her in her own way; and a sort of skirmishing dialogue was usually carried on between them, which would have frequently compelled a smile from any hearers, who had hearts less deeply affected than were those of Sir Edward, Ethelinde, and Montgomery.

Of these, it was impossible to say which was the most miserable: the presence of Miss Newenden by no means satisfied Ethelinde that the world would not equally blame her for residing with Sir Edward; yet whither could she go, or how quit the protection to which her father had consigned her? When Montgomery, who grew so uneasy at her stay in Hanover Square that he could no longer refrain from expressing it, urged her by all the tenderness she had deigned to own for him, and by all his sufferings, to unite her fate with his, and give him a motive for that exertion in regard to making his fortune which he now wanted, she heard him with attention, with tenderness, frequently with tears; but resolutely declined marrying, to carry only indigence and sorrow to the man she loved, and to become a burthen to his mother, who had hardly a sufficiency for herself. Sir Edward had by this time learned that Lady Newenden, in the prospect of marrying Lord Danesforte, wished only that he might obtain the divorce he had meditated; the idea of its being then possible that Ethelinde might be his, flattered the predominant passion of his soul, and he was roused from contemplating a prospect so seducing, only by his tenderness for his children: Lady Newenden was still their mother; and there were moments in which the extreme softness of his temper made him wish it possible to forgive and receive her, whom he had once so tenderly loved, and who was yet endeared to him by those objects of his paternal affection; then he struggled with his reason, and with the sad conviction of her infidelity, to find some palliation of her conduct, and his rage and resentment fell on Lord Danesforte. Nothing but the situation in which on his arrival in London, he had found Colonel Chesterville, had prevented his seeking immediate reparation for the injury he had received from his Lordship. To Colonel Chesterville it was his intention to have applied to accom-

---

Chesterville would have done better to bring back a horse found in Gibraltar than a Spanish wife.

pany him into the field; but his death, and the subsequent distress
and sufferings of Ethelinde, had postponed even his vengeance. It
was, however, so far from being extinguished, that it now blazed
with greater fury than ever: but he carefully concealed his intentions from Ethelinde, who he saw suspected them, and communicated only to young Chesterville the measures he had taken to
obtain, what the laws of honour denominate satisfaction from
Lord Danesforte.

Montgomery usually called once a day on Ethelinde, and
passed many of his hours in the service of her brother. His dejection grew every day deeper and more apparent: sometimes he fancied that the partiality of Sir Edward for Ethelinde, which might
easily be seen even by eyes not sharpened by jealousy, was, if not
returned, at least not displeasing to her; at other times he hated
himself for daring to suspect her; now he determined to execute
his former project of going to India, and now shrunk from the idea
of leaving her in the power of Sir Edward, who, to all the claims
that gratitude gave him over her heart, might soon be in a situation
to obtain her hand. He knew that she esteemed and regarded Sir
Edward as her friend and her benefactor—the benefactor of her
father and her brother; and though he had himself so long gloried
in the certainty that her heart was his own, diffidence of his own
merit rather than any doubt of her affection, made him tremble at
the idea of a long, long separation, in which she would be left only
in the protection of Sir Edward, and when so many motives might
concur to make her forget, or at least sacrifice to her guardian, her
banished and unfortunate Montgomery.

Tormented incessantly with these reflections, his life became
burthensome to him; he no longer pursued any regular plan for
obtaining an establishment; and when Sir Edward mentioned a
renewed hope of being able to procure him a commission in the
service of the East India Company (his first application for which
had failed through the estrangement between him and Mr. Maltravers), Montgomery received the information so coldly, that Sir
Edward could not forbear speaking of it to Ethelinde.—"Believe
me," said he, "I am interested for Montgomery, and will do any
thing that is possible to serve him; but of late he has appeared to
take every thing I have said on that subject rather as an affront than
a kindness. He made himself an application to me for the very post

I have at this time a near prospect of obtaining for him; yet now he seems wholly disinclined to accept it. Ethelinde, I will be ingenuous with you: I believe that the encouragement your poor father gave to this young man not long before his death has destroyed his spirit of enterprise; to quit you he finds impossible: *you* know best, whether unprovided for as he is, you ought to confirm the hopes he entertained; whether you ought, either for your own sake or his, to let him suppose they can be immediately realized."

The changes in Sir Edward's countenance and voice while he made this speech escaped not the observation of Ethelinde, greatly as she was hurt and confused by the purport of it; but her ingenuous nature, incapable of artifice, disdained to affect an indifference which she did not feel; and after a little hesitation, she said—"Sir Edward, I believe you already know, that if I had an independent or even a competent fortune, Mr. Montgomery would be the man to whom I would give it; but situated as we both are, I have told him that we cannot be united, and that the more tenderly I am attached to him, the more resolutely I feel myself able to reject him, and to refuse what would certainly not make him happy; since, were we to marry, situated as we now are, we should feel with redoubled force all the inconveniences of a narrow fortune, or the misery of separating to avoid them. I am not myself afraid of poverty, but much afraid of seeing the fairer prospects of Montgomery blasted by his participating my indigence. I will, with your permission, speak to him on the subject you have to-day named; and I dare venture to say that finally he will not be found negligent of your meditated kindness."

Sir Edward, whose heart glowed with admiration while it ached with the certainty of her steady preference of Montgomery, was ill qualified at that moment to continue the conversation. He left her, therefore, almost immediately; and was soon after summoned to the dining-room by the arrival of Lord Hawkhurst.

His Lordship appeared in mourning, and his countenance expressed something of confusion on the sight of his nephew and his niece, but he seemed struggling to conquer it, and to assume the appearance of cold civility. After sitting a few moments, while, whatever the party thought, none of them seemed disposed to be communicative, Lord Hawkhurst addressed himself to Sir Edward, and desired to be permitted the honor of speaking to him alone. They went immediately into the study, and his Lordship, after a pause, which Sir Edward did not interrupt, thus began—

"Sir Edward, I am well persuaded that you will with the candour, and—I say I am convinced that your natural candour will induce you—to hear—and to hear without being offended, that, which I give you my honor I am very sorry—extremely concerned indeed, to have occasion to trouble you upon."

Sir Edward, though much wondering what could follow such a prelude, coldly assured him that he was prepared to listen, and begged to be honored with his Lordship's commands.

"Mr. Maltravers, Sir Edward, was with me last night; and though I give you my honor nothing is more repugnant to my principles than to interfere—I say, though nothing is more remote from my usual plan than to intermeddle in domestic disagreements; yet really as the matter is represented to me, and as persons are concerned who are related to me, and who even bear my name——"

"Explain yourself, my Lord!" said Sir Edward, impatiently interrupting him, "What has Mr. Maltravers said? and on what has he taken the trouble to address himself to your Lordship?"

"On the unfortunate misunderstanding between you, Sir Edward, and his daughter, Lady Newenden, which he represents as originating solely in you—really, Sir, it is an awkward circumstance to mention—your attachment—your partiality to his (Mr. Maltravers's) niece—who is also my niece—to Ethelinde Chesterville."

Rage, indignation and surprise, stopped, for a moment, the words which Sir Edward would have uttered. "Does Mr. Maltravers dare to affirm so infamous a falsehood?" cried he at length.

Lord Hawkhurst waved his hand in assent; and then pausing to collect his oratorical powers, he spread forth one hand, and laying the other on his breast, went on.—"I am concerned, Sir Edward— much concerned, I give you my honor; I say, I am greatly hurt at the asseverations of Mr. Maltravers, who is much of a gentleman, and my very good friend, on this subject. Palliatives, my dear Sir— palliatives are all we can now apply. Mr. Maltravers seems really solicitous to promote an act of oblivion: he even goes so far as to own that Lady Newenden, irritated doubtless, as is the nature of her sex, by your preference of her relation (a preference either real or imaginary, we will not decide which)—I say Mr. Maltravers is willing to acknowledge, that her Ladyship, piqued as I observed before, *might* possibly resent it by shewing a *little* too much attention to Lord Danesforte: But my dear Sir, do consider the state of facts: her mother, Mrs. Maltravers, was actually with her the whole time, and declares that her daughter was most innocent of every charge which you made against her, when you so hastily and so unkindly left her with threats of pursuing measures which, pardon me, I am sure you must long since have thought better of." Sir Edward was now about to interrupt him, but he said— "Pardon me, Sir Edward; allow me yet a moment to explain, or rather to detail all Mr. Maltravers related to me: he observed then, Sir—I say, Mr. Maltravers observed, that nothing could be a stronger confirmation of the truth of your predilection in favor of Miss Chesterville, than your hastening instantly to London to her; the large sums you immediately advanced for the enlargement of that unhappy and indiscreet young man, her brother (who now by his marriage has completely ruined himself), and your taking her into your house, where I understand she acts as its mistress. Mr. Maltravers (pardon me, Sir Edward, I only repeat his sentiments)— I say, Mr. Maltravers complains, that not satisfied with the large sums you have expended out of your wife's fortune for these purposes, you make her reputation, which is much dearer to her, the victim of this unlucky partiality for, I fear, a very artful young person."

The indignation of Sir Edward was anew trembling on his lips; but his Lordship, who perceived it, again stopped him.—"Yet a moment, Sir Edward—yet a moment of your patience; and I have done. All these charges, my dear Sir—I say all these charges, all these circumstances, will have but an ugly, but a very ugly appearance before the public: I am sure you must, on cool reflection— I say I am well persuaded that on turning over all the relative circumstances in your own mind candidly and coolly, you will allow, that it is best that Mr. Maltravers's offer of a general amnesty be accepted; and an act I say—an act of oblivion on all hands agreed to. I recommend it to you to receive Lady Newenden; I will take care that Ethelinde Chesterville shall be removed to a situation where the affair will not be known: and the world, who are at present, let me tell you; very busy with her fame, will overlook and forget these awkward suspicions, I say——"

Sir Edward could bear any thing better than this reflection on Ethelinde, and his patience, so severely tried, was now exhausted.—"No, my Lord," said he, while fury and disdain animated his features; "say nothing more, I beseech you; for be assured you will obtain no longer hearing to calumny so infamous and proposals so disgraceful. My conduct towards my wife will be justified in another place; it is not to your Lordship, who seems indeed a most prejudiced judge, that I am compelled to give any account of it. As to your niece, my Lord, I should have thought that your paltry desertion of her would have made you blush thus to join in blasting a character which only the malice of fiends could have dared originally to sully. By heaven she is as pure as an angel, and has virtue enough to rescue the rest of the race from perdition. Never shall I be obliged to you, my Lord, while I have a fortune to supply, or an arm to defend her; her father, on his death bed—that death bed where I saw his noble spirit sinking under his cruel relations' neglect, gave his orphan daughter to my care; and never, let the infamous and worthless say what the malice of hell may dictate, never will I give up the sacred trust, or call upon you to relieve me from it; you, who must ever appear to the generous and good,

"The mean deserter of your brother's blood!"[1]

"So much, my Lord, for your Lordship's offer of taking your innocent, your defamed and insulted niece: and as to Mr. Maltravers's part of the message, which you have condescended to deliver, I beg to say in answer to it, that I scorn his ungenerous attempt at retaliation, and that, knowing my own integrity in regard to his niece, I pity, while I must repel once and for ever, his ill-judged experiment to hide the too flagrant infamy of his daughter. If he will apply immediately to myself, he will know more of my intentions about her: your Lordship, I think, will do well to decline appearing again in the negociation." Sir Edward then, without waiting for an answer, left the room; and Lord Hawkhurst, thun-

1 Slightly changed from Pope's "Elegy to the Memory of an Unfortunate Lady," l. 30: "Thou, mean deserter of thy brother's blood."

derstruck with the vehemence of his manner, which his own reproaching conscience secretly justified, immediately quitted the house in confusion and dismay.

END OF THE THIRD VOLUME.

VOLUME IV

CHAPTER I

Ethelinde, though totally unconscious of the purport of her uncle's visit, was extremely hurt at the coolness of his manner towards both her brother and herself. The resemblance he bore to her father encreased the pain which his unkind conduct gave her; but this regret was converted into terror, when Chesterville, to whom Sir Edward, in the first agitation of his spirits, had rashly related the conversation he had held with him, appeared before her, in spite of Sir Edward's remonstrances and entreaties; and with eyes flashing fire, and lips trembling with passion, swore he would that moment go to Lord Hawkhurst and insist on an apology for what he had dared to repeat after Mr. Maltravers. For some moments his rage rendered him so inarticulate and confused, that Ethelinde could not distinctly comprehend the offence of which he complained; but when Sir Edward found himself compelled to explain it, she saw at once all her apprehensions realized, and even exceeded; since the confusion which her brother's application to her uncle must of necessity create, would, instead of stifling a report so injurious to her, more widely and rapidly spread it. Chesterville was, however, as deaf to her entreaties as to the remonstrances of Sir Edward, who insisted very warmly that his interposition was not only needless but improper. An injury received from so near a relation, a wound from an hand that should have been held out in friendship, seemed so insupportable to the fiery and vindictive spirit of Chesterville, that he obstinately adhered to his resolution of seeing Lord Hawkhurst immediately upon it; and all they could obtain of him was to let Montgomery, who had somewhat more influence on him than any other person, attend him.

The young men then went away together; and Ethelinde retiring to her own room, Miss Newenden and her brother were left alone.

"This is a devilish business, Ned," said she, after a short silence. "I am sorry, I think, that you have perplexed yourself with the

Chestervilles. It makes, I can tell you, a confounded uproar; and people think Lady Newenden ill used."

"What people?" asked Sir Edward.

"Oh! all the world that I meet at the riding house or in the park. They say that it is generally understood, your complaints against Lady Newenden are wholly groundless, and originate solely in your wishes to put her cousin in her place. This, I assure you, is the current report of the world."

"I am sorry," cried Sir Edward, indignantly, "that the people you call the world are so malicious and so senseless; but it will make no difference, Ellen, in my attention to Miss Chesterville, whom I hold myself bound in honour to protect as her father."

"Look ye, Sir Edward," cried Miss Newenden, in her sharp tone and quick manner, "I know nothing of love, nor of the fine sentimental stuff sets half the people in the world to make fools of themselves, so I don't pretend to be very quick sighted in such matters; but can you, Ned, lay your hand on your heart; and very seriously and truly affirm, that you have no more partiality for this girl than for any other Miss of your acquaintance; are you no more interested for her than you would have been for Sophy Carlisle or Lucy Althorpe if they had been left under your care?"

"Certainly I am more interested," said Sir Edward, with emotion, "certainly I am much more interested. I loved the Colonel; he had only one fault to detract from a multitude of virtues. He was a man of honour; a man of sense; some of the most agreeable hours of my life have been passed with him, and——"

"And his daughter, his daughter," interrupted Miss Newenden, "inherits all 'her father's wisdom and her mother's charms.' Come, come, brother, it is in vain to deny your regard for her."

"Nor do I," said Sir Edward, angrily, "I rather glory in it. I thought, Miss Newenden, you had more liberality of mind than to join with censorious old women, and envious young ones, in tearing to pieces the character of an innocent person who never can have offended either them or you."

"I join with the cats and the tiffany Misses?[1] not I faith; nor should I have troubled myself to say so much about it now to you, if I did not see you likely to get into a foolish sort of entanglement;

1 Tiffany is a thin gauze muslin; a slang term likening these young women to tiffany; so they are transparently flimsy (shallow). (OED.)

with your wife on one hand, and this girl on t'other. If you like her, with all my heart. I only meant to advise you to quiet the people just at present, by sending her somewhere else. You'll have old Maltravers, and his comely wife, upon you open mouthed; and you'll find it best to take my advice. You know well enough that I give it in mere friendship, and I'm sure nothing else would have made me come up to you now; so don't go to be restive when I coax you to make yourself easy."

She then fancying she had acquitted herself extremely well, left her brother to very unpleasant reflections. He felt more and more the necessity, for her own sake, of parting with Ethelinde; but he could not bear the thoughts of proposing it to her, or even of consenting if she again proposed it, as he saw no other resource for her than marrying Montgomery; he fancied that his love was so disinterested that he could submit to, nay promote any plan that might secure her happiness; but he persuaded himself that in resisting her union with Montgomery, he only opposed what would perpetuate her misfortunes. While contending passions thus distracted him, Ethelinde was taking a resolution to put all end to his difficulties, on her account, by quitting him. She had long seen the necessity of a measure which Lord Hawkhurst's visit hastened; and though she knew not whither to go, she determined to propose several plans to his, to Montgomery's, and her brother's consideration, and to leave them to decide for her; but to refuse with equal steadiness a residence with Sir Edward, or a marriage with Montgomery.

Having brought herself to this determination, and being convinced it was her duty to adhere to it, she prepared to meet with fortitude the disagreeable and painful recital which she expected to hear from her brother and Montgomery when they returned from their visit. Calamity had strengthened her mind in regard to her own sufferings, while it had taught her to feel with keener sensibility for every other person, particularly for those she loved; and in making this resolution the indigence and inconvenience to which it was probable she might be exposed wholly escaped her, while she felt the keenest anguish in reflecting how much her rejection of Sir Edward's friendship might hurt his generosity, and how cruelly her separation from Montgomery must wound his love. These corrosive thoughts she was obliged to brood over in silence, for she had no female friend to sympathize with and console her. Miss Newenden had no idea of pity or affection, and would feel more for a sick horse than for a human being under the severest pressure of mental or bodily affliction. Victorine was gentle, tender hearted, and amiable; but from the difference of her education, and the manners she had been accustomed to, she had no conception of the various species of uneasiness that preyed on the heart of Ethelinde; nor could be made to comprehend why she would not marry Montgomery whom she so passionately loved. The necessity, however, of endurance generally strengthens the power of enduring, (at least till the mind is quite overwhelmed and exhausted) and Ethelinde, having no breast on which to lean, was compelled to exert her own reason, and act from her own principles of rectitude and propriety.

In about three hours after Chesterville and Montgomery had gone out, they returned together. Montgomery, who knew how much the unguarded warmth of her brother frequently distrest her, desired to see her alone in the dressing room where she usually sat. She immediately admitted him; her countenance expressed her anxiety to know the result of the conference they had held, and Montgomery thus related it—

"Be not alarmed," said he, tenderly taking her hand. "Chesterville behaved better than I expected; and upon the whole I am not sorry we saw Lord Hawkhurst. He received us with that sort of air which a great man assumes who suspects that his visitor is come to ask a favour he has no inclination to grant. Chesterville, however, soon made him understand that he waited not on him with a petition but with a remonstrance.

'I came to you, my Lord,' said he, 'to beg you would be pleased to repeat to me what you said to-day to Sir Edward Newenden on the information and at the request of Mr. Maltravers.'

'Repeat it to you, Mr. Chesterville! Certainly—I will repeat it; but you will permit me, Sir, to enquire whether I am to do it at your request or at Sir Edward Newenden's. I—I give you my honour what I said was in pure friendship, and dictated—I say, Sir, it was dictated by no other motive than my regard to the family.'[1]

'Well, my Lord, then you can have no reason to decline repeat-

---

1 Lord Hawkhurst fears that Chesterville will challenge him to a duel and he will have to bear the shame of refusing to rise to this challenge or set forth to be killed or kill. Smith presents both men as as behaving reprehensibly.

ing it, as that will double the obligation. The defamation of my sister is certainly a very kind office from my uncle, and I come to thank him, as soon as I am certain of the extent of his kindness.'

'Really, Mr. Chesterville,' cried his Lordship, reddening at the vehemence with which he was addressed, 'this is rather *brusque*; and I own—I say I own that I am rather surprised that Sir Edward Newenden should misunderstand, or at least misrepresent—I say I rather wonder he could conceive that I meant any other than to serve at once my very good friend, Mr. Maltravers, and Sir Edward Newenden, for whom I have a perfect esteem: I say, my meaning, however ill I have executed my undertaking, most undoubtedly was to use my good offices to conciliate the unfortunate family difference that has arisen; and at the same time, Mr. Chesterville, to serve you and your sister.'

'Here are a great many words, my Lord, which, if I understand aright, mean very little: of any intention to serve me and my sister I own I heard nothing from Sir Edward; of your Lordship's extraordinary repetition of Maltravers's infamous calumny I heard so much, as enforces in my mind the necessity of my noticing it. Mr. Maltravers, my Lord, is very rich; your Lordship is a peer; and ye are both my Uncles. Your ages, my Lord, rather than either your rank, his riches or your mutual relationship, prevent my insisting on the satisfaction which a gentleman in this case feels himself bound to take; but though that is perhaps out of the question, I hold myself equally obliged to demand a recantation of assertions, which coming from you, my Lord, and from Maltravers, may have double influence, and are therefore doubly pernicious.'

'Good God, Sir!' cried his Lordship, in encreasing confusion, 'what is it you would have me say? How can I unsay what I repeated—what I reported, as faithfully as my memory permitted, after Mr. Maltravers?'

'Well, my Lord, but it was not, I understand, after Mr. Maltravers *only*; for I am informed your Lordship asserted that Sir Edward Newenden's having discarded his wife to receive my sister in her place was the common and general conversation of the town. Now, my Lord, among the multitude of persons who are called the town or the world, some one may, nay must, I think, occur to your recollection, who, in your presence, repeated that which you were pleased to call the general and universal report.'

'Some one person, Sir? yes I believe—I rather think many did—so many that just any one particular person may not strike me: and I own I was so hurt, that I had no—I say, I was so hurt at the report, that I rather wished to escape from it than to remark who was in possession of it.'

'What if your Lordship had been kind enough to have defended the character of your brother's daughter, at least till you knew it had merited the odium thus thrown upon it? It would have been more, my Lord, to the honour of your feelings and your humanity than to have taken for granted all that Maltravers has so wickedly and artfully asserted, and which the world, eager after novelty and gratified with scandal, no matter at whose expence, have with so much avidity adopted. But my Lord, to end a conference which may be on many accounts uneasy to you, I beg leave positively to give to any person who dares again repeat the infamous falsehood, the lie direct; and to declare to you, that whenever I can find it in the mouth of any man, who has not his age for his protection, I will give him the lie to his face, and prove him the basest of defamers!' So saying, Chesterville arose; and Lord Hawkhurst, who seemed by an effort to attempt digesting this uncourteous speech, arose also, yet not able to determine whether he should soothe or resent the anger which he could not condemn, he hesitated a moment, and then, just as we reached the door of the apartment, said—'Mr. Chesterville, yet another word with you; Mr. Montgomery, do me the favour to sit down for a moment.' We returned into the room; and after some efforts to speak without betraying his vexation and confusion, Lord Hawkhurst thus addressed your brother—

'Perhaps I should not—I say, perhaps I even ought not to over-look this warmth. But much is due—I say, much consideration is due to your quick sense of honor. I shall rejoice as sincerely as anyone, very sincerely, I give you my honor, at the annihilation of the report; but believe me—I have had some experience in these matters, and you are a young man—believe me it will not do to make a noise about such an affair; 'twill not do; let me advise you—I say let me advise you—suffer it to die; the next topic that arises will put this by, and in a few weeks it will be forgotten. But indeed my dear Sir—it is an impossible project to stop people's mouths—'tis believe me a labour which Hercules himself could not achieve. Well, we'll talk of it no more—I hope you will give yourself no more concern about it: but since I have the pleasure—I say, since I have the pleasure of seeing you here with your friend, Mr. Montgomery, give me leave to enquire a little into your future intentions. You have sold out of the army; that was wrong—very wrong. It would have been in my power to—I say, if you had remained in the army it might—I believe it would—have been possible to have served you.'

'I sold out, my Lord,' said Chesterville coldly, 'under no circumstances that should prevent my purchasing again.'

"Lord Hawkhurst then seemed to feel that he had gone too far. Money was requisite to purchase; and from money it was easy to see his Lordship had no inclination to part. 'You—you have thoughts then of entering the army again?' said he.

'Yes. My friend—that friend who has been so unjustly calumniated because he has acted so nobly by my father, by my sister, and by myself, is now encreasing his unexampled benefits, by treating for a company for me in a regiment stationed in Jamaica. Thither I shall go as soon as the negociation is completed, (which will probably be in the course of a week,) with my wife, whose father is one of the most opulent men on the island.'

"At the mention of this alliance all Lord Hawkhurst's ideas of your brother's situation seemed suddenly to change—'God bless me!' said he, 'I am very glad—sincerely rejoiced indeed—to understand that. Very opulent, is he? I have been misinformed then as to your marriage; I understood it was not altogether so prudent a match. I had an unaccountable notion that your lady was a Spaniard, with whom you ran from a convent. I am extremely glad your prospects are so much more flattering than they have been represented, and I give you my word of honour, my dear nephew, that I not only highly approve your going to Jamaica, but if there is any thing that I can do to assist good Sir Edward in serving you, you may freely command me.'

"Chesterville slightly thanking him, stayed not for a repetition of this new-born and unexpected kindness; but hastening from the house, said to me—'Curse on his mercenary politics! Did you observe how civil he grew when he learned that I was related to opulence? The fellow will lick my feet if at any time I should be possessed of a fortune. How my soul despises him! I will have none of his services! But Montgomery, I must, though I cannot have it from him, have, from somebody, farther satisfaction in regard to Ethelinde. The Maltravers's shall not go about, justifying Lady Newenden at the expence of my sister. I will go myself to old Maltravers——' Here you will, I know, pardon me for having interrupted your brother, and having attempted to dissuade him from a step that in my idea can be attended with no good consequences. Maltravers, bigotted to his daughter, and indifferent to every thing else, will be irritated but not silenced. The breach between him and Sir Edward will then be so far widened as to become incapable of accommodation, which he is now certainly aiming at though he has mistaken the means. It is impossible to help lamenting the unhappiness of Sir Edward; impossible to help wishing that he may have been mistaken in regard to Lady Newenden's culpability. Is it not possible that this division, so fatal to the peace of all the family, may be retrieved and forgotten? You have an heart which would rejoice in such an event, could it be brought about."

"Indeed," answered Ethelinde, "it is, and has, from the earliest intelligence I had of the unhappy misunderstanding, been my first wish to see it at an end; but whenever I have ventured to express that wish to Sir Edward, he has appeared averse to the subject, and has entreated me to drop it. Lady Newenden is of a temper so haughty and unbending, that even if she is innocent of the errors Sir Edward imputes to her, she had rather endure the inconveniences that follow his suspicions than deign to enter into her justification; and the means Mr. Maltravers has so injudiciously adopted, of applying to Lord Hawkhurst, has made all probability of an amicable adjustment more difficult and distant. One step, however, is in my power, and that it is my immediate determination to take.—I will immediately quit this house, and, since I have neither asylum nor support, seek for both the one and the other by getting into some employment."

"Have you then no asylum, Ethelinde?" said Montgomery, looking on her with mournful tenderness; "and can any other situation be so creditable, can any so effectually put an end to the wickedness and folly that has attempted to blast your character, as your taking my mother for your protectress, while you constitute at once her happiness and that of your Montgomery?"

Her deep blushes, her eyes filled with tears, her silent agitation, combined to inspire him with an hope that she heard him not reluctantly. Animated by the idea, he rapidly urged every argument with which his passionate tenderness furnished him, to induce her to consent to an immediate marriage.—"Oh! hear me!" cried he; "soul of my existence, hear me! Argue not with cold pecuniary prudence against my love. Give me but a right to call you mine, irrevocably mine, and I will leave you in the care of my mother, and go whithersoever that beloved hand shall point to me the path of honourable profit. Ah! think of what a man may be capable who knows that his success is to give affluence to a wife so adored, to a mother so revered; and that his return will be welcomed by two beings so worthy of his most arduous exertions. Animated by a certainty so enchanting, I should feel no fatigue! I should fear no peril!"

He was thus proceeding, when Ethelinde, no longer able to conceal what she felt, burst into a passion of tears. For some time utterance was denied her; but at length she said—"Press me no more, Montgomery, on a subject where my duty and my wishes are already but too much at variance. I ought not to hear you, when I know they can never be reconciled. It is not merely pecuniary prudence, but honor itself that forbids my listening to projects which can never be realized but at the expence of your interest."

"Gracious heaven! can any thing be my real interest but my happiness? Would the highest titles, the most unbounded affluence, afford me even the shadow of it without you? Would not the humblest cottage, the remotest obscurity, be a terrestrial paradise *with* you? Ah! Ethelinde! if you loved but half as well as I do, you could not coldly argue on prudence and discretion!"

"Would to heaven there was no necessity for me to do so! The romantic generosity of your character, and your regard for me, which is, I believe, very sincere, now make all inconveniences disappear, which prudence and reason would represent: but I, Montgomery, have seen the anguish that preys on a noble, a feeling mind, in beholding a beloved object exposed to all the uncomfortable circumstances that attend a very narrow fortune. Shall I bring on you this calamity? or could I bear to think, that to escape it you may be impelled alike by your tenderness and courage to expose yourself to a thousand dangers which you would otherwise never encounter? No, Montgomery! pennyless as I am, I will not marry; I will not rob your mother of the little support she now has, nor hazard embittering the life of the man I love with anguish and regret. Had I millions, I would prefer you to all mankind. Having nothing, I determine to tear myself from you. Do not, I entreat you, do not agonize my very soul with ineffectual remonstrances. My resolution may be rendered doubly painful but it cannot be shaken."

"Impossible!" said Montgomery, fixing his eyes most expressively on her's—"Impossible! You cannot have taken such a resolution; nor can you seriously think I will submit to it." Then the idea of Sir Edward's having interfered suddenly occurred to him, and he added—"I do not believe indeed that this opposition is your own. It is not in your nature to be so inconsistent. You deign to own a preference for me; yet are afraid of trusting me with your happiness, afraid that the paltry consideration of money should intrude upon the felicity of a union so perfect as ours would be, if you are indeed sincere."

"*If* I am sincere, Montgomery? Will nothing but that rashness which must inevitably lay up stores for repentance, convince you then of my sincerity? And consider who there is likely to have influence enough with me, to make me a moment hesitate, if my own reason did not tell me I ought to refuse my assent, to the generous but imprudent and impossible plan you have proposed. Are we to think only of ourselves, Montgomery? is your mother to be forgotten?"

"God forbid!" exclaimed he eagerly, "for then I were indeed unworthy of you. No, Ethelinde, I do not forget my mother; but in the proposal I must still warmly press, I think as much of hers as of my own happiness. In leaving you to console her in my absence, I should leave the only person who has the power to make her with cheerfulness sustain it: in leaving you to her tenderness and affection, I should have no fears either for your comfort or your safety: ah! consent then, I conjure you, dearest, most beloved of human creatures! and give not your Montgomery cause for a moment to suppose that you prefer to that dear parent, any other guardian; give me not the pain to——"

"Stop! Montgomery! This is going too far; and I must beg you will tell me what you would allude to by what you just now said of my being influenced by the opinion of others; and have since named, of my preferring any other guardian to your mother.

Suspicion, originally formed on the slightest grounds, is often exaggerated by a warm imagination to a frightful extravagance. Let us therefore suffer no such suspicion to go unexamined. It is undoubtedly to Sir Edward you advert. Yet I think I know you too well to suppose, that you can really believe *he* has on my mind any improper influence, or would use it if he had. My father, with his last breath, gave me to the care of that noble minded, that disinterested friend: my obligations to him, for all he has done for my father and for my brother, are equalled only by what on the same points I owe to you: I have long been accustomed to love him, and he has every claim to my confidence, to my regard, and my esteem. Shall I go inconsiderately to throw off all remembrance of what I owe him, and seek another protection without his concurrence?"

"Inconsistent!" said Montgomery, interrupting her—"Have you not this moment declared that you would quit him in order to silence the calumnies invented by the family of his wife, and go into some employment? Are you sure, then, that to such degradation he would consent, but would oppose your finding an honourable asylum with the mother of your husband?"

Ethelinde, struck with this forcible remark, was unable instantly to reply, and Montgomery thus went on—

"You say, dearest Ethelinde, that suspicion arises frequently from trifles the most inconsequential. My nature is not, I think, suspicious, but

> Who loves must fear:
> And sure who loves like me must greatly fear.[1]

I will candidly tell you all my thoughts. You may securely hear them, for of your angelic purity I never could a moment doubt. Sir Edward is, I acknowledge, all you describe him to be, except that I cannot allow him to be disinterested: no, Ethelinde, I have seen, and so have many others I fear, that he loves you; and his friendship for your father, his generosity towards your brother, was, though not entirely owing to that passion, certainly greatly influenced by it; perhaps almost unknown to himself." He saw anger and impatience rising in the soft eyes and glowing cheeks of his lovely

1 From William Mason, *Elfrida*, lines 264-265.

auditor; but without giving her time to express either, he took her hand, and thus proceeded—

"Have patience. I mean not, I would not for the world offend you. But believe me, Ethelinde, nothing but your innocent unconsciousness of your own attractions could have made you so long blind to what has been visible enough. Sir Edward is but human; he probably thought not of the danger till it was not to be escaped; and the misconduct of his wife helped, while it put all your perfections in too striking a contrast, to persuade him that he was less culpable in indulging the only sentiment that soothed and enchanted him. Far be it from me to suppose for a moment that Lady Newenden's errors have been purposely exaggerated; I am pretty well convinced that she has been greatly to blame, though I think not to the extent which has been represented; but nothing can persuade me that in pursuing a divorce Sir Edward has not in contemplation a future and more happy union."

"Gracious God!" cried Ethelinde, bursting into a flood of tears, "is it then certain that you—that Montgomery can join with the malicious, the invidious world, in imputing the most generous actions to the most unworthy motives? It is time indeed for me to quit the house of my benefactor. But believe me, Sir, your opinion of him will not make me more ready to embrace the proposal you have honoured me with, and this shall be our last conference on the subject."

Thus saying, Ethelinde arose, and still weeping excessively, left the room; whence Montgomery, who had already repented of having said what must give her pain, saw her depart without having courage to detain her, or to attempt making his peace.

CHAPTER II

At the bottom of the stairs, where Ethelinde arrived almost without knowing why she went, or whither she intended to go, she met Miss Newenden.—"Hey day!" cried the latter, "what's the matter now? I never saw such an house in my life. There's Chesterville has been talking himself into a passion below, and you and Montgomery have been *sympathizing* above. It's altogether excessively wearing. Do have done with these perpetual lachrymals; really it hurts even my spirits to hear of nothing but squabbling and sorrowing."

"I am sorry," said Ethelinde, speaking with great difficulty, "that we are destined to give you so much trouble, and sincerely hope it will soon end." Sir Edward, who sat opposite the parlour door, which a servant at that moment opened, now saw Ethelinde, and heard her speak as if she was in tears; starting up, he went to her, took her hand, and enquired earnestly what had thus distressed her. "Nothing, Sir Edward, 'tis nothing indeed but lowness of spirits," replied she, as she attempted to pass him.

"Nay," added he, "there is more in it than that. It is this wrong headed, fiery brother of your's, whose violence overcomes you; but be calm; be satisfied; I have at length persuaded him to let Maltravers alone to me, and to suffer groundless calumny to wear itself out. His commission is signed; he promises to think now only of his departure."

Ethelinde now reassumed presence of mind enough to determine that this hour should decide on her leaving Sir Edward; therefore summoning all her resolution, she said—"If you are not already too much fatigued by listening to or arguing with my brother, extend your kindness a little farther, and let me speak to you in your study."

He led her thither, and shut the door.—"Keep me not in suspense," said he: "what has thus affected you? whence are these tears, and why do you tremble?"

To tell him what Montgomery had said was impossible; she tried therefore to conquer the excess of her emotion, dried her eyes, and sighing, answered that her situation, taken altogether, which she had been resolutely investigating, was such as might surely account for any concern she expressed.

"And has Mr. Montgomery," asked Sir Edward, gravely, "been assisting you in this investigation, and lessening or encreasing your concern?"

"Mr. Montgomery has been with me certainly; but my sorrows *he* cannot lessen, and I am sure he would not willingly encrease them."

The excess of that tenderness she always felt for Montgomery, had already conquered her momentary anger; and her heart told her, that having of late made many remarks on the warmth of

Sir Edward's behaviour to her, she ought not to be offended that the quick sighted and ardent love of Montgomery should have suggested the same. To give peace to an heart which adored her, though she thought it impossible to give happiness, seemed as much her duty, as she thought it to remove from Sir Edward an object which she was afraid he saw with too much partiality, and to put an end at once to the malice of the world, and the apprehensions of the Maltravers's, who had publicly affirmed that she was to become Lady Newenden if their daughter was legally divested of the title.

Arming her resolution with all these considerations, she now prepared to combat all the reasons against her quitting him, which Sir Edward might plead as her friend, or enforce as her guardian. "Sir Edward," said she, her voice faultering through various agitations, "you have already had so much embarrassment, your kindness and generosity to my family have been so much more than I can ever repay, that I almost dread adding any trouble to what has gone before, though it must be the last."

"The last! To what do you allude?"

"To the necessity there is, not withstanding Miss Newenden's presence, that I should immediately quit this house. Every thing concurs to make it necessary; I am sure you must think so yourself, and however your generous wish to accommodate me may make you unwilling to acknowledge, you cannot fail to see it. Suffer me then, Sir Edward, to go—suffer me to go immediately, and remove what appears now to be (however strange that it should be so) considered as an impediment to your re-union with Lady Newenden."

"Yes," answered Sir Edward, his lips trembling as he spoke; "go, Ethelinde, if such is your pleasure. The guardianship with which your father so solemnly invested me, and which I accepted with so sincere an intention to fulfil most religiously, even as I would that some friend should fulfil it to my infant Maria, if at your age she should be left as you are; this trust so dear, so sacred, I resign; for you are weary of my endeavours to serve you, my advice is become importunate, and my friendship a restraint."

"Oh! no! indeed, indeed, Sir Edward, you mistake my meaning entirely. My strongest hope under heaven is in your friendship; but let it be exerted any where rather than under your own roof, since we live in a world where the most generous actions are the most liable to evil interpretations from those who are capable only of base ones. Already have these unworthy insinuations wounded your peace, and my character; already have my brother and my uncle met upon it; and though they parted friends, who knows to what difficulties and terrors the report may hereafter expose me on their account and on your's. Nothing can excuse my incurring the hazard, nothing should induce me to remain a supposed bar in the way of your receiving Lady Newenden."

The mildness of Sir Edward's disposition failed under the agitation of so many conflicting passions as now shook him.—"Receive Lady Newenden?" said he. "Tamely acquiesce in infamy? Never! Were it possible that my passion for her was as warm as when I married her, had I been blind to her faults of temper, and to the thousand provoking instances of her wish to make me unhappy— never, after her behaviour in regard to Danesforte, even tho' I were sure that it amounted only to dauntless contempt of the public opinion, would I again receive her. Name her not, Ethelinde; nor give the foolish and fleeting reports of idleness and malice, which you ought to despise, as reasons for quitting the protection where your father left you, and where, in the eyes of all the estimable part of mankind, you might with propriety remain; but rather own that you wish to give yourself to Montgomery; he is indeed a young man to whom the severest guardian could not object, had he a bare competence, or had you a fortune to enable you to overlook the total deficiency of his. Situated as you both are, I appeal to your own reason and reflection whether I should discharge my duty if I did not point out to you the apparent, the unavoidable inconveniences of such a union, though to prevent it, if you are determined, I shall not even attempt."

With downcast eyes Ethelinde heard him; and then so reasonable did what he say appear, that she felt ashamed of having suspected he had ever entertained for her any other than a brotherly regard; yet her opinion of the necessity of her leaving him was not changed, and she still resolved to adhere to it.

"Nor will I, Sir Edward," said she, "attempt to deny my affection for Mr. Montgomery. I have told him, what I now repeat to you, that had I only a moderate fortune I would be his rather than Empress of the world; but to marry at present is indeed not in my thoughts; I have positively refused, I mean steadily to refuse all his entreaties; but though I go not with him, I must still solicit your permission that I may depart."

Sir Edward, seeing her thus resolute, and conscious that she was right, though he was yet unwilling to own it even to himself, began to consider how he might at once acquiesce in her determination, and yet prevent her being under the necessity of flying for an asylum into the arms of Montgomery.

No project to effectuate this seemed so likely as a proposal that she should go with Miss Newenden, who was, he knew, impatient to return into Dorsetshire, and who, though she cared not for Ethelinde or for any body else, was yet willing enough to oblige her brother when it neither put her to much trouble, or broke in on her favorite pursuits.—"Well, Ethelinde," cried Sir Edward, after turning this thought a moment in his mind, "since such is your determination, will you go into Dorsetshire with Eleanor? There you will still be under my protection, though at so many miles distance scandal itself will hardly be able to make such a residence appear improper. Tell me, shall I name it to my sister?"

"I am afraid," answered Ethelinde, "that my presence might not be desirable to Miss Newenden. It was only a few moments since, that she complained, as I met her, of the air of grief and calamity that reigned throughout the house; to her my tears appear useless, and my wretchedness will be burthensome."

"You mistake her, I believe," replied Sir Edward; "Ellen has not a bad heart, though she has no great sensibility of temper, and may not perhaps enter into a thousand nameless and uneasy sensations which deprive of rest, those who have quicker and keener feelings; but I am persuaded she would be glad to do you any service, and be much happier to have you with her in Dorsetshire than to remain in London, which she generally considers as a punishment."

Ethelinde, without resource, unless from her own relations, the family of the Ludfords, to whom she dreaded applying more than any evil that could befall her, was disposed to acquiesce in this proposal, which might, she thought, procure for her a temporary residence, and give her time to consider what she could do for herself.

Reluctantly, however, she thought of becoming an inmate at the house of Miss Newenden; who was not only incapable of friendship, but of tenderness and pity; and who had no idea either of books or of that sort of conversation in which Ethelinde delighted and excelled. The temptation of possessing the society of Mrs. Montgomery, of uniting her destiny with that of the man she loved, of being freed from the necessity of being burthensome to the family of Sir Edward, or dependent on her own, now forcibly assailed her, and all the objections that could be made to her marriage disappeared, but in a moment all that her father had said of the inconveniences he had himself sustained by marrying without either party having a support for a family, and the misery she should suffer should Montgomery be rendered unhappy and indigent for life, arose to counteract the seducing prospect her fancy drew of living with the two people to whom her heart was most fondly attached, in the lovely solitude of Grasmere.

Sir Edward, who guessed by her countenance the subject which occupied her thoughts, continued to press for her consent to speak to Miss Newenden immediately; which having obtained, he went himself in search of his sister. Glad to escape from London, and not unwilling to oblige her brother (who was the only person for whom she had the least regard) where his gratification broke not in on her particular amusements, she complied without hesitation; and assuring him that Ethelinde should be welcome to her house as long as it suited her to remain there, Sir Edward brought her to the room where Ethelinde remained that she might repeat the invitation personally. This Miss Newenden did with as good a grace as she was capable of, and Ethelinde received it with grace all her own. It was settled then that they should set out together, in three days, for Brackwood Down. The brother and sister departed to give the necessary orders; and Ethelinde retired to her own room to consider how she should take leave of Montgomery, how reconcile him to the resolution she had formed of going where she should see him no more!

The separation between Sir Edward Newenden and his wife, was now become a subject of much conversation, and, as is usual in cases where little or nothing of the truth is known, various reports were circulated; and while some spoke very freely of her Ladyship's attachment, to Lord Danesforte, others affected to pity her, and to assert that to their certain knowledge her indiscreet preference of his Lordship was solely owing to the very improper style in which Sir Edward chose, in her own house, to support her cousin.

Mrs. Royston, who could not forget the mortification she had received from Montgomery, was delighted in every opportunity of declaiming against Ethelinde, to whom she knew he was attached. As fearless in attacking the characters of others as regardless of her own, she related in all companies, with many additions, all she had been able to pick up about Ethelinde. While Montgomery resided with Mr. Royston in Harley Street, she had frequently talked to him of the manner in which he passed his time at Grasmere, and of what he knew of the people in the neighbourhood: by these means she had heard many trifling circumstances in mere conversation which she now ingeniously put together, and said every where, that she knew, from undoubted authority, that the intimacy between Sir Edward and Miss Chesterville had been long understood, and that he had tried to marry her to his ward, Mr. Davenant, in order to blind Lady Newenden, but that the young man was too wise to be taken in.

Royston himself had, among numberless ridiculous foibles, that of being a male gossip: passing half the year at his seat adjoining to one of the boroughs he possessed, he had been accustomed to occupy his politics by studying the family histories of the haberdashers, tanners, woolcombers, braziers, butchers, shoemakers, and chandlers shops, in the little town; and finding his genius extend with his knowledge, he by degrees became acquainted with every thing that happened in the gentlemen's families twenty miles round; by whom, as he was hated for his supercilious insolence, despised for his meanness, and laughed at for his folly, he was seldom admitted to their parties, and the spleen he conceived at their neglect or contempt, he vented in calumny and abuse. Thus he had acquired an habit of retailing, in all companies and on all occasions, scraps of scandal, which were generally not the less eagerly listened to for being oftener false than true; and such a resource is defamation to the vacant head, such a gratification to the malignant heart, that Royston, who was derided as having hardly common sense in other conversation, was eagerly listened to in this; and seldom wanted auditors, when to vilify the character of the unhappy, or to sully the good name of the worthy, was the topic on which he was engaged.

It happened, that the day before that which was now passing, Mrs. Royston had entertained at her table (more remarkable for the variety than the nice selection of its guests) one of those non-descript beings, the fungus production of that rage for trifling novelty and tinsel wit which marks the passing period, a man, who having been what is called *ruined* two or three times, yet contrived by dint of assurance and singularity, to be noticed by a few idle men of fortune; and still found means to make his way among sets of people, who, having no real consequence, none of that respectability which good morals and good manners bestow on affluence, make to themselves a consequence of their own by some affectation either of literary eminence or strange peculiarity. This *gentleman* (for that title, like some in the army, is always retained) had, by saying and defending very impertinent things, passed for a man of courage; and by picking obsolete repartees out of old magazines, forgotten plays, and jest books (which he dressed in a motly and quaint language of his own) for a man of wit. On the strength of these two qualifications, a perfect reliance on his own abilities, and a sovereign contempt for all others, he had some time been a professed genius, "a fellow of infinite jest;"[1] tired, however, of seeing *bon mots* which were not uttered without many a painful research into the dark annals of obscurity, retailed to the *profit* of others, while empty honor alone remained for *him*, he courageously resolved to turn his united talents to account; and nothing doubting but that his sword would awe those whom his pen might perchance offend, he magnanimously determined to consolidate his small remaining stock of money with his new modelled stock of old wit, and became the purchaser, proprietor, and director of a newspaper.

As he began most unmercifully, and gave no quarter, his paper was immediately considered as the principal vehicle of daily scandal; and whoever was solicitous to take away a character through malice, or to acquire one for folly, were sure of exhibiting or being exhibited in "the fashionable paper." This was sometimes carried to such excess, that the proprietor did not find himself quite so easy and unmolested as he had figured to himself he should be: a few who thought themselves too grossly insulted, entered into explanations which generally ended in the proprietor's publicly

1 An allusion to Yorick (Hamlet's line, V: 5, 185), further ironic invective: when we see Yorick he is a skull thrown up by the gravedigger as the gravedigger digs a new grave out of an old one in a common cemetery.

begging pardon, laying the fault on the printer, protesting that no offence was meant, and directly contradicting in the print of Tuesday what had been daringly inserted as an authentic fact in that of Monday. Every body bought what every body execrated as a nuisance; and consoled by the trite but proverbial saying, "let those laugh that win," Mr. Popgun enjoyed his pecuniary success, and a *species* of fame with which he was as well content as if it had been of a more honourable kind.

Such was the man, who having been shut out from all reputable societies, that he might not glean the common occurrences of life to transform for the purposes of his paper, still found a seat at the table of Mrs. Royston: where the scantiness of his fare was well made up by the anecdotes he acquired. Royston, a strange mixture of pride and meanness, of ostentation and avarice, not disliking a numerous circle, whom he fed, however, with as much frugality as possible, and who, though they not unfrequently rose hungry from very little meat, wretchedly dressed in an affectation of French cookery, had yet the glory of eating that little from superb old plate, which looked as if it had been dug out of Herculaneum.[1]

At one of these dinners, on the day before mentioned, the conductor of the newspaper was a guest. Mr. and Mrs. Royston both related all they knew, and much that they had imagined, of the affairs of the Newenden family: they gave particulars of much that passed at the Abbey, and of conversations at Bristol, which made Sir Edward appear as the most worthless and cruel husband to an amiable and unoffending wife; all which duly treasuring up, their guest at the usual hour departed. It happened that the following morning Montgomery and Chesterville were to meet a gentleman with whom the latter had business relative to his commission, at a coffee house in the Haymarket: Montgomery being passed his appointment, Chesterville and the gentleman transacted the business without him, his presence being of no great consequence, and then the other person departing, Chesterville sat down in the coffee room to write a letter while he waited the arrival of Montgomery.

Several persons were in the room talking, to whom he gave no

---

1 An ancient Roman town, destroyed by a volcano and first discovered in 1709, by this time a famous site for archeological discovery. Food from there would be in a sad state.

attention, till a little pale conceited man was heard with an audible voice to read a paragraph in which Sir Edward Newenden and Miss Chesterville were mentioned in a way so scandalously injurious, that an exclamation of disgust was heard from the greater part of the auditors, and, from all, of wonder.

"Upon my soul," cried a young man amongst them, "that is too bad. What! does he mention the names at full length?"[1]

"No," replied Royston, who was present and who had read the sentence, "not so; but I filled up the vacancies, and added to the initials the letters that complete the names; for it was at my table yesterday that Popgun heard the anecdote he has here inserted, and indeed I know it to be true."

"Read it again, Sir," said Chesterville, "and with your own additions, if you please."

The eyes of all present were now turned towards Chesterville, and the countenance of Royston changed to a deadly white: not that he knew Chesterville, but he disliked both his voice and his countenance.

"Read it again, Sir! No, Sir—I shall not, Sir. I have read it once, Sir—and if you have any farther curiosity, here, Sir, is the paper."

"I shall not be able to do it justice, Sir," replied Chesterville, who now approached the little alarmed senator, "since I was not present at your table yesterday; nor can I aver it to be true. Come, Sir, read it again."

"No, Sir—by no means.—I really don't chuse——"

"Not chuse, Sir? when you not only boasted this moment that the scurrilous scoundrel was furnished with the anecdote at your house, but that you know yourself the truth of it? Read it, Sir—read it—and fill up the missing letters."

"Really Sir I think it somewhat out of rule to be called upon; a man in my rank of life, by a young, a very young gentleman, whom I have not the honor to know, to—to—repeat my words, or justify a common newspaper report; I think my figure, my fortune might exempt me——"

"Gentlemen," said Chesterville, turning to the persons in the coffee room, "this fellow, whoever he is, seems to be so con-

1 To avoid a libel suit or a duel a scandal-mongering newspaper and its writers would provide first initials with a row of asterisks; it had the effect of increasing the salaciousness of whatever innuendoes were used.

temptible, that I should content myself with kicking him out of the room, if this were not a matter in which every man who has a character himself, or a female relation whose honor deserves to be defended, was not concerned. Ye have all of you probably a sister, a wife, or a daughter, whom you will not hear basely traduced: the lady whom this animal has dared to make the subject of an infamous libel, is my sister; the daughter of an Englishman—of a soldier who has shed his blood for his country—I appeal to you all, whether this man did not assert that he knew this abusive paragraph to be true?"

The gentlemen unanimously acknowledged that he had said so.

"Then Sir," cried Chesterville, addressing himself to the trembling and dismayed Royston, "I insist upon your instantly acknowledging that you are a lying rascal."

"Good God! Sir," cried Royston, hardly able to speak, "it is impossible you can suppose—impossible you can expect me—upon my honor—upon my soul—surely you can never desire—"

"Look ye, Sir!" said Chesterville—"You are, I see, a paltry insignificant fellow. But it is the sting of a reptile that is often most dangerous. Acknowledge yourself a liar!—instantly acknowledge it!"

"No Sir—indeed Sir—I am very willing to say I might be misinformed—or mistaken—but—"

"That will not do, Sir. Since you decline this avowal, I must enforce my assertion; so I do tell you that you are a liar!—and to prevent any mistake or misinformation on *this* subject, I shall add a memento that will remind you to enquire of me farther." So saying, he seized the terrified Royston with a strong arm, and by an application of his foot sent him, however reluctantly, to the door of the coffee house, where his velocity was stopped by Montgomery, who at that moment being about to enter, stood still in the doorway, greatly surprised at the rapid and involuntary exit which his quondam friend was making. Royston was too much frightened to recollect the friendship subsisting between his adversary and Montgomery; but apprehensive that he should be sent down the Haymarket with as little mercy as he had been compelled to quit the coffee room, he seized Montgomery's arm, and breathless with fear and anger, exclaimed—"My dear friend, I have been cruelly used!"

At the same moment Montgomery heard this, felt Royston's gripe imploring protection, and saw that Chesterville was the man who had been committing the hostilities he complained of, some of the persons round them were trying to prevent Chesterville from proceeding; though he had no intention to pursue an unresisting foe; others attempted to explain the matter to Montgomery. After the tumult a little subsided, Montgomery assured Royston, whom he treated with contemptuous civility, that whatever provocation Chesterville had given he would be ready to justify like a gentleman, and that he would himself wait on him the next morning to receive his commands. Chesterville then wrote his name on a piece of paper, which Montgomery gave to Royston, and the two young men went away together; while Royston, who saw to his utter discomfort, that other consequences were yet to follow, got into a hackney coach, and as it drove towards Harley street, he meditated on means to escape the ignominy of having taken a kicking, without risking the yet more dreadful operation of being shot through the head. All appeared dreary and unpromising. Neither his age, income, his northern coal mines or his southern boroughs, were sufficient defence against the irascible honor of a rash hot headed boy. Often did he wish that he had been giving his silent vote or making an harmless speech in the House of Commons; and frequently did he curse the indiscreet love of babbling about other people's affairs, which had more than once been followed by very disagreeable circumstances. From those which threatened him at present he could see no means to escape; and he made no doubt but the next "fashionable paper" would impale him in an anecdote to which its own falsehood had given ground.

CHAPTER III

Montgomery, though he owned that Chesterville could not have acted otherwise than he did, was vexed that this affair had happened, as he knew it would give new force to the report, and extremely hurt Ethelinde, from whom, however, he determined to conceal it if possible. He was pretty well persuaded that Royston would sooner read a public recantation than meet Chesterville with pistols; but he thought that to let the matter drop with a private apology was the most desirable termination, and this he determined if possible to bring about. Every hour encreased his uneasiness in regard to the situation of Ethelinde. In a few days her brother and his wife were to go to Portsmouth to embark for the West Indies: their departure would make her continuing with Sir Edward infinitely more improper; yet she inexorably continued to refuse to put herself into the only protection which could secure her from the inconveniences of her destiny, and refused it for reasons which he thought unfounded. Though he highly respected and esteemed Sir Edward Newenden, he was by no means content that Ethelinde should remain with him; receiving continually new obligations, deeply impressed with the recollection of those she and her family already owed him: and when he reflected that Sir Edward might possibly obtain a divorce, and be enabled to offer Ethelinde that place which it was evident he would be happy to have her fill, the most uneasy and corrosive apprehensions took possession of his heart: and certain as he was of Ethelinde's affection for him, fear, jealousy, and mistrust, found their way into his liberal mind, and made almost insupportable the idea of quitting England; of which he sometimes thought as a duty he owed his mother, himself, and her for whose sake only he desired independence; and sometimes he fancied that to remain with them, though to share an income hardly sufficient for their support, was more consistent with his tenderness, and with their happiness, than any advantage he might gain for them by leaving them.

At two o'clock the day after the disagreeable meeting in the coffee-house, Montgomery was to go to Mr. Royston to receive his apology on behalf of Chesterville, or an appointment where their differences might be settled. About one he was surprised, at his lodgings in Portland street, whither he had removed to be near Ethelinde, with the following letter:

Harley-street, Feb. 9th, 17—

"My dear Sir,

"Though I may have appeared unmindful of your interest since your abrupt and, give me leave to say, unkind departure from my house, I do assure you I have made it my business to serve you, and have the pleasure to tell you that I have succeeded; my friend, Mr. ——, Chairman of the India Company, having this day informed me that an appointment is now fixed on for you of a nature so advantageous, that I am persuaded you will be satisfied with my zeal for your interest, and will believe me very sincerely,

my dear Sir,

your most faithful servant,

J. ROYSTON."

Montgomery would have been much more amazed at such a letter had he not perfectly understood by this time the character of Royston. That which neither relationship nor friendship would have effected, the fiery and vindictive Chesterville had accornplished, by an insult, which, however it was deserved, no other man would have borne. Royston, with whom self preservation was the leading principle, and who knew that a man who had money and parliamentary interest would always command a certain degree of outward respect, had persuaded himself that it was beneath the dignity of his station to be governed by those chimerical notions of honor which influence such hot headed and romantic boys as Chesterville; yet he was well aware that Chesterville could and probably would force him to fight if he could not persuade Montgomery to appease him, and to prevail on him to accept of an apology, and be content with that and the resentment he had already shewn; but how to make advances to Montgomery he knew not; he had not only treated him with neglect but with rudeness, which, high spirited and haughty from the consciousness of birth and merit, it was improbable he would easily forgive. So active, however, did the impulse of self preservation make Royston, that the wish of Montgomery to go out to India now occurred to him; and as he had lately had an opportunity of serving those who had power in the Company at a contested election for Directors, he determined immediately to apply for preferment for Montgomery. This, as he was again by this time on the side of Ministry, his application immediately obtained; and he lost not a moment in signifying his success. Montgomery, in answer to his letter, sent a verbal message that he would be with him in an hour, and then went in search of Chesterville, to whom he gave the letter he had just received.

Having read it, Chesterville demanded what he intended to do.

"Exactly," replied Montgomery, "as I should have done before the receipt of it: I shall go to Royston, and, as we agreed upon last night, insist either on his meeting you, or publicly unsaying the calumny he publicly asserted."

"Hang the fellow," replied Chesterville, "he appears to be such a coward that he is beneath one's vengeance. Let him send me a written acknowledgment, that he asserted unguardedly what was not true, and leave it to me to make what use I please of the paper; I desire to have no more to do with him unless he has a better appetite for fighting; and since he has it in his power to do you service, my dear Charles, get over the business as easily as you can with him."

"I thank you," answered Montgomery, "but I assure you if he had the power to make me Governor of Bengal, I would not accept it, if the condition was a compromise for words spoken to the dishonor of your sister. Royston must apologize where the insult was given. You may receive it how you please; and even then he is, in my eyes, so very contemptible a fellow, that I know not whether any consideration will induce me to be obliged to him." The young men then parted; and Montgomery went to his appointment.

Royston received him with open arms. "My dear friend!" said he, "how pleased I am to have you under my roof. I am sure we now perfectly understand each other." Montgomery heard all these professions with great coldness; and Royston, finding that all the advantages he had or could offer him had no power to shake that firmness with which he insisted on a recantation being made to Chesterfield, he agreed to undergo the ceremony at an early hour the next morning, at the place where the offence was given. This point being settled, and Royston consoling himself with the sage reflection that it was more noble to acknowledge than defend an error, Montgomery left him, saying coldly that he thanked him for the appointment of which he had procured him the refusal, but must beg leave to consider of it two days; at the end of which he should be enabled to give his answer.

As he walked back to his lodgings, the tumultuous fluctuation of his thoughts returned: should he refuse an appointment which might, in a very few years, raise him to affluence, and give him the power of bestowing every indulgence on the declining age of his beloved mother, of placing the woman he adored in that station to which her merit and her beauty would do so much honor?

Was it for him, thus in early youth to shrink poorly from the duty incumbent on every man to provide for himself, and take from his widowed mother more than half her slender subsistence? These reflections determined him to return to Royston, and by instantly accepting the appointment, put it out of his own power to retract. He stepped back a few yards to execute this resolution; but then came the idea of taking leave of Ethelinde perhaps for ever—of leaving her to forget him, to become the wife of some more fortunate man, possibly of Sir Edward Newenden, while *he* might be employed in accumulating what, without her, was in his mind contemptible dross; and his resolution instantly forsaking him, he again turned and walked towards his own lodgings, glad that he had at least two days to consider of the proposal, and to make another attempt on the inflexible resolution of Ethelinde, whom, if he once could call his, he fancied he could leave with tranquillity, and undertake any employment with a greater power of exertion and greater certainty of success.

Slowly, and still in a perturbed state of mind, he reached the house where he lodged. He was surprised by hearing from the maid who opened the door that a lady was in his dining room. Unable to conjecture who it could be, he ran hastily up; and opening the door, was instantly in the arms of his mother.

So great was his surprise that he was unable to enquire the cause of a journey so unexpected. She saw his agitation; and with that dignity and presence of mind which never forsook her, she said—"You are alarmed, dear Charles, at my sudden appearance, and perhaps guess very truly, that only some disagreeable business would have engaged me to undertake a journey as unpleasant as inconvenient to me. Let me put you out of suspense: Mr. Le Moine, to whom the management of our little property is entrusted, informs me that the great house at Lyons, in which, you know, sixteen hundred pounds sterling of our fund was placed for the sake of receiving better interest, has by some mismanagement been very much shaken in its credit. The concerned are responsible yet, and of undoubted integrity; but still their situation appears to Le Moine so precarious that he advises me to lose no time in withdrawing my property. It is a great deal out of our little all; and as the present state of the French funds makes me unwilling to trust it in them, I shall place it in England if I luckily save it;

but as the removal of it will be attended with some difficulty and perhaps hazard, I have determined to go over myself; and having weighed every thing maturely, I set out from home in a few hours after the receipt of Le Moine's letter; and when I have consulted with you on your present situation, shall proceed as soon as possible to Dover."

Montgomery, equally admiring her firmness of mind and regretting the fatigue and vexation to which his mother might be exposed, now entreated her to suffer him to go immediately to France instead of her undertaking a journey so unfit for her. She told him, however, that she could give no answer to that till she knew his present prospects; but that being a good deal fatigued, they would delay any farther conversation till the afternoon.

Montgomery then left her, at her request, alone; and having procured her an apartment on the first floor in the house where he himself inhabited the second, he ran to Hanover Square to impart to Ethelinde the intelligence of his mother's arrival, and to see whether she would be induced to go to her; for he well knew that he could carry to his mother no satisfaction so great as she would receive from the sight of her.

Ethelinde heard with amazement and concern the reasons of a journey to London, at which she should so much have rejoiced had it been occasioned by any thing but threatened misfortune. She suspected what was indeed true, that Mrs. Montgomery had forborne to tell her son the worst of her apprehensions relative to this part of her fortune, for she thought that nothing but very imminent hazard of its loss could induce her to cross the channel herself when she had in Le Moine an active and trusty agent. This Ethelinde considered as decisive of her fate. The asylum which seemed ever open to her on the banks of Grasmere Water, that dear and tranquil cottage whither she thought that, when every other hope failed her she might always turn her weary steps, and find peace, and protection, in the absence of her lover; now seemed for ever shut against her, and its respected and amiable mistress likely herself to become a wanderer in order to attempt—fruitlessly perhaps attempt, to save almost half of all that she and her son possessed. These mournful ideas filled her heart with anguish and her eyes with tears. She sat silent a moment after Montgomery ceased speaking.—"You will not go then to my mother?" said he, mournfully, "you will not afford me the consolation of seeing you once together before I part with both perhaps for ever."

Ethelinde knew not that he alluded to his going to India almost immediately, which he now believed himself resolutely fixed to do. "Ah! Montgomery," answered she, in a voice broken by tears, "you know that if it *were* possible for me to refuse you any thing I can consistently with your interest, and my own honor grant, it certainly would not be a request in which Mrs. Montgomery is concerned."

"You will go then?" cried he. "Ah! let us not lose a moment."

"But it is necessary to speak to Sir Edward if he is at home," said Ethelinde, "or he may think my going with you extraordinary, and perhaps improper."

"As you judge best," replied Montgomery, piqued, though ashamed of owning it, at finding the deference she was ever inclined to pay Sir Edward. Ethelinde then rang to enquire; but finding Sir Edward gone out, and Miss Newenden not yet returned from Hyde Park, from whence no weather or season detained her, she left a note to inform them that she was gone to pass the day with Mrs. Montgomery, who was unexpectedly arrived in town, and then departed with her lover.

CHAPTER IV

Mrs. Montgomery received Miss Chesterville with transport. The attachments of her warm and sensible heart were now entirely circumscribed to her son and Ethelinde. She loved them with the most warm and anxious fondness; the hopes of seeing them one day united, and enjoying competence if not affluence, animated her courage to embark again in irksome attention to pecuniary business; and in that hope she had reconciled herself to the prospect of parting with her son, if it became necessary for him, to seek his fortune in another hemisphere. The dejection of Ethelinde; the tears she shed in speaking of the parent she had so recently lost; the desolate situation she was in, on which topic, however, she touched but lightly; and the tenderness, that, without acknowledging it by words, it was easy to see she felt for Montgomery; all served to encrease that attachment to her, of which his mother had been sensible on their first acquaintance; and with redoubled pain she reflected, that the circumstances which appeared so threatening to her little fortune, might put it farther than ever from her power to receive into her protection the daughter of her heart.

After dinner the whole party acquired a little more composure; and Mrs. Montgomery, who knew that the sooner she reached France, the greater probability there would be of her recovering the money which appeared so precarious, determined to exert that strength of mind, which in trying exigencies never deserted her, to canvass with her son his prospects; and to help him to form that determination which should seem most consonant to reason and prudence. She considered Ethelinde so much as a party concerned, that she was desirous of having her assist at this conference; and she knew that her excellent understanding would reach her, whatever might be the feelings of her heart, not only to acquiesce, but to advise the execution of any plan by which he was likely to acquire ease and independence.

She began, therefore, by desiring Montgomery to relate to her all the consequences of the various applications he had made since he had been in town. He obeyed her; assigned his reasons for having quitted Mr. Royston, and concluded with shewing her the letter he had that day received from him, and explaining the nature of the appointment thus likely to be within his reach. "I have given," said he, "no answer, and am glad of an opportunity of personally consulting you, Madam, before I return one."

"Since then," replied Mrs. Montgomery, "I am here, and since another person is present, who I hope and believe is also interested in your determination, let me know, my dear Charles, what are your own thoughts?"

"Ah! Madam," answered he, mournfully, "they are far from being pleasant ones. Your little fortune, too inadequate before to your birth and merit, may now perhaps be reduced to less than half. I have been too long a burthen to you; and too long depended on your tenderness for that support which I should have derived from my own exertions. An opportunity now offers, by which I may repair the injustice of fortune towards you; and certainly I ought to embrace it. I will do so, whatever wretchedness I may undergo in tearing myself, perhaps for ever, from all I hold dear on earth—from you and Ethelinde!" He paused a moment to recover the emotion this distressing idea caused, and then in a lower and more tremulous voice went on—

"I had, I own, one hope; and did I yet dare indulge it, the agonies of such a parting would be softened, and I should depart comparatively happy!"

Ethelinde knew he meant her consent to marry him before he went: but the objections to such a union seemed to have become stronger; and silent and sorrowing, she suffered him, without interruption, to proceed.

"That delicious hope is, however, at an end, unless your influence can prevail on Ethelinde not to send me into a long long exile, under the most insupportable of all apprehensions—that of losing her for ever."

Ethelinde, who felt her resolution failing, and dreaded lest the solicitations of Mrs. Montgomery should wholly overturn it, said—"What promise shall I give you, to make you easy on that head? How shall I convince you, that my first wish is for your happiness?"

"Easily, my angelic Ethelinde," cried he, catching eagerly at an expression so favourable to his wishes—"The promise I demand, must be given at the altar; the conviction that you wish to see me happy, I can receive only by your making me so immediately."

"I dare venture," said Ethelinde, "I think I dare venture to appeal to Mrs. Montgomery, whether there are not objections to what you propose so strong, as to render it, if not impossible, at least incompatible with reason and prudence. To enable her to judge fairly between us, I will leave you to urge to her all the arguments you have repeated so often to me; and you must allow me, in my turn, an opportunity of stating to her, when you are not present, those unanswerable reasons against so indiscreet and hasty a step, which I am sure have already occurred to herself."

Ethelinde then arose, and retiring into Mrs. Montgomery's bed-chamber, left the mother and the son together.

"She is an angel," said the former, as she left the room.—"In person and mind she gives me a complete idea of perfection, of which, till I saw her, I doubted the existence."

"Yet you will join with her, Madam, in expecting me to leave her—surrounded by those, who, as sensible of that perfection as I am, will have incessant opportunities of recommending themselves, and erasing from her heart all the impression it may now retain in my favour."

Mrs. Montgomery, affected by the vehemence with which he spoke, and by the tears that filled his eyes, desired him to explain himself, and to tell her from what quarter arose that anxiety which so cruelly agitated him, with what appeared, to her, a groundless fear; Ethelinde's forgetting or forsaking him. He then, with a degree of emotion that encreased the concern of his mother, represented her as wholly dependent on Sir Edward Newenden: he enumerated the obligations she already owed him, and all those ties by which she must consider herself bound to respect and regard him; he described the conduct of Lady Newenden; the irreparable breach which appeared to exist between her and Sir Edward; and the probability there was, that a separation effected by law, would, at some period, perhaps not very remote, leave Sir Edward at liberty to offer his hand where his heart was most undoubtedly so partial. When he had concluded this little narration, his mother said—

"If all you have seen, or rather fancy you have seen, of Sir Edward's particular attachment to Miss Chesterville, really left no question of it, why should you suppose, had he the power of offering her his name and rank, which he never may have, that she would accept that offer to the prejudice of a man whom she undoubtedly prefers now, and who she will then be sensible is absent only to procure a fortune, that he may offer it to her. No, Charles, I can allow much to the anxious solicitude of love like your's, but I cannot allow that you can entertain these suspicions without injury and injustice not only to Ethelinde, but to Sir Edward, whose nobleness of spirit I revere, and am persuaded it is produced by no unworthy motives. That he may admire Miss Chesterville I can easily believe—who that sees and hears her does not? But I think the designs you mention exist only in your warm and apprehensive imagination. That he would act with the tenderest attention, as her brother and her guardian, I have no doubt: why should you join with the ill-judging, the gross and malicious world, and deprive her of such a friend when she has most occasion for his protection?"

Montgomery, almost for the first time in his life, felt a degree of impatience arise while his mother spoke, and he seized the first pause she made to say—"But dearest Madam; you do not know, indeed you do not—"

"Pardon me," cried she, "I do know very well indeed, Charles, that a young man in love sees every object which he fancies opposes his passion, through a false medium, with which sober reason has nothing to do; you magnify the kindness of Sir Edward Newenden to Ethelinde, till you fancy he is as much in love with her as you are yourself; and that therefore she must give her hand to you now, lest she should be compelled hereafter to give it to him: and then, forgetting that you must equally quit her, whether as your wife or your affianced mistress, you conceal from yourself all the inconveniences that it may in the former case befall her; and think only of what may happen to yourself, if she remains in the latter. As your wife, she will be securely your's; but she will no longer have a claim to the protection of Sir Edward, who will, probably, (and with great justice) be disobliged.—You will leave her without any support, but that slender and now uncertain income which she may share with me.—You may leave her in a situation which will aggravate the misery of your absence, and encrease the number of helpless beings, who will have no other dependence but on your life. *I* have learnt how to tremble for her, should she be so circumstanced, by recollecting the terrors I underwent for you, before you saw the light; and what I then endured in the dreaded separation from your father, which I hazarded your life and my own to escape from. Shall I forget all my own sufferings, or be so insensible of those of another, as to desire Ethelinde to risk equal misery? No, Charles, you do not, I am sure, expect it of me. I can bear your absence, since it must be so—at least I will try to bear it with fortitude; but I cannot consent to promote what I think will encrease the unhappiness of Ethelinde, without really promoting your's. Lest, however, you should for a moment believe (yet surely my son will do me more justice than even for a moment to think of it)—that pecuniary motives influence me, I here assure you, that if she will accept so humble an asylum as I have to offer her, nothing will make me so happy as to have your Ethelinde inhabit my cottage, and share my income, whatever it may be."

Montgomery, prevented by a thousand tender emotions from interrupting his mother, now kissed her hand, and bathed it with tears of tender gratitude, mingled however with those of poignant regret, at finding that her ideas, however consonant to the dictates of sound reason, differed wholly from those which the glowing hand of ardent and youthful passion, had impressed on his sanguine and inexperienced mind. A severe internal struggle passed before he could determine to say—"Ah! dearest Madam! I live—I ought to live only to obey you!—And though death appears to me preferable to the cruel necessity of going from you and from Ethelinde, yet, if you think I ought to go—"

"Montgomery," replied his mother, collecting all her fortitude, "do not imagine that there is any consideration on earth but your happiness, that could induce me to think of parting with you. If you believe *that* happiness would be more certainly obtained by remaining in England, and sharing the very little income I shall now probably have, give up all thoughts of going. Ethelinde, I believe, would be content with any lot, however humble, that was your election: but should you, ought you to solicit her to embrace it? The romantic idea of love in a cottage, which has distracted so many young heads, and broken, I fear, many anxious hearts, is too wild and chimerical for you to encourage yourself in dreaming of, or for you to wish that Ethelinde should imbibe.—Brought up in elegance, allied to nobility, and marrying into a family as illustrious as her own, could you, Charles, endure to see your wife, the lovely, delicate, and graceful Ethelinde, employed in the occupations of a laundress or a domestic? It is necessary, my son, to be very sincere with you. My income never exceeded one hundred and fifty pounds a year; to what will it be reduced, if I lose, as I fear I shall, sixteen hundred pounds of the principal that produced it? We shall then have among us about seventy pounds annually. We may indeed *live* upon it: and if my son can submit for himself and for his wife to such a mode of living as an income so narrow must impose, he will not find his mother shrink from the experiment."

"God forbid, Madam," cried Montgomery eagerly, (all the energy of manly virtue, which a violent and predominant passion had awhile stifled in his bosom, blazing forth anew)—"God forbid that your son should act so unworthy of you!—So unworthy of the lovely woman to whom he aspires! Forgive, and think no more of the reluctance I have shewn to perform what is my duty. To have called that angelic creature mine, would, I own to you, have rendered the misery of parting more supportable; but you have convinced me I ought not, for her sake, to think of it; and I should not deserve to carry with me the dear hope of being one day her husband, the soul-soothing certainty of being beloved by her, were I so incapable of real affection, as not to prefer her tranquillity to my own. The more severe this struggle appears, the more I will try to go through it as becomes the son of Montgomery, and of such a mother."——While he spoke however of fortitude, he vainly tried to conquer the anguish which the idea of such a separation occasioned. Mrs. Montgomery had exerted herself to the utmost and fearing lest she should finish the conversation with less firmness than she had shewn during its continuance, she rose and abruptly left the room. Montgomery attempted not to stop her; but leaning his arm on the table, he remained meditating on his situation, and arming himself with all the fortitude which he could collect from pride, reason, and filial duty: the first forbade him to think of placing his wife in a situation so unworthy of her; the second shewed the impracticability of their living on so small an income; and the third represented the cruelty and injustice of depriving his beloved parent of any part of that income, which reduced as he feared it must be, was hardly enough to procure for her the necessaries of life. He now thought himself no longer in danger of relapsing into the weakness he had but a moment before shewn; but then a formidable phalanx of fears arose, which, though they could not shake his determination, made it almost insupportably painful——Sir Edward Newenden! all the obligations Ethelinde owed him; all she must yet receive; his personal merit; his certain attachment; all approaching her in the seducing semblance of disinterested affection! For a moment he felt all the agonies of jealousy: then reflecting on the honor and the principles of Sir Edward; on the delicacy of Ethelinde's mind, and the certainty of her affection for himself, he conquered the hydra he had raised; till the probable length of his absence, the possibility of Sir Edward's becoming free, and the easy transition from gratitude to love, again recurred; and reason, prudence, pride, and ambition could not, though combined to oppose these cruel apprehensions, prevent their tormenting him anew.

In about half an hour, Mrs. Montgomery and Ethelinde returned. Candles were immediately brought, which Montgomery, while he sat alone, had forgot to order; and though Ethelinde drew her hat over her face, it was easy to see by her eyes how truly her heart had sympathized with that of her unhappy lover. Those of his mother bore too traces of the pain she had felt, in communicating to Ethelinde what had passed in their conversation; and that which she was sensible of, in thus being compelled by necessity to advise the separation of two beings, who seemed to be, though now perhaps doomed to meet no more, intended by heaven for each other.

Their hearts were all too heavy to allow them to enter on general conversation, and too full to touch on those topics which engaged their thoughts; deep sighs, therefore, only were exchanged; and as soon as tea was over, Ethelinde desired to have an hackney coach called, to carry her to Hanover Square. Mrs. Montgomery had told her son, that in the morning of the next day she meant to begin her journey for Dover; to which place he intended to accompany her; and even to cross the water with her: and he knew that the journey of Ethelinde with Miss Newenden was so soon to take place, that probably she would be gone before his return to town. Struck, therefore, with the idea that this was to be a final adieu (for the ship in which he should probably sail for India, was to depart in less than three weeks), he had no power to rise to obey her; but sat silent, and yet agitated beyond the power of expression to do justice to the pain he felt.

Again, in a faint voice, Ethelinde repeated—"Will you be so good, Mr. Montgomery, to order a coach for me?"—and again he heard without immediately answering her. At length he said—"You go then!—and we meet no more!"—Ethelinde, to whom this idea was equally insupportable, could utter nothing. Mrs. Montgomery alone had courage to say—"I hope not so!"—"And yet why should any of us hope," said her son, "to meet again? since it is only to give new pangs to a separation more dreadful than that which disjoins the soul from the body.—Why should we say adieu at all—for myself I cannot!"

"Do not then," said Ethelinde: "it is indeed only sentiment refining on misery. All that we feel cannot be expressed; and of what use were it, if it could, but to torture each other." She stopped, rather wondering how she had found courage to say so much than attempting to say more. Montgomery, unable to stay in the room, went down himself to see for a coach, and while

he remained absent, his mother took the opportunity of fortify-
ing the resolution of Ethelinde, though rather needing support
for herself than fit to afford it to another—"You judge rightly, my
best love," said she, tenderly taking her hand; "indeed I know not
whether the intellects of poor Charles will be found equal to the
wretchedness inflicted by parting at all, if you do not exert some
fortitude to enable him to bear it; for my part, I own I dread the
hour when I am myself to say farewel, so much, that I sometimes
doubt whether I shall have strength of mind to encounter it at all. I
did think," continued she, after a short pause, "I did once think of
requesting you to go with me as far as Dover; but what would the
gratification of that wish produce, but fatigue for you, and length-
ened, accumulated anguish for my poor boy!"

"If it will afford you, dearest Madam, any satisfaction," murmured Ethelinde, "think not of either fatigue or pain that it may
give me. I could feel indeed only pleasure in being with you, however it might be embittered by our subsequent separation; but
I own I should doubt whether it might not be too trying to the
resolution, and too destructive to the composure which your son
will require to prepare him for his long, long voyage." The words
died away on her lips; and as inarticulately Mrs. Montgomery
answered—"No, my dear Ethelinde, we will not think of it.—Alas
our separation will be short. When I return from France, I may
again embrace you. But who, oh! my God! who knows whether,
when I have bid farewel to my son, these widowed arms may ever
again enfold their last and dearest blessing."—This idea, so terrible
to the heart of a mother, seemed to conquer all the fortitude which
Mrs. Montgomery had been collecting. A violent passion of tears
relieved her; which she had hardly time to indulge before Montgomery returned with quick steps and wild looks into the room.
He seemed breathless with agitation, and said, in a hurrying way
to Ethelinde—"Miss Chesterville, the coach you desired is there!—
All then ends thus," added he, clasping his hands together—"here,
too probably, terminates for ever all hopes of happiness for me!"

"My dear Charles," said his mother, who now found the necessity of exerting herself—"You do not, I am persuaded, believe
what your distress of mind makes you say. Many smiling years are
yet in store for you; when the consciousness of having deserved
her shall heighten your happiness with the loveliest of women!"

"They *may* be in store for me, Madam; but it is only a possibility. Ethelinde is perhaps destined to make some worthier, some more fortunate man, happy!"

He was proceeding, when Ethelinde interrupted him.—"What shall I say to you, Montgomery, to make you easy on that point?"

"Nothing," answered he, in a tone of mournful despondence, which sunk into her heart; "I would not fetter you by promises which so many circumstances may tempt you to wish you could break. If my distress, if my insupportable torments really moved your compassion, you would become mine irrecoverably, and put it beyond the malice of fate to divide us."

"*If* your distress moved my compassion?" repeated Ethelinde. "Is this then a time to express such a doubt? Cruel Montgomery! Cruel, thus to aggravate sufferings which you see I can hardly support!"

"Forgive me," exclaimed he, "I deserve that reproach—but forgive me; and do you, dear Madam, make allowance for your unhappy son. I am almost as weak as I am wretched! Indulge me, therefore, in one request!——I cannot, Ethelinde, I cannot take my last leave of you to-night, let me therefore see you for only one moment to-morrow! *I*, who just now declaimed against the voluntary misery of a formal parting, now desire to be gratified in misery!"

He seemed to expect an answer.—"Indulge him, my Ethelinde," said his mother, "if you can indulge him without inconvenience; and instead of leaving London early, I will defer my departure till noon."

Ethelinde sighed rather than spoke her acquiescence; and then Montgomery asked leave to attend her home. This was no time to deny him; nor was she able to do it, doubting indeed whether she should have strength to carry her down stairs. She approached, therefore, without speaking, towards Mrs. Montgomery, who, throwing her arms round her, kissed her cheek, on which their tears were mingled; and then turning suddenly away, Mrs. Montgomery cried—"May heaven protect my beloved Ethelinde, and restore to me the daughter of my heart! Farewel! on my return to England we shall meet again!" The idea that then Montgomery would not be there to rejoice in that meeting, stopped her utterance; and Ethelinde, who could not return her adieu by any thing but tears and sobs, hastened to the door, and was led by Montgomery down stairs, and into the coach which was waiting.

When they were placed in the coach, Montgomery still retained her hand, on which, as he pressed it to his trembling lips, the tears incessantly fell during the short time that the coach took in carrying them from Portman street to Hanover Square. Ethelinde attempted not to speak. Her heart seemed ready to burst, from the violence of the pain that oppressed it; and tears failed to give her relief, though they fell in showers on her bosom.

When the coach stopped for directions within a few yards of Sir Edward Newenden's house, Montgomery, having pointed out the door to the coachman, said—"At what time to-morrow may I come?"—"As early as you please," replied Ethelinde.—"Will nine o'clock be agreeable to you?"—"Yes! but would it not be better to spare us both such additional suffering?"

"Do not desire to withdraw your promise, Ethelinde; it is the last kindness, perhaps the very last, that I shall ever solicit!" This plea silenced any farther objection. Montgomery assisted her out of the coach, and led her into the hall; then, only repeating, "Remember nine to-morrow," he left her; and Ethelinde, sending a message to Miss Newenden, who was she found at home, to excuse herself from waiting on her and Sir Edward at supper, retired instantly to her own room.

Sir Edward had been very uneasy at her absence with Montgomery; and her message which signified that she had a cold and head ache, and could eat no supper, did not relieve his concern. He dared not, however, betray it either to his sister or his servants; and therefore, with an heart as ill at ease as was that of the object of his solicitude, he went restless and dissatisfied to his own apartment at an early hour; while Miss Newenden, who had settled with him that evening that she should set out with Ethelinde for Brackwood the next day but one, sat down to write to her servants, that her house and her horses might be ready for her. She had now been ten days in town, in the finest weather for hunting that there had been the whole season; and she saw with pleasure the near termination of a sacrifice to which she had reluctantly submitted.

CHAPTER V

This dreadful morning at length arrived, and brought with it the summons which Chesterville and Victorine had long expected, to set out immediately for Portsmouth, where the West India ship, on board of which they had taken their passage, was arrived, and waited only for a wind.

The pillow of Ethelinde had been all night strewn with thorns, which banished every attempt to sleep, and before six o'clock she was dressed, and ready to receive her brother, who soon after tapped at her door, and told her that they were immediately to depart, having received a message from the commander of the vessel, who was himself setting out for Portsmouth.

Her affection for her brother had neither been deadened by the various sensations she had experienced, or diminished by his own ill conduct, and she heard thus abruptly of his immediate departure with acute sorrow. It seemed as if the same day was to tear from her all that was dear to her upon earth, and her heart recoiled from the severe trial that was before her.

Victorine, though she sincerely loved Ethelinde, was of a gay and volatile temper, and felt much less the pain of separation from every body else since her husband was with her; and she fancied herself returning to her native country, and to a father of whose affluence she had entertained the highest ideas, and of whose kind reception of her she was too sanguine to doubt. Chesterville had taken care to inform himself of every particular relating to Mr. Harcourt; and had learned that he still lived a widower on his estate in Jamaica; that his daughter had married and came to England, where she died the next year, without children; and that his son had been some time in Europe, and was then supposed to be making the tour of France and Italy, after which he was to return to Jamaica, and to accompany his father to England, where he had prevailed on him to make considerable purchases, and where he wished to settle for the rest of his life.

Young Harcourt was described as very gay and expensive, but good natured and generous; and the person that gave Chesterville this intelligence, who was the commander of a Jamaica trader, and knew him well, added—"but as to his gaiety and his expences, they cannot hurt his fortune; and he and his father agree mighty well upon the score of money. To be sure, since he is an only child, there is a great deal of it for him."

This account had inspired Chesterville with the most sanguine expectations; and as he had taken care to procure every testimony that Victorine was the daughter of the unfortunate Anthonietta, he had the warmest hopes of her being received as a daughter by the elder Harcourt; and that the younger would not oppose her having a share of his abundance, since he had now no other sister.

The tears and languor of Ethelinde, on a parting which he thought promised only a speedy and fortunate return to England, seemed more to him than the occasion called for; and he endeavoured to shew it to her in as chearful a light as he saw it in himself. "In a few months, my Ethy," said he, "Victorine and I shall return to you with half a dozen negroes, and a cargo of clayds and muscavados,[1] ginger, aloes and cotton, besides a ship's lading of mahogena enough to furnish an house. We'll have it all consigned to our cousin's, Messrs. Ludford's, of Bristol, who will then, I dare say, be our very humble servants; and when all is happily disposed of, I shall, with the net produce in my pocket, set out to pay first my debt to Sir Edward, and then we will purchase a pretty little freehold, with a manor in some county where there is good pheasant shooting, and you and I and Victorine will live all together as pleasantly as possible."

Ethelinde, though glad to see him so chearful, and that misfortune had wounded him so lightly in its passage, could not forget that not five weeks had yet elapsed since he saw his father expire, whose death his indiscretion had undoubtedly hastened. Montgomery too, the friend to whom he had been in the hour of his adversity so much obliged, seemed to be left out of his arrangement in his visionary prosperity. She was more hurt, therefore, by his apparent want of affection, than relieved by his vivacity,

1 Two forms of sugar: muscavado is raw dark sugar, produced on plantations; clayed sugar is sugar which has been processed by a solution of white clay in water to turn the sugar almost white. The "negroes" Chesterville carelessly refers to may be servants rather than slaves; the context is not precise enough to apply Mansfield's ruling of 1772 clearly. Aloes (used in medicine), ginger and cotton were typical imports. Mahogena is mahogany wood.

and answered, with a deep drawn sigh, and a faint though forced smile—

"You are very good, brother, to admit me into your scheme of felicity; I pray God, that as far as it relates to yourself and my sister, your imaginary good fortune may be realized, and even exceeded."

"Oh! doubt it not," gaily rejoined Chesterville; "that cursed jilt Fortune is weary I know of persecuting me; and now you will see I shall be one of her first favourites. And pray, my sweet Ethelinde, who deserves her partiality better?"

"There are," said Ethelinde, "who deserve it at least as well."

"So there are, upon my soul.—No—I don't say there are, in the plural; but there is *one* dear good fellow who deserves every thing. Yes, I own that Montgomery is truly deserving; and to cease rattling, let me tell you very seriously, my sister, that if ever fortune does smile upon me, I hold myself bound in honor to share every-thing with Montgomery. I hope to live to see him in affluence, and what will make affluence desirable to him, your husband."

This warm praise of her lover obliterated the little displeasure which the too great volatility of her brother had momentarily excited; and while it restored him to her tenderness, redoubled the regret with which she remembered that the globe itself would in a few months be between Montgomery and Chesterville; that her parent and protector was mouldering in the bosom of the earth, and that she should, after the passing day, become desolate and forlorn; relying only on the generous friendship of Sir Edward Newenden, who exerted it not without ill consequence to himself.

So many afflicting reflections were enough to overwhelm stronger spirits, and a firmer heart than Ethelinde possessed. In the dejection which oppressed her, she now wished that she had not so resolutely refuted to unite her fate with Montgomery, and even to accompany him to India; now fancied that it would have been better for her had she determined to have gone to Jamaica with her brother and his wife. She sat in speechless sorrow by the breakfast table, where Victorine now joined her and Chesterville; and where Sir Edward, who was usually a very early riser, soon after appeared.

If the girlish levity of Victorine, elate with hope, and pleased with the thoughts of novelty; and the alacrity inspired by the flat-

tering prospects of her brother, were so painful to the heavy melancholy of Ethelinde, the looks and countenance of Sir Edward
were in perfect correspondence. He seemed hardly able to speak,
while by a painful effort only he kept up a sort of conversation with
Chesterville; received with friendly attention his acknowledgments for all the kindness he had shewn, and gave him excellent
advice for the regulation of his future conduct, and his introduction to Mr. Harcourt, to whom Mrs. Montgomery and her son
had given him letters. The mention of this gave Chesterville occasion to say that he could not go without seeing Montgomery; and
that as soon as he knew he was to set out that morning, he had
informed him of it, and expected him there every moment.

Ethelinde grew paler than before at this intelligence. The
misery of that parting which she felt herself so unable to sustain,
was now to be prolonged, and to be heightened by becoming witness to the previous farewel that Montgomery was to take of her
brother.

She had not, however, time to dwell on the prospect of such
a scene before it was present to her; for Montgomery almost
immediately entered the room. Sir Edward, who had remarked
the change in Ethelinde's countenance at the very mention of his
name, now cast his penetrating looks towards her, and saw, with
anguish, the mournful and heavy eyes which seemed to survey, in
mingled pity, tenderness, and despair, the face of Montgomery,
where on stronger features the same passions were more forcibly
expressed.

Montgomery seemed eager to speak, as if to hide his confusion
and concern; but he hardly knew what he said. In a few moments
the servants, who had been placing the baggage in the chaise which
Sir Edward had lent them, as being more convenient for travelling
than an hired one, came to inform Mr. and Mrs. Chesterville that
every thing was ready.—"Once more then, dear Sir Edward," said
Chesterville, who had now lost his alert gaiety, "once more let me
thank you, though words cannot do it, for all your friendship, and
believe that the first purpose of my life is to shew my gratitude."

He wrung his hand; and Sir Edward advancing to salute Victorine, who thanked him in her broken English, Chesterville turned
towards Montgomery—"My dear Charles!" was all he could say
for a moment: then recovering his voice, he added—"may happi-

ness and health be your's wherever you are! and may the time very soon arrive when the virtue and goodness of Ethelinde shall repay the generous friendship you have shewn to her father and her brother! Sir Edward, till my beloved friend can claim her, to your protection I commend my sister." He stepped forward towards Ethelinde and embraced her, but neither could speak; he gave her hand, while she seemed hardly able to breathe, to Sir Edward, and then ran down stairs, and Montgomery, taking the hand of Victorine, hastily put her into the chaise, and it immediately drove from the door.

Ethelinde heard it; and with a deep sigh and a shower of tears recovering her voice—"they are gone!" said she, faintly.

"But I do not see, my dear Ethelinde," said Sir Edward, who knew not that she was now suffering all the anguish of a parting more terrible, "I do not see indeed why this departure should so heavily afflict you. I rather hope, and there seems to me to be every reason to believe, that what appears now so painful will be attended with the most fortunate consequences."

"Yes, Sir Edward," replied she, "I know all I owe you for having procured poor Harry's re-establishment in the army, and for having sent him where he has such favourable prospects."

"You owe me nothing, Ethelinde. The little I have been able to do would have been infinitely overpaid had it made you easier, or could it make you happy."

Montgomery, after Chesterville's departure, had remained a moment below to recover himself; he now returned into the room. Sir Edward desired him to sit down; and spake of the friends of whom they had just taken leave with great regard. Montgomery, whose soul was torn with sensations of agony hardly to be endured, answered as well as he could; but Sir Edward saw his countenance agitated, and heard his voice tremble; and easily conceiving that he sought an opportunity of being alone with Ethelinde, he after a few moments prevailed on himself to leave, with the woman he adored, a favoured lover.

For some moments after he had left the room, Ethelinde and Montgomery were silent. At length the former, who found that she must either shorten the scene or sink under it, collected courage enough to say—"Does my dear Mrs. Montgomery continue determined to set out to-day?"

"Yes," replied he, "she does; and with her goes the unhappy man who is now come to bid you—ah! too probably, to bid you an eternal adieu!"

"No," answered the faultering and trembling Ethelinde, "we shall meet again: I am persuaded we shall. Providence will protect the son so beloved, and restore him to his excellent mother."

"And what," said Montgomery, interrupting her,—"what shall restore him to happiness if you forget him? Ethelinde! if ever you feel a wish to obliterate from your mind the idea of your banished Montgomery, wish at the same moment that he may never live to know it."

"This is merely distressing me and yourself, Montgomery. If you think me so volatile, so incapable of real attachment, I am unworthy of the affection you profess for me. But you do *not* think it. You know that my heart is—ever must be yours: why must I repeat that it never had, never can have, another affection!"

"Oh! repeat it!" cried Montgomery, "repeat it I beseech you; and let me for one poor moment forget that I am going where I can hear it no more!"

"What shall I say," asked Ethelinde, "to make you as easy under our separation as our situation will admit? Shall I give you the most solemn assurances that I will be yours or die unmarried? If such assurances either spoken or written will afford you one moment's consolation when you think of me——"

"No," replied Montgomery, "I will not ask either. If you continue to love me they will not strengthen my claim to happiness; and if—but I will not think of it—if another should ever become more dear to you—the undone Montgomery would disdain to retain a right to the hand of her whose heart disowns him. Ethelinde! the memorials given and received by common lovers, can do nothing I know towards strengthening an affection like ours: but you will indulge my weakness: there is a picture of you which was your father's; drawn, as I remember hearing him say when you were about fifteen: give me that picture; that when such an immense distance divides us, my eyes may dwell on the faint copy of those features!"

A blush arose on the cheek of Ethelinde; and faultering she said—"Indeed, Montgomery, I would give you the picture with pleasure—but I have not got it."

"Who has it then?" said he eagerly. "Have you given it to Chesterville?"

"No," replied Ethelinde, who by this question had an opportunity of concealing the truth, had she been capable of artifice, "but Sir Edward, who is fond of Meyer's miniatures, and thought that, not only very like but extremely well painted, begged me to give it him."

"And Sir Edward then," cried Montgomery, "has it? Sir Edward wears it?"

"I do not believe he wears it. No, certainly, he has merely put it into a little cabinet where he keeps many others."

" Ask it of him again. It cannot be of the value to him that it is to me. How *could* you so cruelly part with it?"

"How could I refuse it to Sir Edward, to whom I owe so many obligations?"

"Obligations!" exclaimed Montgomery, rising and walking to the other end of the room—"Obligations! Yes, I know their extent but too well! 'Tis these obligations which distract me! A divorce, which I am well informed he intends to sue for, will give you an opportunity of acquitting yourself; and Montgomery, in Indostan,[1] will be recollected only to wonder how you could ever give him hope!"

This was more than poor Ethelinde could sustain. "Cruel! unjust Montgomery! Do you then really think so ill of me? do you really impute the generous conduct of Sir Edward towards us all, to motives which he never, I believe, thought of? I hoped that Montgomery, himself so capable of generous and disinterested friendship, would never have suffered such a misconception of the nobleness exerted by another to enter his thoughts: I hoped that his affection for me was founded so much on his good opinion of my heart and my principles, that it could not give birth to a suspicion and jealousy as unworthy of himself as injurious to me."

Montgomery, who felt himself wrong and unreasonable yet could not conquer the emotions of jealousy which Sir Edward's attention for Ethelinde had always given him, now apologized for what he was willing to allow unreasonable, and now relapsed into discontented murmuring at his fate: but the picture, the picture,

1 India.

like the handkerchief of Othello,[1] was still not to be got over; till
the weeping and distressed Ethelinde was at length compelled to
promise that she would ask Sir Edward for it, and that when he
came back from France he should have it.

Having made her again and again repeat this promise, he
now attempted to obtain her leave to see her then at the house
of Miss Newenden, and to receive it from her own hands. Ethelinde, though she dreaded to think of this interview as the last they
were to have before his sailing for India, yet knew she ought not
to indulge him in this request. She resisted it therefore as long as
she could; till quite overcome by the various emotions of distress
which she had undergone, she heard him only with silent tears. At
length he pretended to believe he had obtained her consent; and
while he eagerly kissed her hand, told her that he by no means considered it as a last adieu; and then, as if willing to quit her while
that hope prevented his relapsing into the frantic expressions of
sorrow in which he had before indulged himself, he hurried away;
and Ethelinde with difficulty reached her own room; where she
remained till dinner, when she tried to appear with tolerable calmness.

But the trials of this day were not yet over. Scarce had the form
of dinner passed, of which only Miss Newenden partook, when
a violent rap at the door surprised them, as it was a very unusual
hour for visitors. Sir Edward and Miss Newenden had given general orders to be denied: but a voice was heard somewhat loud to
echo through the hall, which was immediately known to be that of
Mrs. Maltravers, saying—"Don't tell me; I know he is at home, and
I *will* see him!"

"Good God!" cried Ethelinde, "it is Mrs. Maltravers."

"I declare I won't see her," said Miss Newenden. "I hate her, an
affected, painted old puss."

"There is no occasion for either you or Ethelinde to see her,"
said Sir Edward calmly; "her business is probably with me only."

A servant now entered to say that Mr. and Mrs. Maltravers had
both left their coach and insisted on seeing Sir Edward. He directed

1 Shakespeare's black hero, a Moor, is driven wild with jealousy when he is
told Desdemona has given a handkerchief that Othello gave her to Othello's
lieutenant, Cassio. *Othello* III: 3.

that they should be shewn into his study, and immediately went to them.

Miss Newenden remained a moment with Ethelinde; of whose uneasiness she took however no notice; only said of her brother—"These people are come, I suppose, to see if they can make up matters between Ned and his wife. Poor fellow, he'll be plagued with them, I suppose, the whole evening."

"Would to God," said Ethelinde, "that they might, however, succeed, and that Sir Edward could be prevailed upon to overlook the difference that has arisen between him and Lady Newenden."

"He never explained to me," said Miss Newenden, "what it was that gave him such offence. He was so much in an habit of bearing her insolence and caprice, that I thought he would never have grown restive let her have done what she would. I dare say that all this rearing and kicking, will end in his being quiet again, and submitting to the curb as gently as ever. Ned was always as soft hearted as a girl; and has no notion of taking the bit between his teeth and setting off, as I should have done long ago, if I had been jaded by such a vain, ill tempered, proud doll."

"Do not however," said Ethelinde, "my dear Miss Newenden, oppose a reconciliation if it can be brought about."

"Not I, upon my soul," answered she. "I have not the least intention either to oppose or promote it. I wish Ned very happy; but I have no skill in judging what will make him so. No, I shall never give him any advice about his wife; not even my opinion of her. And perhaps, all things considered, he will be as much plagued in parting with her as in keeping her. I wish him well through it. What have you got to do to-night?" continued she: "if you have much preparation to make you had better do it to-night, as I shall be off in the morning at seven."

Ethelinde, glad to be released from a conversation she was hardly able to support, said she would go to prepare for so early a departure, and retired to her own room to reflect with anguish on the transactions of the day, and with anxiety on the situation of Sir Edward, who remained for some hours in conference with Mr. and Mrs. Maltravers.

CHAPTER VI

At the hour of supper, Ethelinde, whose solicitude for Sir Edward her own extreme unhappiness could not lessen, collected strength enough to go down. She found Miss Newenden alone in the eating parlour, and that her brother's visitors were but just gone. In a few moments he came to them; and Ethelinde, accustomed by the innocent affection she had ever felt for him to study and understand every change of his countenance, saw with infinite concern that he had suffered greatly in a conference which had removed no part of his unhappiness. While the servants waited, however, he affected to talk with his sister of her journey of the next day, and of other indifferent matters; but as soon as the table was cleared, and the servants withdrawn, Miss Newenden, who never had the least notion of checking whatever she had a mind to say, lest it should hurt the feelings of another, asked him very abruptly what the Maltravers's had said to him.

"You may guess," answered he, "that the purport of their visit was to defend, excuse, and falsify the conduct of their daughter; and by endeavouring to prove my opinion of her ill conduct erroneous, to prevail on me to believe I had injured her and induce me to solicit her return."

"And does this come from herself?" enquired Miss Newenden, "or is it only the old folks who desire to make you believe what they please?"

"Really Nelly," answered Sir Edward, "it is an affair in which I feel such distracting contrariety of emotions that I hardly know how to speak upon it."

"Nay I'm sure I don't desire to know more than you have a mind to tell me. You never knew me, brother, teize you with female curiosity."

"I am far from thinking your curiosity teizing, my dear Ellen," said Sir Edward, "but rather thank you for feeling an interest in my unhappiness! nor can I blame the interposition of Mr. and Mrs. Maltravers: the former, either from his excessive attachment to his daughter, or from his wife's management, or perhaps from both, is blind and incredulous when any blame is imputed to her; and as to the old lady, she knows that in her own vanity, folly and levity, her daughter saw at once an example and an excuse; 'tis therefore natural enough for them both to plead for their daughter, and I could forgive them any thing their defence of her might urge them to say of me; but when they forget humanity, truth, candour, and integrity, so far as to assert what they do not themselves believe, and to blast, as far as in their power, the character of the innocent and defenceless, I lose my temper; and could I forgive Lady New-enden's conduct, which is impossible, I would listen to no accommodation till they had publicly vindicated those whom they have so infamously aspersed."

Ethelinde could not be ignorant that this related to her; and harrassed and exhausted as she was, she yet exerted herself enough to reply—"Sir Edward! if you allude, as I apprehend, to what Mr. and Mrs. Maltravers have said of *me*, and if that remains any impediment to a reconciliation between you and Lady New-enden, for God's sake forget it; I trust that the friends who love me never suffered their good opinion to be shaken by a report which those who raised it did not themselves believe. As to the world in general, it has by this time some other object of attention, and certainly cares not what becomes either of me or the report: make therefore no point with Mr. Maltravers about it, but be it suffered to die of itself; while I remain for the rest of my life where I may never again disturb the peace of my cousin and her family."

Sir Edward was extremely affected by the plaintive tenderness of her voice, and by the tears which slowly fell from her eyes while she spoke. "No, Ethelinde!" cried he, taking her hand—"were it in my nature, which it is not, to accept a compromise where my own honor is concerned, I am urged by every motive that ought to have influence with me, to defend yours, and I *will* defend it to my last hour. Speak of it no more, my dear cousin, nor be thus deeply affected; innocence and goodness like yours have nothing to fear; but next in infamy to him who would deprive you of the reality of those virtues, is the despicable wretch who would by falsehood and defamation obscure their lustre and their purity." He found himself too much moved; and unable to command his emotions, he rose hastily, and wishing them both a good night, told them he should be with them at breakfast in the morning, and then left the room.

Ethelinde sat with her handkerchief held to her eyes, leaning on the table. "Come, come," said Miss Newenden, "let's have no more of this sentimental ti tum ti nonsense. I'm really worn to death with it. What signifies crying? old women are always making mischief, and as to that made up antiquity Mrs. Maltravers, she hates you because you are handsomer than either herself or her daughter; and they were both more jealous by half of Lord Danesforte, I dare swear, than ever they were of my brother. Never mind; pluck up a spirit, and shew them you don't care two pence for them, and then they'll be as civil as can be."

"It is not on my own account," sighed Ethelinde, "that I am uneasy, however injurious to me their proceedings have been; but I am miserable when I think in how much trouble and anxiety his great goodness to my father and my brother has involved Sir Edward."

"Well but what good will being miserable do? It can't make things better you know; and you will only fret yourself sick for nothing. If I was you, I would get myself well, that I might look handsome and catch some man of fortune, on purpose to shew Lady Newenden that her malice had done me no harm, and that Ned never had any attachment to you more than because you was her relation."

Miss Newenden was so utterly incapable of entering into the feelings and sentiments of Ethelinde, that she attempted not to convince her that this way of being revenged would make her decidedly miserable: she therefore only thanked her for the interest she took in her welfare, and hastened to bed; where, amidst all the pain she had suffered in the course of the day, that of having parted with Montgomery *for ever* was so much the most severe, that every other anxiety vanished before it. It would indeed have left her no power to have supported herself the rest of the day, if a latent hope that she should once again see him before he left Europe had not lingered in her bosom; and while she wept over their parting as final, she involuntarily flattered herself that he would, notwithstanding her refusal to consent to it, see her on his return from France.

How to ask Sir Edward for a picture which she had given him, and on which she knew he set so high a value, she knew not; yet to disappoint Montgomery after the solemn promise she had given him, was yet more impossible: after much deliberation she determined to ask Sir Edward for it the next morning, that she might leave it in town to be copied. She foresaw that this might introduce a conversation relative to Montgomery, which she wished to avoid; but as no alternative remained, and she could not for a moment support the thoughts of disappointing him or raising anew his uneasiness on the subject of Sir Edward, she fixed on this plan; and as she knew he had never seen the picture above twice, and that she could have it very exactly copied, she believed he would not distinguish it from the original; and should by this means gratify Montgomery without appearing capricious and ungrateful to Sir Edward Newenden.

The various agitations she had gone through during the day, had entirely exhausted her spirits; and in despite of her uneasiness she fell into a slumber, in which however, the image of Montgomery, in distress and in despair, attempting amidst rocks, precipices, storms, and darkness, to reach her, haunted her imagination. Now, she fancied she saw his mother in all the agonies of maternal sorrow, weeping for his death, and accusing her as having been the cause of it; and now, that in the midst of a tempestuous sea she beheld him struggling for life, and holding out his hands towards her and towards his mother, who had neither of them the power to save him. These images had been produced, not only by the perturbation of her mind but by her having recalled to her memory before she slept all the scenes she had passed through with Montgomery, from the first moment of their meeting in the storm on the banks of Grasmere Water, to the last hour of their parting; his saving her when she fell from the boat; his generous friendship to her brother; the sympathizing tenderness with which he attended with her on her dying father; all had been recollected and reviewed with that painful delight that the heart of fond susceptibility feels in dwelling on the excellence it glories in loving, while agonized with the dread of eternal separation.

While sleep gave to Ethelinde only the unrefreshing exchange of vague and imaginary terrors for painful certainties, Sir Edward Newenden, to whom even such a respite from corrosive reflections was denied, was arguing himself into at least the appearance of composure against the next day; when he was to take leave of her, to whom his heart was so fondly attached, that he felt the separation as a deprivation of his existence; and when he was to determine on what conduct he should pursue in regard to Lady Newenden, whom he at once lamented and despised, pitied and scorned; whom he now thought of with tenderness as the mother of his children and now with indignation as her who had disgraced and deserted them.

Neither the behaviour of Mr. Maltravers nor of his wife had served to conciliate and soften Sir Edward. Weak in regard to Lady Newenden, but hard, unfeeling, and severe, towards every body else; elate with the consciousness of immense wealth, and proudly sensible of the consequence it ought to give him with a man whose embarrassed affairs had been retrieved by having married his daughter, Mr. Maltravers had at first assumed with Sir Edward a tone of remonstrance and sharp expostulation: he now resented what was past, now dictated what should be done in future; sometimes defended Lady Newenden, and sometimes allowed that it was possible she might have been driven into some degree of indiscretion by the evident and improper partiality which Sir Edward had shewn to her cousin.

Sir Edward had heard him for the most part with great coolness; but when Ethelinde was so injuriously named he lost his temper. Then Mrs. Maltravers, affecting to believe his warmth arose from his consciousness of the truth of what her husband had said, declaimed against the art and the wickedness of poor Ethelinde till she actually scolded; and nothing but the authority of Maltravers could stop the torrent of female eloquence with which she assailed her son in law, making up in noise and volubility what she wanted in reason and truth.

When Maltravers could prevail upon her to be a moment silent, he with more gravity detailed all the instances Sir Edward had shewn of attachment to the Chesterville family.—"You cannot impose upon *me*, Sir Edward," said he: "I have seen, let me tell you, a great deal of the world, and I think I know mankind well. I cannot therefore listen at all—indeed, Sir Edward, I cannot, to all these pretences of disinterested friendship to your wife's family. Don't I know that nobody cares even for their *own* family, and that a man now won't lend his own brother an hundred pounds with-

out some good that may come of it to himself, nor without security; why then should you so lavishly lend a considerable sum, or
rather give it, for you'll never get it again; no, you'll never see a
guinea of it; why should you give it to the Chestervilles? people
whom you were only distantly connected with: let me tell you, Sir
Edward, you had no right to do it, and it was very plain you considered them more than my daughter's children, though they in fact
have the only claim to it, or than my daughter herself."

"I am very sorry, Sir," said Sir Edward, "that you have seen so
much of the worst side of human nature as to believe that no man
serves a fellow creature in distress but from some selfish motive;
allow me, however, to assure you that had no such person as Miss
Chesterville existed I should equally have done what I did for the
Colonel; and as to the money, if by an arrangement of his affairs
which I hope to get through, I never am repaid it, let me inform
you, Mr. Maltravers, that it was my own, and lay in my banker's
hands out of the produce of my estates, and from the legacy given
by an aunt, as you well know. The money never was your's, Sir, or
your daughter's: Lady Newenden took care to dispose of all she
had any right to, in another manner; mine I chose rather to use in
assisting the worthy in distress, than to lose at play to the vicious
and the profligate."

"*Your* money! the produce of *your* estates, Sir, and the amount
of a legacy! and pray what saved your estates? what but your marriage with my daughter? and what got you a legacy of six thousand pounds from your aunt but your being likely to establish your
family consequence? Had you been poor, you know very well she
would have given all of it, instead of half, to your sister; therefore
in fact you owe even that to your marriage; and to hear you talk
of arranging Chesterville's affairs, and of a probability of being
repaid the money, is really enough to provoke a stone: you know in
your own heart, that he died not worth sixpence, that you buried
him at your own expence, and afterwards bought his son a commission, and now support his daughter, and all for disinterested
friendship! No, no, Sir Edward, such a pretence can take in nobody
but children; these are no times for romantic generosity; and
though you may gain credit for it with boys at college, or boarding
school girls, the world, Sir Edward, knows better, and you can no
more make it believe such a story, than you can make *me* believe

it, who have acquired a tolerable competency by some years of laborious application in India, and know something of the value of money."

Thus, for the greater part of the time, Sir Edward could not make either Maltravers or his wife recede from the prejudice they had taken up as to his motives for having so warmly befriended the family of Ethelinde. Finding, however, that they were incapable of generosity and candour, he alarmed their pride by protesting that their invidious conduct had determined him on a point which had hitherto been doubtful with him, and that he would now attempt that, from which tenderness for his children had hitherto withheld him; and by publicly proving that he complained not without reason of Lady Newenden, vindicate at once his honor and that of the innocent person whom she and her friends and associates had stigmatized to screen or excuse themselves.

Maltravers, while he either was or affected to be blind to the truth, yet could not help feeling the evil consequences to his daughter with which even the attempt to establish her culpability would be attended; and Mrs. Maltravers knew so well that there was foundation for his suspicions, that she thought it too hazardous to dare him to the proof. The steady and cool manner in which he declared his determination, and their knowledge of his temper, which, though mild, cool, and deliberate, was, when thoroughly roused, warm and inflexibly resolute, made them both have recourse to what they should first have tried, soothing and conciliation rather than reproach and invective. All, however, that could be obtained of Sir Edward was, that he would do nothing rashly, and that if Lady Newenden could clear her conduct of the suspicions which rested upon it from her behaviour at Danesforte, Sir Edward would receive her; and that all should be forgotten on both sides that could tend to recall the disagreeable events of the last two months. This concession was rather extorted from Sir Edward Newenden than chearfully granted. They left him, however, when they had obtained it; and had then a much harder task to encounter; which was, to persuade Lady Newenden of the necessity of a reconciliation which she was far from desiring, and which her offended pride, and her disappointed ambition, (that had aspired to a marriage with Lord Danesforte) equally prevented her from soliciting.

The soul of Sir Edward was, during the whole night, the prey of the most torturing reflections. To quit Ethelinde for ever; to be denied even the delight of seeing her, and of being entitled to her gentle confidence and her interesting gratitude; to receive again the woman whose heart he knew was wholly estranged from him, and of whose personal fidelity he had so much reason to doubt; to subject himself again to the uneasiness Lady Newenden's ill temper and rage for dissipation had before involved him in, was a resolution difficult to take, and would be found, he feared, still more difficult to keep. On the other hand, he could not continue to indulge himself with the company of Ethelinde without injury to her; nor had the imperfections and errors of Lady Newenden so entirely erased the tenderness he once felt for her, but that to throw her off for ever would be attended with great pain. While he thought of her, proud, insolent, unfeeling, losing her fame among gamesters and men of intrigue, he fancied he could expel her for ever from his heart and his thoughts; but when the once fair, blooming, artless Maria, who had preferred him to all mankind; when the mother of his beautiful children presented herself in softer colours to his imagination, he was ready to accuse himself of cruelty, and to ask his own heart whether its passion for another had not betrayed him into injustice, and laid him open to suspicion; then, however, all he had seen of her infatuation for the company of Lord Danesforte, of the dauntless effrontery with which she had disdained alike to consult either his peace of mind, or the opinion of the world, occurred to him, and he blamed himself for the facility with which he had long borne it, and despised himself for the pusillanimity with which he but a moment before was persuading himself again to embrace the yoke, and to forget the causes which urged him to throw it off.

CHAPTER VII

The morning brought with it only accumulated anguish for Sir Edward. He attempted to appear gay because he could not be tranquil: but his smile was the forced effort of stifled despair; and while he affected to talk of indifferent matters, the broken and incoherent sentences faultered on his tongue. Ethelinde saw how wretched he was, with concern little short of his own; and dreaded to ask for the picture, which, however reluctantly, her promise to Montgomery compelled her to do. Miss Newenden, however, left them not alone; and Ethelinde, hesitating and fearful, at length said—"Sir Edward, you have a little miniature which was my poor father's: a friend of mine is desirous of having a copy of it. Will you be so good as to lend it me that I may send it to a person who paints miniatures, for that purpose?"

"A friend wants a copy of it? May I ask to whom you mean to grant such an indulgence?"

"Certainly you may ask; and I never will deceive you: the copy is for Mr. Montgomery."

Sir Edward changed countenance; but said, as calmly as he could—"I will fetch the picture, Ethelinde: perhaps you may chuse to give Mr. Montgomery that rather than a copy. If so, I am sure *my* wish to keep it ought to yield to his and your's."

He suppressed a sigh, and arose. Ethelinde, who could not bear to see him unhappy, answered—"No, Sir Edward, if it is of the least value to you as a good miniature I would by no means take it." She was confused, and hardly knew what she ought to say. Sir Edward left the room, but instantly returned with the miniature in his hand.—"Here is the picture, Ethelinde," said he. She took it, and said, in a hurrying voice—"I thank you, I will send it to be copied, and direct that it may be restored to you."

Sir Edward felt that it were wiser not to retain it; but he could not prevail on himself to resign it to Montgomery. He answered not: but again reassuming his place at the breakfast table, forced a conversation on the manner in which his sister would pass the rest of the winter. By this time the chaise was at the door; and the three little Newendens were brought in to take leave of their aunt and Ethelinde.

To the departure of the former, who never shewed them the least attention, they were quite indifferent: but they all were very fond of Ethelinde; and the eldest boy hung about her, and entreated her not to go.—"Pray don't leave us, cousin Ethy, pray don't; but stay and love George, and me, and Maria, now we have no Mama."

"No, dear Edward," answered Ethelinde, while her eyes filled with tears, "I cannot stay now, but I will come another time." She embraced the little boy, who with difficulty could be disengaged from her arms, and kissed tenderly the other two. Miss Newenden saying—"Come, are you ready, Ethy?" she faintly answered—"yes!" and rising, turned towards Sir Edward, who remained as if fixed to his chair, his eyes rivetted on Ethelinde and his boy, and his countenance pale and dejected. "Good bye, dear Ned," said Miss Newenden. He started, arose and kissed her. "A good journey, and health to you, my sister," said he. He would then have approached to salute Ethelinde; but unable to conquer the violence of concern he felt at seeing her thus depart, he was conscious that he should betray it to the servants who were in waiting; he checked himself, therefore, and seizing her hand, pressed it to his lips, and then hastened away, saying in a voice which betrayed all he tried to conceal—"You will both forgive my not attending you to the chaise."

Ethelinde now followed Miss Newenden down, and they immediately departed. The latter, except on particular topics, seldom talked much; and Ethelinde, who could not speak on them, was left at liberty to reflect on her own situation, to carry her thoughts to the travellers who were by this time in France, and with pain to recall the state of mind in which she had just left her friend and benefactor.

Miss Newenden travelled rapidly, and they were soon at Brackwood Down. The mistress of the house welcomed thither her melancholy guest with her usual careless kindness, and then went to inspect into that which interested her most—the condition of her horses. After having satisfied herself in that essential business, she returned into the house; and while their supper passed, questioned the servant who attended, on all the occurrences of the hunts that had passed during her absence. The man, as he waited, described with great exactness the circumstances of each; in what cover they found,[1] whither they ran, and who was in and who thrown out at the death: a detail which seemed to communicate great pleasure to his lady. The conversation ended only with the table cloth; and then, as Miss Newenden was to arise at five the next morning to hunt, she proposed, and Ethelinde most gladly embraced the proposal, to retire immediately to their beds.

The calm tranquillity of the country, and the long fatigue of

---

1 A covert is a hiding place (hole) found by the fox, a thicket; a hunting cover might be shrubs or woodland.

body and mind which Ethelinde had undergone, contributed to procure her a more comfortable sleep than she had long enjoyed. When she awoke the next morning, she found Miss Newenden had been gone above two hours; and glad to enjoy entire solitude, she arose, and having breakfasted alone, went out to survey the environs of her new abode. The habitation of Miss Newenden had been a large farm house, and was awkwardly contrived; but it was well fitted up by its present tenant, and had been sashed,[1] repaired, and furnished with plain but handsome furniture. It stood in a bottom, amid very extensive and unequal downs, which now wore a russet brown except where long lines of wheat broke the dull uniformity of turf in its winter hue; and here and there a scar of chalk, or a spot sown with turnips, and folded with sheep, diversified the landscape. A few ragged hawthorns, bending from the south west, were scattered over the slopes; but other trees there were none, save only two or three old elms which grew about the house. Behind it was a kitchen garden enclosed within a flint wall, and before it a long uninclosed lawn that wound among the hills, and terminated only in the stable yard, about which all that is requisite for the conveniency of horses was amply provided. The stables had been repaired, and part of them new built at a great expence; and they were inhabited by a set of capital hunters, and a proportionable number of grooms and helpers.

This part of Miss Newenden's establishment could give no pleasure to Ethelinde; but in the present state of her mind she was soothed and consoled by the wild and gloomy solitude, where she hoped to have many hours, in which, uninterrupted by the tedious forms of common life, she could dream of happiness and Montgomery.

And in this hope she was not for some time disappointed. Miss Newenden passed almost every morning abroad; came home to dinner about five o'clock; and as she never worked,[2] and very seldom read, she frequently slept on a sopha for some hours in the evening to recover the fatigue of the early part of the day. Thus

1 Provided with sash windows, a window made of movable panes. The carelessness with which this is registered shows the wealth of Miss Newenden.
2 Worked was the common phrase for needlework, sewing, embroidery. Miss Newenden does not sit and sew to pass the time or make garments for others or herself.

Ethelinde was not compelled to exert herself to find conversation, and Miss Newenden was civil without giving her room to think that her company was either a burthen or a pleasure to her.

About half a mile beyond the house the downs rose to a great height, and the horizon this elevated spot commanded was bounded by the sea at the distance of about six miles. This soon became the favorite walk of Ethelinde; and hither she repaired whenever the weather would allow, and seating herself on the twisted root of an old thorn, would contemplate, with a degree of melancholy satisfaction, the ocean which now separated her from Montgomery, and on whose stormy bosom he was so soon to be conveyed to such a fearful distance from her and his native country.

Fondly, however, as her ideas pursued her absent lover, they failed not frequently to turn with grateful solicitude towards Sir Edward Newenden. He had determined at first not to write to her, or ask to hear from her; that by ceasing to study her perfections either in her conversation or her letters, he might try what that self denial could do towards extinguishing a passion that served only to render him miserable; for her affection for Montgomery he now thought so certain, that he no longer dared to dwell on the possibility of her becoming his with any hope that she could become so by choice; and every thing therefore concurred to shew the necessity of his conquering the hopeless tenderness he had too long indulged.

This forbearance, however, was too hard a task for him long to persevere in it: he wrote to Miss Newenden, as usual, short accounts of himself and his children, and contented himself with sending to Ethelinde only affectionate compliments. In answer to these letters he hoped to have some account of the manner of their passing their time, and of the health and spirits of Ethelinde; but Miss Newenden, who hated to write, sometimes entirely neglected it, and when she took the trouble to do it, her letters were so short and unsatisfactory, that Sir Edward became restless and uneasy, and at length broke through the resolution he had formed and wrote to Ethelinde herself. Near a fortnight had now elapsed, and the life of Ethelinde had passed in the same quiet uniformity. She had just received a letter from Mrs. Montgomery, dated from Paris, whither her son had accompanied her,

and informing her that she was then on the instant departing for
Lyons, and Montgomery on his return to England. The same post
had brought one from Sir Edward, relating the farther measures
taken by Mr. and Mrs. Maltravers to effectuate a re-union. Lady
Newenden was with them at their Berkshire house; but had herself given Sir Edward no reason to believe that she was desirous of
the reconciliation which her parents were so anxious to promote.
Having once taken up his pen to write to Ethelinde, he gave way to
the pleasure of indulging that friendly confidence which he loved
to repose in her, and opened to her all his heart so far as related
to the distracting contention which tore it in regard to his wife;
and Ethelinde saw with renewed uneasiness that his mind was
preyed upon by a thousand contradictory passions which he could
neither conquer nor terminate. Her own anxiety was awakened
by the return of Montgomery to England: she trembled at the
thoughts of seeing him again when so certain that it would be the
last time before his long voyage; and yet found that if he did not
come she should be most completely wretched. Every voice she
heard in the house made her heart palpitate; every distant horseman who passed across the wide downs, her eyes eagerly followed;
she trembled when she fancied that she saw in the passing traveller
a resemblance to his figure and his dress, yet when convinced that
the approaching figure was some stranger, she felt mortified, and
turned away to bewilder herself with conjectures, or indulge herself in tears.

The high ground which commanded the sea, presented, on
the other sides, distant views over the country. Thither Ethelinde
now repaired with greater eagerness than ever; and notwithstanding the bleakness of the situation, which exposed her to the severe
winds usual towards the end of February, she passed many hours
every morning there, watching, and at once fearing and hoping
the arrival of him on whom her fancy dwelt with still encreasing
tenderness.

On the third or fourth of these mornings, she saw advancing
towards the house, two gentlemen on horseback, attended by two
servants; and while she fancied, though she was far from them,
that the figure of one of them was known to her, a pack of fox-
hounds, with their huntsman and attendants, issued from behind
a hill in the same direction, and they all proceeded to Brackwood

Down. Ethelinde saw their destination with concern; for she was pretty well persuaded that one of the gentlemen was Davenant. She returned to the house, and found that she was not mistaken; Davenant was in the parlour with Miss Newenden, who almost at the same moment came back from a successless hunt, the morning being frosty and unfavourable. There also was a gentleman his friend, a Mr. Woolaston, well known to Miss Newenden by fame as the completest sportsman in England; and who having gloriously parted with an estate of near three thousand pounds a year, had now nothing to do but to lend his experience in dogs and horses to those who could still afford to keep them in *style*.

Before the entrance of Ethelinde, it had been settled, that Davenant, his friend, his horses and his hounds, should remain a few days at Brackwood. They were passing from his estate in the West to another he possessed in Sussex, where he intended to conclude the hunting season; but the invitation of Miss Newenden delayed their progress; and Ethelinde had the mortification to see her former lover, now infinitely more disagreeable to her than ever, and Mr. Woolaston, who appeared to be confident, presumptuous, and noisy, established for some days at least in the house, of which hitherto quietness had been the sole recommendation.

Though there was, in the opinion of Ethelinde, an evident impropriety in Miss Newenden's receiving such guests, yet, a visitor only, she had no right to object to it; and knew that if she had courage to remonstrate it would avail nothing, as Miss Newenden was as careless of the opinion as insensible to the feelings of others. Nothing remained, therefore, but silent acquiescence; and to arm herself with some degree of pride and coldness against the supercilious airs which Davenant thought proper to assume on meeting her again, and the forward and disgusting freedom with which his friend addressed her.

Miss Newenden, whom their conversation, particularly that of Woolaston, gratified and amused the whole evening, was uncommonly gay and good humoured; and in speaking of their plan for the next day, she said—"Come, Ethy, I have long wished to get you out; 'twill do you fifty times more good, child, than moping at home by yourself. If you've a mind to go with us to-morrow, we shall throw off quite near home, only in Westbourn covers, and about the hangers, and you shall have the Snap mare, who will carry a child of a year old."[1]

"You are very good," replied Ethelinde; "but I am afraid I shall be the means of interrupting your pleasure by an experiment which will afford me none."

"Oh! no," replied Miss Newenden, "'twill not interrupt us, for we shall go on just as if you were not there. Nobody ever stands upon ceremony, you know, in the field; and if you don't like to follow the hounds, James or Frank shall stay with you, and you may come back to the house when you're tired."

Ethelinde, who had been little accustomed to ride on horse-back, still would have declined being of the party; but Miss Newenden, contrary to her usual custom in such cases, seeming to make a point of it, she at length complied, and the Snap mare was ordered to be ready for her in the morning.

Miss Newenden, soon after supper, left the two gentlemen to their wine, and with Ethelinde retired for the night. They were hardly got up stairs before Davenant thus addressed his friend—

"Well, Jack, what dost think of Nelly Newenden?"

"I think her an hard favoured, masculine, disagreeable-looking thing. T'other is as lovely a creature as ever I saw."

"Aye," replied Davenant, "I thought her so once."

"Thought her so once! why—was she ever handsomer than she is now?"

"No, I don't know that she was; but I was a boy, and a fool, and fancied that I should have been proud to have married her. I'm cursed glad that I altered my mind, for I think now I should have been devilish sick of the yoke."

"Egad!" cried Woolaston, "you was more prudent than I should have been. If I could afford to marry at all, I should like her myself. Has she any cash?"

"Not a single sous. No, no, Jack, she won't suit you, believe me. If you want money, look to the lady of the house; she has the yellow boys."[2]

1 A hanger can refer to a wood on a steep hill. A snap mare refers to a horse who descends from an 18th-century thoroughbred horse which won four races and then became a successful stallion. Miss Newenden speaks, thinks, and acts as a horsewoman.
2 "Yellow boys" refers to gold guineas or sovereigns.

"Has she faith?" exclaimed Woolaston. "To what amount, Tom?"

"Oh! to the tune of two or three and twenty thousand pounds, or more for aught I know. She had six or seven given her not long ago by an aunt."

"The devil she has?"

"Yes; and nobody to consult. Suppose, Jack, you try your luck with her."

"Why faith 'tis no bad thought. You know, Tom, how necessary a supply of the ready begins to be to me; but, d'ye think she'd listen to me?"

"Why you may as well try the experiment. If any man succeeds with her, it will be one to whom she can entrust the government of her stud as well as herself."

"Zounds I'd rather take the stud and leave the woman. Why she looks like a stable boy, and talks still more like one. If the lovely Ethelinde now had three and twenty thousand pounds, I should have no qualms."

"But I tell you that the lovely Ethelinde has not three and twenty pence."

"Well; but if I were to swallow the bitter pill of matrimony, gilt with Miss Newenden's gold, d'ye think that sweet girl would remain in the house still by way of humble companion to my spouse?"

"That I cannot tell; but 'tis likely; for you know Sir Edward is supposed to be by no means indifferent to her."

"Oh! then this is the girl that they say has occasioned the parting between Sir Edward Newenden and his wife?"

"The very same."

"Egad I'm glad of that. Perhaps then she is a fixture in the family. But to be in earnest, Tom: d'ye think one might neigh out civilities to this female Nimrod[1] with a likelihood of being heard favourably? Three and twenty thousand pounds would set a man off again without danger of crossing and jostling by d——d impudent troublesome rascals of creditors."

The dialogue ended by Davenant's advising Woolaston to try

1 A term for a powerful hunter; from the Bible, where there are several references, Genesis 10:9, Chronicles 1:10. The connotations are unfavorable, especially when used of a woman.

at least the favourable opinion of Miss Newenden, on which he agreed seriously to reflect; and then pouring out a bumper, he desired Davenant to drink to his future lady, and her lovely companion. Again and again the glasses were filled to the health of the latter; and as the wine mounted into their heads, each talked loudly and lavishly in praise of the personal charms of Ethelinde. The charms of her understanding, and the goodness of her heart, they were incapable of feeling. Davenant, whose former admiration of her beauty the warm encomiums of Woolaston had awakened, began to consider, as well as the present state of his head would give him leave, whether, humbled and reduced as she was, he might not now address her with less honourable views than he had formerly professed, without danger of a repulse; and Woolaston, with equal power of reflection, formed a plan of attack for the next morning. He was now in a situation which afforded him very uncomfortable prospects; and was much struck with the probability of changing those dreary views, and of being re-established in some degree of affluence, if he could marry Miss Newenden: profligate and unprincipled, his connection with Davenant was merely that which interest compelled him to form; and so unstable and unsafe is the friendship of the dissolute, that while Woolaston hoped by means of Davenant to be recommended to an opulent alliance, he with equal avidity considered the probability there might be of engaging Ethelinde as a mistress for his friend; in which case he thought he was secure of obtaining some degree of her favour for himself. With these honourable projects the sportsmen at length retired to their rooms.

CHAPTER VIII

At day-break the party were assembled on horseback in the stable yard, all but Ethelinde, who in a few moments joined them, and was assisted by the grooms to mount the horse provided for her; for Davenant still remained at an haughty distance; and Woolaston, who had now time to arrange and digest his plan, kept close to Miss Newenden, and affected to take no notice of any other person.

They all sallied forth together, towards a copse which edged the hill at about three miles from the house. There, as it was a famous fox cover, they had little doubt of finding; and in a few moments after the hounds entered it, the fox broke the cover, and took over the downs, followed by the pack, by the horsemen, and Miss Newenden.

Ethelinde, who felt no manner of delight in a pursuit that appeared to afford them so much, endeavoured to check the mare she rode, and to prevent her galloping after the rest; but after some ineffectual efforts to this purpose, the creature, who had frequently carried Miss Newenden, and was full of spirit, began to rear and prance: Ethelinde sat it tolerably well; but the groom who was left to attend her assuring her that if she gave the mare her head no harm could come to her, as she would only canter gently, she ceased any attempts to stop her, and in a moment was carried away with the swiftness of the wind.

All she could now do was to exert the little skill she was mistress of, in order to keep the saddle; light and active, she succeeded tolerably well, notwithstanding her fright: but in the midst of her career she was struck by the figure of Montgomery standing near the place where she flew swiftly and involuntarily along. He seemed to gaze on her with astonishment and terror; and his sudden appearance depriving her of all recollection except that which led her to wish herself with him, she disengaged her foot from the stirrup, and letting fall the bridle, threw herself from the saddle; but some part of her dress being entangled on the pummel, and the horse still proceeding with great velocity, she was thrown down with violence, and fell with such force against the ground (which was yet hardened by the frost of the preceding day) that she remained there senseless.

Montgomery, whom she had left about an hundred yards behind her, darted towards the spot in an agony of apprehension not to be described; and lifting her up, he found her face covered with blood, her eyes closed, and the paleness of death on her lips, from which no breath issued to assure him that she yet lived.

Frantic with fear, he wildly called to the servant, entreating him to fly for assistance; but the fellow was already out of hearing; for knowing how angry his mistress would be if any accident happened to the Snap mare, he attended more to the preservation of his place than the preservation of Miss Chesterville. Montgomery then remained alone on a wide down, where no human habitation or human creature appeared, holding in his arms the woman he adored to distraction, who seemed to his terrified imagination to be torn from him for ever.

Stunned by the fall, Ethelinde remained some moments insensible; and Montgomery, who had thrown himself on the ground to support her, in a state of mind bordering on frenzy. He had no means of assisting her recovery: he could not leave her to obtain it, and he saw nobody near him to procure that help for want of which he believed her dying. She began to breathe however, and at length opened her eyes: "Speak to me, Ethelinde," cried Montgomery—"Speak to me, I conjure you; tell me you are not mortally hurt." Her recollection, which the shock had deprived her of, now returned. "I know not," said she faintly, "whether I am hurt to death; but if I am, I die content in your arms, and my last hour will be the happiest of my life."

The trembling and languid voice in which this short sentence was with difficulty uttered, redoubled all the terrors of Montgomery, and the unreserved tenderness it expressed seemed to shew him the value of that life which he believed it was impossible to preserve. At this moment his eyes wildly explored the whole extent of country around him; and at length he saw a human form, but at so great a distance, that it was with difficulty he distinguished it to be a shepherd attending on his flock, and he despaired of making himself heard.

"Let me," cried he to Ethelinde, "let me go to procure, by the means of a man whom I see yonder, a conveyance for you home, that help may be no longer delayed."

"Do not abandon me," replied she, "I am so giddy that I fear my senses are again leaving me: perhaps I am dying; be not too much concerned, dearest Montgomery, if it should be so; remember that this was to have been a separation as cruel, perhaps more cruel than that which death itself can inflict. If I am now to depart, much anxiety, much misery you may escape. Your noble heart, however it may mourn my loss, will no longer in another hemisphere ache with fear or sink with despondence, when you think on your unhappy Ethelinde."

"Distraction!" cried Montgomery. "What shall I do? While I deliberate, she dies. No, think not I would a moment survive you!

Why would you run this risk? Fool that I was ever to part with you!" He now called as loudly as he could to the shepherd, and the wind setting that way, the man at length looked towards them; but having no idea of what was the matter, he contented himself with staring at them a moment, and then went on with wattling his fold.[1]

Montgomery now took off his hat and waved it in the air, again hallowing with all his force; and in a few moments he saw the man striding towards them. As soon as he came within distinct hearing, Montgomery entreated him to make more speed, and as he nearly approached them—"Friend," cried he, "this lady has fallen from her horse, and is much hurt; for God's sake go to Brackwood, and send hither the servants with a carriage to convey her home. Go, instantly go, and I will reward you amply."

The man stood with his hat in one hand, while with the other he scratched his head. "*Fall'd* from his horse, have she," said he in his boorish dialect. "Aye, I wonder they never none of them got a tumble before." "Don't talk, for God's sake," cried Montgomery, whom the least delay rendered distractedly impatient, "but run, and take this for your trouble."

The sight of the money which Montgomery threw towards him had much more effect than the pallid figure of Ethelinde, on the feelings of the rustic; who saying—"Aye, aye, young gentleman, I'll run I warrant you," departed quickly over the hill. "Thank heaven," cried Montgomery, pressing his lovely burthen to his heart, "you will now be removed—you shall be blooded—you will be well." Ethelinde found every attempt to speak attended with great uneasiness: she sighed deeply, and only said—"Be patient, dear Montgomery; the sight of your terror is worse than the pain I feel from the accident."

He saw with fearful apprehension the difficulty with which she spoke:—"I will be patient," cried he; "make no exertion to speak to me." "I will not," replied Ethelinde, again deeply sighing, "for indeed my head feels very confused." She now remained silent; and Montgomery had time to contemplate, while he supported, her almost lifeless form. Her face was bruised: above her temple

1 "Wattle" refers to a material for making fences and walls for shepherd's huts and areas to keep sheep in. Twigs, reeds, and branches are interlaced with poles, rods and stakes.

appeared a cut made by a flint, from which the blood slowly trick-
led down her cheek: her hat had fallen off, and her luxuriant dark
hair spread over her shoulders, and concealed half her face: her
lovely hands, from which he had torn her gloves that he might
chafe them to restore her to life, were of a deathlike hue, and one
of her arms she seemed incapable of moving. While Montgomery,
in the most cruel anxiety, hung over this beloved form, so disfigured yet so dear to his agonized heart, he recalled the time when
he once before held her in his arms to all appearance dying, and
received the first impression of that love which was now become
the first principle of his being. The minutes passed heavily along;
he thought that the people he expected would never arrive; at
length the gardener and one of the helpers, who were the only
servants left at home, arrived with a chaise. Montgomery supported Ethelinde into it, and seated himself by her; but hardly had
it proceeded twenty yards, before, from the revulsion of her blood
or some other cause, Ethelinde fainted, and became lifeless and
senseless in his arms. The men had brought nothing to relieve her
with them; and Montgomery now again fancying she was dead,
was more terrified than before. He stopped the chaise.—"What
will become of me?" cried he; "she is worse than ever—she is dead!
For God's sake send for a surgeon to bleed her; take one of the
horses off and go—ride to the next town for a surgeon. How far is
it now to the house of Miss Newenden?" "How far, Sir," replied the
gardener, "why better than three miles! and as Miss is so bad, had
not your honor better take her to Green's hut, and so send us off
for Doctors?"

"And where is Green's hut? and how soon shall we be there?"

"Lord bless you, why just down in that bottom, behither[1] the
chalk pit—we shall be there in a *minut.*"

To this proposal Montgomery, without knowing whether it
was best or not, assented; and the chaise driving down the hill in
another direction, was immediately at the door of a very small cottage or rather cabin, which, though it consisted only of three little
divisions on the ground, was inhabited by a shepherd, his wife and
five children.

The woman being informed by her husband of the occasion of

1 "On this side of"; *OED* 1711 entry: "the Parlour lies behither, or on this side
the Kitchin."

the strangers' arrival, ran out to help the lady, who, still insensible, was carried into the inner room, and laid on the humble bed which was the only one in the house.

Montgomery now entreated the assistance of the woman to restore her; and she, who had been formerly a servant in a gentleman's family, applied such remedies as she had at hand, and Ethelinde once more opened her eyes. They were turned languidly on Montgomery, who knelt by her with a look most expressive of all he felt, while he grasped her hand in his, and secretly vowed that if she was now restored to his ardent prayers nothing should ever induce him again to leave her. Ethelinde, who from extreme sickness, the usual consequence of fainting, believed herself dying; and from the pain and soreness of her head thought a fracture would prove the occasion of that death which only on Montgomery's account she regretted, exerted herself to speak to him, and tried anew to persuade him that her dissolution was the especial favour of Providence towards them both. "Grieve not immeasurably, my dear friend," said she, "if your Ethelinde is now taken out of a world where happiness, so rarely obtained in a great degree for any, seems never to have been designed in any degree for her. How many circumstances might have befallen me worse than death: I might have lived to have wept for Montgomery; or what would have been infinitely more insupportable, to have heard that he had forgotten me."

"Impossible!" exclaimed Montgomery, "Do not, for mercy's sake, aggravate my fears, which now deprive me of reason. Do not irritate your own sufferings by conversation so affecting, and I hope so unnecessary."

"Lord Sir," said the woman of the cottage, "Miss only makes herself a deal worse by talking about dying and they things; I dare to say the Doctor will be here anon, and will tell you how there be'ent near the danger as you be *afeard* on. Do, Sir, leave Miss along *a me*, and then she'll keep quiet."

Montgomery, who was afraid of yielding in the presence of Ethelinde to the distracting fears which overwhelmed him, was convinced of the propriety of this proposal. "Shall I go," said he, "and await the arrival of the doctor in the next room?"

"As you please," replied Ethelinde: "but do not leave me long."

Montgomery then quitted her; and running out of the house,

threw round anxious looks for the arrival of the surgeon; for he had dispatched the two men different ways, lest either of the nearest should be out. In a very short time the gardener approached with Mr. Greame, a surgeon of the neighbouring town. Montgomery, as soon as he beheld him, ran away to meet him; and entreating him to hasten on, informed him in breathless agitation of the accident that had befallen Ethelinde, and his fears on her account. "Well, Sir, we shall see," said Mr. Greame—"Blows on the head are bad, very bad." He then enquired if the lady had been sick; and hearing she had fainted, he put on a yet more dismal face, and walked solemnly into the house.

As soon as he saw his fair patient he exclaimed—"God bless me, an ugly cut indeed!—a very ugly cut! pray how did it take place?"

Montgomery, who thought that to enquire into the state of it was much more necessary than asking how it happened, answered impatiently that it was probably by a flint. The surgeon then taking out of a case a pair of small scissars, dissevered without mercy a long and beautiful ringlet which hung near the wound, and with as little remorse cut away the locks from the temple, and then with a silver probe he began to examine if the skull had sustained any injury.

Montgomery felt his blood run cold to his heart. The pain this operation seemed to inflict on Ethelinde, and the dread of an unfavourable result to the examination, were together too much for him; and having looked on wildly half a moment, he started away and again ran out of the house.

In the mean time Mr. Greame was with the most perfect composure finishing his enquiry; and then, turning to the woman, he said—"Upon my word a narrow, a very narrow escape—a little deeper—aye, only the fiftieth part of an inch, and trepanning[1] must have taken place."

"Well, Sir," cried the woman, "but what be *we* to do *wi* Miss now?"

"Why she must be blooded immediately, and kept quiet, or a fever of dangerous tendency may take place; for I apprehend, I assure you, a concussion of the brain *has* taken place."

He then prepared to bleed her; but as she could not move to take off her riding dress, he cut it away without ceremony. The

1 It must have perforated, spread, become much wider, with holes forming.

blood was streaming from the lovely arm of Ethelinde, when Montgomery, unable to endure the apprehensions which he was yet afraid to satisfy by enquiry, again entered the room, and heard, that notwithstanding there was no fracture, there was enough to apprehend from the consequence of such a fall; that Ethelinde certainly could not be removed that day; and that she must nei-ther speak nor be spoken to. The operator then, while he bound up her arm, proceeded to give Montgomery reasons for what he had done, and for the necessity of keeping her quiet, without at all attending to the effect which his unfavourable suspicions of her situation, so openly expressed, might have on the feeble spirits of his patient, or the agonies which he saw they inflicted on Mont-gomery.

When he was departed, which he hastened to do as soon as he could, that he might relate at all the other places whither he was going that morning the accident that had happened and the rem-edies he had applied, and that he might inform himself, and conse-quently others, who the handsome young man was who seemed so solicitous for Miss Chesterville, Montgomery began to consider how he could render the place where Ethelinde must for the pres-ent remain, more commodious to her; and after a short delibera-tion, he determined to go to Brackwood, whither he hoped Miss Newenden was by this time returned. He left a strict charge with the woman to be attentive to Ethelinde during his absence; and putting two guineas into her hand as an earnest that whatever trouble and inconvenience she might be put to would be amply repaid, he set forward on one of the horses which had drawn the chaise; for he had himself crossed the country from Dover on post horses, till he came to the nearest post town, and from thence had by choice walked towards Brackwood, which he had been informed was seven miles distant.

On his arrival at the residence of Miss Newenden, he had the mortification to wait above an hour before she returned. At length she appeared with Davenant and Woolaston; and having enquired for Ethelinde and the Snap mare as she entered the stable-yard, she had heard of the accident that had happened to Ethelinde; but had at the same time the satisfaction of finding that the Snap mare had been brought home by Frank, without having sustained any injury.

Elated with her amusements, and flattered by the extravagant praises with which Woolaston had plied her relative to her skill in riding and her judgment in horses, Miss Newenden met Montgomery in gay spirits; and no feeling for the accident or danger of Ethelinde had power to diminish them. "Faith, Charles," cried she, "I'm very sorry though for the foolish girl; but what occasion was there for her to throw herself off? I knew she could not ride worth a farthing, and so put her upon the quietest horse in my stable. It must be quite her own fault; but however don't be frightened, I dare say 'tis nothing but a broken head; only Greame likes to make a fuss with it; she'll be well enough, never doubt it, to come home bye and bye."

Montgomery, with all the frightful circumstances of a concussion of the brain, which Greame had detailed to him, still warm in his imagination, could not agree to this; and Miss Newenden, who wanted to get quit as soon as possible of every thing that was like trouble, ordered her own maid to go down to Green's hut, and take with her such things as Mr. Montgomery directed; and then dismissing all farther care from her mind, she sat down to a late dinner with her guests. Woolaston rose every moment in her opinion; and Davenant took every opportunity to praise him to her when he was for a moment absent, as one of the worthiest fellows that ever lived. While he was gone out after dinner, to his evening inspection of the stable, a duty which he said he always most punctually fulfilled, Davenant began one of these studied encomiums:

"Don't you think," cried he, "that Woolaston is an excellent horseman? There's not a man in England, I'll venture to say, knows an hound better; he understands my dogs now, a devilish deal more perfect than my huntsman."

"Yes," cried Miss Newenden, "and I'll tell you what Tom, he understands now to manage you better than you do how to manage yourself; and from a mere milksop has made a man of you. Why what a poor thing you were when at Grasmere—afraid of the cold, and afraid of the damp, with fifteen or twenty waistcoats on, and half a dozen handkerchiefs round your neck: there's some fire in this fellow: he has cured you of your frivolous whims, and I believe is a man of sense and spirit."

Woolaston heard with great satisfaction the report of this opinion. Unprincipled, unfeeling, and selfish, he was yet very artful, and the keenness with which he still delighted in gratifications his dissipated property could no longer afford him, now urged him to exert every stratagem to secure to himself their continuance, by becoming master of the fortune of Miss Newenden; and having once found the way to an heart which to the usual modes of attack had been invulnerable, he doubted little of his final success.

Every hour now witnessed his fortunate progress. Miss New- enden herself, while hardly conscious of it, found very soon that the hour of his departure would give her pain, and therefore stud- ied how to protract it. She had long piqued herself on living and acting her own way; and when the first idea of securing to herself so valuable a master of the horse as Woolaston occurred to her, she considered that though it would be probably very disagreeable to her brother, occasion much conversation, and make her liable to some blame among her friends, yet she should give the most certain proof of her free agency and liberality of mind. In a few days Woolaston, who saw his advantage, used it so adroitly, that he obtained her consent, and little remained but to prevail upon her to name the day which was to put herself, her fortune, and her stud, in his possession.

CHAPTER IX

While these things were passing at Brackwood, and while Wool- aston in the course of three days had secured the mistress of that mansion, Ethelinde, from the violence of the shock she had received, could not be removed from the cottage of the shepherd. Thither Montgomery had on the first evening conveyed a better bed, and every thing which in his tender solicitude he thought might contribute to her ease and amendment. Trembling for a life a thousand times more precious to him than his own, he could not prevail on himself a moment to leave the cottage; but having borrowed one of Miss Newenden's female servants to attend on Ethelinde in the miserable little apartment where she was obliged to remain, he persuaded the woman of the house, by dint of that most powerful of all arguments, money, to send her children to a neighbour's, in order that the place might be quiet, and then dismissing her and her husband to their repose, he wrapped him- self in his great coat and sat during the night by the cottage fire.

An heavy stupor, the effect of her fall, seemed to hang on Ethelinde, and the symptoms so alarmingly prognosticated by Greame appeared in their full force to his terrified imagination; while Ethelinde herself, finding her head still extremely confused, and her whole frame greatly disordered as well as weakened by the loss of blood which Greame had found it necessary to take, really believed that she was in a few days to die; and far from feeling any regret, she fancied that it was the particular interposition of Providence to save her from keener misery than she had yet experienced. There was something not unpleasant in the languor she was sensible of; and she excused to herself the facility with which she allowed of the constant attendance of Montgomery, by persuading herself that in a few days the hand of death would divide them for ever.

The second day brought with it only increased pain; for the bruises were now more felt than on their being first received. Montgomery, impatient for the arrival of Greame, could not rest any where; while he sat a moment by the bed-side of Ethelinde, and saw on her soft countenance an expression of pain, of which she complained not by words, he found his own anguish insupportable; and without daring to enquire the extent of her sufferings, he flew up to some high point of land, in hopes of seeing the surgeon approach—then he returned to the cottage, listened at the door, fancied he heard her breathe with more difficulty, and again ran away to send somebody for Greame, whom he began to think would never arrive.

Thus past the morning; and about two o'clock Miss Newenden, on whom Greame had called on his way, and who was prevented from hunting by the return of the frost, came down with him and her guests to see the patient, of whose situation the surgeon had given her a very different account from what she had expected. She had none of that tenderness which suffers from the mere representation of the sufferings of another; and her own constitution, from the manner of life she had so early adopted, had, as well as her mind, acquired something of masculine strength and hardness; yet when the situation of Ethelinde was represented to her as hazardous, she expressed some degree of concern; and the two gentlemen, Davenant and Woolaston, encouraged her to consent to Greame's proposal of going all together to the cottage.

When they arrived, Montgomery met them at the door: the disgust he had ever felt towards Miss Newenden, was encreased by Ethelinde's accident, of which she had been the occasion; and he could not see Davenant without recollecting that at Grasmere he had been considered as a lover. There was, in the assured look of Woolaston, (whose figure and appearance was a compound of the dissolute man of the town and the profest jockey), something still more repulsive to the feelings of Montgomery; and he thought the moment he saw the groupe, that to leave Ethelinde among them would give him even more pain than her illness. "Well, Montgomery," said Miss Newenden, as soon as she met him—"what's the matter here? Greame has been talking of I know not what danger that may follow this accident; but he is always a croker[1]—are you not doctor? I dare say Ethy will be well enough in a day or two.— Come, let's go see how she does."

"I am afraid," replied Montgomery, "that the sight of so many persons may fatigue her. Her head is much affected; if you please, therefore, Madam, you and Mr. Greame only shall see her."

They then were admitted into the room; and Greame having declared that she had a good deal of fever, and was not in a state to be removed, Miss Newenden, after expressing as much concern as she was capable of feeling, retired; and promising to send down another servant to relieve in her attendance the maid who was already there, departed with her two friends, equally vexed at the frost and at the trouble this awkward business might bring upon her.

Davenant had always detested Montgomery. The preference that had been shewn him at Grasmere by Ethelinde, the praises then lavished on his figure by the other ladies, as well as by Miss Newenden, who still continued to teize Davenant with encomiums on him, and the real superiority which he possessed in person and in spirit; a superiority that Davenant felt, though he disdained to acknowledge it even to himself; combined to render him odious; and the coldness of Montgomery's behaviour now encreased his aversion. "I don't understand," said he, as he walked home with Miss Newenden, "what sort of footing that young fellow is upon with Miss Chesterville; I suppose, however, that he is an accepted lover."

1 Croaker: someone who foresees evil, who croaks.

"Poor Davenant!" exclaimed Miss Newenden; laughing aloud: —"What! you have not yet forgotten your old *penchant* at Grasmere? Montgomery jockied you, Tom, there; and I believe your chance is still worse now."[1]

"Really you mistake me," answered Davenant, affecting an haughty indifference. "Whatever were then my thoughts of Miss Chesterville, I have since had sufficient occasion to change them; and whatever may be Montgomery's advantages, no interference of mine will lessen their success."

"Faith," cried Woolaston, "he is a fortunate lad to be sole attendant on a young lady: but he appears not to merit his good fortune; I suspect that he is a coxcomb."

"An horrid coxcomb, I assure you: as vain of his person as a girl, and the more vain, perhaps, because he has nothing else to boast of," replied Davenant.

"Pardon me," returned Miss Newenden, who delighted in mortifying Davenant—"He is of a very good family."

"A Scotch family!" cried Davenant, disdainfully—"generally productive of well descended paupers. I suppose that the young man has not fifty pounds a year in the world."

Thus on the indigence of Montgomery, the man of fortune, fortune which he owed not to his own merit, descanted, while Woolaston, whom vice, dissipation, and idleness had impoverished, thought himself at liberty to join in the ridicule, and to irritate the contempt excited by the want of that money, which neither of them knew how to use; and which, they both felt, had not the power to bestow happiness.

The second night Montgomery passed as he had done the first. Ethelinde, however, knew not that he sat up during the whole of it in the peasant's kitchen: for in the evening she had expressed so much uneasiness at his remaining there, that he had promised to leave the cottage and go to Miss Newenden's house till the next day: a promise which he fancied her safety, and his own anxiety would justify his making without his having an intention to keep it.

During the night, a profound silence reigned throughout the humble abode; broken only by the chirping of the crickets which

---

1 Penchant: a strong inclination. Jockied: to play the jockey with; gain advantage by adroit management or trickery; outwit.

ran round the wicker chair he sat on within the low chimney. Sleep was not to be obtained; and his fertile imagination brought before him his future prospects in melancholy perspective.—"Yet a few days, and the sad pleasure yet allowed me, of seeing her, ill and disfigured as she is, will be withdrawn. She will recover; but my miseries will not be removed. I shall see her restored to health; but my peace will not be restored with it. Oh! merciful heaven! how many evils may befall her worse to me than would be her death, terrible as the idea of it appeared only a few hours ago!

"With whom do I leave her, destitute as she is of fortune and of protection? Is Miss Newenden, careless of appearances, harsh in manners, and indelicate in mind, a fit associate and friend for Ethelinde? are these men whom she brings into her house companions for that sensibility and softness so fondly cultivated by Colonel Chesterville? and will she not be perpetually exposed to impertinence and insult? If she removes from among them, whither can she go? To Sir Edward Newenden? Impossible—I can never bear it! Good God! and what is this money in pursuit of which I am to quit her? Am I sure of obtaining it? and if I do, will it make me happy if I lose her; or am I convinced it will make her so, if I return to share it with her?—Ah! no! poor as we are, such a cottage as this would shelter us; and together, we might be happier in it, than the highest affluence could make those who have not hearts like ours. I am young and strong, and why should I be ashamed of supporting her by the humblest labour?—labour which would be comparatively sweet, when I reflected that it saved me from the infinitely more insupportable misery of leaving her."

In these reflections the night, however slowly, wore away, and by the time it was proper for him to make his appearance the next morning, he had persuaded himself that it was consistent with his reason and his duty, as well as flattering to his love, to make another attempt to shake the resolution of Ethelinde, and engage her to consent to their marrying immediately, and going together to Grasmere, there to wait the return of his mother.

He found her, however, so languid and weak, that he dared not hazard it immediately. She was now become conscious of the impropriety of her situation: but while she was very solicitous to be allowed to return to Brackwood, she felt herself by no means able to undergo the removal without suffering great pain: but so

uneasy did her remaining any longer where she was appear to
make her, that on Mr. Greame's arrival she prevailed upon him
to consent to it: it was indeed making his attendance much less
inconvenient to him, and he directed the precautions that should
be taken, all of which Montgomery himself attending to, Ethelinde, on the evening of the third day after her fall, returned to her
own apartment at Brackwood: there too Miss Newenden civilly
requested Montgomery to stay: who could not resist the invitation, though it was not made in his opinion more seducing by the
lady of the house saying, in her thoughtless and boisterous way—
"If this devilish frost continues to get out of the ground, as my
people think it will, we'll be out to-morrow at five, and you, Montgomery, shall have the Snap mare; these two fellows have been
saying that they suppose you cannot ride, and I have told them
you'll throw them out."

Montgomery, though careless of their opinion in this as well
as in more material points, blushed at the idea of their having
spoken of him contemptuously, but he despised them too much
to think them worth notice, and endeavoured, though without
success, to turn the discourse to other topics than the stable and
the field. Woolaston knew his own advantages too well to suffer
the thoughts of Miss Newenden to deviate into reason. The next
day was appointed for his going off to London for a licence; and
he already anticipated the restored, and even encreased figure he
should make at the next Newmarket meeting, when all his former
mischances and mistakes should be remedied by by the possession
of Miss Newenden's five and twenty thousand pounds.

Such was the disposition of the party assembled to supper on
the evening of Ethelinde's return, (who had borne her removal
with much less fatigue than had been expected) when a carriage
was heard to drive furiously up to the door; and there was hardly
time to enquire who it brought, before Sir Edward Newenden
appeared.

He looked wildly round the room; and the persons he saw there
encreased his amazement. "Where is she?" cried he, in a voice that
expressed concern and surprize;—"Where is Ethelinde?—where is
Miss Chesterville?"

"She has had a fall from her horse," said Miss Newenden, (who
was by no means delighted with the sight of her brother) "and is in

bed: but is it her only, Ned, you came to see? in truth all the rest of your friends are much obliged to you."

"I heard she had met with a dangerous accident," replied Sir Edward, trying to recollect himself; "and as her guardian—as her friend—I thought it my duty to see—if if she was—if she was in any hazard."

"Well, and if she had, what good could you have done? D'ye think we don't know in the country how to manage a broken head? But come, sit down. Have you supped? Why, I believe you've fallen off your horse yourself? What's the matter that you wear your arm in a sling?"

"I have hurt it," replied Sir Edward, coldly. "Ethelinde, then," continued he, "is in no danger?"

"Oh! none upon earth! Lord, she was more frightened than hurt; and Mr. Montgomery was glad of an excuse to play the nurse-tender, and so persuaded her, with the help of that old croaker Greame, that she was half killed."

"Have you been long here, Sir?" said Sir Edward, addressing himself with evident concern to Montgomery.

Montgomery, with equal coldness, answered, "I came to this place across the country from Dover, three days ago."

"And how long, Mr. Davenant, have you been at Brackwood?" asked Sir Edward.

"Faith, time has passed so pleasantly to me and my friend Woolaston here, that I have hardly kept an account: if I were to reckon by the common course of time, I believe four days; but so agreeably have they gone, that they have hardly appeared four hours."

Sir Edward, who knew Woolaston only from report, now turned towards him; but he felt no inclination to make any acquaintance with him, and was concerned and amazed to see such a party entertained by Miss Newenden.

His feelings were altogether so unpleasant, that it became impossible for him to exert himself to keep up the conversation: his presence seemed to throw a restraint on the rest of the company; and anxious as he was about Ethelinde, he dared make no farther enquiry unless his sister led to the conversation, which she seemed purposely to avoid. Montgomery, who at once respected him as a worthy man, and dreaded him as one who might perhaps be a fortunate rival, was rendered miserable by his sudden appearance: his manner served to increase this solicitude. Sir Edward was absent and restless, and seemed hardly able to hide the impatience and anxiety under which he laboured. To Davenant's extravagant conversation he listened with disgust and anger; to Woolaston, who was, however, more than usual on his guard, with hardly more temper; and his behaviour towards Montgomery himself was, though rather more civil, so unlike his usual mild and attentive manner, that it was easy to see he was but little pleased by finding him at Brackwood.

As soon as it was possible to withdraw, Sir Edward rose and went to his room; where, as he could not rest without being satisfied as to the situation of Ethelinde, he sent for his servant, and ordered him to bring up to his room the woman who had attended her. From this woman, naturally loquacious, he heard all the particulars of the accident; while she exaggerated, as is the general custom among servants, all the alarming circumstances that had attended it; and all that he heard served only to encrease the anxiety in which he passed the night.

Nor was his solicitude and his affection for Ethelinde the only source of those poignant feelings that robbed him of repose. His family miseries were not abated. Lady Newenden had, in about ten days after the departure of Ethelinde, arrived at her father's house in town. She still disdained to make any advances towards a reconciliation, and affected to scorn the resentment and defy the suspicions of her husband; but her father had prevailed on Sir Edward, before he knew of her arrival, to send the three children thither; and he was to fetch them himself on an evening agreed upon. Maltravers, without communicating his design to his daughter; contrived that he should be introduced to the room where Lady Newenden was, and where her father had purposely placed the little creatures round her. On seeing her thus encircled by his children, Sir Edward forgot for a moment every thing but that she was their mother: the tenderness of his heart prevailed over his resentment; and by the anxious interposition of Mr. Maltravers a reconciliation was hastily brought about; and Sir Edward, who could not resist the tears of the father nor the innocent pleading of the children, in which they had by him been previously tutored, was hurried by this variety of contending passions to promise eternal oblivion, without insisting on any other conditions than that Lady Newenden should go to Denham for some months. She gave a reluctant acquiescence rather than a promise, and testified so little satisfaction at being thus restored to her husband and her children, that Sir Edward, while compelled to make one more effort to save her, trembled at the little prospect there was of his success. Having conquered, however, that violence of resentment which had urged him repeatedly to declare he would never forgive her, he determined to expel from his mind as much as possible all recollection of the reasons he had to complain of her, and to banish at the same time, as far as he could, the idea of Ethelinde, whom for the future he resolved to serve without seeing.

Such, for three days, was his resolution: and so excellent his principles, so truly upright was his heart, that in time his reason would have regained all its strength, and his duty to his children would have supplied what could now never be replaced—his fond affection to his wife: love, once driven away by neglect, or shaken by suspicion so nearly approaching to conviction as his had been, returns no more: but he was yet disposed to pity errors which he knew partly arose from her education and partly from the defects of temper, which she had never been taught to correct; and what he could not wholly forgive he struggled to forget. With such dispositions on his part, peace and honor were yet within reach of Lady Newenden; but unhappily she had loft all relish for the first, and placed the latter in carrying a point very different from that of being restored to domestic happiness.

When Mr. Maltravers had insisted on her quitting Danesforte, after Sir Edward's sudden departure, and going with him and her mother to their house in Berkshire, Lord Danesforte, whose profligacy of character every month of his life rendered more flagitious, was only concerned that the fracas had not made more noise; and he took care that Sir Edward's behaviour should soon be as generally circulated as possible. Though he had not the least affection for Lady Newenden, he was determined that his apparent attachment to her should not be interrupted either by the jealousy of her husband or the precautions of her father. He wrote to her therefore in the style of a man determined not to endure life without her. To Mrs. Maltravers, his sentiments took a still higher flight: and such was her folly and her weakness, that she received his let-

ters for her daughter, and communicated to her the contents of
her own. The heart of Lady Newenden was incapable of love: but
it was inflamed with unappeasable resentment against Sir Edward,
and influenced by vanity and ambition—vanity which made her
glory in the thoughts of being preferred to all those women of
fashion whom Lord Danesforte had before been partial to; and
ambition, which taught her that to be a Countess, with such an
immense fortune as Lord Danesforte still possessed, was more
worthy of her merit than to remain the wife of a Baronet, who had
owed the support of his name only to the fortune she had given
him. No native principles of rectitude, no acquired restraints of
religion, no delicate sensibility of honor, or tender maternal affections, had place in her bosom to counteract the power of these
united temptations; and her mother, instead of checking or discovering, encouraged and concealed them. While, therefore, Mr.
Maltravers was labouring to bring about a reconciliation, his wife
and his daughter, who had formed their own plans, suffered him
to proceed; and Lady Newenden went back to her husband with
no other hope than that she should soon find occasion to break the
chains she so reluctantly submitted to put on. The generous and
manly temper of Sir Edward for some days baffled these projects,
and all her caprices and provoking attempts to move his temper
failed of success. Lord Danesforte, however, to whom they had
not communicated the whole of their plans, was piqued at finding
that notwithstanding the tenderness of her letters to him, Lady
Newenden had consented to a reconciliation with her husband,
which he thought was sincere. His Lordship, determined to interrupt a re-union which was so mortifying to his vanity, hastened
to London, from whence he was at a small distance; and there,
while he meditated how to proceed, he was engaged one evening
in a drinking party, where the fracas that had happened at Danesforte was publicly canvassed; and Lord Danesforte, who though
he could drink a great deal, was deprived of all shadow of reason
when perfectly intoxicated, spoke so disrespectfully of Sir Edward
and so lightly of Lady Newenden, that Mr. Templeton, a relation
of Sir Edward's, who was hardly more sober, took it up. Very high
words arose between them: and though they were parted without
exchanging a mutual challenge, Templeton declared that he considered himself bound to inform Sir Edward of the expressions

that had been used. His Lordship contemptuously answered, with a great oath, that he might take his pleasure: and as this had happened about ten o'clock at night, Templeton, who was young and hot headed, drove immediately to Hanover square; where he told his relation, by way of doing him a kindness, what must inevitably oblige him to take the hazard of destroying Lord Danesforte or losing his own life. Sir Edward, whose unhappiness had been irritated rather than relieved by the behaviour of Lady Newenden during the three days she had been at home, and whose hopeless passion for her cousin was stifled only to prey internally on his heart, was so destitute of happiness, and so lost to hope, that he felt something like a sense of obligation to the young man who gave him at once an opportunity of vindicating his honor and a chance of quitting an existence which was become insupportable. In the first emotion of resentment therefore he wrote to Lord Danesforte a request to meet him the next day, at a place he named five miles from London. Templeton undertook to deliver it that evening: and Sir Edward, who had nothing to settle of his temporal affairs, which he had done some time before, apologized to himself for the step he was going to take by citing those laws of honor from which there is no appeal without infamy; and though he felt the fallacy of that code, he smothered all the remonstrances of his conscience and his principles, and persuaded himself that this was one of those occasions in which a desire of vengeance might be forgiven, even by that Being to whom he was always disposed to consider himself amenable.

He said nothing to Lady Newenden; who was engaged to sup at her father's, with a large company, from whence he had excused himself, and rising at five o'clock the next morning, he ordered his servant to prepare his pistols for a journey, and leaving word that some business called him unexpectedly to Denham, he got into an hired chaise with his gentleman, and was soon at a village near the place of rendezvous; where Templeton, who had eagerly offered to be his second, was arrived a few moments before.

They walked together to the spot, where Lord Danesforte and his second almost at the same moment arrived also.

Sir Edward advancing to his Lordship, repeated the words which Templeton had described him to have said, and asked if he meant to justify them.

"Yes," replied he contemptuously; "what I have said I am ready to repeat. Would Sir Edward Newenden please to hear them again?"

This answer precluding any further conversation, the seconds proceeded to the usual ceremonies. Sir Edward fired, and missed; Lord Danesforte, with a better aim, grazed the arm of his adversary. The seconds then interfered; but neither party being satisfied, Sir Edward fired a second time and Lord Danesforte fell. Shocked as Sir Edward would have been to have had the life of any other human being to answer for, he felt horror rather than compassion and regret; he approached, however, and Lord Danesforte said, with a smile which neither pain nor apprehension robbed of its acrimony—"I believe, Sir, all your qualms on account of your wife may now be over so far as relates *to me*." Sir Edward then, at the request of the seconds, hastened to the village, where a surgeon had been left by Lord Danesforte. He sent him immediately to the spot; where Templeton remained till the wound was inspected; and Sir Edward returned to town; where he shut himself up in his own room; and having had his wound dressed, felt not so much penitence for having disburthened the world of a man so worthless, as concerned at the idea of his lingering long in pain.

Lady Newenden was gone for the day to her father's, and nobody broke in to disturb the indulgence or those numberless uneasy reflections that preyed on his heart, till some of them were mitigated by the arrival of Templeton, who had remained at the village, whither Lord Danesforte had been carried, till the surgeon had extracted the ball; which having been lodged just below the collar bone, had failed of wounding mortally; and as it was with little difficulty extracted, the surgeon declared that unless an unexpected degree of fever came on there was little or no danger.

The report of such a duel could not fail of being soon spread. It was known in town almost as soon as it happened; and Mrs. Maltravers, who was to have a party in the evening, was soon acquainted with it by cards sent by those who were to have been there, but who now excused themselves, as "concluding she did not see company on account of the late unfortunate affair."

Hardly had Sir Edward, therefore, heard that Lord Danesforte was in no danger, before Mrs. Maltravers entered his study, furious as a lioness robbed of her young: her eyes flashed fire; her face was all over as red from nature as her cheeks usually were from art; and in a voice between crying and scolding, she thus (before his gentleman, who began to think his master in more danger from the fury of his mother in law than he had been from the pistol of Lord Danesforte) addressed Sir Edward—

"So! you have done well to be sure! A fine story you have made of it at last. Oh! Sir Edward, Sir Edward, to be so wicked and cruel; and take the life of that poor good dear man, and ruin the reputation of my sweet child! and all for what—for groundless jealousy! oh! I must say you are a base man; and woeful to us I am sure was the hour that ever we suffered our poor dear Maria to throw herself away upon you; she that might have had any body, she that was a match for a prince! I had rather have seen her in a coffin than married to a man who does not know her value: and poor Lord Danesforte too! oh! what will become of us to think we have been the cause of your taking away the life of that excellent, charming man!"

Sir Edward felt his indignation conquered by pity and contempt.—"Be calm, Madam," said he, as soon as he found he had any chance of being heard—"that dear excellent, charming man, is not dead, and I believe in no danger of dying. Go back and console yourself, therefore; and prevail on Lady Newenden to be more careful of that reputation which I have taken some trouble to rescue from the aspersions of your noble favorite."

"'Tis false!" cried Mrs. Maltravers; "an abominable falsehood! He never aspersed her—no never; he admired her too much; and a thousand times, poor dear creature, has he sighed and said to me when we were alone together—'dear Mrs. Maltravers, what a divine resemblance of your divine self is your daughter: and what a happy man is Sir Edward.' Yes! he has said so many times; I don't deny but that he admired Maria—indeed he *has* sometimes breathed a tender wish that he had known her before she was married, or that she had a sister, like herself, or that I was not her mother: all *that* was natural enough; who can help their *penchangs*;[1] but as for any wrong attachment to Maria, I tell you, Sir Edward, 'tis as false as hell!"

Her voice, which had sunk into a whine while she described the platonic passion of Lord Danesforte, now rose again to the clam-

1 Malapropism for *penchants*.

orous shrillness of rage; and Sir Edward, hopeless of appeasing her, had nothing to do but to sit down and attend with patience till her passion had exhausted itself.

Far, however, from finding that it abated for want of opposition, it seemed to gather force in its progress; and she now fell into fits of hysteric crying, now walked about the room with a theatrical air, and ranted like an affronted Empress. Sir Edward began not only to be thoroughly weary of her folly but to feel his arm very painful: any interruption, therefore, was welcome to him, though he foresaw that Maltravers, who now entered the room, would expect a more serious explanation and different reasons for his conduct than what he had thought it necessary to give the lady.

It was, however, some moments before the authority of Maltravers could procure an interval of silence; but when that was obtained, Sir Edward related in a few words what had passed. Maltravers, who had no very strict notions of honor, and a great aversion to the noise this matter would make, heard him with a very discontented air; and telling Sir Edward that he thought he had more prudence and more regard for his family, he bade him sullenly good night; adding that he had left Lady Newenden so very ill in consequence of her alarm, that she would not be able to return home that night. Sir Edward had too much reason to believe that this alarm had not been created by her fears for him, and therefore he suffered her father and mother to depart without expressing any anxiety to see her—a circumstance which the latter exaggerated into the cruellest symptoms of neglect and contempt.

When they were gone, Sir Edward, harrassed in his mind, and suffering pain from his wound, was hastening to bed, when his gentleman, who had served him from a child and was considered more as a friend than a servant, thus began, while he was helping him to undress, from doing which for himself his wounded arm disabled him.

"I wish, Sir, you'd let the surgeon look at it again to-night; do, Sir; indeed it may be of ill consequence. Thank God, however, 'tis no worse. This seems to be quite the week for bad accidents."

"What accidents, Warham?" asked Sir Edward. "This can hardly, I think, be called one."

"It might have been worse, to be sure, Sir; but I mean, besides this ugly affair, poor Miss Chesterville."

"Miss Chesterville!" exclaimed Sir Edward. "What of Miss Chesterville?"

"Lord, Sir!" replied the servant, "I thought to be sure you had known it: Molly Peters spoke of it last night in the housekeeper's room. She had a letter from her brother at Brackwood that mentioned it."

"Mentioned what? You'll torture me, Warham. What has befallen Ethelinde?"

"Why, Sir, what I heard was, that she was out a hunting with Miss Newenden, and got a bad fall, and was carried for dead into a cottage hard by."

"Impossible!" cried Sir Edward, trembling with terror and alarm; "impossible! She never hunts—she hardly ever rides. It must be some mistake."

Warham, however, persisting in his account, Sir Edward, fatigued as he was, entirely forgot himself, and bade him seek the servant instantly who had received the letter, and bring it to him.

This command being obeyed, Sir Edward was soon convinced that there was too much reason for his apprehensions. The letter, which was from Miss Newenden's footman to his sister, was circumstantial, and described not only the day and hour when the accident befel Ethelinde, but the situation in which she at that time remained at the hut of the shepherd, and the opinion Mr. Greame had given of the possible consequences of her fall.

Nothing that merely affected his case had now power to detain the mind of Sir Edward from the bed side of his lovely suffering ward. He saw her in a miserable cabin, without attendants, unsoothed by the consoling voice of friendship and sympathy, for he knew Miss Newenden incapable of either; he represented what she must, in such a situation, suffer; and at length, after a long conflict between his prudence and his solicitude for her, he persuaded himself that he was called upon by every thing dear to the heart of a man of honor and of feeling to fly instantly to her. Love, an auxiliary here too powerful, lent all his sophistry to convince him that he was only acting as a guardian was bound to act: and though in the present circumstances he knew that many objections might with some propriety be raised, his unconquerable tenderness silenced them all. He still, however, wished to have it thought that he was gone no farther than Denham. He left a letter to Mr. Maltravers, saying indirectly that he was gone thither; and at the first dawn of day he stepped into the chaise, which had set him down in the evening at Brackwood.

CHAPTER X

No event could have happened more favorable to the views of Lady Newenden than this expedition of Sir Edward; none that more strongly confirmed the reports that had obtained of Sir Edward's attachment to Ethelinde. The recent duel had drawn all eyes upon him; and that while he was yet uncertain of the life of his adversary, and himself wounded, he should fly to the house where he had placed Ethelinde, could hardly fail of attracting observations as prejudicial to her as corroborating the suspicions which Mr. Maltravers and his family had affected to believe. Of this Sir Edward, as he journeyed towards Brackwood, could not but be sensible: but Ethelinde in danger, and languishing on a sick bed; that lovely face disfigured under painful operations; the grave perhaps opening to receive her; were images which obliterated all the impressions that cold prudence could make. Repeatedly he had promised to her father to defend and protect her; and his generosity, as well as his love forbade his forfeiting that sacred promise lest the worthless and illiberal should cavil at his fulfilling it.

But finding that Davenant, Woolaston, and Montgomery, were witnesses to his arrival, he became more disturbed; and conscious of all he felt, he fancied that every eye could read what passed in his heart. The events of the last week had rendered his accommodation with Lady Newenden less likely to be permanent; and he repented that ever he had consented to an experiment which had served only to convince him that happiness or even content, with her, were not to be obtained. A thousand corrosive reflections followed when he recalled her behaviour and that of her mother; and when his thoughts returned towards Ethelinde, on whom they had once been accustomed to dwell with much pleasure, new and poignant anguish overwhelmed his heart. He knew less than ever how he ought to act in regard to her. His sister, the only female relation to whom he could entrust her, lived rather like an independent man than in the retirement fit for a young woman so situated as

Ethelinde. She continually entertained parties of gentlemen at her house; and far from caring what opinion the world entertained of her actions, she professed a total neglect of the customs of those societies, with which she had no inclination to mix. The very party now with her was a specimen of her contempt for the usual forms observed by single women. Davenant indeed, having been her brother's ward, had some pretence for his visit; but Woolaston was not only a stranger to her but a man of dissolute character, who was known to have subsisted some time by expedients which had placed him among the description of people called black-legs.[1]

He knew that to remonstrate with his sister would not only be fruitless, but that, unaccustomed as she was to controul, she would resent any attempt of his to dictate to her, and would become impatient of the company of Ethelinde if she found it likely to impose on her inclinations the smallest restraint; yet to see Ethelinde, unprotected as she was, in such company, exposed to the impertinence of unprincipled men, distracted him. There appeared, however, no alternative but her marriage with Montgomery, and on that he thought with still greater reluctance.

Unable to rest, he was in the parlour by six o'clock. He took up a book that lay in the window, in hopes of finding something that might divert his thoughts a moment from his various unhappiness; but it was a treatise on hunting, and he laid it down in disgust. He now waited anxiously to see somebody who could give him an account of Ethelinde; but the maids were not yet up, except one whose business it was to prepare breakfast for the hunters. He saw Mr. Woolaston go to the stables and direct the proceedings there with an air of authority, which he remarked, without at all guessing at the right he was so soon to assume. Miss Newenden at length came down herself; and very little pleased with the prospect of her brother's stay, which could not fail to impede all her plans, she spoke to him with a coldness that aggravated his concern; not on his own account, for he knew her too well to expect tenderness and affection from her, but on that of Ethelinde, whose prospects appeared to him every moment more dreary, while he felt himself precluded from the power of rendering them pleasant or even comfortable. After he had asked his sister how she did, he

1 A cheating gambler; swindler.

said—"Have you seen Ethelinde to-day? can you tell me how she finds herself?"

"Lord, brother!" replied Miss Newenden, "d'ye think I have nothing to do but to attend to her? It is enough, I think, if she occupies the whole attention of one of the family."

"You are unkind, Ellen. She occupies no more of my thoughts than every amiable unprotected young woman is entitled to from her guardian."

"Well, I am really as tired as Lady Newenden used to be of hearing of her amiableness and her beauty. She has often said that there was always more fuss with her than with fifty other people; and it's true I think."

"But can you have a person, whether amiable or unamiable, ill in your house, and not be solicitous for their recovery?"

"Dear Ned, she is not ill. If I had met with such an accident I should have put a pledget dipped in Arquebusade to my head, and have got a bottle of Steers's opodeldoc for my bruises,[1] and there would have been an end of it; instead of which, here's fainting, and physicing, and bleeding, and water gruel, and Montgomery running mad, and you not quite in your senses. I suppose the next thing will be that Chesterville will come sailing back from Jamaica, and that you will bring down the college of physicians and the company of surgeons."

Sir Edward now found that he should excite ridicule, but obtain no information from his sister; he dropped, therefore, the discourse, stifling as well as he could the uneasiness and disgust he felt; and Montgomery, Davenant, and Woolaston, after entering the room, they hastily breakfasted; and then all but Sir Edward and Montgomery departed for the chase.

When they were gone, Sir Edward addressed himself to Montgomery, who, melancholy and dejected, had seated himself with folded arms in the window.—"Do you know, Sir, how Miss Chesterville does to-day?"

"I have had no opportunity of inquiring. The servant who attends her is not yet risen."

1 Eau d'Arquebusade (a mix of flowers and herbs in a solution), folk remedy for healing wounds, inflammation of the skin, skin infections and sores. Steers's opodeldoc is a liniment, a mixture of soap, camphor and herbs dissolved in alcohol attributed to Paracelsus

"You saw the accident, I think, Sir; do me the favor to let me understand how it happened?"

Montgomery then recounted all that had passed, in a voice and manner expressive of the lively and tender interest he took in whatever related to the fair sufferer. When he had finished the account, Sir Edward remaining silent, Montgomery paused a moment, and then went on thus:

"You are not unacquainted, Sir Edward, with my long and ardent affection for Miss Chesterville, nor with those cruel circumstances which have compelled me, rather in compliance with the maxims of the world than with my own conviction, to think of quitting her. To you, her father gave a trust of which he, before your arrival, thought me worthy: on your honor and kindness I am convinced she may rely if you can exert them in her favor; but let me ask you, Sir Edward, and forgive the liberty I take, let me ask you whether you *can* afford her the protection for which she has so much occasion? Is her present situation quite what your delicate sense of propriety would suggest for such a young woman?"

Sir Edward foresaw that this conversation would lead to a proposal which he doubted not Montgomery still wished to make—that of marrying Ethelinde immediately. A severe pang seized his heart; yet he could not be angry that Montgomery saw the present circumstances of Ethelinde nearly as he himself considered them.

"No," replied he, "I do not know that it is; I will speak to you, Mr. Montgomery, with frankness. My sister, though without the slightest disposition to do wrong, is not only singular and absurd in her pursuits, but thinks in a manner peculiar to herself; while other women at her time of life, for she is not yet thirty, solicit the function of some older woman; or take the utmost care to observe a punctilious decorum in their company and manners, Miss Newenden has determined to live her own way, and to associate with men, as well as rival them in field sports. 'Tis an unfortunate turn, in my mind, and such as has often given me great concern; but Nelly is her own mistress, and her fortune, her family, and the little pretensions she assumes to rival the ladies in those points wherein they are most anxious to excell, have hitherto prevented her from suffering so much from their report, as many have done who have apparently sacrificed much more to appearances. Miss Newenden's character is, I assure you, unimpeached among them——"

"Far be it from me," said Montgomery, interrupting him, "to doubt it for a moment; but will poor Ethelinde, who, with no fortune, has such eminent beauty, and is not yet nineteen, will Ethelinde as easily escape? I am afraid not, Sir Edward; and to leave her, uncertain even of an home, exposed, perhaps, to insolent proposals, insulted by the cold pity of unfeeling affluence.—Upon my soul, I cannot bear the thoughts of it. The most painful and laborious servitude would be preferable, in my eyes, to the misery I shall endure, under these circumstances, to take a long leave of her; uncertain of what will become of her in my absence, doubting whether I may ever return to her more!"

Torn by a passion as violent and even more hopeless than that which now stifled the voice of Montgomery, Sir Edward could neither conquer his own emotion or appease that of the young and unhappy lover by determining to consent to his wishes. After some hesitation, during which a dreadful conflict passed in his heart, he said—"I thought that all this, Mr. Montgomery, had been settled in town, and that you would not have renewed a conversation on what is to all appearance hopeless to you, and I am afraid very painful to my ward. If indeed your prospects were improved, and Ethelinde chose to unite her fate with your's, I should not, whatever I might think of its prudence, oppose her determination: but as it is——"

"So far from being improved, Sir Edward," said Montgomery, in a tone rather angry, "you know that they are even more reduced: but I am young; I have, I thank God, health to work, and a spirit which would feel no degradation in embracing any honest means to support the woman I adore."

Conscious of the advantage which a project so romantic would give her already beloved Montgomery over such an heart as Ethelinde possessed, Sir Edward liked not to hear it repeated, nor to think that it might be repeated to her.

"My dear Sir," cried he, "you are yet too young to be an adequate judge of what you could do. To talk of labouring for her support is wildness and romance. What is the support she could obtain by your labour? of what labour are you capable?"

Montgomery, naturally warm and impetuous, and now inflamed by lurking but corrosive jealousy, took fire at something of contempt which he fancied this speech implied.—"Sir Edward," cried he, "you may despise me; but I shall never feel myself despicable while my heart tells me I pursue the dictates of natural reason. Whatever I could do for her support, if, humble as my lot must remain, Ethelinde will be content with it, I see not by what usurped authority you can divide us; and give me leave to say, Sir Edward, that if you still attempt to do so, I shall think with the rest of the world, that neither your quality of guardian, nor of a married man, have had power to render you as indifferent as you ought to be to the personal loveliness of Ethelinde."

"You are very young, and I fear very rash," replied Sir Edward, his rising anger being with the utmost difficulty suppressed; "but you are unhappy, and I forbear to retort."

"Forbear nothing on that account, Sir Edward. As men, we are equal—allow me to say too that we are equal as gentlemen; and that it is doing no injury to the family of Newenden to place it on a footing with the house of Montgomery."

Sir Edward had by this time recollected how fruitless and how dangerous any altercation must be; and ashamed of having been betrayed into anger which might be so injurious to Ethelinde, he got the better at once of his emotion, and answered mildly—"We will not talk of our families, Montgomery, nor of ourselves: neither of us, I think, are fortunate enough to have much to boast of in regard to happiness. Let us, therefore, instead of inflaming each other with foolish and useless suspicions and reproaches, consider, as if we were her brothers, what ought to be done for the peace and happiness of her for whom we are both interested."

The noble heart of Montgomery was softened in a moment by candour and generosity—"Pardon me, dear Sir Edward," said he, "I am wrong. I know I have injured you; but I am so completely wretched that my senses seem likely to forsake me. You, who perhaps have loved as I do, though you never could feel what it is like me to love and to despair, will pity and forgive me."

A generous but romantic project now took possession of the mind of Sir Edward. He determined to open his heart and all its weakness to Montgomery; and while he confided to him a secret which he had struggled so frequently to conceal even from himself, to make the jealous and ardent lover the arbitrator between his passion and his honor; and, though he still intended firmly to oppose their immediate marriage, to consult him on the measures

which, during his absence, ought to be pursued to put Ethelinde
at once out of the hazard of improper acquaintance with others,
and of being made liable to an imputed partiality to himself. He
gave himself hardly a moment to consider of the propriety of this
confidence; but seizing on the idea with an enthusiasm which he
believed was the effort of recovering virtue and resolution, he
took the hand which Montgomery held out to him, and said in an
animated tone—

"My dear Montgomery, I do not forgive you because I have not
been offended; but I most sincerely sympathize with you, and as a
proof how much I esteem you, I will now tell you the true state of
a heart infinitely more wretched than your's can ever be."

Montgomery shook his head as if he thought that was not possible; and Sir Edward, hesitating half a moment, went on—

"You did not know me till long after my marriage, or it would
be unnecessary for me to assure you that my affection was then
Lady Newenden's. Her person is now as lovely, perhaps, as it was
then; I know not whether it is not even more so. I was of an age
to be charmed with mere personal beauty; her character was not
formed; she appeared gentle and amiable; she preferred me to
men who would have, in the eyes of an ambitious woman, more
advantages; fancy augmented every perfection; her beauty would
have rendered even her defects pleasing to me, if love had suffered reason to discover any. We married; and for a little, a very
little while, I thought myself happy; but by degrees I discovered
that Maria was merely a pretty woman; and that there were many
hours when a rational companion was more necessary to my happiness than a fine lady, who, careless whether I was pleased or displeased, was at least determined to please herself, by obtaining
that general admiration which so highly gratified her vanity, and
which she thought had not been shewn before only because she
had never before been seen.

"When my eldest boy was born I flattered myself that new
sentiments would be awakened; but Maria had never the heart
of a mother: and I saw, with stifled anguish, that she was more
solicitous to make her appearance with undiminished beauty,
than about the child, whose birth would have doubly endeared
her to my heart. By the excessive fondness of her father, and the
silly adulation of her mother, she had acquired an early habit of

believing that no woman was an object of so much consequence as herself. I saw this disposition in a thousand nameless instances. I tried—vainly tried not to see it. I still loved her; and though I could not esteem her as I wished to have done, she knew not that my expectations of permanent felicity declined almost unconsciously; for whatever were my mortifications my behaviour to her was unchanged. You have often heard me say how partial I have from a boy been to the country, particularly to my native country; but I could seldom prevail on Lady Newenden to go even to Denham, unless for a few days with parties of company. To go to Grasmere she positively refused; and the birth of my other two children, which happened within the three following years after that of Edward, made me delay from time to time to insist upon it. At length the urgent occasion there was for my presence, a hope that such a journey might yield her a salutary respite from perpetual company, late hours, and deep play, and a foolish idea that the scenes of sublime and beautiful nature might awaken in her mind a taste for simple and domestic pleasures, united to make me press for her going to Grasmere. Her mother, with her usual absurdity, encouraged her opposition to my wishes; but I found means to engage Mr. Maltravers on my side, and finally we succeeded.

"The dread of solitude, rather than any love for her cousin, induced her to ask the company of Ethelinde Chesterville. I had seen her very frequently, but generally in mixed company. Her beauty was striking; but it seemed to me not more conspicuous than that of my wife. Alas! I knew not, till I had continual occasion to converse with her, the power of a lovely form, animated by a soul like her's. Considered as a married man, as her near relation, I had a thousand opportunities of observing the charms of her understanding and the unaffected goodness of her heart. All that Maria wanted, Ethelinde seemed to possess: candid, ingenuous, and humane; warm in her affections; with all her advantages of form, unconscious that she possessed any; and with a strong, lively, and cultivated understanding, as modest as if she had known nothing. Involuntarily I was making perpetual comparisons; alas! Lady Newenden gave me perpetual cause to make them; yet I endeavoured—very earnestly endeavoured to check in its infancy a passion as improper as it was hopeless. That I have succeeded so ill is now the torment of my life.

"I need not relate to you, Montgomery, its irresistible progress. Davenant's proposals, which at first I thought I could encourage, soon gave me sensations that made a narrow examination of my heart necessary. I found too certainly that I now knew, for the first time, what it was to love. I condemned myself for not having fled before from the dangerous unconscious object who had inspired it; but as it was then too late, I persuaded myself that as the violence of my attachment exceeded not its purity, I might, however wretched myself, continue to see, and acquire a kind of happiness in serving her whom I could perceive no prospect of ever calling mine.

"Such was the disposition of my mind when Ethelinde left Grasmere Abbey. I found that even at that early period her heart, which repulsed the addresses of Davenant with scorn, was by no means indifferent to you. I tried at least to accustom myself to endure what was inevitable—her preferring another; for I could myself claim no preference as a lover: yet I will candidly own that my passion revolted perpetually against my reason; and though I knew I could never expect her to love me, otherwise than as her friend and her guardian, there were times, when all your merit and the hopelessness of my own situation were insufficient to reconcile me even for a moment to the idea of your possessing her heart.

"In her absence I attempted anew to argue myself out of a predilection which was at least prejudicial to my own happiness and could be productive only of distress to its object; but in making this experiment I had occasion to experience the truth of that maxim which says, that 'absence which destroys a slight degree of love, augments a violent and serious passion, as the wind extinguishes a feeble flame but encreases a strong fire.'[1] Though I saw her no longer, my imagination dwelt on her perpetually; Lady Newenden's careless indifference making it turn towards her with still encreasing fondness; yet let me say, that whatever were my internal conflicts, I carefully avoided betraying them by any alteration in my behaviour to my wife; I would have even redoubled, if it had been possible, my boundless indulgence; nor did she, I

---

1 L'absence diminue les mediocres passions & augment les grands; comme le vent éteint les bougies et allume le feu. *Rochefaucault.* [Smith's note.] François de La Rochefoucauld (1613-1680) *Maximes* (302b). Smith did not provide the French translation and note in the first edition of *Ethelinde.*

am persuaded, discern that the attention I shewed her came not from the heart. Alas! her own was incapable of so nice a distinction; and she studied my happiness too little to know whether I was indeed what I affected to appear. Then it was, that every resolution to conquer my attachment, was at once overcome by the circumstances of my boy's illness. His mother, occupied entirely in a circle she had formed at Scarborough, affected to be unable to undertake the journey which appeared necessary if ever we hoped to see him alive. Shocked at her unfeeling excuse, and frantic with fears for the life of my child, I arrived at Denham—I arrived, not to weep over the darling of my heart, but to find that the tenderness, the attention of Ethelinde, had snatched him, under Providence, from the grave; and that supplying to him all the tenderness of a mother, she had preserved his life at the hazard of her own.

"Had I not loved her before, I must have loved her then; but to the great judge of hearts I dare appeal whether, as my love encreased, it became not more sacred. She was then, she is still idolized as an angel; and I protest that if the sacrifice of my life would conduce to the happiness of her's I would resign it with delight.

"Yet, Montgomery, I will not deny that there have been times when suffering all the misery inflicted on me by Lady Newenden's insupportable temper, and having too frequently reason to doubt whether she has not dishonoured me as well as made me wretched, I have harboured dangerous ideas—I have dreamed that a release from a union, once the happiness but now the torment of my life, was possible, and then the image of Ethelinde has intruded itself in seducing colours: yet these enchanting visions have been instantly dissolved when I have reflected that were I at liberty to-morrow to offer my hand to Ethelinde, I know that she would not accept it, for that heart is your's. This conviction, which ought for ever to put an end to all hope, has not, I own, been received without many a severe pang; yet so truly do I love her, that were I sure she would be happy I think I could give her to you, and bury for ever in my heart, if I could not eradicate, this tyrannical and fatal attachment. Judge, Montgomery, whether this candid confession, which I was under no necessity of making, is not a proof of the purity of my love, and whether, in making a favored lover the confidant of my hopeless passion, I do not give him the

best security for its disinterested tenderness. Let us not then consider ourselves, but what should be done for the present support
and content of Ethelinde. Montgomery, hear me when I declare to
you, that would a provision out of my fortune enable you to live
happily together, I think I could put it apart for her use on those
conditions; but besides that I know you to be too noble minded
to accept it, I will own to you that I have very little in my power
to offer. When I married Lady Newenden my estates were greatly
incumbered. Her fortune cleared them; and I for three years lived
within the income they produced: but since that period Lady Newenden's card money has made a great diminution, and as I have
paid for poor Chesterville all the ready money I had of my own, I
should now be getting deeply into debt if Mr. Maltravers had not
voluntarily made a considerable addition to our income, which, as
I consider it as entirely appropriated to Lady Newenden, I make
it a point never to interfere with. You know your own situation;
ask yourself whether you ought to involve Ethelinde in its inconveniences, and answer the question not like a mere lover, but like
him who to the real interest of a beloved object, is noble enough to
sacrifice his own immediate happiness: let me not suppose, Montgomery, that I am more disinterested than you are, only because I
have less to hope."

The various emotions with which Montgomery had listened
to this extraordinary confession are not to be described. Tho' he
in fact knew all that Sir Edward had told him, his avowal did not
appear the less astonishing; and he knew not, when he ceased
speaking, what reply to make. Various and tumultuous sensations kept him for some moments silent. He saw that Sir Edward
expected of him, a sacrifice of all his hopes, while he appeared
willing to encrease the remoter one of his marrying on his return
from India; and that he asked his advice on the disposal of her,
while he was absent; a point, which he could not settle in his own
mind, on any plan except that of her going down to Grasmere, and
remaining with his mother. The confusion and indecision of his
thoughts was visible in his countenance. Noble minded himself,
he knew none of that narrow mistrust which renders the integrity
of another doubtful; but to hear Sir Edward Newenden, on whom
she must be left so entirely dependent, avow his love for her, and
own that there had been moments when he had meditated on

making her his, gave him a sort of uneasiness which he could neither repress or acknowledge.

"I do believe, Sir Edward," said he, at length, "that notwithstanding the attachment you have owned, and of which I was not before ignorant, I might confide safely in your honor, and fearlessly leave Ethelinde to your protection; but will the world, that knows not the firmness of that honor, see her left, without comments as injurious to her fame, as to your peace? Too much has already been said of your partiality to her; and pardon me if I say, that with all your endeavours to conceal it, she herself is the only person who has remained ignorant of it. Judge, therefore, whether she ought to continue with your family, and be supported by your bounty? Allow me, Sir Edward, to say with the same candour which you have used, and I doubt not expect, that nothing I have heard has served to make me relinquish my opinion; on the contrary, I think your own peace, as well as her's and mine, demand that even if I leave her, I leave her as my wife."

"I deserve more confidence, Montgomery, than you seem to place in me. Be assured, my friend, that I do not mean to mortify or distress you when I remind you that you have nothing on which to support her: and would you submit to have that assistance given her as Mrs. Montgomery which I can with greater propriety offer to her while she remains the unprotected daughter of my deceased friend, left to my guardianship. However my own feelings and my attention to her's would make me wish in either case to keep such assistance secret, yet the prying and inquisitive world would in either case decide that it was so, for they know her situation—they know your's."

Montgomery was struck with this remark; and feeling that his whole soul revolted from the idea of having his wife pensioner on the bounty of another, cried eagerly—"Repeat it not, Sir Edward, for heaven's sake, and suffer me to leave you a moment. I am too wretched!"

"Hear me out, however," replied Edward: "hear at least what I have to offer Ethelinde. Though her situation with Miss Newenden is not, I own, the most eligible, yet, as I have nothing better to suggest, I would propose her remaining here till Mrs. Montgomery returns; then, if she prefers going down to her, as I doubt not she will, I wish to have her happy, and surely shall not oppose it. In either case; I will pay her quarterly thirty guineas, and I will endeavour to make it appear even to her as arising from what I have been able to save out of the wreck of her father's fortune; and surely, Montgomery, you are too liberal minded to doubt the disinterested motives on which I will thus act. To put an end, however, to every doubt, and to convince you that I shall not even see her, I protest to you that it is my intention to quit England for some years, and pass into Italy; *with* Lady Newenden, if she can determine to quit her country rather than her honor; *without* her, if the hold that her dissolute connections have on her heart is too strong to be broken by maternal affection or duty to me. The disagreeable affair I have been involved in with Lord Danesforte, the uneasy doubts which that affair has served rather to heighten than remove, and my resolution to break Lady Newenden's acquaintance with him, or quit her for ever, all serve to strengthen this determination; and whatever struggles it may cost me, I now mean to take leave of Ethelinde. Her peace, her happiness require that I resign the dangerous indulgence of seeing her; and I swear to you, Montgomery, that there is no sacrifice I would not make for her. I shall be every where equally wretched; my lot is cast, and must be, I know, endured; but unhappy as I am destined to be, I shall derive a source of comfort and gratification in knowing I have communicated none of my misery to Ethelinde."

Tears were in his eyes when he ceased speaking. Montgomery, equally affected, could only wring his hand; and say—"You are generous, Sir Edward, I own it. Ethelinde deserves such a friend; but allow me to see and speak to her before we converse farther on what is to be done hereafter. I came hither to take leave of her. How I shall execute my purpose, I know not: her fall, her illness, the terror of losing her for ever, and the unsettled state in which I am to quit her, have united to unnerve my resolution; yet my promise to my mother is passed; she believes that I am even now embarked; an almost certain fortune attends me whither I am going, if I live; and if I die, I hope I am not a coward, yet to die and see her no more!—if it should be so——no! I will not, I cannot pursue the train of ideas that such a thought leads to."

"We have both need of solitude and reflection, my dear friend," said Sir Edward: "we will therefore part; but allow me before I go to state to you that I must return to London this evening. I left my

house in confusion; Lady Newenden ill at her father's; and could I
have commanded myself when Ethelinde was in danger, I ought
not in prudence to have come. Try, my dear friend, if you cannot
determine to return to London with me. Receive my honor as a
pledge that I will see Ethelinde no more. Do *you*, with prospects
full of hope, make that exertion which *I* make in despair. I resign
the gratification of seeing her that I may not give occasion to calumny to hurt her delicacy; do you resign it for a little time only in
the delightful hope of returning to enjoy with her uninterrupted
happiness. Reflect how much your fate is likely to be preferable to
mine, and you have surely too much spirit to lament it."

Montgomery could only beg an hour or two to consider what
he *could* do. They then parted: Sir Edward went out to walk alone,
and Montgomery to seek the servant who attended Ethelinde;
from whom he learned that she had passed a very good night, had
very little remains of pain, and was already dressed. Montgomery
then sent to beg he might see her, and was immediately admitted
to her room.

CHAPTER XI

Sir Edward Newenden, in his solitary walk, was endeavouring to
strengthen the resolution he had taken to deny himself for the
future the sight of Ethelinde; and if he could not conquer his passion for her, to prove its purity by consulting only her happiness.
He was anxious, however, that Montgomery might be equally disinterested, and very desirous that she might be spared that painful
hesitation and cruel struggle which his remaining longer at Brackwood might occasion to her; but he persuaded himself that it was
merely solicitude for her repose, and no lurking jealousy of Montgomery, that made him thus impatiently await the hour of their
separation.

The combat between what he saw to be his duty, and what he
felt to be his inclination, was most severely renewed in the breast
of Montgomery. All the arguments he had heard, and all that his
own reason had suggested to him on the side of his going to India,
were light when opposed to the dread of leaving Ethelinde never
perhaps to return. The confession of Sir Edward had left on his

mind a confused sensation of confidence and uneasiness. Generous and candid himself, and having seen numberless instances of
Sir Edward's noble spirit, he could not doubt but that he was at the
moment perfectly sincere; but what reliance could be placed on
the resolution and integrity of the firmest and most upright mind
under the influence of a passion so violent as that he had acknowledged; a passion which had recently drawn him into a step so
inconsiderate as that of quitting London under the circumstances
he had done, to fly down to Ethelinde on the vague report of her
accident. He knew, by what had passed within his own bosom,
how unstable are the wisest determinations when counteracted
by a predominant and tyrannic affection: and while he did justice
to the candour of Sir Edward, and mistrusted not his honor, he
trembled involuntarily, to leave Ethelinde, so situated as to be still
compelled to accept a support from him in addition to the numerous obligations she already owed him.

Yet if he could prevail on her to quit the protection to which
her father had consigned her, and unite her fate with his, how
could he support her? Mr. Royston, so eager to provide for him
abroad, would do nothing for him in England. He had no interest, therefore, and no provision but his mother's slender and probably reduced income, and again the idea recurred of distressing
that beloved mother, of seeing Ethelinde languishing in indigence,
surrounded perhaps by a family of lovely well-born beggars, and
of living to reproach himself with having poorly shrunk from the
duty he owed to her, to his mother, and himself; this reflection
seemed to restore his firmness, and he thought he could rather
quit her, than hazard, by his stay, to realize a prospect which would
be as distressing to his feelings, as unworthy the courage and
steadiness of a man.

Thus amid the fluctuation of uneasy thoughts, Montgomery
was introduced to the room where Ethelinde was at her breakfast.
She appeared much better, and complained very little of her head.
Her spirits were also much amended; and while she expressed
much surprise at the unexpected arrival of Sir Edward, she seemed
very anxious to know what had brought him so suddenly to Brackwood, and where he had left Lady Newenden: though nothing
could be more natural than her solicitude, Montgomery, liberal
and candid in every thing else, was made restless and half angry by

the tender interest she seemed to take in whatever related to him, and as soon as he answered such enquiries as he thought necessary to satisfy without alarming her, either on account of the noise which the duel would make, (of which he said nothing) nor on Sir Edward's rash journey, he said—"Sir Edward returns to London this evening. He has offered to take me with him. Ethelinde, I will own that I am compelled to appeal to you to determine for me, for of myself I cannot—no, it is impossible for me to resolve to leave you."

Ethelinde turned pale at the information as well as at the manner in which he gave it: but thus called upon to strengthen his faultering resolution, she stifled by an effort of reason and virtue the pang that seized her heart; and while it throbbed with anguish, she called up a faint forced smile, and answered—

"Surely, Montgomery, we have not to argue over again the necessity of that measure, distressing as it ever must be to us both, that has so long and so properly been determined upon. This second parting, with all its pain, we have brought upon ourselves; let not *your* fortitude, which ought to strengthen mine, sink under it. To you I look for support: disappoint me not by shewing that he on whom I rely, is even weaker than I am."

"Ah! rather say," cried Montgomery, eagerly interrupting her, "that your calmer temper, your milder feelings, suffer you not to love to the excess I do, and that you can look with resignation on that horrible necessity that drives me to despair and to madness."

"My dear Montgomery," answered Ethelinde, "you know not, nor do I wish you should know, half the anguish of that heart which you call calm and resigned. Believe me, your Ethelinde, though less loud and less impatient, feels as severely as you do the cruel stroke to which she must submit. I know, however, I have long known, that I must be wretched; but as my miseries hitherto have not originated from my own faults, so I will yet try to evade the severest sting of those which may be to come, by keeping free at least from self reproach; and surely I should have much wherewith to upbraid myself hereafter, if, because to bid you farewell makes me endure the bitterest anguish that any circumstance in this life can inflict, I were to evade it at the expence of your honor, suffer you to break your promise to your mother, and resign an establishment that may with honor raise you to the affluence, to which your birth and merit give you so just a title."

"My birth!" exclaimed he, "what is my birth but a curse to me? and the merit you impute to me, what has it obtained but an honorable exile? Had I been more humbly born I should not have been told that to use my health and youth to acquire a support for her I adore in my own country, was degrading and dishonorable. Oh, Ethelinde! the humblest peasant that traverses these bleak hills, and retires at night to his clayey and thatched cottage, is to me an object of envy. He labours for a small stipend; but it is certain; and he shares it with his wife and his children: surrounded by all that is interesting to the heart of man, he feels not that poverty to which he has always been accustomed; he fears nothing for to-morrow; and when he dies, his children are secure of being able to live as he has lived: but an illustrious beggar, as I am, must cringe at home to people who are raised, by acts which *I* should blush to practice; to mushroom greatness; on men who

> 'Fish up their dirty and dependent bread,
> From pools and ditches of the common wealth
> Sordid and sickening at their own success.'[1]

or must be sent to extort from the helpless natives of another hemisphere—gold, the curse of mankind; that having plundered a distant country he may return to corrupt his own. Alas! as I sat by the scanty embers of the shepherd's fire those two nights when you lay so ill in the adjoining cabin, how did I wish that we had both been born to a destiny as humble as his, and that even now you could learn to prefer the quiet comfortable cottage on the border of Grasmere Water, to long long years of separate misery, terminated perhaps by death, perhaps by affluence, for which we may find too late that happiness and health have been sacrificed."

The eyes of Ethelinde were filled with tears, and her heart with redoubled anguish, while he thus spoke. Loving him so tenderly, to bid him leave her; to seem fearful of enduring the humble life which he was for her sake willing to submit to; to undergo the misery of parting from him, and that of being left to contemplate

1 Cowper, *The Task*, III: 808-810. From a long passage detailing the corruption of Parliament and jobbery.

the dangers to which he must be exposed from the long voyage and the unpropitious climate; and on the other hand to reflect on the happiness which with him she must find in the deepest obscurity! her resolution was shaken; she could not at that moment exert any of that virtuous fortitude of which she had been but a moment before serenely conscious; but overwhelmed by tenderness, she dissolved into tears, and could only in broken murmurs say—"Did you then, Montgomery, sit up in the cottage those two nights? why would you do so? Ah! why thus aggravate all the anguish I must endure? why make me drink to the dregs this bitter cup?"

"Resolve then," cried Montgomery, with equal emotion, "resolve to dash it from you, and let us dare to be poor and happy. Let me quote, since the language is superior to any I can use, a sentence of an enchanting author, applicable to our situation: '*Soyons heureux et pauvres; ah! quel trésor nous aurons acquis! J'ai des bras, je suis robuste; le pain gagné par mon travail te paroitra plus delicieux que les mets des festins. Un repas appreté par l'amour, peut-il jamais être insipide?*'[1]

"Alas!" replied Ethelinde, "you need no other eloquence than your own to prevail on one whose feeble heart is ready to aid rather than to contend against your arguments. Spare me, dear Montgomery, spare me the repetition of those reasons which still, in my opinion, are so strong for your departure, and which would make my acceding to your stay, however I might wish it, as contrary to my duty as to your interest. Let us not, my dear friend, be the slaves of passion, but exert our reason and our prudence to save us from future repentance. Happiness we cannot command; it will perhaps elude our grasp in the moment that we have sacri-

---

1 Rousseau. [Smith's note.] Jean-Jacques Rousseau, *Julie, ou La Nouvelle Héloïse*, ed. René Pomeau (Paris: Garnier, 1960): Première Partie, Lettre XXVI, p. 67. As translated by Philip Stewart and Jane Vache, *Julie; or The New Heloise: Letters of Two Lovers Who Live in a Small Town at the Foot of the Alps* (Hanover: University Press of New England, 1997): Part One, Letter 26, p 76: "Let us be happy and poor, ah! what riches we will then possess . . . I have good arms, I am strong; the bread earned by my labor will seem more delicious to you than the fare of feasts. Can a meal prepared by love ever lack savor?" Montgomery omits the second sentence of the passage: "*Mais ne faisons point cet affront à l'humanité et croire qu'il ne restera pas sur la terre entière un asile à deux amants infortunés,*" as translated: "But let us not affront humanity by believing that there will remain no asylum in the whole earth for two unfortunate Lovers."

ficed every duty to obtain it. Let us, therefore, do what is right, and leave the event to Providence, who knows better than we do how it may finally be obtained."

The faultering voice, broken by frequent sighs, in which this sentence was pronounced, betrayed, notwithstanding all her struggles to conceal it, the violent internal conflict that Ethelinde underwent: Montgomery, unable to bear it, rose and walked with hurried step about the room; his heart oppressed with unutterable anguish; he could neither controvert the justice and truth of what she had said, nor could he bear the thoughts of leaving her; and among all the confused and impracticable wishes he formed, the only distinct one seemed to be that they might both die, if they could not live together.

"What shall I do?" exclaimed he; "how shall I tear myself away? my soul recoils from the attempt. Let me, before I torture myself by allowing its necessity, let me wait to hear from my mother; perhaps the loss which she had so much reason to apprehend may not have happened; on her undiminished income we could live; why should I anticipate agonies, compared to which those of death would be pleasurable."

Ethelinde, though she had very little hope that Mrs. Montgomery would save her property, yet caught at a bare possibility when it seemed to soften the horrors of parting by holding out a hope that it might not be final. Her weakness of body, her softness of mind, equally rendered her incapable of bearing the sight of Montgomery's wretchedness, and she felt herself every moment ready to consent to beg with him round the world rather than to part with him for a few years.

She continued, however, silent; and Montgomery, approaching her, eagerly took advantage of it.—"Do you," cried he, "do you consent that I should wait to hear from my mother?"

"Alas!" replied she, "you must judge for yourself. The ship, perhaps, which is now ready to sail, may depart without you."

"I can go then in another."

"The appointment may be lost."

"No, of that I am secure. Let me then suppose that it is yet possible you will go down to Grasmere; that you will, if we have indeed wherewithal to exist together with that dear parent who will rejoice in our happiness, forbid my leaving you; and suffer me, instead of embarking for India, to return hither, and take you from hence to humble but lasting felicity."

Ethelinde could not oppose him; she murmured out an incomplete acquiescence, rather to appease the violence of his agitation than because she felt it right, or entertained any hope that the little income of his mother remained undiminished. He was kissing her hand in the wild transports of gratitude when Sir Edward Newenden entered the room.

"I do not leave her," cried Montgomery, before Sir Edward could speak: "she consents to go down to Grasmere, if the little fortune we have still is found to be ours, as I dare venture to believe it will be."

A faint blush tinged the cheek of Ethelinde, from whence illness and anxiety had driven even the pale roses that bloomed there in her happier days; she turned her languid eyes on Sir Edward, who changed countenance, but seemed by an effort of resolution to recover himself; and sitting down by her, took her hand, and with a smile said—

"If this impetuous lover, Ethelinde, would give me leave, I would tell you how truly it rejoices your guardian and your friend that you are so well recovered of the effects of your accident."

"You are always most kind to me, Sir Edward," replied she; "always in truth I have found you my guardian and friend."

"As such, Sir Edward," cried Montgomery, who, though he could not blame the gratitude of Ethelinde, was alarmed by the tenderness with which she expressed it, "as such, as the guardian and friend of Ethelinde, I apply to you to ratify her consent: it is indeed but conditional; but let me now take leave of her in the hope that I may in a few days return to claim the promise she has given me."

"Montgomery," replied Sir Edward, still endeavouring to stifle his increasing emotion, "it has ever been, it will ever be my purpose to fulfil religiously the sacred trust which Colonel Chesterville reposed in me, and to promote the welfare of his daughter. None can know better than I do the inefficacy of riches to constitute happiness; and I shall not oppose what she herself believes will make her happy, however I may regret the hazard she will incur of finding that if money secures not felicity the total want of it will be attended with inconveniences which she is, I fear, ill calculated to contend with."

"Be it mine," said Montgomery, in the most animated tone, "be it mine to save her from every inconvenience. Ah! can any lot be so delightful as to live only for her service—" He was going on when Sir Edward gravely said—

"I understood indeed that you thought so when you determined with such proper spirit to execute that service the most effectually by seeking in India a fortune worthy of her."

"But if Ethelinde will be happier on the little we have, why should I leave her?"

"I thought," replied Sir Edward, "that all this had been before discussed. I have said, and I repeat, that as the guardian of Miss Chesterville I will oppose nothing she thinks will make her really happy; as her friend only I will give her my opinion, and that is surely my duty to do, even though I feel that it may be probably painful and certainly fruitless."

Ethelinde, sinking under the long continued conflict of her own heart, could not bear this. Faint and breathless, she leaned her head on the table before her, and said with a deep sigh—"Ah! dear Sir Edward, why will you suppose I disregard your opinion?"

"I am grieved," replied he, while all his features expressed the excess of his agitation—"I am grieved to see you so affected; and will shorten a conversation so painful to us all. Montgomery has very naturally represented to you only the summer view of the prospect which he desires you to contemplate with pleasure. I will not, with the gloomy pencil of a careful guardian sketch out the reverse. You have so much sense that it were needless; but I will appeal to your own judgment, to that excellent understanding which love itself is, I think, incapable of misleading, whether the other plan is not much more rational in itself, worthier of his spirit and of your approbation." He paused a moment as if collecting courage to go on. Neither Ethelinde or Montgomery spoke, and at length in a firmer voice he proceeded—"It has been said, Ethelinde, that I am, that I have been too fond of your company. I never denied that I preferred your conversation to that of every other human being. You will recollect, however, that this partiality has never exceeded that of a brother for a favorite and beloved sister."

"Oh never!" sighed Ethelinde. She seemed to be attempting to say more, but Sir Edward gave her not time.

"Do not however, my dear Ethy, nor do you, Montgomery, suppose, that innocent as this indulgence has ever been, I oppose your marriage to gratify myself by its continuance. Whatever may be your decision, it is in either case mine to quit England with my children in few days, and to remain at least some years on the continent of Europe. This determination must, Montgomery, convince you, were it possible you could entertain any other idea of me, that my advice is wholly disinterested. As I must consider Ethelinde as my ward, I cannot justify it to myself were I to acquiesce in her marrying indiscreetly without representing to her its probable consequences, and pointing out to her the alternative in her choice, that she may not fancy herself compelled by her situation to marry, and by a sophistry usual with lovers impute that to necessity which is indeed the effect of inclination."

"Name your alternative, Sir Edward," said Montgomery impatiently.

"It is her remaining with my sister or with your mother till your return, which will in all probability, with the advantages you have, happen in a very few years. From the remainder of Colonel Chesterville's fortune I hope and I believe I shall save about an hundred and twenty pounds a year, which I will take care shall be punctually paid her. You will, therefore, have nothing to apprehend for her. When your mother returns, she may, if she prefers it, live with her, and without the painful circumstance of being wholly dependent on her small fortune. Till then this house, though not perhaps the properest or most desirable, is yet a secure and creditable asylum. I must go from hence," added Sir Edward, "in an hour: decide therefore, Montgomery, whether you will go with me; and you, my dear Ethelinde, calm your spirits, I beseech you; and remember that whatever be your determination you will ever have in me a friend and a brother."

He now hastily rose and left the room, having exerted his resolution to the utmost. When he was gone, Montgomery, whose love was still too powerful for his reason, again addressed himself vehemently to Ethelinde, from whom the affectionate and friendly solicitude of Sir Edward had again drawn those tears which the extreme pain she had before felt had checked for a moment.

"Speak to me, Ethelinde," cried he eagerly; "speak to me, I conjure you: tell me that nothing Sir Edward has said will make you revoke your permission. I cannot part with you—upon my soul I cannot—for months—for years—perhaps for ever. I am a coward—I sink into childish weakness at the idea. Oh! deliver me from the cruel necessity of undergoing such torture, unless you can teach me to endure it."

"How can I lend you fortitude, Montgomery, who want it myself? Do you think I suffer less than you do? Or am I better able to support it? Alas! no! Sir Edward has assuredly reason on his side, but reason will not prevent my being desolate and miserable when you are gone: and as to pecuniary considerations, if there is indeed a probability that out of the wreck of my father's fortune something may be saved, will it not enable us better to live together? And should it be brought in aid of the motives that are to part us?

Montgomery knew too well that so far from any residue being likely to remain in the hands of Sir Edward, there was not enough to pay him a tenth part of what he had lent the Colonel and paid for his son; and that he had thus represented it to Ethelinde only to spare her the pain of receiving new obligations; yet would not Montgomery undeceive her, because he had promised secrecy to Sir Edward; otherwise he was too noble to let even jealousy tempt him to any thing like a mean suppression of merit in a rival, whatever fears he might entertain concerning the influence of that rival over the gratitude of his mistress.

Montgomery, therefore, without seizing, as Ethelinde expected, the idea that the impediments to their union might be in a great measure removed by this circumstance, contrived only to press her to adhere to the promise he had drawn from her before Sir Edward came to them; and he, in his turn, assured her that with the hope of seeing her again so soon, of meeting her to part no more, he would bid her adieu with calmness and resolution. This promise was particularly consoling to Ethelinde, as she dreaded the effect of that agitation of spirits into which the excess of his passion had frequently thrown him—agitation the more alarming as he was usually mild and rational, and his passions on no other point were capable of obscuring his reason. She wilfully shut her eyes to the little probability there was that Montgomery would receive in town the favorable accounts with which he sanguinely flattered himself, and was as wilfully forgetful that even if these expectations should be realized she was now overlooking or misrepresenting the same difficulties which she had before summoned all her prudence and reason to behold in their true colors.

No alteration, unless for the worse, had happened either in her circumstances or in those of Montgomery; but her love, which seemed before hardly capable of augmentation, had encreased; she had found the former separation from Montgomery, and his uncertain absence, even more intolerable in the reality that her lively fancy had represented them; and seeing from daily experience in the house of Miss Newenden, as she had done in that of Sir Edward, that it was possible to be very affluent yet very unhappy, she had gradually reconciled her mind to the deprivation which she knew she must submit to with Montgomery of all the elegancies and many of the comforts of life, and had convinced herself that to live for and with him, whom she so tenderly loved in a situation that barely afforded its necessaries, would be without comparison a more fortunate lot, than the most exalted or brilliant situation that could be offered her, on condition of parting from him for a few years.

Under this conviction, the arguments she had used in the former part of this scene, to induce Montgomery to quit her, were the forced efforts of virtue and resolution, supported by her promise to Mrs. Montgomery; but they were too painful, and her heart revolted too much against them to suffer her obstinately to defend them; and weak and exhausted as she was by the sight of Montgomery's sufferings as well as her own, all her remaining fortitude was hardly sufficient to save her from the additional imprudence of going with him at all events, and becoming his wife whether his mother's income was or was not sufficient for their support.

CHAPTER XII

Montgomery, while he tried to stifle every suggestion which arose in his mind that he was perhaps groundlessly sanguine, was collecting resolution to bid farewell to Ethelinde with calmness, as only for a short time. Sir Edward felt with almost equal poignancy, the pain he was yet compelled to undergo of parting from her

also; and in order that her future situation might give him as little
uneasiness as possible, at least while she remained with Miss Newenden, he determined before he went to speak to his sister fully,
and endeavour to convince her of the regard she owed to the opinion of the world, without hinting that the presence of Ethelinde
made that attention more requisite. He had not the least suspicion
of the designs entertained by Woolaston: but he proposed talking
to Davenant, which as his former guardian he thought he had a
right to do, to beg that he would not bring visitors to Miss Newenden's house, whose characters rendered them improper companions for two single women.

But while he formed this design, the party who had so strong
an interest in deceiving him, were taking measures to preclude
its necessity. Miss Newenden, who grew every moment more
attached to Woolaston as his various knowledge unfolded itself
itself in the stable, the field, and the kennel, had too firmly determined to reward his merit to suffer any remonstrances of her
brother to shake her resolution; but still she was willing to avoid
hearing them, and she contrived to make Davenant and Woolaston understand that it would be better for them to depart before
Sir Edward, if he staid longer than that evening, and if he did not,
to say before him that they were immediately going into Sussex.
To any proposal of her's they both readily agreed, and it was
settled among them that they should take leave of her that day
at dinner, and as soon as Sir Edward was gone to the Continent,
as he had informed his sister he intended, that Woolaston was to
return and become master of Brackwood and its spirited lady. This
arrangement was very satisfactory to him; as he dreaded much the
influence of Sir Edward, and was afraid if he suspected his intentions he would represent to this sister the imprudence of marrying a man so situated, and of putting herself entirely in his power,
in so strong a light, that his hopes would too probably be blasted
forever.

When they met, therefore, at dinner, Woolaston was extremely
guarded in his behaviour. Davenant affected to be out of humour
at the little sport they had found, and declared his resolution of
going towards home that evening. Miss Newenden assumed her
usual careless ease; and it required no great exertion to deceive Sir
Edward, occupied as he was by his own poignant uneasiness. He

eat nothing, and hardly spoke; while the wretchedness that corroded his heart could only be exceeded by that suffered by Montgomery. Ethelinde still remained in her own room; and had she not had a pretence to do so from the effects of her late accident, she would have found it impossible to go through a scene in which she beheld her lover and her best friend suffer so cruelly on her account.

An uncomfortable dinner being thus passed, a chaise was heard at the door, and a servant informed Sir Edward that it was his; he started up, and in evident confusion left the room. Montgomery, who fancied he was gone to speak to Ethelinde, was tempted to follow him: but ashamed of shewing any suspicion of the conduct of such a man, he sat still, yet in such apparent uneasiness, that Davenant, who enjoyed every opportunity of mortifying him, began to talk to him of Sir Edward's great goodness to his new ward, and of the extraordinary kindness he had shewn to her father. This conversation was insupportable. Montgomery bore it a moment or two, and then without answering, abruptly quitted the room, and walked hastily backwards and forwards in the hall, dreading the moment when he was to say adieu, yet thinking every moment an age while he believed Sir Edward prevented his being admitted to Ethelinde, for he could not bear that a third person, and above all others that Sir Edward, should be witness to a parting, which, however transient he endeavoured to persuade himself it would be, appeared more terrible to his imagination than any other species of torture.

At length Sir Edward came down stairs; and seeing Montgomery in the hall, he asked in an eager and hurried voice if he was ready. Montgomery, in a tone of equal agitation, answered—"I shall be ready as soon as I have spoken to Ethelinde."

"Go then," replied Sir Edward, "go, for she expects you, Montgomery. As you love that dear unhappy girl, spare her weak and exhausted spirits. Do not, I beseech you, lengthen by fruitless complaints a scene so distressing."

"No, Sir Edward," cried Montgomery, "whatever I suffer——" He would have said more, but his voice was choaked, and he hastened away.

Sir Edward had at first been attempting to soothe and tranquillize Ethelinde; telling her how he intended to settle her pecuniary concerns during his absence, and recommending it to her to remain with Miss Newenden at least till Mrs. Montgomery's return. He would not again touch on her marriage, but contented himself with entreating her to do nothing material without consulting him. Drowned in tears, and unable to speak, she held out her hand in token of giving him this promise. He took it; and as he pressed it to his trembling lips, he besought her to take care of her health; on no account to venture again on horseback; and then adding—"And ever remember, Ethelinde, that till you have otherwise disposed of this dear hand, you are accountable for your care of yourself to him on whom the precious trust devolved on your father's death—to him, who has hitherto, however inadequately he has succeeded, endeavoured to fulfill it, and who would not, but for the most cruel circumstances, a moment resign the sacred pleasure of executing in person the office of your guardian, your brother, your protector, your friend!"

"May heaven reward you, Sir," said Ethelinde, in a voice hardly audible, "for all your goodness!"

"I ask no reward," replied he, "but the knowledge that you are happy—could I know that, I could endure all my own miseries. But I know not what I would say.—Once more, dearest Ethelinde, farewell! May heaven protect you!" He then turned hastily away, and left the room.

Sir Edward's generous efforts to conceal what it was impossible for her not to see, and the evident struggle he underwent, as well as his endeavours to make her easy as to a support without wounding her delicacy, could not but greatly affect Ethelinde; nor did the more acute anguish which now awaited her, blunt the poignancy of her distress on his account. That of Montgomery, however, was so severe that all his attempts to persuade himself that even this third parting would not be the last, failed entirely of softening its pangs. Instead of exerting any portion of that courage he had but a moment before tried to promise, he no sooner entered the room, and saw Ethelinde, her face concealed by her handkerchief, and her head reclined on the arm of a sopha on which she sat, than he threw himself on his knees before her; and in a voice tremulous and almost convulsed, he cried—"Behold, Ethelinde, your unhappy Montgomery once more prepared to receive at your hands his sentence. Ah! dares he hope to live with you—to live for you—or is banishment and lingering death to be his portion?"

Grief and tenderness had not so entirely overcome Ethelinde, depressed as she was, but that she was yet able to recall in some degree that fortitude which the stronger mind of Montgomery seemed entirely to want.—"If you indeed love me," cried she, "spare me, dear Montgomery, this cruel repetition. Can I say more than I have already said? Ought I indeed to have said so much? I refer myself wholly to your mother. If her letters authorize you to relinquish the voyage you have undertaken, I am your's whenever you come to claim me; if on the contrary——"

"Name it not," cried he, eagerly interrupting her, "I cannot bear the supposition; but tell me, if I must leave you—and yet I will not, cannot think of it—will you go to my mother's—and will you remain with her; shall I believe that you are together; and wretched as I must be, will one dear spot of earth contain all that can restore me to happiness?"

"It shall, my dear friend. Whether absent or present, whether in England living for me in obscurity, or generously encountering perils for me in another quarter of the globe, your Ethelinde is equally and irrevocably your's. Dictate to me in regard to your mother what I shall do, and I will place all my little remaining comfort in obeying you."

"Promise me then, that whether I go or stay you will suffer no persuasions to detain you from my mother, but that as soon as she returns you will go with her to Grasmere."

"I do promise it; and when you look on this testimony of my obedience to a former request, you will not, my dear Montgomery, suspect that I can hesitate a moment in fulfilling a promise that by affording me your beloved mother's society and protection, will give me the only consolation I shall be capable of tasting if you are torn from me."

She then gave him the picture which she had reserved for the moment of his departure, though he had often before solicited it. He took it eagerly, kissed it, and put it in his bosom; then seeing Ethelinde pale and faint from contending passions, and feeling that the longer he staid with her the more terrible it became to tear himself away, he arose, and pressing her in his arms, said—"I *must* go. Almighty God! preserve her, and may our separation be short!

Ethelinde, I rely on your promises—I know they are sacred. The person of Montgomery may be driven from you by the cruelty of his destiny; but his heart, his soul, his existence, are with you: remember that, and preserve him in attending to our own health and life."

Ethelinde could only press his hand. Sir Edward, who was during all this time agitated by the most distressing conflict between reason, propriety, and passion, now found the latter so much too strong for the other two, that he hastily ran up stairs, and approached the door of Ethelinde's apartment. Montgomery, hearing his step, was roused from the delirium of grief and love, and starting at once away, hastened to the door, where Sir Edward, seizing his arm, cried—"Come, dear Montgomery, you will destroy Ethelinde."

"God forbid!" replied he, not knowing what he said; "it were better I were myself destroyed."

Sir Edward, who felt an undeniable mixture of envy and compassion, led him down stairs, and they both got without speaking into the chaise that was in waiting; Sir Edward having before taken leave of his sister and her guests, and Montgomery finding it impossible for him to command himself enough to take leave of them at all.

Ethelinde, in that sort of tumultuous yet hopeless anguish that precludes almost the power of reflection, listened to their steps as they descended the stairs together; she heard the door shut, the chaise drive away, and as the last faint sounds of the wheels died away on her ear, hope seemed to be excluded from her heart. Struck forcibly with the idea that Montgomery was gone for ever, an idea which she had hitherto combated, she found herself strangely tempted to give way to shrieks, cries, and all the agonies which despair extorts from the impatient sufferer under cureless misfortune; but her weakness of body checked more than her reason, these violent transports. She could weep, however, no longer; but fixing her eyes on the door where last she saw the departing form of Montgomery, she sat for some time stupid and motionless, till she was awakened from this state of torpid sorrow by again hearing the sound of wheels which seemed to approach the door. Her heart beat violently. "Is it possible?" said she, "that they can be returned?" She yet moved with difficulty; but the possibility that Montgomery might again be in the house affected her so much that she was insensible of pain; and rising, she opened the door of her room and listened. There were several persons in the hall, but she heard not the voices of those whom she fancied might be returned. At length a loud laugh from Miss Newenden, and the harsh toned voice of Woolaston in conversation with her and Davenant, made her believe she was mistaken; and in a few moments she distinctly heard these two gentlemen take leave of Miss Newenden, step into a chaise, and depart also.

At any other time their departure would have been grateful to her; but now, wholly absorbed in one painful idea, she felt nothing but the misery of having bidden farewell to her lover; though his return could only have renewed all the sufferings she had just before with so much difficulty sustained, she felt new pangs from having been thus deceived, and with difficulty returned to her seat, where her senses seemed entirely to forsake her; and where, though she yet breathed and beheld the surrounding objects, she was really unconscious of what she was about, of the lapse of time, and of what she ought to do to fulfill the promise she had so recently given Montgomery to take care of her health.

In this situation Miss Newenden found her, when about half an hour after the departure of her visitors she went up to enquire after her merely because she had nothing else to do.—"Well, Ethy," cried she, as she entered the room, "and how do *you* do? So! we have lost all our men at once. Lord! child, what's the matter with you? you look like a wax figure, with your fixed heavy eyes and pale face. Come prythee have a little more spirit. *You* a soldier's daughter, and intend to be a soldier's wife? why you are fit for nothing."

Though startled by such an address from her gloomy reverie, it was the soothing voice of sympathy and tenderness only that could melt Ethelinde into tears, and soften the intense pain that oppressed her. She turned her languid eyes on Miss Newenden, and with a smile of anguish and a deep drawn sigh answered, without having any precise idea of what had been said—"I am much obliged to you."

"Pooh!" answered Miss Newenden, "obliged to me; for what? will you have any supper? what shall I send you?"

"I am going to bed, I thank you, and have no appetite," answered Ethelinde with a little more recollection.

"Well, well, but you must eat. Why one would think you were starving for a match. I believe you don't weigh now above a feather. I shall send you up a cold chicken, and I desire you will eat it. What sort of figure will you make when your pretty fellow returns laden with rupees if you set out with fasting and weeping before he is gone? You'll be as thin as a forest horse in a hard winter; and then you'll lose your beauty, and will wonder that he regrets his yellow women and his dancing girls."

To this unfeeling though well meant raillery, Ethelinde could give no answer. Miss Newenden left her, and soon after sent up her supper by the servant who attended her. Ethelinde, hardly conscious of what she did, had some idea that it was right to eat; she tried, but found it impossible; and desiring the maid to give her a glass of wine and water, and to take away the supper, she began to undress herself, and fancied that on her pillow she might find some respite from the extreme pain which throbbed in her heart; but Montgomery, gone for ever, was a sentence to which every pulse beat in agonizing responses. She addressed herself to heaven, she besought strength of mind to endure this affliction, and even heavier if heavier should be inflicted; and while she prayed most fervently for his preservation she with equal fervour desired to become worthy of him. This appeal to heaven, this confidence in the only power who could preserve and restore her beloved Montgomery, or enable her to endure his absence, relieved her oppressed heart; and finding herself more composed, she believed her prayers were heard; and at length was released, though only by a short and agitated slumber, from the recollection of the agonies she had gone thro' in parting from Montgomery, and from the remembrance of Sir Edward's distress, which, powerful and overwhelming as was the predominant sentiment of her heart, could not escape her, or fail to be remembered with concern.

VOLUME V

CHAPTER I

Sir Edward Newenden and Montgomery journeyed rapidly towards London, but neither of them were inclined to conversation, and as they approached the town their mutual uneasiness and anxiety seemed to increase: Sir Edward remembered the strange situation in which he had left his family; his wife absent, mourning over the effects of that vengeance which he had been compelled to take on Lord Danesforte, his children without their mother, his own actions perhaps misrepresented; while his conscience, unaccustomed hitherto to allow him any great latitude, represented to him in forcible colours the error he had committed in yielding to the first impulse of ungovernable affection, and hastening at such a time to Ethelinde. The reproaches he made himself on this head served however to strengthen the resolution he had made, not to conquer his passion for her, for that he felt to be out of his power, but to preclude the possibility of its doing her farther injury, by quitting the only satisfaction he ever promised himself, that of seeing her and loving her in silence, reserving only the right of a guardian to serve and befriend her by the interposition of others.

Montgomery, whose heart was agitated between faint hopes and tormenting apprehensions, was eager to get to his lodgings, where he expected to find letters from his mother, on the contents of which his fate depended. He leaped out of the chaise, therefore, the moment it stopped in Hanover Square; and hardly staying to take leave of his fellow traveller, he hurried to his lodgings in Portland Street, whither he had desired his letters to be directed.

Sir Edward, on entering his own house, learned of his servants that their lady had returned to it that morning, that her mother was with her, and that physicians had been sent for to attend her, as she was extremely ill. Numberless uneasy and distressing reflections now crouded on the mind of Sir Edward. He knew not how to refuse receiving his wife, for nothing on her part had occurred since their last meeting to make him wholly decline it: yet the contemptuous and disgraceful conversation repeated to him by Templeton; the speech Lord Danesforte had himself made on receiving his wound; her violent concern, and the general style of her conduct since their reconciliation; all contributed to impress more deeply on his mind the suspicions before too strong of her misconduct. He had not time long to consider how he should act, before Mrs. Maltravers, hearing he was returned, sent to desire to speak with him; and though he foresaw how disagreeable the interview would be, he could not refuse to admit her.

Her conversation, mingled with tears, lamentations, and reproaches, tended to persuade him that he had cruelly injured Lady Newenden, and most unjustly gratified, on Lord Danesforte, vengeance which he ought not to have conceived. She represented her daughter's situation as very dangerous; and as being occasioned solely by her fears for her husband and for her own reputation.—"And yet" cried she, "you could be so hard hearted, so unfeeling as to leave her, and go out of town. Oh! Sir Edward, who would have thought that you could use Maria so cruelly. I assure you she feels it, though, poor soul, she is not surprised at it; if she had been dying, to be sure you must have gone to Brackwood on *such a pressing occasion.*"

Sir Edward, vexed and confused to understand that the reason of his journey was known, was yet too ingenuous and spirited to deny it.—"Madam," answered he, with as much calmness as he could assume, "you will, I hope, allow me to be master of my own actions. Be assured that any such reflections as you have now thrown out are so far from being likely to produce the effect you seem to expect from them, that they can serve only to convince me of the badness of that cause which can be defended only by the despicable devices of malignity and falsehood. Let Lady Newenden convince me she has never forfeited her right to my exclusive affection; having done that, which, however open to conviction I am, she will, I fear, find very difficult, let her continue, by a very different conduct from what she has lately assumed, to shew me that I have misunderstood her, and she will never find that my affection for her cousin is of a nature to give her any cause of complaint. To a candid, a generous, a liberal mind, it must ever have appeared what it really is; but I am sorry to say that your daughter possesses little of those qualities. I hope, however, that she judges not of my conduct, of my attachments, by her own; and in doing justice to her principles and passions, supposes her cousin equally culpable."

The calm severity of this retort seemed to be particularly cutting to Mrs. Maltravers; whose subsequent harangue on the virtues, beauty, and fortune of her daughter, and on her own consequence and perfections, was very loud and very long. Sir Edward, seeing it was not likely soon to conclude, was leaving her in possession of his apartment, when Maltravers himself entered the house, and having peevishly ordered his wife to leave them together, he with more coolness entered into conversation with Sir Edward; and after discussing many points with more candour than he expected with him, (candour which originated in the dread he had lest his daughter's conduct should ill bear the investigation with which it was threatened if an absolute separation should happen) he agreed to enforce with all his power the plan which Sir Edward proposed—of immediately going with Lady Newenden and his family to Paris, and from thence to Italy, to remain at least a twelve month. Their going abroad together immediately after the duel would at least put an end to the report of its being occasioned solely by her Ladyship's attachment to Lord Danesforte: the reflections made on Sir Edward's partiality to Ethelinde would be forgotten; and Maltravers saw so many advantages in it, that he warmly encouraged the proposal. It was only his authority that had compelled Lady Newenden to return to the house of her husband a second time, though he carefully concealed that circumstance from Sir Edward; and he now, in pursuance of this arrangement between them, so effectually urged the necessity of immediate compliance, that Lady Newenden, who was in a few days tired of the farce of affecting to be sick when she was really in perfect health, dismissed her physicians; and no impediment remaining, the whole family, with Mr. and Mrs. Maltravers, set out for Dover in about a week after Sir Edward's visit to Brackwood, and proceeded directly to Paris. Lady Newenden, tho' she behaved with haughty and sullen coldness towards Sir Edward, yet seemed to have forgotten the violent friendship she had professed for Lord Danesforte, who was before their departure out of all danger, and gone to his Gloucestershire house. Neither Mrs. Maltravers or her daughter now ever named him, though he used to be the eternal theme of the former; and Sir Edward, though very miserable, endeavoured in change of scene to find amusement, and in the tender caresses of his children consolation. The image of Ethelinde, however, pursued him every where; and hardly conscious of his motive, he lingered at Paris longer than he originally intended, because he there hoped to hear of her more quickly and more frequently than it was possible for him to do when he removed to a greater distance from England.

Montgomery, on arriving at his lodgings, found only one letter from his mother, which informed him merely of her arrival at Lyons, and that from the complicated nature of the engagements of that house to which her money had been lent, she had not yet been enabled to get information whether her money would or would not be safe. Montgomery thought the whole letter written in despondence which she seemed anxious to conceal; and the suspense in which it left him redoubled his wretchedness. Royston, having left two or three messages at his lodgings during the last week of his absence, now called upon him to let him know that his appointment was made out; and that the vessel on which it was necessary for him to embark lay ready to sail, her departure from the river being absolutely fixed to happen in about ten days. Thus circumstanced, it became necessary for him to determine either to stay or go; and the contending passions with which he was agitated grew almost too painful to be endured without the deprivation of reason.

Sometimes he thought himself resolutely fixed to undertake a voyage which his courage, his honor, his reason, equally forbade his relinquishing; then the image of Ethelinde, in all its seducing charms, presented itself to him; he figured to himself all the happiness of living with her and his mother at Grasmere, and the enchanting picture of such society, their perfect confidence, their tender friendship, and their unbounded love for him: and he forgot for a moment that he had not the means of affording to these two beings, so tenderly beloved, the necessaries of life.

In the mean time, Royston, who was very proud of the service he had done him, and who had been complimented on the merit of his young relation by all those to whom he had presented him, bustled about in his service with a zeal for which Montgomery knew not how to account. He himself delayed from day to day to make the last preparations, still willing to hope that he might not be compelled to quit the country which contained all that gave value to his existence.

A week passed thus; and at the end of that time Sir Edward took leave of him before his departure for the Continent. Sir Edward spoke but little to Montgomery of his voyage to India; but seemed to consider it as fixed; and of Ethelinde he only said that he had taken measures to have her supplied quarterly with the money he had named, and that he hoped she would pass her time between the house of his sister and that of Mrs. Montgomery. At parting, however, he wrung the hand of Montgomery, and said with a deep sigh—"Farewell, dear Charles! Your voyage, however long, your absence, however tedious, will, I doubt not, be fortunate. In me your situation excites envy; for if there is any thing more delightful than living with the object of our affection, it is living for them in the hope of being one day united, and in the consciousness of doing that which may promote that union. All these flattering prospects are your's. See them in their true colours, and you will be comparatively happy."

Montgomery could not reply; and tho' he felt the force of Sir Edward's observation, he could no where find any sensation in his own breast at all allied to happiness. He was glad, however, that Sir Edward Newenden was not to be in the same country with Ethelinde; and while hardly daring to own to himself the uneasy jealousy he sometimes felt, he could never prevail upon himself to reflect, without uneasiness, on the friendship which Ethelinde so openly avowed for Sir Edward Newenden, or on that tender affection he had acknowledged himself sensible of for her.

While Montgomery remained in his torturing suspense, still eagerly clinging to an hope which grew every hour more feeble, Ethelinde passed the greatest part of her time alone; for Miss Newenden, as the hunting season drew near its close, pursued that amusement with encreased avidity. Ethelinde, however, far from finding this solitude tedious, was extremely glad to be so little under the necessity of conversing; and as her thoughts dwelt on Montgomery, it was pleasant to have so little occasion to affect an interest for others. Miss Newenden, though still very civil to her, appeared more than usually occupied in affairs of her own; and Ethelinde observed that she often received and answered letters, a circumstance hitherto unusual with her; but this might in so many other ways be accounted for, that Ethelinde was far from suspecting they came from a favoured lover.

Sir Edward Newenden, however, being now in France, his sister, though determined to reject any advice he might give, was yet unwilling to hear it, and therefore prepared to execute her matrimonial project before her design could reach his ears. Some days, however, wore away; on the part of Miss Newenden in a sort of bustle which seemed to portend some change in the family; and in that of Ethelinde in deeply participating all the melancholy anxiety so forcibly expressed in the letters she received from Montgomery. Every post day this distress was renewed and increased; and the terms in which he described the sufferings inflicted by his painful uncertainty were faithful pictures of her own anguish and regret. At length a heavy pacquet was delivered to her: with an unusual foreboding of evil, with trembling hands, and a beating heart, she opened it, and read thus.

London, March 11, 17—

"Before you read a letter, which I write in a state of mind not to be described, peruse that which I enclose to you from my mother."

Ethelinde, hardly knowing what she did, unfolded the second letter, which ran thus.

Lyons, Feb. 28, 17—

"My dear Charles,

"Not doubting but that this will find you still in London, it would have been most gratifying to me to have given you a pleasing account of our business. Judge, my son, of what I suffer in being compelled to inform you, that, having at length been present at the investigation of the affairs of Messrs Du Chesne, I find that above a thousand pounds are absolutely lost, and the remaining six hundred there is so little probability of recovering that I cannot but consider it as gone also. Mr. Le Moine, however, advises a process to be commenced, to which I have reluctantly consented; not only because it appears to me that the expence attending the suit will be entirely thrown away, but because I must of necessity await the issue of it here, instead of returning to England. Alas! my dear Charles, my wishes to hasten thither have no longer that motive which has ever since your birth influenced all my inclination. In returning to my country I shall not embrace him who alone has the power to make that or any other part of the globe pleasant to me; but deprived as I must be of this first delight of my life, I had formed in my imagination another, and pleased myself with the fond hope of receiving there your other self—the lovely, amiable, interesting Ethelinde. Collecting at Grasmere all you loved; having in her a being to whom I could continually speak of my son, and to whose heart he is as precious as to mine, I thought I should less severely feel the cruel deprivation to which I must submit; and in contemplating the perfections of her who will, I still trust, crown our future days with happiness, I believe that those which were passing in this dreaded but necessary absence, would be rendered less insupportable.

"Weeks and months must now elapse before I shall press to my anxious heart the darling of your's. They will, however, heavily, be passed, and the moment it is possible I will hasten back to her. Tell her then, my son, to preserve her health, as she would wish to make me, when we *do* meet, as easy as in your absence I can be; tell her that she is accountable to me for the felicity of my dear Charles, and that I am sure she will enable me to discharge a trust so dear and welcome to me.

"For yourself I have little to say, since I commit your safety to that Providence which preserved you amid many perils to be the blessing and consolation of your mother, while you were yet so young that she knew not how invaluable the blessing was: and I have surely nothing to add on the subject of advice; I need not recommend any virtue to him who so eminently possesses them all, whose steady religion, and unsullied conscience gives him fortitude, whose noble and undaunted spirit is inherited from a long line of ancestors, to whose illustrious name he lends new glory, and whose heart has all the tenderness of a woman blended with the firmness of an hero.

"Write to me, dear Charles, by every possible conveyance, and imitate not the weakness I feel, while doing what on your account I know to be right, in thus consenting to and promoting your voyage. Ah! nothing but that conviction could make me submit to the anguish I now suffer. I would, I ought to conceal it, but the blotted paper betrays what passes in my heart while my hand is employed in bidding you, my beloved Charles, adieu! May heaven

preserve and restore you to the ardent payers of your affectionate
mother,

CAROLINE MONTGOMERY."

With difficulty Ethelinde finished this letter; and before she
could attempt to read that of Montgomery, she sat down and
gave way to a violent passion of tears. "It is all over then," said she;
"every hope is gone; yet what did I expect? All that this fatal letter
tells me, I had before every reason to believe would happen!" Thus
arguing with herself, she at length acquired courage to go on with
Montgomery's letter.

"Having read what I have received from the best of parents
and of women, you see, my Ethelinde, that your unhappy lover is
destined to be exiled from you and from her. The lingering hope I
had nourished in my heart is gone for ever.—I submit—I cannot
bear to think of my mother's situation; for her sake, as well as in
the hope of becoming as much more worthy of you as pecuniary
advantages can make me, I must go! Ah! what did I not before owe
that dear parent; and what an infinite increase of obligation I feel,
in the tender solicitude she expresses, for that beauteous being so
dear to this agonized heart. If ever I return—if I return and find
you both such as my anxious fondness will incessantly represent
you, what boundless happiness will be mine; but if——Ethelinde!
I cannot finish the sentence! Oh! thou beloved possessor of the
very soul of Montgomery! remember that he acquires courage to
doom himself to certain present misery, only in the hope of being
one day happy; and that his happiness, his very existence depend
on you. Let my mother's letter speak more coherently than I can
do of what we both expect of you. Ah! do not—do not disappoint
us. I cannot write. Why indeed should I betray my own weakness
while I recommend fortitude to you? I am beset by people who
congratulate me on my appointment, and display the advantages
that await me. Ah! they would find reason rather to condole with
and pity me, could they see the tortures of my soul. How much I
envy the lowest mechanic who bows to me for orders, and how
ardently I wish it were possible for me to become the last retainer
of my noble house amid the rude mountains of the North if I
could live with those I love!

"But all this is the mere garrulity of helpless despair, in which I

ought not to indulge myself. I will repress then these fruitless murmurs to which even your tender spirit rises superior. Pardon me if
I have already said too much—ah! pardon the wild effusions of a
heart bursting with anguish, of a spirit at war with itself. Two days
hence I will write again: then I shall be embarked in that element
which is to convey me from you; but I must go while I have yet
resolution; if I think too deeply I shall be again unnerved. Write
to me, however; tell me you are well; and tell me my weakness
excites your pity without diminishing the love you deign to own—
that tender love which constitutes the sole felicity that either now
or hereafter can render, in this world, life desirable to your devoted

                    CHARLES ARCHIBALD MONTGOMERY."

   Ethelinde, being quite unfitted for any sort of society by the
emotions to which these letters had given rise, complained of
being ill, and went early to bed, where, for some hours her tears
incessantly flowed; but by degrees her natural good sense conquered this immeasurable and useless grief; she considered how
little the indulgence of it would avail, and how prejudicial it must
be to that health so dear to Montgomery. In the power of constituting his felicity she felt her own value, and for him wished to preserve, unblemished by the destructive hand of sorrow, that form
which had first attracted his eye, as well as she assuredly should
that heart which had secured his affection. She waited with trembling impatience the arrival of the second letter, which at length
arrived, dated from the Nore; and amid all the incoherence of
passion, informed her that the ship was then getting under weigh
to proceed to the Downs,¹ from whence he said he should write
again.

---

1 The Nore is a sandbank at the mouth of the Thames estuary, where the
river meets the North Sea, it became the site for a "mutiny" (a strike asking
for better conditions and pay) because of its use as a place for anchorage. The
Downs are an area in Kent stretching to the cliffs of Dover, which includes the
harbour of Deal in the Dover district of Kent. Montgomery's second letter
suggests his ship will leave from this route.

CHAPTER II

Ethelinde now found a new employment, full of melancholy anxiety, in viewing the distant ocean from her favorite eminence, and fancying every vessel which appeared but as a spot in the grey horizon might possibly bear Montgomery within it. However content she had hitherto been to find herself alone, she now wished for somebody who could tell her which of the ships she saw passing were East-India men.[1] She watched the weather; and made enquiries which nobody heeded; for the people around her were no otherwise solicitous about the wind than as the various points from which it blew produced a cold scenting[2] morning, or was favourable to their pursuit. Ethelinde, therefore, still indulging her mournful contemplations, wandered about all day on the hills, wishing for intelligence, yet unable to obtain it. The letter promised from the Downs came not; yet five or six days had passed. She knew not all the various delays which occur before a ship actually leaves the river: and she fancied that Montgomery had already quitted the Coast of England.

Still she found a gloomy satisfaction in surveying the sea on which he was embarked; and this she continued to enjoy without interruption. Miss Newenden seldom enquired how she passed her time, and they met only at dinner and supper. It was at the end of about ten days, that Ethelinde, on entering the eating room, found the table set out with an unusual air of preparation: five plates were placed on it: Miss Newenden seemed extremely reserved and extremely restless; and went so frequently to the window, that Ethelinde at last ventured to enquire whether she expected company?

She answered yes; but gave her no farther information. In a few moments, however, her suspense was at an end: Woolaston, and a

---

1 Probably refers to the East India Company; a ship owned and/or used by the East-India Company. See Wikipedia article which differentiates this from other companies as well as the phrase "East-Indies" for an area in India (which includes West Bengal). http://en.wikipedia.org/wiki/East_India_Company
2 A wind bad for hunting; it prevents the dogs from scenting their prey.

young man with him, who appeared to be a clergyman, appeared in a new phaeton and four, and Davenant followed in his with six.[1] Ethelinde, with some surprise, and more uneasiness, beheld this arrival. She had been present so little during the last visit that she had no idea of the footing Woolaston was upon; but it now needed little explanation. He was evidently expected; he was as evidently welcome; and though the event of the next day was not openly mentioned that evening, so little pains were taken to conceal it, that Ethelinde felt hardly any astonishment when at nine o'clock the next morning Miss Newenden's maid, who sometimes assisted in her room, came in and told her, with the air of a person who is in possession of an important secret, that her lady was then actually gone to church to be married to Mr. Woolaston.

Ethelinde went down as usual to the breakfast parlour; where in a few moments the party came in from the ceremony, and Woolaston introduced his wife to Ethelinde in form. Mrs. Woolaston made no apology for the mystery she had observed, as seeming to think herself accountable to nobody; and her change of situation seemed to make no alteration either in her behaviour or the style of the house, except only that Mr. Woolaston became at once its acknowledged master. Two or three days after the marriage, Mr. Borlace, the young clergyman who had married them, departed, and a *parté quarrè*[2] remained of Mr. and Mrs. Woolaston, Davenant, and Ethelinde.

Ever since she had declined the addresses of Davenant, he had affected to consider himself as affronted, and to look upon her as a silly ignorant girl who was blind to her interest, and not worth his farther attention. Ethelinde, who had always beheld him with a mixture of contempt and aversion, hoped and believed that this coldness on his part would continue; and by avoiding him as much as possible, she endeavoured to convince him that the change in her own situation had made none in her opinion of him. Unhappily, however, for the peace of the deserted Ethelinde, Davenant was now induced by a variety of motives to pursue her with less

1 Showy and expensive forms of phaetons (itself a sort of equivalent of today's luxury speed automobiles. The extravagance of both are meant to impress Miss Newenden.

2 A foursome, the use of the French term suggests more than two couples: Davenant is intended as Ethelinde's sexual partner while Woolaston is now Miss Newenden's. The more accurate term is *parté carrée*.

honourable views than those he once entertained. Her beauty
he had always admired: but never so much as since he had heard
Woolaston praise it: his mean and ungenerous spirit found a
malignant and unworthy gratification in believing that, subdued
as she now was, he could obtain as a mistress her who had refused
to become his wife; and that he should finally triumph in bearing her away on his own terms from him whom he had always so
inveterately hated—the handsome, gallant, favoured Montgomery. Sir Edward Newenden, in acquitting himself of his trust as his
guardian, had given him some advice on his future conduct, which
Davenant, so far from being grateful for, remembered with sullen
anger. Obstinacy, generally the companion of ignorance, would
never suffer him to own himself in the wrong; and though he
knew that he had, in consequence of not attending to Sir Edward's
admonitions, sunk above thirty thousand pounds of his fortune,
he rather disliked him for having foreseen than owned any obligation to him for having tried to prevent it. He reflected, therefore,
with satisfaction on the mortification which the marriage of Miss
Newenden would occasion to Sir Edward, and would have found
double pleasure in succeeding with Ethelinde, from the certainty
that it would be to him a still more cruel blow.

The sullen resentment, and insolent contempt which he had
shewn towards Ethelinde, it was difficult to quit. By degrees,
however, he pretended attention and tenderness; but so ill was his
temper and manners calculated to play the lover, that his attention appeared to her troublesome officiousness, and his tenderness impertinence, which only served to drive her from him with
disgust and even terror. Having once, however, engaged in the
attempt to subdue, what he could not but perceive, her coldness
and dislike, he resolved, with all the hard immovable obstinacy
and pride of his character, that she should not escape him; and
he had in the worthless and unprincipled Woolaston an assistant,
who, with all the inclination, had now all the power to promote his
ungenerous designs.

The hunting season was almost at an end, and Mrs. Woolaston
went out less frequently than during the winter. Whenever she did
go, however, her husband only went with her; and Davenant found
some pretence or other to remain in the house, where he had often
the pleasure of passing the morning alone; for Ethelinde, who

found that he pursued her every where else, usually took refuge in her own room, and locked the door.

As even her native complaisance had never been able to conceal the disgust with which Davenant always inspired her in the former part of their acquaintance, she now attempted not by any effort of civility to obliterate that impression, but whenever Woolaston left them alone, which he took perpetual opportunities of doing, she seized the first moment in her power to quit the room also. It happened that about a week after Mrs. Woolaston's marriage, she was herself giving some orders in her stables; and Woolaston, in pursuance of his promise to his friend, affected to recollect something about one of the horses, and starting from his seat he ran away after her to the stables. The circumstance of her being left with Davenant had now happened so often that it was impossible to believe it was accidental. Ethelinde, however, determined it should be fruitless; and eager to go for her morning walk, for in consequence of having seen in the ship news of a paper, which she now anxiously perused, that the East India ship on board which Montgomery was, had three days before passed by Deal, and proceeded with a fair wind, she fancied that as the wind still continued in the same quarter, she might now see it; and however remote, however imaginary this melancholy pleasure might be, she still found a delight in indulging it, with which she could not bear that Davenant should interfere. Woolaston therefore had no sooner left the room, than she rose from the table, round which they had been sitting, and was opening the door, when Davenant, who had not had time to arrange the speech he meditated to detain her, rose hastily, and as with one hand she opened the door, he seized the other.

"Pray now," cried he, as if he had a right to be heard, "what occasion is there for all this hurry?"

Ethelinde, struggling to get her hand from him, answered in visible displeasure—"I am going out, Mr. Davenant."

"Going out are you? Oh! then I'll go with you, I want a walk."

This was even more disagreeable than remaining in the house with him; and Ethelinde was now compelled to say in some confusion that she should not walk, but was going to her room to write letters.

"What is the use of writing letters?" cried he, seizing the other hand, and drawing her towards a chair. "'Tis of no use to write them to-day, for I can tell you Woolaston does not send to the post. So come and sit down—I want to ask you about Sir Edward." Ethelinde now thought that it was better to sit a few moments with him than to let him suppose she feared him; she therefore sat down; but said impatiently—"I beg you will not detain me long, as I really have letters to write."

"Pooh, pooh," cried he, contemptuously, "we all know who you write to; but 'twill be time enough if the dear creature receives your packet in a fortnight after he gets to Bengal. Let the poor fellow sail in peace after his Nabobship,[1] and do you think now a little of your old friends. I dare say by the time he gets to the end of his voyage that he'll be thinking like Uncle how to make the most of himself and of his pretty person, unless he happens to pick up a Yarico by the way.[2] Nay don't sigh so; but if he *should* happen, as he's so very handsome, you know, to bring home some governor's widow, or the yellow daughter of some rich factor[3]—I dare say your affection for him is so perfect that you'd rejoice in his good fortune."

Ethelinde, who was at first disposed to cry, now felt her indignation conquer her vexation.—"Mr. Davenant," said she, "your talents for ridicule are so very slender that really your attempts excite only pity. If you mean by what you have said to speak of Montgomery with contempt, know that it recoils on yourself, and that notwithstanding the advantage which you suppose your fortune gives you over him, he, in my idea, possesses in regard to you all the superiority which every natural and acquired perfection of mind and person can give a man over him who has no obligations

1 A sneer: a nabob was the slang term for a man who had become conspicuously rich by going out to India to work. Davenant means to degrade Montgomery by referring to him this way: as someone doing dirty work, born without wealth, in a ship filled with similar men.

2 The story of Inkle and Yarico was told by various writers, from Richard Steele (*Spectator*), to Francis Thynne Seymour, Lady Hertford (a poem, circulated in manuscript), to George Colman the Younger (a comic opera, 1787). The point of the allusion is betrayal: Yarico, an Indian girl, helps Inkle, an English trader, to leave the West Indies, where he is shipwrecked; when she returns with him to society, he sells her into slavery, and marries a woman who will give him the status he wants. Davenant is tormenting Ethelinde.

3 A factor is an agent or manager for a mercantile or colonial business. Farming (collecting rents especially) is a form of business.

but to that capricious chance which bestowed on him money he does not deserve, and which he knows not how to use."

A blush of rage and shame now rose on the dull countenance of Davenant. He tried, but ineffectually, to force a smile; and hesitated to consider what he should say that should not betray how severely he was hurt, while it expressed yet more bitter contempt against this fondly preferred rival, of whom he could not think with patience; but Ethelinde, who had repented the patience she had shewn in listening to him a moment, had already left the room.

She hastened trembling to her own, where a flood of tears relieved her.—"Oh! Montgomery," exclaimed she, "where art thou? Why is not thy generous, thy gallant spirit, sensible of the insults, of the miseries to which thy desolate Ethelinde is exposed? Even the last poor and mournful gratification that remained is denied me—even now perhaps the ship on whose prosperous voyage more than my existence depends, is hovering on this coast. Those eyes, where every passion is so forcibly expressed, are turned with fond and fruitless regret towards the hills of Dorsetshire, and vainly, very vainly searched for some trace of that poor, forlorn, deserted being, whom thou canst no longer protect." This stroke of self pity quite overwhelmed her; she remained for a moment in an agony of grief, while the cruel sense of what had passed within the last eight months pressed on her recollection— her father!—her brother!—her lover!—all, all taken from her. The first certainly gone for ever; the other two never perhaps to return. She felt as if deprived of every thing valuable in life; it required an effort of resolution to determine to live; and her heart seemed so oppressed that she fancied she should be suffocated if she did not immediately go into the air. The fear of meeting Davenant however was not conquered by this paroxysm of sorrow. She stepped out therefore on the staircase to listen if he was still walking in the parlour, and after standing there a moment breathless, she was relieved by hearing Woolaston enter, and propose to him to ride to the market town on some commission Mrs. Woolaston wanted to have executed that morning; she found he consented, and soon afterwards seeing them on horseback together, she hurried on her things and fled to her seat under her beloved old thorn.

There she felt the violent oppression abate; she breathed more freely; she gazed on the extensive view; where the faint verdure, hardly perceivable, was yet enough to mark the approach of Spring. Above her head—

> "The vault was blue,
> Without a cloud.————————"[1]

And before her the sea appeared so clear that she fancied she could distinguish the gentle undulation of the waves. Numberless small vessels were scattered on its calm surface; the white sails of some caught the full rays of the sun, others were in shadow, and appeared like dusky specks hanging in the air. No human being appeared on the whole extent of the open country between her and the sea. Scarce a cottage or a haystack arose as a sign that it was inhabited; and Ethelinde sat in a mournful yet not unpleasant reverie, till she almost fancied herself alone on a desert coast, watching for the vessel on which all her hopes of liberty and life depended. Her real situation was indeed hardly less forlorn. Young, beautiful, indigent, and friendless, the world was to her only as a vast wilderness, where perils of many kinds awaited her; and England contained not now one being solicitous for her happiness, not one friend to whom she could appeal for pity and protection.

As these melancholy reflections passed through her mind, she felt almost disposed to repent that she had, by refusing all his proposals, compelled Montgomery to leave her.—"If his voyage should be successless! if he should perish in it, how bitter will be the reproaches I shall make myself, if indeed remorse, insupportable remorse robs me not of all recollection. Yet why should I indulge such gloomy apprehensions? Why doubt that Providence to which his mother, whose tenderness for him is not less than mine, with confident hope resigns him. I have done what she thought, what I myself felt to be my duty; and shall I doubt the justice of heaven in rewarding a sacrifice so exquisitely painful, that only the great judge of hearts knows how much it cost me." In reflections like these some hours past away; and in this appeal to heaven her mind had acquired composure, which was assisted by the tranquillity of every thing around her. No sounds but the wind sighing through

1 Cowper, *The Task*, Book 6, lines 62-63. The tense is changed.

the leafless hawthorn under which she sat, or the whistling of the
Stone Curlew, the wild and solitary inhabitant of open countries,
broke the silence of perfect seclusion. Suddenly however from the
dip of an hill which concealed part of the road from Brackwood
to the neighbouring town, an horseman appeared riding furiously
towards her; and she had hardly time to regret the interruption,
and to endeavour by flight to escape it, before her uneasiness, and
alarm were encreased by perceiving it was Davenant.

He gallopped towards her with a degree of velocity that made
her step back from the approach of his horse, whose side was
bathed in blood by the spurs of his savage master, who, as he yet
came closer to her, shewed her a large pacquet he held in his hand.
"I have it," cried he in a voice that left Ethelinde in yet greater consternation: "I have this letter, so long, so anxiously expected. Your
itinerant lover has at least found a messenger for his dispatches
who spares not speed; but"—and he added an horrid oath—"I
must be paid for my trouble before I deliver my billet doux."

He now leaped from his horse; and holding the letter from
her with one hand, he threw the other arm rudely round her. She
started from him in terror and amazement, for she now perceived
by his inflamed eyes and flushed cheeks, that tho' he had not yet
dined he had been drinking.

"What do you mean, Mr. Davenant?" cried she, hastening
from him with trembling feet towards the house; "leave me this
moment: and if the letter is mine give it me."

"Not so fast, Miss Chesterville—not so fast, if you please; you
have escaped me once to-day; here it is not so easy. I ask however
only a little civility. Surely a dear sweet letter from the dear creature *who has every advantage over me but in that fortune which I do not
deserve,* is worth a kiss."

Hurried and alarmed as Ethelinde was, it occurred not to her
immediately that he had taken up this letter at the post house. The
idea of his having seen Montgomery was raised by the expression he had used of—"your itinerant lover;" yet she remembered
instantly that it was impossible; but before she could conquer the
confused and uneasy sensation it created, Davenant had again
rudely seized her, and again demanded his reward before he delivered the letter.

Collecting, however, all her presence of mind, she said resolutely—"Your bringing it, Sir, was quite undesired, and I am far from considering myself obliged to you. As a man of honour, as a gentleman, you will certainly not be guilty of so unworthy an action as detaining a letter addressed to another."

While she said this, she still, trying to disengage herself, walked on towards the house; but Davenant, in whom profligate and unprincipled society had quite conquered the natural diffidence of his character, was now not easily repulsed; and all the odious and malignant passions of his heart were depictured on his countenance, while with another oath, and something between a grin and a smile, he swore thro' his shut teeth that he would compel what he asked, and if obliged to do so she should never have her letter at all.

Ethelinde, though extremely terrified, had courage enough to determine that she would not purchase the letter of Montgomery by a concession which he would never endure that she should make; yet afraid of giving her persecutor a pretence for greater impertinence and brutality, she answered as calmly as she could.— "Well, Sir, carry the letter home then. It will be soon enough for me to receive it when we get there. It is time to return, or our friends will wait dinner."

"Look ye, Miss Chesterville," cried Davenant, whose intoxication now became more frightfully evident—"I have once in my life been fool enough to offer to marry you; you'll never catch me at that again; but I'll do a more sensible thing; for d— me if I don't settle six hundred a year upon you; and I think that's a devilish handsome price for a girl that has not a sixpenny piece in the world, and a little crack in her character with that story of Sir Edward. Come, come, don't affect all these violent airs; but remember 'tis not an offer you'll have every day. 'Tis not every body has the spirit or the cash to make it."

The fears of Ethelinde were now conquered by anger, contempt, and detestation.—"This is an insult, Sir," said she, "which even your present condition cannot excuse. As I consider myself, while in his house, as under the protection of Mr. Woolaston, I shall certainly——"

"Certainly do what?" interrupted Davenant in a taunting voice. "You'll tell Woolaston, will you? To spare you the trouble, my coy shepherdess, know that Jack Woolaston is not only aware of my intentions, but encourages them; he has offered to put you wholly in my power; and faith if he had had any qualms he is so much in mine, that I should have known how to have quieted them. He owes me a pretty little sum; but as I have put his frosty faced wife and her cash into his hands, he has sworn to pay me the principal out of the first money he touches, and I forgive him the interest in consideration of his using interest with you in my favour."

Shocking as this intelligence was, it seemed like a flash of lightning to the mind of Ethelinde; which, however terrifying in itself, served to shew the precipice on the brink of which she stood. To escape the insolent grasp which still rudely detained her was however her first and most difficult task, as the brutality of Davenant was likely to subject her to insufferable rudeness, which she might not long have been able to have repelled if two of his grooms had not now approached them in haste. When he dismounted he had let his horse go, who had immediately made his way to the stables, where the men seeing him arrive without their master, had enquired of Mr. Woolaston what was become of him; and Woolaston, who knew that he was more than half drunk in consequence of a morning repast which they had partaken with some friends they had met at the inn, concluded that instead of finding Ethelinde, as he proposed when they parted on the downs, he had fallen from his horse. He directed his servants therefore to go in search of him. The men no sooner approached than Davenant, with dreadful imprecations, bade them return as they came: but Ethelinde, dreading nothing so much as being left alone with him again, caught the arm of one of them, and said—"James, your master has been drinking—I cannot go home with him indeed—I insist on your not leaving us."

The man, amazed at her terror, stood with his hat off, staring at his master, who now lifted up the end of his whip, and swore that if he did not immediately go he would knock him down. Ethelinde, however, continued to cling to him and implore his protection; and the servant, convinced that she had reason for her fears, and who, humble as his station was, had English spirit enough to resist a tyrant in defence of innocence, very calmly told his master that he might strike if he pleased, but that he should not let Miss be frightened by the best man in England.

The fury of Davenant now exceeded all bounds. He levelled a

violent blow at the groom, who caught on his arm what would otherwise have been fatal; the other servant, far from taking part with his master, now stepped forward, and though little more than a boy, wrenched the horse whip from his hands and threw it away. Ethelinde in the mean time hurried on in terror not to be described, pursued by Davenant, absolutely raving with passion. He uttered against his servants the most incoherent execrations; and swearing he would instantly discharge his men he added—"and as for this letter from that beggarly puppy, curse me if you shall ever have it at all." Thus saying, he tore it to pieces and threw it away; while Ethelinde, in breathless agony, was almost carried into the house by James; and Davenant staggered after; where he related to Woolaston what had passed his own way; and sending for his upper groom ordered him instantly to discharge the two others, whom he notwithstanding threatened with personal chastisement.

Woolaston dared not blame a conduct of which it was easy to foresee that the consequences would be frightening away Ethelinde, and rendering all their plans abortive. Too much in the power of Davenant, and compelled to keep up appearances with his wife, of whose ready money he was in a few days to be put in possession, he tried to palliate what could not now be remedied. He went himself to Ethelinde's room; and having with difficulty obtained admittance, he endeavoured to soothe and appease her by imputing Davenant's rude behavior entirely to intoxication, and entreating her to forget and forgive it. Ethelinde, not yet recovered from the tremor into which she had been thrown, answered very little; and Woolaston found it would be still necessary for him to apologize to his wife.

This however was no difficult task. Mrs. Woolaston could see no ill in the conduct of any body whose company gratified him. Her attachment to her husband was indeed such as she had never appeared capable of feeling, and now, he no sooner began to excuse Davenant, and express his regret for the confusion which his indiscretion had made, than she said—"Dear Jack, make no speeches to me; I am not at all angry with Tom Davenant, nor indeed much surprised; for that foolish girl is the veriest prude in nature; yet with so much silly vanity that she fancies every man that looks at her is mad for her. Lord! what signified it if Tom did kiss her. I'm sure I wish with all my soul he'd marry her, and then there would be no more plague with her, and Ned would be quit of the guardianship that he fancies he has undertaken. If she complains to me, I assure you I shall tell her my mind pretty freely. Such a racket indeed! as if a little romping could hurt her."

Woolaston, well pleased to find that all the blame of the fracas would rest on the prudery of Ethelinde, went down to Davenant, and when they had diverted themselves a little at her expence, and laughed at the consternation the loss of Montgomery's letter would occasion, which they thought an excellent joke, they attended Mrs. Woolaston in the dining room. Ethelinde, however, appeared not; and on a message being sent to her she excused herself, saying that her long walk had fatigued her. Mrs. Woolaston, not without some severe remarks on her folly, sent up her dinner. As soon as their own was over, and the lady withdrawn, which she seldom did till it was very late, Davenant and his host set in to drinking; and though the latter, who had a stronger head, contrived to walk out of the room at one in the morning, Davenant was long before that time so entirely brutalized, that after his servants had with difficulty got him into his own room, they were obliged to exert all their strength to prevent his rushing in the fury of complete intoxication towards that of Ethelinde, on whom he vented the most illiberal abuse for her prudery and folly.

CHAPTER III

The unhappy Ethelinde had hardly been allowed time to recover from the immediate terror of Davenant's ferocious behaviour before she had been compelled to hear the excuses of Woolaston for his friend; and when she hoped to be alone the rest of the evening, was to undergo the sharp remonstrances of his wife, who however disinclined to give herself any unnecessary trouble, yet as she saw her husband, or fancied she saw him made uneasy by the behaviour of Ethelinde to his friend Davenant, she determined to speak to her about it in terms that should convince her of her disapprobation.

Entering the room, therefore, where the disconsolate Ethelinde sat, ruminating on her wayward destiny, she began by enquiring why she would not come down to dinner.

"I was fatigued with my walk, Madam. I was terrified and flurried by Mr. Davenant's very extraordinary behaviour to me."

"Really, Miss Chesterville, these conceited airs, this affectation of excessive delicacy is *mighty tiresome*. I thought as you saw more of the world you would get rid of such squeamish folly—a mighty matter indeed! what Davenant asked for a kiss?"

"Mr. Davenant, Madame, was extremely rude; and so little master of the little reason he usually has, that he appeared capable of any insults. Surely I have reason to complain, when he has taken from me a letter of consequence, and torn it to pieces."

"Poor Ethy," exclaimed Mrs. Woolaston, loudly laughing. "So he tore your love letter. Well that was really a sad thing; but I'll devise a punishment for him which will give you ample revenge: make him write you another."

"*He* write another?" cried Ethelinde.

"Aye why not? Why one love letter you know is nearly as good as another; and I dare say with taking scraps out of novels, and a little of Woolaston's help, who is quite a dab at it, he'd produce you now in a day or two, his dictionary being well consulted, as pretty a love letter as a sentimental Miss need desire to read in an arbour."

"I am sorry, Madame," said Ethelinde, extremely piqued, "that you make so very light of what is in my mind a most ungentlemanlike and unmanly action; but assuredly if Mr. Davenant possessed greater powers of entertainment than those you allow him, I should receive his letters only as an additional insult, and should spurn them as resolutely as I would the most brilliant offers he could make me."

"Faith, Ethy, as to offers I am afraid he'll never give you another opportunity of refusing them; and I am sorry, upon my soul, for it; for notwithstanding all these fine sentiments, and your anger and indignation, I cannot conceive you'd be such a fool as to let them go by if he did."

"You must then, Madam, think me worse than a fool: a wretch without principle, feeling, or honor, if you supposed, that engaged as I am to Mr. Montgomery, I would accept Mr. Davenant had he as many attractive as I think he has disagreeable qualities."

Another loud laugh from Mrs. Woolaston interrupted her—

"Lookee, my dear romantic Princess," cried she, "I've now lived so long in the world that I trust not to *professions*. I've heard all these sentiments before, and I've seen young ladies as disinterested as you are, consider better of the matter, and discover, when the first lover was out of sight, that a second with a great fortune was no bad substitute. I'll lay twenty to one, that before next grass, when you'll be rising twenty, and have picked up a little more sense, you'll make a match with Davenant."

"Never!" exclaimed Ethelinde, "I had rather perish."

Mrs. Woolaston now left her, having laughed and talked herself out of the slight anger she felt on her entering the room; and Ethelinde, who had been interrupted by her appearance from a contemplation on the means to recover her letter, or at least the fragments of it, rejoiced at her departure; and as soon as she was convinced from enquiries she made of the servants, that Davenant and Woolaston were set in to drinking, she went, though it was now dark, softly down stairs, and gliding out of the house by a way which led to the back of the stables, she went towards the place where the letter had been torn.

The wind had dispersed it, and a few only of the largest portions remained on the spot. These she put into her bosom, and fancied that they acted as a talisman to soothe its throbbing anguish. The night was mild and calm; and as the moon now appeared through the fleecy clouds that were gathered over the sea, she hoped if she waited a little it would afford her light enough to recover the remaining fragments of this precious manuscript. In this she was not deceived. In about half an hour, a lovely clear moon was unveiled; and wandering in every direction round the spot, she collected the remaining pieces, which Davenant in his fury had not torn very small, and at length believing she had them all, she was returning home free from every apprehension, for she feared nobody but Davenant, when she suddenly saw two men mounting the hill, and knew that as there was no covert near, to escape them was impossible.

She walked therefore, though with a palpitating heart, towards the house as quickly as she could. The men approached; and her fears were immediately relieved by finding that they were the two grooms who had rescued her from their master's insolence.

They pulled off their hats as they passed her, and wished her health and happiness. "I hope," said she, imagining immediately that they were discharged—"I hope I have not been the means of your losing your places."

"Yes, Ma'am," replied James, "Master ordered us to be discharged, and so Mr. Mash has paid us off; but I assure you that if 'twas to do again I should do just the same. I can get another place; but I could not have answered it to my conscience to have left you with Mr. Davenant. I'm sorry to say it, Miss; and sorry to fright you; but you ben't in good hands."

"Not in good hands!" cried Ethelinde, terrified and amazed. "Do, good James, if you have reason to believe so, explain yourself."

"Why then, Miss, I'll tell you what I know. Mr. Davenant makes no secret among us in the stable, especially when he's a little in liquor, of any thing as he've a mind to; and of late he has said more than once that some time ago he would have married you; but now he knew better; as your father was dead, and you'd no money, your pride must come down to other terms. Mash, the head groom, is quite in his favor, and I've heard discourse between them that I cannot repeat—I'm sure they did not talk like honest men; and Mash for his own ends encourages Mr. Davenant in worser doings than he would think on himself. For my part, I'm not much better than other folks, but it makes me stare again sometimes to see the rate they goes on at; and I know that Mash have said to Master that he should get you away down to one of his own houses, and shew you what fine places he have, and what great estates."

"Is it possible," said Ethelinde, trembling, "that such a design can have been conceived?"

"Lord, Miss," answered the man, "that's nothing. Mash fears neither God nor man, nor devil; and if Master Davenant will but pay him well would run the hazard of being hanged as soon as not. 'Twould make a stone speak, to hear him tell the wickedness he helped to do at his last place at Lord Danesforte's."

"Lord Daneforte's!" cried Ethelinde, whose terror was excited by the very name.

"Yes, Miss; and Mr. Davenant got him from my Lord by doubling his wages. To be sure he has a great place; but there—'tis money got, as one may say, with a rope round one's neck."

"And have you ever heard of any design in particular against me?"

"I can hardly tell that. I've heard Mr. Davenant swearing and complaining that he could make nothing of you, and I've heard Mash say in answer, that his honour never would till his advice was taken; and then often and often they have gone and consulted together."

"I am very much obliged to you, James, said Ethelinde, "for this information; but indeed I am greatly concerned that your generous defence of me should have thrown you out of your bread. To make you adequate amends is not in my power; accept however of this trifle; and do you, Peter," addressing herself to the other, "allow me to offer you this."

She would then have put a guinea into the hand of each; but the elder refused it, and held the hand of the other, who was a mere lad.—"No, no, Miss," said he, "what we did was not for lucre or gain. We've a good deal of wages in our pockets, and places are more plenty than parish churches. I'd scorn to take fee or reward for saving a fine young lady like you from such a man as 'Squire Davenant. I think he've enough on 'em already."

Ethelinde, while the man was yet speaking, was meditating how she should act. To stay at Brackwood appeared at once to be impossible; yet whither could she fly? She gave herself no time however, to digest two or three plans that arose confusedly in her mind, only determining to go, without considering whither, she said, after a moment's pause—

"James, the circumstances you have mentioned make me determine to quit Mrs. Woolaston this evening. Can you at three o'clock in the morning, procure me a chaise on the road to Dorchester?"

James answering in the affirmative, and offering to come with it himself, Ethelinde again offered her little present, which the man still resolutely refused, but consented that his comrade should receive what she wished him to take. Such terrors now possessed her that she dreaded returning to the house; but that being unavoidable, she desired James to accompany her to the door, which he did without being perceived. He then left her to make the best of his way to the town from whence he was to procure the chaise; and Ethelinde, with light steps, and a heart filled with tumultuous fears, stole to her own room, where she locked herself in; but it was sometime before she could acquire composure enough to consider steadily the step on which she had hastily determined.

Montgomery's letter, however, the fragments of which she had folded up in a sheet of paper, and put into her bosom, she now anxiously took up; but too much agitated to attempt to re-adjust the pieces, and decypher it, she could only kiss the torn relicts, and bathe them with tears, which seemed to relieve her heart of great part of the anguish and terror that weighed upon it.

She then attempted to recall and consider the conversation of Davenant's servant. Every thing ill she could readily believe of a man so unprincipled as he now appeared to her, yet though she doubted not his disposition to evil, she could hardly conceive that he would venture on any, where personal hazard could be incurred; yet what or whom had he to fear in insulting her? Not Sir Edward, for he was absent in the South of Europe; not her brother, who was she knew not where, for no intelligence of him had yet been received; not Montgomery, for he was gone where her injuries would not reach his knowledge till they might be without remedy, and from whence he might never return. Her heart fainted within her at this retrospect of her forlorn situation. She looked in vain for pity and protection from Woolaston or his wife: they were too evidently inclined to favor Davenant in his designs, whatever those designs might be; and Mrs. Montgomery, the only friend to whose protection she could fly, was not yet in England; nor had she one person whom she could venture to believe would receive and befriend her till the period of that dear friend's return secured her an asylum. She ran over in her mind every expedient, but could find none satisfactory; she even doubted whether any alarm was sufficient to authorise her to quit the asylum where Sir Edward had placed her; yet the change in Mrs. Woolaston's family, of which Sir Edward was not even yet apprized, made a great difference in the necessity of her obedience to his wishes; and she was sure that his opinion of Davenant was such as would secure her his approbation of any step which should free her from the insolence of his pretensions.

Thus in the severest perturbation of mind some hours passed; she now put together a few of her clothes; now desisted, and determined to trust to Providence for protection, and to remain where she was; now she sat down to write to Mrs. Woolaston, to thank her for her civilities, and account for her departure; and then again trembled at the step she was about to take, and shrunk from launching alone and unprotected into a world of which she knew but little, and nothing that did not tend to encrease the terror with which she contemplated it.

While she thus doubted and hesitated, the sound of Davenant's voice on the stairs, apparently in contention with Woolaston, who seemed trying to appease him, gave new force to her fears. She listened; she heard her name repeated amid a volley of the most horrid oaths; and fancying that he would even then force his way into her room, she double locked it, while her trembling hands attempted to make it more secure by their feeble pressure against it.

After a moment, however, the tumult appeared to cease; the house became quiet; but the alarm of Ethelinde's spirits subsided not so easily; and this last terror determined at once her wavering resolution. She was convinced that what Davenant had himself told her was true; and that Woolaston was wholly in his power. She was equally certain that the man who had delivered her from his insults had more ground than mere conjecture for the interpretation he had put on the frequent consultations between his master and the upper groom; and what she had just heard was a specimen of what Davenant was capable of when inflamed by wine, of which he was now accustomed to swallow such quantities that he could hardly ever be said to be perfectly sober.

Her indecision thus ended, she put up such of her cloaths as were immediately necessary in a small caravan trunk; and sealing up the rest, she sat down to direct them; but then remembered that she when she quitted the house she was then in, she knew not whither to go; nor even where she could ask the slight favour of room for the trunks that contained her apparel. Her mind in this distress glanced towards her own relations; but except Clarinthia Ludford, there was not among them one from whom she had ever received the least attention; and from the idea of encountering the vulgar importance and humiliating pity of her aunt, and the impertinent familiarity of her little pert cousin Rupert, her whole heart recoiled. Her elder uncle, she had never seen, she had no other family connections on her mother's side; and from Lord Hawkhurst she expected nothing. With whatever reluctance

therefore, she was compelled to determine to remain at Dorchester, where she proposed to procure a private lodging, and wait the
answer of Clarinthia Ludford, to whom she proposed to write,
requesting the protection of her aunt till the return of Mrs. Montgomery.

Having once determined, she became more composed, and sat
down to write to Mrs. Woolaston: when she very candidly confessed that Mr. Davenant's behavior had compelled her to quit a
place where she might be again made liable to such treatment.
She thanked her in the warmest terms for the kind protection she
had so long afforded her; and concluded with many wishes for her
health and happiness.

Then being convinced that the house was perfectly quiet, and
the moon, though almost down, affording her a faint light, she
took the trunk in her hand, and softly gliding down stairs, she
opened the door which led towards the stables, crossed the stable
yard, and ascended the hill; her heart beating violently, and her
spirits failing her at every step she took. The pale and uncertain
light lent by the last rays of the moon, now sinking in the sea;
the stillness of every thing around her; the hazard she was incurring in trusting herself at such a time and in a place so remote,
to a man she knew nothing of; all contributed to overwhelm her
with terror: but to remain where Davenant was master, after all
she had suffered and all she had reason to apprehend, appeared so
much more terrible, that though slowly and with faltering steps,
she still found in her fears courage to go on. At length she arrived
at the spot where she expected the chaise, and where she began
to doubt whether she should find it. But James had been punctual
to his appointment; and no sooner saw her than he approached
and informed her that the chaise, which had been above an hour in
waiting, was only a few yards lower on the hill. Ethelinde, breathless with many fears, was incapable of thanking her conductor, but
followed him, though not without increased agitation. The chaise
however soon appeared, and part of her alarm subsided. She was
soon placed in it; James mounted behind; and in a very short time
she reached Dorchester. In her way thither she had time to reflect
that Weymouth, a place the continual resort of strangers, was
much properer for her than Dorchester, as she would there be
much less liable to observations which might be unfavourable to

her; as it must appear singular that so young a woman should fix
alone in a place where she was wholly unconnected. It was further
also from Brackwood; and these united reasons determined her
merely to change horses at Dorchester, and go on immediately.
She communicated this resolution to James when she arrived at
the inn, and begged to be allowed to reward him for his services;
but he not only again refused her money, but desired leave to see
her safe to the place where she intended to remain. Ethelinde was
now convinced of his honesty: and as he assured her that it would
not be at all out of his way, as he was going back into Devonshire,
his native country, she consented to accept his farther attendance:
and without any accident arrived about twelve at noon at Weymouth, where she was immediately accommodated with a private
lodging; and after the extreme fatigue and alarm she had undergone, within the last four and twenty hours, she found herself in a
place of safety; and enjoyed quiet and refreshing repose.

The next morning, before Ethelinde could determine to write
her letter to Clarinthia Ludford, she began with painful pleasure
to put together the fragments of Montgomery's letter, which had
been written on several sheets of long paper. Some pieces were
still wanting; but these Ethelinde by her imagination supplied, and
read with satisfaction, that as his departure became inevitable his
mind had acquired courage to bear his separation from her with
more calmness, and that his first wish was, to hear of her once
more before he lost sight of the coast of England. The rest of his
letter contained the warmest entreaties that she would take care
of her health; repeated exhortations to go directly to his mother
as soon as she arrived; and concluded with presages of their future
meeting in happiness and security more sanguine than any he had
before appeared to entertain.

The animated description which he gave of his feelings on
embarking were not wanting to depress and melt her. Not knowing whether the ship on board which he was had certainly passed
the coast of Dorset, she felt a mournful pleasure in believing it
yet possible that she might see it; and in this idea she proposed
passing most of the hours she should remain at Weymouth on
the beach.

But before she began to indulge this romantic but soothing
weakness, it was necessary for her to write to Miss Ludford: it was

a task which she reluctantly undertook, but at length she finished and sent away the following letter—

"You will I believe, my dear Miss Ludford, be much surprised at receiving a letter from me; but the marriage of Miss Newenden and other reasons making my continuance with her inconvenient, I am persuaded that Mrs. Ludford, who before I was so unfortunate as to lose my father, obligingly offered to receive me for a few months, will now allow me the pleasure of being with you and of paying my respects to her, till the return of Mrs. Montgomery, who is detained in France longer than she expected. If, however, my aunt will be at all incommoded by granting me this favor, I am sure I have no right to ask it, and I beg, my dear cousin, that you will in an early answer inform me without reserve whether such a visitor for about three weeks will be agreeable to all your family: to whom allow me to offer compliments and respects; and let me assure you that I am, my dear Miss Ludford,

very affectionately your's,

ETHELINDE CHESTERVILLE."

Weymouth, March 24, 17—.

Ethelinde, having altered her letter half a dozen times, sealed and sent it at last without being satisfied with what she had written. Her dislike to her aunt, from the little she had seen of her, was invincible; and she felt so great a repugnance to asking any favour of her, and so great an aversion to become an inmate in her house, that she sometimes wished she might be refused, and might in the repulse of the only relation to whom she could apply, find an excuse for remaining alone in the lodgings where she now was till Mrs. Montgomery's return.

While she waited the letter from Bristol, which was to determine her, she lived, notwithstanding the very cold March winds, on the sea shore; and whenever she descried a large ship, in making eager enquiries. After two days, however, thus spent, she learned from the papers that the vessel about which she was anxious was seen off Plymouth proceeding with a fair wind. All hopes, therefore, of enjoying the chimerical and gloomy satisfaction of supposing she beheld the distant sail that wafted her lover from her, was at an end: but in the sublime yet melancholy scenes which the

rocks and sands afforded, she still found a pensive and not unpleasing occupation; and still she loved——

> "To stray along the beach,
> Asking of every surge that bathed her foot,
> If ever it had touch'd the ship's tall sides."[1]

In this way, and in reading over a hundred times all the letters
she possessed from Montgomery, particularly the last, the time
passed, though in entire solitude, not unpleasingly, till she was
roused from the mournful tranquillity by receiving the two following letters with the Bristol post mark under a franked cover.
That from the elder lady, which she first opened, ran thus.

"Dear niece,
"I have seen your letter to Miss Ludford; and since you have
now no home, shall be willing to receive you till such time as the
person you mention (whom I do not know) can take you. I must
say I should have taken it kinder if you had given a preference to
your relations before you were forced to it. However, your remiss-
ness shall make no difference; as I make it a rule to be as kind as I
can to my family who want it of me: I bless God they are but few,
and those who are able should help the rest. I have ordered one
of my footmen to be at the Bear at Bath on Tuesday next, and he
will take a post chaise from the inn there for you to come on, as I
should not chuse my relation should be seen to come to Bristol in a
stage coach. I am, dear niece,

Your well-wisher, and sincere friend,
DOROTHY LUDFORD."
Bristol, March 31st.

Disgusted, mortified, and almost wholly deterred from any farther thoughts of being under the smallest obligation to her coarse
minded aunt, Ethelinde now read the second letter, which was to
this effect.

1 Three lines of Cooper's, speaking of Omni, a title altered to suit the circumstance. [Smith's note.] Cowper, *The Task*, Book 1, lines 654-656: in the original: "Methinks I see thee straying on the beach, / And asking of the surge that
bathes thy foot / If ever it has wash'd our distant shore."

"You cannot conceive, my dearest creature, the excessive delight which your sweet letter inspired. I am charmed to a degree with the thoughts of seeing you; pray lose no time, for you cannot guess at my immense impatience, my lovely Ethelinde, to embrace you; and I am absolutely enchanted with the notion of your staying with us. Alas! my angel, you have no idea of the excessive want I am in at this period of a dear confidential friend like your amiable self, to whom I can unveil all the embarrassments and secrets of my bosom in tender sympathy. I long too for a tender and reciprocal communication from you. I have so much to tell you that we shall never have done. I am half wild with pleasure, and our Rupert is not less exquisitely pleased at the idea of our beauteous visitor. My mother regulates your journey; and I have only to repeat that I conjure you, my love, to hasten to your most affectionate and impatient

CLARINTHIA!"

The romantic warmth of the second letter was hardly less displeasing to Ethelinde than the frigid and reluctant style of the first. Again she deliberated whether she should accept an asylum that promised only mortification on one side from her aunt, and on the other folly and absurdity from Clarinthia, if not impertinence from Rupert. After some reflection, however, she considered that the necessity of her staying with them could exist no longer than till Mrs. Montgomery's return; and that if that wished-for period was delayed beyond a fortnight or three weeks, and her stay with her aunt was found as irksome in reality as it appeared in prospect, she could at any time quit a house where nobody had power to enforce her continuance, and might retire to a lodging. She had about thirty guineas in her possession, which Sir Edward had sent to her before his departure; and that would, she thought, be sufficient to support her, if, after a trial which prudence directed her to make, the abode at Mrs. Ludford's was found even for so short a time insupportable. She resolved, therefore, to go; and having written to Sir Edward, stating very frankly her reason for quitting his sister, and her present intentions, she departed in a post-chaise for Bristol, early on the next morning but one after she had received her aunt's and cousin's answer.

Nothing material occurred on the road; and at Bath she met the servant sent by her aunt, who had already provided a chaise, in which she soon reached the end of her journey.

The carriage no sooner stopped at the door than Clarinthia flew down to receive her, and embraced her with a thousand affectionate professions which she had hardly left herself breath to make. Ethelinde was a poor dissembler, and knew not how to put on the semblance of that affection for her cousin which she did not feel; but her native sweetness and elegance of manners, left no deficiency visible in the eyes of Clarinthia, who was no very accurate observer, and generally so occupied by her own fancied sensibility, that if she could prevail upon any dear friend to listen to its effusions, she thought very little of their real sentiments. Having at length exhausted the first violence of her delight, Ethelinde was conducted up stairs, where Mrs. Ludford sat in form to receive her; her son, half reclining on a sopha, with a book in his hand, repeated as she entered—

"So from the dappled east the morning breaks."

He then sauntered towards her; saluted her with great freedom, and led her to his mother, who, hardly rising, said—"So! child, how d'ye do?" Fatigue, anxiety, and a recollection which at that moment arose, of other journeys she had made when a father's arms had protected her or were eagerly extended for her reception, altogether conquered the firmness with which Ethelinde had been trying to meet this disagreeable moment. She attempted to return her aunt's cold enquiry by expressing some pleasure at seeing her; but her tongue refused its office; her eyes filled with tears; and she was forced to take out her handkerchief, and sit down.

Mrs. Ludford, far from being affected, was offended; and impatient to impress on her niece all her own consequence, and a proper sense of the obligation she owed to her, she said in a very ungracious way—"I hope, niece Chesterville, that what has happened to you since you last visited Bristol, has made you reflect on your *situation*; and corrected the little unbecoming pride, which, as your relation, child, I thought myself obliged to tell you of. So! your poor father, I find, died insolvent at last?"

Ethelinde, feeling most sensibly all the cruelty of this address, could only answer with her tears; and her aunt unfeelingly proceeded—

"I always knew indeed how it must be—I am really extremely concerned. However, child, you will find me and Miss Ludford extremely kind to you as long as you continue to deserve it. Pray, who is that Mrs.——what d'ye call her?—some Scotch name—Clarinthia, my dear, what was the name that Ethy mentioned?"

"Montgomery, Madam."

"Aye, true, Montgomery; pray, niece, who is she?"

Had not Ethelinde been disabled from answering this question by the tears and sighs which the mortifying contrast between her former and her present prospects excited, she would have found it very difficult to have answered without betraying some part of the resentment which this affectation of forgetfulness, and contemptuous manner of speaking of her friends and of her beloved father, raised even in her gentle bosom: but the pain she endured was too acute; and fortunately Clarinthia, who, though she professed much more feeling than she had, was not entirely void of it, relieved her by saying—"Dear Ma'am, I believe my cousin is too much fatigued to enter into conversation this afternoon. My dear Ethelinde, had you not rather retire?"

"If you please," sobbed the unresisting sufferer, who dreaded nothing so much as the coarse interrogatories or harsh remonstrances of her insensible and haughty aunt. She then slightly curtseying to the mother and the son, (who during this disgusting reception had gazed on her with a degree of impertinent freedom as offensive as the insulting questions of his mother) left the room, and was shewn by Clarinthia into the apartment prepared for her, which was a neat room adjoining to her own. As soon as she reached it, she threw herself into a chair and yielded to the excess of anguish that oppressed her. She already bitterly repented having put herself in the power of Mrs. Ludford; and the conversation in which Clarinthia already attempted to engage her was not likely to reconcile her to an abode where only a comfortless vicissitude between arrogance and folly seemed to await her. Clarinthia besought her to compose herself, brought her a glass of water with drops in it, and seemed really solicitous for her recovery from the agitation of spirits into which her mother's harsh manners had thrown her; but Ethelinde no sooner became more tranquil, than Clarinthia was so eager to take advantage of it, that it appeared as if she had been less solicitous for the relief of her cousin than for some body to listen to those narratives which she had such a vio-lent inclination to relate, and of which she was herself the heroine.

"I am so glad, my sweet girl," said she, "that you are come, for I have been dying to see you! 'Tis so difficult to find a tender sympa-thetic friend worthy of one's confidence! You cannot imagine how ill and deceitful Miss Nelson behaved; so I have quite broke with her: she told every where of an affair that I entrusted her with; and it was with the greatest difficulty I could prevent it from coming to papa's knowledge. In your gentle and faithful bosom I am sure I may repose all my sorrows."

"Of sorrows," replied Ethelinde, faintly, "I should hope and believe you, my cousin, could not have many."

"Ah! you little know, my fair Ethelinde," replied Miss Ludford, putting on an air of despondency, "you little know the embarrass-ments of a tender, a too susceptible heart; wishing to obey paren-tal commands, yet involuntarily and devotedly attached to another beloved object."

Ethelinde felt less than ever disposed to become the confident of her romantic cousin, when she found that whatever attach-ment she had was contrary to the approbation of one if not of both her parents; but to avoid it was impossible; and she was not now in a state of mind calm enough to consider how she should act, whether hear in silence, or remonstrate if she found, as she greatly feared, that the greatest charm Clarinthia found in having an *attachment*, was in having so placed it, as to be sure of an oppo-sition from her family, and to have laid a plan for such imaginary miseries as might establish her in her own opinion the "heroine of a tale of sympathy," not unworthy the place she contemplated with the most pleasure—a modern circulating library.

Ethelinde, compelled therefore to listen to a long and romantic history of feeling and sentiment, could not obtain a release till she had promised to give her cousin her sincere opinion of her situa-tion the next day; and then fatigued and unhappy, she was suffered to retire to her bed, Clarinthia undertaking to make her excuse for her not appearing at supper.

CHAPTER IV

The next morning, Ethelinde was constrained to hear a long and insulting harangue from her aunt, who ostentatiously displayed her own great kindness in thus receiving her when she had lost all those friends on whom she preferably depended; and concluded with a lecture on the prudence necessary to young women who were destitute of fortune.—"You are still I see in mourning, child," said she at the end of this tedious discourse; "I forget how long your unfortunate father has been dead?"

"Not yet three months, Madam: but had more time elapsed since that regretted period, I should not have changed my dress."

"Why perhaps you are right, niece. It is convenient, as I suppose you have no great change of cloaths. However as to that Miss Ludford will assist you when you are out of mourning, so as that you may appear properly when we go in the summer to Southampton, and I will be very willing myself to make you some little elegant additions to your dress. I dare say we shall do mighty well together; for though we are not people of title, such, you know, as you have been used to; yet I make it a rule to have the best of every thing; and to have all such little matters fashionable and genteel about me, so that I should not chuse to have *my* niece appear otherwise."

"There is, I flatter myself, no danger of my disgracing you, Madam," said Ethelinde, with all the spirit she could assume. "While my father lived, his tenderness supplied me with more cloaths of every kind than I had occasion for. I am not a bad œconomist; and I have still a much more extensive wardrobe than I am likely to have occasion for. At Grasmere, where I hope to be before the end of the summer, dress is very immaterial, and the simplest will suffice me, as it does my beloved friend, who, in such plain apparel as is usually worn by Quakers, retains, with true elegance of appearance, manners which would do honour to the most refined society."

"What, do you tell *me*," said Mrs. Ludford, frowning with contempt and anger, "of your quakers and your refined societies.

You've got a young fellow in your head, and are grown careless, I see, of the opinion of everybody else but those that belong to him. A Scotch woman, without money, is mighty likely indeed to have an elegant appearance. However, Miss, if you have no more discernment, I am sure you are mighty welcome to seek your highland friends, and to wrap yourself up in a plaid, and live on oat cakes if you please; I have done my duty; I have acquitted myself; and all the world will do me the justice to say, that let what will befall you, I have acted the part of a generous and kind relation; but there is some people one cannot serve; so whenever or wherever you chuse to go, I wash my hands of the consequences."

Ethelinde, whose spirits the slightest effort exhausted, could give no other reply to this cruelty than tears; but Clarinthia, who had been absent during the greatest part of this dialogue, now returned; and appeasing her mother as well as she could, who had indeed almost talked herself out of breath, she carried the desolate Ethelinde away with her to undergo a new species of persecution in being consulted on a love epistle which she was composing to the "dear youth," with whom she carried on in despite of Ethelinde's remonstrances a clandestine correspondence.

Thus, between the gross and unfeeling insults of her aunt, and the weak and dangerous confidences of her cousin, many days passed heavily along. The latter she determined never to encourage, though she did not think herself justified in betraying them; and for the former, she endeavoured to bear them with patience, in reflecting that the time now approached when the arrival of Mrs. Montgomery in England would release her from such irksome dependence for ever.

The disagreeable circumstances of her situation were, however, soon encreased by the return of Rupert Ludford from London, whither he had gone the day after Ethelinde's arrival at Bristol. He seemed to have brought with him a reinforcement of the vanity and affectation which had before rendered him so extremely disgusting to Ethelinde; nor did he possess one virtue to palliate his numerous follies. Brought up by a mother coarse minded and selfish, as an only son, he had imbibed all her narrowness of spirit; and his boundless opinion of himself, made him look on half the world as beings who were without consequence if they contributed not in some way or other to his gratification; and on the other half as

people with whom Nature designed him to be on a level, though
he was unfortunately a step below them by being connected with
trade. Every journey he made to London rendered the name of
a merchant at Bristol more odious to his ears, and encreased his
desire for the arrival of that period when he should be enabled to
throw off all his mercantile connections and give his talents to the
cultivation of poetry and the fine arts, and his time to those noble
friends, who, however reluctantly he admitted the idea, he was
now tempted to suspect, were frequently more accommodated
by the money they occasionally borrowed of him, than gratified
by his conversation. Among an extensive acquaintance, he had no
chosen friend but Emmersley, who with a small fortune had taken
to the bar, where, having too little genius to advance without close
attention, and being too idle to apply, he sauntered away life without getting at all forwarder; and while he found an excellent table
at Ludford House during every vacation, was content with the
name of a barrister, to retain only the pertness which sometimes
adheres to the character; which pertness an unblushing confidence
in his own intellectual advantages, made him fancy was wit. If he
was not witty himself, he was the cause of wit in others; for he
acted occasionally as the sharpener or the butt of that which Mr.
Rupert was incessantly labouring to produce; and whenever they
were in company together, the attention of the whole circle was
usually engrossed by their play upon each other, to the great edifi-
cation of the hearers, and to the delight of Mrs. Ludford, who generally laughed immoderately at the sprightly sallies which were in
these dialogues exhibited.

Old Ludford, though he was much less delighted with his
son's acquirements, was yet too much accustomed to submit in
many instances to his wife to dispute that judgment, which had
directed his education, and which now with so much complacency contemplated its effects. He saw, with pleasure, that in the
main point Bobby (he had not yet learned to soften his name to
Rupert) adhered to excellent maxims, and continued to love
money, though he declined to assist in acquiring it. With some
of the loans he had made to his great friends, his father had been
acquainted, and had seen good security taken; others, where that
could not bear very close inspection, Mr. Rupert had kept to himself, and raised the money on his own credit unknown to the old

gentleman: and if at any time the father remonstrated on his current expences, which sometimes ran high, he knew how to pique
his pride by representing the necessity there was for a man whose
father was known to be so opulent, to appear respectable; and he
awakened his avarice, while he put his apprehensions to sleep, by
talking of contracts and agencies to be procured by the interest of
the personages to whose society the figure he made obtained him
admission. Old Ludford was of a plodding heavy temper, but not
without ambition of making his name of consequence, nor insensible to that sort of pride which makes a man value himself on a
large fortune of his own acquiring. If therefore he occasionally suffered some pain from his son's expences, his ambition and vanity
immediately healed the wound; and he forgave his dissipation in
favour of his genius and abilities, which his wife often assured Mr.
Ludford were such as must, whenever Rupert obtained a seat in
parliament (which it was in contemplation to procure for him)
raise him to the first notice, and probably the first posts.

Ethelinde had seen enough of her cousin Rupert and of his
friend Emmersley to dread their arrival as a misfortune which
almost counterbalanced the satisfaction she felt at the removal of
the family from Bristol to Ludford House. It was now the middle
of April; and in the country Ethelinde hoped to have a few hours in
which, amid the enchanting progress of spring, she might be suffered uninterruptedly to think of Montgomery, and offer up her
prayers to heaven for his preservation. At Bristol, she was hardly
ever a moment alone, unless in the hours usually given to repose;
for her aunt always insisted on her appearing in company, when
she failed not to hint at the indigent condition to which her niece,
though the granddaughter of an Earl, was reduced, and at her own
goodness in protecting her. This, which was usually delivered in
an half whisper, drew the eyes of the company on the blushing
and mortified Ethelinde; and could she have doubted of what her
aunt had been saying, the humiliating and affected pity which the
generality of the hearers afterwards threw into their behaviour
towards her, would have convinced her of the tenor of Mrs. Ludford's conversation. If ever the elder ladies were so deeply engaged
at cards that she could escape unperceived by them to her own
room, it was impossible to elude the vigilance of Clarinthia, who
had always some sentimental sorrow or sympathetic embarrass-

ment to relate; while she appeared quite insensible of the real and
heavy distresses of her cousin. Much of their time passed in visiting people, who, amid great affluence, were so ignorant and under
bred, that Ethelinde shrunk from their society with a dislike that it
was impossible for her to conquer, and difficult for her to conceal.
She saw that the matrons despised her for being poor, hated her for
being nobly born, and imputed her melancholy to pride: while the
Misses eyed her with disdain as a dependent on their equal Clara
Ludford, and as such affected to treat her; while they were not
without apprehensions of her engrossing the favour of Rupert, for
whose partiality many of them had hitherto contended with so
little decided preference, that he had occasionally celebrated all;
and each had a *sweet copy of verses* to shew, wherein she was the
Amoret, Phillida, or Amaryllis, that had employed the amorous
muse of this mercantile and versatile poet.

Amid society so utterly unpleasant to her, Ethelinde had nothing either to divert or sooth her settled sorrow, or her present anxiety for Mrs. Montgomery's return, of which she yet heard nothing.
At Ludford House, whither the family now removed for a few
weeks, she flattered herself that she should be more at liberty to
be wretched; and not compelled, while her heart was breaking, to
attend to scandalous anecdotes about people of whom she knew
nothing; or frivolous details of dinners given, or fashions arrived,
or servants discharged; which, with a few other equally uninteresting topics, composed the usual conversation she was condemned
to hear. This removal would not, she knew, relieve her either from
the barbarous taunts which she occasionally endured from her
aunt, from the harrassing secrets of her intriguing cousin, or the
mixture of feigned admiration and insulting compassion, with
which, on her first arrival, Rupert had received her. Fortunately,
however, the ton which he had last acquired in London, was that
of indolence and apathy. He found himself fatigued with every
thing, was amazed how he could ever have found any satisfaction
in dancing, or walking, or riding, and declared that the first and
only acquirement worth the attention of a man of sense or fashion
was to be perfectly at ease.

Ethelinde felt, in the respite which this new mode of being fashionable gave her from his rhymes and compliments, the only comfort she had long known; and a few days after she was settled at

Ludford House, she had the much greater satisfaction of receiving a letter from Sir Edward Newenden, in which he highly approved of her reasons for quitting Mrs. Woolaston (at whose marriage he expressed a mixture of displeasure and concern) and besought her to remain with Mrs. Ludford till the return of Mrs. Montgomery. He enclosed her an order for money, and a letter of credit on his Banker in London for any amount that she might want before he wrote her again, as he informed her that he was now removing towards Italy. To this letter, which was filled with expressions of paternal tenderness for her, he added, that as to himself, he was well, "and not more unhappy than usual." He gave a pleasing account of his children, on whose daily improvement he dwelt with fondness; but Lady Newenden he only named as being, together with her father and Mrs. Maltravers, in good health. And Ethelinde, gratified as she was by his approbation of her conduct, and unfailing friendship, could not without bitterness perceive, that, deserving as he was of affection, gratitude and esteem, he was yet unhappy in that quarter whence he had the greatest right to expect felicity.

CHAPTER V

Another fortnight passed, and still no intelligence arrived of Mrs. Montgomery—The depression of Ethelinde's mind grew hourly greater; and her health proportionably suffered. Deprived of every thing that could render life desirable; and doubting whether she ever should be restored to those friends, without whom it would become a burthen; compelled to affect a tranquillity she could not feel, or be exposed to reproaches for pride, coldness and affectation; she had no respite but in sleep; which, though often broken and disturbed, yet afforded her sometimes more pleasing images than her waking hours presented: and she now never beheld the dawn of the day without regretting its return, and entering reluctantly on a scene of painful dissimulation and continual internal uneasiness.

Clarinthia's wild and romantic turn created one of the daily difficulties she had to encounter. Ethelinde found, that far from having any steady affection for the young officer with whom she clandestinely corresponded, she had discarded her former lover whom she once preferred, only because her father who had at first opposed his pretensions, at length encouraged them, in consequence of the death of an elder brother, by which he became heir to a considerable fortune. This young man, whose name was Southcote, still visited at the House, and having really conceived an early attachment to Clarinthia, her caprice and ill treatment had not yet divested him of his passion.—But Clarinthia had found out that there was more heroism in giving herself to a man who had nothing, than in acceding to the mercenary views of her Father; and when Ethelinde attempted to argue with her on this subject, she was silenced by Clarinthia saying, "Nay, my dear Ethelinde, did you not refuse Davenant and engage yourself to Montgomery, who is not richer than my beloved Rivers; and surely, if you with all your prudence would do this, I have at least as much pretension to prefer the man I love. My father will be angry at first perhaps, but I know, that marry how I will, he will give me twenty thousand pounds."

While they remained at Bristol, Clarinthia contrived easily to receive letters from her lover, and the only tax she levied then on Ethelinde was obliging her to read them, and to hear her answers: but now she expected of her another concession; which was, to suffer the Captain's letters to be directed under cover to her. This Ethelinde absolutely refused, and a coldness arose from thence on the part of Clarinthia, which was soon aggravated into absolute hatred. Mr. Southcote had not for some months been at Bristol; but business, relative to his West India property, now bringing him thither, he came over to Ludford House to pass some days, and was still considered by the old gentleman as the lover of his daughter. He had not however been three days in the company of Ethelinde, before his attachment to her cousin was entirely eradicated; and he very frankly told her, that being now convinced he had nothing to hope, he had determined to persecute her no more with his passion: but being still desirous of connecting himself with a family he so highly esteemed, he entreated her interest with her amiable cousin.

Clarinthia, who had listened to this speech with amazement and mortification, burst into a convulsive laugh of mingled spite and contempt. "O! yes Sir," replied she—"Yes! you may depend upon my interest with my amiable cousin; only, as unluckily she is engaged, I am afraid neither my interest nor your own extraordinary merits will have any effect."

Southcote now eagerly desired an explanation; but Clarinthia, though resolute before to reject him, was now so piqued at his resignation of her, and preference of Ethelinde, that she answered him only with contemptuous raillery, and no sooner quitted him than she sought her cousin, who had escaped from the breakfast table to wander in a coppice at a small distance from the house; where as Mrs. Ludford had hitherto forborne to exercise her taste, she found quiet and some degree of pleasure in contemplating the beauties with which nature lavishly embellishes the most rustic spots towards the end of April. Seated on the turf, she was lost in the pensive pleasure of reading over Montgomery's letters, when Clarinthia, who knew her usual haunts, interrupted her, and with an air which extremely excited her surprise, cried as she approached—"I beg pardon, Miss Chesterville, I hope I don't disturb you? but I could not delay wishing you joy."

"Joy of what, my Cousin?"

"Oh, you don't know I dare say—or else lovers are with you such common acquirements, that one or two more or less, are not worth your attention."

"Upon my word, Clara, I am quite ignorant of your meaning."

"So! I admire the *sang froid* of some people.—What, you don't know that Southcote is in love with you and gives me up?—To be sure, he is much in the right, and my *discarded* lover does well to console himself with your gentle attractions.—I told him however you were engaged."

"You did well; and I hope, that whether this story originates in some raillery of his, or merely from some misunderstanding of yours, that I at least shall hear no more of it."

"That would be a pity," retorted Clarinthia with encreasing acrimony; "No, pray have the glory of refusing a man who was once thought not unworthy of *me*; and boasts of having for the sake of the dear Montgomery, discarded two men, both of fortunes superior to what even *I* have a right to expect."

"Surely, Clarinthia, you are out of humour this morning, or something has strangely changed you. When did I ever boast of having discarded any lover? or what reason have I ever given you to suppose that I should be gratified by the addresses of Mr. South-cote? If however that were really the cause, why should you be angry, since he is, as you acknowledge, discarded by you?"

"Oh, I beg you won't fancy neither," cried Clarinthia, in a tone between a laugh and a cry—"I beg you won't fancy, child, that I care about him; so far from it, I am sure I should be glad if you were to have him to-morrow."

Ethelinde easily perceived that her cousin was weak and vain enough to desire to retain in her chains, him, whom she would through perverseness reject, and was angry that she had not been able to secure one of those attachments, at once violent and hope-less, of which she had read so much, and by which the romantic coquettishness of her mind would have found itself particularly gratified; she was therefore rather concerned than angry, and with great gentleness remonstrated with her cousin on the unreason-able offence she seemed to have taken, assured her that Mr. South-cote had never addressed her, and that in all probability what he had said was merely a finesse which he had used to try if his Clar-inthia could be awakened to any return of affection for him, by the apprehension of seeing him prefer another: and she added, that should he be serious, which she did not believe likely, she should give him at once her reasons for declining to hear more of addresses, which she was very willing to allow offered her advan-tages, to which she had no pretensions.

The mildness, humility and sweetness of her answer, together with the idea she had started that Mr. Southcote had used her name merely to alarm the jealousy and awaken the latent love of his former mistress, appeased the unreasonable and capricious anger of Clarinthia for that time; but when Southcote a few days afterwards actually addressed her, and applied openly to Mr. and Mrs. Ludford for their approbation and interest, all her animosity against the innocent and unhappy Ethelinde was again excited. It was in vain that Ethelinde immediately, yet with great politeness, assured Mr. Southcote that her heart was irrevocably another's, and that in consequence of that assurance he immediately left the house. Confusion and ill humour remained in it, in consequence of this unfortunate overture, which rendered it infinitely more insupportable than ever. Old Ludford, who had hitherto seen Ethelinde with great indifference, now looked upon her with dislike, as having been the means of his Clarinthia losing a match he so highly approved; (for her other entanglement was a secret to him). Mrs. Ludford could not bear that any man should prefer her dependent niece to a daughter whose person resembled her own, whose education she considered as the most exquisite that could be given, and who had twenty thousand pounds. While Clarinthia was humbled, mortified and enraged, to be at length convinced, that instead of living single, or what would have been still better, dying for love, Southcote had not only broken her chains for ever, but had seriously intended to marry the indigent Ethelinde.

Severe as these heartburnings were, they were on all parts restrained from breaking forth in absolute rudeness towards the lovely and unhappy being who had excited them, by this consideration; that, if they treated her too harshly, she would quit them before the return of Mrs. Montgomery, and by that means might very probably be thrown in the way of Southcote, and being quite without protection and support be compelled to accept him. This the whole family united in wishing to prevent. The father, because he still hoped while Southcote remained single that the match with Clarinthia might be brought about; the mother, through mere envy and malignity; and Clarinthia, because she was no sooner convinced that he had really conquered his former affection, than she felt an invincible desire to engage him again in a passion for her, that she might then sacrifice him to another, as the compleatest triumph she could enjoy over her too lovely cousin, and her faithless admirer. Such were the politics at Ludford house, which saved Ethelinde from being driven out of it by such rudeness and insult as all her native gentleness, added to her wishes of obeying Sir Edward as far as she could, would not have enabled her to have borne. It had however some good effects: Clarinthia now no longer persecuted her with violent friendship or troublesome confidences; Mrs. Ludford no longer insisted on her appearing, whatever company were present; but she was suffered with very little notice to pass the greater part of her time either in her own room or the gardens, and to employ herself in writing, drawing or work, without enquiry or remark. Thus, with less actual misery than in the former part of her residence with her aunt, three weeks passed. Rupert was little at home; and when he was, he no longer seemed to consider her as worth the fatigue he should incur by being polite to her; but treated her with a kind of indolent contempt, as a girl to whom he could undoubtedly become acceptable whenever he chose to give himself the trouble.

Ethelinde had now been seven weeks with the Ludfords, and except the letter she had received from Sir Edward, had in all that time heard nothing of any of those friends on whom her thoughts perpetually dwelt. Chesterville had now been gone long enough to allow her to expect to hear from him; he had promised to write from the Madeiras, but no letter had arrived; and Mrs. Montgomery had not written, though Ethelinde had acquainted her with her change of situation, and had told her without reserve all the reasons she had to be more than ever solicitous for her return. Of Montgomery himself it was not yet possible for her to have any intelligence—but,

> "Her fancy follow'd him through foaming waves
> To distant shores; and she would sit and weep
> At what a sailor suffers."[1]

And oftener in beholding the luxurious and useless follies in which Rupert Ludford more than ever indulged himself, she would painfully reflect on the strange disposition of the goods of fortune, which, while they enabled such a being as her little conceited cousin to enjoy all the real and artificial pleasures which wanton wealth has to bestow, were so totally denied to the nobly born and nobly minded Montgomery; that with all his merit, all his advantages of understanding, figure and birth, he was compelled to seek even an uncertain and precarious support by quitting Europe, and becoming in an unwholesome climate, and amid continual hazard, a candidate for a small portion of Asiatic wealth, which, after all, he might not obtain. The oftener she made this mortifying comparison the more her spirits and her hopes were depressed; yet, with all her remaining strength of mind, she endeavoured to look forward to a day of retribution even in this world; and consoled by the recollection of his worth and goodness and of her own adherence to her duty throughout her hitherto unhappy life, she tried to acquire fortitude to bear present evils, from her reliance on the final though long delayed justice of Heaven.

1 Cowper, *The Task*, Book 6, lines 539-541.

CHAPTER VI

The family of Ludford had been accustomed to pass part of every summer at Southampton, and as the young man to whom Miss Clarinthia believed herself attached was quartered in that neighbourhood, she was extremely eager that they might go thither earlier in the year than they had usually done. Nothing was easier than to affect a nervous complaint. Her father was as fond of her as his nature permitted him to be of any thing, and readily assented to her wishes. Mrs. Ludford too, who loved to shew herself and her coach and four where they attracted more observation, as novelties, than they could possibly find in the neighbourhood of Ludford House, was not less condescending to the desires of her daughter. They all would have been willing to have left Ethelinde behind them: but as that would have been hazardous on account of Southcote, whose West India connexions brought him frequently to Bristol, it was determined that she should go with them. But Clarinthia, whose natural good humour was lost in her insatiable desire to monopolize admiration, now no longer pressed her to go to public places; but Ethelinde contented herself, after a slight invitation which she invariably refused, to walk, read or otherwise divert herself; while her cousin, either on horseback in a morning, or at parties in the evening, had opportunities to carry on her clandestine love, without being suspected either by her father or her mother.

The situation of Ethelinde therefore was very little changed by this removal to a place of public resort. But every week and every day that passed encreased the uneasiness and anxiety with which she thought of the long protracted return of Mrs. Montgomery, from whom she received not even a letter, to relieve her mind from any part of this tormenting suspence.

A thousand uneasy conjectures now distrest her: sometimes she fancied she was ill in France, or that the world no longer boasted of one of its brightest ornaments; and sometimes she supposed that since her affairs were only more embarrassed, she forbore to write what could give only pain to her already unhappy correspondent. But every supposition by which Ethelinde could account for her silence was unsatisfactory, and the more she attempted to investigate its cause, the more reason she found to be disturbed and alarmed.

Time, however, heavily passed on, the end of June arrived; the place was filled with a croud of company, all eager for amusement. But Ethelinde, who had no delight in what attracted them, and who saw herself considered only as a dependent on the Ludfords, lived more than ever alone. In her solitary and pensive walks, which generally lay towards the pleasant common across which the road goes to the town, she had frequently been overtaken or met by a gentleman who appeared to be in a very ill state of health, and to be oppressed with melancholy as deep as her own: he was, as well as herself, in mourning, and ill health or sorrow, rather than time, had given an appearance of infirmity to a manly and graceful figure, and of sallowness and languor to the fine features and expressive eyes. He had frequently gazed on Ethelinde with an earnestness that from any other person would have distrest if it did not alarm her; but there was something in the look and manner of this stranger which excited her confidence rather than her fear; she fancied that there was in his face a great resemblance to features always present to her mind—to those of Montgomery; yet she knew that he had no father living, nor any very near relation; and she checked this idea as being merely a chimera, formed by her imagination on some slight similitude, hardly perceivable by another. They had thus met several times: the stranger, though he always seemed disposed to speak, had hitherto contented himself with bowing as he passed her, and sometimes when he thought she did not perceive him, turning to look after her, till she was no longer within his view. Ethelinde, though she fancied he was unhappy, and was involuntarily interested for him for that reason, and because of his imaginary likeness to Montgomery, could not speak first.

It happened however, that early one morning she went muffled up in a great cap and long cloak, to get from the library the second volume of a book she was reading; the stranger whom she had so often observed, sat reading in a corner so intent on his book that he perceived her not; but when she asked the person who waited to serve her, for the book she wanted, and heard it was not at home, she expressed her disappointment, and at the sound of her voice the stranger looked up and took not his eyes from her while she remained in the shop; when she had left it, he enquired of the bookseller who she was?

"I really cannot inform you, Sir: she is I think a sort of companion to some ladies of great fortune from Bristol, who come here every year."

"And her name?"

"There, Sir," said the master of the shop, shewing her name in his subscription book—"That is her name, written by herself."

"Chesterville!" exclaimed the stranger—"Good God! and can you tell me to what family of that name she belongs, what relations she has, and for whom she is in mourning? and whether she is married, or a widow?—yet, she is so young—surely—I wish I knew." The man professing himself incapable of answering all these enquiries, the stranger in great apparent anxiety went forth to make them elsewhere; but he could not describe Ethelinde otherwise, than as a tall young lady in mourning, who was generally with Mrs. Ludford. Mrs. Ludford and her daughter were perfectly well known by the various tradesmen to whom he applied for information, but the young lady in mourning had either never been at their shops, or having laid out no money there, had passed unnoticed: no intelligence would therefore be gained; and Ethelinde, who intended the first time she had an opportunity to ask at the library who the stranger was, went for her evening walk alone as usual, quite unconscious of the tumultuous anxiety which the knowledge of her name had occasioned. The evening was warm, and she had left the house sooner than usual to avoid the racket and confusion of the universal dressing for a ball, in which every body but herself were engaged. She had been disappointed of the second volume of the book she had begun, which was the beautiful and pathetic Julia de Roubigné, but she had taken another simple and natural story, Fatal Obedience, or the History of Mr. Freeland;[1]

1 *Julia de Roubigné* (1777), Henry Mackenzie's (1745-1831) tragic novel of sensibility where the heroine is murdered by her husband in a plot-design resembling *Othello*; the hero is a Montgomery type and expends himself in Martinique in humanitarian efforts on behalf of slaves. *Fatal Obedience, or The History of Mr. Freeland* (1769), anonymous. This omniscient narrative is another story of a young couple who without money enough to live an upper middle class life are persuaded to wait while Savile, the young hero, attempts

and having found a seat on the grass, in the shade formed by one of the clumps of fir planted on the common, she had escaped a moment from her own unhappiness, and was absorbed by her concern for the lovely unfortunate Gertrude, when her attention was suddenly called off, by the hasty approach of the stranger she had so often seen. He pulled off his hat, but seemed breathless and confused: "Will you, Madam," said he inarticulately, "will you forgive this rude intrusion from a man deeply interested in the question which he hopes you will allow him to ask?"

Ethelinde, though somewhat alarmed and surprized by such an address, arose hastily, and with her usual ease and sweetness replied, though not without some appearance of confusion, "that she should consider herself much honoured by his commands."

"Your name, Madam, I am informed, is Chesterville. May I enquire whether it is your family name?—or—" he stopped and hesitated, and Ethelinde took that opportunity to reply.

"Certainly, Sir, it is the name of my family."

"Be so good then, Madam, as to tell me—have you brothers, and are any of them married?"

"I have, Sir, one brother, who is married."

"And—pray pardon my curiosity—you will I am sure, when I tell you from what it arises—whom did he marry?"

"A native of Spain, who was however the daughter of an English gentleman."

"Gracious God!—I thank thee!" exclaimed the stranger with clasped hands, and a countenance strongly expressive of emotion. —"I have then some traces of my lost Victorine:—dearest young lady, by your countenance, a countenance which the moment I beheld it became most interesting to my heart; you I am sure will pardon and pity the anxiety of a father who seeks his only remaining child, and whose troubled mind is haunted by remorse and anguish when he persuades himself, that for having too long abandoned *her*, avenging heaven has robbed him of the rest."

Ethelinde, amazed as she was, had yet presence of mind enough left to attempt appeasing the excessive agitation of Mr. Harcourt, whom she now clearly perceived in the interesting stranger. She

to secure a fortune; his nature and the world's corruption stand in the way, and Gertrude, the heroine, dies before they can marry. It is told by the young man now turned recluse.

besought him to be more tranquil, for he appeared ready to faint, and to forbear any farther conversation till he could speak with less pain.

"Lovely, considerate creature!" cried he, gazing on her with eyes which now filled with tears—"I will endeavour to recover myself—Yet one question more.—Where is my Victorine?—When can I press her to this throbbing heart, and implore her pardon for my cruel, my unnatural neglect."

Had Ethelinde been a stranger under such evident distress she would have been much affected, but when she considered Mr. Harcourt as the uncle of Montgomery, the brother of his beloved mother, and the father of Victorine, she forgot that she had never before spoken to him, and felt as if she was herself his daughter. When therefore the violent and encreasing agitation of his spirits seemed to convulse his whole frame, she intreated him to lean on her arm, and to hasten home before he made any farther efforts to acquaint himself with circumstances that might give him pain. —"I have met with an angel," cried Harcourt, "who seems sent by Heaven to speak peace to my soul.—I will endeavour to follow your advice, lovely Miss Chesterville, because I will neither terrify nor trouble you.—Tell me only where my daughter is, and I will suppress as much as I can every other emotion but gratitude to Providence which has preserved, and will restore her."

He then, collecting all his strength, walked, but with slow and faltering steps, towards the town; and after a moment acquired courage to renew the question he had asked, of where Victorine then was?

Ethelinde found it necessary immediately to satisfy him; and therefore, tho' with difficulty and in a low voice, she related without disguising any part of the truth, the situation of her brother when he returned from Gibraltar; and the consequences of his return. But when she came to that part of her narration where it was necessary to mention the death of her father, the sad and tender recollections that crouded on her memory, choaked her utterance; and, unable to proceed, she was compelled to accept from Mr. Harcourt that support which she had a moment before offered him.

"Do not," cried he, much affected by her distress—"do not I beseech you gratify my anxious enquiries at this expence to yourself; let me waive a conversation too affecting to us both till we are better able to bear it.—Where are you?—May I be allowed to wait on you home?"

Ethelinde, believing that the Ludford family, if not already departed to the ball, were too much engaged to be very inquisitive after her visitor, and knowing that the dining parlour was at that hour usually vacant, ventured to invite thither her new acquaintance. As soon as he was seated she went herself to fetch him refreshment, which he appeared so much to need; and having taken it, he seemed to have got over the tremor and faintness which had so much alarmed her. In a few moments he became still more tranquil; and Ethelinde finished, in as few words as she could, the little history of those embarrassments which had made it necessary for Chesterville and his wife to depart for the West-Indies; which they were only enabled to do by the generous and disinterested friendship of Sir Edward Newenden.

Mr. Harcourt severely blamed himself for his neglect: "Oh my poor deserted child," cried he, tears again filling his eyes—"to what difficulties was not your infancy exposed, what must you have thought when you were old enough to think, of your father? And now, when the rigid but just hand of destiny has by severe chastisement awakened him to a sense of his neglected duties, he finds you gone in search of *him* who ought to have protected and provided for her: and if he is not already sufficiently punished, thy innocent life may perhaps be demanded to fill up the measure of vengeance."

Ethelinde now again endeavoured to console and reassure him on the fate of Victorine. He heard her with attention and gratitude; and when she ceased speaking, he said, with a deep sigh, —"you are very good thus to endeavour to reconcile me to myself; had I indeed been quite forgetful of my poor Victorine, nothing I think could quiet the reproaches of my own heart: but though I did not enough, I made many, but successless enquiries, both of the person who succeeded to her grandfather's property, and in Spain, I could gain no intelligence of her; and as I proposed this year to come to England for the rest of my life, I then hoped to trace her out by the indefatigable research, which I intended in person to make. Alas! he who had the greatest influence in bringing me to the resolution I formed of quitting Jamaica—my son! he for whom alone I enjoyed in imagination the purchases I had made in England and the great affluence which I possessed, is gone! To that very affluence which enabled him to indulge without restraint his passion for pleasure and dissipation, he fell a martyr, in his nineteenth year: and if I have lost Victorine, I am without a child to inherit what I shall leave, when I follow him, as I shall soon do, to the grave!"

Ethelinde could answer nothing: and Mr. Harcourt, after a moment, in which the remembrance of his son deprived him of the power of utterance, thus proceeded—

"At the age of forty I return to England; which though I was born in France, I consider as my native country. I return, but as a stranger and an alien, without a certainty of finding one person who may be interested for me, who may be induced by the tender ties of blood to render the rest of my life easy. I had a sister—but I have not heard from her these many months; and buried in obscurity as she was, the letters and the remittances I lately sent to her, may never have reached her or her son, whom, if he still lives, I shall consider as my own."

The emotion of Ethelinde now exceeded all description; to find, that if Montgomery had remained a few weeks only in England, the arrival of his uncle would have rendered his voyage unnecessary; to reflect on all the sufferings which a little patience would have spared them, and that now he was out of the reach of his benefactor, and might never return to enjoy the prosperity which awaited him, quite overwhelmed her. Harcourt imagined that she was merely affected by pity for him, or by the interest which her brother's relationship to him gave her in his narrative; while she was endeavouring to acquire voice to tell him where his sister and his nephew were, he thus went on—

"It is now two years since my poor boy returned to me from England, where he had been educated at a public school.—I soon after received intelligence of his sister's death who had gone the year before with her husband to England; and my son became doubly precious to me. He was, in figure, in temper, and in accomplishments, every thing a fond father could wish: but his vivacity was boundless: he was gay, animated, and generous to an excess; and Jamaica, a residence which long habit and great prosperity had rendered pleasant to me, was too confined a scene for his volatile spirit; he easily persuaded me to do what would be agreeable to him, and he obtained from me a commission to make considerable purchases in England, and I agreed to dispose of all my West-India estates, except two, which were not only the most certain in their produce, but the most easily managed in the absence of their proprietor. After about three months stay he went back to Europe, and laid out the money with which I had entrusted him, to great advantage in a western country. Having settled every thing to his wish, he wrote to me to say, that as he knew it must be many months before I could settle my affairs and quit Jamaica, he proposed employing the intermediate time in making the tour of Europe. I had letters from him from time to time from the different Italian towns he visited, and looked forward to the period which now approached, when we should meet in England to live together like friends; for as his friend I had always taught my son to consider me. Such were my hopes—ah! vain and fallacious hopes! —It is now four months since, having arranged all my affairs so as to quit the West Indies for ever, I waited at Kingston to embark on board a merchant man which I had freighted with such of my effects as remained to be transported to Europe: a ship came in from England; it belonged to the merchant to whom the produce of my estates were usually consigned; eagerly and impatiently I expected the first boat which came on shore, and which I hoped brought me a packet from my son, who transmitted his letters by means of my correspondent in London. Judge of the feelings of a father, who, instead of tidings of the health and happiness of a son so beloved, saw that son himself, arrive on shore, not such as he left me, in all the pride of youth and health, but emaciated, pale, and to all appearance in the last stage of a consumption; unable to walk, he was borne from the boat in the arms of the negroes, who would have put him into mine—but speechless with grief and amazement, I stood heartstruck and immovable, while they placed the sort of litter in which he had been brought, before me. Exhausted with the fatigue of being removed from the ship, my poor boy could not for a moment speak to me—Oh! God! The altered but still pleasing countenance which he turned towards me in that moment of speechless agony, is ever present to my mind —sleeping or waking, I see before me the faint smile which sat on those pale lips and sunken cheeks. When having recovered a little breath he took my hand, and said in a hollow and tremulous voice: 'My father, I obtain my wishes, and am come to die in your arms.'

"Somebody, I know not who, who possessed their senses, which I did not, directed us both to be conveyed to the house of an intimate friend, where every thing was done for my son that was supposed likely to be useful to him, and where after a few hours, of which I have no recollection, my friend prevailed upon me to listen to the Mulatto servant who had accompanied my son, and from whose relation it was possible we might learn what had occasioned this fatal change, and from thence know what remedy might with hopes of success be applied.

"Remedy I too well knew there was none—but in the sullen hopelessness of despair, I listened to the account Carlos gave of his master: he said, that he got into parties whose whole business was pleasure, and that he had several times been confined with dangerous fevers in consequence of these excesses, and that his general state of health was extremely hurt—that Carlos had often ventured to remonstrate with him, but in vain; his volatility made him turn his advice, as well as that of some friends, who saw his constitution gradually giving way, into ridicule; and, when he was told the consequence of this wild career, he answered, that if he could not enjoy life like a man of spirit, he had rather not keep it.

"At length he was seized at Marseilles with an ardent fever, which left him in a state of almost infantine weakness; Carlos took that opportunity of introducing a Physician traveling with an English family, who advised his immediately returning by sea to England, as the only chance of conquering the ill effects of his past indiscretions, and removing him from scenes where he was too likely to commit others when he recovered. To England he returned; but the mischief was done; his ruined constitution nothing could restore; he remained a few weeks with my correspondent, who treated him like a son, and had the best advice for him: but it was evident to all the Physicians who were consulted, that nothing could save him. He felt it by that time himself, and felt it without any other measure of regret, than what arose from his knowledge of the pain it might give me.

"His wishes to see me once again, made him press them to tell him whether it was probable that he might live till my arrival in England, which I had fixed to be at the end of five months from that time. They owned that they feared not. He then, with that vivacity which had not yet forsaken him, determined to hire a ship and come to me: and with a firmness of mind very extraordinary in so young a man, he ordered on board a leaden coffin, and necessaries to preserve his remains if he should die on the voyage, that they might be interred with those of his mother.

"Neither my friend in London or the medicinal people whom he had summoned, could prevail upon him to relinquish this project. The latter indeed, seeing him so resolute, soon ceased to oppose it; and though there remained hardly any hope of his recovery, it was barely possible that the voyage to his native climate might be of more use than medicines. But his decline, though slow, was yet too perceivable during the voyage; and when Carlos concluded his narrative, I was but too much confirmed in the sad conviction that a few hours, or at the most a few days, would consign my only hope to a premature grave.

"Dreadful as was this certainty, the remonstrances of my friend restored to me resolution enough to attend him while he yet lived; I stifled the anguish of my heart; I affected to entertain hopes, and tried to speak chearful; but the dear departing being, who had, with all his volatility, more fortitude than his unhappy father, besought me not to deceive myself. 'I die, dear sir,' cried he, as he held my hand, 'and die perfectly easy, if you have but forgiven me for the pain I have occasioned to the best father that ever man had! Think not of my loss with such bitterness; perhaps it is better for us both; my days have hitherto, through your goodness, been all pleasant ones; I have enjoyed every moment of my life, though it has been short; a long life equally fortunate I could not expect, and by quitting it now, I perhaps escape from many sorrows and calamities, while I have nothing to regret on earth but leaving you.' I affect you, dearest Miss Chesterville, too much; forgive me! I have a mournful, a severe delight, in dwelling on the last scene of a life so dear to me, and with how few do I dare indulge the sad luxury of speaking of it."

A silence of a few moments now intervened, which was broken only by the convulsive sobs of Mr. Harcourt and the deep sighs of Ethelinde. The former then continued.—"Let me hasten to close a relation that is I see too distressing to your tender bosom. A few hours before he closed his eyes for ever, I was placed by the chair where he sat, being unable to breathe in a bed; he looked at me a moment earnestly, and then said, as well as his extreme weakness permitted, 'My dear sir, there is yet one thing on which I wish you to listen to me. I have often heard you mention with regret the daughter born to you in Spain, and have often lamented the little success of your endeavours to discover her. When the fever which has been attended with these tedious consequences, seized me at Marseilles, I was meditating a journey to Barcelona, where I intended to have made personal enquiries for my sister, and dare venture to believe I should have succeeded, for by means of a merchant at Marseilles, I had already procured intelligence of her, though it is not such as I wish at this moment to give you.' —'Give it me however,' cried I.—'It is,' replied my son, 'that being obliged to quit the convent where she was brought up, she became a sort of humble companion to the daughters of a merchant, from whom she went away with a young Englishman: to England they imagine, but they refused through resentment of her conduct to give any particulars about her. You will soon, my dear sir, have no other child. I need not I know urge you to seek out and receive this unfortunate sister, wheresoever she may be. She is yet so young that her errors cannot have been numerous; perhaps they were involuntary. May she prove worthy of you, my father, and heal those wounds which I see my loss will inflict. Let her and that nephew of whom you have so often spoken, and whom while I was a school boy, I used to love, though I saw so little of him; let them together share the princely fortune you possess; unless, as you are yet but in the middle of life, a second marriage should give you other sons, more deserving of your tenderness than I have been.' —There was something so affecting in the firmness with which so young a man contemplated his approaching dissolution, and looked back to the world only to find future comforts for the only person who made him wish to live, that had he not been my child, this conversation would have been insupportably distressing.— Think then, of what I suffered?—I remember only, that I promised my poor boy never to rest till I had found the dear deserted girl whom he so generously recommended to my care; and then the thoughts of all I was on the point of losing, and the impossibility that any thing could make me amends for the cruel stroke which levelled all my fond hopes with the dust, robbed me for a while of

the painful consciousness of my misery; I fell from wild and frantic exclamation into a stupor, from which when I recovered it was
only to relapse again into distracted ravings. The interval lasted
but till I heard and understood that my son was gone for ever. I will
say nothing of what became of me afterwards. To the unwearied
attention of a friend I owe it, that I yet live. It was this friend, and
his wife, one of the best women in the world, who awakened me
to a sense of my duty: they taught me resignation by restoring to
my mind a sense of that religion I had too much neglected; but
even those consolations were embittered by the reflections they
bought with them on my past conduct. I regretted, ah how deeply,
the little restraint I had ever put on the inclinations of my son. I
imputed to my boundless indulgence the destruction of all my
happiness. I had made him his own master at an age when other
boys are still at school, and trusting to the goodness of his understanding and the brilliancy of his faculties, had neglected to give
him those principles, without which understanding is useless, and
brilliant faculties only as fatal auxiliaries to the headlong passions
of youth.

> 'The poor fond parent, humbled in the dust,
> Now owns in tears, the punishment was just.'[1]

Yet, alas! we do not always bear best the calamities to which we are
ourselves accessary. The reflection, that with a more careful and
stricter education, my son might now have been living, happy himself and constituting my happiness, perpetually haunts me, and
adds bitterness to the regret I must incessantly feel through life,
where not an incident occurs but what reminds me of my irreparable loss. As soon as I was in a condition to undertake the voyage,
I embarked, not for England, as I originally intended, but for Barcelona, where I employed myself in obeying the last desires of my
son, and the dictates of my own sorrowing heart: I there learned,
that my poor Victorine had left the family who had taken her upon
charity, with an English officer of the name of Chesterville; I had
the consolation of believing she set out for England as his wife,
and thither I immediately followed them; but illness, the effect
of accumulated sorrow and anxiety, detained me for some weeks

1 Thomas Parnell (1679-1718), *The Hermit*, lines 232-233.

at Paris; and as soon as the dangerous weakness, occasioned by a bilious fever, would permit, I came hither from Havre.[1] I wrote immediately to London, to engage various persons in enquiries after my daughter and her husband: and I wrote also to my sister, whose residence is in the North of England. From my first letters I have yet received no satisfactory intelligence; and to the latter, those to my sister and my nephew, I have had no answers at all. —Yet, I will not, I ought not, to yield to that heavy despondence which too frequently threatens to annihilate my courage and my faculties; I will rather consider my fortunately meeting with you, Madam, as an earnest, that Heaven accepts my repentance, and will restore to me my long lost Victorine. An attraction too powerful to be resisted, seemed to impel me towards you; yet it was not the loveliness of your form, or the sweetness of your countenance, enchanting as they are, that created this fortunate fascination; it was that soft yet deep melancholy which appeared to possess you, and that look which seemed to promise the tenderest pity for the miseries of others; you were always alone—you were in mourning —you were about the age of the daughter I sought—it was even possible you might be that daughter. I clung to an idea so soothing to my sick heart, and mistook perhaps the power of beauty for the force of blood. But however desirous of speaking to you, I was still afraid of alarming, or of offending you; and I know not how long my painful silence would have lasted, had I not learned in the library this morning that your name was Chesterville. New tumults of hope and expectation then seized me; they became too violent to be long endured, and compelled me to follow and to address you: thus commencing, however abruptly, an acquaintance which promises to be the most fortunate I can now make, rendered at present most soothing by the interest you generously take in my sorrows, and promising hereafter to be the means of restoring me to all of happiness I can now taste on earth."

"And yet," said Ethelinde, "you know not all of which it is in my power to acquaint you." She then informed him of what she knew relative to Mrs. Montgomery and her son, omitting only the affection which had so long subsisted between Montgomery and herself. Mr. Harcourt heard her with anxious concern. The inconveniences to which his sister had been, and was still exposed,

1 The second largest port in France.

the involuntary absence of a nephew whom he had the power to render independent, and the uncertainty whether he might now ever return to possess independence, were united to the concern with which he reflected on the situation of his daughter: and such complicated anxiety drew from him tears, of which Ethelinde, who wept with him, could not stop the course; when they were suddenly interrupted by the entrance of Miss Ludford, drest for the ball. She flounced into the room, and was walking up to the glass which afforded her a survey of her whole person, when she saw, not only Ethelinde, (whom she would hardly have noticed,) but a gentleman with her. "I did not know, Miss Chesterville, that you had company."

Ethelinde then introduced Mr. Harcourt by his name.—It sounded well, and Clarinthia having nothing else to do, deigned to enter into conversation with him, till he, finding himself almost exhausted by the various emotions he had experienced within the last few hours, and seeing it improbable that he should have any farther opportunity of conversation with Ethelinde that night, withdrew to his lodgings, having obtained leave to wait on her again the next day.

CHAPTER VII

Mr. Harcourt had no sooner withdrawn, than Miss Ludford enquired who he was. "He is," replied Ethelinde, "the half brother of Mrs. Montgomery, and the father of Mrs. Chesterville."

"And pray where did you met him? Lord! it is vastly odd he should come to see you without waiting on papa. He comes, I suppose, from Scotland."

"No, from Jamaica; where he has lately lost an only son; in consequence of which my brother's wife becomes heiress to all his immense fortune."

This was intelligence that could not but be interesting to Mrs. Ludford, who at that moment entered the room, and to whom Clarinthia immediately communicated it. Nothing was to her so mortifying as to suppose that any other family, and still more those branches of her own whom she considered as dependant and impoverished, should be possessed of affluence superior or even equal to that from which she derived her own consequence. Her ample visage flowed with the sudden emotion of surprise and pain this intelligence gave her; and turning haughtily towards Ethelinde, she said—"A great fortune? Truly that's a likely story. Pray, child, is this an invention of the person who has been here, or your own?"

"Neither, Madam," replied Ethelinde with some spirit. "To what end should he invent, or should I repeat a falsehood so ridiculously useless, and so easily detected."

"It is impossible it should be true, however," returned Mrs. Ludford: "for I am sure if there had been any such man of large fortune in Jamaica, Mr. Ludford must have known him. He that has such great consignments from the Island! Call your father, Clary, I'm determined to know, however."

Ethelinde, the agitation of whose spirits this conversation was ill calculated to soothe and compose, would willingly have escaped from the room; but as she arose to depart, Mr. Ludford waddled into the room; and his wife eagerly put the question to him whether there was any such person as a Mr. Harcourt of very great property in Jamaica?"

"Aye to be sure there is," replied he; "and what then?"

Mrs. Ludford, again changing countenance, informed him of what Ethelinde had told her; and had hardly concluded her account, before the eager desire of accumulating money, the latent but strongest principle in the heavy mind of old Ludford, was suddenly roused—"Bless my soul," cried he, rubbing his hands, "has Mr. Harcourt himself been here? I wish I had seen him. His consignments are very considerable—I wish I could have paid my respects to him. His consignments, I know, are very capital indeed —very capital—and not a shilling advance ever expected from his merchant. I heartily wish, my dear, you had called me down."

"Lord, papa," said Clarinthia, "what signifies his consignments; I am sure you have business enough; and for my part I wish you'd have done with it quite, instead of slaving always for more money. Come now don't let us stay talking about such things, I desire of you; but let us go to the rooms. The coach has been waiting this half hour."

Ludford had now Harcourt's consignments, and the probability of his getting them transferred to his own house, so strong in

his head, that instead of complying with the wishes of Miss Clarinthia, or attending to her impatience, he was meditating how to
insinuate himself immediately into the favor of the rich planter.
—"Suppose, love," said he, addressing himself to his wife, (who sat
fanning herself, half out of breath at the prospect of the hitherto
indigent Ethelinde and her brother being raised to affluence by
this newly discovered relation)—"Suppose, love, we send a com-
plaisant card, and invite Mr. Harcourt to dinner to-morrow. It will
be but common civility, you know, and I dare say he will take it
kind. Bless me, I wonder I never heard of his landing—I wonder
what ship he came in; but we will invite him to dinner, Dolly—
shall we?"

"With all my heart, Mr. Ludford," said the lady indignantly,
"with all my heart, if you mean as one gentleman to another out
of hospitality; but I hope you don't think of cringing to him for
consignments. I bless God, you are now in a *sitiation* not to need
any such proceeding; and I am sure my son Rupert would not
approve of your letting yourself down to ask favours of the King
himself."

"Not ask favours?" cried Ludford, whose pride yielded to his
avarice. "I am sure your son Rupert spends money fast enough
and he ought not to be above any honest means of getting it.
Besides I've always wished for the consignments of that estate;
they're the best on the Island; and if I could get them, more sugars
would be entered at the port of Bristol, consigned to Ludford and
Company, than there is for Grubworth, Grinder, Still, Manchineel
and Company;[1] and let me tell you, Dolly, that is a thing not to be
despised."

Ethelinde now silently withdrew to her room, leaving them to
settle this matter as they would. The dialogue had, however, forcibly brought to her mind the speech which her brother just before
his departure made on the attention he should meet with from the
Ludfords when he obtained a share of Harcourt's fortune; and she
could not but reflect with thankfulness on the certainty there now
was that her brother was not only secure of affluence, but would
be enabled to discharge his pecuniary obligations to Sir Edward;

1 Manchineel is one of the most poisonous trees in the world; it's found in the
Caribbean. A still is an apparatus used to distill liquid mixtures. The company's
name is appropriately allegorical.

and that Mrs. Montgomery had no longer any occasion to remain in France waiting the precarious issue of a law suit; but then the uncertainty whether Chesterville or Montgomery might ever return to enjoy the fortune which now awaited them, struck cold on her heart, and destroyed all the agreeable visions which her late acquired friend had raised in her mind. A thousand projects now suggested themselves to her; but they all ended in the painful conviction that she could do nothing to expedite the return of her brother and her lover, except writing to every place where it was possible letters might reach them; and on that subject, as well as on sending a messenger to Lyons, at which Mr. Harcourt had hinted the evening before, she determined to consult him the next morning, when he had engaged her to meet him early on their usual walk. So various were the emotions that this sudden change of fortune had given rise to in the mind of Ethelinde, that she could not sleep; but at the dawn of day was dressed, and waiting with impatience for the hour of rendezvous. Before its arrival, however, Ethelinde, to her infinite satisfaction, received (forwarded from Brackwood, from whence it had been long in its passage) a letter from Mrs. Montgomery, informing her that, hopeless of a speedy determination of her law-suit, and uneasy at the situation of her beloved Ethelinde, which, from the two letters she had received from her, was, she found, far from pleasant, she had determined to hasten to England; and desired her to prepare, in pursuance of the wishes and parting injunctions of their mutually dear Montgomery, for entire sequestration at Grasmere.

With this welcome letter in her hand, Ethelinde hastened to meet Mr. Harcourt. She found him apparently in weaker health than the day before; but the sight of his sister's hand seemed to revive him.—"I have not then lost every thing," said he. "After an absence of so many years, I shall embrace my Caroline, and enjoy at least the satisfaction of placing her above the inconveniences she has too long so nobly struggled with. Let us, loveliest Miss Chesterville, let us consider this as the omen of our future good fortune, and let us soothe our otherwise insupportable anxiety by the hope that Victorine, Montgomery, and Chesterville, will before many months are lapsed—" He paused a moment, sighed, and then in a lower voice said—"Ah! dreamer than I am! Thus it was that I fondly, anxiously watched the return of him, who did indeed return, not as my sanguine expectation painted him, but to have his premature grave watered by the tears of a father, who can now never expect happiness! Should my daughter, should my nephew, be destined so to meet me! Pardon me, dearest Miss Chesterville," continued he, seeing Ethelinde extremely affected by this dreadful idea—"pardon me, I ought not, I know, to sink my own spirits, or disturb yours by images so painful; but I have suffered so much—my nerves are so shaken, that they intrude upon me in spite of myself. I have been long a lonely wanderer, and have fancied myself a being to whom nobody would attend but through mercenary motives, nobody listen, but in hopes of some advantage from the calamities I deplored, and now, when I have found in your gentle pity a balm for my wounded spirit, I seem to find relief from communicating the terrors which in spite of reason still haunt me."

Ethelinde, who, from the excess of her tenderness for Montgomery, was easily alarmed, felt that these terrifying apprehensions were indeed communicated most painfully to her anxious bosom, but she endeavoured to conceal the effect they had upon her, and to speak chearfully. She succeeded so well as to turn Mr. Harcourt's mind again towards his sister; and on consulting the date of her letter, they found that she was probably already in London, or would be there in a very few days.

The impatience with which they both desired to accelerate a meeting so long wished for, made them equally averse to the delay which must be created by Mr. Harcourt's accepting the invitation to dinner, so officiously made by Mr. Ludford; but on reflection, Ethelinde considered that her going with Mr. Harcourt, to whom she was almost a stranger, to Mrs. Montgomery's lodgings, where she might not yet be arrived, would be imprudent, and that it would be better only to write thither, and to wait till they heard from Mrs. Montgomery, before they left Southampton. In the mean time, Mr. Harcourt, with whatever reluctance, determined to accept the politeness of Mr. Ludford. The sordid soul of the money-loving trader, never more evidently appeared than in the behaviour of Mr. Ludford towards his newly made acquaintance, whom he treated with fatiguing and fawning civility; as well as towards Ethelinde, with whom he had till now hardly exchanged ten words since she became resident in his house. He now affected to call her his niece; while Mrs. Ludford, not able to conquer the envy and malignity of her narrow and selfish heart, could no farther command herself than to refrain from treating Ethelinde with her usual haughty asperity. Still, however, she affected for her contemptuous pity, more difficult either to be borne or repelled than actual rudeness. She spoke to her with that kind of forced condescension with which the rich and prosperous frequently chuse, under the semblance of goodness, to insult those who, having been once equal or superior, are by some caprice of fortune thrown accidently below them in pecuniary circumstances. Mr. Harcourt, who was exactly that kind of man to whose lively sensibility, and generous attention to the feelings of another, such behaviour was calculated to disgust and even render uneasy, grew towards the hour of tea extremely restless. The whole day had been to him a day of tortures: but they were not yet at an end: Miss Clarinthia had somehow contrived to introduce a long sentimental discourse on friendship and fine feelings, which at length her mother thus interrupted, Ethelinde having for a moment left the room.

"Yes, Clarinthia, my dear; you have indeed very excellent notions of friendship. I bless God I have always brought you up not to consider so much the difference of people's stations as their merit: and your regard for my niece, poor thing, is a proof of it. It were to be wished indeed poor Ethy had been more lucky in the world: however, Providence you see, Mr. Harcourt, has raised her up friends, and I hope, poor thing! she will do well."

To Harcourt, this canting jargon would have been altogether unintelligible, had he not understood from Ethelinde, the situation in which her father died, and from his observation on the manners of the family she was now with, conceived the utmost dislike to them, and regret that she was compelled a moment longer to be obliged to them.

When Mrs. Ludford, therefore, concluded her last speech, all his complaisance prevented him not from casting on her a look of mingled disdain and anger.—"You hope Miss Chesterville will do well, Madam? doubt it not. If the most exalted, the most unaffected merit, entitles its possessor to good fortune, who has so just a claim? On the caprice of fortune, however, she will now no longer depend: for her brother will have property which will enable him to secure to her such a provision as she deserves, and till his arrival it shall be my care, that she feel none of the inconveniences to which she has hitherto I fear been too much exposed."

"If Ethelinde has complained of her *sitiation*, Sir," said Mrs. Ludford, colouring, "she is, I must say, very ungrateful. I have treated her like my own child, though she knows very well that she never would accept my invitation while any other of her relations would receive her. I overlooked it because she was my niece, and an orphan, poor thing; but otherwise it must be owned that it was rather grating to think that my own sister's daughter should prefer other people. For my part, Mr. Harcourt, I am sure I would not say a word for the world to prejudice you against her. No, very far from it; but this I must say——"

Ill health, misfortune, and a long habit of seeing all around him obedient to his commands, had given to the temper of Harcourt a degree of asperity and impatience, when people he disliked thwarted or fatigued him; and he now could not forbear interrupting the eloquent harangue, by which Mrs. Ludford seemed disposed to display her own goodness, with—"Dear Madam, excuse me; I *can* hear nothing that can prejudice me against Miss Chesterville; my opinion of her is fixed for ever. It is very possible that you have been very kind to her; but allow me to say, that in my mind you derive more honour from such a niece than any other circumstance either of situation or fortune. A stranger cannot behold her with indifference. What then ought to be the effect of such perfection on the hearts of those who are so happy as to be her relations."

This speech silenced the two ladies for a moment, while they tried to conquer the spleen it excited; and Harcourt dreading the arrival of Ludford and his son, who were summoned to tea, took the opportunity afforded by this interval to rise, and wishing them a good night, he hastened away.

"There!" cried the elder lady, as soon as he was gone; "there! This is the return I get for my generosity. Proud of *her* indeed! Yes to be sure; I wonder for what?"

"Of her beauty, Mama," cried Clarinthia, with a laugh forced to conceal a disposition to cry. "Don't you see that her beauty is the thing. Mr. Harcourt, dismal and deplorable as he is, is not so old but what Miss has known how to throw out her lure for him. If she had not been a beauty, we should have heard neither his fine praises nor his fine promises."

"What do you mean," exclaimed Mrs. Ludford. "You don't suppose surely that Mr. Harcourt would marry such a girl as Ethy. Besides, is she not engaged to that fellow, that young Scotchman that is gone on a wildgoose chase to *Ingee*?"

"Well, what signifies that? He may never come back, you know, or if he does, his complaining will signify nothing when his uncle has carried away his fair one. Oh! you don't know, Mama, indeed you don't, the deceit some people are capable of. I am sure I had once a very different opinion of Ethelinde, but some late circumstances have convinced me that the sympathetic tenderness of my own heart has again deceived me. Yet I wish her well, I am sure; and if she does marry this rich West Indian, I heartily hope she will be very happy."

"She shall not, I am determined she shall not marry Mr. Harcourt. Am I not her nearest relation? and shall I suffer such a thing? no, I'll take care——"

"Well; but, dear Ma'am, consider Sir Edward Newenden only has power over her. He is her guardian; and if you suspect any such thing, had you not better write to him. He is much belied, you know, if he has not some interest in keeping her single."

While these ladies were thus canvassing the future possible advantages of Ethelinde, and wishing to counteract them, she was writing the letters which had been agreed upon between her and Mr. Harcourt to Montgomery and her brother; and sending forth impatient wishes for the return of Mrs. Montgomery. Three or four days, however, wore away, before the welcome letter arrived which informed her that she was in London, and anxiously expected her lovely young friend to join her there, and accompany her to Grasmere.

Mr. Harcourt and Ethelinde now lost not a moment in preparing for their departure; while Mrs. Ludford, mingling the bitterest sarcasms with affected kindness, was compelled to see her niece withdrawn from her ostentatious protection, and Clarinthia felt at once relieved by the absence of one whose superior attractions threatened a diminution of that admiration she desired to monopolize; and mortified by believing that her hitherto indigent and dependent cousin would be enabled to move in a sphere superior even to her own.

Ethelinde took leave of them with her usual sweetness, and thanked them with as much grateful sensibility as if she had never had reason to complain of their reluctant and sometimes insulting good offices. Harcourt was much relieved by the certainty of his sister's safe arrival; and though he was still languid and low, the tears which he shed were those which the warmth of reviving hope draws from an heart, that has long felt only the cold apathy of torpid despair.

Their journey was rapidly performed; but a few miles before they reached London, Ethelinde concerted with her fellow traveller a little plan to prevent Mrs. Montgomery's being too much surprised by the sight of a brother from whom she had been so many years divided.

On their arrival in Portland-street, as it was summer, and not more than six o'clock, Mrs. Montgomery, who expected Ethelinde with impatient solicitude, came down herself to the door on hearing the chaise stop. Ethelinde, springing out, was immediately in her arms, and they went together into the parlour, where she endeavoured to recover her emotion enough to announce Mr. Harcourt without doing it abruptly; but the pale and altered figure of her friend, the faded yet interesting likeness to that face ever strongly present to her imagination, had struck her with a variety of sensations so painful, that she was entirely without power to do it; and Mrs. Montgomery perceiving something unusual in her manner, was alarmed by an idea, ever too forward to present itself to her anxious heart, that some unfavourable accounts had been received of the vessel in which Montgomery was embarked. "You know nothing of Charles?" said she, fixing her penetrating eyes on those of Ethelinde with a look of uneasy enquiry—"Have accounts been received of the ship's touching at Madeira?[1] Have any accounts come——" She stopped, as if hardly daring to ask more. "Alas! no!" replied Ethelinde, who caught her alarm instantly; "why do you ask? Surely you have heard nothing? Has there been any report of——"

"I hope not," replied Mrs. Montgomery: "but I thought by your

1 A Portuguese archipelago in the north Atlantic ocean, north of Teneriffe, the Canary Islands.

looks that you had something to relate. I am too easily alarmed. God knows how I, who cannot a moment take my thoughts from my son, shall be able to endure the long long exile to which he is condemned. Ah! Ethelinde, should he do otherwise than well, how shall I regret having consented to, and even advised his voyage. I feel however that if that should happen, my anguish, though it must last to the end of my life, will be of short continuance." Overwhelmed by tenderness and sorrow, Mrs. Montgomery now gave way to a flood of tears; but Ethelinde, while she accompanied her, acquired courage to say—"My dear Madam, you guessed truly that I had something to relate; but my intelligence is such as to give you only pleasure."

"Relates it to my son then?"

"Not immediately to him: but you have other relations—other friends—of whose health and arrival in England you would certainly rejoice to hear."

"Other relations! Alas no! I *had* indeed a brother; but it is now long since I heard from him. He is, if not dead, lost to me. Another climate, other connections, a different mode of life, have obliterated from his mind the memory of his country, and that affection for his sister which he never had indeed many opportunities of indulging."

Ethelinde then informed her that the brother whom she supposed had forgotten her, was at that moment waiting impatiently at her door. The joy and surprise of this intelligence almost deprived Mrs. Montgomery of her recollection: nor were the feeble spirits of Mr. Harcourt less agitated in embracing a sister whom he had not seen for so many years. As soon as they became a little more composed, Harcourt would have entered on his own melancholy history and have spoken of his son;—a subject from which his thoughts were never long detached. But Ethelinde, who knew how ill he could sustain the recollection of circumstances so painful, and how distressing the recital would be to the harrassed mind of Mrs. Montgomery, prevailed upon him to leave it to her to inform his sister of all those particulars of which she was ignorant: and at length saw them separate for the night with more composure than she had supposed they could have known after the tumultuous and painful pleasure of a meeting so unexpected.

CHAPTER VIII

Early the next morning Ethelinde attended at the bed side of Mrs. Montgomery, related to her the circumstances by which Mr. Harcourt became deprived of his children, and sought in Victorine and Montgomery heirs to his immense possessions. The tears which the distress of her brother drew from her, were mingled with those of the deepest regret for the departure of her son; which she now accused herself of having rashly precipitated. She attempted with her usual firmness of mind to check the excessive pain this idea gave her; but Ethelinde saw it through all her endeavours to stifle it; she saw with astonishment that it took every moment stronger possession of her mind, and that something like a presentiment of evil hung heavily on her spirits, which neither her reason, nor her reliance on heaven, could enable her to shake off. She said indeed but little; and sought to excuse her tears and her dejection by the part she took in the deep concern and declining health of her brother: but Ethelinde, who from the fears that possessed her own heart was too well enabled to judge of those that corroded the heart of Mrs. Montgomery, found that the strength of mind which had in so many trials supported her, sunk entirely before the fearful idea of having sent her son from her to return no more; and that the affluence which was now assured to her, far from giving her any satisfaction, was rendered not only tasteless but painful, since it had arrived too late to save her from a sacrifice which she now perpetually accused herself of having needlessly made.

Her mind, relieved from the necessity of any attention to pecuniary matters, had leisure to dwell incessantly on that one object; and her imagination, warm and tender, was perpetually employed in representing every mode by which misfortune might reach the dear object of her solicitude, of whom she now hardly ever spoke without tears; and to think on whom without interruption she would frequently shut herself up for many hours in darkness, being at times unable to bear even the company of Ethelinde, which had been once so soothing to her; or to hear the sighs of her brother, whose cureless sorrows for an only son seemed to represent those she was so soon to experience. In about a week this melancholy party set out for Grasmere; where Mrs. Montgomery languished to be: and whither Mr. Harcourt was glad to accompany her, to await what he could not yet expect for some months, the arrival of Victorine and her husband. Ethelinde, oppressed as she was by her fears for Montgomery, which his mother's dreadful despondence rendered so terrible to her, was compelled to exert herself to direct every thing for their journey and to support them on their way: for Mr. Harcourt's health became every day more uncertain; and the mind of his sister seemed in the pain of incertitude to have lost at once all its vigour; she could no longer bestow any attention on the common business of life; and on more material points, if Harcourt ever consulted her, she would declare herself incapable giving any advice. "If Charles was here," she would say, "he would do every thing. If Charles was in England, you, my brother, would have the best and most active agent. But he, perhaps, may revisit England no more!" The private and various uneasiness which Harcourt felt, and the pressure of bodily infirmity, was increased by observing this sickly despondence obscure the elevated mind of his sister: but his own spirit, broken by sorrow and pain, could make no successful effort to chear her; and without the gentle and incessant attentions of Ethelinde they would both have sunk under their sufferings before it was possible for any of those persons to arrive who occasioned their solicitude.

Ethelinde gave herself up to the melancholy but not unpleasing task with equal heroism and tenderness. Harcourt was often so ill as to make an attendant necessary both night and day; and while he became so habituated to her assistance that he would receive his medicines from no other hand, she was, for many nights, when his complaints recurred with great violence, obliged to watch by his bed side, not without frequent fears that the deep melancholy into which Mrs. Montgomery had fallen, would be rendered incurable by the accumulated sorrow that the death of her brother would inflict. From his chamber, it was her daily occupation, during five or six weeks that he lay dangerously ill, to go to that of Mrs. Montgomery, (who, when he was worse, had not courage to visit him,) to represent his situation in the most favourable light, and to chear her spirits with hopes of good news from India: and this she often executed with a frame exhausted with fatigue, and all that sickness of the heart which arises from hope long delayed. When both Mrs. Montgomery and her brother were in more supportable health, she read to them whole days, and found that books alone were capable of detaching their thoughts a moment from their anxieties. This redoubled her zeal, and lightened her fatigue; and if at any time she found her spirits sinking, she remembered that she was the sole dependence of Montgomery's mother and uncle, and from that reflection she acquired new courage. Thus past the months of September, October, and November: Chesterville and his wife had been gone ever since February: the letters which Mr. Harcourt and Ethelinde had dispatched to them in June, had probably reached them at Jamaica in August; and if, as it was most likely, they directly took shipping to return, they might now be in London. But the month of December and part of January elapsed, before a letter from Chesterville, dated at Portsmouth, informed Mr. Harcourt (who had desired him to direct to his merchant in London, who now forwarded the letter,) that he was landed in England, with Victorine, and a little boy, of whom she had been delivered before they embarked.

This welcome intelligence seemed to give new life to Mr. Harcourt. He pressed his sister and Ethelinde to accompany him instantly to London. But Mrs. Montgomery, though she sincerely shared his felicity, could not determine to be present at a meeting with would serve only to remind her of that which she so much more ardently desired, and Ethelinde, however rejoicing in the good fortune of her brother, would on no account leave her. Mr. Harcourt therefore departed alone for London, where he met his daughter with emotions of mingled pain and pleasure so violent, as threatened to shatter his weakened frame to its dissolution. The transition from that indigence which had been relieved only by the friendly interposition of Sir Edward Newenden, to affluence exceeding his most sanguine hopes, had, on the warm unsteady temper of Chesterville, an intoxicating effect. Harcourt, pleased with his figure, his vivacity, and that air of fashion which bespoke him at once well born and well educated, saw none of his faults; and the beauty and sprightly simplicity of his daughter inspired him with the tenderest sensations of paternal fondness. He thought he could never do enough to make up to her the long neglect he had been guilty of, nor be grateful enough to Chesterville for having snatched her from precarious poverty and mortifying dependance. He took therefore an house for them in Portland Place,[1] which he furnished in a superb taste, purchased for Victorine carriages, cloaths, and jewels; and he delighted to contemplate her thus adorned, and to trace in her lovely figure, and animated countenance, the resemblance to her mother, whom he had once fondly loved, and with whose premature death he frequently reproached himself. He beheld Chesterville with almost equal regard. That mixture of thoughtlessness and spirit, the easy gaiety which the difficulties he had encountered had not diminished, and which while it became his age and figure, did not appear to lessen the susceptibility of his heart, was sufficient to secure him Harcourt's attachment; but when with so many outward perfections, he considered him as having loved and rescued Victorine, this regard arose to infatuation, which even the errors that he could not long conceal were insufficient for some time to cure; for even those errors were converted into perfections by the transmuting power of that partiality which Harcourt had conceived for him; and tho' his expences soon exceeded the ample sum which his father-in-law had assigned to his use, they were considered only as instances of proper spirit and commendable pride, which made him very naturally desirous of returning into that rank of life wherein he had a right to appear, while at the same time he did honour to his benefactor.

Victorine, as thoughtless and lively as her husband, entered with all the avidity of her age and character into scenes which from their novelty became irresistibly attractive. Her youth, her beauty, her utter ignorance of the world, and the foreign accent that added a peculiar charm to the simplicity of her conversation, drew round her a multitude of admirers. She was pleased with their flattery, and being naturally a coquet, encouraged it; while her female acquaintance made at random, and consisting chiefly of young married women as volatile as herself, were but little calculated to check her giddy career. For the first two or three months her father rather encouraged than repressed that rage for amusement, which kept her at her toilet till dinner, in company from that time till five or six the next morning, and invisible to him till the dinner of the

1 An unusually wide, very fashionable and expensive street laid out in the later 18th century London Marylebone district.

following day. Towards spring, however, he had another severe attack of the bilious complaint which had so soften reduced him to the brink of the grave: and then it was that he missed the sympathizing softness of Ethelinde. His daughter indeed loved him, and enquired tenderly after him two or three times a day; but his only constant nurse was an old housekeeper, who consulted her own ease much more than the alleviation of his infirmities; who would frequently busy herself in putting his apartment to rights when he was disposed to sleep, and who, when he lay restless and in pain, was much oftener snoring in her chair than attentive to the means of his relief; so, that the fatigue of awakening her being more than he could encounter, he sometimes missed his medicines; and sometime became so low, from this defection of Victorine, that when he did take them, they lost their efficacy.

Chesterville had by this time been initiated anew into those scenes where he had formerly been so great a sufferer. He was now less a dupe; but their effects on his morals and his temper were more likely to be permanent. He played with greater caution; but the love of play took faster hold of his heart. He plunged into expences which he knew Harcourt's fortune could support him in: but by degrees the love of money, or rather of those luxuries and indulgences which nothing but the possession of it could secure him, blunted his feelings. He had not yet seen his sister since his return to England. He had talked indeed frequently of going down to Grasmere, since she could not be prevailed upon to come to London; but something or other always happened to delay his journey.—The weather was dreadful; or Victorine had made an engagement; or Mr. Harcourt was ill:—and by degrees he grew weary of excuses; losing, with the inclination to see his sister, even the wish to conceal his neglect and unkindness by plausible pretences: and with all the outward appearance of a man of the very first ton, he gradually acquired the callous and selfish insensibilty which are supposed too often to accompany boundless prosperity and uncontrouled gratification. Ethelinde, who knew her brother too well, had dreaded this relapse: and her suspicion that all her fears were realized, increased when, after many evasions of his long promised visit, Chesterville at length informed her, in the only letter he had written to her for two months, that it would be impossible for him to see her for some time, unless she could resolve to come to London; for that Mr. Harcourt, who was now somewhat recovered of a tedious illness, had determined to go as soon as he was well enough to the seat he had purchased in Worcestershire, where he had never yet been; and that they should be established there for the rest of the year. The whole letter was cold, and Ethelinde thought haughty and boasting.—It spoke of improvements and expensive alterations intended to be made at this superb place: and mentioned eight or ten thousand pounds which Mr. Harcourt intended to expend in enlarging a piece of water, and removing a hill that intercepted the view of it from the house: and he added—"You see, dear sister, how difficult it will be for me to find time for a journey into the north this summer; and I wish you could make it convenient to come to us, and that Mrs. Montgomery could accompany you: a wish in which my wife very sincerely joins with, dear Ethy, your's affectionately, though in great haste,

H. CHESTERVILLE."

Over this letter, which Ethelinde would not shew to Mrs. Montgomery, she shed the bitterest tears which had fallen from her eyes since the death of her father. In all her other trials—in the comfortless society of the Woolastons, and vulgar insults of the Ludfords—in her own indigent circumstances—even in the absence of the man she adored—there was something not unpleasing mingled with her sorrow—But here, in the neglect and ingratitude of her brother—of him whom she had so tenderly loved—for whom she had unrepiningly suffered—there was anguish, to the endurance of which her resolution was quite unequal. She saw in his behaviour to her more than neglect—she saw, with great reluctance, that while he could not well avoid giving her a cold and barely civil invitation, it was not his intention she should accept it. He had discovered that Mr. Harcourt's fortune, splendid as it was, was not at all more than he should himself have occasion for: and he did not wish that Montgomery, of whom his uncle spoke with great affection; or Ethelinde, whom he professed to love as well as his own daughter; or Mrs. Montgomery; should possess a large or indeed any share of what he so well knew how to dispose of. But lately, conscious of this narrow principle himself, he had not been able to disguise it even in the short letter he wrote to this sister; both so rapid and irresistible is the progress of selfish avarice when once it seizes on the human heart, that Ethelinde had hardly received the letter, sooner than Chesterville had persuaded himself of the justice of what he desired.—"What claim," cried he, as he argued the matter with himself—"what claim has Montgomery to any part of Harcourt's fortune? he is only the son of his half sister, and certainly ought not to deprive my wife of any share of her inheritance. Besides, 'tis ten to one if ever he returns from the East Indies. As to his mother, what use has an old woman for money: if Harcourt gives her a little decent annuity it is quite enough. As to Ethy indeed, I should be glad to be sure to have her properly provided for; and if Harcourt has a mind to make her a present of a thousand or fifteen hundred pounds it may not be amiss; but as she intends to mope away her life in that out of the way place with Montgomery's mother, I see no sort of use in her having more; and I cannot think it otherwise than an unjust robbery of my son, who has surely the best right to all his grandfather has, that I do not want: besides, I may have a large family, and 'twill be hard to have that money given to others which ought to be a provision for my younger children."

Thus urged the man, who had only a few months before received his sister's jewels, and disposed of them for his support; who had been obliged to Montgomery for his maintenance while in prison; and who now frequently hazarded, at games of chance, more than four times the sum which he thought a sufficient provision for that sister; and too much for that generous disinterested friend, of whose death he thought with indifference, and whose unwearied friendship he had forgotten.

Ethelinde, while she felt and deplored in silence this cruel change in the heart of her brother, made no effort to counteract the effect his artifice had on Mr. Harcourt. She knew that he had given his sister on their first meeting three Bank bills of a thousand pounds each, to make up, he told her, at once, her loss in France. This sum Mrs. Montgomery had immediately laid out in the stocks; and it made Ethelinde easy as to her future support. If Montgomery returned even without fortune, it was enough to secure them all competence in that retirement which every hour endeared to her; if he returned successful, they should have more than they wanted; and if he never returned—an idea which too often forced itself on her trembling heart—if he never returned —of what use would be the riches of the world to his mother or to herself.

Ethelinde therefore suffered her brother and his wife to proceed in monopolizing entirely the present favour and the future fortune of Mr. Harcourt. Mr. Harcourt himself, however, relinquished less willingly the delight which, from their first interview, he had received from the company of his sister and her fair friend; and as soon as he arrived at his house in Worcestershire, he wrote pressingly to them to come to him. But Mrs. Montgomery, whose health anxiety had cruelly shaken, could not determine to quit the tranquil scenes of Grasmere for the tumultuous abode of gaiety and splendour; for such Victorine, unconscious of his motives, had, at Chesterville's desire, described Mr. Harcourt's house to be in her letters to Ethelinde. The improvements that were in progress, the amusements she partook, and the variety of company she saw, she described with as much vivacity as she enjoyed them; narratives which Ethelinde read with pity and concern, and from which the sick heart of Mrs. Montgomery recoiled with distaste.

Very differently did *they* pass those days, which, fond as they were of each other and of the solitude they inhabited, would have passed in serene satisfaction, had not every one in its progress been embittered with anxiety. At length however they were rendered comparatively happy, by receiving letters from Montgomery that he was arrived at Bengal. But, grateful as his mother was to heaven for this intelligence, the idea of the fearful distance between them, and the dangers to which (since Mr. Harcourt's return) she had needlessly permitted him to be exposed, hung heavy on her heart; and Ethelinde had often occasion to shew an appearance of confidence and courage she was far from feeling, to sustain the spirits of her venerable and beloved friend.

CHAPTER IX

While Ethelinde was watching over the declining health, and soothing the painful solicitude of Mrs. Montgomery, many weeks passed—not indeed happily, but in that state of satisfaction which the consciousness of doing her duty, of acquitting herself towards heaven and earth, has alone power to bestow. This resigned and chearful confidence was confirmed, when other letters were received form Montgomery.—These gave an account of his health having received less injury from the climate than is common to Europeans during the their first abode in it: the letter to his mother was particularly chearful, and its perusal gave her at first more plea- sure than her heart had, since his departure, been capable of feel- ing; but after she began to study it, as she did for many days, all her anxiety returned, though not to so painful an excess. She reflected that eight months had passed since that letter was written; and her tenderness made her so ingenious in tormenting herself, that she was perpetually considering all the circumstances which might have since that period have occurred to retard or prevent his return. It was still worse when she read his letter to Ethelinde. The ardour of his affection for her, had rendered him less capable of dissim- ulation; and forgetting the probability there was that his mother would see his letters, he related the disasters of his voyage, which had been tedious and unhealthy; and there appeared a languor and despondence in the style, a dread of being separated form her for ever, which he could not disguise. Of his actual situation he said, that it might be extremely lucrative to some other man: but that he had found it so impossible with his principles and his feelings to fill it, that he had solicited and obtained a removal to a distant settlement; where his knowledge of languages would be of great service to the company, and whither he should go in a few weeks from the date of his letter. He spoke in his letter to his mother of the same intention, but to her he described it as a matter of choice and of probable advantage. Now however it appeared, not only as removing him farther from her, and making it much longer before the letters of recall which she had sent out would reach him; but as a measure to which he was compelled by the unpleasantness of that situation which had been so differently described to him; and magnifying all her apprehensions, she soon relapsed into the depressing anxiety from which the first perusal of these letters had roused her.

Ethelinde, tender and timid as she was, was yet so much tranquillized by having good accounts of his health, and so gratified by those expressions of unalterable, and if possible of increased attachment with which his letters were filled, that her

heart seemed again open to the lively impressions of hope; and
the future appeared to her in softer colors. Spring was not far
advanced, and the season contributed to soothe her mind and to
aid her representation of future happiness, when Montgomery
should return; and relieving her from every sorrow and solicitude,
give to the beautiful scenes of Grasmere their greatest charm.

Every spot about the cottage was endeared to her by some recollection of him.—The row of laurels in the court, he had himself planted when he first came thither with his mother; they were
now large trees; and beyond them, next the water, was a weeping willow, under which he had been used to sit with a book, on
a bench he had made himself. Several drawings he had done of
rocks and little pieces of scenery about the lake, hung in the parlour; and over his mother's chair was a picture of him painted in
France when he was a boy. On these memorials Ethelinde had
with melancholy pleasure gazed during the long winter; now
she looked at them with renewed sensations of hope and delight.
Montgomery was well; his love was undiminished; his absence,
now no longer necessary, was likely to terminate many years
sooner than her most sanguine expectations had represented.
She thought with delight on the moment when she should give
him an account of the manner in which she had passed her time
since his departure: in attending on his beloved mother; in perfect-
ing herself in those accomplishments he delighted in; in studying the books he loved; and as she was dressing, she beheld, with
conscious satisfaction, a face and figure which had lost none of
their charms during his absence. When any apprehension of accidents or delays occurred to her, she repulsed and stifled them as
much as possible, and endeavoured to impart some portion of her
own confidence and hope to the bosom of Mrs. Montgomery;
for whom she not only felt as being the mother of her lover, but
with the same tenderness as if she had been her own. *She* seemed
indeed to have filled that vacancy in her soft heart which the loss
of her father had left; but time diminished nothing of that filial
tenderness with which she had loved him, and now cherished
his memory. Towards the middle of May she received from her
brother, who now very seldom wrote, a cold letter in answer to
several of her's. He seemed out of humour, without knowing, or
at least being willing to own, why he was so: he named the per-

petual ill health of Mr. Harcourt in a way that Ethelinde thought unfeeling, and added, "his idea is now to have Mrs. Montgomery and you with him at Clare Park this summer.—You may do as you please, but trust me you will find it far from pleasant." Ethelinde felt hurt, not only by the general coldness of the letter, but by the desire it expressed to keep her and Mrs. Montgomery at a distance from Mr. Harcourt. A confused idea of his motives mingled itself with her reflections.—"Is it possible," said she, "that Harry can suppose our presence could be prejudicial to him?—Surely he cannot harbour of me—of Mrs. Montgomery—any suspicions that we are capable of injuring his interest, even if it were in our power!—I will rather suppose that the reluctance, which, however distantly expressed, is evident enough, arises from consciousness that he has again embarked in indiscreet expences. He fears I may remonstrate with him; he loves not to hear advice; solicitous only to forget the past that he may enjoy the present; he would evade the representations of his sister who remembers too much of one, to enter with equal avidity into the pleasures offered by the other; and who may, he thinks, disturb his gaiety by setting before him what he is so desirous of recollecting no longer." A few posts after the receipt of this letter, Mrs. Montgomery received one from Mr. Harcourt, which ran thus—

Portland Place, May 17, 17—

"What can be the reason, my dear sister, that I hear so seldom from you, and that, since the letter which informed me of the favourable intelligence you have received of our dear Charles I have not had one line from you or from Ethelinde. While you fondly count the moments that are yet to elapse before you can embrace your son, do not forget, dear Caroline, that you have a brother equally anxious for the arrival of that fortunate period; and who has, alas! no son of his own. Mrs. Chesterville is desirous of staying in London some time longer—she must be indulged. Of Mr. Chesterville, I of late see so little that I cannot say much; —he is I know as fond of London as my daughter is, at this gay season; but my health and my inclination equally urge me to go immediately into Worcestershire. Contrive, I beg of you, to meet me there. Change of scene will benefit your health; nothing can be of so great advantage to mine, as your's and Ethelinde's company;

nothing else indeed has power to mitigate the pains of body and mind which are frequently to be endured your ever affectionate

W. HARCOURT."

To this letter Ethelinde prevailed on Mrs. Montgomery to give an answer of assent. They had no business in London; and therefore fixing their departure at the distance of a week, when they knew Mr. Harcourt would be in Worcestershire, they joined him there by slow journies. Ethelinde left Grasmere with regret, but still in the delightful hope of revisiting it soon with Montgomery. The journey afforded her pleasure, from the novelty of the scenes it presented to her: she saw with satisfaction that Mrs. Montgomery's thoughts, though never to be diverted from their principal object, took a more chearful turn; and though after her arrival at Clare Park, she declined being much in company, she became more chearful than she had been for many months before. There were yet very few families in the neighbourhood, as it was the season when London was full of attractions; but, in the company of his sister and of Ethelinde, Mr. Harcourt found new reason to delight in the tranquillity which was, in the absence of Chesterville and Victorine, restored to his house.

Chesterville was very little pleased with the party who were now so well pleased with each other; but he was too deeply immersed in the pursuit of those pleasures which London only afforded, to prevail upon himself to quit it in order to counteract the influence he apprehended. He was politic enough therefore to affect content he was far from feeling; and Victorine, inattentive to every thing but amusement, considered very little about her father; or when she thought of him, rather rejoiced that the company of Mrs. Montgomery and Ethelinde would preclude the necessity of her early attendance on him in the country. Her child, of whom he was extremely fond, was with him, and that she thought sufficient security against any other partiality. The natural tenderness of Ethelinde's heart made her also much attached to the little boy, and gave her new character, new charms, in the eyes of Harcourt; who could not reflect without pain on the different disposition of Victorine. Whenever he involuntarily made this comparison, he instantly reverted to his own conduct; and asked himself whether the faults of Victorine were not rather owing to his former neglect of her, than to her natural disposition; and, while he blamed his own former errors, he endeavoured to excuse those in the present conduct of his daughter, to which could he not be blind, while the endearing manners of Ethelinde perpetually reminded him of a contrast so mortifying.

In every soothing attention to him and to his sister, in the practice of every virtue and the cultivation of every talent that gives dignity and lustre to the female character, Ethelinde passed in retirement near three months, before Chesterville and his wife came into the country. Her walks, though solitary, were not unpleasing; for the image of Montgomery was ever present to her, and the sanguine hope of his return soothed and tranquillized her mind.

But this calm was at an end when, in the month of August, Chesterville and Victorine came down. He could not live an hour without company, play, and the highest luxuries of the table: she had no other pleasure in coming into the country, than that which she was to derive from the splendour they were to exhibit before the neighbouring families; who no sooner heard of their arrival, than they began a round of dinners, in which, all, whether they could afford it or not, emulated the luxury and magnificence of Clare Park. Mrs. Montgomery had been reconciled to her long absence from her beloved cottage by seeing how much her brother was gratified by her abode with him; but now she became very anxious to return to it; for though she usually declined appearing in company, the whole style of the house was become unpleasing to her; and she saw with silent concern that Mr. Harcourt was rendered unhappy by a manner of life which he yet wanted resolution to break through.

Ethelinde was yet more unhappy than either of them: for, in addition to the desultory, confused, and generally disagreeable society, which broke in upon her time and fatigued her with pertness and insipidity, she had occasion to remark, almost on their first interview, the strange alteration which prosperity had made in her brother. He was now no longer the gay and amiable, though thoughtless Chesterville, who was at once blamed and beloved:— but his manners partook of the change that had happened in his heart. The ambition which was now a leading feature in his character, had irritated rather than checked that love of play that had before been so fatal to him: but it had taught him caution, reserve, and artifice. He had of late passed all his time between the cabals of party, and the vigils of the gaming-house; and his vivacity and his feeling had vanished together. Hardness and carelessness of manner had succeeded; and though he was still on his guard before Mr. Harcourt, he no longer took any pains to conceal from the rest of the world, the sentiments he had adopted, or the life he pre-ferred. Amid all his former errors, Ethelinde had ever depended on the natural goodness and rectitude of his heart; and fondly hoped, that his innate generosity and tenderness would finally conquer the defects of his character: but when she found him become proud, reserved, and ungrateful, avaricious, ambitious, and osten-tatious; valuing himself on his birth, which never before seemed to have been considered enough, and displeased at every expence Mr. Harcourt engaged in, which contributed nothing to the grati-fication of his vanity, Ethelinde could deceive herself no more, and was convinced too certainly that she had no longer a brother. Among the people of high fashion, with whom only he was accus-tomed to live, Ethelinde heard him, with some surprise, mention Lord Hawkhurst.

"Of whom do you speak, Harry?" enquired she: "of my father's brother?"

"Certainly," replied he. "I know no other of the name."

"And you have often seen his Lordship?"

"Very often. He and the family are coming to his house in this country in a few days, in order to be near us the rest of the summer. We are to be a good deal together."

Ethelinde, however unwilling to mortify him, could not help saying gravely—"You have forgotten then, or at least forgiven the offence you once took, when you thought that Lord Hawkhurst neglected my father and insulted me."

"Oh, as to that," replied he coldly,—"it was merely misrepre-sentation; what could he do, you know, for other people when he has so large a family of his own.—That is, you know—that among people of a certain rank—in short, it is impossible that in a certain style of life the same attention can be given to relations as mid-dling folks can give, who may have, perhaps, nothing else to do."

"Not if the relations of these people in a certain style are dis-tressed," replied Ethelinde.—"But in affluence, in prosperity,

there is no occasion to remind them of the ties of blood.—Lord
Hawkhurst could forsake and neglect his brother in penury; in
the confines of a prison; but to his nephew, possessed of Mr. Harcourt's income, Lord Hawkhurst feels himself related."

"Natural enough," said Chesterville carelessly.—"It is the way
of the world, child, and if you are determined to quarrel with
every body who does the same, you had better return again to
Grasmere, for you will hardly find elsewhere any such sentimental
folks as you seem to desire."

"I wish I was at Grasmere," sighed Ethelinde, her eyes filling
with tears, "or rather with that beloved parent, who, but for such
detestable doctrine, might still have been alive."

"*Vous etes la Maitresse Madame*,"[1] cried Chesterville, yawning.

This was rather too much; the gentleness of Ethelinde gave
way to a moment of indignation she could not suppress.—"Good
God! Mr. Chesterville," cried she, "is it thus you receive the mention of a father—of such a father—whose death——"

"Lookye, sister," interrupted he very abruptly, "I have now
the means of being happy, and happy I am determined to make
myself. What is the use of croaking over past troubles? 'twill mend
nothing; and now they are over, why should we think about them?
Come, have done whimpering, child, and go dress yourself for
dinner. Some Frenchman, Voltaire, is it not, says, '*que les maux ne
sont bon que pour oublier*.'[2] Faith I am quite of his mind; and of that
of some other honest fellow, a poet of our own, I forget who, who
says—

> "Curst by no slavish rules, our wisest plan
> Is sure—to be as happy as we can."[3]

1 In modern English: "You are your own mistress" becomes "you can do what
you please" or it's your choice, it's up to you.
2 The only thing to do with evil is dismiss it from your mind. This is my free
translation, to indicate how Chesterville is reading the passage he identifies
with Voltaire. It does not seem to be by Voltaire.
3 Horace was in the era identified with a complacent contentment whose
standard text is that of Pomfret's "The Choice" (1700); these lines come from
an imitation of Horace (Book 2, Satire 6) as translated by Edward Burnaby and
Mr. Fawkes, found in *The Works of Horace in English Verse*, by J. Duncombe et
al., 2nd edition, London 1767, Vol. 3, p. 209). Chesterville is making twisted use
of the fable of the town and country mouse; see Pope's ironic translation in his
Imitations of Horace, III: vi.

Believe me, Ethy, a pretty woman, (and upon my soul you are sometimes divinely handsome) a pretty woman never mistakes her interest more than when she affects to be wise and sententious. If you would but be a little ridiculous, put on a good deal of rouge, and talk a reasonable quantity of nonsense, I should not doubt seeing you so much the fashion that you might form some high connection."

"I have no such ambition, Sir," said Ethelinde; "surely among other things that you have suddenly forgotten, are your obligations and my affection for the generous——(he is not indeed rich, and therefore I must not perhaps call him your friend)—the generous, noble minded Montgomery."

"No upon my soul I have a great regard for Montgomery; I have faith; but what good does it do, you know, to a fellow so many thousand miles off, and who, perhaps, may never come back. I'll answer for it he thinks but little of this violent affection that you fancy you have for him. Upon my life, Ethy, I wish you happy, and therefore I wish you could get this whining romantic nonsense out of your head about inviolable friendship and everlasting love: stuff that you have picked up from the novels and story books you are eternally reading. In real life such *things are not*.[1] Why now only consider for a moment how excessively silly you will look, if after pining and peaking away twelve or fourteen years of your best looking days in the hopes of the dear youth's return to fulfil his vows, he imports an Asiatic wife and half a dozen little yellow children; you of course will die of despair; *c'est la regle*,[2] you know: and so poor Charles, who of course thinks you have more sense than to wait for such distant contingencies, will be hurt and unhappy, and all that, perhaps for the rest of his life."

This image, however ludicrously represented, was insupportable. Ethelinde, incapable of answering, rose and left the room: and her brother, careless of the pain he had thus wantonly

1 A sarcastic allusion to typical subtitles of reformist works, perhaps particularly to Elizabeth Inchbald's *Such Things Are* (1787). Chesterville would not have sympathized with such reformist perspectives; later "jacobin" novels (the term is a modern critical one) sometimes had similar titles: Robert Bage's *Man as He Is* (1792); *Hermsprong, or Man as He Is Not*, or Godwin's *Things as They Are; or The Adventures of Caleb Williams* (1796)

2 It's the rule. Chesterville means "this is the way things work in the world."

inflicted, went out at another door, humming a tune, and calling to his gentleman to attend him in his dressing room.

Ethelinde, after this dialogue, avoided as much as possible being alone with her brother, which was by no means difficult; for before he and Victorine were visible in a morning, she had usually made breakfast for Mrs. Montgomery and Mr. Harcourt, had read to them for three or four hours, and had retired to her music or her books.

Chesterville rose late, and then drove or rode out for the rest of the morning, returned only time enough to dress for dinner, at which he had generally company; and as soon as coffee was over, play filled up the interval, till supper, at three or four in the morning, broke up the tables.

Discontent and disappointment preyed on the health and spirits of Mr. Harcourt; and their effect was the more severe, because his tenderness for his daughter prevented his remonstrating with her or her husband. His fortune was so ample that their expences, great as they were, had not yet hurt it. He was content that they should expend his income; and when he felt himself disposed to murmur at the little consideration they seemed to have for him in the manner of their doing it, he still endeavoured to repress his dissatisfaction, and to persuade himself it was unreasonable that two young people, who possessed all the advantages of nature and fortune, should submit to that confined manner of life, which misfortune and ill health had rendered desirable to his sister and himself.

Mrs. Montgomery saw, but was too generous and too considerate to notice or encourage, uneasiness which could only be productive of a coolness, perhaps of a breach between him and his children: she endeavoured, therefore, to divert his attention from the scenes of dissipation that passed in one part of the house by forming a little society in the other, where, under the pretence of being herself indisposed, her brother might, in her apartment, enjoy his own amusements and his own hours.

CHAPTER X

The family of Lord Hawkhurst was now arrived at Abersley, the seat of his ancestors, an old but magnificent house of about ten miles from the seat of Mr. Harcourt. They sent immediately to enquire after the family at Clare Park; and his Lordship, in a very affectionate letter to his nephew, expressed a wish that, among persons so nearly related, all ceremony might be waved; and proposed with Lady Hawkhurst and his daughters to have the honor of dining with Mr. Harcourt the following Thursday.

Chesterville, who, well born as he was, had lately acquired a passion for nobility, and had learned to value himself on his descent, was pleased with this letter; and Mr. Harcourt, desirous of shewing every attention to the uncle of Victorine's husband, desired him to express his pleasure at the proposal, and to give orders for such an entertainment as would do honor to the fortune of the visited and the rank of the visitors.

Thus commissioned, Chesterville failed not to acquit himself well. Every delicacy that money could purchase was procured in profusion. The superb service of plate; the elegant decorations of the table: the numerous attendants, and fashionable luxuries that were displayed; all served to impress on his guests the conviction of Harcourt's boundless fortune, which in London was less exhibited and less remarked.

Mrs. Montgomery, conquering on this occasion her reluctance to mix with company, sat at table, of which Victorine did the honours; and Ethelinde, more beautiful than ever, took her seat below, the youngest of the Lady Chesterville's; who all affected to be highly gratified by thus meeting her, though so few months had passed since they neglected and slandered her.

Lady Hawkhurst, however, though she now studiously concealed it, was not less sensible of the pain she had always felt in being compelled internally to acknowledge the superiority her personal charms had over those by which she hoped her daughters would long since have obtained affluent establishments. None of them were yet married. By a change of ministry her Lord had lost his places; and his fortune was so conditioned as to leave it little in his power to provide for his daughters in a manner suitable to their rank. It had been the study of her Ladyship's life to get them well married; but in this important object she had hitherto failed, probably from the ill judged avidity with which she pursued it.

The day passed with all that unmeaning politeness which so ill supplies the place of confidence and affection. Harcourt exerted himself as much as he could; Mrs. Montgomery had ever all the ease and unaffected elegance of real fashion. The young ladies were sprightly and talkative, and conversed with Victorine on what they had seen and done in London after she had left it; and Lady Hawkhurst dropped the usual haughty superiority of her manner for a sort of fawning politeness, extremely disgusting to Mrs. Montgomery and Ethelinde, but such as her Ladyship thought exactly calculated to impress the whole company with ideas of her goodness and condescension; while Lord Hawkhurst addressed himself principally to Mr. Harcourt; and among many encomiums on his generosity to his dear nephew, he spared not to speak of that dear nephew in very high terms, to talk very much at large of the family interest, and to propose bringing him into parliament for one of his own boroughs. Chesterville was now no longer the giddy unfortunate boy, of whom he never augured any good; but his dear Harry, his only nephew, the second hope of his family. Ethelinde, who, except her brother, was alone sensible of this extraordinary change, could hardly repress the dislike and contempt that she felt. She was civil, however, but silent; and heartily rejoiced when the whole party, after inviting Mr. Harcourt, and all his family to dinner the following week, returned home. Lady Hawkhurst was no sooner seated in her coach, and driven from the door, than she thus began—"Either this Mr. Harcourt has a mine, or he is a madman. Pray, my Lord, does he always make the figure he did to-day?"

"Yes, I believe so," replied Lord Hawkhurst; "and why should he not? he has a very great fortune."

"So I always understood, but I had no idea *how* great a fortune. I figured to myself too that he was an old man; why he is yet in the middle of life."

"About three and forty, I believe; though ill health and a residence in a hot climate, make him, I think, look older than he is."

"And pray, my Lord, what do you judge his fortune really to be?"

"The estate in this country is a good four thousand five hundred a year after all deductions. He had made, I understand, a very advantageous purchase in Staffordshire of upwards of three. He has a very great estate still in Jamaica, and I have been credibly informed not less than sixty thousand pounds in the funds."

"And will your nephew, will Chesterville be possessed of all this?"

"I suppose so; yes certainly, unless he married again."

A silence of some minutes ensued. "Unless he marries again," repeated Lady Hawkhurst to herself; "and why should he not? What a match for Lady Belle or Lady Helen. What signifies age? besides he is not so old." From this moment, the idea that it was possible to bring this about, took such strong possession of her Ladyship's imagination that she could think of nothing else. "Four thousand five hundred a year here; three more in Staffordshire; as much again in Jamaica, and sixty thousand pounds in the funds!" repeated she, as she was undressing; "and all to go to a natural daughter, that little black Spanish girl, while my daughters may drag out their lives in the honourable indigence of necessitous nobility, and live all together pining on a poor four or five hundred a year, with a job coach,[1] two maids and a footman."

"I have been thinking, my Lord," said she to her husband the next morning, as she made tea for him in her dressing room, "I have been thinking what a pity it is that Mr. Harcourt does not marry again. He is an agreeable man—I really think him very agreeable; and what a fortune! I declare I should not be sorry to hear he had taken a fancy to Lady Arabella."

"Nor I, I give you my honor, Madam. I wonder, that anxious as you justly are on that point, it never occurred to you before."

"Why I had fancied him an old decrepid creature; and as to his fortune, I never imagined it so splendid."

"Well, Madam, since you now see him and his fortune in another light, try what can be done to make him look upon either of your daughters as a desirable party for him: but let me give you one piece of advice; the girls have lost two or three very good matches, and I suspect that you don't fish with art enough; before the prey is well hooked you draw your line. Excuse me; you understand the terms of angling; the artificial fly will not do here; it must be a ground bait;[2] and remember that it is the interest of so many to spoil your sport, that you must have all your eyes about you."

1 A coach which you rent as you need it.
2 She must begin slowly: ground bait is bait thrown to the bottom (the ground) of whatever water you are fishing in to attract fish to the site in the first place.

"Pooh! my Lord, I am serious."

"I give you my honour, Madame, so am I; perfectly serious; and therefore Lady Hawkhurst it is that I bid you beware of Mrs. Montgomery, of Chesterville and his little hawk-eyed wife, and above all of my demure, but very pretty, and as I suspect, very sly niece Ethelinde."

"Surely you don't think she has the same plan herself?"

"No; she is said to be engaged, you know, to young Montgomery; but there is no—I say, Madam, there is no knowing—money —money, Lady Hawkhurst, does every thing in this world." This polite and noble couple soon after parted; and her Ladyship retiring to her *boudoir*,[1] sat down to consider how she should open the campaign against the heart of poor Harcourt, in whose park and house, plate, jewels, equipage, and fortune, she saw so many charms.

Lady Arabella, brought up to consider a great establishment as the only good worthy of her ambition, and now in her twenty fifth year, had seen, not without much severe mortification, many of her acquaintance who had, she thought, no better pretensions than herself, disposed of to men of fortune. The mercenary maxims in which she had been educated made her entirely indifferent as to the accomplishments of the person she might marry; and Mr. Harcourt's fortune being adequate to her expectation, she readily entered into the plan her mother suggested, and became immediately, in consequence of this arrangement, so extremely attached to Victorine and Ethelinde, that she could not resist the pleasure of visiting them twice on horseback before the day when they were to meet again; and contrived so adroitly to flatter Victorine, that she became quite charmed with her company, and much of her thoughts and conversation dwelt on the good humour, vivacity, elegance, and fashion of Lady Belle.

The day at length arrived when the family at Clare Park were to fulfil their engagement at Abersley. Mrs. Montgomery, who really was ill, was allowed to decline going. Ethelinde felt the necessity of her attendance, and however reluctantly, was obliged to comply; but she was now going to visit for the first time the paternal seat of her ancestors—the place where her father had passed his youth, and which she had often heard him describe with

1 A lady's private sitting room.

that melancholy delight which a sensible mind feels in recalling the scenes of those gay hopes and early enjoyments that return no more. To this house, his profession, and the coolness which had, in consequence of his marriage, long alienated him from his brother, had occasioned him to be many years a stranger. He had often expressed to his daughter a wish to revisit it with her; and now! she was, by a chain of unexpected events, to go thither—not as a daughter of the family, but as a mere visitor; and to recall the image of her father only to recollect that he was in his coffin in the neighbouring church; which, like many of those in remote counties, yet adjoined the old family mansion of the Chestervilles.

With spirits extremely depressed, Ethelinde sat out.[1] They were not raised by observing the careless indifference of her brother, who, occupied entirely by present plans and pleasures, seemed not to have the least recollection of the circumstance that so deeply affected his sister. Their noble hosts received the whole party with expression of civility bordering on adulation. Lady Hawkhurst addressed herself with marked attention to Mr. Harcourt: she placed him next to herself; conversed with him about his improvements, which she highly commended; softened her voice when she enquired about his illness, and asked with all the affectation of tender solicitude what advice he had had, and from what medicines and regimen he found most benefit? Harcourt, utterly unconscious of the meaning of all this solicitude, answered her enquiries and cajoleries with the air of a man who felt himself obliged, and fatigued by well meant but irksome civilities. At length the tedious dinner ended, and by the ladies retiring he was released.

Lady Hawkhurst left the young ladies for a few moments; and then, as the Lady Chestervilles and Victorine had nearly exhausted the topics that were common between them, one of them proposed going to the billiard room till tea time; to which Victorine assented: but Ethelinde, whose melancholy reflections unfitted her for play or conversation, begged to be excused; and when she saw them engaged she left them, and walked along through the spacious apartments and galleries of the house. At the end of a gallery she came into a room that seemed to have been forsaken by the family. It had received no alteration for many years; and was darkened by cedar wainscoting and rich arras, on which hung

1 To stay to the end of something extremely unpleasant.

several family pictures. She was struck instantly with that of her father, in the uniform of his regiment while an ensign. The likeness was so strong, that it gave her instantly the idea of him as she remembered him: it seemed to look pensively upon her, while she gazed at it with indescribable emotion and melted into tears.

It was the second week in September; the sun was already sunk amid deep red clouds, and the little light he yet lent, was lessened by a rookery of elms which were between that part of the house and the church yard. The long old fashioned windows in ponderous frames, admitted the twilight reluctantly, while the tapestry hangings, and curtains of purple mixed damask, gave to the whole room, every part of which retained its ancient massy magnificence, that gloom and obscurity which inspired and encouraged the most melancholy thoughts. Ethelinde remained gazing on the picture of her father till the canvas no longer received any rays of light; but her tears still flowed, though the object that had excited them faded in surrounding darkness. When she could distinguish his features no longer, she slowly moved towards one of the windows and turned her eyes toward the spot where the form, which was there represented in youth and health, was mouldering into dust.

Beyond the chancel of the church, and appearing indistinctly through the trees, a kind of mausoleum was erected over the family vault. The imagination of Ethelinde had by the sudden sight of this picture powerfully recalled the recollection of her father, and now, while she fixed her eyes on his monument, ran over the scenes which passed immediately before his death; the tenderness he had shown for his son even at the moment he was precipitated to the grave by his ill conduct; his fond attachment to her; and the charge he had given in her behalf to that brother who now seemed to have forgotten it all;—and contrasting with this mournful remembrance those scenes she every day saw, with the coldness, ingratitude and profusion, to which she was a reluctant witness; and with her own deserted and dependant situation; she fell at length from the slow languor of sorrow into an agony of tears; and uttering aloud an apostrophe to her father, she invoked his tender and benign spirit to soothe and console her.

Suddenly a gust of wind rushed through the long gallery which divided these apartments from those where she had left the company; and the door, which had not been quite closed, heavily opened before it. Ethelinde shuddered. "He hears me," cried she; "surely he hears me, and comes from his grave to meet me!" Her reason a moment checked the idea; but fancy, so long busied in restoring his countenance, his voice, and gesture, had already the superiority. She looked fearfully towards the slowly opening door, and she figured to herself her father standing there and beckoning to her to follow him. She stepped forward from the window as if she would have sprung towards the phantom she had thus raised; but without feeling what impeded her, she fell suddenly on her knees, and losing all powers of action and recollection, she remained in that posture with her head leaning against the gilt iron work of a large marble table that was between the windows. There she would probably have remained, for she seemed to be totally forgotten by the rest of the company, if a violent storm, of which the sudden gust of wind had been the forerunner, had not shaken the whole building. The housekeeper came round the rooms to see if the windows were shut against the torrents of rain which were falling. She had a candle in her hand; but on entering the room, she saw a figure in white kneeling between the windows, and without giving herself time to think of any thing but the stories of ghosts and apparitions, with which the servants in old and seldom inhabited houses, delight to terrify each other, she let the candle fall, and hastened back in great terror to her own room.

Fear now possessed the other servants; to whom she related, that by a flash of lightning she had seen a spirit in the north drawing room. This end of the house, from its being little used by the family, and so near the church yard, had always the reputation of being haunted. After a few moments of debate, it was agreed that her own footman should communicate this singular circumstance to Lady Hawkhurst, for Mrs. Perkins declared that for her own part she was too nervous and ill to stir out of her chair for all the world; and she questioned if ever she should be her right self again as long as she lived. While hartshorn, therefore, and drops were applied by the female servants, the footman marched up to his lady, looking behind him at every step; and entering the room where her Ladyship was with Victorine and her daughters, he informed her in a whisper that Mrs. Perkins was taken in fits from having seen a spirit in the north apartment.

Sensible of very little fear from the inhabitants of this world, Lady Hawkhurst was still less apprehensive of those of another. "Seen a spirit?" cried she, indignantly; "seen a fool! What does the ridiculous old woman mean?"

"Indeed, my Lady," replied the man, "I don't know; but to be certain she is very much frighted, and there is not one of the maids as will go to that side of the house, tho' it rains so, and many of the windows, my Lady, are open."

"Go then, and shut them yourself," cried her Ladyship, "and trouble me no more with such supreme folly." The man, quite as fearful as the old housekeeper herself, now stood aghast, till Lady Hawkhurst, who, after a moment's pause, found more to laugh than to be offended at, took a candle herself, and desiring Victorine and her daughters to follow her, she went to the room, where Ethelinde, the cause of all this alarm, was found on the floor. Lady Hawkhurst, on speaking to her, was surprised to find her almost senseless; they raised her, however, and placed her on a sopha; where, after some time, she was able only to say, that she believed a flash of lightning had struck her down, (which was really the case) that she was suddenly sensible of giddiness and stupor, as if she had received a violent blow; and though she appeared not to have sustained any injury from fire, her eyes were much affected, and her head still greatly confused. She was still so faint and ill that it was impossible for her to return to Clare Park that night; Lady Hawkhurst, therefore, had her put to bed; and it was proposed to Mr. Harcourt that he also should stay, as Chesterville and Victorine had before agreed to do, the former being engaged to go on a shooting party with his uncle; but Harcourt, who knew Mrs. Montgomery would be much alarmed, and who on account of his ill health was unwilling to sleep out of his own house, declined staying, notwithstanding the pressing instances of Lady Hawkhurst, and the gentleness with which Lady Belle besought him to consider the length of his journey in weather so unfavourable. He visited Ethelinde before his departure; and though he had been at first very much alarmed at the strange accident that had befallen her, he left her in less uneasiness, as she spoke to him calmly, and assured him that from whatever cause so sudden an indisposition had arisen, it was not likely to be of any consequence; but that she should probably be well enough to accompany him home the next morning, when he promised to return early to fetch her.

When he was gone, however, and when Ethelinde had prevailed
on the youngest of the Lady Chestervilles to leave her, the idea of
having seen her father recurred again to her mind with all its force;
and far from thinking of it with terror, she cherished the soothing
melancholy it impressed. "He came not," said she, "to alarm and
terrify, but to soothe and console me. To give me, perhaps, inti-
mation of some approaching calamity, or to strengthen my mind
against present regret." Untinctured with any shade of supersti-
tion as her mind was, it yet received with avidity an impression
soothing to that tenderness with which she cherished the memory
of her father, and insensibly sleep stole upon her, which, though it
shut not out the images that had employed her waking thoughts,
refreshed and relieved her; and at a very early hour in the morning
she awoke, feeling little or no remains of the giddiness and stupor
which she had been so sensible of the preceding evening, and just
in that state, when she thought a quiet walk would entirely restore
her.

She arose therefore, and dressing herself in a morning gown
and cap, with which her cousins had accommodated her, she went
down stairs. All the inhabitants of the house were yet in their beds,
and on going out, she found only a labourer mowing the grass, by
whom she was directed through a shrubbery to the church yard, as
she desired more nearly to view the place.

"Where all her buried ancestors were pack'd."[1]

Sitting down on a rustic and half ruined tomb, she contemplated
with mournful pleasure the picturesque appearance it made
adjoining the church, which was very antique, and its narrow windows half hid by mantles of ivy; while from among the mouldering buttresses young ash trees waved their light leaves, and the
fern, and the wall flower, with variety of lichens and mosses, were
scattered about the broken grey stone of the roof, and among
the inequality of the arches and windows. A group of yew and

1 *Romeo and Juliet*, IV: 3, 41: "where all my buried ancestors are pack'd." Ethelinde is likened to Juliet: both look at the vaults where their family corpses lie.
This kind of scene, the heroine returning to a grave of her father, is found in
later 18th and early 19th century sentimental and gothic novels, e.g., Sophie
Cottin's *Amélie Mansfield*.

cypress, relieved with their spiry forms, the more solid and regular mass of stone which composed the mausoleum; and beyond the church, as well as on one side of it, an extensive wood of very ancient elms formed a dark and magnificent back ground, and was the habitation of innumerable rooks, who, with owls and daws that had found dwellings about the church itself, mingled their cries at this early hour of the morning, with the wind, murmuring hollow among the ruinous building and surrounding trees.

CHAPTER XI

After a pensive ramble of above two hours, Ethelinde returned to the house. Only the inferior servants were yet risen; and Ethelinde, having in vain wandered over several rooms in search of a book, to amuse her in the long interval she yet had to pass before breakfast, was at length shewn by one of the house maids into a small dressing room, where the young ladies were accustomed to sit in a morning, and where the servant assured her there were variety of books. Books, however, there were none, but two or three novels which Ethelinde had already read; but under the harpsichord were several French news papers scattered among the music books which lay there. Ethelinde took them to read, and seeing, in one of those of the latest date, East India news, it immediately caught her attention.

It contained an account brought by a French ship to Bordeaux which had touched at the Mauritias, and said, that a few weeks before an English vessel in its passage from Calcutta to Madrass, had been driven by a tornado out of her course, and after beating about many weeks without being able to regain it, had, after suffering every inconvenience of famine and fatigue, at length approached so near the harbour on the Isle of Bourbon, that they were in hopes of gaining it:[1] but in consequence of a squall of wind

1 Mauritias is Mauritius, an island in the Indian ocean, southeast of Africa; Calcutta, now Kolkata, is capital port of West Bengal, principal city of East India; Madrass is Madras, nowadays Chennai, a capital port city off the Bay of Bengal, southeast Asia; the Isle of Bourbon (first taken by the French) is now Réunion, an island in the Indian Ocean east of Madagascar, and was an important stopover for East India trade. The economic perspective of *Ethelinde* has global reach.

which overtook them, they were violently driven towards a rocky part of the coast beyond; and the sailors and passengers, enfeebled by famine and fatigue, had many of them perished, while only a few reached the shore to relate their complicated disasters.

This detail, heightened by many circumstances of horror, extremely affected Ethelinde, though it related the calamity of persons who were, as she supposed, strangers to her. What then was the agony of her mind, when in a list of about half a dozen names of persons who were passengers, she saw that of Montgomery among those who were lost.

The paper fell from her trembling hand. The room seemed to turn round with her. She no longer wept; she was incapable of weeping; but heartstruck, she seemed deprived, by the shock, of all power of reflection of enquiry. When she could breathe, which was not for some minutes, she again took up the paper, and again the fatal paragraph appeared. The remembrance of what Montgomery had said of his intended departure to another settlement, rushed then upon her mind, and instantly confirmed the probability of this dreadful account.

She would have given the world at that moment to have had somebody near her to whom she could communicate this fearful intelligence, in hopes of their bringing arguments to render this truth doubtful; but had any of the family been visible, they knew not Montgomery, and were little of a disposition to embarrass themselves about the fate of a stranger. Ethelinde had seen too many instances of their inattention to the calamities of others, even where they could have assuaged those calamities, not to be very certain that she should fatigue them by complaints, without obtaining any of that patient pity of which her sick heart stood so much in need. Her brother was the only person to whom she could apply on such a topic; and while she traversed the room with trembling steps, listening to hear if his voice was distinguishable in the hall; now attempting to lessen her terrors by recollecting how often false reports arise, and her soul now sinking under the dread that it might be true; she felt a secondary apprehension in remembering how little her brother had of late seemed to think of his absent friend, and in doubting whether, occupied as he now continually was in pleasures and pursuits of his own, she should even from him meet with tenderness and sympathy.

The circumstances of the preceding evening, the heavy presentiment of impending evil which she in vain had endeavoured to throw off, all seemed to form to her oppressed and alarmed imagination, a kind of internal evidence of the truth of this fatal intelligence, and amid undescribable wretchedness, she passed near two hours before a servant came to inform her that breakfast was ready.

With a countenance so much affected by the pain she endured that it gave her the appearance of having recently arisen from the bed of sickness, she followed the servant down, and entered a room where gaiety was visible even to extravagance. The young ladies were tittering at something which was a secret to every body but themselves and Victorine; Lady Hawkhurst was entertaining, with a flow of eloquence peculiarly her own, one of the visitors who were with them; the other and Chesterville were listening to his Lordship relating a bon mot of his own on some election matters, at which, as was expected of them, both his auditors immoderately laughed. On the entrance of Ethelinde, whose heart sunk still more at the sound of mirth so discordant to her feelings, each of the party enquired in the usual way after her, and expressed satisfaction at seeing her well enough to come down to breakfast, but none of them observed or were enough interested in her looks to remark the eyes, filled with expressive concern, nor the pale and trembling lips with which she returned their compliments.

Breakfast over, Chesterville, who was going out to shoot with his uncle, rose to leave the room. Ethelinde then acquired courage to say—"Brother, may I speak with you before you go?"

"Ha," replied he, "to be sure you may; but make haste, Ethy, because you see my Lord waits for me." He then withdrew to a window. Ethelinde wished he would quit the room, but however followed him, and said, taking the French paper from her pocket —"Here is a newspaper which has almost killed me; read it, and you will not wonder at my terror and concern."

"A newspaper! what about?" He took it, however, and hastily ran over the sentence she pointed out. "Oh!" cried he, when he had read it, "'tis not worth while, child, to make yourself uneasy about this: there are a hundred people of the name, I dare say, in that part of the world. Never fret about it, because it is a thousand to one if it is Charles; and if it should be, your teazing yourself will be of no manner of use. Hang the paper; I wish it had been burnt. Depend upon it, however, that it is not authentic. Do not be frightened about it; and I would advise you neither to think of it yourself, or to speak of it to Mr. Harcourt or Mrs. Montgomery. We shall have nothing but boring conjectures and lamentation; and after all, I dare swear there's not a word of truth in it."

Then with an air which made it too evident that he cared not whether there was or no, so long as his own enjoyments were not flattened or impeded by being obliged to affect concern he did not feel, he turned away; and apologizing to Lord Hawkhurst for having detained him, he left the room. Little reason as Ethelinde lately had to expect tenderness and feeling from her brother, she was quite overwhelmed by his new instance of his careless ingratitude. She would have gone back to her room, there to indulge her tears; but after an attempt to cross that where she was, she sat down in the first chair she reached, and fell into an agony of tears.

This immediately drew towards her the attention of Lady Hawkhurst, the young ladies, and Victorine, who, with more eagerness than interest, enquired what was the matter. She might easily have imputed her tears to the effect of what had happened to her the evening before; but she was in no condition to reflect on consequences, and pointing to Victorine the account which had so alarmed her, she besought in broken accents the younger of her cousins to assist her to her room.

When she was gone, Victorine read the paragraph, and explained to the ladies who remained, the engagements between Ethelinde and her cousin Montgomery. She spoke of his loss, as she really felt it, with concern that dissolved her also in tears; while Lady Hawkhurst, shrewd, discerning, and ever alive to what might promote her favourite views, saw, after a moment's consideration, all the advantages which the grand project she now had in hand might derive from this circumstance. Harcourt was every moment expected. The probability that he had lost his nephew, for whom he had told her he destined a large share of his fortune, made her success at once more probable and more desirable; and the tender sympathy which Lady Belle might express, would open to his imagination a compensation for present grief in the future society of so tender hearted and amiable a young woman.

Struck with these ideas and totally regardless of the pain she might inflict either on Ethelinde or the object of her experiment, she began in flowing accents to lament the unhappy catastrophe, of which she would suffer nobody to raise the least doubt. Her affected concern redoubled the sobs of Victorine; and Lady Belle, who perfectly understood her part, saw Mr. Harcourt's carriage drive up to the door, and was drowned immediately in such tears as a good actress can with little effort produce.

Harcourt was shewn into the room by the servant, but stopped at the door in amaze and concern, for he saw his daughter leaning against Lady Helen in an agony of sorrow, while Lady Hawkhurst held salts to her nose; and on the other side of the room her eldest daughter reclined her head on a table, and seemed equally overwhelmed with grief.

"Good God!" exclaimed Harcourt, "what has happened? Victorine are you ill? is Ethelinde worse? Where is she? I beseech you keep me not in suspence!"

"Oh, Sir! oh, Mr. Harcourt!" exclaimed Lady Hawkhurst, in a theatrical tone, "how shall we relate a circumstance which has truly pierced all our hearts!"

"Speak for God's sake," cried Harcourt impatiently; "speak; is Ethelinde living and well?"

Lady Belle, who thought she could now appear to advantage, rose with an affectation of weakness; and approaching Harcourt, she held with one hand her handkerchief to her eyes, and laid the other gently on his arm—"Dear Sir," cried she, "be patient. Ethelinde, my lovely, my beloved cousin is well, and will, I hope—I sincerely hope, survive the severest blow a sensible heart can feel; that of losing the dear object of its tenderness!" As if this idea was too terrible, she now retreated, and sat down; while Harcourt, more and more astonished and terrified, could only in an hurried and inarticulate way again implore them all to explain themselves. This at length Lady Hawkhurst did; and Harcourt, trembling as he read the paper which she put into his hands, grew extremely sick when he had finished it, and said in a voice hardly audible—"It is, I fear, too true. So fade for ever all my fond hopes from that quarter! Oh! my poor sister!"

The change in his countenance now gave an opportunity to Lady Hawkhurst to insist on his swallowing a cordial she brought him, which Lady Belle presented with her own hand, and sighing as she did it, cried—"Why does fate thus persecute the amiable and worthy! I am told that the dear friend you lament was every thing that can delight the eye or charm the heart of woman."

"He was more, Madam," said Harcourt; "he was all that a parent could ask of heaven; the pride of his family, of his country, and of human nature."

"Like *you* too in his figure," interrupted Lady Hawkhurst. "Oh! Heaven, what a cruel blow!"

Harcourt was unfitted to return the compliments they intended him; he was indeed hardly conscious of where he was, but sat silent and motionless, till Victorine, whose concern was real, approached him—"Look not so distressed my dear father," cried she, as she threw her arms round him. He pressed her to his breast; and bursting into tears, felt himself so much relieved that he was able to rise and ask leave to retire with her for few moments into another room.

At the door, however, he met Ethelinde, who had passed the short time she had been absent in a very different manner. She had called off her thoughts a moment from herself to the mother and uncle of Montgomery; and in feeling with such poignancy her own anxious terrors, forgot not those which would overwhelm them, and probably be fatal to one or both. Her genuine love for *him*, made all he had loved doubly dear to her in that moment of distress; and she had determined, however difficult and painful the effect might be, to conceal from them the anguish that preyed on her spirits, at least till confirmation of the mournful news made dissimulation impossible.

But though she had collected fortitude enough to descend with some composure to receive Mr. Harcourt, it vanished at once, when on meeting him she saw expressed in his countenance that he had already learned all she wished to conceal from him. It struck her immediately that he had had it authenticated by some other means; and the faint hope which had hitherto supported her van-ishing at once, her spirits could contend no longer; a mortal pale-ness was on her face; her eyes closed; and she would have fallen on the ground, had he not stepped towards her and supported her to a chair. It was, however, some minutes before she recovered, and many more before he could convince her that he knew noth-ing of Montgomery but what he had learned of the ladies who had received him. This conviction seemed a little to relieve her; and as it was still possible to keep the circumstance a secret from Mrs. Montgomery, Ethelinde again summoned her resolution, and taking the drops and other remedies which Lady Hawkhurst liberally administered, she found herself at the end of about half an hour well enough to desire Mr. Harcourt would hasten their departure. Lady Hawkhurst urged him with equal earnestness to stay, and her eldest daughter, in a tender tone, besought him not to venture out while he was yet so affected. Ethelinde, however, who doubted every moment whether her resolution to appear calm before Mrs. Montgomery would not give way, was very solicitous to have their meeting over. Victorine now desired to return with him, though she had proposed staying some days at Abersley; but to this Ethelinde objected, not only because it might appear singular to Mrs. Montgomery, who knew of her intended absence, but because she really much doubted of Victorine's discretion. Victorine, whose feelings were rather lively than deep, easily acquiesced, and after a great deal of exclamation and cajolerie from Lady Hawkhurst, and a few more tears from the fine eyes of Lady Belle, Mr. Harcourt and Ethelinde were suffered to depart.

As they went, Harcourt, though never very sanguine, and though his mind was still under all the agitation of concern, yet endeavoured to soothe and console his fair companion by suggesting all the possibilities there were that the news they had received was unfounded. He perfectly agreed with her in the necessity there was for keeping it a secret from Mrs. Montgomery; and she now rather rejoiced that he himself knew it, since she could find the relief of speaking to him on a subject that must weigh so dreadfully on her heart; and since she saw, that while he considered his sister's tranquillity, he checked the darker fears to which he was naturally inclined to yield, and endeavoured to flatter himself that his nephew still lived.

Ethelinde, however, engrossed by one predominant concern, could not, as she passed over the events of the morning in her mind, help remarking the behaviour of Lady Hawkhurst and her eldest daughter. She knew their general character so well, and had, even in the little she had seen of them, so often observed their coolness and insensibility to the misfortunes of others, and the inattention and even disgust which they discovered when any distressing or melancholy object was presented to their minds, that she could not help being surprised at the extraordinary interest they seemed to take in the reported misfortune of Montgomery, to whom they were strangers, and at the great attention they shewed Mr. Harcourt. A confused notion of their real motive occurred to Ethelinde, but other contemplations prevented her thinking steadily of any matter less interesting, and her more immediate anxiety was to appear before Mrs. Montgomery with fortitude and apparent chearfulness. When they met, however, Mrs. Montgomery was struck with the change she saw in her, and remarked it with great concern; but Ethelinde assuring her that it was merely the consequence of the violent head ache and giddiness that had been occasioned by her accident of the preceding evening, she at length became easier; and Ethelinde, whose exertion was too painful to be long supported, hastened to her own room.

On the table she found a letter from Sir Edward Newenden. She expected only the usual remittance which, since Mr. Harcourt's arrival, she had earnestly entreated him not to send; but as he still continued to do it, she concluded this packet contained it. Her conjecture was true; but her concern and regret found a new object, in reading the following letter.

Naples, July 18, 17—

The crisis of your unfortunate friend's fate is at length arrived; and the disgrace which he has endured so much to ward off from his children, has fallen upon them. Lady Newenden is gone with Lord Danesforte, and now nothing remains for me but to return to England, and do what I ought long since to have done. Mr. and Mrs. Maltravers (the former of whom I sincerely pity) are already on their return to England with my two younger children. I shall follow them with Edward in a few days. The conduct of Lady Newenden will soon be so publicly known, that it is as unnecessary as painful for me to dwell on it to you. For myself, I am too certainly very wretched; but I have infinite consolation in reflecting that I endeavoured to save her, and that I deserved to succeed. Freed, therefore, from all self reproach, I can encounter with firmness the uneasy task before me. The ensuing winter will disengage me from an unhappy woman, whom I still think of with pity, and the rest of my life must be dedicated to those beloved children who

are not less dear to me than if their mother had deserved my affection. May I not say, my lovely friend, that I have also much soothing consolation in expecting from *you* that gentle pity which only
friendship can give to my sick heart; and which, pure and angelic as
it is, your happy Montgomery will himself allow you to bestow, on
your unfortunate and faithful

E. NEWENDEN."

The uneasiness of Ethelinde was greatly encreased by this intelligence. It seemed as if calamity was ever to overwhelm, in some
form or other, those she most loved, and who most merited her
affection. She passed some hours alone in the most melancholy
reflections. Mrs. Montgomery then sent up to beg to see her; and
she wiped the tears from her eyes, and endeavoured to hide the
traces of that anguish which preyed on her spirits. The letter, however, of Sir Edward Newenden, it was necessary to communicate
to her friend; and to her friendship and concern for him, the uneasiness which Ethelinde found it impossible wholly to disguise, was
in a great measure imputed.

When she was alone with Mrs. Montgomery, the part she was
obliged to sustain was rendered sometimes almost insupportable by continual conversation about Montgomery; who, as he
occupied all his mother's thoughts, engrossed also her discourse.
Sometimes desponding and representing every thing that might
happen to him in the most melancholy light, she accused herself
of rashness and folly for having promoted his voyage; at other
times she seemed to wish to be shewn more agreeable visions, and
to have the great probability of his return represented to her: while
she indulged herself in dwelling on the transports with which she
should embrace him; the happiness which would crown her latter
days in seeing him united to Ethelinde; and how much the close of
her life, amidst a family of his, would repay her for all her sufferings through many years of affliction.

When visions so enchanting possessed her imagination, Ethelinde, who grew every day more convinced of their fallacy, found
all her resolution giving way before the shocking idea of a mother
thus flattering herself with fond hopes of happiness with him
who was already gone for ever; dwelling with pride and exultation on those virtues which had long since received their reward

in heaven; and tenderly tracing on her mind the changes which
time and climate might have made on that form and those features
which were notwithstanding

> "Perhaps under the 'whelming tide
>   Visiting the bottom of the monstrous world."[1]

Still, whatever it cost her, Ethelinde guarded carefully against
betraying what she felt on hearing this conversation. But the effort
was too great to be sustained long without a visible alteration in
her health. Her only relief was the melancholy resource of talking
about Montgomery with Mr. Harcourt, who had written to every
quarter from which information was likely to be obtained, and
who now awaited answers with the most painful impatience. But
in this she seldom dared indulge herself lest it should raise suspicion; and opportunities every day became more rare; for Lord and
Lady Hawkhurst and their family had obtained such a footing, that
they seemed to form only one society with the inhabitants of Clare
Park. Chesterville, always out on parties, had not yet discovered
the motive of his uncle's extraordinary attachment to Mr. Harcourt, and Victorine was too little acquainted with the arts of such
a woman as Lady Hawkhurst to guess at all what she was about:
but Ethelinde, though she gave up the greatest part of her time
to Mrs. Montgomery, saw enough to convince her of the nature
of her Ladyship's views; and she saw too, not without uneasiness
on behalf of her brother, that Harcourt was much more sensible
of their attention than on their first acquaintance: and when they
were alone, he sometimes spoke of Lady Arabella in terms which
made her apprehend it very likely that he might be brought, by no
very slow degrees, to console himself for his former misfortunes
by a second marriage. Lady Belle wore no rouge; she had taken
quite a grave and retired turn; talked only of domestic comforts
and the pleasure of improving such a beautiful place as Clare
Park; expressed virtuous disgust at the dissipation and abandoned
morals of modern young men; and declared that happiness in
her idea consisted in living in elegant retirement, with a man of
sense, who had passed the summer of life and whose mind was

---

1 Milton, *Lycidas*, lines 157-158: "Where thou perhaps under the whelming
tide / Visit'st the bottom of the monstrous world."

softened and refined by that knowledge of the world which too often hardens and corrupts it: and when she had drawn a picture of Mr. Harcourt, she would look at him tenderly, sigh deeply and then, as if conscious of what she had done, leave the room in confusion. Her person was fine, and her manners very insinuating; and Ethelinde every day beheld the progress she made in the heart of Harcourt—an heart, which feeling every hour more severely the vacancy made in it by the death of his son, by his daughter's dissipated turn, which made her incapable of filling it or returning his affection, and now by the too probable loss of his nephew, naturally sought some other object on which to repose; and could hardly fail of being flattered in believing he had met that object in the form of an handsome and amiable woman. His fortune was so large that he thought he might marry without injustice to his daughter, on whose child he proposed making very large settlements; and to this idea he by degrees familiarized his mind, till he determined to consult his sister and Ethelinde on it; for on their advice, judgment, and disinterested affection, he had such reliance that he would take no step of such consequence as that of opening his intentions to Lord Hawkhurst till he had consulted them. The first opportunity, therefore, that he had of being alone with Ethelinde he took occasion to complain of the continual absence of Chesterville, and his enormous expences—"I would not pain *you*, my dearest Ethelinde, for the world: but in very truth, my fortune, large as it is, must soon be considerably injured, and I am sure you think that were I to suffer this to go on I should be guilty of great injustice to little Harry, to his mother, and to myself; to say nothing of my sister and of our beloved Montgomery, who, as I will still hope, may yet return to us."

"Certainly," replied Ethelinde, "I do think so; and I have often regretted the incurable passion which my brother seems to have for expensive pleasures."

"'Tis less," continued Harcourt, "what comes usually under the denomination of pleasures that I regret, than his constant attendance at gaming tables; of which, though pains have been taken to conceal it from me, I am well informed. I know, that notwithstanding the large sums with which he has been supplied by my order, he has raised money by those methods which have been fatal to so many young men. I own this information has made me very uneasy; nor does it indeed much contribute to my comfort to see the avidity with which Victorine enters into a style of life as injurious to her as displeasing to me. I am often ill; I expected in her to find a nurse, who, from love and gratitude, would have delighted to attend me. I am often low spirited, and oppressed with that sort of melancholy which the soft and consoling voice of affection can alone remove. Does my daughter attend or console me? Alas no! She is either out on some party of pleasure or surrounded at home by giddy creatures like herself, and idle young men, who would ridicule any attention she shewed to her father; yet she has not a bad heart; she does not want feeling; and Chesterville might have rendered her as lovely in her mind as her person."

Ethelinde assented to this; and then Harcourt proceeded to tell her that ill health made a London residence so unfit for him that he had resolved to remain in the country; that Mrs. Montgomery having declined taking her residence wholly with him, he should then be left quite alone; and in short that he had very serious thoughts of marrying Lady Belle Chesterville; as he believed, that notwithstanding her high birth and education, she had all that composure of mind and all those sentiments which would render him happy—"And," continued he, "it seems to me that this step is not only likely to secure me an easy and tender companion for the remainder of my days, but will also be the most certain means of convincing your brother of his error before he has farther involved himself. When I am married, he will find it more difficult, if not impossible, to raise money on the prospect of inheriting my estate, and I shall take care that before the affair is concluded, such a part of it shall be settled on his son, and such a part on Victorine and himself during their lives, as shall secure to them, even if I should have a second family, a very sufficient and even splendid income. On my sister also I shall settle one of the farms I have in Staffordshire, which produces a clear four hundred a year, and I shall invest in the stocks ten thousand pounds in the names of trustees whom I shall appoint for her and her son."

Ethelinde, though before well convinced, from many observations, that Mr. Harcourt had thought much on this subject, was however surprised to find he had so thoroughly arranged his plan. He ceased speaking, and seemed to expect her answer; she was by no means prepared to give it; and remaining some time silent, he at length said—"Tell me, Ethelinde, what are your sentiments?"

"That you have an undoubted right, Sir, to form any connection which appears to you likely to render you happy."

"Give me then," answered he, "with your usual sincerity, your opinion whether your cousin Lady Belle is likely to make such a wife as I expect."

Ethelinde was now cruelly distressed: she knew that her cousin had, to carry her point, been acting a part altogether unlike her own character, which was spirited, arrogant, volatile and dissipated; she knew that in town she passed whole nights at the card-table, and was the first in the circle of fashion and gaiety; she knew her incapable of real affection, selfish, and ambitious; and that she was extremely artful her present success evinced. Ethelinde, however, was very unwilling to say all or any part of what she knew; she was equally unwilling to say what she did not think; and yet to evade such a question was difficult, without giving Harcourt reason to believe that she was either disingenuous or interested.

Again she paused; but Harcourt again pressing her to speak, she said, that never having been much with her cousins she was incompetent to judge of their characters, but that Lady Arabella appeared at present very amiable; then hastening from a point on which she could not speak to her own satisfaction, she asked whether his conversation with her was in confidence or whether she was at liberty to speak of it.

"You may mention it if you please," replied he; "I mean to speak of it myself to my sister; and for the rest of the family I think it will come less aukwardly from you than from me."

Mr. Harcourt then went up to the apartment of Mrs. Montgomery, and Ethelinde into the park to consider what she should do. Her brother was forty miles from home; Victorine was also absent on a visit; the return of both was uncertain, and she well understood that there was no time to be lost. She determined, therefore, to write instantly to Chesterville; and having done so, and sent her letter away express, she returned to Mrs. Montgomery, whom she found very uneasy at the conversation she had had with her brother.

"You know me, my Ethelinde, too well," said she, "to make it necessary for me to declare to you that my sentiments on this matter are wholly disinterested; but this Lady Belle—shall I tell you very simply that I do not like her? She seems to me to suffer a perpetual struggle between her real and her assumed character; and then Lady Hawkhurst is so haughty, so loud, so dictatorial, so much of the veteran woman of fashion—she seems to have no principle, if I may so express myself, but interest, and to have no feelings but those of pride and ambition. Even her affections for her children have taken this turn; and I am convinced that she would rejoice to see them great, though certain they were miserable. What will become of my poor brother, if he finds himself deceived; and, when it is too late, discovers that instead of a dove he has purchased a bird whose fine plumage covers the spirit of a vulture."

"Indeed," replied Ethelinde, "I greatly dread it." She then told Mrs. Montgomery her real opinion of the character of Lady Belle; and they agreed that unless Chesterville managed better than they expected he would do, Mr. Harcourt would certainly fall into the snare prepared for him. "As for myself," said Mrs. Montgomery, "I am determined to return as soon as possible to Grasmere. There I am—not happy indeed—for happiness and I are perhaps divided for ever; but I am at least easier than here; where, indulgent as my brother is to my love of solitude, I am exposed to frequent interruptions from persons who, as they mean only civility, I cannot offend by refusing their society. I am unwilling also to appear busy in regard to this marriage. If my brother is determined upon it, as I believe he is, my opposition will incur only his dislike, and that I cannot bear; I shall certainly become hateful to Lady Belle, who will probably obtain influence enough over him to deaden all other affections; and therefore, Ethelinde, I shall fix on next Tuesday to begin our journey."

Ethelinde assured her that her wish had long been to return to Grasmere. She knew that before the day Mrs. Montgomery had named Chesterville would return, and that she should have acquitted herself as far as possible in giving him an opportunity of attempting at least to prevent a marriage so fatal to the prospects his ambition had laid out before him: for the rest, had she been convinced that Lady Belle would have made Mr. Harcourt happy, she would have thought it inexcusable to endeavour, liberal as his intentions were in regard to her brother, to have dissuaded him from the marriage.

The rage and agitation of Chesterville on his return are not to be described. It was with the utmost difficulty that Ethelinde could prevent his going to expostulate in very unguarded terms with Mr. Harcourt. On Lady Hawkhurst he lavished every term of dislike which his anger and threatened disappointment dictated; and instead of considering what he should do to counteract her projects, he continued to rail against her for having formed them; while Ethelinde, sorry as she was for his uneasiness, could hardly help thinking he was in some measure justly punished for the avidity with which he had cultivated acquaintance and friendship with the family who had neglected his father in the bitter hour of adversity, and had apparently forgotten, when he himself most needed their friendship, those claims of kindred which they assiduously renewed the moment that they saw him in the sunshine of fortune. This, however, was no time to remind him of the folly of his conduct; and all Mrs. Montgomery and Ethelinde could do, was to endeavour to appease him, and point out to him the means to prevent what he feared. All his jealousy and mistrust of them, which had made him so cold and indifferent even to his sister, now vanished; and he besought Mrs. Montgomery, with an earnestness almost abject, to stay and assist Victorine in dissuading her father from this dreaded marriage: but this she positively though politely refused; and on the day she had settled to go, she took an affectionate leave of Mr. Harcourt (to whom, in a private conference, she had insisted much on the necessity of being well informed of the real character of her to whom he mean to entrust the peace of his future life) and then with Ethelinde departed for her cottage at Grasmere, notwithstanding all the entreaties of Chesterville and Victorine that they would stay, and the reluctance of Mr. Harcourt to part with them.

CHAPTER XII

In the quiet solitude of Grasmere, where every object served to bring before her the image of Montgomery and the happiness which she once hoped to enjoy in living there with him—hopes that she now believed were vanished for ever—the spirits of Ethelinde seemed likely wholly to forsake her. To conceal her terrors from Mrs. Montgomery was a task which every hour became more difficult and more painful; but she reflected that she was by this dissimulation saving from insanity or from death one so dear to him; and she besought heaven to give her strength to repress and conceal her own sorrows so long as she could fulfil any duty towards the mother of him she adored.

That mother, with a mind strong beyond her sex, and with all the resources of comfort offered by religion, was yet hourly sinking under the anguish which uncertainty inflicted. Often she accused herself of having hastily sacrificed him to unworthy motives; and whenever she had courage to speak upon the subject, which she could not always do, she lamented her precipitation in terms of the bitterest regret. Her anxiety for letters now become excessive; and Ethelinde was alarmed by every one she opened lest she should receive news of fatal import. Mrs. Montgomery, often unable to contend with the dreadful pain of anxiety, was compelled to have recourse to opiates to obtain sleep, and sometimes preferred entire solitude even to the company of Ethelinde.

For some days the uneasiness she was in about her brother added greatly to the distress of Mrs. Montgomery, as well as to that of Ethelinde. Its object was then changed by their hearing that he had been seized with a return of his usual illness, which had been so violent for some time as to reduce him to the point of death, and that in consequence of his physician's advice he was going to Bath. The accounts they afterwards received from thence spoke only of his amending health; and the tenderness Victorine had shown towards him seemed to have had its effect in detaching his mind at least for the present from thoughts of a marriage so fatal to her interest, and probably to his own repose.

The situation of Sir Edward Newenden was an additional weight on the mind of Ethelinde. Lady Newenden's conduct was now become matter of discussion in the newspapers. Ethelinde had a short letter from him to inform her he was arrived in London: he was unhappy; and her soft heart bled for his unhappiness amidst the superior calamities that oppressed her. Whenever Mrs. Montgomery desired to be wholly alone, Ethelinde, who never otherwise left her, wandered away to those scenes where she could indulge herself most in the sad luxury of recalling Montgomery forcibly to her mind. Sometimes she sat under the

willow she had been so fond of; its withered leaves were now falling, and its long branches, as they waved in the wind around her,
seemed to whisper only sorrow; but her most frequent walks were
along the edge of the lake, now often ruffled by wild gusts from
the hills, and darkened by heavy clouds; to the creek where Montgomery had snatched her from death. A group of alder and birch
grew near it; and when she last left Grasmere, they had afforded a
delicious shade over its grassy borders; but now the little foliage
they retained was of a faint yellow, forming a mournful but not
unpleasing contrast with the dark hollies and half leafless oaks that
started from the mass of rocks which arose behind them. Here she
frequently lamented that she had not perished. "Had I died then,"
said she, "how much of suffering had I escaped! Oh! Montgomery! why did you rescue me from death to survive my father, to see
my friends wretched, and now to weep over the memory of happiness lost for ever! But for your fatal affection for me you might
now have been the support of your widowed mother. 'Tis I have
destroyed you; yet I live to believe it, and may linger many years
vainly to lament you!"

   Another of her melancholy wanderings was longer; it was to
the seat which Sir Edward Newenden had made in the cliff above
Grasmere Park, where she met Montgomery in the first days of
their attachment. It was endeared to her by a thousand tender recollections. There Montgomery had first told her he loved her; and
there, after he left Grasmere to attend on her father, he had been
accustomed to sit and think of her. The seat was a little cave in a
soft sand rock; over its unequal arch, the ivy, mingled with clem-
atis, wild hop, briony,[1] and woody nightshade, formed festoons
which half concealed the entrance: within was a rude table, on
which Montgomery had told her he had written those little pieces
of poetry which she had with so much pleasure heard him repeat;
and there yet remained a memorial of his usual way of passing his
time in this sequestered spot, for on one of the masses of rock he
had engraved her cypher. On this she perpetually gazed, leaning
her head on the oak table before her. The waterfall, which was
now swelled by autumnal rains into a rapid torrent, gushing from
the alpine heights above, and seeking its way to the lake among
the rocks immediately near her, at once encreased and soothed

1 Briony: a flowering gourd plant with large leaves and small flowers.

her sadness. Amid the rushing of the torrent, and the hollow sighing of the wind that swelled its sound, she often sunk into such absence of mind, and yielded so entirely to the impressions of fancy, that she believed she really heard the voice of Montgomery.

In these reveries she was sometimes so absorbed, that neither the threatened storm nor the approach of night had power to awaken her from them; but the necessity of attending Mrs. Montgomery, to whom she generally read an hour or two before she went to her bed, made her, before night fall, quit this scene of sorrowful contemplation, which, as she left, she usually uttered an apostrophe to Montgomery.—"I go," cried she, as if he really heard her—"I go to acquit myself of my duty to your mother. Oh! come with me, beloved of both our hearts! And in dreams at least let me see thee, though we in this world may meet no more!"

Thus passed the month of October. The dreary weather of the following month, tho' it often wrapped in blue mists the scene she so much loved, and choaked with leaves the narrow way that wound among the rocks towards it, prevented not her solitary rambles. The very horrors of the surrounding landscape now afforded her the only gratification she was capable of tasting, and thus in the words of an exquisite modern poet, she sometimes addressed the wild and forlorn scene around her—

"To this sad soul more welcome are thy glooms,
    Than Spring's green bowers, or Summer's gaudy blooms,
    Nor asks an heart that only breathes to sigh,
    A warmer mansion—or a kinder sky."[1]

It was now, however, near the end of the month; and the frosts, which were often severe, threatened to make her beloved spot inaccessible by spreading sheets of ice over the mountain path.

[1] Miss Seward's Louisa. [Smith's note.] Anna Seward (1747-1809), *Louisa: A Poetical Novel* (1784), lines 219-222. An epistolary verse narrative whose story and perspective are appropriate: a heroine and hero of strong sensibility, Louisa and Eugenio, were in love, but Eugenio's father coerces him into marrying Emira, who is wealthy but turns out to have a character like that of Maria Lady Newenden: mercenary, worldly, cold to her children. Eugenio writes an exculpatory letter and Louisa forgives him, but she remains tragically alone (Seward has Pope's Eloisa in mind). They write to Emma, who is at first living in the East Indies, so the poem has the *Ethelinde* colonialist perspective.

This approaching deprivation made her with more avidity enjoy her favorite scene, while it was possible; and cold as it was, she had placed herself there early one morning, when her eyes were suddenly struck with an unusual volume of smoak ascending from the chimneys of Grasmere Abbey, which lay immediately beneath her. The house had appeared till now hardly inhabited; the windows were seldom opened, and no fire seemed to be made but in the housekeeper's room at one end of it. Ethelinde had sent several times, since her present abode at the cottage, to enquire after Mrs. Dickenson, but had avoided going thither because her spirits were unequal to the questions which she knew the good woman would ask. She had now no other idea than that the rooms were airing on account of the damp weather; but as she thought it possible that Mrs. Dickenson might have heard of Sir Edward and the children since she had, she determined to go down to the house to enquire. She descended, therefore, by the way that led towards the abbey, crossed the lawn, and entered by a glass door which opened into a parlour. She traversed it, and hearing some body move in the study adjoining, she concluded it to be the housekeeper, and opening the door was struck by the sight of Sir Edward Newenden himself, pale and emaciated, sitting in his dressing gown at a table, on which he was writing. He lifted not up his eyes on her opening the door. The room was long and somewhat dark; and as she almost involuntarily approached him, he said in a low voice, still without moving his eyes from the paper—"Dickenson, let Matthew get ready to carry this letter to Mrs. Montgomery."

"Sir Edward!" said Ethelinde, in a faint tone.

At the sound of her voice he dropped his pen, started up, and crying as he advanced—"My Ethelinde! my angel! He clasped her to his heart. The suddenness of the interview, and the pale and dejected figure of her benefactor, were together too much for her feeble spirits, and she almost fainted in his arms.

He placed her on a chair; and as soon as she seemed restored to her senses, he, who appeared not entirely to possess his own, cried —"You know then the circumstance of which I thought it would be my lot, unwillingly, and with an aching heart, to inform you; but oh why would you in such a state of mind come so far!"

"Know what?" faultering, asked Ethelinde.—"What do you suppose I know? Lady Newenden? is it of her?" Then the idea that what he alluded to related to Montgomery, confusedly entered her mind—"or is it," continued she, "is it—I dare not ask—the French account about which I wrote to you—the confirmation—the——"

She struggled for breath to go on, but could not. Her eyes were fixed with a look of wildness and horror on Sir Edward. She grasped one of his hands eagerly in hers.—"Tell me," cried she, "tell me, I conjure you. Certainty, however dreadful, I could, I think I could better bear than this terrible suspense."

"The information that paper contained, my Ethelinde, is unhappily too true. When I received your letter, I made enquiry at Paris. The accounts I have from thence leave no doubt——"

"It is enough—it is enough," cried Ethelinde, "I cannot hear particulars." A deadly paleness was on her face, a shuddering convulsive sigh burst from her heart; but she was incapable of shedding tears; and Sir Edward beheld with terror the wild and glazed look with which her eyes seemed to follow round the room some imaginary figure. More alarmed by this still and silent horror than he would have been at the most violent expressions of grief, he endeavoured to awaken her from the heavy shock which seemed to have locked up her senses.

"Ethelinde," cried he, "for mercy's sake recollect yourself: what have I told you that you did not before know, at least that you had not too much reason to suspect? Remember, I beseech you, what you owe to the mother of him you lament!—of him to whom your sorrows are now useless. Remember what you owe to yourself, and to your surviving friends. There is one at least to whom the sight of you, in your present state, is more dreadful, more insupportable than his own misfortunes."

Unconscious of what he had said, unknowing what she answered, Ethelinde now with the same wild look gazed a moment on the face of Sir Edward; and repeating his last words, cried —"Misfortunes! what misfortunes? is anybody unfortunate but me? no! no! Mrs. Montgomery and I bear them all between us!"

"Indeed, Ethelinde," said he, "I cannot support this!" He left her, and walked to the other end of the room. "Good God!" whispered he to himself, "what shall I do with her? If I could provoke her to tears—to exclamation—any thing were better than this alarming stupor."

He now again walked towards her.—"I thought, Ethelinde,"

said he gravely, as he again approached her.—"I thought you had
some regard for me. I find I was cruelly mistaken. You will not even
allow me the privilege of weeping with you. You forget that Montgomery was my friend? that I loved him as my brother; admired
his character, and honored his virtues. Would to God his fate had
been more fortunate, or rather would I could have exchanged my
destiny for his. Life to *him* was of value, for *you* loved him; to me
it is a torment, for I am bereft of everything that rendered it desirable, except those dear unfortunate and motherless little ones, for
whom I hoped to have found a friend in you. But you reject us and
forget us all."

The first intelligence, conveying the certainty of what she
dreaded, had given a blow to the heart of Ethelinde, which had
stunned all her senses. In a few moments, recollection, roused by
the sorrowful vehemence of Sir Edward's manner, returned, and
a violent burst of tears relieved her. Sir Edward, glad to see her
weep, attempted not to check the course of her tears, but as her
heart seemed as if it would burst, he thought it better to call the
housekeeper, and quit her himself till the violence of her grief
subsided. He therefore went himself and sent in Mrs. Dickenson,
who sat silently by her; and after a dreadful fit of crying, she sunk
into a more quiet state, and recollected that Mrs. Montgomery
would probably be alarmed at her stay. She enquired the hour;
and being told that it was about one o'clock, she desired to see Sir
Edward, who immediately attended her. As he approached her,
she held out her hand to him.—"My dear Sir Edward," said she,
with as much steadiness of voice as she could acquire, "I believe I
have been ungrateful. Pardon me; I am too wretched to excite any
thing but pity. You are not angry with me?"

"Angry, my dear Ethelinde," replied he, pressing her hand to his
lips. "Is it possible you could for a moment suppose it? I thank God
that you are calmer; exert not yourself to talk, but endeavour to
bear with patience an inevitable misfortune. Nothing is so useless
as the consolation usually offered—I attempt not to console you.
—I cannot if I would!" A deep and convulsive sigh rendered almost
inarticulate the answer of Ethelinde.—"Ah! Sir Edward, there is
another person to console whom it will be *as* difficult. Poor Mrs.
Montgomery!—thus ends then that miserable uncertainty which
you have been so little able to bear; thus ends the last hope of your

days. How shall I tell her! Sir Edward I feel it to be impossible.—I can never relate to her a catastrophe of which she has yet no idea —I should die in the attempt!"

"Do not then attempt it," said he. "And yet," interrupted Ethelinde, "to whom can I entrust it?—Now, perhaps at this moment, she wonders at my stay.—She will mistrust something, let me therefore return immediately."

Sir Edward, glad to find she had now her perfect recollection, sat down by her; and after consulting a moment with the old housekeeper, they determined, that, as she so anxiously desired to return, he would take her to the cottage in his post chaise, and there be governed by the situation in which he found Mrs. Montgomery whether he should discover to her her misfortunes, or send for Mr. Harcourt to be with her before he overwhelmed her with tidings so insupportable. To this plan Ethelinde agreed: Sir Edward withdrew to give orders for the chaise, and Mrs. Dickenson assisted Ethelinde to prepare for going; her own trembling hands and streaming eyes being but of little use to her. She then tottered down stairs, and was put into the carriage. The coach way was near three miles round; and as they went Sir Edward had time to exhort Ethelinde to preserve, as much as she could, the appearance of composure before the unhappy mother. "Remember," said he, "that a very sudden shock may deprive her of life, or of her senses; you consider her health and repose as sacred deposits left you by Montgomery; you will not therefore consult them less now than while you had yet hopes of rendering to him an account of your trust." Ethelinde acknowledged that she ought to do as he directed, and, though trembling and faint, assured him she would try at it. Nothing served so much to recall her own fortitude as the recollection that, without it, she must see her venerable and beloved friend sink under her misfortunes without being able to help her; and this consideration induced her to restrain, though it could not diminish, the anguish of her heart.

When they arrived at the cottage, they found Mrs. Montgomery at first a little surprised by seeing a carriage at her door so unexpectedly. The countenance too of Ethelinde would have alarmed her, had not she supposed that the change she observed there was owing to the unexpected arrival of Sir Edward, for whom she knew that Ethelinde felt so tender an interest.

Though relieved by the apparent composure of Mrs. Montgomery from that immediate dread of the future which had weighed so heavily on the spirits of Ethelinde, the painful remembrance of the past quite conquered her strength; and as soon as Sir Edward was gone, who had engaged Mrs. Montgomery in conversation relative to his own affairs, she went up to her chamber, saying only, that her walk, the cold, and the sudden sight of Sir Edward Newenden, had made her ill. Alone, and in her bed, the certainty—the dreadful certainty that she had lost Montgomery for ever, returned in all its force. Inevitable evils, it is said, are always borne the best; but Ethelinde, amidst all that anxiety which had reduced her mind to the tenderest weakness, and exposed it to all the terrors of fancy, had yet, in the bottom of her heart, cherished an hope that he still had escaped, and would return to her such as her affection delighted in representing him. That latent hope was now destroyed; the happiness of her life was blasted for ever by the very means which she had fondly flattered herself would secure it; and she had now no comfort but in thinking that she had done her duty, rather than yielded to her inclination, when she reluctantly consented to his going. There is, in extreme distress, no other source of consolation but in reflecting that duties strictly executed will finally be rewarded, though here, for some reasons we are unable to penetrate, misery is too frequently the portion of those who most religiously adhere to them: the tender mind of Ethelinde now sought from heaven that comfort which nothing on earth could give her; and determining to consecrate the rest of her life to the beloved memory of him who was thus snatched from her, she found some degree of courage gradually return, and meditated how to soften the dreadful blow that was yet to fall on her dear unhappy friend.

Her intended precautions were however useless. The next day after her interview with Sir Edward, Mrs. Montgomery opened a letter which contained the fatal information. The sorrows of those advanced in life are silent; but prey deeply on the heart, if it is not yet hardened by long and repeated calamity. Mrs. Montgomery felt, or fancied she felt, that she should survive only a very short time, him for whom alone she had lived—for whose sake only life had any charms; and Ethelinde saw with astonishment, that she bore the certainty of the loss of all she loved with more outward calmness than she had often shewn while she merely apprehended what had now actually happened. Nothing seemed to distress her so much as any attempt to console her, or to persuade her that her own dissolution was distant. She thought of death with that sort of delight which a journey would have given her at the end of which she was sure of meeting her son: and when Ethelinde, with tears and entreaties, often implored her to take medicines prescribed for her, she took them indeed, but smiled at their inefficacy and sometimes asked Ethelinde "why she wished her so ill as to desire her life?" In a little time she desired to see Sir Edward Newenden, who, after the first interview, came to her, at her request, almost every day; Ethelinde frequently left them together, and went out alone to the wildest spots, where she could weep unseen, and call, unheard, on the beloved name of Montgomery.—She imagined she saw Mrs. Montgomery sinking rapidly to her grave; and believed that she should very soon follow her. Her constitution, never very strong, had been greatly injured by repeated shocks; and she hoped that her youth alone would not support her against the last, and that she should not be left alone in a world where, after the loss of Mrs. Montgomery, she thought she should have nothing for which it would be supportable to live.

Returning from one of these walks, she was surprised to see the post-chaise of Sir Edward Newenden at the door of the cottage, at an hour when he did not usually visit it. On entering the parlour she saw him leaning against the wainscot, with his handkerchief to his eyes, and Mrs. Montgomery seemed mildly remonstrating with him. Seeing it was Ethelinde who entered, he started from the posture he was in, and hurried by her, without speaking, into the garden. "What is the matter with Sir Edward, my dear Madam?" said Ethelinde in great astonishment. "Lady Newenden," replied Mrs. Montgomery, "is dead; and, whatever reason he had to detest her, the account of her death, attended with some shocking circumstances which he is unable to relate, has quite overwhelmed him. I have been trying to argue him into a more composed state of mind; but you see the way he is in."

Shocked and amazed, Ethelinde enquired whether she should go to him.—"No," replied Mrs. Montgomery, "he seems particularly hurt at the sight of you. It is yet, I fear, no time to attempt to soothe him, or to reason with him: go therefore, my love, up to your own room, and I will send for him in; for in the present state of his mind he should not be alone."

Mrs. Montgomery then went herself into the garden, and Sir Edward, affected by the interest she took in his sorrows, notwithstanding the heavy pressure of her own, became, on her account, able to command himself; and she had the satisfaction to see him return home more composed than, from the first violent emotions of his grief, was probable. Though the sudden death of a woman he had once loved, of his children's mother, had at first been a severe shock to Sir Edward, his reason soon conquered his concern; and he reflected on the event in a few days as on a stroke of providence in his favour, and in that of his children, who must have suffered had the separation by law taken place to which her conduct would have obliged him to recur, and in which he was indeed occupied at the time he received the intelligence from Italy that rendered all his measures unnecessary.

But though he soon subdued his first sorrow, and felt in all its force the comfort his conscience brought to him, which assured him that he had acquitted himself towards his wife with the most perfect integrity, indulged her foibles, and even overlooked her misconduct to a degree of weakness for which his friends had often reproached him, but of which he now thought with pleasure, he could not determine to quit Grasmere or go to London; but, anxious to see his children, he wrote to entreat Mr. Maltravers, in whose care they were left, to send them down to him. The unhappy father of Lady Newenden, who was now taught so severely to repent of his fatal indulgence to her, had not yet recovered the tidings of her death. Without resources but from present objects, he had lost the idol to which he had been so many years offering incense, and knew not how to submit to the blow. His wife, to whom he imputed much of the ill conduct of his daughter, was become hateful to him: and he shut himself up in his own apartment, where disappointment and grief incessantly preyed upon his soul. In sending his grandchildren to their father, he wrote a letter with which Sir Edward was much affected. It acknowledged all his kindness to the lost Maria, and recommended her children to his care.—"In the will, a copy of which I enclose to you," said he, "You will see that I have amply provided for each of your children—Take care of your girl; she will be as

lovely as her unhappy mother.—Give her a better education. They
will all be independent of you.—I hope you will so bring them up
as that their independence may not make them less worthy. For
yourself, Sir Edward, feeling as I do your worth, I have given you
what I once intended should be at the disposal of my daughter.
Mrs. Maltravers is sufficiently provided for; never suffer your children to be with her.—You will probably marry.—I hear that the
young man to whom my niece Chesterville was engaged, is dead.
—I wish your choice may be directed to her.—She is a good girl,
and deserves to be happy—you will make her so; and she will be
tender of your children.—I believe I was less kind to her than I
ought to have been.—Repentance on that, and many other points,
is too late.—I have given her a thousand pounds, and sincerely
wish you happy with her;—I shall hardly live to see it, as I think
you will not marry till the mourning for the late Lady Newenden
is expired."

To unite himself for ever with Ethelinde—with her who had
been so long the possessor of an heart which dared not acknowledge the affection he could not conquer, had been the first and
most soothing idea that Sir Edward had entertained after he recovered from the first shock which his wife's death gave him. But with
whatever delight he cherished this idea, he had not yet ventured
to breathe an hint of it even to Mrs. Montgomery. Every day, however, he went to the cottage; the children usually accompanied
him, and all the fondness which had formerly subsisted between
them and Ethelinde was renewed, and even augmented. She
found the only pleasure she was capable of tasting in their innocent mirth; and when they were too noisy for Mrs. Montgomery,
she took them into her own room, or out to walk with her, leaving Sir Edward to sit with her friend, whose greatest gratification
seemed to be in talking about her son; a conversation to which
the spirits of Ethelinde were so unequal, that whenever his name
was mentioned she was obliged to leave the room. So capricious is
grief, that she could not endure to hear the name pronounced by
another which she incessantly repeated to herself; and if ever he
was spoken of, the languor and sadness which usually hung over
her gave way to a momentary impatience, and she fled from the
persons by whom he was named, as if they had done her an injury.

Mr. Maltravers survived only a fortnight after having disposed

of his affairs in the manner he had mentioned to Sir Edward.—
He gave to his two grandsons their thirty thousand pounds each
in money, and to his granddaughter twenty; and, leaving to the
eldest of the boys the reversion of half his estates in land, he gave
the rest, (with the exception only, of a thousand pounds to Ethelinde and a few inconsiderable legacies,) to Sir Edward Newenden;
bequeathing to his wife only the seven hundred a year which he
had settled on her at her marriage and a legacy of five hundred
pounds for mourning. With this, however, though full of bitterness and resentment, she went to Bath, where she lived at the card
table, and got a set of friends in whose society she soon recovered the loss of her husband and her daughter; and in a very few
weeks was as gay and as much at ease as if no such misfortune had
befallen her. She had no trouble about her grandchildren, whose
very existence she would not have been sorry to have forgotten;
and in her dress and manner was soon so young and fashionable,
that nobody, unless they very narrowly examined her face, would
have believed that she owned the venerable title of grandmother.

Mrs. Montgomery, in everything her opposite, was evidently
though very gradually declining; she had no complaint but universal languor, and her face

> "As beauty lingering left its loved abode."[1]

was still most interesting; though so pale that the blood seemed
wholly to have forsaken it, except where deep blue veins gave a
yet more pallid hue to her temples and forehead. Her hair was
quite white, a change occasioned rather by sorrow than age; and
her eyes had lost their vivacity but not their sweetness: incurable
grief, softened by patient resignation, was the character her countenance had taken:—all its animation and spirit was gone; or, if
ever it returned for a moment, it was when she spoke of her near
approach to that period, when, disengaged from this earth, she
should rejoin her two dear Montgomerys—her husband and her
son.

Nothing seemed to interest her in the world but the situation

1 From *A Collection of Poems in Six Volumes. By Several Hands* (London: Dodsley,
1758), "The Dowager," Vol. 6, p. 122, line 28. The poem is a portrait of an exem-
plary widow who lives in rural retirement with a beloved daughter.

of Ethelinde, and of this she now sometimes spoke to Sir Edward; who, gazing on her with tender veneration, and considering her already as a saint, heard her, with mingled pain and pleasure, thus address him on that subject, about a month after the death of Mr. Maltravers.

"I have been unusually ill to-night, my good friend, and I believe my trial will soon be over: you, who know what I have possessed and what I have lost, will not wonder that I feel these symptoms with delight. There is but one point, in my near prospect of death, that distresses me; it is, the condition in which Ethelinde will be left when I am no more.—Her beauty, her sensibility, the soft-ness of her temper, all combine to fill me with uneasiness lest her future life should be even less tranquil than that portion of it that has passed.—I consider her as my daughter; as the sacred trust left me by my son; and I shall meet him in heaven with an allay of my joy if I leave Ethelinde unhappy and unprotected."

This was an opportunity beyond the hopes of Sir Edward, who had long meditated how to speak on this subject, but was ever checked by his fears of finding Mrs. Montgomery averse to what he so ardently desired. He now, not without all the tremulous hesi-tation of doubt and anxiety, related to her his long though hopeless attachment to Ethelinde; the pain it had cost him to conceal what he had vainly attempted to subdue; and that his going abroad was not less on account of Lady Newenden's indiscreet conduct, than to detach himself from the dangerous indulgence of seeing her, whom he then could not wish to call his without a double crime. —"Believe me, however, dear madam," continued he, "that, incur-able as my passion for her is, I would, if our dear Montgomery had lived, have promoted their union: for she loved him, and he was worthy of her love.—They would have been happy! and such is my affection for Ethelinde, that her interest, her felicity, are dearer —far dearer to me than my own.—Yes, I dare assert that what I feel for her is true love; so true, that though the internal conflict has been now above two years preying on my heart, I would have car-ried my sorrows to the grave in silence, had their communication been likely to wound her sensibility or her husband's peace."

The tears of Mrs. Montgomery testified how deeply Sir Edward's little narrative had affected her: they were both silent a moment, and then he reassumed his discourse.—

"Heaven has disposed otherwise of events than was very lately probable. The heart of Ethelinde, deeply wounded by the loss of him who deserved all her tenderness, will never perhaps again be sensible of love such as she felt for the dear, regretted Montgomery; but her tender esteem is, I believe, mine; if you, dear Madam, do not oppose my hopes, she may perhaps, when her present grief is a little softened by time, give me that hand which I consider as the first blessing on earth, and as much of that tender heart as depends on sympathy and friendship."

"No, Sir Edward," replied Mrs. Montgomery, after a deep sigh —"I love Ethelinde too well—I esteem you too much, to oppose your hopes. It has, indeed, been part of my mournful contemplations to promote them; and to see her, before I die, in the protection of her best friend. As I feel daily the slow, but certain approach of the hour when we must part, and am well convinced that it cannot long be delayed, I have often been on the point of telling my lovely friend my sentiments on this subject; but hitherto time, instead of meliorating her anguish, seems to have encreased it; and frequently when I begin to speak to her, she flies from me, or throws herself into an agony of tears which precludes all possibility of conversation. The resignation which I am enabled to shew, from the certainty only of soon meeting all I regret, to be separated no more, seems to her I believe to arise from coldness; for I can see that she is often offended and surprised at the calmness with which I speak of my son, and would I think love more me more if I expressed what I suffer, instead of sacrificing my grief to God! and submitting with patience to his irrevocable though heavy decree.—Judge therefore, whether while she is in such a temper of mind, I can name to her a proposal which she would think an injury to the memory of her lover—I will however try what is to be done; and believe me, Sir Edward, that you are the only man on earth to whose protection I would give Ethelinde, the only one who is in my eyes worthy of a place in that heart which has been occupied by the image of Charles Montgomery."

Too much affected to continue the conversation, she now left the room. Faithful however to her promise, and dreading lest death, which seemed inevitable, should prevent her executing what she thought her duty towards her friend, she seized the first moment they were alone and composed, to relate to Ethelinde the conversation she had had with Sir Edward Newenden.

Ethelinde, recollecting all that had formerly passed, had very little doubt of Sir Edward's views before Mrs. Montgomery undertook to be his advocate, but so fondly was her whole soul dedicated to the idea of Montgomery, that she had long since determined never to listen to any proposals of marriage, but to pass her whole life as his widow. She was shocked, as Mrs. Montgomery had foreseen, at the first mention of Sir Edward's proposal, and even felt resentment against her for having listened to it. "You know, dear Madam," said she, as soon as she recovered her voice, "you know how sincere a friendship I have for Sir Edward—you know all the obligations I owe him: to his care my dying father gave me! to him I am indebted even for my subsistence since I became fatherless. I love him as the tenderest, best of brothers—had he been really my brother I could not more affectionately love him. But feeling as I feel for another, who, though dead, is not less the object of my everlasting attachment, can I think of giving my hand to Sir Edward Newenden? Since indeed, I have not a heart to bestow, and he deserves to possess one undivided by any other affection. Renew not then again the only conversation which I can listen to from you without pleasure." Discouraged by this answer, which was immediately communicated to him, but not despairing of an alteration in her sentiments, Sir Edward long forbore to speak himself to Ethelinde on the subject nearest his heart: but the silent dejection into which he sunk, affected Ethelinde more than the most studied eloquence exerted in his favour could have done. She sometimes, in seeing how greatly he was changed, accused herself of ingratitude towards a man whose genuine love and unwearied friendship deserved that she should sacrifice to him at least the appearance of that regret which she felt would last for ever; but then the idea of Montgomery who had perished, only because he sought to acquire fortune for her, returned in all its force, and she fancied she heard him reproach her in mournful accents for thinking even a moment of giving to another that faith which had been solemnly given to him: and her whole soul recoiled from the thoughts of entering into another engagement, even with Sir Edward Newenden.

Four months passed, during which Sir Edward found that far from losing any part of that sorrow which the loss of Montgomery had immediately occasioned, Ethelinde felt it rather heavier. His love increased by this proof of her steady affection, knew no bounds; and had arisen to an height that in a less regulated mind might have amounted to frenzy. The suspense he was in between hope, that time might produce some alteration in his favour, and fear lest Ethelinde should continue obstinately to reject him, preyed incessantly on his health, and totally altered his temper: he now sought only solitude; sick disgust overtook him in all society where Ethelinde was not; and where she was, he found in her looks, her tone of voice, her gentle attention to him, fewel[1] for the fire that consumed him. His affairs called him to London: he left his children in the care of Ethelinde; and hastening thither, tried to lose in the hurry of business, and among the friends with whom he used to live, the acuteness of his pain. But he found every body troublesome and fatiguing.—Business appeared unusually tedious and intricate, and society insupportably insipid. The meeting he was obliged to have with Woolaston's creditors, who had seized every thing and left Mrs. Woolaston in extreme distress, contributed to harass his mind and exhaust his spirits. He contrived, however, to rescue some part of his sister's fortune from the talons of the vultures who had taken possession of it; and having fixed her at his own house at Denham, and so settled with her husband that he was never again to molest her, (for, not content with robbing her of her fortune, he had treated her extremely ill,) and having secured her an income sufficient for her support in the way she chose to live in, he hurried over the other matters that called him to London as quickly as possible, and returned to Grasmere Abbey;—more thoroughly convinced than ever that he could not exist without Ethelinde and determined to bring his fate to a crisis the first opportunity he should have of speaking to her alone.

CHAPTER XIII

With this disposition Sir Edward Newenden went early the next morning after his arrival at Grasmere to the cottage of Mrs. Montgomery. He found her greatly changed in the fortnight he had been absent: she was sensible of it herself; and repeated to him

1 An obsolete spelling of "fuel."

her concern that she should quit the world without seeing the two persons happy for whom she was most solicitious. "I have a letter," continued she, "from my brother, who is, I thank God, so much recovered from his illness that he promises me a visit, and Victorine and Chesterville come with him. He at length tastes of some tranquillity, and I shall embrace him before I die. He joins with me, dear Sir Edward, in wishing that Ethelinde may be yours; perhaps the united voice of all her friends may influence her to reward the merit of the living, since the dead are not to be recalled. I am persuaded that my Montgomery himself, if happy spirits are conscious of what passes in this world, would approve of her giving to you her hand; and that he would not consider his memory injured by its being cherished in the breast of your wife."

Sir Edward, encouraged by this conversation, enquired where he might speak with Ethelinde? "I know not exactly," replied Mrs. Montgomery, "as after having given an hour this morning as usual to your children in her own room, she put on her hat, and told me she was going for her walk, as the day promised to be uncommonly fine. I was pleased to see her look more chearful than she generally does, but I made no enquiry as to the course of her walk. It usually, as you well know, is towards the seat on the rock, and there it is very probable you may find her."

Thither, with a palpitating heart, Sir Edward bent his steps; he found Ethelinde sitting in the cave, where she had of late passed so many hours. A book lay before her on the oak table, and a few flowers, the earliest of the year, were scattered round it: the notes of the birds that towards the end of March begin their first songs, and the lulling murmur of the torrent now just gurgling down the rock, had soothed her mind into a state of soft and pensive melancholy. The approach of Sir Edward awakened her from it, not without adding some degree of apprehension to her surprise, for he had never joined her there before: she now knew not of his return to the abbey; and perturbation, hurry, and uneasiness, expressed on his countenance, could not have escaped a less interested observer.

When he spoke to her, the idea that something unusual had happened to him, or that some particular uneasiness pressed upon him, was more forcibly renewed. She waited a few moments in expectation of his telling her what had occasioned the trouble she observed; but as he briefly answered every question she asked him on the subjects which she knew had engaged his time and attention in town, and that he even seemed to have settled his sister's affairs better than, at his departure, he expected, she at length said —"Are you not well, my dear Sir, or has any thing occurred to give you unusual pain?"

"My pain," answered he, "is not unusual, Ethelinde; but it is at length become insupportable. *You* see it without pity, but *I* can sustain it no longer. Determine, therefore, to be mine, or to see him who has so long adored you, fly from you, merely to hide from your sight the consequences of that anguish which you refuse to remove."

More alarmed than surprised at the vehemence of his manner and purport of his words, Ethelinde tried to collect courage enough to speak; but before she could acquire it, Sir Edward went on—

"You know how ardently I loved you even when there were between us barriers that appeared insurmountable; when I was united to another, when your heart was solely occupied by that fortunate young man, whose fate I must ever contemplate with envy; you know that then I never offended you by a declaration of sentiments which it would have been as improper for you to listen to as fruitless for me to avow; you know, or you ought to know, all my silence cost me—all that I suffered—when every hour gave me occasion to contemplate perfections which I thought could never be mine; yet so entirely did I love you even then that had the happy Montgomery lived, I should have supported life by contemplating your felicity, and have been, however internally wretched, resigned; but now, that destiny itself has broken that union, shall I, with equal resignation, see you wearing out, in fruitless grief, that life which alone can give value to mine, and sacrificing your youth, your health, your talents, your virtues, to a vain, a chimerical idea of attachment to him who is no more! Have you for me neither pity or esteem? have you no wish to restore me to peace? to render my future days as happy as those you have hitherto seen me pass have been miserable? Have not my children, those lovely unfortunate little ones, a claim upon you, to give them a yet stronger title to your affection, and to restore to them a mother who truly feels more real tenderness for them than she had who gave them birth?

Have the wishes of your venerable, your beloved Mrs. Montgomery no influence? who declares that she shall leave the world without regret, if you, the sole remaining object of her solicitude, are no longer exposed to the dangers which surround youth, beauty, and sensibility like your's. Alas! if these motives have no power to awaken your tenderness, can I hope that the misery of your friend will excite your pity. You have seen me in lingering tortures for weeks, for months; you would continue to see me still in them, if I had not determined that this shall be the period in which my fate shall be decided. Give me then hopes that you will be less inflexible, or let me, while I have yet strength to remove myself from you, bid you adieu forever."

"Sir Edward," replied Ethelinde, after a short but expressive pause, "I am not, I hope, either insensible of your merit or ungrateful for all your goodness to me. If gratitude, if affection, if esteem, if the tenderest solicitude for your happiness, were enough to make you happy, I should think that I ought to sacrifice my reluctance to marry, and to give you my hand; but if I may judge of your sentiments, they are so delicate, that you would be unhappy unless your wife could repay them with her whole heart. The tenderest affections of mine are buried in the grave of Montgomery. Every hour in its passage convinces me that it will be ever impossible for me to recall them to any other object. Should I then, in justice to you Sir Edward, undertake engagements which it will not be in my power to fulfill? shall I at the altar promise to love you only, conscious as I am that great as is my esteem, my affection, my gratitude towards you, the image of Montgomery, lost as he is for ever, is as potent in my heart as if he really existed. I know that to the generality of men this would be considered as sentimental declamation, the effect of romantic enthusiasm; but it is not from Sir Edward Newenden I fear to excite ridicule on such a topic; you have an heart to which I dare appeal for my sincerity when I say that my attachment to Montgomery is so interwoven with my existence, that it never can end but with life; in conquering it, if to conquer it were possible, I should become contemptible in my own eyes, and certainly should gain nothing in your's."

Sir Edward heard her in silence, with clasped hands, and eyes fixed with mournful earnestness on her face. He seemed afraid of breathing, lest he should interrupt discourse which yet wounded him to the soul.

"Let us, therefore, my dear Sir Edward," continued she, "let us think no more of a measure which would assuredly not make you happy, because it would render me miserable. Deprive me not of the only pleasures I can now enjoy—those of weeping at liberty without a breach of duty, and of remaining the most attached and grateful of your friends."

"Grateful!" exclaimed Sir Edward, his voice trembling in his throat, "grateful, Ethelinde, for what? for paltry pecuniary assistance, too contemptible for you to recollect, and such as I should have rejoiced in having the power to administer to a daughter of any man of honor, my friend, even though that friend had not been Colonel Chesterville, even though that daughter had been as destitute of attractions as you are attractive. But why do I prolong a conversation which is, I see, painful to you? You have decided, and I must submit. My presence is uneasy to you, since you can feel only concern in seeing me wretched. I go therefore and——"

He arose, and would have left the place abruptly, with wildness and agitation of manner that terrified Ethelinde: she caught his hand, and cried in a voice that expressed how much she was affected—"Sir Edward, my dear Sir Edward——"

"Dear!" answered he, endeavouring gently to disengage himself—"*Am* I dear to you, Ethelinde, and *can* you condemn me to perpetual misery? Oh! embitter not your cruelty by dissimulated kindness; preserve at least your sincerity. If I were *indeed dear* to you could you——"

"Hear me, Sir Edward.——I have, in being very ingenuous with you, done what I think my sincerity as well as your esteem for me demands. Good God! is it to *you* I should use dissimulation? Surely no! I have told you that in giving my hand to any other man than Montgomery, whatever may be his merit, I shall be unhappy. I feel that time will with me fail of its usual effect, and that years will pass away without diminishing the regret with which the loss of Montgomery will recur to me. What would be your uneasiness to see this—to be every day sensible, that though I stifled my sentiments, I still felt them in all their force; to see the slow, but certainly destructive hand of sorrow, preying on an heart which you would suppose ought to be yours only, and my health declining, perhaps my temper injured, by the restraint I should think myself obliged to impose, when, as your wife, I might ineffectually try, if not to obliterate at least to weaken the powerful and corrosive recollection of those days when I had hopes of being the wife of Montgomery. How many amiable and deserving women are there to whom——"

"Stop, Ethelinde," said Sir Edward, "I have heard you hitherto with calmness; but I cannot continue to do so, when you speak of the possibility of my transferring to another that heart which has so long been your's. Believe me, my attachment to you, hopeless as you determine it shall be, is as unchangeable as your own to Montgomery. If you were a better judge of your own attractions, you would know that he who has so long had an opportunity of studying, with a disposition to understand and admire those perfections, can feel little inclination to follow the advice which you seem disposed to offer. Your happiness, and not my own, has been, shall still be the first and fondest object of my wishes. I have often said, and I hope with sincerity, that had Montgomery lived to have become, in being your husband, the most enviable of human beings, I could have witnessed his felicity, not perhaps without envy, but at least without any of those malignant sentiments which usually accompany that passion; since Providence has taken him from us, I have fatally for myself, indulged those hopes which I before made it a point of honor to suppress: but since you say your happiness is inconsistent with mine, let *me* alone suffer for having yielded to those hopes; let me again study the hard lesson of silent suffering, again try what absence will do—ah! painful, fruitless, hopeless experiment!"

Again he would have turned away; but Ethelinde, more deeply affected, said—"No, Sir Edward, you shall not go: stay, I beseech you, and let me be still your ward, your sister, your friend! So you generously say you should have considered me had Montgomery lived: by an effort of virtuous resolution then, to which your noble spirit is more than equal, learn to think of him as still living."

"Rather behold him really so!" cried a voice which struck motionless its auditors. Ethelinde, uttering a faint shriek, held by the arm of Sir Edward in amazement, while he, with equal surprise, beheld a man, who rushing from a thicket which grew near their seat, threw himself on his knees before her, and eagerly seizing her hands, pressed them to his forehead and his eyes in frantic rapture, crying—"Behold, my Ethelinde, behold that Montgomery so fondly regretted—so faithfully beloved!—he, who has been betrayed by the utmost tormenting jealousy into an action unworthy of him, and has listened to that discourse which has convinced him he has wronged you, and the worthiest of friends and men. Look not, my angel, so terrified; but speak to me, I conjure you."

Ethelinde, however, was unable to speak, and Sir Edward with difficulty prevented her falling. Distressed at the condition he saw her in, he said, not without some appearance of displeasure —"Why would you, Sir, be thus rash? Why thus abruptly appear before her?"

"Pardon, dear Sir Edward," replied the half frantic Montgomery—"pardon the transports of a man, who believing he had lost every thing, finds himself still possest of Ethelinde's love, and of such a friend as you are. She is mine," continued he, straining her to his bosom—"she is mine! Believing me dead, she loved me still! I come, shipwrecked and a beggar, to my country; but am richer than fortune could have made me, in the possession of that dear, dear heart! Heaven give me strength to bear such excess of happiness—forgive my precipitancy, and speak to me, my Ethelinde; 'tis Montgomery! your long lost Montgomery, whose arms enfold you!"

"Montgomery!" sighed Ethelinde. "Good God!"

The sudden surprise seemed for a moment to have deprived her of her senses. Sir Edward saw with concern that she could not recover herself. He feared she would faint—"You will destroy her if you are not more calm," said he. "Surely it was very ill judged thus to surprise her."

"Again, dear Sir Edward!" answered he—"again I beg your pardon. I came under such depression that my reason fails under the intoxicating influence of joy. But I will be calm; speak to me, Ethelinde, and I will try to be calm."

"Montgomery, ever dear Montgomery!" repeated Ethelinde. She gave him her cold hand; but could articulate no more, nor shed a tear, though, from her deep and broken sighs, her heart seemed bursting.

"Let us go," said Sir Edward, "to my house; and do you, my dear Ethelinde, endeavour to recollect yourself."

"I will," replied she faintly, "indeed I will! Poor Montgomery!
—is it possible?"

"Poor indeed," cried he—"poor in every thing but love! This
garb, this altered countenance, may tell you that Montgomery is
changed in every respect but in his heart."

He was going on; but Sir Edward besought him not to talk to
her till they got to the abbey.—"You see," said he, "how much she
is still affected. Lean upon me, Ethelinde, and let Montgomery
support you on the other side."

She obeyed; and while they slowly led her along, Montgomery
continued to utter disjointed sentences, expressive of the tumultuous transports of his soul; while, her eyes continually fixed on
his face, she seemed still to doubt whether her happiness was real.
On their arrival at the abbey, Ethelinde, relieved by tears, became
more composed; and the stupor and faintness which had so much
alarmed Sir Edward, having in a great degree subsided, he left her
with Montgomery, and retired to his study to compose a mind
hardly less ruffled than his had been, though from a very different
cause.

The hopes he had been indulging of calling his the woman he
adored, were vanished for ever. A dreadful pang attended this conviction: but his generous and disinterested nature prevailed, after
a short but severe struggle, over all considerations that merely
affected himself. Determined to find his felicity in that of those he
loved, he rejoiced in the restoration of a beloved son to a tender
mother, a valuable man to his country, and felicity to Ethelinde.
After a short absence, he returned with apparent serenity to the
room where he had left her with Montgomery; and taking her
hand, he said, with an half mournful and forced smile—"Well, my
dear Ethy, if you have now forgiven your wanderer for his abrupt
appearance, would it not be well to consider how we shall introduce him to his mother, for whom, in her present languid state, I
should apprehend very ill consequences from the effect of such a
surprise as his appearance to-day gave you."

"We have been trying to talk of it," replied Montgomery; "but
do you, dear Sir Edward, who are so much more capable, determine for us."

"And soon, Sir Edward," said Ethelinde; "for it is already past the usual hour of my return, and I fear Mrs. Montgomery may be alarmed."

"Do you find yourself," answered he, "equal to the meeting, or rather are you able to conceal what you know."

"I am afraid not; but I will at least attempt it. I carried for many weeks, in my agonized bosom, the fatal secret of his supposed death: I will try if, for a few hours, for longer it will be impossible, I can conceal the transporting certainty of his life."

Montgomery, tenderly solicitous for his mother, and greatly distressed by the account Ethelinde had given him of the state of her health, was ready to submit himself wholly to the guidance of Sir Edward; and it was determined that he should carry Ethelinde home in his post-chaise; saying only that she had walked further than usual, and being tired, had called at the abbey to be conveyed home by that means to the cottage; that he should stay there with her himself, and in conversation gradually open to her, first the possibility, and afterwards the assurance that her son was living, who, when Sir Edward thought her sufficiently prepared, was, at a signal agreed upon, to appear.

This being settled, Sir Edward and Ethelinde departed together. They hardly spoke the whole way: Sir Edward silently revolved the events of the day, and meditated how he might best acquit himself to his own satisfaction, and with the least risk to the feeble frame of Mrs. Montgomery; while Ethelinde, overwhelmed as she was with the sense of her own unexpected happiness, felt her admiration of his greatness of mind mingled with pain from the certainty of how much it cost him. As they approached the house, the recollection of all she owed him, from her father's first embarrassments till the present moment, pressed on her mind; and almost involuntarily she lifted his hand to her lips: a tear fell upon his hand; he kissed it off, sighed deeply, but said nothing till the chaise stopped at the door, when in a voice that he meant should be firmer than it was, he desired her to try to compose her countenance that Mrs. Montgomery might have no cause to suspect she had met with any extraordinary occurrence.

CHAPTER XIV

Sir Edward and Ethelinde easily accounted to Mrs. Montgomery for their stay; but the latter, finding herself quite unequal to any share of the task Sir Edward had undertaken, hastened away as soon after dinner as she could? while he entertained Mrs. Montgomery for some time on indifferent subjects. As soon, however, as a pause in the conversation gave her leave, she enquired, with that appearance of tender interest which she always felt on the subject of Ethelinde, whether he believed that she should, before she died, be made easy by leaving her his wife. "I have a letter to-day," said she, "from my brother, and I am glad to find that though Lady Hawkhurst followed him with her family to Bath, the marriage she so artfully meditated has wholly failed. It is difficult to sustain long an assumed character, and Bath was of all others the place where it was to Lady Arabella the most difficult. My brother fortunately discovered her true one, and is thankful that he discovered it before he had engaged himself in irremediable wretchedness. Chesterville and Victorine have seen the danger, and I hope profited by it, as he mentions being well satisfied with their conduct. This on his account is most satisfactory to me; yet, my dear Sir Edward, it has lessened but little my anxiety in regard to this adopted daughter of my heart. Chesterville can never be the friend, the brother *she* deserves, for his heart is incapable of it. If she goes to reside with them, she will not complain, but she will undoubtedly be unhappy. Naturally of a pensive turn, and her heart cruelly wounded by an irreparable loss, *their* style of life will be painful to her; and her melancholy, all soft and interesting as it is, will ever be a restraint upon them; besides that my brother's partial fondness for her, will be but too likely to excite discontent in his daughter and her husband. Whither then can she go? and what will be her destiny?"

"I believe," said Sir Edward, collecting all his fortitude, "that the generous interest you take in my favour, added to her friendship for me, would make some change in her resolution, if she had not of late taken up a notion that he whom she regrets as dead may yet be living. I could not combat an idea on which she dwelt with so much fondness: she brought indeed numberless instances to confirm its probability; and certainly it is not impossible."

Convinced as Sir Edward had been after the most assiduous enquires that Montgomery had really perished by shipwreck at the Mauritius, he had never before encouraged the unhappy mother to dwell on a possibility that could, he thought, answer no other purpose than to lengthen or renew her sufferings. She now turned on him those eyes that had long ceased to look towards any object in this world with hope or pleasure. They seemed as if they would penetrate his inmost thoughts.—"What do you mean, Sir Edward," said she, in a solemn tone, "and why do you seem to encourage such wild—oh! God!—such hopeless imaginations."

"Be calm," replied he, "and I will tell you that a sailor has been seen in London who was in the vessel in which Montgomery was supposed to be lost: and this man says that he believes it is very likely your son escaped."

"Almighty God!" exclaimed she, starting from her chair, "there then remains an hope! Where, and when can I see this man? Send for him, dear Sir Edward: or rather let me go in search of him that no time may be lost, for many days of suspence I shall not survive. Oh! merciful heaven, if it be thy pleasure," continued she, clasping her hands, "if it be thy pleasure to restore him to his widowed mother!" The idea seemed a moment to animate her whole frame, but then fear of a disappointment checked her transports.—"Oh! No, I dare not hope it. He is gone, he is lost for ever; for had he been living he would have been in England as soon as this mariner." She sat down and seemed grasping for breath. "My dear Madam," said Sir Edward, assuming a chearful tone, "you are needlessly agitated. Consider that if the intelligence is groundless, it will make no real difference, because, believing the worst already, you can learn nothing more to fear, while it is possible, nay probable, that you have much to hope. For my own part I own I have very sanguine expectations, but I will not say a word of them till I see that you can hear me with more composure."

"Sanguine expectations, Sir Edward! you know then more than you have communicated. Sanguine expectations! tell me, I conjure you, from whence they arise?"

"Command yourself then, my dear good friend, and I will obey you. I *have seen* the sailor, who is positive that your son by swimming gained the shore. Can you hear the rest?"

Mrs. Montgomery bowed her head, but could not speak. "That rest is only a continuation of good tidings. The same person tells me that he not only has no doubt of your son's having escaped death, but that he is now in England, perhaps hastening to you!"

She held out her hand to Sir Edward in speechless transport; but he found her pulse sinking, her eyes closed, she fell lifeless in her chair. He rang in terror; the servants and Ethelinde ran to her assistance; and Montgomery, who waited only at the corner of the house, was alarmed at the confusion he heard, and fearing that it was occasioned by his mother's indisposition, he rushed into the room, and was on his knees before her before either Sir Edward or Ethelinde had the power to restrain him.

For some moments they believed her dead; and the cruel alteration sickness and sorrow had made in her figure and countenance, confirmed Montgomery in this dreadful idea. He deplored, in accents of piercing distress, that he had arrived only to witness the last sighs of the best of parents. He now ran out for assistance; then remembering that no medical help could there be obtained, he flew back to the room, and walking about in an agony of grief and apprehension, was afraid of looking at his mother lest he should see her expire.

Feeble, languishing, and even in the last stage of a decline as Mrs. Montgomery seemed to be, she had yet more strength than her appearance indicated; the remedies Ethelinde administered had their effect, and in a few moments she was enough restored to be sensible that her beloved Charles was not only living, but was actually embracing her knees, and shedding tears of the tenderest filial affection on the hands she put forth to bless him. The first emotion of her heart, after the return of her senses, was gratitude to the Being who had preserved and restored him. After having silently but fervently offered up her thanks she pressed her son fondly to her heart; and having taken some refreshment, reposed on a sopha; while her son, whom her eyes followed incessantly, seemed disposed to gratify the curiosity which the whole company must, he knew, feel to know the particulars of his life since his quitting England. Sir Edward Newenden, however, soon after

Mrs. Montgomery was tolerably recovered, took his leave for the evening and returned home.

The altered looks of Montgomery, as well as his dress, which was that of a common sailor, gave his mother and Ethelinde painful impressions of all the sufferings and hardships he had undergone. With the tenderest expression of pity, love, and solicitude, the eyes of both seemed to ask a detail of his adventures. He saw that they would be relieved and gratified by hearing it, and thus began.

"I will not describe to you the horrors of storms in the tropical regions, or attempt to give you an idea of that which after many weeks of famine and fatigue, during which we were driven by a succession of hurricanes quite out of our course, threw the vessel I was in on a rock near the Isle of Bourbon. As it was evident she must soon go to pieces, those, who, aided by the desperation of their circumstances, found courage to brave the almost equal peril of the tremendous surf which broke on the shore, threw themselves into the water; I was among these; and trusting to my skill in swimming, and to my personal strength, I left the ship; and under the protection of Providence, found myself, though with some severe bruises, on shore on the island. I had plunged into the sea in the cloaths I had on board but my purse, (in which was some money and two small diamonds,) a little parcel of linen, and two miniatures I always wore about me. The people, however, among whom I was, with five others, cast, were not inhospitable. By a ship going to India, three of my fellow sufferers returned thither. My hope was to get a passage to Europe. After ten tedious weeks, an American ship came into the port of St. Denys[1] on her return to that country. America was comparatively near England, and I eagerly enquired for a passage; but the master, who was a species of animal I had never seen before, would not receive me without money, of which, though I had saved my purse, I had now very little left. I was obliged, therefore, to agree to work for my passage; and in that situation I arrived at Boston, after a long voyage, in which I suffered some fatigue and hardship, which I bore however

1 St. Denys is a port city on the northern coast of the Isle of Bourbon (now called Réunion, a French overseas department located in the Indian Ocean, east of Madagascar.)

without murmuring when I reflected that every league brought me nearer to the objects of all my solicitude; and at night, or whenever my watch was over, I kissed the two dear pictures I had preserved of my mother and my Ethelinde: their beloved images soothed my short slumbers, and I awoke indeed to new toil, but to toil lightened by the hope of soon embracing the beloved originals.

"In about six weeks after I landed at Boston, where I with great difficulty subsisted, I got a passage for Ireland, but still as a common sailor; from thence I landed at Bristol; and as soon as I touched English ground, my anxiety to hear of you both became insupportable. I recollected the family of the Ludfords, and determined to apply to them, without however discovering how deeply interested I was in the intelligence I asked. They were at their house a few miles from the city; I walked thither, and approached the door in my jacket and trousers, which I own were not in very good order, my whole ambition being to have cleaner linen than usually found under such habiliments, and I had been obliged to sell a ring and a small diamond I had in my purse, to furnish myself till this time with that indulgence and the necessaries of life. When I reached the door, I found a coach in readiness to take the ladies out. I was ordered by the laced footman of Mrs. Ludford to retire. 'What do you do here, fellow?' demanded the insolent domestic. 'We suffer no such people to come to the door.' I answered that I was just come from India, where I had seen a friend of Mrs. Ludford's, and wished to be allowed to speak to her. The man, however, would have repulsed me with insult, if at that moment the lady of the house, leaning on the arm of a young woman, who appeared to be a kind of companion, had not appeared in all the unwieldy splendor of recent wealth, and self-created importance. I approached her with my hat in my hand, and in the humble phrase which seemed to become my condition, began to speak. She stopped, and turning to her footman, said—'What is the reason you do not obey my orders? Why are you beggars suffered to come to this door?' 'I am no beggar, madam,' said I, smiling at the ridiculous air of dignity the lady assumed; 'but having lately arrived from India, I waited on you at the desire of Mr. Montgomery to enquire after Miss Chesterville.' 'I know nothing about her,' replied she, passing by me, without deigning to look at me again; 'but if you apply to the Newendens, I suppose you may learn more.' The lady then seated herself in her coach, her companion followed her and she was driven from the door.

"I now ventured to ask the footman for intelligence of Miss Chesterville. The upper servants condescended not to hold converse with a person of my appearance, and shut the door in my face; but from an inferior female servant, who came to it soon afterwards, not yet arrived to the dignity of supreme insolence, I learned that Miss Clarinthia had married a young officer against the consent of her father, and was gone with him to join his regiment; and that Mr. Rupert had some time before departed from his paternal compting house to make the tour of Italy, from whence he sent such accounts of his parties with Princes and Princesses, such verses, such curiosities, as reconciled his mother to his absence, though it much discomposed the old gentleman: that as to Miss Chesterville, she had left their family a long time before with a rich gentleman, whose name the girl could not remember, and that she had since been married to him or some other great 'Squire or Lord, as had been told in their kitchen. Astonished and alarmed by this intelligence, vague and disjointed as it was, I hastened from Ludford house to Bath, intending to proceed directly to London; but on my arrival there, I saw on the door of a splendid house in one of the new streets the name of Maltravers, and ventured to knock at it. There again my appearance had nearly precluded me from all intelligence; but after assuring the servant that I wanted nothing but some information that would give him no great trouble, he vouchsafed to tell me that the Mr. Maltravers I enquired after had been some time dead, and that the house I now saw belonged to his widow. I asked after Lady Newenden. Lady Newenden too was dead: and 'Sir Edward,' said I; 'pray where is he?' 'Indeed,' replied the footman, 'I don't know. I don't think that my lady ever hears of him.' I told him that it was very material to me to know where to find him; that I had letters also, and a message of consequence to deliver to Miss Chesterville, a niece of his Lady's, and that it would be doing me a great service if he would go up to his Lady to enquire where I might see either of them. Probably he delivered his message imperfectly; and the name of Sir Edward Newenden, united with that of Miss Chesterville, excited the malignant curiosity of the lady; for after a moment the footman came back and told me, that though his lady was engaged with company, she would see me herself. I followed the footman to the door of a room, where, though it was yet morning with them, a party were at cards. Mrs. Maltravers, whom I hardly recollected, and who did not know me, bade me approach; and turning half round, she said—'What do you know, friend, of Sir Edward Newenden and Miss Chesterville? My servant informs me you have something to say about them.' I replied that the servant then had been mistaken, for that I merely took the liberty to beg a direction to either of them, having letters from India for them. 'Is that all?' cried she, with visible ill humour; 'and pray who directed you to me?' I answered that knowing the connection of the families, I had presumed—'Presumed indeed,' replied the lady. 'People are continually plaguing me for an address to Sir Edward Newenden, as if *I* had any knowledge of him. I assure you, young man, and all whom it may concern, that I am quite a stranger to Sir Edward Newenden. The man hides himself, I believe, in the Hebrides, or under the North Pole; and then his former acquaintance are teazed for his address.'

"I humbly represented that I had letters to deliver from India to him and Miss Chesterville: 'to whom, perhaps Madam,' said I, 'you will be so good as to give me a direction, though you cannot to Sir Edward Newenden.' 'Oh! as to that,' cried she, sneeringly, 'I can as easily do one as the other; for undoubtedly they are together. Reports says they are married. I know nothing of that; but however, friend, they have an establishment together, that is certain, so you will have only one trouble in delivering your letters; but do understand, and let it be generally understood, that I am wholly unconnected with Sir Edward Newenden. Here, John, shew this person out.' I retired in greater uneasiness than I entered; every circumstance seemed to confirm my apprehension, and in an increasing agony of suspense I reached the Devizes[1] the same evening by means of a return chaise. There, however, I was compelled to stop for the night, as no conveyance within reach of my slender finances was likely to offer till the next day.

"At the inn where the chaise put me down, I observed a phaeton

---

[1] Devizes was and is a center for banks and solicitors, a market town (nowadays shops) in central Wiltshire; in the 18th century a coaching stop between Bristol and London, a sort of hub for travellers.

with arms on it, which being somewhat remarkable, I remembered to be those of Davenant. On enquiry, I heard that the carriage belonged to him; the waiters told me he had lived there almost a month. I sought his servants; but they had not been long with him, and knew not even the names of those for whom I was so painfully anxious. I determined therefore to address myself to their master. This, however, was not very easy; for I discovered that Davenant, by excessive drinking, dissolute connections, and low company, had greatly impaired his fortune, and was now so apprehensive of his creditors that he was unwilling to hold converse with strangers. By means, however, of his servants, whom I treated at the expence of almost half the money I had left, the *lady* who lived with Davenant was prevailed upon to direct that I might be admitted. It was near nine o'clock in the evening before I obtained this favour; but Mr. Davenant had not risen from his dinner table, which was covered with wine and bowls of punch, and surrounded by an exciseman, a feeder of fighting cocks, a celebrated bruiser,[1] and the woman who was his present favourite.

"The bloated figure and inflamed countenance of Davenant excited my compassion. He seemed, however, not to have the least recollection of me; but with half shut eyes, and a voice rendered almost inarticulate by intoxication, he accosted me by the name of honest Jack, I suppose from my sailor's dress, and in coarse phrase asked what I wanted with him. I told him that I came lately from India, and being entrusted with letters of consequence to Sir Edward Newenden, which I wished to deliver myself, I took the liberty of desiring a direction to his present residence. 'And how the devil,' said he, 'd'ye think I know any thing of such a parson in a coloured coat, as that queer old guardian of mine. Faith, friend, I don't keep such company. You may enquire about him of the next methodist preacher, who is much more likely to know than I am where to find him.' It would be disgusting to repeat the oaths with which this unfortunate being interlarded all the intelligence I could gain from him, which was, that he had heard that Sir Edward lived entirely at Grasmere, and that you, my Ethelinde, resided

1 The point is Davenant now dines with people hired to catch smugglers (they are responsible for collecting the excise tax) and prize-fighters, those who make money off blood sports. He has fallen from his gentlemanly world altogether.

with him, 'Some say,' added he, 'they are married, and I hope they
are, with all my soul, because I know what a devilish jilt the girl is,
and the starched knight will stand a good chance of being served
by his second as he was by his first wife. Rat me if I should not
be cursed glad to hear it.' I turned from the profligated ideot with
disgust, but all my uneasiness was redoubled. I hardly doubted
any longer of Ethelinde's marriage, and to the night I passed in
consequence of this persuasion, that which threw me desolate
and shipwrecked on the Isle of Bourbon was comparatively happy.
Sleep was no longer in question. On top of one of the night stages
I proceeded to London. I hurried to the town house of Sir Edward
Newenden. He had left it only the preceding morning to return
to Grasmere. I questioned the maid who had the charge of it, and
her answers served only to persuade me that all I apprehended
was certain, that Ethelinde was married, and that I was undone.
I cannot if I would describe the state of mind in which I now proceeded to the north. My money was so nearly expended, that I was
obliged sometimes to walk, at others to procure a conveyance for
a few miles in some chance carriage; and thus I was, notwithstanding the impatience which devoured me, six days in performing a
journey, which had I had money I should have made in two. Last
night about eight o'clock I arrived on the borders of the lake; the
moon was trembling on its clear surface; and from among floating clouds her rays fell on the white chimnies of my mother's cottage. Good God! what were my feelings when I first beheld them? I
dared not enter; for I felt that the absolute certainty of Ethelinde's
marriage I was utterly unable to sustain. Hardly knowing what I
did, and afraid to enquire of myself what I meant to do, if I was
really as wretched as my fears represented me to be, I traversed
those well-known paths that led to the cottage with undescribable
terror; now hastening as if determined to know the worst, now
stopping for breath, and to recover that resolution which seemed
every moment on the point of giving me up to the phrenzy of
despair. I threw my eyes wildly round me, and remembering the
spots where we had first met, all my agonies were redoubled.
There! cried I, turning my eyes towards the creek, there I snatched
her from death, she who now lives for another! As I did this, I saw
distant lights through the trees, and the abbey seemed to have
candles in every window. Good God! said I, there she is! no longer

my Ethelinde, but the bride of Sir Edward Newenden; there, surrounded by splendor and elegance, she drives from her heart for
ever the memory of the indigent, unhappy wanderer, who had
nothing to give her but an heart; and *you* my mother! could *you*
suffer this? but you perhaps were not consulted; sinking under
concern and regret, your feeble remonstrances were unheard or
unregarded when ambition and interest solicited. Oh! forgive me,
dearest Ethelinde, continued he, forgive me that I thought thus of
you. Be not thus affected, my angel; I cannot bear your tears."

Ethelinde, smiling through them, promised to be more composed, and Montgomery, kissing her hands, and then those of his
mother, proceeded—

"The night grew cold and stormy; and the moon was no longer
visible; when I reached the court of the cottage, about half past ten
o'clock; every thing was silent round it; I opened the little gate as
softly as I could, and a thousand tender recollections crowded on
my mind. I trembled, and was obliged to lean against it a moment
for breath, when the old pointer, of which I had been so fond from
a boy, ran out to me, and instead of barking, as is his custom to
strangers, jumped up and licked my hands. *You* have not forgotten me, Vigo, said I: and I know not why, but I burst into tears.
My heart seemed relieved: I was able to consider what I should do
for the night; and thinking that my sudden appearance at such an
hour might too much alarm my mother, I determined to seek a
lodging in some of the out-houses. I easily found one filled with
straw, where I lay down, and my faithful dog remained by me. I
had often slept sound in a much worse lodging; but now to sleep
was impossible, notwithstanding the great fatigue I had undergone for several preceding days.

"Before day break, I left my straw, and went into the village,
as well for food as to ask questions which I trembled to have
answered. The people of the small ale house, which supplied me
with a coarse breakfast, had no recollection of me in this dress, and
answered my enquiries as those of a stranger, who, travelling into
Scotland to his friends, had missed his way. The woman, who was
not unwilling to talk, gave me the history of her good master, as
she called Sir Edward Newenden, and told me how he had been
vilely used by his first lady, who, as good luck would have it, died
in parts beyond the sea, and now how he was going to be married

out of hand to a sweet pretty lady as lived in their village, one Miss Chesterville. Going to be married, cried I, with emotion which would have betrayed me to any more observing person, are they *not* married then? She replied that it was the general opinion of the neighbourhood that they were, though for some reason or other it had been kept a secret. 'To be sure, for my part,' said she 'as I says to my husband, 'I think how they *be* married; for there, Miss, she have had ever so long the care of his honour's children, and is as fond on 'em as if they were her own; and Master himself lives as 'twere at Madam Montgomery's.' This account rather corroborated than diminished my fears; and finding my soul sicken under their influence, I could not collect strength to have them confirmed; but abruptly quitting my talkative landlady, I wandered away through the woody paths of the north fell, again to consider what I should do. As I sat on the roots of the old thorns and hollies of the rock that hang over the foot-way leading from the abbey, I heard voices swell in the breeze, and looking down thro' the yet leafless branches, I saw Sir Edward Newenden followed by two of his servants with something in their hands. He seemed to be giving them directions. I thought, tho' I could not see his face, that he had, in his air and manner, all the alertness of hope, if not of happiness, and at that moment I felt disposed to rush upon him and stab him to the heart.

"This gloomy and dreadful idea yet possessed my mind after I lost sight of him, whom I considered as the destroyer of all my happiness; but then the recollection of my mother, the cruelty I should be guilty of towards her, towards that tender and dear parent who had lived but for me, came fortunately to soften the fury with which I was inspired, and again I wept like a woman.

"Thus between stupor and phrenzy, which I cannot describe, I passed above an hour; and then without having come to any resolution, I went up towards the cave where I first told my Ethelinde of my love, and where I used to sit whole hours to think of, or write to her. What were my emotions when I saw her there; lovely indeed as ever, but paler and thinner than I had left her; she had a book in her hand, but she seemed rather to meditate than read. I was within a few yards of her, hidden by the thick brush-wood that grew round the foot of the rock. I heard her sigh; I fancied that she repeated the name of Montgomery, and I was on the point of rushing out of my concealment to know my destiny, perhaps to die at her feet, when the appearance of Sir Edward Newenden drove me back to my covert in an agony of such terrible suspense as I cannot even now recollect without shuddering."

Montgomery concluded his narrative by describing the sensations he felt while he listened to the dialogue between Ethelinde and Sir Edward; again he apologized to her for the imprudence of his abrupt appearance; "but who," added he, tenderly embracing her, "ah who that had feared, so justly feared that he was undone, and found himself at once the happiest of mankind, could have borne such transcendent felicity with a more equal mind?"

It was now time to separate for the night. Montgomery, whose reflection returned, was anxious that neither his mother or Ethelinde, who had suffered so much agitation during the day, should be fatigued by sitting up late. Mrs. Montgomery kissed her son; a silent tear spoke how much she was affected with those emotions to which words cannot do justice, when beneath her own roof, in health and safety, she bade good night to the darling of her heart.

Early the next morning Ethelinde received from Sir Edward Newenden the following letter—

"Let me, dearest Miss Chesterville, again congratulate you and Mrs. Montgomery on the events of yesterday—I do most sincerely; but mine is one of those situations where to fly for a short time from those I most sincerely love, is perhaps best on their account and certainly so on my own.

"I go, therefore, to-morrow morning, before you can receive this, towards London with my eldest boy; and from thence, in a very few days (which will be employed in visiting Mrs. Woolaston, and settling my pecuniary concerns) to Dover, where I shall embark for France, and go immediately to Geneva: there it is my present purpose to continue twelve or fourteen months.

"Within less than as many days I conclude you will give your hand to the only man who entirely deserves such a blessing. You will continue, I know, to honor me with that sisterly affection that has hitherto been at once a pleasure and a torment to me. I will endeavour henceforth to learn the art of making it only the former; and I beg of you and your dear Montgomery to forgive, to pity, and, if possible, to *forget* my weakness. Before I return to England, I will learn to conquer it wholly, and will not present myself to my sister till I am worthy of being called her brother.

"In leaving my two little ones to your care, I know that they are in the hands of the best and tenderest of friends. If you remove to London take them with you—you will love them, for your heart is formed for love. They are amiable—they are motherless—they are mine! Any of those circumstances would recommend them to your compassionate bosom—all those circumstances united, secure for them the protection and tenderness of Ethelinde and Montgomery.

"Assure, my respectable, and now most happy friend, of my true regard; and now loveliest, dearest, best of women, adieu! May the blessing of heaven be upon you. Remember, and I know Montgomery will remind you of it, remember to write to the most faithful of your friends,

E. NEWENDEN."

Ethelinde shed tears over this letter; and when Montgomery went to call her for an early walk, he found her still weeping. His gallant heart sympathized in her sorrow: he would have gone instantly to the abbey to have attempted detaining in England a friend so justly dear to them both; but Ethelinde informed him that the servant who brought the letter, and to whom she had spoken, had assured her that his master, who had not been in bed all night, had departed before day break for London with his eldest boy.

Ethelinde and Montgomery went, however, instantly to the abbey to fetch the two younger children; and in giving to them attention truly maternal, she found the only alleviation of that concern, which, in despite of the happiness she enjoyed, she could not help feeling for the sufferings inflicted by hopeless love on one of the noblest hearts in the world.

Mrs. Montgomery felt the effect of the painfully delightful scene she had gone thro' more afterwards than she had done the evening it happened. The languor of which she was sensible, made her again believe her death not very distant, and she desired to have her son and Ethelinde united, and then she said she should leave the world without one wish unfulfilled.

Her's and Montgomery's importunities left Ethelinde no

excuse to delay her marriage, and within a week after Montgomery's return, she gave him her hand at the village church, only Mrs. Montgomery, Mrs. Dickenson, the housekeeper at Grasmere Abbey, and two other servants, being present.

Their marriage made no alteration in their simple domestic arrangement. The happy Montgomery would have thought himself in a state of felicity too great for humanity, had not fears for his mother's health sometimes made him remember how easily it might be diminished. As the summer advanced, however, Mrs. Montgomery, whose heart was relieved of all those cares which had so greatly hurt her health, grew much better; and towards autumn, her son, who dreaded a relapse if she continued in the north during the winter, prevailed on her to go to Bristol for those months. Thither he accompanied her with Ethelinde and the two little Newendens.

There they saw Lord Danesforte; who, after every other expedient to retrieve a ruined constitution, came thither to die. He appeared to be a walking skeleton; but was still surrounded with persons whose business it was to keep off the approaches of reflection and remorse, if they could not retard those of death. He was persuaded to the last moment that he should recover; and much as he deserved to suffer, Ethelinde could not hear of his decease, which soon happened, without being greatly shocked, and reflecting with a mixture of pity and horror on all the misery he had brought, not only on the family of Sir Edward Newenden, but on those of many other persons, though he now unrepentingly was gone where all his crimes were registered.

Mr. Harcourt came to his sister at Bristol, and added to her happiness. His health was much amended; his daughter was no longer careless of his ease, or ungrateful for his tenderness; and Chesterville himself, who, with Victorine, passed a month with them at Bristol, was much changed in consequence of the alarm which Mr. Harcourt's proposed marriage had given him. He was still rather too much a man of the great world, but Ethelinde loved him, and overlooked his faults, because she wished neither to remember or discover them. He had now two children, and seemed really to consider the necessity of providing for them as well as pleasing himself, out of the ample income paid him by Mr. Harcourt.

Whatever were his real feelings as to the generosity of his

father-in-law towards Montgomery and his sister, he carefully concealed them, and even affected pleasure at the presents he made to them and Mrs. Montgomery. Montgomery, however, always the most generous and disinterested of men, would absolutely accept of no more money than Mr. Harcourt had already settled on himself and his mother. "It is enough, my dear uncle," said he, "for all my wants, and all my wishes, for neither Ethelinde or I have any intention to quit the dear tho' humble abode on the banks of Grasmere Water, where we have found happiness, and where we enjoy

"That best seclusion from a jarring world,"[1]

which, young as we both are, we have both learned to covet. We shall be rich there with what your generosity has already done for us. It would only give us pain to deprive of more, those who have a right to all your fortune. Come in the course of the summer, my dear Sir, come and see if we can be happier than the bounty of Providence and your bounty has already made us."

The happiness enjoyed by Mrs. Montgomery, whose health was completely re-established, and by her son and daughter, was such as admitted indeed of no addition but what it received by the birth of a daughter, in whose infant features Montgomery delighted to trace the mingled resemblance of his mother and her own; and by the arrival of Sir Edward Newenden, who, after an absence of something more than twelve months, returned to Grasmere, with his heart as partial as ever to his charming friend, but divested of all the painful sensations which had formerly attended that partiality. He employed himself between the duty he owed his country, and the education of his children, fondly fancying that the time might come when his eldest boy, whose life Ethelinde had once been, under heaven, the means of saving, might become the fortunate husband of the infant cherub whom he saw at her breast. Thus in present content, and with hope of future happiness, the life of this amiable man was restored to serenity, and those days which he passed at Grasmere were always the happiest of the year. Montgomery and Ethelinde, delighted to see that sorrow no longer

1 Cowper, *The Task*, Book 3, line 675: "Oh, blest seclusion, from a jarring world..." The passage takes into account all that has gone before in the novel, e.g., "Retreat/Cannot... Restore/Lost innocence, or cancel follies past/But it has peace, and much secures the mind..."

596 ETHELINDE

corroded the heart of him to whom they owed so many obligations, were, as well as Mrs. Montgomery, grateful to Providence
for the unmixed blessings they thus enjoyed, and endeavoured to
deserve by the practice of every virtue, the continuation of felicity
so seldom tasted on earth.

FINIS.